Before long, all twenty — — — — — — — — — — eir mounts. The wing had a paper str— — — — — — — nd hadn't been anywhere close to it since the opening — — of the war against Unkerlant. *Stretched too thin*, Sabrino thought again. He whacked the beast with an iron-tipped goad. With a scream of fury, the dragon sprang into the air, batwings thundering.

Orosio's image appeared, tiny and perfect, in the crystal Sabrino carried. "There's the bridge, sir," he said. "On the bend of the river, a little north of us."

As Sabrino guided his dragon into a dive toward the bridge, the Unkerlanters on the ground started blazing at him. He was the lead man: he drew the beams. He could hear raindrops and sleet sizzling into steam as beams burned through them. When one passed close, he smelled a breath's worth of lightning in the air.

He released the eggs under his dragon's belly, then urged the beast higher into the air once more. He saw the flashes of sorcerous energy and heard the roars as the eggs burst behind him. More flashes and roars said his dragonfliers were striking the bridge, too.

He twisted in his harness, trying to see what had happened. He let out a whoop on spotting what was left of the bridge: three or four eggs had burst right on it. "You bastards will be a while fixing that!" he shouted.

TOR BOOKS BY HARRY TURTLEDOVE

Into the Darkness
Darkness Descending
Through the Darkness
Rulers of the Darkness
Jaws of Darkness
Out of the Darkness
The Two Georges (by Richard Dreyfuss and
Harry Turtledove)
Household Gods (by Judith Tarr and Harry Turtledove)
Between the Rivers
Gunpowder Empire: Crosstime Traffic

(Writing as H. N. Turteltaub)
Justinian
Over the Wine-Dark Sea
The Gryphon's Skull
The Sacred Land
Owls to Athens

OUT OF THE
DARKNESS

HARRY TURTLEDOVE

TOR®
fantasy

A TOM DOHERTY ASSOCIATES BOOK
NEW YORK

This is a work of fiction. All the characters and events portrayed in this book are either products of the author's imagination or are used fictitiously.

OUT OF THE DARKNESS

Copyright © 2004 by Harry Turtledove

All rights reserved, including the right to reproduce this book, or portions thereof, in any form.

Edited by Patrick Nielsen Hayden
Map by Ellisa Mitchell

A Tor Book
Published by Tom Doherty Associates, LLC
175 Fifth Avenue
New York, NY 10010

www.tor.com

Tor® is a registered trademark of Tom Doherty Associates, LLC.

ISBN 0-765-34362-2
EAN 978-0765-34362-8

First edition: April 2004
First mass market edition: April 2005

Printed in the United States of America

0 9 8 7 6 5 4 3 2 1

Dramatis Personae
(* shows viewpoint character)

ALGARVE

Adonio	Constable in Tricarico
Almonte	Major; sorcerer near Pontremoli
Balastro	Count; Algarvian minister to Zuwayza
Bembo*	Constable in Eoforwic
Botelho	Mage in Ruuivaes, Lagoas
Clarinda	Serving woman in Trapani
Dosso	Jeweler in Trapani
Fiametta	Courtesan in Tricarico
Frontino	Gaoler in Tricarico
Gismonda	Count Sabrino's wife in Trapani
Lurcanio*	Colonel formerly occupying Priekule
Mainardo	Former King of Jelgava; Mezentio's brother
Mezentio	King of Algarve
Mosco	Captain in Priekule; Brindza's father
Norizia	Baroness; Gismonda's friend in Trapani
Oberto	Baron; mayor of Carsoli
Oldrade	General in Trapani
Oraste	Constable in Eoforwic
Orosio	Captain of dragonfliers outside Psinthos
Pesaro	Constabulary sergeant in Tricarico
Pirello	Mage in Trapani
Prusione	General in southern Algarve
Puliano	Lieutenant in Plegmund's Brigade in Yanina
Sabrino	Count and colonel of dragonfliers outside Psinthos
Saffa	Sketch artist in Tricarico
Salamone	Soldier; father to Saffa's son
Santerno	Captain in western Valmiera

Sasso	Constabulary captain in Tricarico
Spinello*	Colonel in Eoforwic
Tibiano	Injured civilian in Tricarico

FORTHWEG

Aldhelm	Bodyguard in Gromheort
Beornwulf	King of Forthweg
Brorda	Baron in Gromheort
Ceorl*	Soldier in Plegmund's Brigade in Valmiera
Conberge	Ealstan's sister in Gromheort
Doldasai	Courtesan in Gromheort
Ealstan*	Bookkeeper in Eoforwic; Vanai's husband
Elfryth	Ealstan's mother in Gromheort
Ethelhelm	Musician in Eoforwic
Grimbald	Conberge's husband in Gromheort
Hengist	Hestan's brother in Gromheort
Hestan	Bookkeeper in Gromheort; Ealstan's father
Kaudavas	Kaunian refugee in Zuwayza
Nemunas	Kaunian refugee in Zuwayza
Osferth	Official in Gromheort
Penda	King of Forthweg; in exile in Lagoas
Pernavai	Kaunian in Valmiera; Vatsyunas' husband
Pybba	Pottery merchant in Eoforwic
Saxburh	Ealstan and Vanai's daughter in Eoforwic
Sidroc*	Soldier in Plegmund's Brigade in Yanina
Tamulis	Kaunian from Oyngestun in Gromheort
Trumwine	Forthwegian minister to Zuwayza
Vanai*	Kaunian in Eoforwic; Ealstan's wife
Vatsyunas	Kaunian in Valmiera; Pernavai's husband
Vitols	Kaunian refugee in Zuwayza

GYONGYOS

Alpri	Istvan's father in Kunhegyes; cobbler
Arpad	Ekrekek (ruler) of Gyongyos
Balazas	Ekrekek Arpad's Eye and Ear in Gyorvar
Batthyany	Istvan's great-uncle in Kunhegyes; deceased

Diosgyor	Corporal near Gyorvar
Frigyes	Captain; captive on island of Obuda; deceased
Gizella	Istvan's mother in Kunhegyes
Gul	Baker's son in Kunhegyes; Saria's fiancé
Horthy	Gyongyosian minister to Zuwayza
Ilona	Istvan's sister in Kunhegyes
Istvan*	Sergeant; captive on island of Obuda
Korosi	Sentry in Kunhegyes
Kun	Corporal; captive on island of Obuda
Maleter	Villager in Kunhegyes
Petofi	Captain in Gyorvar
Saria	Istvan's sister in Kunhegyes
Szonyi	Captive on island of Obuda; deceased
Vorosmarty	Mage near Gyorvar

JELGAVA

Ausra	Talsu's sister in Skrunda
Donalitu	King of Jelgava
Gailisa	Talsu's wife in Skrunda
Krogzmu	Olive-oil dealer in Skrunda
Kugu	Silversmith in Skrunda; deceased
Laitsina	Talsu's mother in Skrunda
Mindaugu	Wine merchant in Skrunda
Pumpru	Grocer in Skrunda
Talsu*	Tailor in Skrunda
Traku	Tailor in Skrunda; Talsu's father

KUUSAMO

Alkio	Theoretical sorcerer in Naantali district; Raahe's wife
Elimaki	Pekka's sister in Kajaani
Heikki	Professor of sorcery, Kajaani City College
Ilmarinen*	Theoretical sorcerer in Naantali district
Juhainen	One of the Seven Princes of Kuusamo
Lammi	Forensic sorcerer on the island of Obuda

Leino*	Sorcerer in Jelgava
Linna	Serving girl in Naantali district
Nortamo	Grand general in Jelgava
Olavin	Elimaki's estranged husband
Paalo	Sorcerer in Ludza, Jelgava
Pekka*	Theoretical sorcerer in Naantali district; Leino's wife
Piilis	Theoretical sorcerer in Naantali district
Raahe	Theoretical sorcerer in Naantali district; Alkio's husband
Ryti	Language instructor in Yliharma
Tukiainen	Kuusaman minister to Jelgava
Uto	Pekka and Leino's son in Kajaani
Valamo	Tailor in Yliharma
Waino	Captain of the *Searaven*

LAGOAS

Araujo	Marshal in southern Algarve
Brinco	Grandmaster Pinhiero's secretary
Fernao	Theoretical sorcerer in Naantali district
Pinhiero	Grandmaster of the Lagoan Guild of Mages
Sampaio	Fernao's uncle in Kajaani
Simao	Major in Algarve
Xavega	Sorcerer in Jelgava

UNKERLANT

Addanz	Archmage of Unkerlant
Akerin	Alize's father in Leiferde
Alize	Peasant girl in Leiferde
Andelot	Lieutenant near Eoforwic
Ansovald	Unkerlanter minister to Zuwayza
Bertrude	Alize's mother in Leiferde
Curneval	Soldier near Gromheort
Dagaric	Captain in western Unkerlant
Dagulf	Peasant in Linnich
Drogden	Captain in Yanina

Garivald*	Sergeant near Eoforwic
Gurmun	General of behemoths near Eoforwic
Joswe	Soldier in Gromheort
Leudast*	Lieutenant in Yanina
Leuvigild	General in Eoforwic
Merovec	Colonel in Cottbus; Rathar's adjutant
Noyt	Soldier near Trapani
Obilot	Peasant woman near Linnich
Rathar*	Marshal of Unkerlant in Patras
Swemmel	King of Unkerlant
Vatran	General in Patras

VALMIERA

Baldu	Algarvian collaborator near Carsoli; playwright
Bauska	Serving woman in Priekule
Brindza	Bauska's daughter in Priekule
Enkuru	Collaborationist count near Pavilosta; deceased
Gainibu	King of Valmiera
Gainibu	Krasta's son
Gedominu	Merkela's first husband; deceased
Gedominu	Skarnu and Merkela's son
Krasta*	Marchioness in Priekule; Skarnu's sister
Kudirka	Midwife in Priekule
Latsisa	Peasant woman near Pavilosta
Marstalu	Duke of Klaipeda
Merkela	Underground member in Priekule; Skarnu's fiancée
Povilu	Peasant near Adutiskis
Raunu	Sergeant near Pavilosta
Sigulda	Algarvian collaborator near Carsoli; Smetnu's companion
Simanu	Collaborationist count near Pavilosta; deceased
Skarnu*	Marquis in Priekule
Skirgaila	Woman in Priekule

Smetnu	Algarvian collaborator near Carsoli; editor
Sudaku	Soldier in Phalanx of Valmiera in Yanina
Valmiru	Butler in Priekule
Valnu	Viscount and underground member in Priekule
Vizgantu	Major in southern Algarve
Zemaitu	Peasant near Pavilosta
Zemglu	Peasant near Adutiskis

YANINA

Iskakis	Yaninan minister to Zuwayza
Mantzaros	General in Patras
Tassi	Iskakis' wife; Hajjaj's companion
Tsavellas	King of Yanina
Varvakis	Merchant in Patras

ZUWAYZA

Hajjaj*	Foreign minister of Zuwayza in Bishah
Ikhshid	General in Bishah
Kawar	Crystallomancer in Bishah
Kolthoum	Hajjaj's senior wife
Lalla	Hajjaj's former junior wife
Maryem	Palace servant in Bishah
Mundhir	Captain in Bishah
Qutuz	Hajjaj's secretary
Shazli	King of Zuwayza
Tewfik	Hajjaj's majordomo

OUT OF THE
DARKNESS

Great Northern Sea

E Q U A T

West

ZUWAYZA

Cape Hadh Far's

BISHAH
NAJRAN
SAMAWA
Wadi Ugeiqa
JURDHAN
Bay of Ajlun
SAB ABAR
GLOGAU

UNKERLANT

Elsung/Kisung Mts.

Kleis R.
Regen R.
WIRDUN
EOFORWIC
WIHTGARA
HWINCA
VOLKACH
ONGESTUN
GROMHEORT
TRICA
SOMMERDA
PEREUM
WALDSOLMS
GOZZO
PFREIMD
UBACH
COTTIGGORO
WRIELEN
GOLDAP
HWITERNE
DORO
LAUTERTAL
MIDLUM
FORTHWEG
LEHESTEN
ALGAR
Cottbus R.
COTTBUS
TANNRODA
THALFANG
ORTAH
AVA
ASPANG
Yf. Rugen
GYONGYOS
D
E
I
R
TRAPANI
KUNHEGYE
HAGENOW
Bfe. Rottum
JANINA
GYOVAR
PA
DUBSWALDEN
ELTHWIM
FORK
HOHENRODA
WEINBERGE
LEIFERDE
D
PRESSECK
BRANNA
OSGINCH
PLUNG
PILNU
ANDLAU
LOHR
PIANKENFELS
BALATON ISLANDS
GULINGEN
KUFTU
PATRAS
TOLK
MANDELSLO
MAUROMOUN
PRAMSEN
Mamming Hills
DUCHY of
GRELZ
RYSUM
Narrow Sea
LAND of the ICE PEOPLE
HESHBON
Barrier Mountains

One

Ealstan intended to kill an Algarvian officer. Had the young Forthwegian not been fussy about which redhead he killed, or had he not cared whether he lived or died in the doing, he would have had an easier time of it. But, with a wife and daughter to think about, he wanted to get away with it if he could. He'd even promised Vanai he wouldn't do anything foolish. He regretted that promise now, but he'd always been honorable to the point of stubbornness, so he still felt himself bound by it.

And he wanted to rid the world of one of Mezentio's men in particular. Oh, he would have been delighted to see all of them dead, but he especially wanted to be the means by which this one died. *Considering what the whoreson did to Vanai, and made her do for him, who could blame me?*

But, like a lot of rhetorical questions, that one had an obvious, unrhetorical answer: *all the other Algarvians in Eoforwic.* The Algarvians ruled the capital of Forthweg with a mailed fist these days. Ealstan had been part of the uprising that almost threw them out of Eoforwic. As in most things, though, almost wasn't good enough; he counted himself lucky to remain among the living.

Saxburh smiled and gurgled at him from her cradle as he walked by. The baby seemed proud of cutting a new tooth. Ealstan was glad she'd finally done it, too. She'd been fussy and noisy for several nights before it broke through. Ealstan yawned; he and Vanai had lost sleep because of that.

His wife was in the kitchen, building up the fire to boil barley for porridge. "I'm off," Ealstan said. "No work for a bookkeeper in Eoforwic these days, but plenty for someone with a strong back."

Vanai gave him a knotted cloth. "Here's cheese and olives and an onion," she said. "I only wish it were more."

"It'll do," he said. "I'm not starving." He told the truth. He was hungry, but everyone in Eoforwic except some—not all—of the Algarvians was hungry these days. He still had his strength. To do a laborer's work, he needed it, too. Wagging a finger at her, he added, "Make sure you've got enough for yourself. You're nursing the baby."

"Don't worry about me," Vanai said. "I'll do fine, and so will Saxburh." She leaned toward him to kiss him goodbye.

As their lips brushed, her face changed—literally. Her eyes went from brown to blue-gray, her skin from swarthy to pale, her nose from proud and hooked to short and straight. Her hair stayed dark, but that was because it was dyed—he could see the golden roots, which he hadn't been able to do a moment before. She seemed suddenly taller and slimmer, too: not stubby and broad-shouldered like most Forthwegians, including Ealstan himself.

He finished the kiss. Nothing, as far as he was concerned, was more important than that. Then he said, "Your masking spell just slipped."

Her mouth twisted in annoyance. Then she shrugged. "I knew I was going to have to renew it pretty soon, anyhow. As long as it happens inside the flat, it's not so bad."

"Not bad at all," Ealstan said, and gave her another kiss. As she smiled, he went on, "I like the way you look just fine, regardless of whether you seem like a Forthwegian or a Kaunian. You know that."

Vanai nodded, but her smile slipped instead of getting bigger as he'd hoped. "Not many do," she said. "Most Forthwegians have no use for me, and the Algarvians would cut my throat to use my life energy against Unkerlant if they saw me the way I really am. I suppose there are other Kaunians here, but how would I know? If they want to stay alive, they have to stay hidden, the same as I do."

Ealstan remembered the golden roots he'd seen. "You should dye your hair again, too. It's growing out."

"Aye, I know. I'll take care of it," Vanai promised. One way the Algarvians checked to see whether someone was a sorcerously disguised Kaunian was by pulling out a few hairs and seeing if they turned yellow when removed from the suspect's scalp. Ordinary hair dye countered that. The

Algarvians being who and what they were, thoroughness in such matters paid off; Vanai kept the hair between her legs dark, too.

Carrying his meager lunch, Ealstan went downstairs and out onto the street. The two blocks of flats across from his own were only piles of rubble these days. The Algarvians had smashed both of them during the Forthwegian uprising. Ealstan thanked the powers above that his own building had survived. It was, he knew, only luck.

A Forthwegian man in a threadbare knee-length tunic scrabbled through the wreckage across the street, looking for wood or whatever else he could find. He stared up in alarm at Ealstan, his mouth a wide circle of fright in the midst of his shaggy gray beard and mustache. Ealstan waved; like everyone else in Eoforwic, he'd spent his share of time guddling through ruins, too. The shaggy man relaxed and waved back.

Not a lot of people were on the streets: only a handful, compared to the days before the uprising and before the latest Unkerlanter advance stalled—or was allowed to stall?—in Eoforwic's suburbs on the west bank of the Twegen River. Ealstan cocked his head to one side. He didn't hear many eggs bursting. King Swemmel's soldiers, there on the far bank of the Twegen, were taking it easy on Eoforwic today.

His boots squelched in mud. Fall and winter were the rainy season in Eoforwic, as in the rest of Forthweg. *At least I won't have to worry much about snow, the way the Unkerlanters would if they were back home,* Ealstan thought.

He spotted a mushroom, pale against the dark dirt of another muddy patch, and stooped to pick it. Like all Forthwegians, like all the Kaunians in Forthweg—and emphatically unlike the Algarvian occupiers—he was wild for mushrooms of all sorts. He suddenly shook his head and straightened up. He was wild for mushrooms of almost all sorts. This one, though, could stay where it was. He knew a destroying power when he saw one. His father Hestan, back in Gromheort, had used direct and often painful methods to make sure he could tell a good mushroom from a poisonous one.

I wish the redheads liked mushrooms, he thought. *Maybe one of them would pick that one and kill himself.*

Algarvians directed Forthwegians hauling rubble to shore up the defenses against the Unkerlanter attack everyone in the city knew was coming. Forthwegian women in armbands of blue and white—Hilde's Helpers, they called themselves—brought food to the redheads, but not to their countrymen, who were working harder. Ealstan scowled at the women. They were the female equivalent of the men of Plegmund's Brigade: Forthwegians who fought for King Mezentio of Algarve. His cousin Sidroc fought in Plegmund's Brigade if he hadn't been killed yet. Ealstan hoped he had.

Instead of joining the Forthwegian laborers as he often did, Ealstan turned away toward the center of town. He hadn't been there for a while: not since he and a couple of other Forthwegians teamed up to assassinate an Algarvian official. They'd worn Algarvian uniforms to do it, and they'd been otherwise disguised, too.

Back then, the redheads had held only a slender corridor into the heart of Eoforwic—but enough, curse them, to use to bring in reinforcements. Now the whole city was theirs again . . . at least, until such time as the Unkerlanters chose to try to run them out. Ealstan had a demon of a time finding the particular abandoned building he was looking for. "It has to be around here somewhere," he muttered. But where? Eoforwic had taken quite a pounding since he'd last come to these parts.

If this doesn't work, I'll think of something else, he told himself. Still, this had to be his best chance. *There* was the building: farther into Eoforwic than he'd recalled. It didn't look much worse than it had when he and his pals ducked into it to change from Algarvian tunics and kilts to Forthwegian-style long tunics. Ealstan ducked inside. The next obvious question was whether anyone had stolen the uniforms he and his comrades had abandoned.

Why would anybody? he wondered. Forthwegians didn't, wouldn't, wear kilts, any more than their Unkerlanter cousins would. Ealstan didn't think anybody could get much for selling the clothes. And so, with a little luck . . .

He felt like shouting when he saw the uniforms still lying

where they'd been thrown when he and his friends got rid of them. He picked up the one he'd worn. It was muddier and grimier than it had been: rain and dirt and dust had had their way with it. But a lot of Algarvians in Eoforwic these days wore uniforms that had known better years. Ealstan held it up and nodded. He could get away with it.

He pulled his own tunic off over his head, then got into the Algarvian clothes. The high, tight collar was as uncomfortable as he remembered. His tunic went into the pack. He took from his belt pouch first a small stick, then a length of dark brown yarn and another of red. He twisted them together and began a chant in classical Kaunian. His spell that would temporarily disguise him as an Algarvian was modeled after the one Vanai had created to let her—and other Kaunians—look like the Forthwegian majority and keep Mezentio's men from seizing them.

When Ealstan looked at himself, he could see no change. Even a mirror wouldn't have helped. That was the sorcery's drawback. Only someone else could tell you if it had worked—and you found out the hard way if it wore off at the wrong time. He plucked at his beard. It was shaggier than Algarvians usually wore theirs. They often went in for side whiskers and imperials and waxed mustachios. But a lot of them were more unkempt than they had been, too. He thought he could get by with the impersonation—provided the spell had worked.

Only one way to learn, he thought again. He strode out of the building. He hadn't gone more than half a block before two Algarvian troopers walked by. They both saluted. One said, "Good morning, Lieutenant." Ealstan returned the salute without answering. He spoke some Algarvian, but with a sonorous Forthwegian accent.

He shrugged—then shrugged again, turning it into a production, as Algarvians were wont to do with any gesture. He'd passed the test. Now he had several hours in which to hunt down that son of a whore of a Spinello. The stick he carried was more likely to be a robber's weapon than a constable's or an officer's, but that didn't matter so much these days, either. If a stick blazed, Mezentio's men would use it.

Algarvian soldiers saluted him. He saluted officers.

Forthwegians gave him sullen looks. No one paid much attention to him. He hurried west toward the riverfront, looking like a man on important business. And so he was: that was where he'd seen Spinello. He could lure the redhead away, blaze him, and then use a counterspell to turn back into his proper self in moments.

He could . . . if he could find Spinello. The fellow stood out in a crowd. He was a bantam rooster of a man, always crowing, always bragging. But he wasn't where Ealstan had hoped and expected him to be. Had the Unkerlanters killed him? *How would I ever know?* Ealstan thought. *I want to make sure he's dead. And who has a better right to kill him than I do?*

"Where's the old man?" one redheaded footsoldier asked another.

"Colonel Spinello?" the other soldier returned. The first man nodded. Ealstan pricked up his ears. The second Algarvian said, "He went over to one of the officers' brothels by the palace, the lucky bastard. Said he had a meeting somewhere later on, so he might as well have some fun first. If it's anything important, you could hunt him up, I bet."

"Nah." The first redhead made a dismissive gesture. "He asked me to let him know how my sister was doing—she got hurt when those stinking Kuusamans dropped eggs on Trapani. My father writes that she'll pull through. I'll tell him when I see him, that's all."

"That's good," the second soldier said. "Glad to hear it."

Ealstan turned away in frustration. He wouldn't get Spinello today. Braving an Algarvian officers' brothel was beyond him, even if murder wasn't. He also found himself surprised to learn Spinello cared about his men and their families. But then he thought, *Well, why shouldn't he? It's not as if they were Kaunians.*

For four years and more, the west wing of the mansion on the outskirts of Priekule had housed the Algarvians who administered the capital of Valmiera for the redheaded conquerors. No more. Occupying it these days were Marquis Skarnu; his fiancée, Merkela; and Gedominu, their son, who was just starting to pull himself upright.

Skarnu's sister, Marchioness Krasta, still lived in the east wing, as she had all through the occupation. She'd had an Algarvian colonel warming her bed all through the occupation, too, but she loudly insisted the baby she was carrying belonged to Viscount Valnu, who'd been an underground leader. Valnu didn't disagree with her, either, worse luck. That kept Skarnu from throwing Krasta out of the mansion on her shapely backside.

He had to content himself with seeing his sister as little as he could. A couple of times, he'd also had to keep Merkela from marching into the east wing and wringing Krasta's neck. The Algarvians had taken Merkela's first husband hostage and blazed him; she hated collaborators even more than redheads.

"We don't know everything," Skarnu said, not for the first time.

"We know enough," Merkela answered with peasant directness. "All right, so she slept with Valnu, too. But she let the redhead futter her for as long as he was here. She has to pay the price."

"No one ever said she didn't. No one ever said she won't." While Skarnu was out in the provinces, he'd got used to thinking of himself as being without a sister after he'd learned that Krasta was keeping company with her Algarvian colonel. Finding things weren't quite so simple jolted him, too. He sighed and added, "We're not quite sure what the price should be, that's all."

"*I'm* sure." But Merkela grimaced and turned away. She didn't sound sure, not even to herself. Doing her best to recover the fierceness she'd had when fighting Algarve seemed futile, she brushed blond hair back from her face and said, "She deserves worse than this. This is nothing."

"We can't be too hard on her, not when we don't know for certain whose baby it is," Skarnu said. They'd had that argument before, too.

Before they could get deeply into it again, someone knocked on the door to their bedchamber. Skarnu went to open it with more than a little relief. The butler, Valmiru, bowed to him. "Your Excellency, a gentleman from the palace to see you and your, ah, companion." He wasn't used to having Merkela in the mansion, not anywhere close to it, and treated her as he might have treated any other dangerous wild animal.

Her blue eyes widened now. "From the palace?" she breathed. Gentlemen from the palace were not in the habit of calling on farms outside the hamlet of Pavilosta.

"Indeed," Valmiru said. His eyes were blue, too, like those of Merkela, of Skarnu, and of almost all folk of Kaunian blood, but a blue frosty rather than fiery. Over the years, his hair had faded almost imperceptibly from Kaunian blond toward white.

Merkela pushed at Skarnu. "Go see what the fellow wants."

"I know one thing he wants," Skarnu said. "He wants to see both of us." When Merkela hung back, he took her hand, adding, "You weren't afraid to face the redheads when they were blazing at you. Come on." Merkela glanced toward Gedominu, but the baby offered her no excuse to hang back: he lay asleep in his cradle. Rolling her eyes up to the ceiling like a frightened unicorn, she went with Skarnu.

"Good day, your Excellency, milady." The man from the royal palace bowed first to Skarnu and then, just as deeply, to Merkela. He was handsome and dapper, his tunic and trousers too tight to be quite practical. Skarnu had outfits like that, but he'd come to appreciate comfort in his own time on a farm. Merkela's tunics and trousers were all of the practical sort needed if one were to do actual work in them. Instead of working, the functionary handed Skarnu a sealed envelope, then bowed again.

"What have we here?" Skarnu murmured, and opened it. Someone who practiced elegant calligraphy instead of working had written, *To the Marquis Skarnu and the Lady Merkela: the pleasure of your company is requested by his Majesty, King Gainibu of Valmiera, at a reception this evening to honor those who upheld Valmieran courage during the dark days of occupation.*

"I trust you will come?" the palace functionary said.

Skarnu nodded, but Merkela asked a question that sounded all the sharper for being so nervous: "Is Krasta invited?" She gave Skarnu's sister no title whatever.

Voice bland, the functionary replied, "This is the only invitation I was charged to bring here." Valmiru sighed when he heard that. All the servants would hear it in short order. So would Krasta, and that was liable to be ugly.

But Merkela nodded as sharply as if her family had been noble for ten generations. "Then we'll be there," she declared. The functionary bowed and departed. Only after the butler had closed the door behind him did Merkela let out something that sounded very much like a wail: "But what am I going to *wear*?"

"Go out. Go shopping," Skarnu said—even he, a mere man, could see why she might be worried.

But he couldn't guess how worried she was. In something like despair, Merkela cried, "But how do I know what people wear to the palace? I don't want to look like a fool, and I don't want to look like a whore, either."

Valmiru coughed to draw her notice, then said, "You might do well to take someone who is knowledgeable in such matters with you—Bauska, perhaps."

"Bauska?" Merkela exclaimed. "With her half-Algarvian bastard?"

"She's Krasta's maidservant," Skarnu said. "She knows clothes better than anyone else here."

"She knows what I think of her, too," Merkela said. "She'd probably get me to buy something ugly just for spite."

"Whatever she suggests, bring it back and try it on for me first," Skarnu said. "I know enough not to let that happen. But Bauska's the best person you could choose . . . unless you wanted to go out with Krasta?" As he'd thought it would, that made Merkela violently shake her head. It also persuaded her to go out with the maidservant. Skarnu hadn't been so sure that would happen.

Gedominu woke up while his mother was on her expedition to Priekule. Proving he'd been away from his servants for a long time, Skarnu changed him himself and fed him little bits of bread. The baby hummed happily while he ate. Skarnu wished he himself were so easy to amuse.

A peremptory knock on the door warned him he was

about to be anything but amused. He thought about ignoring it, but that wouldn't do. Sure enough, Krasta stood in the hallway. Without preamble, she said, "What's this I hear about you and . . . that woman going to the palace tonight?"

"It's true," Skarnu answered. "His Majesty invited both of us."

"Why didn't he invite *me*?" his sister demanded. Both her voice and the line of her jaw seemed particularly hard and unyielding.

"I have no idea," Skarnu said. "Why don't you ask him the next time you see him?" And then, his own temper boiling over, he asked, "Will he recognize you if you're not on an Algarvian's arm?"

"Futter you," Krasta said crisply. She turned and stalked away. Skarnu resisted the impulse to give her a good boot in the rear to speed her passage. *She* is *pregnant,* he reminded himself.

"Dada!" Gedominu said, and Skarnu's grim mood lightened. His son made him remember what was really important.

When Merkela returned festooned with boxes and packages, he waited to see what she'd bought, then clapped his hands together. The turquoise tunic and black trousers set off her eyes, emphasized her shape without going too far, and made the most of her suntanned skin. "You're beautiful," Skarnu said. "I've known it for years. Now everyone else will, too."

Despite her tan, she turned red. "Nonsense," she said, or a coarse, back-country phrase that meant the same thing. "Everyone at the court will sneer at me." Skarnu answered with the same coarse phrase. Merkela blinked and then laughed.

On the way to the palace, she snarled whenever she saw a woman shaved bald or with hair growing out after a shaving: the mark of many who'd collaborated horizontally. "I wonder if Viscount Valnu will have his hair shaved, too," Skarnu remarked.

Merkela gave him a scandalized look. "Whatever he did, he did for the kingdom."

"I *know* Valnu," Skarnu told her. "He may have done it

for the kingdom, but that doesn't mean he didn't enjoy every minute of it." Merkela clucked but didn't answer.

When they pulled up in front of the palace, Skarnu handed Merkela down, though he knew she was used to descending for herself. The driver took out a flask with which to keep himself warm. A flunky checked Skarnu and Merkela's names off a list. "Go down this corridor," the fellow said, pointing. "The reception will be in the Grand Hall."

"The Grand Hall," Merkela murmured. Her eyes were already enormous. They got bigger with every step she took along the splendid corridor. "This is like something out of a romance, or a fairy tale."

"It's real enough. It's where King Gainibu declared war on Algarve," Skarnu said. "I didn't see him do it; I'd already been called to my regiment. But the kingdom didn't live happily ever after, I'll tell you that."

At the entry to the Grand Hall, another flunky in a fancy uniform called out, "Marquis Skarnu and the Lady Merkela!" Merkela turned red again. Skarnu watched her eyeing the women already in the Grand Hall. And, a moment later, he watched her back straighten as she realized she wasn't out of place after all as far as looks and clothes went.

Skarnu took her arm. "Come on," he said, and steered her toward the receiving line. "Time for the king to meet you." That flustered her anew. He added, "Remember, this is why he invited you."

Merkela nodded, but nervously. The line moved slowly, which gave her the chance to get back some of her composure. Even so, she squeezed Skarnu's hand and whispered, "I don't believe this is really happening."

Before Skarnu could answer, the two of them stood before the king. Gainibu had aged more than the years that lay between now and the last time Skarnu saw him; the red veins in his nose said he'd pickled as well as aged. But his grip was firm as he clasped Skarnu's hand, and he spoke clearly enough: "A pleasure, your Excellency. And your charming companion is—?"

"My fiancée, your Majesty," Skarnu answered. "Merkela of Pavilosta."

"Your Majesty," Merkela whispered. Her curtsy was awkward, but it served.

"A pleasure to meet you, milady," the king said, and raised her hand to his lips. "I've seen Skarnu's sister at enough of these functions, but she was always with that Colonel Lurcanio. Some things can't be helped. Still, this is better."

"Thank you, your Majesty," Merkela said. She had her spirit back now, and looked around the Grand Hall as if to challenge anyone to say she didn't belong there. No one did, of course, but anyone who tried would have been sorry.

Skarnu glanced back at Gainibu as he led Merkela away. Gainibu, plainly, had not had an easy time during the Algarvian occupation. Even so, he still remembered how to act like a king.

The dragon farm lay just outside a Yaninan village called Psinthos. Sleet blew into Count Sabrino's face as he trudged toward the farmhouse where he'd rest till it was time to take his wing into the air and throw the dragonfliers at the Unkerlanters yet again. Mostly, the mud squelched under his boots, but it also had a gritty crunch that hadn't been there a couple of days before.

It's starting to freeze up and get hard, Sabrino thought. *That's not so good. It means better footing for behemoths, and that means King Swemmel's soldiers will come nosing forward again. Things have been pretty quiet down here the last couple of days. Nothing wrong with that. I like quiet.*

He opened the door to the farmhouse, then slammed it and barred it to keep the wind from ripping it out of his hands. Then he built up the fire, feeding it wood one of the dragon-handlers had cut. The wood was damp, and smoked when it burned. Sabrino didn't much care. *Maybe it'll smother me,* went through his mind. *Who would care if it did? My wife might, a little. My mistress?* He snorted. His mistress had left him for a younger man, only to discover the other fellow wasn't so inclined to support her in the luxury to which she'd been accustomed.

Count Sabrino snorted again. *I wish I could leave me for a younger man.* He was nearer sixty than fifty; he'd fought as a footsoldier in the Six Years' War more than a generation before. He'd started flying dragons because he didn't want to get caught up once more in the great slaughters on the ground, of which he'd seen entirely too many in the last war. And so, in this war, he'd seen plenty of slaughters from the air. It was less of an improvement than he'd hoped.

Smoky or not, the fire was warm. Little by little, the chill began to leach out of Sabrino's bones. *Heading into the fourth winter of the war against Unkerlant.* He shook his head in slow wonder. Who would have imagined *that,* back in the days when Mezentio of Algarve hurtled his army west against Swemmel? One kick and the whole rotten structure of Unkerlant would come crashing down. That was what the Algarvians had thought then. They'd learned some hard lessons since.

Joints clicking, Sabrino got to his feet. *I had a flask somewhere.* He thumped his forehead with the heel of his hand. *I really am getting old if I can't remember where.* He snapped his fingers. "In the bedding—that's right," he said aloud, as if talking to himself weren't another sign of too many years.

When he found the flask, it felt lighter than it should have. Of that he had no doubt whatever. *If that dragonhandler gives me wood, I don't suppose I can begrudge him a knock of spirits.* He yanked out the stopper and poured down a knock himself. The spirits were Yaninan: anise-flavored and strong as a demon.

"Ah," Sabrino said. Fire spread outward from his belly. He nodded, slowly and deliberately. *I'm going to live. I may even decide I want to.*

At that, he was better off than a lot of Algarvian footsoldiers. Psinthos was far enough behind the line to be out of range of Unkerlanter egg-tossers. How long that would last with the ground freezing, he couldn't guess, but it remained true for the time being. And the furs and leather he wore to fly his dragon also helped keep him warm on the ground.

Someone knocked on the door. "Who's there?" Sabrino called.

The answer came in Algarvian, with a chuckle attached: "Well, it's not the king, not today."

King Mezentio *had* visited Sabrino, more than once. He

wished the king hadn't. They didn't see eye to eye, and never would. That was the reason Sabrino, who'd started the war as a colonel and wing commander, had never once been promoted. He opened the door and held out the flask. "Hello, Orosio. Here, have some of this. It'll put hair on your chest."

"Thanks, sir," Captain Orosio said. "Don't mind if I do." The squadron commander drank while Sabrino shut the door. After drinking, Orosio made a horrible face. "Burn the hair off my chest, more likely. But still, better bad spirits than none at all." He took another swig.

"What can I do for you?" Sabrino asked.

"Feels like a freeze is coming," Orosio said as he walked over to stand in front of the fire. He was in his late thirties, almost as old for a captain as Sabrino was for a colonel. Part of that came from serving under Sabrino—a man under a cloud naturally put his subordinates under one, too. And part of it sprang from Orosio's own background: he'd had barely enough noble blood to make officer's rank, and not enough to get promoted.

But that didn't mean he was stupid, and it didn't mean he was wrong. "I thought the same thing myself, walking back here after we landed," Sabrino said. "If the ground firms up—and especially if the rivers start freezing over—the Unkerlanters will move."

"Aye," Orosio said. The single word hung in the air, a shadow of menace. Orosio turned so that he faced east, back toward Algarve. "We haven't got a lot of room left to play with, sir, not any more. Before long, Swemmel's bastards are going to crash right on into our kingdom."

"Unless we stop them and throw them back," Sabrino said.

"Aye, sir. Unless." Those words hung in the air, too. Orosio didn't believe it.

Sabrino sighed. He didn't blame his squadron commander. How could he, when he didn't believe it, either? The Derlavaian War was far and away the greatest fight the world had ever known—big enough to dwarf the Six Years' War, which the young Sabrino who'd served in the earlier struggle would never have imagined possible at the time—

and Algarve, barring a miracle, or several miracles, looked to be on the losing end of it, just as she had before.

King Mezentio promised miracles: miracles of sorcery that would throw back not only the Unkerlanters but also the Kuusamans and Lagoans in the east. So far, Sabrino had seen only promises, not miracles. Mezentio couldn't even make peace; things being as they were, no one was willing to make peace with him.

What did, what could, a soldier trapped in a losing war do? Sabrino strode over and set a hand on Orosio's shoulder. "My dear fellow, we have to keep doing the best we can, for our own honor's sake if nothing else," he said. "What other choice have we? What else is there?"

Orosio nodded. "Nothing else, sir. I know that. It's only . . . There's not a lot of honor left to save any more, either, is there?"

After we started massacring Kaunians to gain the sorcerous energy we needed to beat Unkerlant? After we mixed modern sophisticated sorcery and ancient barbarism and still didn't get everything we wanted because Swemmel was willing to be every bit as savage as we were and an extra six inches besides? No wonder no one wants to make peace with us. I wouldn't, if I were our enemies.

But he couldn't tell Orosio that. He said what he could: "You know my views, Captain. You also know that no one of rank higher than mine pays the least attention to them. Let me have that flask again. If I drink enough, maybe I won't care."

He hadn't even raised it to his lips, though, when someone else knocked on the door. He opened it and discovered a crystallomancer shivering there. The mage said, "Sir, I just got word from the front. Unkerlanter artificers are trying to throw a bridge over the Skamandros River. If they do . . ."

"There'll be big trouble," Sabrino finished for him. The crystallomancer nodded. Sabrino asked, "Aren't there any dragons closer and less worn than this poor, miserable wing? We just came in from another mission, you know."

"Of course, sir," the crystallomancer said. "But no, sir, there aren't. You know how thin we're stretched these days."

"Don't I just?" Sabrino turned back to Orosio. "Do you think we can get them into the air again, Captain?"

"I suppose so, sir," the squadron commander answered. "Powers above help us if the Unkerlanters hit us with fresh beasts while we're in the air, though—or even the Yaninans."

"Or even the Yaninans," Sabrino echoed with a sour smile. Tsavellas' small kingdom lay between Algarve and Unkerlant. He'd taken Yanina into the Derlavaian War as Algarve's ally—not that Yaninan soldiers had covered themselves with glory on the austral continent or in Unkerlant. And, when Unkerlanter soldiers poured into Yanina, Tsavellas had switched sides with revoltingly good timing. With another sour smile, Sabrino went on, "As we said, we have to do what we can. Let's go do it."

His dragon-handler squawked in dismay when he reappeared. His dragon screamed in brainless fury—the only kind it had—when he took his place once more at the base of its long, scaly neck. More handlers brought a couple of eggs to fasten under its belly. It didn't claw at them, though Sabrino couldn't figure out why.

"Keep feeding it," he told the handler, who tossed the dragon chunks of meat covered with crushed brimstone and cinnabar to make it flame hotter and farther. Algarve was desperately short of cinnabar these days. Sabrino wondered what his kingdom would do when it ran out altogether. *What will we do? We'll do without, that's what.*

Before long, all twenty-one dragonfliers were aboard their mounts. The wing had a paper strength of sixty-four, and hadn't been anywhere close to it since the opening days of the war against Unkerlant. *Stretched too thin,* Sabrino thought again. He nodded to the handler, who undid the chain that held the dragon to an iron stake. Sabrino whacked the beast with an iron-tipped goad. With another scream of fury, the dragon sprang into the air, batwings thundering. The rest of the men he led followed, each dragon painted in a different pattern of Algarve's green, red, and white.

With low clouds overhead, the wing had to stay close to the ground if it wanted to find its target. *You can't let Unkerlanters gain a bridgehead.* Sabrino knew that as well as every other Algarvian officer. King Swemmel's men were too cursed good at bursting out of such abscesses in the front when they judged the time ripe.

Orosio's image appeared, tiny and perfect, in the crystal Sabrino carried. "There's the bridge, sir," he said. "On the bend of the river, a little north of us."

Sabrino turned his head to the right. "Aye, I see it," he said, and guided his dragon toward it. "The wing will follow me in the attack. With a little luck, the rain will weaken the beams from the Unkerlanters' heavy sticks." They would know the Algarvians had to wreck a bridge if they could, and they would want to stop Mezentio's men from doing it. That meant blazing dragons from the sky, if they could manage it.

As Sabrino guided his dragon into a dive toward the bridge snaking across the Skamandros, the Unkerlanters on the ground did start blazing at him. He was the lead man: he drew the beams. He could hear raindrops and sleet sizzling into steam as beams burned through them. When one passed close, he smelled a breath's worth of lightning in the air. Had it struck . . . But it missed.

Below him, the bridge swelled with startling speed. He released the eggs under his dragon's belly, then urged the beast higher into the air once more. He saw the flashes of sorcerous energy and heard the roars as the eggs burst behind him. More flashes and roars said his dragonfliers were striking the bridge, too.

He twisted in his harness, trying to see what had happened. He let out a whoop on spotting what was left of the bridge: three or four eggs had burst right on it. "You bastards will be a while fixing that!" he shouted, and turned his dragon back toward the farm in what passed for triumph these days. Only eighteen dragons landed with his. The bridge had cost the other two, and the men who flew them. It was, unquestionably, a victory. But how many more such "victories" could Algarve afford before she had no dragonfliers left?

Lieutenant Leudast stared glumly east across the Skamandros River. The river, running harder than usual because of the late-fall rains and not yet ready to freeze over, had stalled Unkerlant's armies longer than its commanders would have wanted. Artificers were supposed to have bridged it by now, but Algarvian dragons had put paid to that. Now the artificers, or those of them the attack from the air hadn't killed, were trying again.

Captain Drogden came up to Leudast. Drogden was a rugged forty; like Leudast himself, he'd seen a lot of war. He headed the regiment of which Leudast commanded a company. Both of them wore hooded capes over their tunics, and both of them had the hoods up to fight the freezing rain. Both of them also wore wool leggings, wool drawers, and stout felt boots. Cold was one thing Unkerlanter warriors knew how to beat.

"Maybe we'll get it across this time," Drogden said, peering through the nasty rain at the artificers at work.

"Maybe." Leudast didn't sound convinced. "But not if the stinking redheads send more dragons and we haven't got any on patrol. That wasn't what you'd call efficient." King Swemmel had tried mightily to make efficiency Unkerlant's watchword. His subjects mouthed his slogans—inspectors made sure of that—but they had a good deal of trouble living up to them.

Captain Drogden rubbed his nose. Like Leudast—like most Unkerlanters—he boasted a fine hooked beak, one that was sometimes vulnerable to cold weather. He said, "I hear there's a new commander at the closest dragon farm. The old commander's gone to a penal battalion."

"Oh," Leudast said, and said no more. Once in a while, the men who fought in a penal battalion escaped it by conspicuous, death-defying heroism. Far more often, they simply died softening up tough Algarvian positions so the soldiers who followed them in the attack got a better chance of success.

"Chief dowser almost went with him," Drogden added.

"Rain must have saved the mage," Leudast said. His superior nodded. Dowsers spotted dragons at long range by sorcerously detecting the motion of their wingbeats. Finding that motion in the midst of millions of raindrops taxed dowsing rods, spells, and the men who used them.

A gang of Yaninan peasants squelched by, carrying timbers for the Unkerlanter artificers and their bridge-building. The Yaninans were as swarthy as Unkerlanters, but they were mostly lean men with long faces, not stocky men with broad cheekbones. They grew bushy mustaches, where Leudast and his countrymen shaved when they got the chance. They wore tight tunics, trousers so tight they were almost leggings, and, absurdly, shoes with pompoms on them. They also wore unhappy expressions at being shepherded along by a couple of Unkerlanter soldiers with sticks.

"Our allies," Leudast said scornfully.

Drogden nodded. "As long as we don't turn our backs on them, anyhow. Powers below eat them for kicking us when we were down, and for getting away with switching sides when they did. We could have smashed them right along with the redheads."

"Probably, sir," Leudast agreed. "But the way I look at it is like this: their whole fornicating kingdom is a penal battalion these days. And they know it, too—look at their faces."

The regimental commander thought about that, then laughed and nodded and slapped Leudast on the back. "A penal kingdom," Drogden said. "I like that, curse me if I don't. You're dead right. King Swemmel will find a way to make them pay."

"Of course he will," Leudast said. Both men took care to speak as if they were paying the king a huge compliment. No one in Unkerlant dared speak of Swemmel any other way. You never could tell who might be listening. One of the oldest sayings in Unkerlant was, *When three men conspire, one is a fool and the other two are royal inspectors.* It held a lot of truth under any king who ruled from Cottbus. Under Swemmel, who'd had to win a civil war against his twin brother before taking the throne, and who scented plots whether they were there or not, it might as well have been a law of nature.

A few eggs burst, perhaps a quarter of a mile away: Algarvian egg-tossers, feeling for the new bridge. The bursts weren't particularly close to it, either. A couple of the Yaninans in the work gang dropped the log they were carrying and made as if to run. One of the soldiers with them blazed a puff of steam from the wet ground in front of them. They probably didn't understand his curses, but that message needed no translation. They picked up the log and went back to work.

"Surprised he didn't blaze 'em," Drogden remarked.

"Aye," Leudast said. "Back when the war was new— when we moved into Forthweg, or we'd just started fighting the Yaninans—I'd've taken cover when I heard bursts that close. I know better than to bother now. Those dumb buggers don't."

"You've been in it from the start?" Drogden asked.

"I sure have, sir," Leudast answered. "Before the start, even—I was fighting the Gongs in the Elsung Mountains, way out west, when Algarve's neighbors declared war on her. I was in Forthweg when the redheads jumped on our back, and I've been trying to kill those whoresons ever since. They've been trying to kill me, too, but they only blazed me twice. Add it all up and I've been pretty lucky."

"Matter of fact, they've got me twice, too," Drogden said. "Once in the leg, and once—" He held up his left hand. Till he did it, Leudast hadn't noticed he was missing the last two joints of that little finger.

"Were you in from the very beginning, too?" Leudast asked him.

"I've been in the army since then, aye, but I only went to the front a year and a half ago," Drogden said.

"Really?" Leudast said. "You don't mind my asking, sir, how did you manage to stay away so long?" *Who kept you safe?* went through his mind. So did, *Who finally got angry enough at you to make you come work for a living like everybody else?*

But Drogden said, "For a long time, I was in charge of one of the big behemoth-breeding farms in the far southwest. It was crazy there, especially after the redheads started overrunning so many of the farms here in the east. We were getting breeding stock and fodder out as best we could, and sending the animals and everything else across the kingdom so we could go on breeding them in places where the enemy's dragons couldn't reach. We did it, aye, but it wasn't easy."

"I believe *that*," Leudast said. There had been plenty of times, the first year and a half of the war, when he'd wondered if the kingdom would hold together. There had been more than a few times when he'd feared it wouldn't. He went on, "You had an important job, sir. What are you doing here?"

With a shrug, Drogden replied, "They replaced me with a man who knew behemoths but who'd lost an arm. He couldn't fight any more, but he could be useful in my old slot. That freed me up to go into battle. Efficiency."

"Efficiency," Leudast echoed. For once, he didn't feel like a hypocrite saying it. The move Captain Drogden described made good sense, even if he might have preferred to stay thousands of miles away from the war. On the other hand . . . "Uh, sir? Why didn't they put you in among the behemoth-riders, if you were in charge of a breeding farm?"

"Actually, I trained as a footsoldier," Drogden answered. "Raising behemoths was the family business. I joined the army because I didn't feel like going into it." He laughed a brief, sardonic laugh. "Things don't always work out the way you plan."

"That's true enough," Leudast agreed. A couple of more Algarvian eggs burst. These were a little closer, but not enough to get excited about. He went on, "If things had worked out the way the redheads planned, they'd have marched into Cottbus before the snow fell that first winter of the war."

"You're right," Drogden said. "From what I've seen, Mezentio's men are almost as smart as they think they are. That makes them pretty cursed dangerous, on account of they really are a pack of smart buggers."

"We've seen *that,* curse them," Leudast said.

His regimental commander nodded. "Sometimes, though, they think they can do more than they really can. That's when we've made 'em pay. And now, by the powers above, they'll pay plenty."

"Aye." Savage hunger filled Leudast's voice. Like almost

all Unkerlanter soldiers who'd seen what the Algarvians had done with—done to—the part of his kingdom they'd occupied, he wanted Algarve to suffer as much or more.

Drogden looked up to the dripping sky. A raindrop hit him in the eye. He rubbed at his face as he said, "I hope the weather stays bad. The worse it is, the more trouble the Algarvians will have hitting that bridge—and however many others we're building across the Skamandros."

"When the bad weather comes, that's always been our time." Leudast started to say something more—to say that, if not for Unkerlant's dreadful winters, the redheads might well have taken Cottbus—but held his tongue. Drogden might have reckoned that criticism of King Swemmel. The fewer chances you took, the fewer risks you ran. Leudast looked across the Skamandros again. Facing the enemy, he had to take chances. Facing his friends, he didn't.

Sunshine greeted him when he woke up the next morning. At first, he took that with a shrug. But then, remembering Captain Drogden's words, he cursed. The business ends of some large number of heavy sticks poked up to the sky on the west bank of the Skamandros. Any Algarvian dragons that did dive on the bridge wouldn't have an easy time of it. Mezentio's dragonfliers hadn't had it easy the last time they attacked, either, but they'd wrecked the bridge.

Leudast ordered his own company forward, all the way up to the edge of the river. The beams from their sticks couldn't blaze a dragon from the sky without the wildest luck, but they might wound or even kill a dragonflier. That was worth trying. "The Algarvians will throw everything they've got at us," he warned his men. "They can't afford to let us get a foothold on the far side of the Skamandros."

As if to underscore his words, a flight of Unkerlanter dragons, all painted the same rock-gray as his uniform tunic and cloak, flew low over the river to pound the Algarvian positions on the eastern side. The soldiers nodded approvingly. If the redheads were catching it, they would have a harder time dishing it out.

And when the Algarvian strike at the bridge came, Leudast didn't even notice it at first. One dragon, flying so high that it seemed only a speck in the sky? He was tempted to laugh at Mezentio's men. A few of the heavy sticks blazed at it. Most didn't bother. They had no real hope of bringing it down, not from that height.

He didn't see the two eggs the dragon dropped, either, not till they fell far enough to make them look larger. "Looks like they'll land on the redheads," one of his men said, pointing. "Serve 'em right, the bastards."

But it did not do to depend on the Algarvians to be fools. As the eggs neared the ground, they suddenly seemed to swerve in midair, and those swerves brought them down square on the bridge over the Skamandros. A long length of it tumbled into the river. "What sort of sorcery is that?" Leudast howled.

He got no answer till that evening, when he put the same question to Captain Drogden. "The redheads have something new there," the regimental commander replied, with what Leudast reckoned commendable calm. "Steering eggs by sorcery is hard even for them, so they don't do it very often, and it doesn't always work."

"It worked here," Leudast said morosely. Drogden nodded. The Unkerlanters stayed on the west bank of the Skamandros a while longer.

Hajjaj was glad to return to Bishah. The Zuwayzi foreign minister was glad he'd been allowed to return to his capital. He was glad Bishah remained the capital of the Kingdom of Zuwayza, and that Unkerlant hadn't chosen to swallow his small, hot homeland after knocking it out of the Derlavaian War. But, most of all, he was glad to have escaped from Cottbus.

"I can understand that, your Excellency," Qutuz, his secretary, said on the day when he returned to King Shazli's palace. "Imagine being stuck in a place where they wear clothes all the time."

"It's not so much that they wear them all the time," Hajjaj replied. Like Qutuz, he was a lean, dark brown man, though his hair and beard were white rather than black. And, like Qutuz, like almost all Zuwayzin, he wore only sandals and sometimes a hat unless meeting with foreigners who would be scandalized at nudity. He groped for words:

"It's that they need to wear them so much of the time, that they would really and truly die if they didn't wear them. Until you've been down to the south, you have no idea what weather can do—none, I tell you."

Qutuz shuddered. "That probably helps make the Unkerlanters what they are."

"I wouldn't be surprised," Hajjaj answered. "Of course, other Derlavaians, ones who don't live where the weather's *quite* so beastly, wear clothes, too. I wouldn't care to guess what that says about them. And the Kuusamans have a climate every bit as beastly as Unkerlant's, and they are, by and large, very nice people. So you never can tell."

"I suppose not," his secretary said, and then, in musing tones, "Kuusamans. We haven't seen many of them in Zuwayza for a while."

"No, indeed," Hajjaj agreed. "A few captives from sunken ships, a few more from leviathans killed off our shores, but otherwise . . ." He shook his head. "We'll have a lot of closed ministries opening up again before long."

"Ansovald is already back at the Unkerlanter ministry," Qutuz observed.

"So he is," Hajjaj said, and let it go at that. He despised the Unkerlanter minister to Zuwayza, who was crude and harsh even by the standards of his kingdom. He'd despised him when Ansovald served here before Unkerlant and Zuwayza went to war, and he'd despised him down in Cottbus, when Ansovald had presented King Swemmel's terms for ending the war to him. Ansovald knew. He didn't care. If anything, he found it funny. That only made Hajjaj despise him more.

"Kuusamans," Qutuz repeated. "Unkerlanters." He sighed, but went on, "Lagoans. Valmierans. Jelgavans. New people to deal with."

"We do what we can. We do what we must," Hajjaj said. "I've heard that Marquis Balastro did safely reach Algarve."

"Good news," Qutuz said, nodding. "I'm glad to hear it, too. Balastro wasn't a bad man, not at all."

"No, he wasn't," Hajjaj agreed, wishing the same could be said of the cause for which Algarve fought.

Having the Algarvian ministry standing empty felt as

strange as imagining the others filled. Not even Hajjaj could blame Swemmel of Unkerlant for requiring Zuwayza to renounce her old ally and cleave to her new ones. He'd never liked many of the things Algarve had done; he'd loathed some of them, and told Balastro so to his face. But any kingdom that could help Zuwayza get revenge against Unkerlant had looked like a reasonable ally. And so . . . and so Zuwayza had gambled. And so Zuwayza had lost.

With a sigh, Hajjaj said, "And now we have to make the best of it." The Unkerlanters had made Zuwayza switch sides. They'd made her yield land, and yield ports for her ships. They'd made her promise to consult with them on issues pertaining to their dealings with other kingdoms—that particularly galled Hajjaj. But they hadn't deposed King Shazli and set up the Reformed Principality of Zuwayza with a puppet prince, as they'd threatened to do during the war. They hadn't deposed Shazli and set up Ansovald as governor in Bishah, either. However much Hajjaj disliked Swemmel and his countrymen, they might have done worse than they had.

And they would have, if they weren't still fighting hard against Algarve—and not quite so hard against Gyongyos, Hajjaj thought. *Well, if they've chosen to be sensible, I won't complain.*

One of the king's serving women came into the office and curtsied to Hajjaj. "May it please your Excellency, his Majesty would confer with you," she said. But for some beads and bracelets and rings, she wore no more than Hajjaj and Qutuz. Hajjaj noticed her nudity more than he would have if he hadn't just come from a kingdom where women shrouded themselves in baggy, ankle-length tunics.

"Thank you, Maryem," he replied. "I'll come, of course."

He followed her to Shazli's private audience chamber. He enjoyed following her; she was well-made and shapely. *But I don't stare like the pale-skinned foreigners who drape themselves,* he thought. *We may scandalize them, but who really has the more barbarous way of looking at things?* He chuckled to himself. If he hadn't studied at the University of Trapani in Algarve, such a notion probably never would have occurred to him.

"Your Majesty," he murmured, bowing as he came into King Shazli's presence.

"Always a pleasure to see you, your Excellency," Shazli replied. He too was nude, but for sandals and a thin gold circlet on his brow. He was a slightly plump man—nearing forty now, which startled Hajjaj whenever he thought about it—with a sharp mind and a good heart, though perhaps without enormous force of character. Hajjaj liked him, and had since he was a baby. "Please, sit down," the king said. "Make yourself comfortable."

"Thank you, your Majesty." Zuwayzin used thick rugs and piles of cushions in place of the chairs and sofas common elsewhere in Derlavai. Hajjaj made himself a mound of them and leaned back against it.

Shazli waited till he'd finished, then asked, "Shall I have tea and wine and cakes sent in?"

"As you wish, your Majesty. If you would rather get down to business, I shan't be offended." Zuwayzin wasted endless convivial hours in the ritual of hospitality surrounding tea and wine and cakes. Hajjaj often used them as a diplomatic weapon when he didn't feel like talking about something right away.

"No, no." Shazli hadn't had a foreign education, and clung to traditional Zuwayzi ways more strongly than his much older foreign minister. And so another serving girl fetched in tea fragrant with mint, date wine (Hajjaj actually preferred grape wine, but the thicker, sweeter stuff did cast his memory back to childhood), and cakes dusted with sugar and full of pistachios and cashews. Only small talk passed over tea and wine and cakes. Today, Hajjaj endured the rituals instead of enjoying them.

At last, the king sighed and blotted his lips with a linen napkin and remarked, "The first Unkerlanter ships put in at Najran today."

"I hope they were suitably dismayed," Hajjaj remarked.

"Indeed," King Shazli said. "I am given to understand that their captains made some pointed remarks to the officers in charge of the port."

"I warned Ansovald when I signed the peace agreement that the Unkerlanters would get less use from our eastern ports than they seemed to expect," Hajjaj said. "They didn't seem to believe me. The only reason Najran is a port at all is that a ley line runs through it and out into the Bay of Ajlun." He'd been there. Even by Zuwayzi standards, it was a sun-blazed, desolate place.

"You understand that, your Excellency, and I also understand it," Shazli said. "But if the Unkerlanters fail to understand it, they could make our lives very unpleasant. If they land soldiers at Najran . . ."

"Those soldiers can make the acquaintance of the Kaunians who managed to escape from Forthweg," Hajjaj said. "I don't know how much else they could do. Even now, when the weather is as cool and wet as it ever gets, I can hardly see them marching overland to Bishah. Can you, your Majesty?"

"Well, possibly not," the king admitted. "But if they want an excuse to revise the agreement they forced on us . . ."

"If they want such an excuse, your Majesty, they can always find one." Hajjaj didn't often interrupt his sovereign, but here he'd done it twice in a row. "My belief is that this is nothing but Unkerlanter bluster."

"And if you are wrong?" Shazli asked.

"Then Swemmel's men will do whatever they do, and we shall have to live with it," Hajjaj replied. "That, unfortunately, is what comes of losing a war." The king grimaced but did not answer. Hajjaj heaved himself to his feet and departed a little later. He knew he hadn't pleased Shazli, but reckoned telling his sovereign the truth more important. He hoped Shazli felt the same. And if not . . . He shrugged. He'd been foreign minister longer than Shazli had been king. If his sovereign decided his services were no longer required, he would go into retirement without the slightest murmur of protest.

Shazli gave no sign of displeasure. Hajjaj almost wished the king had, for the next day Ansovald summoned him to the Unkerlanter ministry. "And I shall have to go, too," he told Qutuz with a martyred sigh. "The price we pay for defeat, as I remarked to his Majesty. Given a choice, I would sooner visit the dentist. He enjoys the pain he inflicts less than Ansovald does."

Hajjaj dutifully donned an Unkerlanter-style tunic to visit Ansovald. He minded that less than he would have in high summer. *Calling on the Jelgavans and Valmierans means wearing trousers,* he thought, and imagined he was breaking out in hives at the mere idea. Another sigh, most heartfelt, burst from him.

Two stolid Unkerlanter sentries stood guard outside the ministry. They weren't so stolid, however, as to keep their eyes from shifting to follow good-looking women going by with nothing on but hats and sandals and jewelry. With luck, the sentries didn't speak Zuwayzi—some of the women's comments about them would have flayed the hide from a behemoth.

Ansovald was large and bluff and blocky. "Hello, your Excellency," he said in Algarvian, the only language he and Hajjaj had in common. Hajjaj savored the irony of that. He had little else to savor, for Ansovald bulled ahead: "I've got some complaints for you."

"I listen." Hajjaj did his best to look politely attentive. Sure enough, the Unkerlanter minister fussed and fumed about the many shortcomings of Najran. When he finished, Hajjaj inclined his head and replied, "I am most sorry, your Excellency, but I did warn you about the state of our ports. We shall do what we can to cooperate with your captains, but we can only do what we can do, if you take my meaning."

"Who would have thought you ever told so much of the truth?" Ansovald growled.

Staying polite wasn't easy. *I do it for my kingdom,* Hajjaj thought. "Is there anything more?" he asked, getting ready to leave.

But Ansovald said, "Aye, there is."

"I listen," Hajjaj said again, wondering what would come next.

"Minister Iskakis tells me you've got his wife—Tassi, I think the bitch's name is—at your house up in the hills."

"Tassi is not a bitch," Hajjaj said, more or less truthfully. "Nor is she Iskakis' wife: she has received a divorce here in Zuwayza."

"He wants her back," Ansovald said. "Yanina is Unkerlant's ally nowadays, and so is Zuwayza. If I tell you to give her back, you bloody well will."

"No," Hajjaj said, and enjoyed the look of astonishment the word brought to the Unkerlanter's face. He also enjoyed amplifying it: "If Iskakis had her back, he would use her as he uses boys, if he used her at all. He prefers boys. She prefers not being used so. Unkerlant is indeed Zuwayza's ally, even her superior. I admit it. But, your Excellency, that does not make *you* into *my* master, not on any individual level. And so, good day. Tassi stays." He enjoyed turning his back and walking out on Ansovald most of all.

Every now and again—more often, in fact, than every now and again—Istvan felt guilty about being alive. It wasn't so much that he remained a Kuusaman captive on the island of Obuda. Gyongyosians reckoned themselves a warrior race, and knew that captivity might befall a warrior. But to have stayed alive after his countrymen sacrificed themselves to harm Kuusamo . . . That was something else, something harder to bear in good conscience.

"We knew," he said to Corporal Kun as the two of them chopped wood in the midst of a chilly rain. "We knew, and we didn't do anything."

"Sergeant, we did what needed doing," Kun answered. His next stroke buried his axehead in the ground, not in the chunk of pine in front of him. Maybe his conscience bothered him, too, in spite of his bold words. Or maybe he just couldn't see what he was doing: he wore spectacles, and the rain couldn't be doing them any good. Indeed, he muttered, "Can't see a cursed thing," before going on, "We didn't get our throats cut, either, and that puts us ahead of the game. Or will you tell me I'm wrong?"

"No," Istvan said, though he didn't sound altogether convinced. He explained why: "Half of me feels we should have told the Kuusamans what was coming, so our comrades would still be alive. The other half . . ." He shrugged. "I keep wondering if the stars will refuse to shine on my spirit because I didn't do everything I could to hurt the slanteyes."

"How many times have we been over this?" Kun said patiently, as if he had the higher rank and Istvan the lower. "Did Captain Frigyes really hurt the Kuusamans? Not bloody much. You can tell by looking—well, you could if it weren't raining." His precision was a hint that he'd been a mage's apprentice in Gyorvar, the capital, before getting conscripted into Ekrekek Arpad's army.

Istvan sighed. Kunhegyes, his home village, lay in a mountain valley far in distance and even further in ideas from Gyorvar. He clung to the old ways of Gyongyos as best he could, not least because he hardly knew any others. He was a big, broad-shouldered man with a mane of tawny yellow hair and a thick, bushy beard a shade darker. Like a lot of his countrymen, he looked leonine. So did Kun, but he made a distinctly scrawny lion even when he wasn't wearing his spectacles. Though he dwarfed the Kuusaman guards, he was neither tall nor wide by Gyongyosian standards, and his beard had always been and probably would always be on the patchy side.

With another sigh, Istvan said, "A pox on it. Let's just work. When I'm chopping wood, I don't have to think. Since everything happened, I don't much feel like thinking."

"Aye, I believe that," Kun answered. In a different tone of voice, the words would have sounded sympathetic. Instead, as usual, Kun only sounded sardonic.

"Ahh, go bugger a goat," Istvan said, but his heart wasn't in the curse. Kun was as he was, as the stars had made him, and no one could change him now.

"You two lousy Gongs, you talk too much," a Kuusaman guard yelled in bad Gyongyosian. The guards didn't usually give their captives as much leeway as Istvan and Kun had; the patter of the rain and the curtain of falling drops must have kept them from noticing what was going on for a while. "To work harder!" the small, dark, slant-eyed man added. He carried a stick, which meant the Gyongyosians had to pay heed to him, or at least pretend they did.

After a while, the wood-chopping shift ended. The Kuusamans collected the axes from the detail, and carefully counted them before dismissing the captives. They tried to take no chances—but they'd let the Gyongyosians turn loose a sorcery that had wrecked big stretches of Obuda, all through not paying quite enough attention to what their captives were up to. Kun said, "You've got your nerve, Sergeant, talking about goats to me."

Istvan looked around nervously before answering, "Oh, shut up." His voice was rough and full of loathing. Goats were forbidden beasts to Gyongyosians, perhaps because of their lasciviousness and habit of eating anything. Whatever the reason, forbidden they were; it was perhaps the strongest prohibition the folk of Gyongyos knew. Bandit bands and perverts sometimes ate goat to mark themselves off from ordinary, decent people—and when they got caught at it, they were most often buried alive.

Kun, for a wonder, did shut up. But he held out his left hand, palm up and open, so the rain splashed down onto it. Along with a woodcutter's calluses, he had a scar on the palm, between his second and third fingers. Unwillingly, Istvan held out his hand, too. His palm bore an identical scar. He had a scar on the back of his hand, too, as if a knife had gone all the way through. It had. Kun bore a like scar there, too.

"We're the only ones left now, I think," Istvan said. Kun nodded somberly. Neither one said what they were left from. Istvan wished he could forget. He knew he never would, not to his dying day.

Back when the squad he'd led were fighting in the great pine woods of western Unkerlant, they'd ambushed some Unkerlanters in a little clearing, not least so they could take the stew Swemmel's soldiers were cooking. It turned out to be goat stew. The whole squad had eaten of it before the company commander came up and realized what it was.

Captain Tivadar would have been within his rights to blaze them all. He hadn't done it. After they'd stuck fingers down their throats to puke up their appalling meal, he'd cut every one of them to atone for their inadvertent sin. Not a man had cried out. They'd all counted themselves lucky. To be known as a goat-eater in Gyongyos . . . Istvan shuddered. He hadn't done it on purpose, but how much difference did that really make? He still often wondered if he was accursed.

Tivadar was dead, killed in those endless woods. So far as Istvan knew, he'd never said a word about what he'd done there in the clearing. The other men in the squad had died in other fights. Szonyi, as good a fighting man as any Istvan had known, had chosen to let his throat be cut here on Obuda. Istvan hadn't been able to talk him out of it.

Only Kun and me, sure enough, Istvan thought. His eyes slid toward the ex-mage's apprentice. He wished no one else knew what he'd done. He wished it with all his soul. But, on the other hand, how much difference did a wish like that make? *He* knew he'd had goat's flesh on his tongue, and its mark scarred his spirit as Tivadar's knife had scarred his hand.

Perhaps deliberately changing the subject, Kun said, "Just as well the Kuusamans didn't ask us too many questions after Frigyes loosed his spell."

"Why should they have?" Istvan returned. "We didn't have anything to do with it. We'd both come down with the runs hours before it happened."

Kun walked a little straighter for a couple of paces. He'd found the leaves that turned their guts inside out. But then he said, "If I'd been the one picking up the pieces after that sorcery, I'd've wondered why a couple of men just happened to get sick right then. I'd've wondered whether they knew more than they were letting on."

"By the stars, you've got a nasty, suspicious mind," Istvan said.

"Thank you," Kun answered, which spoiled the insult. Kun went on, "If I'm the fellow investigating something like that, I'm *supposed* to have a nasty, suspicious mind, eh?"

"Maybe," Istvan said. "I guess so. Somehow, I get the feeling Kuusamans aren't as suspicious as they ought to be."

"You may be right." Kun thought it over as they neared their barracks. "Aye, sure enough, you may be right. It doesn't mean they're not dangerous, though."

"I never said it did," Istvan replied. "We fought them here on Obuda, you and I, but it's their island now. Most of the islands in the Bothnian Ocean are theirs now."

"I know," Kun said. "I can't help but know, can I? And what does that tell you?"

"What, that you know? It tells me you're not a complete fool—just mostly."

Kun gave Istvan a sour look. "You're being stupid on purpose. You're not nearly so funny when you do that as when you're stupid because you don't know any better. What does it tell you that the Kuusamans hold most of the islands in the Bothnian Ocean, and that we aren't taking any back the way we would when the war was new?"

The barracks loomed ahead: an ugly, leaky building of raw timber. The cots inside, though, were better and less crowded than had been the cots in the Gyongyosian barracks where Istvan had stayed before while stationed on Obuda. But that wasn't why the barracks felt like a refuge now. If he got inside, maybe he wouldn't have to answer his comrade's question.

Kun coughed sharply. Again acting as if his rank were higher than Istvan's, he said, "You know the answer as well as I do. Why won't you say it?"

"You know why, curse it," Istvan mumbled.

"Is the truth less the truth because you don't name it?" Kun asked inexorably. "Do you think it will go away? Do you think the stars won't shine their light on it? Or do you just want me to have to do the dirty work and say it out loud?"

That's exactly what I want. But Istvan didn't want anyone to say it out loud, because he did feel that somehow made it more real. But if he'd gone forward against the Kuusamans, if he'd gone forward against the Unkerlanters, couldn't he go forward against the truth, too? Almost as if he were attacking Kun, he shouted into the smaller man's face: "They're taking the fornicating islands because we're losing the fornicating war! There! Are you fornicating happy now?"

Kun gave back a pace—a couple of paces, in fact. Then he had to rally, and he did. "You're honest, at any rate," he said. "The next question is, what do we do if we keep on losing?"

"I don't know," Istvan answered. "And you don't know, either. It's been a long time since Gyongyos lost a war." He spoke with the pride to be expected of a man from a warrior race.

"That's because we haven't fought a whole lot of them lately," Kun said. "When you think about what all's gone on in this one, that's not so bad, is it?"

Istvan started to reply, then realized he had no good reply to give. What was the point of being a man from a warrior race without any wars to fight? On the other hand, what was the point of fighting a war and losing it? Shaking his head and muttering to himself, Istvan went into the barracks.

Some of the captives already inside nodded to him. Most of the men he'd known best, the men from his own company, were dead thanks to Captain Frigyes. Most of the faces here now, the men lounging on cots, the fellow putting more wood on the stove, were strangers to him. But they were of his kind. They looked like him. They spoke his tongue. Maybe in a captives' camp he was a sheep among sheep with them, not a wolf among wolves. Still, he was with his own. That would do. It would have to.

Two

Bembo strutted through the ravaged streets of Eoforwic twirling his bludgeon by its leather strap, as if he were the king of the world. Once upon a time, Algarvians on occupation duty in Forthweg might as well have been kings of the world. The constable sighed, pining for the good old days. He put on his show at least as much to keep up his own spirits as to impress the Forthwegians around him.

From behind him, somebody called out in pretty good Algarvian: "Hey, tubby, the Unkerlanters'll press you for oil when they cross the Twegen!"

By the time Bembo and his partner, Oraste, had whirled, nobody back there looked to have opened his mouth. None of the Forthwegians on the street so much as smiled. That left the constable with nobody to blame. "Smartmouthed son of a whore," Bembo said. He started to set his free hand on his belly, as if to deny he had too much of it. Then, as if afraid the gesture would call attention to his ample flesh, he left it uncompleted.

Oraste, unlike Bembo, was not the typical high-spirited, excitable Algarvian. He was, in fact, dour as an Unkerlanter most of the time. But he was laughing now, laughing at Bembo. "He got you good, he did."

"Oh, shut up," Bembo muttered. He didn't say it very loud. Oraste had a formidable temper, and Bembo didn't care to have it aimed at him. One of the reasons he enjoyed being a constable was that it meant he could dish out trouble without having to take it.

All that had broken down during the Forthwegian uprising here. Constables and soldiers had fought side by side then, what with the rebels giving almost as much trouble as they were getting. And, with the Unkerlanters indeed just on the other side of the river, nobody could feel safe at night— or, for that matter, during the daytime. If they started tossing eggs again . . . Bembo looked around for the closest hole into which to jump. As he'd expected, he wouldn't have to run far. Eoforwic, these days, was little but holes and rubble.

He and Oraste turned a corner. A couple of Forthwegians had been shouting at each other. When they saw the constables, they abruptly fell silent. Bembo let out a small sigh. He might have had the chance to shake them down if they'd kept squabbling. Oraste sighed, too. He probably would sooner have beaten them up than put a bribe in his belt pouch, but no accounting for taste.

A squad of Algarvian soldiers tramped by, on their way down to the Twegen. One of them pointed to Bembo and Oraste and called, "You constable bastards thought you were lucky, all safe and comfy back here in Forthweg away from the western front. Well, now the Unkerlanters have bloody well come to you since you didn't have the balls to go to them." His pals laughed.

There were a dozen of them. Because there were a dozen of them, Bembo replied in a whisper only Oraste could hear: "If you soldier bastards hadn't got run out of Unkerlant, *we* wouldn't be worrying about Swemmel's buggers now."

His partner grunted and nodded and said, "If I ever see that particular son of a whore by himself, he'll be sorry his mother let the next-door neighbor in for a quickie whenever her husband went to work."

Bembo guffawed. A couple of soldiers looked back suspiciously. "Come on, you lugs, get moving," called the corporal in charge of them. "What do we care about a couple of fornicating constables?"

"I wish I was a fornicating constable right now," Bembo said. "It'd be a lot more fun than what I am doing."

Oraste laughed less than Bembo thought the joke deserved. That made Bembo sulk instead of strutting as he and Oraste paced off their beat. A lot of Algarvians would have jollied him along till he was in a good humor again. Oraste, a sullen fellow himself, didn't care—indeed, didn't notice—what sort of humor the people around him were in.

"They ought to send us all back to Algarve," Bembo said after a while, looking for something new to complain about. "All us constables, I mean."

That made Oraste laugh, but not in the way Bembo had intended. "Oh, aye, the soldiers would really love us then," he said. "Wake up, fool. Sleepy time's over."

"But what good are we doing here?" Bembo demanded. Now that he'd started, his complaints made perfect sense—to him, at least. "This whole miserable city is under military occupation and martial law. What are constables good for, then?"

"For whatever soldiers don't feel like doing," Oraste answered. "I know what's eating you, old pal. You can't fool me. You just don't want to be here when Swemmel's bastards finally get around to swarming over the Twegen."

"Oh, and you do?" Bembo retorted. "I'll just bet you do, sweetheart."

Oraste didn't answer that. Because he didn't, Bembo concluded he had no answer. There was no answer. No Algarvian in his right mind—probably no crazy Algarvian, either—wanted to be in a town the Unkerlanters overran. If you were in there then, either you wouldn't come out or you'd come out a captive. Bembo wondered which was worse. He hoped he wouldn't have to find out.

A Forthwegian labor gang went by, herded by a couple of Algarvians with sticks. "Wonder how many of those whoresons are Kaunians in sorcerous disguise," Bembo said.

"Too many," Oraste answered. "One'd be too many. However this stinking war turns out, we've got rid of a whole great raft of blonds. That was worth doing."

Bembo shrugged. Back before the war, he hadn't thought much about Kaunians one way or the other. A few blonds had lived in Tricarico, as a few—sometimes more than a few—had lived in a lot of cities in the north of Algarve: reminders of where the Kaunian Empire had once stretched. But they'd been taken away while the war was new. Bembo supposed that made sense. How loyal would blonds in Algarve be when King Mezentio was at war with Jelgava and Valmiera, both Kaunian lands, and with Forthweg, a kingdom where blonds had more than their share of money and power?

His own notions about Kaunians had changed after the Derlavaian War broke out. He remembered that, now that he thought about it a little. How could they have helped but change, when the bookstores were filled with romances about the slutty blond women of imperial days and other choice bits, and when every fence and wall sprouted broadsheets telling the world—or at least the Algarvian part of it—what a pack of monsters Kaunians were?

He blinked. "You know something?" he said to Oraste. "We were *made* to hate the blonds. It didn't just happen."

His partner's shoulders, broad as a Forthwegian's, went up and down in a businesslike shrug altogether different from the usual Algarvian production. "Speak for yourself," Oraste said. He jabbed a thumb at his own chest. "Me, I never needed any help."

A lot of Algarvians—and, from everything Bembo had seen, even more Forthwegians—felt the same way. "Before the war," Bembo began, "what was the—?"

He didn't finish, for bells began clanging all over Eoforwic. "Dragons!" Oraste exclaimed. "Futtering Unkerlanter dragons!" He looked around, his eyes wild, as did Bembo. "Now where in blazes is a cellar?"

"I don't see one." Bembo wasn't the least ashamed of the fear in his voice. Most, almost all, the buildings hereabouts were wrecks, their cellars, if they'd ever had them, buried under rubble. He moaned. "But I see the dragons."

They flew low, as they usually did on raids like this, only a couple of hundred feet above the waters of the Twegen. The rock-gray paint Swemmel's men gave them made them all the harder to spot, but Bembo could see how many of them there were, and that no Algarvian beasts rose to challenge them. One or two tumbled out of the sky, hit by beams from heavy sticks, but the rest came on, eggs slung under their bellies.

"No cellars," Oraste said as some of those eggs began to fall and to release bursts of the sorcerous energy trapped inside them. "Next best thing is the deepest hole in the ground we can find." He started to run.

So did Bembo, his belly jiggling. Oraste jumped into a hole, but it was plainly too small for a pair of good-sized men. Bembo kept running, while the roars from bursting eggs came closer and closer as the Unkerlanter dragons penetrated deeper and deeper over Eoforwic. Bembo spotted a likely hole and dashed towards it. He was only a couple of strides away when an egg burst much too close—and then he wasn't running any more, but flying through the air.

It wasn't anything like his dreams of flying. For one thing, he had no control over it whatever. For another, it didn't last more than half a heartbeat—and when he hit a pile of rubble, he hit hard. He felt something snap in his leg. He heard it, too. That was almost worse—at least till the pain reached his mind, which took a couple of extra heartbeats.

Somebody close by was screaming. Whoever he was, he had to be close by: Bembo could hear him through the din of the eggs. After a moment, he realized those screams came from his own mouth. He tried to make them stop, but it was like trying to recork a fizzing bottle of sparkling wine—once that stopper was out, no getting it in again. He bawled on and on, and hoped an egg would burst on him and kill him. Then, at least, it would be over.

No such luck. *What did I ever do to deserve this?* wondered some small part of his brain still able to think. Unfortunately, he had no trouble coming up with answers. Few Algarvians who'd served in Forthweg would have.

The dragons kept dropping eggs for what seemed like forever. Bembo kept screaming all that while, too. And he kept screaming after the Unkerlanter dragons flew back toward the west.

"Oh, shut up," Oraste told him. "Let's have a look at you." He did, with rough competence, the accent being on *rough*. When he finished, he said, "Well, Bembo my lad, you are one lucky son of a whore."

That startled Bembo enough to make him stop screaming for a moment. "Lucky?" he howled. "Why, you—" He called Oraste every name he knew. Considering the decade or so he'd spent in the constabulary, he knew a lot of names.

Oraste slapped him in the face. "Shut up," he said again, this time in a flat, angry voice. "I said lucky, and I meant fornicating lucky. You're hurt bad enough, they won't keep you around here, on account of you won't be good for a fornicating thing for a long time. That means you won't be here when the Unkerlanters finally do come over the Twegen. And if that's not lucky, what in blazes is? You want me to try splinting your leg, or you want me to wait for a healer?"

Bembo cursed him again, not quite so savagely as before. Then the pain made everything blurry for some little while. When he fully returned to himself, someone he didn't recognize was leaning over him, saying, "Here, Constable, drink this."

He drank. It tasted nasty—a horrible blend of spirits and poppy seeds. After a bit, the pain ebbed—or he felt as if he were floating away from it. "Better," he mumbled.

"Good," the healer said. "Now I'm going to set that leg." *Go ahead,* Bembo thought vaguely. *I won't care.* But he did. The decoction he'd drunk wasn't strong enough to keep him from feeling the ends of the broken bone grinding against each other as the healer manipulated them. Bembo shrieked. "Almost done," the healer assured him. "And you'll be going back to Algarve to get better after that. They'll take good care of you."

"Oraste was right," Bembo said in drowsy, drugged wonder. A couple of Forthwegians put him on a litter—and hauled him off toward the ley-line caravan depot. When he got there, another healer poured more of the decoction down him. He never remembered getting carried aboard the caravan. When he woke up, he was on his way back to Algarve.

Outside the royal palace in Patras, a blizzard howled. Marshal Rathar had little use for the palace or for the capital of Yanina. He wore a heavy cloak over his knee-length rock-gray tunic, and was none too warm even with it. "Why do you people not heat your buildings in the wintertime?" he growled at King Tsavellas.

The king of Yanina was a skinny little bald man with a big gray mustache and dark, sorrowful eyes. "We do," he answered. "We heat them so we are comfortable. We do not turn them into ovens, as you Unkerlanters like to do."

Both the King of Yanina and the Marshal of Unkerlant spoke Algarvian. It was the only tongue they had in common; classical Kaunian was much less studied in their kingdoms than farther east on the continent of Derlavai. Rathar savored the irony. Tsavellas had had no trouble talking with his erstwhile allies, the redheads. Now he could use his command of their language to talk with the new masters of Yanina.

"If you are indoors, you should be warm," Rathar insisted. He enjoyed telling a king what to do, especially since Tsavellas had to listen to him. King Swemmel . . . This time, Rathar's shiver had nothing to do with the chilly halls through which he walked. The King of Unkerlant was a law unto himself. All Kings of Unkerlant were, but Swemmel more so than most.

"Warm is one thing," Tsavellas said. "Warm enough to cook?" His expressive shrug might almost have come from an Algarvian.

Rathar didn't answer. He was eyeing the painted panels that ornamented the walls. Yaninans in old-fashioned robes—but always with pompoms on their shoes—stared out of the panels at him from enormous, somber eyes.

Sometimes they fought Algarvians, other times Unkerlanters. Always, they were shown triumphant. Rathar supposed the artists who'd created them had had to paint what their patrons wanted. Those patrons had lost no sleep worrying about the truth.

He couldn't read the legends picked out in gold leaf beside some of the figures on the walls. He couldn't even sound them out. Yanina used a script different from every other way of writing in Derlavai. Rathar reckoned that typical of the Yaninans, the most contrary, fractious, faction-ridden folk in the world.

"Here we are," Tsavellas said, leading him into a room with more Yaninans painted on the walls and with maps on the tables. A Yaninan officer in a uniform much fancier than Rathar's—his short tunic over kilt and leggings glittered with gold leaf, and even his pompoms were gilded—sprang to his feat and bowed. Tsavellas went on, "I present to you General Mantzaros, the commander of all my forces. He speaks Algarvian."

"He would," Rathar rumbled. He was hardly fifty himself—burly, vigorous, and dour. Any man who'd spent so much time dealing with King Swemmel had earned the right to be dour. When he held out his hand, Mantzaros clasped his wrist instead, in the Algarvian style. Rathar raised an eyebrow. "Have you forgotten whose side you're on these days, General?"

"By no means, Marshal." Mantzaros drew himself up to his full height, which was a couple of inches less than Rathar's. "Do you seek to insult me?" Yaninans were some of the touchiest people on earth, too, without the style Algarvians brought to their feuds.

"No. I seek to get some use out of the rabble you call an army," Rathar said brutally.

That made both Mantzaros and King Tsavellas splutter. The general found his voice first: "Our brave soldiers are doing everything they can to aid our allies of Unkerlant."

"You have not got more than a handful of brave soldiers. We saw that when you were fighting against us," Rathar said. Ignoring the Yaninans' cries of protest, he went on, "Now that you are on our side, you had better get your men moving against the cursed redheads. That was the bargain you struck when you became our allies"—*our puppets,* he thought—"and you are going to live up to it. Your men will spearhead several attacks we have planned."

"You will use them to weaken the Algarvians so you can win on the cheap," Tsavellas said shrilly. "This is not war. This is murder."

"If you try to go back on your agreement, your Majesty"—Rathar used the title with savage glee—"you will find out what murder is. I promise you that. Do you understand me?"

Tsavellas and Mantzaros both shivered and turned pale beneath their swarthy skins. The Algarvians killed Kaunians for the life energy that powered their strongest, deadliest sorceries. To fight back, Swemmel ordered the deaths of criminals, and of the old and useless of Unkerlant. But, now that his soldiers held Yanina in a grip of iron, what was to stop him from killing Tsavellas' folk instead? Nothing at all, as anyone who knew him had to realize.

"We are . . . loyal," Tsavellas said.

"To yourselves, perhaps," Rathar answered. The king looked indignant—indeed, almost shocked. No Yaninan would have dared speak to him so. But Marshal Rathar was no Yaninan—for which he thanked the powers above—and had to deal with a king ever so much more fearsome than Tsavellas. He went on, "King Swemmel still recalls how you would not turn over King Penda of Forthweg to him when Penda fled here early in the war."

General Mantzaros said something in Yaninan. If it wasn't, *I told you so,* Rathar would have been mightily surprised. Tsavellas snapped something pungent in his own language, then returned to Algarvian: "King Penda escaped my palace. I still do not know how he came to Lagoas."

On the whole, Rathar believed him. But that had nothing to do with anything. In a voice like sounding brass, he said, "But you had Penda here in Patras, here in your palace, and you would not give him to Swemmel when my sovereign demanded his person."

"He was a *king,*" Tsavellas protested. "He *is* a king. One does not surrender a king as one does a burglar."

"Is a king who has no kingdom still a king?" Rathar asked. "I did not give him to Mezentio of Algarve, either, and he wanted him, too."

Rathar's shrug held a world of indifference. "You did not surrender him to King Swemmel. Swemmel reckons that a slight. I speak no secrets when I tell you King Swemmel's memory for slights is very long indeed."

Tsavellas shivered again. "It is easy for your king to have a long memory. He is strong. For a man who rules a small kingdom, a weak kingdom, trapped between two strong ones, things are not so easy."

"Unkerlant was—is—trapped between Gyongyos and Algarve—and Yanina," Rathar said. "You may redeem yourself, but you will pay whatever price King Swemmel demands. If you balk, you shall not redeem yourself, and you will pay much more. Do you understand that, your Majesty?" Once more, he enjoyed using the king's formal title as he dictated to him.

King Tsavellas wilted. Rathar had expected nothing less. The King of Yanina found himself in an impossible situation. He'd saved his throne by switching sides at just the right moment, but he'd left himself a hostage to Unkerlant in doing so. If he didn't obey, Swemmel could easily find some pliant Yaninan noble—or an Unkerlanter governor—who would. "Aye," Tsavellas said sullenly. "Tell us what you require, and we shall do it. Is it not so, General?"

"It is so," General Mantzaros agreed. "It will bleed our kingdom white, but it is so."

"Do you think Unkerlant has not been bled white?" Rathar said. "Do you think Yanina did not help bleed Unkerlant white? This is what you bought, and this is the price you will pay for it. You know the Algarvians are holding along the line of the Skamandros River?"

"Aye," the king and his general said together.

Rathar wasn't so sure how much they knew, but accepted their word for the time being. He said, "I intend to throw Yaninan armies across the river here and here"—he pointed to the spots he had in mind—"in three days' time. You will have them ready, or it will go hard for you and your kingdom."

"In three days?" Mantzaros croaked. "That is not possible."

"This is your last chance to keep Yaninan armies under Yaninan officers, General," Rathar said coldly. "If you do not move the men as we require, we shall do it for you. That will be the end of your army as an army. We will use it as part of ours—as a small part of ours. Have you any questions?"

"No," Mantzaros whispered. He spoke in Yaninan to King Tsavellas, who replied in the same tongue. Mantzaros dipped his head, as Yaninans usually did in place of nodding. Returning to Algarvian, he said, "We obey."

"Good. That is what is required of you, no more—and no less." He turned his back on the general and the king and strode out of the map room. The painted Yaninans on the hallway walls stared reproachfully from their big, round, liquid eyes. He ignored them, as he had ignored the king and the general once they gave him what he wanted. He also ignored the anxious Yaninan courtiers who tried to get him to tell them what was going on. After fawning, they cringed.

Rathar's carriage waited outside the palace. "Take me to our headquarters," he told the driver. The soldier, a stolid Unkerlanter, nodded and obeyed without a word. That suited Rathar fine.

The headquarters was an appropriated house, quite fine, in a district full of fancy shops—certainly fancier than any in Cottbus. The Yaninans couldn't fight worth a lick, but they lived well. When Rathar walked in, he smelled a pungent, smoky odor he'd never met before and heard General Vatran coughing. "Powers above, what's that stink?" he demanded.

"I'm breathing the smoke of these leaves I got from the grocer across the street," Vatran answered between wheezes. He was stocky and white-haired, almost twenty years older than Rathar: one of the few truly senior officers to have survived a generation of Swemmel's rages, but a solid soldier nonetheless. "Varvakis says they come from some island in the Great Northern Sea, and the natives there all swear by them."

"For what?" Rathar asked. "Fumigation?"

"No, no, no. Health," Vatran said. "None of these natives ever dies before he's a hundred and fifty years old, if you believe Varvakis. And even if you cut what he says in half, that doesn't sound too bad to me." He coughed again.

So did Rathar. "Nasty stench," he said. "If you have to breathe this cursed smoke all the time, I think I'd sooner die. It'll probably rot your lungs. And if these natives are so bloody wonderful, why do they belong to some Derlavaian kingdom nowadays? All those islands do, you know."

"You haven't got the right attitude," Vatran said reproachfully.

"I don't care," Rathar answered "I'll tell you this, though: Tsavellas and Mantzaros would agree with you."

"I'll bet they would," Vatran said. "You got what you wanted from them, I expect?"

"Of course I did," Rathar told him. "It was that or pull this kingdom down around their ears. We'll throw Yaninans over the Skamandros till they bridge it with their bodies if we have to. Then we'll clean out the stinking redheads ourselves." He paused. "They don't stink any worse than those leaves."

"Sorry, sir." Vatran didn't sound sorry. He was grinning. So was Rathar. Why not, when they were pushing the Algarvians back?

Rain blew out of the west, into Colonel Spinello's face. *It could be worse,* the Algarvian officer thought as he peered from his riverfront hole in the ground in Eoforwic across the Twegen toward the Unkerlanter positions on the west bank.

When he said that aloud, one of the men in his brigade gave him an odd look. "*How* could it be worse, sir?" the trooper asked, real curiosity in his voice.

"For one thing, it could be snowing." Spinello had no trouble coming up with reasons. He'd seen the worst the Unkerlanters and the weather could do. "Down in the south, it *would* be snowing. It probably is, right this minute. And Swemmel's whoresons could have us surrounded, the way they did down in Sulingen. They could have snipers as close to us as you are to me. One of those bastards blazed me down there, straight through the chest. I'm lucky I'm here. So you see, things aren't so bad."

He was a prancing, handsome little gamecock of a man, one who stayed dapper even when things were at their worst. As always, he spoke with great conviction. He believed what he was saying when he said it, and usually made others believe it, too. That was one of the reasons he had such good luck with women. *That and technique,* he thought smugly.

Every once in a while, of course, even conviction didn't pay off. The trooper said, "Oh, aye, some luck, sir. You were so lucky, they got you repaired and sent you up here to give the Unkerlanters another chance at doing you in. You can call that luck if you want, but it's the kind of luck you can keep, if you ask me."

"Well, who did ask you?" Spinello said. But that was a gibe, not a reprimand. Freeborn Algarvians, even common soldiers, *would* speak their minds. That was part of what made them better soldiers than Unkerlanters, who were liable to end up sacrificed if they talked out of turn.

And if we're such splendid soldiers, what are we doing fighting way back here in the middle of Forthweg? he asked himself. He knew the answer perfectly well: enough indifferent soldiers could overwhelm a smaller number of good ones. They could, aye. But, when King Mezentio ordered the Algarvian army into Unkerlant, who had imagined that they might? Mezentio hadn't. Spinello was sure of that.

Shouldn't he have? Spinello wondered. *He just assumed Unkerlant would fall to pieces, the way all our other enemies did when we hit them.* He peered across the river again. He couldn't see any Unkerlanter soldiers stirring about, but he knew they were there. *It didn't work out quite the way Mezentio and the generals thought it would. Too bad.*

A few eggs burst on this side of the Twegen, but not close enough to make him do anything but note them. It was, on the whole, a quiet day. Before long, he feared, Swemmel's men would burst out of their bridgeheads north and south of Eoforwic. They would probably try to cut off and surround the city, as they had with Sulingen. He wondered if the battered Algarvian forces in the neighborhood could stop them. He had his doubts, though he would have gone on the rack before admitting as much.

And if the Unkerlanters do cut us off? Well, then things will be . . . pretty bad.

Motion he caught out of the corner of his eye made him whirl, stick swinging up ready to blaze. But it was only a couple of Hilde's Helpers, the Forthwegian women who worked hard to keep the Algarvians in Eoforwic fed. Some of them—not all—kept the Algarvians happy other ways, too. But a man had to listen if one of them said no. Offending them might mean going hungry, and that would have been very bad.

They wore hooded cloaks over their long, baggy tunics. One of them came up to Spinello and the trooper in the hole with him. She took a loaf from under the cloak and gave it to Spinello. "Bread with olive," she said in bad Algarvian. "I myself to bake."

"Thank you, sweetheart." Spinello bowed as if she were a duchess. He tried talking with her for a little while, but she didn't speak enough of his language to follow much, and he had next to no Forthwegian.

We could probably get along in classical Kaunian, he thought. He was fluent in the language of scholarship and sorcery, and in Forthweg, as nowhere else, it remained a living language, too. Many Forthwegians had learned it to deal with their Kaunian neighbors.

But Spinello didn't try it. Most Kaunians who had lived in Forthweg were dead by now, slain to fuel Algarve's sorcerous onslaught against Unkerlant. And most Forthwegians weren't particularly sorry about that. Had they been, the Algarvians would have had a much harder time doing what they'd done. So no, classical Kaunian didn't seem like a good idea.

He tore the loaf in half and gave one piece to the soldier in the hole with him. They both ate greedily. "Powers above, that's good!" Spinello exclaimed. The trooper nodded, his cheeks as full of bread as a dormouse's could get full of seeds.

The clouds were thick enough that nightfall took Spinello by surprise. He hadn't expected it to get dark for some little while yet, and hadn't seen anything in the least resembling a sunset. "Have to keep our eyes open," he called to his men. "Swemmel's buggers are liable to try to sneak raiders across the river." They'd done that a couple of times lately, and created more chaos than the small number of soldiers who'd paddled across the Twegen should have been able to spawn.

But, a couple of hours later, two Algarvians came up to the river not far from where Spinello still kept his station. When he climbed out of his hole to find out what they were doing, one of them shook his head. "You haven't seen us," the fellow said. "We've never been here."

"Talk sense," Spinello snapped. "I command this brigade. If I say the word, you bloody well *won't* have been here."

Muttering, the man who'd spoken stepped closer to him, close enough to let him see the mage's badge on the fellow's tunic. "If you command this brigade, get us a little rowboat. I have work to do," he said. "And if you try interfering with me, you'll end up envying what happens to the cursed blonds, I promise you."

Spinello almost told him to go futter himself. Outside the army, he would have. He'd come close to a couple of duels in his time. But discipline and curiosity both restrained him. "What are you going to do?" he asked.

"My job," the mage answered, which stirred Spinello's temper all over again. "Now get me that boat."

"Aye, your Highness," Spinello said. The wizard only laughed. Spinello called orders to his men. They came up with a rowboat. It was, undoubtedly, stolen from a Forthwegian. Spinello cared nothing about that. He bowed to the mage and to the fellow with him, who'd said not a word. "Welcome to the Royal Algarvian Navy."

He got not even a smile, let alone a laugh, and set them down for a couple of wet blankets. The mage began to incant. Some of his charms were in old-fashioned Algarvian, others in classical Kaunian, still others in what sounded like Unkerlanter. Spinello could follow the first two, not the third. The mage finished, cocked his head to one side, and nodded. "The confusion spell should hold for a while—

they aren't expecting it," he said. "Now let's tend to you."
His comrade only nodded. He got to work again, this time
with a simple charm in classical Kaunian. Before Spinello's
eyes, the silent Algarvian's appearance changed—he took
on the seeming of an Unkerlanter. He then stripped off his
own uniform and took from his pack that of an Unkerlanter
major. He got into the rowboat and started rowing west
across the Twegen.

"Good luck," Spinello called after him. "Bite somebody
hard." Why send a man in sorcerous disguise into
Unkerlanter-held territory if not to bite somebody hard?

From the boat, the fellow gave back the only three words
Spinello ever heard from him: "I intend to." Then he vanished from sight, sooner than Spinello expected. *The confusion spell,* he thought. He looked around for the mage to
show off his own cleverness, but the fellow had already
disappeared.

Spinello wondered if the disguised Algarvian would return to his stretch of the riverfront, but he never saw the
man again. The next day, the Unkerlanters stirred and
milled around in a way that made him hope the fellow had
accomplished something worth doing, but no one to whom
he talked seemed to know.

More of Hilde's Helpers came by to give the Algarvians
dishes they'd cooked. A rather pretty girl—*pity she's got
that blocky Forthwegian build,* Spinello thought—with a
blue-and-white armband gave him a bowl with a spoon
stuck in it. He sniffed and nodded. "Smells good, darling.
What's in it?"

"Barley. Olives. Cheese. Little sausage," she answered in
halting Algarvian. Her voice was sweet, and might have
been familiar.

Laughing, Spinello wagged a finger at her. "I'll bet you
put some mushrooms in, too, just to drive me mad."

He had to repeat himself before she understood. When
she did, she jerked in surprise, then managed a nod of her
own, a halting one. "Aye. For to taste. To *flavor.* Chop very
fine." She mimed cutting them. "Not to notice. Only for to
taste. For to taste good."

Spinello considered. After some of the things he'd had to

eat in Unkerlant, what were a few mushrooms? He grinned at the girl. "Kiss me and I'll eat 'em."

She jerked again, harder than she had before. He wondered if some other Algarvian had given her a hard time, who could guess when? *You've got to be careful with Hilde's Helpers,* he reminded himself. *Treat 'em like noblewomen, even if they are just shopgirls.* This one, though, hesitated only a moment. She nodded and leaned toward him. He did a good, thorough job of kissing her. "Now," she said, "you to eat."

Eat he did. "It *is* good," he said in some small surprise after the first mouthful, and wolfed down the rest of the bowl. The Forthwegian girl was right; except for the flavor they added, he hardly knew the mushrooms were there. He'd dreaded biting into some big, fleshy chunk, but that didn't happen at all. When he'd eaten every bit of the stew, he got to his feet, bowed, and made a production of returning bowl and spoon. "Another kiss?" he asked.

She shook her head. "Go to make more. For others." She hurried off.

A crystallomancer shouted, "Hey, Colonel, I've just picked up some emanations from the fornicating Unkerlanters. Sounds like somebody just bumped off General Gurmun. I bet that was our pal last night."

"I bet you're right," Spinello breathed. "And I bet they'd trade a couple of brigades of ordinary men for that Gurmun whoreson, too. He was far and away the best they had with behemoths."

The confusion on the other side of the Twegen continued the whole day long. The Unkerlanters hardly bothered harassing Eoforwic. Spinello didn't take that for granted. His guess was, they would start pummeling the city hard when they began to recover. But he enjoyed the respite while he had it.

His own respite didn't last so long as Eoforwic's. He woke in the middle of the night with belly pains and an urgent need to squat. "A pox!" he grumbled. "I've come down with a flux." But squatting didn't help, and the pain only got worse.

When morning came, his men exclaimed in horror.

"Powers above, Colonel, get to a healer," one of them said. "You're yellow as a lemon!"

"Yellow?" Spinello stared down at himself. "What's wrong with me?" He scratched his head. He didn't argue about going to a healer; he felt as bad as he looked, maybe worse. "I wonder if it was those mushrooms. Plenty of reasons we don't eat them, I bet."

He got a powerful emetic from the healers. That just gave him one more misery, and did nothing to make him feel better. Nothing the healers did could make him feel better, or even ease his torment. It ended for good three days later, with him still wondering about those mushrooms.

Vanai splashed hot water, very hot water, water as hot as she could stand it, onto her face again and again, especially around her mouth. Then she rubbed and rubbed and rubbed at her lips with the roughest, scratchiest towel she had. Finally, when she'd rubbed her mouth bloody, she gave up. She could still feel Spinello's lips on hers even after all that.

But then she snatched Saxburh out of her cradle and danced around the flat with the baby in her arms. Saxburh liked that; she squealed with glee. "It was worth it. By the powers above, it *was* worth it!" Her little daughter wouldn't have argued for the world. She was having the time of her life. She squealed again.

"Do you know what I did?" Vanai said. "Do you have any *idea* what I did?" Saxburh had no idea. She chortled anyhow. Still dancing, ignoring the sandpapered state of her lips, Vanai went on, "I put four death caps in his stew. Not one, not two, not three. Four. Four death caps could kill a troop of behemoths, let alone one fornicating Algarvian." She kept right on dancing. Saxburh kept right on laughing.

Fornicating Algarvian is right, Vanai thought savagely. Her mouth was sore, but she didn't care. *I'd've put my lips on his prong to get him to take that bowl of stew. Powers below eat him, why not? It's not as if he didn't make me do it before. Teach me tricks, will you? See how you'll like the one I just taught you!*

Spinello, without a doubt, felt fine right now. That was

one of the things that made death caps and their close cousins, the destroying powers, so deadly. People who ate them didn't feel anything wrong for several hours, sometimes even for a couple of days. By then it was far too late for them to puke up what they'd eaten. The poison stayed inside them, working, and no healer or mage had ever found a cure for it. Soon enough, Spinello would know what she'd done.

"Isn't that fine?" Vanai asked Saxburh. "Isn't that just the most splendid thing you ever heard in all your days?" The baby didn't have many days, but, by the way she gurgled and wriggled with glee, it might have been.

All Forthwegians hunted mushrooms whenever they got the chance. In that, if in few other things, the Kaunians in Forthweg agreed with their neighbors. No one—not even Algarvian soldiers, not any more—paid much attention to people walking with their heads down, eyes on the ground. And who was likely to notice what sort of mushrooms went into a basket? One thing Vanai's grandfather had taught her was how to tell the poisonous from the safe. Everyone in Forthweg learned those lessons. This once, Vanai had chosen to stand them on their head.

"And so you too have some measure of revenge, my grandfather," she whispered in classical Kaunian. Brivibas would never have approved of her saying any such thing to him in mere Forthwegian.

Saxburh's eyes—they would be dark like Ealstan's, for they were already darkening from the blue of almost all newborns' eyes—widened. She could hear that the sounds of this language were different from those of the Forthwegian Vanai and Ealstan usually spoke.

"I will teach you this tongue, too," Vanai told her daughter, still in classical Kaunian. "I do not know if you will thank me for it. This is a tongue whose speakers have more than their share of trouble, more than their share of woe. But it is as much yours as Forthwegian, and you should learn it. What do you think of that?"

"Dada!" Saxburh said.

Vanai laughed. "No, you silly thing, I'm your mama," she said, falling back into Forthwegian without noticing she'd done it till after the words passed her lips. Saxburh babbled more cheerful nonsense, none of which sounded like either Forthwegian or classical Kaunian. Then she screwed up her face and grunted.

Knowing what that meant even before she caught the smell, Vanai squatted down, laid Saxburh on the floor, and cleaned her bottom. Saxburh even thought that was funny, where she often fussed over it. Vanai laughed, too, but she had to work to keep the corners of her mouth turned up. She wouldn't have used Forthwegian so much before she started disguising herself. It really was as if Thelberge, the Forthwegian semblance she had to wear, were gaining at the expense of Vanai, the Kaunian reality within.

Even if the Algarvians lose the war, even if the Unkerlanters drive them out of Forthweg, what will it be like for the blonds left alive here? Will they—will we—go on wearing sorcerous disguises and speaking Forthwegian because it's easier, because the Forthwegians—the real Forthwegians—won't hate us so much then? If we do, what happens to the Kaunianity, the sense of ourselves as something special and apart, that we've kept alive ever since the Empire fell?

She cursed softly. She had no answer for that. She wondered if anyone else did, if anyone else could. If not, even if the Algarvians lost the Derlavaian War, wouldn't they have won a great battle in their endless struggle against the Kaunians who'd been civilized while they still painted themselves strange colors and ran naked through their native forests throwing spears?

The familiar coded knock Ealstan used interrupted her gloomy reverie. She snatched up Saxburh and hurried to unbar the door. Ealstan gave her a kiss. Then he wrinkled his nose. "I know what you've been doing," he said. He kissed Saxburh. "And I know what *you've* been doing, too." He took her from Vanai and rocked her in his arms. "Aye, I do. You can't fool me. I know just what you've been doing."

"She can't help it," Vanai said. "And it's something everybody else does, too."

"I should hope so," Ealstan answered. "Otherwise, we'd all burst like eggs, and who would clean up after us then?"

Vanai hadn't thought of it like that. When she did, she giggled. Ealstan went on, "And what did you do with your morning?"

Before Vanai realized she would, she answered, "While Saxburh was taking a nap, I put on a blue-and-white armband and went out and pretended I was one of Hilde's Helpers."

"Powers above, you're joking!" Ealstan exclaimed. "Don't say things like that, or you'll make me drop the baby." He mimed doing just that, which made Vanai start and made Saxburh laugh.

Vanai said, "I really did. And do you want to know why?"

Ealstan studied her to make sure she wasn't kidding him. What he saw on her face must have satisfied him, for he replied, "I'd love to know why. The only reason that occurs to me right now is that you've gone crazy, and I don't think that's right."

"No." Vanai said that in Forthwegian, but then switched to classical Kaunian. "I wore the armband because I wanted to give a certain officer of the redheaded barbarians a special dish—and I did it."

"A special dish?" Ealstan echoed in his own slow, thoughtful classical Kaunian. "What kind of—? Oh!" He didn't need long to figure out what she meant. His eyes glowed. "How special was it?"

"Four death caps," she answered proudly.

"Four?" He blinked. "That would kill anybody ten times over."

"Aye. I know." Vanai wished she could have killed Spinello ten times over. "I hope he enjoyed them, too. People who eat them say they're supposed to be tasty."

"I've heard the same thing," Ealstan answered, falling back into Forthwegian. "Not something I ever wanted to find out for myself." He carefully set Saxburh in her little seat, then came back and took Vanai in his arms. "You told me not to take chances, and then you went and did this? I ought to beat you, the way Forthwegian husbands are supposed to."

"It wasn't so risky for me as it would have been for you,"

she answered. "I just gave him the food, took back the bowl, and went on my way. He still feels fine—I'm sure of it—but pretty soon he won't. What was I to him? Just another Forthwegian." *Just another wench,* she thought, remembering the feel of his lips on hers. *But the last wench, the very last.*

"It's a good thing you did get the bowl—and the spoon, too, I hope," Ealstan said. Vanai nodded. He went on, "If you hadn't, the Algarvian mages could have used the law of contagion to trace them back to you."

"I know. I thought of that. It's the reason I waited for them." Vanai didn't tell Ealstan about the couple of quizzical looks Spinello had sent her while he ate her tasty dish of death. Had he half recognized, or wondered if he recognized, her voice? Back in Oyngestun, they'd always spoken classical Kaunian. Here, of course, Vanai had used what scraps of Algarvian she had. That, and the difference in her looks, had kept Spinello from figuring out who she was.

"Well, the son of a whore is gone now, even if he hasn't figured it out yet. Four death caps?" Ealstan whistled. "You could have killed off half the redheads in Eoforwic with four death caps. Pity you couldn't have found some way to do it."

"It is, isn't it?" Vanai said. "But I got rid of the one I most wanted dead." That was as much as she'd ever said since Ealstan found out about Spinello.

Ealstan nodded now. "I believe that," he said, and let it go. He'd never pushed her for details, for which she was grateful.

Saxburh started to cry. Ealstan joggled her, but this time it didn't restore her smile. "Give her to me. I think she's getting fussy," Vanai said. "She's been up for a while now." *And I've been dancing with her, dancing because of what I just did to Spinello. And I still feel like dancing, by the powers above.*

She sat down on the couch and undid the toggles that held her tunic closed. Ealstan reached out and gently cupped her left breast as she bared it. "I know it's not for me right now," he said, "but maybe later?"

"Maybe," she said. By her tone, it probably meant aye.

As Saxburh settled in and began to nurse, Vanai wondered why that should be so. Wouldn't seeing Spinello have soured her on men and anything to do with men? Till she first gave herself to Ealstan, she'd thought the Algarvian had soured her on lovemaking forever. Now . . . *Now I just fed him four death caps, and I want to celebrate.* "Come on, sweetheart," she crooned to Saxburh. "You're getting sleepy, aren't you?"

Ealstan, who'd gone into the kitchen, heard that and laughed. He came back with a couple of mugs of something that wasn't water. He gave Vanai one. "Here. Shall we drink to . . . to freedom!"

"To freedom!" Vanai echoed, and raised the cup to her lips. Plum brandy slid hot down her throat. She glanced toward Saxburh. Sometimes the baby was interested in what her mother ate and drank. Not now, though. Saxburh's eyes started to slide shut. Vanai's nipple slid out of the baby's mouth. Hoisting her daughter to her shoulder, Vanai got a sleepy burp from her, then rocked her till she fell asleep. Saxburh didn't wake up when she set her in the cradle, either.

Her tunic still hanging open, Vanai turned back to Ealstan. "What were you saying about later?"

He raised an eyebrow. She wasn't usually so bold. *I don't kill a man I hated every day, either,* she thought. Back in the bedchamber, she straddled Ealstan and rode herself—and him with her—to joy with short, hard, quick strokes, then sprawled down on his chest to kiss him. *I wish I did, if only it would make me feel like this every time.* Even the afterglow seemed hotter than usual. Laughing, she kissed him again.

Winter roared into the Naantali district of Kuusamo as if it were part of the land of the Ice People. The blizzard outside the hostel howled and shrieked, blowing snow parallel to the ground. Pekka's home town of Kajaani didn't usually get quite such wretched weather, even though it lay farther south: it also lay by the sea, which helped moderate its climate.

Pekka had hoped to be able to experiment in the scant hours of daylight that came here, but scrubbed the idea when she saw what the weather was like. No matter how much Kuusamans took cold, nasty weather in stride, everything had its limits.

And it's not as if I've got nothing else to do, she thought, brushing a lock of coarse black hair back from her eyes as she waded through paperwork. The greatest drawback she'd found to running a large project was that it transformed her from a theoretical sorcerer, which was all she'd ever wanted to be, to a bureaucrat, a fate not quite worse than death but not enjoyable, either.

Someone knocked on the door to her chamber. She sprang to her feet, a smile suddenly illuminating her broad, high-cheekboned face. Any excuse for getting away from that pile of papers was a good one. *And it might be Fernao.* That idea sang in her. She hadn't expected to fall in love with the Lagoan mage, especially when she hadn't fallen out of love with her own husband. But Leino was far away—in Jelgava now, battling against the Algarvians' bloodthirsty magic—and had been for a long time, while Fernao was here, and working side by side with her, and had saved her life more than once, and. . . . She'd stopped worrying about reasons. She just knew what was, knew it and delighted in it.

But when Pekka opened the door, no tall, redhaired Lagoan with narrow eyes bespeaking a touch of Kuusaman blood stood there. "Oh," she said. "Master Ilmarinen. Good morning."

Ilmarinen laughed in her face. "Your lover's off somewhere else," he said, "so you're stuck with me." With Master Siuntio dead, Ilmarinen was without a doubt the greatest theoretical sorcerer in Kuusamo, probably in the world. That didn't keep him from also being a first-class nuisance. He leered and laughed again at Pekka's expression. The few wispy white hairs that sprouted from his chin—Kuusaman men were only lightly bearded—wagged up and down.

Getting angry at him did no good. Pekka had long since learned that. Treating him as she did Uto, her little boy, worked better. "What can I do for you?" she asked, as sweetly as she could.

Ilmarinen leaned forward to kiss her on the cheek. That was going too far, even for him. Then he said, "I've come to say goodbye."

"Goodbye?" Pekka echoed, as if she'd never heard the word before.

"Goodbye," Ilmarinen repeated. "To you, to this hostel, to the Naantali district. It took some wangling—I had to talk to more than one of the Seven Princes of Kuusamo— but I did it, and I'm free. Or I'm going to be free, anyhow, as soon as this ghastly weather lets me escape."

"You're *leaving*?" Pekka said. Ilmarinen nodded. She wondered if her senses were failing her or if, more likely, he was playing one of his horrid practical jokes. "You can't do that!" she blurted.

"You'd better revise your hypothesis," Ilmarinen said. "I'm going to falsify it with contradictory data. When you see that I'm gone, you will also see that you were mistaken. It happens to us all now and again."

He means it, she realized. "But why?" she asked. "Is it anything I've done? If it is, is there anything I can do to change your mind and make you stay?"

"No and no," the master mage answered. "I can tell you exactly what's wrong here, at least the way I look at things. We're not doing anything new and different any more. We're just refining what we've already got. Any second-rank mage who can get to ten twice running when he counts on his fingers can do that work. Me, I'd sooner look for something a little more interesting, thank you kindly."

"What is there?" Pekka asked.

"I'm going to the war," Ilmarinen answered. "I'm going to Jelgava, if you want me to be properly precise, and I'm sure you do—you're like that. If those fornicating Algarvian mages start killing Kaunians and aiming all that sorcerous energy at me, I aim to boot 'em into the middle of next week. Time to really *use* all this sorcery we've dreamed up. Time to see what it can do, and what more we need to do to fancy it up even more."

"But . . ." Pekka floundered. "How will we go on without you?"

"You'll do pretty well, I expect," the master mage said.

"And I'll have a chance to play with my own ideas. Maybe I really *will* figure out a way to knock the Algarvians into the middle of next week. I still say the potential for that lies at the heart of the experimental work we've done."

"And I still say you're out of your mind," Pekka answered automatically.

"Of course you do," Ilmarinen said. "You're the one who opened this hole in the ice, and now you don't want to fish in it for fear a leviathan will take hold of your line and pull you under."

"Those *are* the kinds of forces you're talking about," Pekka said. "Even if you were right—and you're not, curse it; you almost killed yourself and took half of Kuusamo with you because you'd miscalculated, if you recall—even if you were right, I tell you, you'd never be able to come up with a usable sorcery. Paradoxes would prevent it."

"Whenever a mage says a spell is possible, he's likely right," Ilmarinen replied. "Whenever he says a spell is impossible, he's likely wrong. That's an old rule I just made up, but it covers the history of pure and applied sorcery over the past hundred and fifty years pretty well, I think."

He had a point, though Pekka didn't intend to admit it. She said, "I think you're being very foolish. You were talking about second-rank mages, Master. What will you be able to do in Jelgava that any second-rank mage can't?"

"I don't know," he answered cheerfully. "That's why I'm going there: to find out. I know everything I can do here and"—he yawned with almost as much theatrical flair as an Algarvian might have—"I'm bored."

"That shouldn't be reason enough to abandon something of which you're such an important part," Pekka insisted.

"Maybe it shouldn't, but for me it is." Ilmarinen's foxy features donned that leer once more. "If I happen to run into your husband while I'm in Jelgava, what shall I tell him?"

Not a thing! Not a fornicating thing! Pekka wanted to shout. Just before she did, she realized that was the worst thing she could possibly say. With studied indifference, she answered, "Tell him whatever you please. You will anyway."

That took the leer off his face. It got her what might have

been a respectful glance. "You're cooler about the whole business than I thought," Ilmarinen said.

Pekka, just then, felt anything but cool. Letting him know that, though, didn't strike her as a good idea. She said, "If you're bound and determined to do this, powers above keep you safe."

"For which I thank you," Ilmarinen said. "I will miss you, curse me if I won't. Your heart's in the right place, I think, even if I can't imagine what you see in that overgrown Lagoan mage."

"He's not overgrown!" Indignation crackled in Pekka's voice. "And you're a fine one to talk. What do *you* see in Linna the serving girl?"

"A pretty face and a tight twat," he answered at once. "I'm a man. Men aren't supposed to need any more than that, are they? But women, now, women should have better sense, don't you think?"

Actually, Pekka did think that, or something like that, anyway. But Ilmarinen was the last person with whom she wanted to talk about it. Instead of talking, she hugged him hard enough to make him wheeze as the air came out of him. Then, for good measure, she kissed him, too. "I still think you're being a fool, but you're a fool I'm fond of."

"You're stuck with me a while longer," he said, "till this accursed weather eases up. But then I'm flying—or more likely sailing—north for the winter." Off he went down the hallway. Pekka wondered why she'd even tried to change his mind. He was no more inclined to listen to her than she was to pay attention to the advice she got from a clerk at a grocer's shop. He did what he wanted, and reveled in it.

If he wants to tell Leino, I'll kill him, she thought. But that worried her less than it had when he first asked his sardonic question. Had Ilmarinen really intended to blab to her husband if he saw him, he wouldn't have teased her about it first. She was sure—well, she was pretty sure—of that.

Still shaking her head in astonishment, she went back to the paperwork. A few minutes later, another knock on the door interrupted her. This time, it *was* Fernao: tall and redheaded and, but for his eyes, most un-Kuusaman looking.

Even the neat ponytail in which he wore his hair shouted that he was a Lagoan.

But, over the past couple of years, he'd got pretty fluent in Kuusaman. "You'll never guess what," he said now. He even had something of a Kajaani accent, which only showed he'd done a lot of talking and listening to Pekka.

"About Ilmarinen disappearing?" she said, and watched his jaw drop. "He came to me first," she told him. "How did you find out about it?"

"He's in the refectory, pouring down ale and boasting about the wires he pulled to get away," Fernao answered.

"That sounds like him," Pekka said sourly.

"He's really off to Jelgava?" Fernao asked.

"That's what he says," Pekka replied. "He has connections with the Seven Princes that go back longer than either one of us has been alive, so I suppose he is. I haven't seen the paperwork, but he wouldn't carry on like that without it."

"No, he wouldn't." Fernao didn't sound particularly happy. After a moment, he showed Pekka why: "If he goes to Jelgava, if he sees your husband there, will he talk? You Kuusamans are such a straitlaced folk, I fear he might."

"We're no such thing!" Pekka exclaimed. Then, a little sheepishly, she asked, "Is that how Lagoans see us?"

"A lot of the time, aye," he said. "You . . . often take such things too seriously."

"Do we?" Pekka suddenly remembered fleeing his bedchamber in tears after the first time they'd made love. "Well, maybe we do. But I don't think Ilmarinen will talk too much to Leino. He's not an ordinary Kuusaman, you know."

"Really?" Fernao's voice was dry. "I never would have noticed. What did you do, tell him you'd put a lifetime itching spell on his drawers if he ever opened his mouth?"

Pekka giggled. "It's a pretty good idea, but no. If I'd threatened him, he *would* blab to Leino if he ever saw him. He may not see him, of course. He probably won't, in fact—Jelgava is a good-sized kingdom. But when he teased me about it, I told him to do whatever he wanted, so he won't feel he *has* to run off at the mouth."

"Good thinking." Fernao quirked up an eyebrow. "And what do *you* want to do?"

"It's more fun than paperwork," Pekka said. Realizing a heartbeat too late how imperfect that was as praise, she did her best to show him—and herself—exactly how much more fun than paperwork it really was.

A new broadsheet went up all over the Jelgavan town of Skrunda. Talsu read a copy pasted to the front wall of the crowded block of flats where he and his family had moved. EXCHANGE OF CURRENCY, the headline read. Below it, in almost equally large characters, it declared, *All coins bearing the impress of the false king, usurper, and vicious tyrant, Mainardo the cursed Algarvian, must be exchanged for those minted under the auspices of his glorious Jelgavan Majesty, Donalitu III, by*—the date named was less than two weeks away. The broadsheet continued, *Any attempt to pass the monies of the false king and vicious tyrant after the date aforesaid shall be punished with the greatest possible severity. By order of his glorious Jelgavan Majesty, long may he reign.*

Talsu, his wife Gailisa, his younger sister, and his mother and father shared one room, none too large, and a tiny, cramped, kitchen. Bathroom and toilet were at the end of the hall. That was, Talsu supposed, better than sharing a tent, as they'd done after a Lagoan or Kuusaman dragon raid burned down Traku's tailor's shop and the rooms above it where the family had lived. Still, it did produce its share of friction.

When Talsu climbed the stairs to the flat, he found his father doing some hand stitching on a pair of trousers before using a spell to extend the stitchery down along the entire length of the hem. Traku set the work down when Talsu came in. "Hello, son," he said in his gravelly voice: he looked—and sounded—more like a bruiser than a tailor. "What's new in the outside world? I don't get to see it much."

"A new broadsheet went up," Talsu answered, and explained what was on it.

From the kitchen, his mother called, "That's good. That's very good, by the powers above. If I never see Mainardo's cursed pointy nose on another piece of silver,

I'll stand up and cheer. The faster we forget the redheads ever conquered us, the happier I'll be."

"I don't know, Laitsina," Traku said. "Did you hear what Talsu said they'll do to you if you make a mistake? We'll have to sift through all our silver. I don't want to spend a stretch in the dungeons just because I was careless."

"King Donalitu is still King Donalitu," Talsu said, and he didn't mean it as praise. "If the redheads had picked one of our nobles instead of Mezentio's brother, they would have had an easier time getting people to put up with them."

"They didn't care a fart whether we put up with 'em or not," Traku said. "They thought they had the world by the short hairs, and that what we thought didn't matter. What were we? Just a pack of Kaunians. That's why the arch on the far side of the square isn't standing any more, even though it had been there since the days of the Kaunian Empire."

"That's right," Talsu said. "I was taking some clothes across town when the redheads wrecked the old arch. They said it insulted them, because it talked about how the Kaunians of long ago beat the old-time Algarvians."

"They did things like that all over Jelgava—all over Valmiera, too." Traku lowered his voice. "And they did a lot worse to the Kaunians of Forthweg, by what everybody says."

Talsu's sister Ausra came out of the kitchen wearing an apron over her tunic and trousers and said, "What do you want to bet they find some way to cheat us when we turn in the money the Algarvians issued?"

"I wouldn't be surprised," Talsu said.

"Neither would I," Traku agreed. "I'm glad we don't have King Mainardo and the redheads running things any more, but I'd be almost gladder if we didn't have Donalitu back."

That was treason. If anybody besides his family heard it, Traku might end up in a dungeon regardless of whether he exchanged Mainardo's coins for Donalitu's. Back before the Algarvians ran Donalitu out of Jelgava, his dungeons had had an evil reputation all over Derlavai. He wasn't a madman or the next thing to it, as Swemmel of Unkerlant was said to be, but no one loved him.

Wistfully, Talsu said, "The Kuusamans have seven princes. Maybe they could spare one for us? The Kuusaman soldiers I dealt with when I was with the irregulars were all good people. They didn't act like they were afraid of their officers, either."

"Neither did the redheads, come to that," Ausra said.

"No, they didn't," Talsu admitted unhappily. "But they had other things wrong with them—starting with thinking everybody who had yellow hair was fair game. Donalitu's bad. They were worse."

Neither his sister nor his father argued with him. Traku said, "They aren't gone yet, either, the whoresons. They're still hanging on in the western part of the kingdom. The sooner we're rid of them forever, the better."

"But if they leave, they know the Lagoans and Kuusamans will follow them right into Algarve," Talsu said.

Traku grunted. "Good. I wish we'd gone deeper into Algarve, back before we got beat. Then maybe all this never would have happened to us."

For a long time, Talsu's father had blamed him almost personally for Jelgava's lost war against Algarve. Traku had been too young to fight in the Six Years' War, and didn't know what the army—especially the Jelgavan army—was like. Talsu said, "If our officers had been any good, we would have gone deeper. But if our officers were any good, a lot of things about this kingdom would be different." That was about as much as he cared to say about that, even in the bosom of his family.

Ausra said, "They're putting together a new army for the kingdom, now that we have our own king back again. That was the last set of broadsheets, before this one about exchanging Mainardo's money."

"I saw it," Talsu said. "It won't be a new army—you wait and see. It'll be the same old army, with the same old noble officers who don't know their—" He broke off before using a phrase from that same old army in front of his sister. In spite of having to stop, he'd got out what had been wrong with the Jelgavan army in which he'd served. As in most armies, nobles held almost all officers' slots . . . and Jelgavan nobles, from King Donalitu on down, were some of the most hidebound, stubborn, backwards-looking men the world had ever seen.

Gailisa came into the flat then. Talsu was glad to break off and give her a hug and a kiss. She returned them a little absently. She hadn't been quite the same since her father got killed when Kuusaman and Lagoan dragons dropped eggs on Skrunda about a week before the Algarvians had to clear out of the town for good. Talsu had shown Kuusaman footsoldiers and behemoths an undefended way through the redheads' lines. He wished he'd done it sooner. Maybe the islanders' dragons wouldn't have flown that night.

His late father-in-law had been a grocer. Gailisa had helped him. These days, she was working for another grocer, one named Pumpru, whose shop had survived. She said, "Do you know about the new money-changing decree?"

"We were just talking about it a few minutes ago," Talsu answered. "I saw the broadsheets on my way home from delivering a cloak."

"It's a cheat," Gailisa said.

"What? Have they turned out light coins that are supposed to be worth the same as the older, heavier ones?" Talsu asked. "That's what Mainardo did. Donalitu's not too proud to steal tricks from an Algarvian, eh?"

"Close, but not quite," Gailisa said. "Pumpru took some of Mainardo's money in to be changed as soon as he saw one of the broadsheets. If King Donalitu told everybody to jump off a roof, he'd do that just as fast—he's one of those people. But he wasn't happy when he came back to the store. He wasn't happy at all."

"What's wrong with the new money?" Traku asked.

"It *is* new money." Gailisa nodded. "If they'd given old silver, weight for weight, that would have been fair. But all the coins Pumpru got are shiny new. And they're too hard, and they don't sound right when you ring them on a counter. You don't have to be a jeweler to figure out there's not as much silver in them as there's supposed to be."

"And Donalitu puts the difference in his pocket," Talsu said. Gailisa nodded again. Talsu made as if to pound his head against the wall of the flat. "What a cheap trick! He didn't waste much time reminding people what he is, did he?"

"He's the king, that's what he is," Traku said. But he didn't blindly follow King Donalitu, the way Pumpru the grocer did, for he went on, "And if you get on his wrong side, you'll find yourself in a nice, cozy dungeon cell, too, so watch what you say."

"I will, Father," Talsu promised. "I've already spent more time in a dungeon cell than I ever want to."

"But that was for making the Algarvians angry, not the proper king," Ausra said.

"Same dungeon," Talsu replied dryly. "And it wasn't the redheads running it, either—it was Jelgavans just like you and me. They'd worked for Donalitu before Mainardo came in. One of them said he'd go back to working for Donalitu if Mainardo ever got thrown out. He meant it."

"That's terrible!" his sister exclaimed.

"Son of a whore ought to be dragged out of his fornicating dungeon and blazed," his father growled.

"Of course he should," Talsu said. "But what do you want to bet he was right? What do you want to bet he's still just where he always was, except now he's making things hot for people who got in bed with the Algarvians instead of for people who wanted us to get our own rightful king back?"

Slowly, one at a time, Gailisa, Traku, and Ausra nodded. Talsu's wife said, "Ausra's right. That *is* terrible. It isn't the way the world's supposed to work."

"Do you know what the worst part of all is, though?" Talsu said. This time, his family shook their heads. He went on, "The worst part of all this is, none of you argued with me. No matter how terrible it is, you think it's pretty likely, too, the same as I do."

"It *shouldn't* be this way," Gailisa insisted. But then her courage wilted. "It always seems to be, though—here in Jelgava, anyhow. The people who have a lot keep grabbing more and more."

"That's the story of this kingdom, sure enough," Traku said. "Always has been, just like you said, Gailisa. Powers below eat me if I think it'll ever change. And it's likely the same way everywhere. When Mezentio's buggers were

holding us down, they weren't shy about grabbing everything they could get their hands on."

"From what I saw of the Kuusamans, they're different,"
Talsu said. "Their officers and men seemed to be friends,
and the ones with the higher ranks didn't ride roughshod
over the ordinary soldiers. Come to think of it, I even had
one regimental commander like that, back when we were
still in the war."

"What happened to him?" Gailisa asked.

"Colonel Adomu?" Talsu said. "About what you'd expect—he actually went out to do some real fighting, so he
got killed pretty quick. I never knew another officer like
him: not in *our* army, anyhow." The Algarvians had had a
fair number of that stripe, too, but he didn't care to say so
out loud. He didn't want to praise the redheads, not after
everything they'd done.

"Supper's ready!" his mother called, and that gave him
something happier to think about.

Three

⟨separator⟩

"Bauska!" Marchioness Krasta shouted from her bedchamber. "Powers below eat you, Bauska, where have
you gone and hidden?"

"Coming, milady," the maidservant said, hurrying in—
and panting a little, to show how much she was hurrying. She
dropped Krasta a curtsy. "What can I do for you, milady?"

"At least you sound properly respectful," Krasta said.
"Some of the servants these days . . ." She made a horrible
face. The servants didn't come close to giving her the respect she deserved. They all took their lead from her
brother and that hateful cow of a farm girl he'd brought
home with him. There were times when Krasta almost
wished the Algarvians had managed to hunt Skarnu down.

Then he wouldn't have had the chance to rub his virtue in her face.

Bauska's answering smile was bleak. "Well, milady, we're in the same boat, you and I, aren't we?"

"I should say not," Krasta answered indignantly. "Your snot-nosed little brat has an Algarvian papa, sure as sure. One look at her would tell that to anybody. Viscount Valnu is father to my child." She firmly believed it these days.

"Of course, milady," Bauska said. The words were right. The tone called Krasta a liar—oh, not quite blatantly enough to let her bound up and slap Bauska's face, but it did, it did. The maidservant went on, "And even if that's so . . ." She broke off, not quite in the nick of time. *Even if that's so,* she didn't say, *everybody knows you opened your legs for Colonel Lurcanio for years and years.*

Krasta tossed her head. "So what?" she said, as if Bauska had made the accusation out loud. But the rest of her impassioned defense was silent, too. *What if I did? The Algarvians looked like winning the war. Everybody thought so. I was better off with a redhead in my bed than I would have been without. I wasn't the only one. I wasn't even close to the only one. It seemed like a good idea at the time.*

It had been a good idea at the time. Krasta remained convinced of that. Once she got an idea—which didn't happen all that often—she clung to it through thick and thin. But she'd never expected times to change so drastically. Taking an Algarvian lover didn't look like a good idea any more. What it looked like these days, in a Valmiera no longer occupied, was something very much like treason.

With her own sandy-headed little bastard, Bauska couldn't very well say that. She had to count herself lucky that she hadn't had her head shaved and her scalp daubed with red paint, as had happened to so many Valmieran women who'd given themselves to Mezentio's soldiers. With a sigh, the maidservant repeated, "What can I do for you, milady?"

"My trousers don't fit me any more," Krasta said peevishly. "Hardly any of them even come close to fitting any more. Look at me! I'm still in these summery silk pyjamas with the elastic waist, and I'm about to freeze my tits off.

Maybe I ought to get a great big long loose tunic to cover all of me, the kind Unkerlanter women wear." She shuddered at the mere idea.

But Bauska's voice was serious as she answered, "Maybe you should, milady. The Unkerlanters have done so much to fight the Algarvians, everything about them is stylish these days. One of their tunics might be just the thing for a woman with child to wear."

"Do you think so?" Krasta asked, intrigued. She considered, then shook her head. "No, I don't want to. I don't care whether their clothes are stylish or not. They're too ugly to stand. I want trousers, but I want some that fit me properly."

"Aye, milady." Bauska sighed. But that sigh wasn't aimed at Krasta, for she went on, more to herself than to the marchioness, "Maybe you're right. When I think about Captain Mosco, I don't suppose I want to see Unkerlanter-style clothes catch on here in Valmiera."

Mosco had been Colonel Lurcanio's aide—and was father to Bauska's bastard daughter. He'd never seen his child by her, though. Before Brindza was born, he'd gone off to fight in Unkerlant. He was one of the first Algarvians pulled west by the ever more desperate battle against King Swemmel's men, but far from the last. He'd never sent so much as a line back once ordered away from Priekule. Maybe that meant he'd been a heartbreaker from the start. Maybe, on the other hand, it meant he'd died almost as soon as he made the acquaintance of warfare so much more savage than any that had washed over Valmiera.

With a sniff, Krasta said, "Remember, you silly goose, he had a wife somewhere back in Algarve."

"I know." Bauska sighed again. What that meant was, she didn't care. Had Mosco walked into the mansion right then—assuming he could have come anywhere close to it without getting blazed by vengeful Valmierans—she would have greeted him with open arms and, no doubt, open legs. *Fool,* Krasta thought. *Little fool.*

Lurcanio had a wife somewhere back in Algarve, too. He'd never denied it or worried about it. Krasta hadn't cared. Men, in her considerable experience, got what they could where they could. She'd never imagined herself in love with Lurcanio, as Bauska had with Mosco. He'd given her skill in bed and protection from other redheads, and she hadn't really looked for anything more.

Now that Lurcanio was gone from her bed, gone from Priekule, gone—she thought—from Valmiera (though he could have been one of the Algarvians hanging on in the rugged country of the northwest), there were times when Krasta missed him. Now that he was gone, she remembered with a warm glow what he'd been able to do for her . . . and she conveniently forgot how he'd frightened and intimidated her. He being the only man who'd ever managed to do that, forgetting came all the easier.

But she couldn't forget how even these pyjama bottoms were starting to grow cruelly tight. "Where in blazes do I go to find clothes I can wear?" she demanded. "As far as I know, there was only one shop on the whole Boulevard of Horsemen that catered to pregnant women, and it's been closed up with NIGHT AND FOG scrawled across the window for two years now."

The Boulevard of Horsemen was, far and away, the toniest street of shops in Priekule. That meant it was the only one Krasta cared about. Going anywhere else would have been stepping down in class, and she would sooner have been buried alive. But if the Boulevard didn't have what she needed, she could look elsewhere without social penalty.

Bauska said, "I found the clothes I needed on Threadneedle Street, milady. Plenty of such shops there, some cheap, some not so."

"Threadneedle Street," Krasta echoed. She remembered Bauska's clothes as being ugly. *She* could do better, though. She was sure of it. She had more taste and more money. How could she go wrong? Musingly, she said, "I've never been down to Threadneedle Street."

"Never, milady?" Bauska looked astonished. "But everybody buys clothes there."

"I don't do what everybody else does," Krasta said in lofty tones. *And if I hadn't taken an Algarvian lover when so many other women did . . .* But it was much too late to worry about that.

After some rummaging, Bauska found her a pair of trousers she could at least wear. Her tunics were getting tight, too, both at what was left of her waist and at the chest. She reckoned only part of that a drawback; the rest was an asset, especially when dealing with men.

Her driver gave her a bleary look when she told him she wanted to go out. He was drinking much too much these days. Krasta couldn't even yell at him, the way she wanted to. Who could guess what would happen if she antagonized the servants? They were liable to go to her brother, and she had enough trouble with Skarnu as things were.

The day was clear and cold and crisp as the carriage rattled into the heart of Priekule. People on the streets looked shabby, but they looked happy, lively, in a way they hadn't when the Algarvians held the city. Krasta still wasn't used to not seeing redheads strolling along and taking in the sights. When Algarvian soldiers in Unkerlant got leave, they often came east to rest and relax in the capital of a kingdom that had, at least for a while, truly yielded to them.

No Valmieran wore kilts these days, either. They'd grown moderately popular among those who wanted to curry favor with the occupiers or just wanted to show off shapely legs. No more, though. Now, if the Algarvian-style garments weren't thrown out, they lay at the bottom of clothes chests and in the back of closets. For a Valmieran to put on a kilt today might well be to risk a life.

"Threadneedle Street, milady," Krasta's driver said glumly. "Best you get out now, so I can find a place to put the carriage."

"Oh, very well," Krasta said. The street *was* crowded, not only with carriages but also with goods wagons and with a swarm of foot traffic. *Tradesmen and shopgirls and riffraff like that,* Krasta thought scornfully. *If these are the people Bauska thinks of as* everybody, *powers above be praised that I have some idea of what true quality is worth.*

But her maidservant had been right: plenty of the cramped little shops along Threadneedle Street sported names like FOR A MOTHER and CLOTHES FOR YOU BOTH and even—dismayingly, as far as Krasta was concerned—MAYBE IT'S TWINS. She rolled her eyes. She didn't particularly want one baby. If she were to have two . . . She wondered if Valnu could have sired one and Lurcanio the other. Wouldn't *that* be a scandal? She had no idea if it were possible, and even less idea of whom to ask. Not asking anyone struck her as a pretty good plan.

Shopping here, she rapidly discovered, was different from shopping on the Boulevard of Horsemen. No fawning shopgirls guided her from one elegant creation to the next. Instead, clothes were crammed onto racks. In shops with SALE! painted on their windows, getting anything took harder fighting than most of what the Valmieran army had done. Commoner women much more extravagantly pregnant than Krasta elbowed her aside to get at a pair of loose-fitting trousers or a baggy tunic they wanted. She didn't need many lessons along those lines. Before long, she gave as good as she got, if not better. After all, wasn't elbowing commoners aside a proper sport for a noblewoman?

The clothes were cheaper than she'd expected. They were also none too sturdily made. When she complained about that to a shopkeeper, he said, "Lady, use your head. You think you're gonna be in 'em long enough to wear 'em out?"

What he said made good sense, but his tone infuriated her. "Do you know who I am?" she demanded.

"Somebody trying to waste my time, and I ain't got it to waste," he answered, and turned to a woman holding out some trousers to him. "You like these, darling? That's two and a half in silver. . . . Thank you very much."

Krasta didn't buy anything there: the only revenge she could take. She did get what she needed, and she hunted down her driver, who stowed away his flask when he saw her coming. "Home," she said, and escaped Threadneedle Street with nothing but relief.

Back at the mansion, though, Merkela happened to be walking outside when Krasta came up the drive. The farm woman's son toddled beside her, holding her hand for balance. "What have you got in the sacks?" Merkela snapped, as if suspecting Krasta of smuggling secrets to the Algarvians.

"Clothes," Krasta answered shortly. She had as little to

do with Merkela as she could. It was either that or claw her, and Merkela would delight in clawing back.

She clawed now, with words instead of nails: "Oh, aye, for your bulging belly. At least I know who my son's father is. Don't you wish you could say the same?" Krasta snarled an unpleasantry at her and stalked—as well as a pregnant woman could stalk—into the mansion.

Fernao's head ached. Like a lot of the mages at the hostel in the Naantali district, he'd had too much to drink bidding Ilmarinen farewell the night before. He looked at the mirror above the sink in his room—looked at it and winced. "Powers above," he muttered. "My eyes are as red as my hair."

Pekka came up beside him. The bed they'd shared was narrow for two to sleep in, but they'd both poured down enough spirits to keep them from moving much. Pekka also winced. She said, "My eyes are red, too, and I haven't even got red hair."

He draped an arm around her shoulder. "I like what you have," he said. "I like everything you have."

"Including red eyes?" She made a face at him. "I don't like that, and I don't care what you think. I need strong tea, maybe with just a splash of spirits in it, to take the edge off."

"That sounds wonderful." Fernao limped over to the closet and chose a tunic and kilt. He would limp for the rest of his life, and one shoulder wasn't everything it might have been, either. He'd almost died down in the land of the Ice People, when an Algarvian egg burst much too close to him. For quite a while, he wished he had. No more. Time—and falling in love—had changed that.

Pekka kept a couple of outfits in his closet these days, as he had a couple in hers. That helped them spend nights together and maintain the polite fiction that they were doing no such thing. She changed her clothes while he got his cane. He wasn't an old man—far from it. Not so long before, he would have shaken his head in sorrow at the sight of someone his age who needed a cane to get around. Now, he counted himself lucky. For a long time, he'd been on crutches. Compared to that, a single stick didn't seem so bad.

After running a brush through her hair, Pekka looked in the mirror again. "It will have to do," she said sadly.

"You always look good to me," Fernao said.

"I hope you have better taste than that," Pekka said. "My one consolation is, everybody who was at the farewell will be feeling the same way we do."

"I have trouble believing Ilmarinen is really gone," Fernao said as he went to the door. "The project won't be the same without him."

"That's why he left—he said the project already wasn't the same," Pekka answered. "It won't be the same for me now, I'll tell you that. With Master Siuntio dead, with Master Ilmarinen gone . . ." She sighed. "It's as if the adults had all left, and now things are in the children's hands." She walked out into the hallway. Fernao followed and closed the door behind them.

As they headed for the stairs that would take them to the refectory, he said, "We aren't children, you know."

"Not for everyday things," Pekka agreed. "In this, next to Siuntio and Ilmarinen—what else are we?"

"Colleagues," Fernao answered.

Pekka squeezed his hand. "You do sound like a Lagoan," she said fondly. "Your people have their share of Algarvic arrogance."

"I wasn't thinking about me so much," Fernao said. "I was thinking about you. You were the one who made the key experiments. Siuntio knew it. Ilmarinen knew it. They tried to give you credit. I honor them for that—a lot of mages would have tried to steal it instead." Several of his own countrymen sprang to mind, starting with Grandmaster Pinhiero of the Lagoan Guild of Mages. He doggedly plowed ahead: "But you don't seem to want to take it. What's the opposite of arrogance? Self-abnegation?" The last word, necessarily, was in classical Kaunian; he had no idea how to say it in Kuusaman.

Pekka started to get angry. Then she shrugged and laughed instead. "Kuusamans see Lagoans as one thing. I don't suppose it's any surprise that you should see us as the opposite. To a mirror, the real world must look backwards."

Irked in turn, Fernao started to growl, but checked himself and wagged a finger at her. "Ah, but who is the mirror—Lagoans or Kuusamans?"

"Both, of course," Pekka answered at once. That made Fernao laugh. He'd never known a woman who made him laugh so easily. *Must be love,* he thought. *One more sign of it, anyhow.*

When they walked into the refectory, he saw right away that Pekka had known whereof she spoke. All the mages already there looked subdued. Some of them looked a good deal worse for wear than merely subdued. No one moved very fast or made loud noises of any sort. When a mug slipped off a serving girl's overloaded tray and shattered, everybody flinched.

Fernao pulled out a chair for Pekka. She smiled at him as she sat. "I could get used to these fancy Lagoan manners," she said. "They make me feel . . . pampered, I think, is the word I want."

"That's what they're for," Fernao agreed. His leg and hip yelped as he too went from standing to sitting. Little by little, he was getting used to the idea that they would probably do that as long as he lived.

After a quick nod, Pekka frowned. "Maybe you have them and we don't because we have an easier time with the idea that women and men can mostly do the same jobs than you Lagoans do. Do the fancy manners and the deference men show your women help keep them from thinking about things they can't have?"

"I don't know," Fernao confessed. "I haven't the faintest idea, to tell you the truth. I never would have thought of connecting manners and anything else. Manners are just manners, aren't they?" But were they just manners? Now that Pekka had raised the question, her remark made a disturbing amount of sense.

Before he could say so, one of the serving girls came up and asked, "What would you like this morning?"

"Oh, hello, Linna," Fernao said. "How are you today?"

"My head hurts," she answered matter-of-factly. She'd been at Ilmarinen's farewell celebration. For all Fernao knew, she'd given the master mage a special farewell of her own once the celebration wound down. Fernao wondered just what Ilmarinen had seen in her: to him, she wasn't especially pretty or especially bright. But Ilmarinen had bristled like a young buck whenever anyone else so much as gave her a *good day*. Now she sighed and went on, "I'll miss the old so-and-so, powers below eat me if I won't."

"He'll miss you, too," Pekka said.

"I doubt it," Linna replied with casually devastating cynicism. "Oh, maybe a little, till he finds somebody else to sleep with him up in Jelgava, but after that?" She shook her head. "Not likely. But I *will* miss him. I've never known anybody like him, and I don't suppose I ever will."

"There *isn't* anybody like Ilmarinen," Pekka said with great conviction. "They only minted one of that particular coin."

"You're right there," Linna said. "He's even good in bed, would you believe it? I finally told him aye as much to shut him up as for any other reason I can think of. He'd been pestering me for so long—I figured we might as well get it over with, and then I could let him know I wasn't interested any more. But he fooled me." She shook her head again, this time in slow wonder. "Once he got started, I never wanted him to stop."

Fernao coughed and looked down at his hands. That was more than he'd expected or wanted to hear. Kuusamans—especially their women—were a lot franker about some things than Lagoans. Casting about for some sort of answer, he said, "Ilmarinen would be good at anything he set his mind to."

"He probably would," Pekka agreed.

Linna didn't say anything, but the look on her face did argue that Ilmarinen had indeed been good at something. Recalling herself—she needed a moment to do so—she said, "What can I bring you? You never did tell me."

"Tea. Hot tea. Lots of hot tea, and a jar of spirits to splash into it," Fernao said.

"Same for me," Pekka added. "And a big bowl of tripe soup to go alongside." Linna nodded and hurried off toward the kitchens.

"Tripe soup?" Fernao echoed, wondering whether he'd heard right. But Pekka nodded, so he must have. He gave her an odd look. "Do Kuusamans really eat things like that? I thought you were civilized."

"We eat all sorts of strange things," Pekka answered, a twinkle in her eye. "We just don't always do it where foreigners can see us. Chicken gizzards. Duck hearts. Reindeer tongue, boiled with carrots and onions. And tripe soup." She laughed at him. "Turn up your nose all you like, but there aren't many things better when you've had too much to drink the night before."

"I've had tongue," Fernao said. "Beef tongue, not reindeer. They sell it smoked and sliced in fancy butcher's shops in Setubal. It's not bad, as long as you don't think about what you're eating."

The twinkle in Pekka's eye only got more dangerous. "You've never had brains scrambled together with eggs and cream, where what you're eating thinks about you."

Fernao's stomach did a slow lurch, as it had been known to do when waves started pounding a ley-line ship on which he was serving. *Only one way to deal with this,* he thought. When Linna came back with the tea and the strengthener and a big steaming bowl of soup, he pointed to it and said, "Let me have some of that, too."

Pekka's eyebrows flew up like a couple of startled blackbirds. Linna just nodded. "Good for what ails you," she said, "though who would've thought a Lagoan had wit enough to know it?"

"Are you sure?" Pekka asked, pausing with a spoonful of soup—and a chunk of something thin and grayish brown in the bowl of the spoon—halfway to her mouth.

"No," Fernao answered honestly. "But if it's nastier than I think, I don't have to eat it all." He spooned honey into his tea, and poured in a splash of spirits, too. Hot and sweet and spiked, the brew did make him feel better. He gulped it down.

Pekka drank fortified tea, too, but concentrated on the soup. Linna brought Fernao's bowl back almost at once. "Cook did up a big pot of it this morning," she said, setting it down in front of him. "After what all went on last night, he figured people would need it. I had some myself, back in the kitchen."

Looking around the refectory, Fernao saw several Kuusamans with bowls like his in front of them. *If it doesn't hurt them, it probably won't kill me, either,* he thought. Pekka eyed him inscrutably as he picked up his spoon.

Of all the things he'd expected, actually liking the soup was among the last. "That's good!" he said, and sounded suspicious even as he spoke: as if he suspected someone of tricking him. But it *was*. The broth was hot and greasy and salty and full of the flavors of garlic and chopped scallions. And the tripe, while chewy, didn't taste like much of anything. His headache receded, too. Maybe that was the tea. But, on the other hand, maybe it wasn't.

He beamed at Pekka. "Well, if this is barbarism, who needs civilization?" She laughed. Why not? Her bowl was already empty.

Like all the Forthwegians in Plegmund's Brigade, Sidroc hated winters in the south. This was the third one he'd been through, and they got no easier with practice. He didn't think Yanina was quite so cold as southern Unkerlant had been, but it was a lot worse than Gromheort, his home town. There, snow had been a curiosity. It was nothing but an eternal nuisance here.

He remembered throwing snowballs with his cousins, Ealstan and Leofsig, one day when white did cover the ground up there. He'd been perhaps nine, the same age as Ealstan, with Ealstan's older brother in his early teens. Sidroc grunted in his frozen hole in the ground. No more playing with them. Ealstan had done his best to break his head, and he himself *had* broken Leofsig's—broken it with a chair. *Whoreson gave me one hard time too many,* Sidroc thought. *Good riddance to him. The whole family's a pack of filthy Kaunian-lovers.*

Somebody called his name—an Algarvian, by the trill he put in it. "Here, sir!" Sidroc sang out, speaking Algarvian himself. Even now, after more than two years of desperate fighting, there wasn't a Forthwegian officer in Plegmund's Brigade—nobody higher than sergeant. The redheads reserved the top slots for themselves.

Lieutenant Puliano wasn't an Algarvian noble, though.

He was a veteran sergeant who'd finally become an officer for the most basic and desperate reason of all: there weren't enough nobles left to fill the places that needed filling. All but invisible in a white snow smock, Puliano slithered along the ground till he dropped into the hole next to Sidroc. "I've got something for you," he said. "A present, you might say."

"What kind of present?" Sidroc asked suspiciously. Some of the presents officers gave, he didn't want to get.

Puliano laughed. "You weren't born yesterday, were you?" With his gravelly voice and no-nonsense attitude, he sounded like a sergeant. In fact, he put Sidroc in mind of Sergeant Werferth, who'd been his squad leader—and, without the rank, his company commander—till he got blazed outside a Yaninan village. That village didn't exist any more; Sidroc and his comrades had slaughtered everybody there in revenge for him. Puliano went on, "It's nothing bad. No extra sentry-go. No volunteering to storm the enemy bridgehead over the Skamandros singlehanded."

Sidroc just grunted again. "What is it, then?" He remained suspicious. Officers didn't go around handing out presents. It felt unnatural.

But Lieutenant Puliano dug into his belt pouch and gave Sidroc a straight cloth stripe for the shoulder straps of his tunic and two cloth two-stripe chevrons for the tunic sleeve—Forthwegian and Algarvian blazons of rank. Men of Plegmund's Brigade wore both when they could get them, though the Algarvian insignia were more important. "Congratulations, Corporal Sidroc!" Puliano said, and kissed him on both cheeks.

Sergeant Werferth never would have done that. "Well, dip me in dung," Sidroc said, startled into Forthwegian. He was more polite in Algarvian: "Thank you, sir."

"You are welcome," Puliano said. "And who knows? You may make sergeant yet. You may even make officer yet."

That startled Sidroc. In fact, it startled him right out of politeness. "Who, me?" he said. "Not fornicating likely— uh, sir. I *am* a Forthwegian, in case you had not noticed."

"Oh, I noticed. You're too ugly to make a proper Algarvian." Puliano spoke without malice, which didn't necessarily say he meant it for a joke. Before Sidroc could sort that out, the redhead went on, "If they made *me* into an officer, who knows where they'll stop?"

He had something there. The only kingdom that really didn't care whether its officers were noblemen or not was Unkerlant. Swemmel had got rid of old nobles much faster than he'd created new ones. If the Unkerlanters hadn't let commoners become officers, they wouldn't have had any.

Puliano grinned and pointed west. "Now, *Corporal*"— Sidroc didn't care for the way the redhead emphasized his shiny new rank—"we have to see what we can do about that bridgehead on this side of the Skamandros."

"What, you and me and nobody else?" Sidroc said. The Unkerlanters had spent lives like water to force their way across the river after being balked for some considerable while. Most of the lives they'd spent forcing the crossing were those of Yaninans. *That'll teach Tsavellas to turn his coat,* Sidroc thought savagely.

"No, lackwit," Puliano answered. "You and me and everything the fellows in the fancy uniforms can scrape together." He might have been reading Sidroc's mind, for he went on, "It's not the nasty little whoresons in the pompom shoes in the bridgehead any more. I wish it were; we could deal with *them*." He spat in fine contempt. "But it's Unkerlanters in there now, Unkerlanters and as many stinking behemoths as they can cram into the space. And if we wait for them to bust out . . ."

Sidroc made a very unhappy noise. He'd seen too often what happened when the Unkerlanters burst from their bridgeheads. He didn't want to be on the receiving end of that again. But he asked, "Have we got any real chance of flinging them back across the river?"

Puliano's shrug was as theatrical as his scornful spitting. To a Forthwegian's eyes, Algarvians overacted all the time. "We have to try," he said. "If we don't try, we just sit here waiting for them to futter us. If we try, who knows what might happen?"

He had a point. Most of the time, the Unkerlanters were as stubborn in defense as any general could want. Every so often, though, especially when they got hit at a time or from a direction they didn't expect, they would panic, and then the men attacking them got victories on the cheap.

"We have enough behemoths of our own to throw at them?" Sidroc persisted. "We have enough Kaunians to kill to put some kick in our attack?"

"Behemoths?" Puliano gave another shrug, melodramatic and cynical at the same time. "We haven't had enough behemoths since the battles in the Durrwangen bulge. This won't be any different from any other fight the past year and a half. Blonds . . . Powers above, we're even short on blonds." But his battered features didn't seem unduly disheartened. "Of course, since Tsavellas isn't on our side any more, we don't have to worry about what happens to these stinking Yaninans. Their life energy works as well as anybody else's."

"Heh," Sidroc said. "I would sooner kill Kaunians. I never did like Kaunians. We are better off without them. But nobody will miss these Yaninan bastards, either."

"Just so," Puliano agreed. "Kaunians are the great enemies of Algarve, of real Derlavaian civilization, always and forever. But, as you say, the Yaninans betrayed us. They'll pay for it. Indeed they will." He clapped Sidroc on the back one more time, then went off to spread the news elsewhere.

Sidroc waited in his hole, wondering if the Unkerlanters would spend some more Yaninans, or even some of their own men, in a spoiling attack to disrupt whatever the Algarvians had in mind. It didn't happen before his relief came to take his place. "Hullo, Sudaku," he said. "Everything is pretty quiet there for now. It won't last, though, not if the lieutenant has the straight goods."

"We have to take out the bridgehead," Sudaku answered seriously. "If we do not, the Unkerlanters will come forth and take *us* out."

They both spoke Algarvian. It was the only tongue they shared. Sudaku was no Forthwegian. He and a good many others like him had attached themselves to Plegmund's Brigade in the grim fighting during the breakout from the Mandelsloh pocket in the eastern Duchy of Grelz. No one had bothered to detach them since; the Algarvians had more important things to worry about. By now, some of the men from the Phalanx of Valmiera could curse fluently in Forthwegian.

And, by now, Sidroc had stopped worrying about the obvious fact that Sudaku and his countrymen were tall and blond and blue-eyed—were, in fact, every bit as Kaunian as the blonds from Forthweg whom Mezentio's men massacred whenever they needed to. He did sometimes wonder why the Valmierans fought for Algarve. The reasons they'd given didn't seem good enough to him—but then, his own probably looked flimsy to them, too. All he really worried about was whether he could count on them in a tight place. He'd seen, again and again, that he could.

Sudaku asked, "Do we hear right? Are you promoted?"

"Oh. That." Thinking about assailing the Unkerlanter bridgehead, Sidroc had almost forgotten about his new rank. "Aye, it's true."

"Good for you," the Valmieran said. Sidroc shrugged. He didn't know whether it was good or not, not really. Then Sudaku smiled a sly smile and added, "Now you will be able to tell Ceorl what to do."

"Ah," Sidroc said, and smiled. He hadn't thought of that. He and the ruffian had been giving each other a hard time for a couple of years. Now, at last, he had the upper hand. Of course, if he rode Ceorl too hard, he was liable to end up dead in the attack on the bridgehead regardless of whether the Unkerlanters blazed him. Neither the Phalanx of Valmiera nor Plegmund's Brigade worried overmuch about keeping hard cases from their ranks.

When Sidroc got back to his squad—*his* squad indeed, now—Ceorl greeted him with, "Well, here's a fine outfit ruined."

"Plegmund's Brigade's been in trouble ever since it took you in," Sidroc retorted. But he went on, "We may be ruined, if we really do have to try and smash the Unkerlanter bridgehead. It won't be easy. That job never is."

Lieutenant Puliano hadn't been joking. Sidroc wished it were otherwise. He didn't get so much as the chance to sew his new insignia of rank to his tunic before he and the men with him got ordered forward. Some behemoths came with them. The beasts wore snowshoes to help them get over and through the drifts: an Unkerlanter notion that had dreadfully embarrassed the Algarvians the first winter of the war, and that Mezentio's men had since stolen. Seeing behemoths with Algarvians aboard them raised Sidroc's spirits. It proved the redheads were serious about this attack.

They also brought up egg-tossers to pound the Unkerlanter positions on the east side of the Skamandros. The pounding didn't last long. All too soon, officers' whistles shrilled. "Forward!" Puliano shouted, along with his fellow commanders. To his credit, he *went* forward, too. Algarvian officers led from the front, one reason Mezentio's men needed so many replacements.

Sidroc ran past a few dead and dying Unkerlanters whose blood stained the snow. For a heady moment, he thought the attack might have surprised Swemmel's soldiers. Then they struck back. Dragons—some of them painted Yaninan red and white—streaked over from the west side of the river. The Algarvians didn't have nearly enough beasts in the air to hold them off. Despite the Algarvian behemoths stiffening the attack, far more Unkerlanter animals trudged forward to oppose them. As always, the Unkerlanters turned a bridgehead into a spiky hedgehog as fast as they could.

This time, they didn't wait for the Algarvians to start killing Kaunians or Yaninans before striking back in kind. The ground shuddered beneath Sidroc's feet. Violet flames shot up from it. Men shrieked. Behemoths bellowed in mortal agony. And, when the Algarvian mages did resort to their own murderous magic, it was to defend against what Swemmel's sorcerers were doing, not to aid in the attack.

Crouching behind a great gray stone, Sidroc called out to Puliano: "We cannot do this."

"We have to," the Algarvian lieutenant answered. "If we don't, they'll futter us later."

"If we do, they will futter us now," Sidroc retorted.

He hoped Puliano would tell him he was full of nonsense, but the redheaded veteran only grimaced. Another attack did go in. The Unkerlanters held it off and beat it back. After that, sullenly, the Algarvians—and the Forthwegians and Valmierans and Grelzers and the handful of

Yaninans who couldn't stomach serving Swemmel—drew back. Sidroc knew what that meant. It meant trouble; Puliano was dead right. *And it means we aren't strong enough to stop the trouble,* he thought. He shrugged a broad-shouldered shrug. He'd been in a lot of trouble in this war. What was once more?

In all his life, Garivald had never gone through—had, in fact, never imagined—a winter without snow. He came from a little village called Zossen, down in the Duchy of Grelz. Blizzards there were so much a fact of life that every peasant hut had its doorway facing north or northeast, away from the direction from which the bad weather was likeliest to come. Even in his time as an irregular in the woods west of Herborn, the Grelzer capital, he'd known no different winters.

Zossen, these days, no longer existed. The Algarvians had made a stand there when Unkerlanter armies fought their way back into Grelz, and nothing was left of the village or of the family Garivald had had there. And Swemmel's impressers, a few months later, had efficiently dragged him into the army, even though he and Obilot, the woman with whom he'd taken up while in the irregulars, were working an abandoned farm well away from any other village.

An Algarvian egg burst, not too far from Garivald's hole in the ground in the Unkerlanter bridgehead south of Eoforwic. No snow here: just rain through the fall and into the winter. People had told Garivald it would be like that, but he hadn't believed it till he saw it himself.

Another egg burst. He saw the flash as all the sorcerous energy trapped inside the egg was released at once, and the fountain of mud and dirt that rose. The redheads had tried several times to drive the Unkerlanters back across the Twegen River, tried and failed. They hadn't mounted any full-scale attacks against this bridgehead lately, but they didn't let the Unkerlanters rest easy here, either.

From the rear, somebody called, "Sergeant Fariulf!"

"I'm here," Garivald answered. Swemmel's impressers hadn't been perfectly efficient when they swept him into their net. They'd got him into the army, but they didn't know who they had. As Fariulf, he'd just been one peasant recruit among many. As Garivald the leader of an irregular band, the composer of patriotic songs, he was a target. He'd led men, he'd influenced men, without taking orders directly from King Swemmel. That made him dangerous, at least in Swemmel's eyes.

"Lieutenant Andelot wants you, Sergeant," the soldier said.

"I'm coming," Garivald told him. A couple of more eggs burst in front of his hole as he scrambled out and went back toward his company commander. Even had the Algarvians been pounding the bridgehead just then with everything they had, he still would have had to go. No one in Swemmel's army got away with disobeying orders.

"Hello, Sergeant," Andelot said. He was several years younger than Garivald, but he was an educated man, not a peasant, and spoke with a cultured Cottbus accent. Garivald liked him as well as he could like anyone set in authority over him.

"What can I do for you, sir?" Garivald asked now.

Andelot set his hand on some papers. "I just wanted to say, this report you wrote after the last time the redheads tapped us is quite good."

"Thank you, sir." Garivald grinned his pleasure at the praise.

With a chuckle, Andelot said, "Anyone could tell you're new to having your letters. Once you've been writing for a while, you'll come to see what a nuisance putting reports and such together can be."

"It's your own fault, sir, for teaching me," Garivald replied. Only a handful of people in Zossen had been able to read and write; the village had had no school, and not much of anything else. He'd shaped and carried all his songs in his head. He still did, for that matter—putting them down on paper would have put Swemmel's inspectors on his trail faster than anything else he could think of.

"I don't think we'll have the leisure for reports and such for very much longer," Andelot said.

"Ah?" Garivald leaned toward him. "Are we finally going to break out?"

Andelot nodded. "That's the idea."

"Good," Garivald said. "I'm sick of looking at this same little chunk of Forthweg day after day—especially since it gets more torn up every single day." His nostrils flared. "If it weren't winter—or as close to winter as they get around here—we wouldn't be able to stand the stink. It's pretty bad even so."

"Mezentio's men have hurt us," the company commander agreed. "But we've hurt them, too, and we're going to hurt them more. When we do break out of here—and out of our other bridgehead north of Eoforwic—the city will fall."

"Aye, sir." Now Garivald nodded. "That's what I thought."

But Andelot hadn't finished. "And that's not all, Fariulf," he went on, as if Garivald hadn't spoken. "Once we break the hard crust of their line, we storm eastward with everything we've got. And do you know what? I don't think they can stop us, or even slow us down much, this side of the Algarvian border."

"The Algarvian border," Garivald echoed in dreamy tones. Then he asked a question that showed his ignorance of the world outside Zossen and the Duchy of Grelz: "How far is it from here to the Algarvian border?"

"A couple of hundred miles," Andelot answered lightly. Garivald gaped, but only for a little while. Even though he'd been dragged into the army relatively late, he'd seen how fast it could move when things went well. Andelot went on, "We strike them at sunrise day after tomorrow. Have your men ready."

"Aye, sir." Garivald saluted and went up to his muddy hole in the ground once more. He knew dismissal when he heard it.

Behemoths came forward that evening under cover of darkness. Some of them sheltered under what trees still stood. Others stayed out in the open, but with great rolls of mud-colored cloth spread over them to make them harder for Algarvian dragons to spot from the air. The deception must have worked, for the redheads flung no more eggs than usual at the bridgehead the next day. The following night, still more behemoths tramped up toward the fighting front.

And, some time in the dark, usually quiet hours between midnight and dawn, that calm was shattered when every Unkerlanter egg-tosser in the bridgehead suddenly started hurling eggs at the Algarvians as fast as it could. The din, the flashes of light, the quivering of the earth beneath Garivald were all plenty to terrify him. What they were doing to the redheads among whom the eggs were landing was something he didn't care to think about. *The worse they get hit, the better,* did go through his mind. The worse the Algarvians got hit at the beginning, the more trouble they would have fighting back.

As dawn stained the sky ahead with pink, officers' whistles shrilled. "Forward!" The cry echoed all through the bridgehead.

"Forward, men!" Garivald yelled at the top of his lungs. "Forward! Urra! King Swemmel! Urra!" And then he added a new cry, one that had just occurred to him: "On to Algarve!"

"On to Algarve!" the men in his squad echoed. Moving on to Algarve was easier when whole regiments of behemoths thundered forward alongside the footsoldiers.

Here and there, Algarvian resistance was tough. Garivald had discovered that, however much he hated them, the redheads made brave and resourceful foes. Wherever they hadn't been smashed flat, they clung to strongpoints, held on, and pushed back the advancing Unkerlanters as best they could. That was what the behemoths advancing with his countrymen were for. The egg-tossers and heavy sticks they bore on their backs made short work of positions the footsoldiers couldn't possibly have cleared by themselves.

"Come on! Keep moving!" Garivald shouted till he grew hoarse. "We've got to keep up with the behemoths."

In spite of the pounding the egg-tossers had given the Algarvian lines, the first day's advance went slowly. Mezentio's men had put as many rings of fieldworks around the rim of the Unkerlanter bridgehead as they could, and had to be dug out of them one battered set of trenches at a time. Whatever reserves they had close by, they threw into the

fight. They knew what was at stake here no less than the
Unkerlanters did.

Toward evening, Garivald found himself huddled behind
a burned-out barn only a few feet from Andelot. He
couldn't quite remember how he'd got there. All he could
feel was relief that nobody was blazing at him for the moment. Panting, he asked, "How do you think we're doing,
sir?"

"Not too bad," Andelot answered. "I think we might be
better off if they hadn't managed to murder General Gurmun. He was one of our good ones, our really good ones.
But we have room to spare, and the redheads don't."

"How *did* they do that, sir?" Garivald asked.

"Nobody knows, because we never caught the whoreson
who killed him," Andelot answered. "My guess is, they did
something like what they tried to do here in the bridgehead,
only you caught it and Gurmun's guards cursed well
didn't."

"They sent in a redhead sorcerously disguised as a Forthwegian, sir?" Garivald asked.

"Maybe. More likely, though, they sent in an Algarvian
disguised as one of us," Andelot said. "We don't look much
different from Forthwegians, and they have people who
speak our language. Somebody like that could get in to see
Gurmun without much trouble. He'd come out and disappear—and after a while, somebody would have gone in and
found Gurmun dead. I don't *know* that's how it happened,
mind you. I'm just a lieutenant—nobody tells me these
things. But it's my best guess. We'll go slower than we
would have with Gurmun in charge. I'm sure of that."

Garivald snatched a little sleep in the dubious shelter the
barn gave. Screeching whistles roused him well before
dawn. He got his men up and moving. Beams from the
business end of Unkerlanter and Algarvian sticks flashed
and flickered like fireflies.

He wondered if Mezentio's men would loose their fearsome, murder-based magic. They didn't. Maybe the Unkerlanter attacks had killed most of their mages or wrecked the
camps where they kept Kaunians before slaughtering them.

He knew less about that than Andelot knew about how General Gurmun had died, but it seemed a reasonable guess.

What Garivald did know was that, midway through the second day of the breakout, Unkerlanter men and behemoths smashed past the last prepared Algarvian positions and out into open country. "Come on, boys!" he shouted. "Let's see them try and stop us now!" He trotted east, doing his best to keep up with the behemoths.

Peering west, Leino had no trouble seeing the Bratanu Mountains, the border between Jelgava and Algarve. On the Algarvian side of the border, they were called the Bradano Mountains. But, since the Kaunian ancestors of the Jelgavans had given them their name, the Kuusaman mage preferred the blonds' version.

Looking ahead to the mountains made him wistful, too. "See?" He pointed to the snow that, at this season of the year, reached halfway down from the peaks. "You can find winter in this kingdom, if you go high enough."

He spoke classical Kaunian, the only language he had in common with Xavega. The Lagoan sorcerer tossed her head, sending coppery curls flying. "So you can. But we are still down here in the flatlands. And powers above only know when we shall drive the cursed Algarvians back beyond their own frontier."

"Patience." Leino stood up on his toes to give her a kiss; she was taller than he. "It was only this past summer that we came ashore on the beaches near Balvi, and here we are at the other side of the kingdom. I do not see how the Algarvians can keep us from crossing the mountains. They do not have the men, the behemoths, or the dragons to do it."

"Patience." Xavega spoke the word as if it were an obscenity. "I have no patience. I want this war to be over and done. I want to go back to Setubal and pick up the pieces of my life. I hate the Algarvians as much for what they have done to me as for what they have done to Derlavai."

"I believe that," Leino murmured; Xavega was invincibly self-centered. He hadn't been going to bed with her because he admired her character. He didn't. He'd been going

to bed with her because she was tall and shapely, somewhere between very pretty and outrageously beautiful, and
as ferociously talented while horizontal as anyone looking
at her vertical could have hoped. With a small sigh, he said,
"I want to go back to Kajaani and start over, too."

"Kajaani." Xavega sniffed. "What is a Kuusaman provincial town, when set beside Setubal, the greatest city the
world has ever known?"

The capital of Lagoas was indeed a marvel. Leino had
gone there a couple of times for sorcerers' convocations,
and had always been amazed. So much to see, so much to
do . . . Even Yliharma, Kuusamo's capital, couldn't really
compare. But Leino had an answer with which even short-
tempered Xavega couldn't quarrel: "What is Kajaani? Kajaani is home."

He missed Pekka. He missed Uto, their son. He missed
their house, up a hill from the ley-line terminal stop. He
missed the practical magecraft he'd been doing at Kajaani
City College.

Would he miss Xavega if the chances of war swept them
apart? He chuckled under his breath. Some specific *part* of
him would miss her; he could hardly deny that. But the
rest? He ruefully shook his head. Xavega didn't even *like*
Kuusamans, not as a general working rule. That she made
an exception for him was almost as embarrassing as it was
enjoyable.

And how would he explain her to his wife? If the powers
above were kind, he'd never have to. If they weren't? *I'd
been away from you for a long, long time, sweetheart,* was
about as good as he could come up with. Would Pekka
stand for that? She might; Kuusamans did recognize that
men and women had their flaws and foibles. But she
wouldn't be very happy, and Leino didn't see how he could
blame her.

He almost wished she were carrying on an affair of her
own—nothing serious, just enough so that she couldn't beat
him about the head and shoulders with tales of glistening,
untrammeled virtue. He didn't find that likely; he didn't really think his wife was the sort to do such things. And he
didn't really wish she were that sort. Just . . . almost.

Kuusaman dragons, eggs slung under their bellies, flew by heading east to pound the Algarvian positions in front of the Bratanu Mountains. Aye, Kuusaman and Lagoan dragons ruled the skies over Jelgava. The Algarvians had a lot of heavy sticks on the ground, but those didn't help them nearly so much as dragons of their own would have done.

Painted sky blue and sea green, the Kuusaman dragons were hard to spot. Kuusamans had never believed in unnecessary display. Kuusamans often didn't believe even in necessary display. Algarvic peoples, with their love for swagger and opulence, had a different way of looking at things. Algarvian dragons were painted green, red, and white; the colors of Sibiu were red, yellow, and blue; and those of Lagoas red and gold. Algarvian soldiers had gone into the Six Years' War in gorgeous, gaudy, impractical uniforms. The slaughter in the early days of that fight, though, had forced pragmatism on them in a hurry.

Before long, the muted roar of eggs bursting in the distance came back to Leino's ears. In an abstract way, he pitied the Algarvian soldiers who had to take such punishment without being able to give it back. But, as a practical mage, he knew abstraction went only so far. He much preferred dishing out misery to taking it.

When he said that aloud, Xavega nodded. "Against the combined might of Lagoas and Kuusamo, they are all but powerless to resist," she replied.

The combined might of Lagoas and Kuusamo here in Jelgava was two or three parts Kuusaman to one part Lagoan. The Kuusamans were also fighting, and winning, a considerable war against Gyongyos across the islands of the Bothnian Ocean. Xavega didn't like to think, didn't like to admit, that the short, swarthy, slant-eyed folk she looked down on both metaphorically and literally were a good deal more powerful than her own countrymen. Few Lagoans did. And, because Lagoas looked west and north across the Strait of Valmiera toward Derlavai while the Kuusamans concentrated on shipping and trade, they didn't often have to. Leino smiled. *Often* was different from *always*.

But then his smile slipped. "The Algarvians cannot

match us in men or beasts, no. But in magecraft . . ." By the time he finished, he looked thoroughly grim.

Xavega scowled, too. "Aye, they are murderers. Aye, they are filthy. But that is why we are here, you and I. The magecraft we learned can make their own wickedness come down on their heads, not on those against whom they aim it."

"Indeed." Leino had to work to hold irony from his voice. It wasn't that Xavega hadn't told the truth. It was just that, as she had a way of doing, she turned things so they looked best to her. The sorcery she was talking about came from Kuusamo, not Lagoas. If fact, unless Leino was entirely wrong, Pekka had had a lot to do with devising it. She hadn't said so—but then, she hadn't been able to talk about what she was doing for quite some time. The few hints Leino had picked up all pointed in that direction.

Before his thoughts could glide much further down that ley line, a crystallomancer burst out of a nearby tent and came running toward him and Xavega. "Master mages! Master mages!" the fellow cried. "One of our dragonfliers reports that the Algarvians are stirring at their special camp near the mountains."

"Are they?" Leino breathed. Mezentio's men called the camps where they kept Kaunians before killing them by an innocuous name, not least, Leino suspected, so they wouldn't have to think about what they did. Names had power, as any mage knew. And the Algarvians' enemies had adopted this euphemism, too, not least so they wouldn't have to think about what the Algarvians were doing, either.

"What is he saying?" demanded Xavega, who'd stubbornly refused to learn any Kuusaman. There were days when Leino found himself surprised she'd ever learned classical Kaunian.

He explained, adding, "You would think they would have learned their lesson."

"Algarvians are arrogant," Xavega said. By all the signs she gave, she'd never noticed her own arrogance. She went on, "Besides, their murderous sorcery is the strongest weapon Mezentio's men have. If they use it when no mages are in position to strike back at them, they can work no small harm. Here, I would say, they judge the risk to be worth it."

"I would say you are right," Leino answered. "I would also say we are going to teach them they have miscalculated."

The crystallomancer seemed to follow classical Kaunian only haltingly. He spoke to Leino in the Kuusaman that was their common birthspeech: "Shall I tell the men at the front that they *will* have sorcerous protection?"

"Aye, you can tell them that," Leino answered, also in Kuusaman. The crystallomancer saluted and dashed back to his tent. Leino fell back into classical Kaunian: "This time, at least, we have some little warning. That must have been a sharp dragonflier. Usually, we have to start the counterspells when we feel the jolt as the Algarvians start killing."

Xavega nodded. She put her arms around Leino and gave him a long, thorough kiss. When at last they broke apart, she murmured, "Use my strength as your own when we give them what they deserve."

Heart pounding, Leino nodded, too. On the cot and in matters magical, Xavega gave of herself without reserve. Everywhere else, she was as spoiled a creature as had ever been born. Leino knew that. He could hardly help knowing it. But it didn't make any difference to what he would do now. Here, he almost had to lead, for the spells were in Kuusaman; no one had yet had the leisure to render them into classical Kaunian or Lagoan. Xavega had learned the rituals well enough to support him, and she did that very well.

"Before the Kaunians came, we of Kuusamo were here," he murmured in his own tongue, a ritual as old as organized magecraft in his land. "Before the Lagoans came, we of Kuusamo were here. After the Kaunians departed, we of Kuusamo were here. We of Kuusamo are here. After the Lagoans depart, we of Kuusamo shall be here." He'd used the traditional phrases whenever he incanted in Jelgava, even though they weren't strictly true here, as they were back in his homeland.

Once they'd passed his lips, he went through all the preliminary phases of the spell he would hurl at Mezentio's sorcerers. Xavega nodded approval. "Good," she said.

"Very good indeed. As soon as they start killing, as soon as they reveal their direction and distance, we shall drop on them like a pair of constables seizing a band of robbers."

"They *are* robbers, by the powers above," Leino said. "And what they steal cannot be made good, for who can give back a life once lost?"

A few minutes later, he sensed the disturbance in the world's energy grid as the Algarvians began killing Kaunians. He took savage pleasure in casting the rest of the spell and flinging it at the mages who had gone back to the most barbarous days of wizardry to try to support their kingdom in a losing war. Xavega's hand rested on his shoulder. He felt her strength flowing into him, flowing through him, and flowing out of him against the Algarvians. And he felt the power Mezentio's men had unleashed now crumpled, bent back, turned against them.

"This is easy!" Triumph filled Xavega's voice. "It must be because we were ready in advance."

"I suppose so," Leino said when he could snatch a moment between cantrips. "It almost feels . . . too easy?"

Xavega laughed and shook her head. But suddenly, as Leino began a new charm, he felt another upsurge of sorcerous energy from the west, this one far stronger than the one before. *I've been outfoxed,* he thought as the ground shuddered beneath him. Xavega screamed. *The Algarvians used one sacrifice to get us to show where we were, then had more Kaunians and more mages waiting to strike us when we revealed ourselves. Now how do we get out of this?*

Red-purple flames shot up all around them. The crystallomancers' tent caught fire. Xavega screamed again. Cracks in the ground yawned wide beneath her and Leino. Leino screamed, too, as he felt himself falling. The cracks slammed shut.

Ilmarinen's bones creaked as he got off the ley-line caravan in the western Jelgavan town of Ludza. Carrying a carpetbag heavier than it might have been because it was full of papers and sorcerous tomes, he descended to the platform. The depot was battered but still standing, which proved the Algarvians hadn't turned and fought here, as they'd done in a good many places he'd seen on his journey across King Donalitu's realm.

A Kuusaman mage about half Ilmarinen's age stood waiting on the platform. "Welcome, Master!" he exclaimed, hurrying forward to take the carpetbag. "It's a great privilege to make your acquaintance, sir. I'm called Paalo."

"Pleased to meet you," Ilmarinen answered. "You have a carriage waiting?"

"I certainly do, sir," Paalo said. "And we may speak freely as we go. My driver is cleared to hear secrets."

"I'm so sorry for him," Ilmarinen murmured. Paalo gave him a puzzled look. Ilmarinen stifled a mental sigh. *Another bright young man born without a funny bone,* he thought. *Too many of them these days.* But he would have to deal with this one, at least for a while. "I heard in—Skrunda, was it?—that something had gone wrong up here. What can you tell me about it?"

"I'm afraid that's right, sir," Paalo said. "It doesn't do to depend on the Algarvians to keep trying the same thing over and over. They caught a couple of our mages—well, actually, one of ours and a Lagoan—in as nasty a trap as you'd never want to see."

"Started killing Kaunians for a lure, then killed a bunch more once we'd begun the counterspell, the second time aiming at our mages?" Ilmarinen asked.

"Er—aye." Paalo frowned. "Did you hear that back in Skrunda, sir? They weren't supposed to know that much about it. If somebody back there is asking questions where he isn't supposed to, I want to know who. We'll put him someplace where he can ask questions of the geese that fly by, and of nobody else."

"No, no, no—nothing like that." Ilmarinen shook his head. "I had all that time to think while I was sailing up from Kuusamo. One of the things I was thinking about was, if I were one of fornicating Mezentio's mages, how could I get back at the nasty Kuusamans and Lagoans who were giving me such a hard time?"

Paalo stared. "I hope you won't be angry at me for saying so, sir, but you seem to have outthought the entire sorcerous high command of our army and that of the Lagoans, too." He slung Ilmarinen's carpetbag in the carriage, then turned to see if the master mage needed a hand getting in himself. When he discovered Ilmarinen didn't, he asked, "How did you do that?"

"I suspect it wasn't very hard," Ilmarinen answered, and Paalo's narrow, slanted eyes got about as wide as they could. Ilmarinen went on, "No doubt all the army mages were so full of themselves—and so full of what their fancy spells could do—that they never bothered thinking about what the other bastards might do to them. Stupid buggers, but I don't suppose it can be helped."

"Er . . ." Paalo said again. Ilmarinen realized he might have sounded too harsh; criticizing military mages to another military mage was almost bound to prove a waste of time. Perhaps to disguise what he was feeling, Paalo gave the driver minute instructions on how to get back to a place he'd surely come from. Then, sighing, he went on, "I wish Leino and Xavega had foreseen such consequences as accurately as you did, Master Ilmarinen."

"They probably should have—" Ilmarinen broke off. "Leino?"

"That's right." Paalo nodded. "Did you know him, sir?"

"I've met him a few times." Ilmarinen shook his head in bemusement. "I've done a good deal of work with his wife, though. They had—they have—a little boy." *And what will Pekka and her Lagoan lover do when they find out about this? I wish I were back there in the Naantali district, so I could see for myself. A better piece of melodrama than most of the playwrights come up with, by the powers above.*

"His . . . wife?" Paalo said. "Are you sure, sir?"

"I've been to their home. I've met their boy. He looks like his father," Ilmarinen replied. "I never saw them naked in bed together and screwing, if that's what you mean, but I have no doubt they were guilty of it. Why?"

Paalo turned as red as a golden-skinned Kuusaman could. "I don't wish to speak ill of the dead, but. . . ."

"But you're going to," Ilmarinen said. "After a buildup like that, my friend, you'll blab or I'll turn you into a sparrow and me into a sparrowhawk. Talk!"

Instead of talking, Paalo suffered a coughing fit. "Well, sir, it's only that . . . Anyone who knew Leino and Xavega here in Jelgava knew they . . . they . . ."

"Were lovers?" Ilmarinen suggested.

Paalo nodded gratefully. "So they were. And so we all assumed Leino had no, ah, impediments that would have kept him from . . ."

"Screwing her," Ilmarinen supplied, and got another grateful nod from Paalo, who struck him as a very straitlaced man. "Xavega," Ilmarinen murmured. "Xavega. I saw her at a sorcerers' colloquium or two, I think. Bad-tempered woman, if I recall, but pretty enough to get away with it a lot of the time."

"That's her," Paalo said. "Drawn straight from life, that's her."

Ilmarinen hardly heard him. "And put together?" he added, his hands shaping an hourglass in the air. "I wouldn't have thrown her out of bed, even if I'd been married to two of my wives at the same time." He eyed Paalo, who'd gone from red to a color not far removed from chartreuse, and patted him on the back. "There, there, my dear fellow, I've upset you."

"It's nothing, sir," the other wizard said stiffly. He was plainly lying through his teeth, but Ilmarinen rather admired him for it here. After a moment, gathering himself, Paalo added, "You aren't . . . quite what I expected in a master mage, if you don't mind my saying so."

"I'm a raffish old son of a whore, is what I am," Ilmarinen said, not without a certain pride. "What you expected was Master Siuntio—but even he had more juice in him than people who didn't know him would guess. But, juice or no juice, plaster or no plaster, he's dead now, and you're bloody well stuck with me. And if I don't match what you think a master mage should be—I *am* a master mage, so maybe you'd do better revising your hypothesis."

"Er . . ." Paalo said yet again. He laughed a nervous laugh. "You *aren't* what I expected, not at all."

"Too bad." Ilmarinen leaned forward to tap the driver on the shoulder. "How much longer till we get where we're going?"

"Half an hour, sir," the fellow answered, "if the Algarvians don't go and drop any eggs on our heads."

"Are they in the habit of doing that?" Ilmarinen glanced at Paalo. "Your head still looks moderately well stuck on."

He'd expected the younger mage to go, *Er,* for the fourth time. Instead, solemnly, Paalo said, "I do begin to wonder, the more I sit by you." That startled a laugh out of Ilmarinen. Paalo went on, "No, the Algarvians haven't got many dragons in the air here. We rule the skies. They're trying to hold our beasts on Sibiu away from Trapani and the south, and most of their dragons that aren't doing that are fighting the Unkerlanters."

"Ah, the Unkerlanters," Ilmarinen said. "Swemmel's paid the butcher's bill for this war, even if we islanders may come out of it looking better than he does. I'm sorry for him. I'd be even sorrier if he weren't such a nasty, miserable bastard in his own right. An ally, aye, but a nasty, miserable bastard all the same."

"Best thing that would happen would be for Mezentio's men to wreck Unkerlant as badly as Swemmel's men wreck Algarve," Paalo said. "Then we wouldn't have to worry about either one of them for a generation."

That fit in quite well with Ilmarinen's view of the world. But all he said was, "How likely is it? The things we want most, the things we need most—those are the things we're least likely to get."

"What do we do, then?" Paalo asked, his tone not far from despairing.

Ilmarinen set a hand on his shoulder. "The best we can, son. The best we can." He cocked his head to one side. "Do I hear eggs bursting up ahead? The first thing we'd better do is, we'd better finish whipping the Algarvians. What *they* think is the best thing that could happen isn't what *we* want, believe you me it isn't."

"I know that," Paalo said. "Every single Kuusaman has known it since they used their filthy magic against Yliharma."

"And ever single Kuusaman *should* have known it since they started using their filthy magic against the Unkerlanters," Ilmarinen said. "Killing people for the sake of their life energy is just as nasty aimed at the Unkerlanters as it is when it's aimed at us."

"I suppose so," the other mage said. "It doesn't hit home the same way, though. I guess it should, but it doesn't." Since he was right, Ilmarinen didn't argue with him.

The carriage rolled past olive trees and almonds and the oranges and lemons the Jelgavans used to flavor their wine and the vineyards in which they raised the grapes for that wine. None of those crops would have grown in Kuusamo. Oh, a few cranks raised a few grapes on north-facing hills in the far, far north of Ilmarinen's homeland, and in warm years they got a few bottles of thoroughly indifferent wine from those grapes. They were proud of themselves. That didn't mean they weren't cranks.

Ilmarinen enjoyed the spicy, aromatic scent of the citrus leaves. Even in wintertime, birds hopped here and there through the trees, searching for bugs. That would have been plenty to tell the master mage he wasn't home any more. Pink-flowered oleanders added their sweet, slightly cloying scent to the mix. Then the breeze shifted a little. Ilmarinen's nose wrinkled.

So did Paalo's. "Dead behemoths," he explained. "The Algarvians had a few around here. We surrounded them and pounded them with dragons, and that's what you smell. They're very good with the beasts. Our own behemoth crews go on and on about that. They've had plenty of practice fighting the Unkerlanters, I suppose. But all the practice in the world won't help you if you're as outnumbered as they were and if you haven't got any dragons of your own overhead."

"Good," Ilmarinen said. "Nobody ever said the Algarvians weren't fine soldiers. Nobody ever said they weren't brave soldiers. That doesn't mean they don't need beating. If anything, it means they need beating more than ever, because it makes them more dangerous than they would be otherwise." He pointed ahead, to a ragtag collection of tents. "Is that where I go to work?"

"It is, sir, aye," Paalo said. "I'm sorry. I wish it were finer."

"Don't worry," Ilmarinen said. "Let the Algarvians worry instead." He hoped they would.

Four

When the knock on the door to Fernao's chamber came, Pekka and he had just finished putting on their clothes. In a low voice, one that, with luck, wouldn't carry out into the hallway beyond, Pekka said, "It's a good thing he didn't get here a few minutes ago."

"I think it's a very good thing, sweetheart," Fernao replied as he headed for the door. His voice was so full of sated male smugness, Pekka started to stick out her tongue at his back. But she was feeling pretty well sated herself, and so she didn't. Fernao opened the door. "Aye? What is it?"

"I'm sorry, sir," the crystallomancer in the hallway said. "I need to speak to Mistress Pekka. I checked her chamber first, and she wasn't there, and . . . well, this is the next place I looked. Is she here?"

"Aye, I'm here," Pekka answered, coming up to stand beside Fernao. That the two of them spent all the time they could together was no secret from the folk at the hostel in the Naantali district. If it still was a secret in the wider world, it wouldn't stay one for long. Sooner or later, word would get to Leino. Pekka would have to deal with that . . . eventually. For now, she just asked, "And what's gone wrong, or what does somebody think has gone wrong?"

"Mistress, Prince Juhainen would speak to you," the crystallomancer said.

"Oh!" Pekka exclaimed. She stood on tiptoe to kiss Fernao—no, no secrets here, not any more—then said, "I'll come, of course." A call by crystal from any of the Seven would have got her immediate, complete attention, but Juhainen's domain included Kajaani and the surrounding districts—he was *her* prince, or she his particular subject. "Did he say what he wanted?"

"No, Mistress Pekka," the crystallomancer replied. She

turned and started down the corridor. Pekka hurried after her. She looked back over her shoulder once. Fernao waved and blew her a kiss before shutting the door. She smiled and went on after the crystallomancer.

"I hope he won't be angry because he's had to wait," she said when she and the crystallomancer reached the chamber that kept the hostel linked to the outside world no matter how beastly winter weather in the Naantali district grew.

"He shouldn't be," the other woman replied. "He's been prince for a while now; he knows how these things work." Juhainen's uncle, Joroinen, had preceded him as one of the Seven, and had died in the Algarvian attack on Yliharma three years before. Joroinen was one of the main reasons her project had gone forward. Juhainen backed her, but not the way his uncle had.

His image looked out of the crystal at Pekka. "Your Highness," she murmured, and went to one knee for a moment, a Kuusaman gesture of respect from a woman to a man that had a long and earthy history behind it. "How may I serve you, sir?"

Prince Juhainen was younger than she. He'd looked it, too, on first succeeding Joroinen, but didn't any more. Responsibility was having its way with him. Pekka knew that weight, too, but Juhainen had more of it on his shoulders than she did. He said, "Mistress Pekka, I would give a great deal not to be the bearer of the news I have to give you."

"What is it, your Highness?" Alarm flashed through her. Had the Seven somehow decided the project wasn't worth continuing after all? That struck Pekka as insane, when magic she and her colleagues had created was used in Jelgava every day, and was one of the most important reasons the Kuusaman and Jelgavan armies had driven across the kingdom in less than half a year. She thought first of the project; that Juhainen's news might instead be personal never crossed her mind.

Tiny and perfect in the sphere of glass in front of her, Juhainen's image licked its lips. *He doesn't want to go on,* Pekka realized, and fear began to edge its way into her alongside astonishment. The prince sighed and looked down at a leaf of paper on the table in front of him. Then, with another sigh, he said, "I regret more than I can tell you that, in operations west of the town of Ludza, your husband Leino fell victim to a sorcerous attack from the Algarvians. He and the mage with whom he was partnered both perished. They were resisting one sorcerous assault from the enemy when another, this one aimed specifically at them, struck home. For whatever they may be worth to you, Mistress Pekka, you have my deepest personal condolences, and those of all the Seven Princes of Kuusamo. We knew the work your husband did before the war; thanks to the behemoth armor he helped devise, many crews and many footsoldiers who might have died still live."

Pekka stared at him. "No," she whispered: not so much disagreement as disbelief. She'd hardly heard anything Juhainen said after he told her Leino was dead. Much more to herself than to the prince, she said, "But what will Uto do without his father?"

"What amends the Seven of Kuusamo can make, we will," Juhainen promised. "Your son shall not lack for anything material. When the time comes for him to choose his course in life, all doors will be open to him. Of this you have my solemn vow."

"Thank you," Pekka said, almost at random. She felt as if she'd walked into a closed door in the dark: stunned and shocked and hurt, all at the same time. She believed Juhainen now, where she hadn't a moment before. Disbelief was easier. Here, for once, she would have been happier not knowing the truth.

Ilmarinen would not approve, she thought dizzily. She knew her wits weren't working the way they were supposed to: she knew, but she couldn't do anything about it. People in accidents often behaved so; she'd heard as much, anyway. She wished she weren't experiencing it for herself.

"Is there anything I can do for you, Mistress Pekka?" Juhainen asked.

"No," Pekka said, and then remembered herself enough to add, "No, thank you."

"If ever there is, you know you have only to ask," the prince said.

"Thank you, your Highness," Pekka said. Prince Juhainen's

image vanished from the crystal as his crystallomancer cut the etheric connection. Pekka got to her feet, vaguely surprised her legs obeyed her will.

"Are you all right, Mistress Pekka?" asked the crystallomancer who'd brought her to this chamber.

"No," Pekka answered, and walked past her. She would have walked through her if the crystallomancer hadn't scurried out of her way.

The next thing Pekka knew, she was standing in front of the door to her own room. She went inside and barred the door behind her. She hadn't run into anyone on the way—or if she had, she didn't remember it. She threw herself down on the bed and started to weep. All the tears she'd held back or been too numb to shed came flooding out.

Fernao will wonder where I am, wonder what's happened, she thought. That only brought on a fresh torrent of tears—these, tears of shame. *Powers above, if the knock on the door had come a few minutes earlier, we'd have been making love. Wouldn't that have been a perfect way to find out Leino was dead?*

"It was only because you weren't here," she said aloud, as if her husband stood beside her listening. But Leino didn't. He wouldn't, not ever again. That finally started to strike home. Pekka wept harder than ever.

After a while, she got up and splashed cold water on her face. It did no good at all; looking at herself in the mirror above the sink, she saw how puffy and red her eyes were, and how much she looked like someone who'd just staggered out of a ley-line caravan car after some horrible mishap. Even as she dried her face, tears started streaming down her cheeks once more. She threw herself down on the bed again and gave way to them.

She never knew how long the knocking on the door went on before she noticed it. Quite a while, she suspected: by the time she did realize it was there, it had a slow, patient rhythm to it that suggested whoever stood out there in the hallway would keep on till she gave heed.

Another splash of cold water did even less than the first one had. Grimly, Pekka unbarred and opened the door anyhow. It might be something important, something she had to deal with. Dealing with anything but herself and her own pain right now would be a relief. *Or,* she thought, *it might be Fernao.*

And it was. The smile melted off his face when he saw her. "Powers above," he whispered. "What happened, sweetheart?"

"Don't call me that," Pekka snapped, and he recoiled as if she'd struck him. "What happened?" she repeated. "Leino. In Jelgava. The Algarvians." She tried to gather herself, but had no great luck. The tears came whether she wanted them or not.

"Oh," Fernao said softly. "Oh, no. I'm so sorry."

Are you? she wondered. *Or are you just as well pleased? Why shouldn't you be? Your rival is out of the way. How convenient.* Nothing she'd ever seen from Fernao, nothing he'd ever said, made her believe he would think, did think, like that. But she wasn't thinking very clearly herself right then. Sometimes, she did think clearly enough to understand that.

Fernao started to come into the room. Pekka stood in the doorway, blocking his path. He nodded jerkily, then bowed, almost as if he were an Algarvian. "All right," he said, though she hadn't said anything aloud. "I'll do anything you want me to do. You know that. Tell me what it is, and I'll do it. Only . . . don't shut me away. Please."

"I don't want to have to think about that right now," Pekka said. "I don't want to have to think about anything right now." But she couldn't help it; what ran through her mind was, *Oh, powers above—I'm going to have to let Uto know his father isn't coming home from the war.* That was another jolt, almost as bad as hearing the dreadful news from Juhainen. "For now, can you just . . . leave me be?"

"All right," he said, but the look in his eyes—so like a Kuusaman's eyes in shape, set in an otherwise purely Lagoan face—showed she'd hurt him. "Whatever you want me to do, or don't want me to do, tell me. You know I'll do it . . . or not do it."

"Thank you," Pekka said raggedly. "I don't know what the etiquette is for the wife's lover when the husband dies."

Spoken in a different tone of voice, that might have been a joke. She meant it as a statement of fact, no more.

Fortunately, Fernao took it that way. "Neither do I," he admitted, "at least not when—" Several words too late, he broke off. *At least not when the lover has nothing to do with the husband's demise,* he'd been about to say: that or something like it. Lagoans weren't quite so touchy or so much in the habit of taking other men's wives for lovers as Algarvians, but some of the romances Pekka had read suggested they did have their rules for such situations.

She didn't want to think about that now, either. In the romances, the wife was often glad when her husband met his end. *She* wasn't glad. She felt as if a ley-line caravan had just appeared out of nowhere, run her down, and then vanished. Leino had been one of the anchors of her world. Now she was adrift, lost, at sea. . . .

Had Fernao chosen that moment to try to embrace her, in sympathy either real or something less than real, she would have hit him. Maybe he sensed as much, for he only nodded, said, "I'll be here when you need me," and went down the hall, the rubber tip of his cane tapping softly on the carpet at every stride.

Pekka had never imagined she would have to compare a dead husband and a live lover. She found she couldn't do it, not now. She dissolved in tears again. Tomorrow—perhaps even later today—she would start doing everything that needed doing. For the time being, grief had its way with her.

Colonel Sabrino had been at war more than five years. In all that time, he could count on the fingers of one hand the number of leaves he'd got. The ley-line caravan glided to a stop. "Trapani!" the conductor called as he came through the cars. "All out for Trapani!"

Grabbing his duffel bag and slinging it over his shoulder, Sabrino left the caravan car. No one waited for him on the platform: no one here knew he was coming. *I'll surprise Gismonda,* he thought, and hoped he wouldn't surprise his wife in the arms of another man. That would prove embarrassing and complicated for all concerned. One thing—he wouldn't surprise his mistress in the arms of another man. That would have proved even more embarrassing and complicated, but Fronesia had left him for an officer of footsoldiers who she'd thought would prove more generous. Absently, Sabrino wondered if he had.

The depot had seen its share of war. Planks stretched across sawhorses warned people away from a hole in the platform. Boards patched holes in the roof, too, and kept most of the cold rain off the debarking passengers and the people waiting for them. The sight saddened Sabrino without surprising him. All the way back from eastern Yanina, he'd seen wreckage. Some of it came from Unkerlanter eggs; more, by what people said, from those dropped by Kuusaman and Lagoan dragons. Now that the islanders were flying off the much closer islands of Sibiu, they could pound southern Algarve almost at will.

Our dragonfliers are as good as theirs, Sabrino thought bitterly. *A lot of our dragonfliers are better than any of theirs. Anyone who's stayed alive since the beginning has more experience than a Kuusaman or a Lagoan could hope to match. But we haven't got enough dragons, and we haven't got enough dragonfliers.*

Stretched too thin. The words tolled like a mournful bell inside Sabrino's mind. Algarvian dragons had to be divided among the west—where King Swemmel's men swarmed forward yet again—Valmiera, Jelgava, and the defense of the south against the air pirates flying out of Sibiu. How was one kingdom supposed to do all those jobs at the same time? It was impossible.

If we don't do all those jobs, we'll lose the war.

That was another painfully obvious truth. It had been obvious to soldiers since the battles of the Durrwangen bulge, perhaps since the fall of Sulingen. Any civilian with eyes to see would surely have noted the same thing after Kuusamo and Lagoas gained their foothold on the mainland of Derlavai in Jelgava. Now armies came at Algarve from the west and from the east. *On which front will we lose ground faster?*

Outside the depot, cabs waited in neat ranks, as in the old days. Sabrino waved to one. The cabby waved back. He hurried toward the cab. The driver descended, opened the door for him to get in, and asked, "Where to?"

Sabrino gave his address, or rather half of it, before stopping and staring. The cabby's black uniform was the one he remembered, from heavy shoes to high-crowned cap with shiny patent-leather brim. But . . . "You're a woman!" he blurted.

"Sure am," the cabby agreed. She was middle-aged and dumpy, but that wasn't why he'd needed a moment to know her for what she was. Smiling at his confusion, she went on, "You haven't been home for a while, have you, Colonel?"

"No," Sabrino said numbly.

"Plenty of women doing all kinds of things these days," the driver told him. "Not enough whole men—or crippled men, come to that—left to do them, and they've got to get done. Hop in, pal. I'll take you where you're going. You want to tell me again where that is, without choking this time?"

Still astonished, he obeyed. When he got into the passenger compartment, she closed the door behind him, then scrambled up to her seat. The cab began to roll. Sure enough, she could manage a horse.

Streets were rougher than Sabrino remembered. That wasn't the cab's elderly springs; it was poorly repaired holes in the roadway. Some of them hadn't been repaired at all. Jounces made his teeth click together.

Everything seemed more soot-stained than Sabrino remembered, too. The reason for that wasn't hard to find, either. Charred ruins were everywhere, sometimes a house or a shop, sometimes a block, or two, or three. The air stank of stale smoke. Just breathing made Sabrino want to cough.

There was the jeweler's shop where Sabrino had had a ring—booty he'd taken in Unkerlant—repaired for his mistress. No, there was the block where the shop had stood, but only wreckage remained. He hoped Dosso had got out. He'd been doing business with the jeweler since just after the Six Years' War.

Most of the people on the street were women. Sabrino had seen that on earlier leaves. It stood out even more strongly now. Even some of the constables were women.

The rest were graybeards who looked to have been summoned from retirement. Most of the men not in uniform limped or went on crutches or had a sleeve pinned up or wore a patch over one eye or had some other obvious reason for not being at the front. Everyone seemed to be wearing somber clothing—some the dark gray of mourning, others shades of blue or brown hard to tell from it in the sad winter light. Women's kilts had got longer, too. Sabrino let out a silent sigh.

The cab rattled to a stop. "Here you go, Colonel," the driver said. Sabrino got out. The driver descended to hand him his bag. He tipped her more than he would have if she were a man. She curtsied and climbed up again to go look for her next fare. Sabrino went up the walk and used the brass knocker to knock on his own front door.

When a maidservant opened it, she squeaked in surprise and dropped him a curtsy more polished than the one he'd got from the cabby. "Your Excellency!" she exclaimed. "We had no idea . . ."

"I know, Clarinda," Sabrino answered. "It's not always easy to send messages from the front. But I'm here. The Unkerlanters haven't managed to turn the lady my wife into a widow quite yet. Is Gismonda at home?"

Clarinda nodded. "Aye, my lord Count. Nobody goes out as much as we did . . . beforehand. Let me go get her." She hurried away, calling, "Lady Gismonda! Lady Gismonda! Your husband's home!"

That brought servants from all over the mansion to clasp Sabrino's hand and embrace him. The last time he'd had such a greeting, he thought, was when he'd managed to escape the Unkerlanters after they blazed down his dragon.

"Let me through," Gismonda said, and the cooks and serving girls parted before her as if she were a first-rank mage casting a powerful spell. Sabrino's wife gave him a businesslike hug. She was a few years younger than he; she'd been a beauty when they wed, and her bones were still good. She would have hated being called handsome, but the word fit her. After looking Sabrino up and down, she nodded in brisk approval. "You seem better than you did the last time they let you come home."

"I was wounded then," he pointed out. "You look very good, my dear—and you don't look as if you were about to go to a funeral." Gismonda's tunic and kilt were of a bright green that set off her eyes and the auburn hair that, these days, got more than a little help from a dye jar.

Her lip curled. "I don't much care for what people call fashion these days, and so I ignore it. Some fools do cluck, but the only place I care about hens is on my supper plate." She turned to the head cook. "Speaking of hens, have we got a nice one you can do up for the count's supper tonight?"

"Not a hen, milady, but a plump capon," he replied.

Gismonda looked a question to Sabrino. His stomach answered it by rumbling audibly. As if he'd replied with words, Gismonda nodded to the cook. He went off to get to work. Gismonda asked Sabrino, "And what would you like in the meanwhile?"

He answered that without hesitation: "A hot bath, a glass of wine, and some clean clothes."

"I think all that can probably be arranged," Gismonda said. By the look she gave the servants, they would answer to her if it weren't.

Sabrino was soaking in a steaming tub—luxury beyond price in the wilds of Unkerlant or Yanina—when the bathroom door opened. It wasn't a servant; it was his wife, carrying a tray on which perched two goblets of white wine. She gave Sabrino one, set the other on the edge of the tub, and went out again, returning a moment later with a stool, upon which she perched by the tub. Sabrino held up his goblet in salute. "To my charming lady."

"You're kind," Gismonda murmured as she drank. Their marriage, like most from their generation and class, had been arranged. They never had fallen in love, but they liked each other well enough. Gismonda sipped again, then asked a sharp, quick question: "Can we win the war?"

"No." Sabrino gave the only answer he could see.

"I didn't think so," his wife said bleakly. "It will be even worse than it was after the Six Years' War, won't it?"

"Much worse," Sabrino told her. He hesitated, then went on, "If you have a chance to get to the east, it might be a good idea." He didn't elaborate. He didn't want to think about the Unkerlanters' coming so far, but couldn't help it. Gismonda's thoughtful nod told him she understood what he meant.

Her eyes glinted. "Since you're unfortunate enough to find yourself in Trapani without a mistress, would you like me to scrub your back for you—or even your front, if you're so inclined?"

Before he could answer, bells started ringing all over the Algarvian capital, some nearer, some farther. "What's that?" he asked.

"Enemy dragons," Gismonda replied. "The warning for them, I mean. The dowsers are skilled, not that it helps much. Get dressed—quickly—and come down to the cellar. We can worry about other things later." She sighed. "The capon will have to go out of the oven and into a rest crate. We will get to eat it eventually."

The only clothes Sabrino had in the bathroom were his uniform tunic and kilt and a heavy wool robe. Without hesitation, he chose the robe. Even as he tied it shut, eggs began falling on Trapani. He'd delivered attacks and been under attack from the air, but he'd never imagined a pounding so large and sustained as this. And it went on and on, night after night after night? Gismonda did not have to hurry him down the stairs. He marveled that any of Trapani was left standing.

The cellar hadn't been made to hold everyone in the mansion. It was cramped and crowded and stuffy. Even down here underground, the thuds and roars of bursting eggs dug deep into Sabrino's spirit. Everything shook when one came down close by. If one happened to land on the roof, would everyone be entombed here? He wished he hadn't thought of that.

After a couple of hours, he asked, "How long does this go on?"

"All night, most nights," Clarinda answered. "Some of them fly away, but more come. We knock some down, but . . ." Her voice trailed away.

All night long? Sabrino thought with something approaching horror. *Every night? We never could have done that, not at the height of our strength.* The height of Algarve's strength seemed very far away now, very far away indeed. *We are going to lose this war, and then what will become of us?* The eggs kept falling. They gave no answer, or none Sabrino wanted to hear.

For the first time since the middle of summer, Ealstan couldn't hear any eggs bursting. The fighting had passed east from Eoforwic. Algarvians no longer swaggered through the streets of Forthweg's capital. Now Unkerlanters stumped along those cratered, rubble-strewn streets. If they'd expected to be welcomed as liberators, they were doomed to disappointment. But they didn't seem to care one way or the other.

"Just another set of conquerors," Ealstan said one afternoon, when he got back to the flat he shared with Vanai and Saxburh. "They look down their noses at us as much as the Algarvians ever did."

"Powers above be praised that we're safe and that this building is still standing, so we have a roof over our heads," his wife replied. "Past that, nothing else really matters."

"Well, aye," Ealstan said reluctantly. "But if we rose up against Swemmel's men, they'd squash us the same way the Algarvians did. That's . . . humiliating. Is Forthweg a kingdom, or is it a road for its neighbors to run through any time they choose?" Almost as soon as the question was out of his mouth, he wished he hadn't asked it. Too many times in years gone by, Forthweg had proved to be nothing but a road.

But Vanai surprised him by answering, "I don't know. And do you know something else? I don't care, either. I don't care at all, if you want to know the truth. The only thing I care about is, the Unkerlanters don't march through the streets yelling, 'Kaunians, come forth!' And if I go outside and my sorcery slips—or even if I go outside without my sorcery—they won't drag me off to a camp and cut my throat. They don't care about Kaunians one way or the other, and you have no idea how good that feels to me."

Ealstan stared. Maybe because Vanai had looked like Thelberge for so long, he'd let himself forget—or at least not think so much about—her Kaunianity. The Kaunians in

Forthweg often found Forthwegian patriotism bewildering, or even laughable. That was one reason, one of many, Forthwegians and Kaunians rubbed one another the wrong way. And he couldn't blame Vanai for thinking the way she did, not after everything she'd been through. Still . . .

A little stiffly, he said, "When the war is finally over, I want this to be our own kingdom again."

"I know." Vanai shrugged. She walked over and gave him a kiss. "I know you do, darling. But I just can't make myself care. As long as nobody wants to kill me because I've got blond hair, what difference does it make?" Ealstan started to answer that. Before he could say anything, Vanai added, "Nobody but a few Kaunian-hating Forthwegians, I mean."

Whatever he'd been about to say, he didn't say it. After some thought, he did say, "A lot of those people went into Plegmund's Brigade—my cursed cousin Sidroc, for instance. I don't think they'll be coming home."

"That's good," Vanai admitted. "But there are always more of those people. They don't disappear. I wish they did, but they don't." She spoke with a weary certainty that was very Kaunian indeed.

The day was mild, as even winter days in Eoforwic often were. They had the shutters open wide to let fresh air into the flat. A couple of daggerlike shards of glass remained in the window frames, but no more. *Now, maybe, I can think about getting that fixed,* went through Ealstan's mind. *Maybe, in spite of everything, this city will come back to life again now that the Algarvians are gone.*

Motion down on the street drew his eye. He went to the window for a better look. Through much of the summer and fall, he wouldn't have dared do any such thing—showing himself would have been asking to get blazed. A couple of Unkerlanters, recognizable by their rock-gray tunics and clean-shaven faces, were pasting broadsheets on still-standing walls and fences. "I wonder what those say," he remarked.

"Shall we go down and find out?" Vanai replied. "We can do that now, you know. *I* can do that now, you know." To emphasize how strongly she felt about it, she switched from the Forthwegian she and Ealstan usually used to classical Kaunian.

"Why not?" Ealstan replied in the same language. Vanai smiled. Though she was more fluent in Forthwegian than he was in the tongue she'd most often used back in Oyngestun, he pleased her whenever he used classical Kaunian. Maybe it reminded her that not all Forthwegians hated the Kaunians who shared the kingdom with them.

Ealstan scooped Saxburh out of the cradle, where she'd been gnawing on a hard leather teething ring. She smiled and gurgled at him. Her eyes were almost as dark as his, but her face, though still baby-round, promised to end up longer than a pure-blooded Forthwegian's would have. Vanai threw on a cloak over her long tunic. "Let's go," she said, and really did sound excited about being able to leave the flat whenever she wanted.

As usual, the stairwell stank of boiled cabbage and stale piss. Ealstan was resigned to the reek these days, though it had distressed him when he first came to Eoforwic. Back in Gromheort, his family had been well-to-do. He hoped they were well, and wondered when he would hear from them again. *Not till the Unkerlanters run the redheads out of Gromheort,* he thought. *Soon, I hope.*

Vanai pointed to the front wall of a block of flats a couple of doors down. "There's a broadsheet," she said.

"Let's go have a look," Ealstan said. Here in the street, another stink filled the air: that of dead meat, unburied bodies. The Algarvians hadn't fought house by house in Eoforwic, not when it became plain the city would be surrounded. They'd got out instead, saving most of their men to give battle elsewhere with better odds. But a good many of them had perished, and some Unkerlanters—and, almost surely, more Forthwegian bystanders than soldiers from both sides put together.

The broadsheet's headline was bold and black: THE KING WILL SPEAK. Ealstan stared at those astonishing words. Vanai read the rest, " 'The King of Forthweg will address his subjects before the royal palace at noon on' "—the date was three days hence. " 'All loyal Forthwegians are urged to come forth and hear their sovereign's words.' "

"King Penda's back?" Ealstan's jaw fell in astonishment. He grabbed Vanai and kissed her. "King Penda's back! Hurrah!" He felt like cutting capers. He did cut a few, in fact. From Vanai's arms, Saxburh stared at him in astonishment. He kissed the baby, too. "King Penda's back! I never thought the Unkerlanters would let him show his face in Forthweg again."

"I'm glad you're pleased." By Vanai's tone, the news didn't excite her nearly so much.

"Let's go hear him when he speaks!" Ealstan exclaimed. His wife looked as if that wasn't the thing she most wanted to do, but she didn't say no. She might not share his patriotism, but she'd learned better than to argue about it with him.

And so, on the appointed day, Ealstan and Vanai and Saxburh with them went to the square in front of the palace. Ealstan wore his best tunic, not that it was much better than the others. Vanai hadn't bothered putting on anything special.

Blue and white ribbons and streamers and banners—Forthweg's colors—did their best to enliven the battered square and even more battered palace façade. In front of the palace stood a new wooden platform with a speaker's podium at the front. Unkerlanter soldiers stood guard around it. More soldiers, these probably of higher rank, stood on it with a personage in fancy robes.

Ealstan got up on tiptoe, trying to see better. "Is that King Penda?" he said, almost hopping in his excitement. "Who else could that be but King Penda?" He took Saxburh from Vanai and held her up over his head. "Look, Saxburh! That's the king!"

"I don't think she cares," Vanai said pointedly.

"Not now, but she will when she's older," Ealstan said. "She's seen the king!"

The king did not come to the podium at once. Instead, one of the Unkerlanter officers strode forward. "People of Forthweg!" he called in accented but understandable Forthwegian. "I am General Leuvigild, King Swemmel's commander for Forthweg." *What does that mean?* Ealstan wondered. Before he could say anything, Leuvigild went on, "People of Forthweg, I give you a king who has struggled side by side with us to free your kingdom from the Algarvian invaders, a man who has fought alongside Unkerlanter soldiers rather than fleeing his kingdom for a life of ease and luxury, safe in Lagoas. People of Forthweg, I give you King Beornwulf I! Long may he reign!"

In dead silence, Beornwulf came up to the podium. *A puppet,* Ealstan thought bitterly. *Nothing but an Unkerlanter puppet.* Back before the war, he'd heard of Beornwulf a few times: the man was an earl or count with estates in the west of Forthweg. *The man is a whore, naked in King Swemmel's bed, and he prostitutes his kingdom along with himself.*

"People of Forthweg, I will make you the best king I can," Beornwulf said. "We are allied with Unkerlant in the tremendous struggle against accursed Algarve. We shall follow our ally's lead, and in so doing regain our own freedom. So long as we do that, we shall stay great and free. I expect all my subjects to recognize the importance of this alliance, and to do nothing to jeopardize it, as I shall do nothing to jeopardize it. Together, Unkerlant and Forthweg will go forward to victory."

He stepped back. More silence followed: no curses, no boos, but no cheers or applause, either. Quietly, Vanai said, "Well, it could be worse, you know."

And she was right. Swemmel could simply have annexed Forthweg. Maybe rule from a puppet would prove better than direct rule by a puppet-master like the King of Unkerlant. Maybe. Ealstan wondered if he dared hope for even that much.

People started filing out of the square. They had to file past more Unkerlanter soldiers, men who hadn't been there when the square filled. "What are they doing?" Vanai said, alarm in her voice. "They can't be checking for Kaunians. They don't do that . . . do they?"

"Your spell is fine," Ealstan told her, and squeezed her hand. "And you dyed your hair not so long ago. You'll get by."

Not everyone got by. The Unkerlanters—there were a surprising lot of them—pulled people out of the crowd and let others through. They didn't listen to the cries of protest that started rising. But nobody did more than shout. The

Unkerlanters all had sticks, and likely wouldn't hesitate to use them. Most people seemed to get through. Having no choice, Ealstan and Vanai went forward.

An Unkerlanter soldier looked Ealstan up and down. He paid Vanai no attention whatever. In what was probably his own language rather than Forthwegian, he asked, "How old are you?"

Ealstan got the drift; Forthwegian and Unkerlanter were cousins. "Twenty," he said.

"Good." The Unkerlanter gestured with his stick. "You come here with us."

Ice ran through Ealstan. "What?" he said. "Why?"

"For the army," the Unkerlanter answered. "Now come, or be sorry."

"King Beornwulf will have an army?" Ealstan asked in surprise.

"No, no, no." The Unkerlanter laughed. "King *Swemmel's* army. Plenty of Algarvians to kill. Now come." By the way he gestured with the stick this time, he'd use it if Ealstan balked. Numbly, Ealstan went. He didn't even get to kiss Vanai goodbye.

Colonel Lurcanio had spent four happy, useful years in Priekule, helping to administer the occupied capital of Valmiera for King Mezentio of Algarve. He'd seen a great many other Algarvians leave Valmiera to fight in Unkerlant, a fate not worse than death but near enough equivalent to it. After the islanders landed in Jelgava, he'd seen other countrymen go north to fight there.

At last, with the Valmierans ever more restless under Algarvian control, there simply weren't enough Algarvians left to hold down the occupied kingdom any more. And so Mezentio's men had withdrawn from most of it, the bargain being that the Valmieran irregulars wouldn't harass them so long as they were pulling back. Both sides had stuck to it fairly well.

And so I've become a real soldier again, Lurcanio thought. A tent in the rugged upland forests of northwestern Valmiera was a far cry from a mansion on the outskirts of

Priekule. If he wanted his cot warmed, he could put stones by the campfire and wrap them in flannel. They were a far cry from Marchioness Krasta. Lurcanio sighed for pleasures now lost. Krasta hadn't a brain in her head, but the rest of her body more than made up for that. Not for the first time, Lurcanio wondered if she was indeed carrying his child.

He had no time to dwell on the question. Instead of keeping Priekule running smoothly for Grand Duke Ivone, he had command of a brigade of footsoldiers these days. And they were about to strike. As soon as the Algarvians abandoned the northern coast of the Strait of Valmiera, Kuusamo and Lagoas promptly started pouring men and behemoths and dragons across the arm of the sea separating their island from the Derlavaian mainland. Algarvian dragons and leviathans did what they could to hinder that, but what they could was less than their commanders had expected—less than they'd promised, too.

"As if anyone with sense would believe our promises nowadays," Lurcanio muttered. Too many of them had been broken. And so Kuusaman and Lagoan soldiers rampaged west through southern Valmiera, a few brigades of Valmierans with them. They were heading straight for the border of the Marquisate of Rivaroli, which had been Algarvian before the Six Years' War, Valmieran between the Six Years' War and the Derlavaian War, and was now Algarvian once more. How long it would stay that way . . .

Is partly up to me, Lurcanio thought. He turned to his adjutant, Captain Santerno. "Are we ready?"

"As ready as we can be, sir," Santerno answered. He was a young man, with perhaps half Lurcanio's fifty-five years, but he wore two wound badges and what he called a frozenmeat medal that showed he'd fought in Unkerlant through the first dreadful winter of the war there. He had a scarred face and hard, watchful eyes. "Now we get to find out how good the islanders really are."

His tone said he didn't expect the Lagoans and Kuusamans to be very good. After what he'd seen in the west, his attitude proclaimed, nothing the islanders did was likely to impress him. And his eyes measured Lurcanio. He didn't say, *You've been sitting on your arse in Priekule, screwing blond women and living high on the hog, but what kind of warrior do you make?* He didn't say it, but he thought it very loudly.

What kind of warrior do *I make?* Lurcanio wondered. After four years of being a military bureaucrat, he was going to find out. "Do you think we can slice south through them, all the way to the sea?" he asked.

"We'd cursed well better, wouldn't you say, Colonel?" Santerno replied. "Cut 'em off, chew 'em up. That'll buy us the time we need here, maybe let us set things right against the Unkerlanters." He didn't sound convinced. A moment later, he explained why: "We've scraped a lot together to make this attack. We might have done better to throw it all at Swemmel's bastards."

"How would we stop the islanders then?" Lurcanio asked.

"Powers below eat me if I know, sir," his adjutant said. "All I can tell you is, we haven't got the men in the west to keep the Unkerlanters out of Algarve the way things are. I got to Valmiera just a couple of weeks before we pulled back. That was supposed to free up more men for the west, but they've been sucked up into Jelgava, or else they're here in the woods. Seems like we can't stop everybody." He rolled his eyes. "Seems like we can't hardly stop *anybody.*"

Stretched too thin, Lurcanio thought sorrowfully. Safe and warm and cozy in Priekule, he'd wondered about that. He'd sometimes even wondered about it lazy and sated in Krasta's bed. But he'd been only a military bureaucrat, and so what was his opinion worth? Nothing, as his superiors had pointed out several times when he'd tried to give it.

"Tomorrow morning," he said, "we'll see what we can do."

"Right," Santerno said, and gave him that measuring stare once more. *What will you do, Colonel, when you really have to fight?*

They moved south out of the forest a little before dawn, under clouds and mist. The Lagoans and Kuusamans still hadn't got accustomed to fighting in Valmiera. They hadn't realized how big a force the Algarvians had built up, there in the rugged northwest of the kingdom, and had only a thin screen of pickets warding the men moving west on what they reckoned more important business. Bursting eggs and trampling behemoths and dragons painted in green and red and white announced that they'd miscalculated.

"Forward!" Lurcanio shouted all through the first day. Forward the Algarvians stormed, just as they had in the glorious early spring of the war when Valmiera fell. Disgruntled Lagoan and Kuusaman captives went stumbling back toward the rear, disbelief on their faces. Algarvian soldiers relieved them of whatever money and food they had on their persons. "Keep moving!" Lurcanio yelled to his men. "We have to drive them. We can't slow down."

"That's right, Colonel," Santerno said. "That's just right." He paused. "Maybe you haven't done a whole lot of this stuff, but you seem to know what's going on."

"My thanks," Lurcanio said, on the whole sincerely. He didn't think Santerno paid compliments for the sake of paying them—not to a man twice his age, anyhow.

That first day, the Algarvians raced forward as hard and as fast as any of Mezentio's generals could have hoped. *A spear driven into the enemy's flank,* Lurcanio thought as he lay down in a barn to snatch a few hours' sleep. *Now we have to drive it home.*

The roar of bursting eggs woke him before sunup the next morning. The bursts came from the south: Algarvian egg-tossers already up into new positions to pound the enemy. "You see, sir?" Santerno said, sipping from a mug of tea he'd got from a cook. "The islanders aren't so much of a much."

"Maybe you're right," Lurcanio answered, and went off to get some tea of his own.

Things went well on the second day, too, though not quite so well as they had on the first. Algarvians slogged forward through snow that slowed both footsoldiers and behemoths. "We've got to keep going," Santerno said discontentedly. "The faster we move, the better our chances."

But the Kuusamans and Lagoans, no longer taken altogether by surprise as they had been when the attack opened, fought back hard. They also wrecked every bridge they could as they retreated, making Mezentio's artificers spend precious hours improvising crossings. And the enemy seemed to have endless herds of behemoths, not the carefully hoarded beasts the Algarvians had accumulated with so much labor and trouble. They weren't so good on the behemoths as the veterans who rode the Algarvian animals, but they could afford to spend their substance freely. Lurcanio's countrymen couldn't.

On the third day, the sun burned through the low clouds earlier than it had on the first two of the attack. "Forward!" Lurcanio shouted once more. The Algarvians had pushed about a third of the way down to the Strait of Valmiera, fairly close to the distance their plan had prescribed for the first two days. Lurcanio was more pleased than not; no plan, he knew, came through battle intact.

He was also weary unto death. He felt every one of his years like another heavy stone on his shoulders. *I have had a soft war,* he thought as he splashed south through an icy stream. *A good thing, too, or I'd have fallen over dead a long time ago.* Someone blazed at him from the trees beyond the stream as he came up onto the bank. The beam boiled a puff of steam from the snow near his feet. He threw himself down on his belly with a groan. *I wish I could just lie here and go to sleep.* Not far away, Captain Santerno sprawled behind a tree trunk. Lurcanio noted with a certain amount of relief that the hard-faced youngster looked about as haggard as he felt himself.

A couple of Algarvian behemoths lumbered up out of the stream. The egg-tossers on their backs made short work of the enemy footsoldiers in the trees. Lurcanio heaved himself to his feet. "Forward!" he yelled, and then, more quietly, spoke to Santerno: "Who would have thought it? We may really do this."

"Why not?" his adjutant answered. "These Kuusamans and Lagoans, they're not so tough. If you haven't fought in Unkerlant, you don't know what war's about."

Lurcanio had heard that song before. He began to think Santerno was right, though. Then, toward the afternoon, his brigade surrounded a town called Adutiskis. The road the

Algarvians really needed to use ran through the town. The Kuusamans holed up inside threw back the brigade's first attack, killing several behemoths Lurcanio knew his countrymen couldn't afford to lose. He sent in a message under flag of truce to the Kuusaman commander: "I respectfully suggest you surrender your position. I cannot answer for the conduct of my men if they overrun the town. You have already fought bravely, and further resistance is hopeless."

In short order, the messenger returned, bearing a written answer in classical Kaunian. It said, *Powers below eat you.* Lurcanio and Santerno stared at that. The hard-bitten adjutant swept off his hat in salute and said, "The man has style."

"Aye," Lurcanio agreed. "He also has Adutiskis, and it's a cork in the bottle." He led another attack. It failed. Mages brought up blonds to kill—maybe Kaunians from Forthweg, maybe. Valmierans scooped up at random. Lurcanio asked no questions. Winning overrode everything else. But Kuusaman wizards in the town threw the spell back on their heads. "We *have* to get through," Lurcanio raged. "They're crimping the whole attack."

The fourth morning dawned even brighter and clearer than the third had, and swarms of Kuusaman and Lagoan dragons flew up from the south. Eggs crashed down on the Algarvians' heads. Dragons flamed behemoths one after another till the stink of burnt meat filled Lurcanio's nostrils. The Kuusamans in Adutiskis held against a third attack, and then he had to turn men away from the town to try to contain an enemy thrust bent on relieving it. By the slimmest of margins, he did.

Even more enemy dragons were in the air the next morning. Every so often, one would get blazed out of the sky and smash down into the snow, but two or three fresh beasts always seemed to take its place. The Algarvian advance stumbled to a halt. "Did you ever see anything like *this* in Unkerlant?" Lurcanio asked Santerno.

Numbly, the younger officer shook his head. "We have to fall back," he said. "We can't stay out in the open like this. We'll all get killed." The Algarvian commanders took three days longer to realize the same thing, which gained them little ground and cost them men and beasts they could not spare. Adutiskis never did fall. *And the way into Algarve lies open for the enemy,* Lurcanio thought grimly.

Leudast had no trouble figuring out when he crossed the border from Yanina into Algarve. It wasn't so much that the buildings in the villages changed, though they did—the Algarvians were given to vertical lines enlivened with ornamental woodwork that struck the Unkerlanter lieutenant as busy. It wasn't even that redheads replaced small, skinny, swarthy Yaninans. More than anything else, it was the roads.

In Unkerlant, cities had paved streets. Villages didn't. Often, good-sized towns didn't. Roads between cities were invariably dirt—which meant that, in spring or fall, they were invariably mud. That mud had gone a long way toward slowing the Algarvian advance on Cottbus the first autumn of the war.

Yanina hadn't seemed much different from Unkerlant, not as far as roads went. Oh, there was one paved highway leading east from Patras, but Leudast hadn't been on it very long. Everywhere else, the rules he knew held good: paved streets in cities, dirt in villages and out in the countryside.

In Algarve, things were different. Every road was topped with cobbles or slates or concrete. Every single one, so far as Leudast could see. "Powers above, sir," he said to Captain Drogden. "How much does it cost to pave over a whole cursed kingdom?"

"I don't know," Drogden answered. "A lot. I'm sure of that."

"Aye." Leudast clicked his tongue between his teeth. "I always knew the redheads were richer than we are. They have a lot more crystals than we do, their soldiers eat better food and more of it, they use supply caravans that put anything we've got to shame. But seeing their kingdom . . ." He shook his head. "I didn't know they were *that* much richer than we are."

"It doesn't matter," Drogden said. "It doesn't fornicating matter. The whoresons aren't in Unkerlant any more, trying to take away what little we've got. Now we're here—and by the time we're through with them, they won't be so fornicating rich any more. Most of 'em'll be too dead to be rich."

"Suits me, sir," Leudast said. "Suits me fine. I just don't want to end up dead with 'em. They pushed us back till they could see Cottbus. I've come this far. I want to see Trapani."

"So do I," Drogden said. "Bastards fight for every village like it was Trapani, too." He spat. "They haven't got enough men left to stop us, though."

Leudast nodded. "Some of that last batch of captives we took look like they were too old to fight in the last war, let alone this one."

"Some of 'em won't be ready to fight till the next one, either." Drogden spat again. "Little buggers like that are dangerous, too. It's like a game to them, not anything real. You and me, we're afraid to die. Those kids, they don't think they can. They'll do crazy things on account of it."

"They're Algarvians," Leudast said. "That means they're all dangerous, as far as I'm concerned."

"Something to that—something, but not everything," Drogden answered. "The women, now . . . Mezentio's whoresons had fun with our girls when they came into Unkerlant. Now it's our turn. Redhaired pussy's as good as any other kind."

"I expect it would be," Leudast agreed. Drogden sounded as if he was speaking from experience. No one among the Unkerlanters' commanders would say a word if their soldiers and officers raped their way through Algarve. Leudast hadn't indulged himself yet. He didn't know whether he would or not. Go without long enough and you didn't much care how you got it.

"They're all sluts anyway—Algarvian women, I mean," Drogden said. "They deserve it—and they're going to get it, too."

"A lot of 'em are running away from us as fast as they can go, for fear of what we'll do to them," Leudast said.

"That's fine. I don't mind a bit." Drogden had a nasty chuckle when he chose to use it. "The more they clog their nice paved roads for their own soldiers, the more trouble they end up in. And when our dragons fly over, don't they have fun?"

"Don't they just?" Now Leudast spoke with the same savage enthusiasm as his regiment commander. "The redheads would do that to our peasants and townsfolk when they jumped on our back. Nice to let 'em know what it feels like."

Funny, he thought. *I don't mind seeing Algarvians torn to pieces by sorcerous energy from our eggs or flamed into charcoal by our dragons. I don't mind that at all, except for the stink of the burnt meat. So why am I squeamish about throwing a woman down and stabbing her between her legs with my lance?*

Before he could dwell on that, eggs burst close enough to make him flatten out on the ground like a snake. "They do keep trying to hit back," Drogden said. "Well, they'll pay for it. They'll pay for everything."

He was soon proved right. The Unkerlanters had many more egg-tossers up near the fighting front than the Algarvians did, and soon pounded the redheads into silence again. The push into western Algarve went on—till the redheads made a stand in a town called Ozieri. Instead of swarming into the town and fighting house to house, as they would have done earlier in the war, the Unkerlanters swept around it—a lesson they had learned from their Algarvian foes. Once Mezentio's men inside Ozieri were cut off from help, the Unkerlanters could pound them and their strongpoint to bits at leisure and at minimum expense.

That didn't bring out the Algarvian defenders. They'd learned their lessons in the long, bitter war, too. Their soldiers dug in among the ruins. Sooner or later, they would make the Unkerlanters pay the price for winkling them out. *Sooner or later, we'll throw second-line soldiers at them,* Leudast thought. *Losing those fellows won't matter so much—and we'll get rid of the Algarvians.* Sometimes the game had steps almost as formal as a dance.

But the Algarvian civilians in Ozieri didn't understand how the game was played. They'd never expected to have to learn; they'd left that lesson for the people of all the kingdoms bordering their own. When eggs started bursting among the homes and shops they'd cherished for generations, many of them didn't know enough to go down to their cellars and try to wait out the attack. Those people grabbed whatever they could and fled east with it in their arms or on their backs.

What they didn't realize was that it was too late for such flight. By the time the eggs started falling heavily, the Unkerlanters had already surrounded Ozieri. Civilians fleeing the place found themselves in just as much danger as soldiers would have—if anything, in more, because they couldn't blaze back and didn't know how to take cover.

Leudast blazed an old man with a duffel bag slung over one bent shoulder. He wasn't happy about doing it, but he didn't hesitate. For all he knew, the old Algarvian was one of the soldiers recently dragooned into the army, and the canvas sack was full of those nasty little throwable eggs the redheads had got so much use from the past few months.

Somebody blazed at him a moment later, from the direction from which the old man had come. He rolled behind a hedge, wishing the Algarvians hadn't manicured their landscapes so neatly. A shriek from that same direction a moment later argued that some other Unkerlanter had taken care of the redhead with the stick.

Another shriek came from behind Leudast. This one was torn from a woman's throat. By the way it went on, and by the laughs that accompanied it, he didn't think she'd been wounded by an egg or a stick.

Sure enough, when he went back to check, he found three men holding her down and a fourth, his tunic hiked up, pumping away on top of her. The soldier grunted, shuddered, and pulled out. One of his pals took his place. "Hello, Lieutenant," said the fellow on her right leg. "You want a turn? She's lively."

"She's noisy, is what she is," Leudast answered.

"Sorry, sir," said the fellow who had her arms. "She bites whenever you put a hand over her mouth. We don't want to get rid of her till we've all had a go."

"Shut her up," Leudast said. "She's liable to bring redheads down on you, and you aren't exactly ready to fight." That got the soldiers' attention. A rough gag didn't stop the woman's screams, but did muffle them. The man who was riding her drove deep, then sat back on his haunches with a satisfied smirk on his face.

"You going to take her, Lieutenant?" asked the soldier who had her arms. "Otherwise, it's my turn."

There she lay, naked—or naked enough—and spreadeagled. Would it make any difference to her if five men had her, or only four? *Do I care?* Leudast wondered. *She's only an Algarvian.* "Aye, I'll do it," he said, and bent between her thighs. It didn't take long. He hadn't thought it would. And what had her brothers or husband—maybe even her son; he thought she was close to forty—done in Unkerlant? Nothing good. He was sure of that.

He didn't feel particularly proud of himself afterwards: not as if he'd take a step toward overthrowing Mezentio. But he wasn't sorry, either. *Just . . . one of those things,* he thought.

"Behemoths!" The shout from ahead came in Unkerlanter, so Leudast supposed the Algarvians east of Ozieri had mustered a counterattack. They kept striking back whenever they could, even with the odds dreadfully against them. Here, if they could fight their way into the town, they might bring some soldiers out with them, and that might help them make a stand somewhere else.

As always, the Algarvians fought bravely. Their footsoldiers knew how to use behemoths to the best advantage. With skill and bravado, they pushed the Unkerlanters back about half a mile. But skill and bravado went only so far. Against dragons and many more behemoths and many more men, the counterattack faltered short of its goal. Sullenly, the Algarvians drew back.

Leudast waited for Captain Drogden to order the regiment forward again. That was Drogden's way: to hit the redheads hard when they weren't ready for it. But no orders came. "Where's the captain?" Leudast asked.

An Unkerlanter pointed over his shoulder. "Last I saw him, he was going off behind that fancy house there. He had a redhead with him." The soldier's hands shaped curves in the air.

Leudast went after Drogden without hesitation. Fun was

one thing, fun at the expense of the fight something else. "Captain?" he called as he went around the house, which was indeed a great deal fancier than any he'd seen in his own village. "You there, Captain?"

Amidst the yellowish brown of dead grass, rock-gray stood out. There lay Drogden, his tunic hiked up to his waist—and a knife deep in his back. There was no sign of the woman he'd had with him, or of his stick. Leudast scrambled away in a hurry—she might be lying in wait, ready to blaze whoever came after Drogden. But no beam bit or charred grass near Leudast. Still, he shook his head in blank dismay. *Drogden was a careful fellow,* he thought, *but this once he wasn't careful enough.* He shivered. *It could have been me.*

Skarnu found himself restless and discontented in Priekule. He'd thought that, when he came back after the Algarvians abandoned his beloved city, he would simply resume the life he'd led before the Derlavaian War called him into King Gainibu's service. But going to one feast after another palled fast. He didn't mind drinking a bit, but getting drunk night after night seemed a lot less enjoyable, a lot less amusing, than it had in peacetime.

And, of course, he'd gone to those feasts not least looking for some pretty girl or another with whom he might spend the rest of the night. Plenty of pretty girls still came to those affairs. Several all but threw themselves at him: almost all women with reputations for having slept with one Algarvian or another during the occupation. *Maybe they think they'll look better by going to bed with me,* he thought. *Or maybe they just want to make sure they've taken care of both sides.*

These days, though, Skarnu wasn't looking for a pretty girl. He'd found one—and one with a temper a good deal sharper than his own. "Thank you, my dear," he told one noblewoman whose offer had left nothing to the imagination, "but it's about even money whether Merkela would blaze you or me first if I did that."

Her laughter was like tinkling bells. "You're joking," she said. Before Skarnu could even shake his head, she read his eyes. "You're not joking in the slightest. How very . . . barbaric of your . . . friend."

"My fiancée," Skarnu corrected her. "She's a widow. The Algarvians executed her husband. She hasn't got much of a sense of humor about these things." The noblewoman didn't lose her bright smile. But she didn't hang around long, either.

A mug of ale in her hand, Merkela came up to Skarnu a moment later. "What was that all about?" she asked, a certain hard suspicion in her voice.

"About what you'd expect." He put his arm around her. "I know who I'm going home with tonight, though, and I know why."

"You'd better," Merkela said.

"I know that, too." Skarnu chuckled. "I told Skirgaila you'd come after her—or maybe me—with a stick if she didn't leave well enough alone. She didn't believe me. Then she did, and turned green."

"I ought to give her something to remember me by now," Merkela said, with the same directness she'd used while hunting redheads.

Before she could advance on Skirgaila, Viscount Valnu came up, the usual mocking smile on his bony, handsome face. "Ah, the happy couple!" he said, and contrived to make it sound almost like an insult.

"Hullo, Valnu," Skarnu said. Valnu didn't seem to mind the endless rounds of feasts. But then, he'd been coming to them all through the Algarvian occupation, too. Aye, he'd been in the underground. Still, Skarnu was sure he hadn't let that keep him from having a good time.

His arrival distracted Merkela. She didn't know what to make of Valnu. *But then, a lot of people don't know what to make of Valnu,* Skarnu thought. Skirgaila, meanwhile, had practically painted herself to the chest of another nobleman who hadn't collaborated with the Algarvians. Skarnu nodded to himself. *She wants to repair one sort of reputation, sure enough, and she doesn't care about the other sort.*

With peasant bluntness, Merkela demanded, "Are you *really* father to the child Krasta's carrying?"

Valnu's blue, blue eyes widened. "*Am* I, milady? I don't

know. I haven't looked inside there to tell." That was bluntness of a sort Merkela wasn't used to; she flushed. Chuck-
ling, Valnu went on, "*Could I be* that father, though?
Without a doubt, I could be." He fluttered his eyelashes at
Skarnu. "And now I'll have the poor girl's outraged brother
coming after me with a club."

"You're impossible," Skarnu said, at which Valnu bowed
in delight. Even Merkela snorted at that. With a sigh,
Skarnu went on, "I hope you are. All things considered, I'd
not have the family dragged through too much dirt."

"You're no fun at all," Valnu said. "I know what your
problem is, though—I know just the disease you've
caught."

"Tell me," Skarnu said, raising an eyebrow. "What sort
of slander will you come up with? If it's vile enough, I'll
haul you before the king."

"It's pretty vile, all right," Valnu said. "You poor fellow,
you've caught . . . responsibility. It's very dangerous unless
you treat it promptly. I came down with it myself for a
while, but I seem to have thrown it off."

"I believe *that*," Skarnu said. But he couldn't stay too annoyed with Valnu. No matter how much fun the viscount
had had here in Priekule during the occupation, he'd played
a hard and dangerous game. Had the Algarvians realized he
was anything more than a vacuous good-time boy, he would
have suffered the same nasty fate as had so many men—
and women—from the underground.

No sooner had that thought crossed Skarnu's mind than
Valnu said, "You know, it's possible you're being too hard
on your poor sister."

"And it's possible we're not, too," Merkela snapped before Skarnu could answer. "That cursed redhead was hard
whenever he was alone with her, wasn't he?"

"Lurcanio? No doubt he was," Valnu replied. The bow he
gave Merkela was distinctly mocking. "And you're learning
cattiness fast. You'll make a splendid noblewoman, no
doubt about it." He grinned. She spluttered. He went on,
"But I still mean what I said. Krasta held my life in the hollow of her hand. She *knew* what I was, knew without the
tiniest fragment of doubt after the late, unlamented Count

Amatu met his untimely demise after dining at her mansion. Yet even if she did know, neither Lurcanio nor any of the other redheads learned of it from her. More: she helped make them believe I was harmless. So I beg both of you, do have such patience with her as you can."

He sounded unwontedly serious. Merkela's eyes blazed. Getting her to change her mind once she'd made it up was always hard. Skarnu said, "We have a while to think about it. Her baby's not due for another couple of months. If it looks like you—"

"It will be the handsomest—or loveliest, depending—child ever born," Valnu broke in.

"If it's a little sandy-haired bastard, though . . ." Merkela's voice was as cold as the winter winds that blew up from the land of the Ice People.

"Even then," Valnu said. "There's a difference between going to bed with someone for love and doing it from . . . expediency, shall we say?" By his tone, he was intimately acquainted with every inch of that debatable ground.

But he didn't persuade Merkela. "I know how far I will go," she said. "I know how far everybody else will go, too." She didn't quite turn her back on Valnu, but she might as well have.

And Skarnu thought she was likely to be right. In a newly freed Valmiera where everyone was doing his best to pretend no one had ever collaborated with Mezentio's men, bearing a half-Algarvian child would not be tolerated. The only reason Bauska had had as little trouble over Brindza as she'd had was that her bastard daughter seldom left the mansion. A servant and her child could hope to remain obscure. A marchioness? Skarnu doubted it.

"A pity," Valnu murmured.

"How much pity did the Algarvians ever show us?" Merkela said. "How much did they show anyone of Kaunian blood? Did you ever meet any of the Kaunians from Forthweg who got away from them? You wouldn't talk of pity if you had."

Valnu sighed. "There is some truth in what you say, milady. Some. I have never denied it. Whether there is quite so much as you think . . ."

Merkela took a deep, angry breath. Skarnu didn't want to see a quarrel—no, more likely a brawl—erupt. Maybe that was the disease of responsibility, as Valnu had said. Whatever it was, he had to move quickly—and delicately. Calming Merkela when her temper was high had the same potential for disaster as trying to keep an egg from bursting after its first spell somehow failed. Mistakes could have spectacularly disastrous consequences.

Here, though, he thought he had the answer. He said, "Shall we set our wedding day for about the time when Krasta's baby is due? Whatever happens then, we'll upstage her."

That distracted Merkela, as he'd hoped. She nodded and said, "Aye, why not?" But she wasn't completely distracted, for she added, "It will also help quiet the scandal if she *does* have a little redheaded bastard."

"Maybe some," said Skarnu, who'd hoped she wouldn't think of that.

Merkela's frown was thoughtful now, not angry—or not so angry. "As far as Krasta's concerned, we shouldn't muffle the scandal. We should shout it. As far as you're concerned, though—"

"As far as the whole family is concerned," Skarnu broke in. "Whoever that baby's father is, it's first cousin to little Gedominu, you know."

His fiancée plainly hadn't thought of that. Neither had Skarnu, till this moment. "They'll have to live with it all their lives, won't they?" Merkela murmured. Skarnu nodded. A bit later, and more than a bit reluctantly, so did she. "All right. Let it be as you say."

"Do invite me," Valnu cooed. "After all, I may be an uncle."

Merkela hadn't thought of that, either. Skarnu said, "We wouldn't think of doing anything else. We'll need someone to pinch the bridesmaids—and maybe the groomsmen, too."

"You flatter me outrageously," Valnu said. And then, pouring oil on the fire, he asked, "And will you invite the aunt, too?"

Skarnu wanted to hit him with something. But Merkela

merely sounded matter-of-fact as she answered, "She wouldn't come anyhow. I'm only a peasant. I don't belong. I could be a traitor, so long as I had blue blood. That wouldn't matter. But a farm girl in the family . . ."

"Is the best thing that ever happened to me." Skarnu slipped his arm around her waist.

Valnu said, "Nobles wouldn't be nobles if we didn't fret about such things. It could be worse, though. It could be Jelgava. Jelgavan nobles make ours look like shopkeepers, the way they go on about the glory and purity of their blood."

With a certain venomous satisfaction, Merkela said, "It didn't keep their noblewomen from lying down for the red-heads, did it?"

"Well, no." Valnu wagged a finger at her. "You're almost as radical as an Unkerlanter, aren't you? When Swemmel's nobles turned out not to like him, he just went and killed most of them."

"And the Unkerlanters threw Algarve back," Merkela replied. "What do you suppose *that* says, your Excellency?" She used the title with sardonic relish. Valnu, for once, had no comeback ready.

Five

When people spoke of walking on eggs, they commonly meant the kind hens or ducks or geese laid. These days, Fernao felt as if he were walking on the sort egg-tossers flung and dragons dropped. Anything he said, anything he did, might lead to spectacular disaster with the woman he loved.

And even if I don't do anything, I can be in trouble, he thought. If he left Pekka alone, she was liable to decide he was cold and standoffish. If he pursued her, she might decide he didn't care about anything but getting between her legs. When word first came back that Leino had died, he'd wondered if he really ought to be sorry. After all, her husband, his own rival, was gone now. Didn't that leave Pekka all to him?

Maybe it did. On the other hand, maybe it didn't. He hadn't realized how guilty she would feel because she'd been in his chamber, because they'd just finished making love, when she got summoned to learn of Leino's death. If she'd been somewhere else, if she'd never touched him at all, that wouldn't have changed a thing up in Jelgava. Rationally, logically, anyone could see as much. But how much had logic ever had to do with what went on in people's hearts? Not much, and Fernao knew it.

In the cramped hostel, he couldn't have avoided Pekka even had he wanted to. Everyone gathered in the refectory. He felt eyes on him whenever he went in there. *Powers above be praised that Ilmarinen's in Jelgava,* went through his mind once—actually, rather more than once. If anybody could be relied upon to start bursting the eggs under one's metaphorical feet, Ilmarinen was the man.

Pekka didn't automatically come sit by him, as she had before the Algarvians killed Leino. But she didn't go out of her way to avoid him, either, which was some solace, if not much. One evening about a month after the news got back to the Naantali district, she did sit down next to him.

"Hello," he said carefully. "How are you?"

"I've been better," Pekka answered, to which he could only nod. When a serving girl came up and asked her what she wanted, she ordered a reindeer cutlet, parsnips in a reindeer-milk cheese sauce, and a lingonberry tart. The girl nodded and briskly walked away toward the kitchen as if the request were the most ordinary thing in the world.

Fernao couldn't take it in stride. To a Lagoan, especially to a Lagoan from sophisticated Setubal, it seemed a cliché come to life. He didn't smile the way he wanted to, but he did say, "How . . . very Kuusaman."

"So it is," Pekka answered. "So I am." The implication was, *What are you going to do about it?*

"I know," Fernao said gently. "I like what you are. I have for quite a while now, you know."

Pekka tossed her head like a unicorn bedeviled by gnats. "This isn't the best time, you know," she said.

"I'm not going to push myself on you," he said, and paused while his serving girl set his supper before him: mutton and peas and carrots, a meal he could easily have eaten back in Lagoas. He sipped from the mug of ale that went with it, then added, "I think we do need to talk, though."

"Do you?" Pekka said bleakly.

Fernao nodded. His ponytail brushed the back of his neck. "We ought to think about where we're going."

"Or if we're going anywhere," Pekka said.

"Or if we're going anywhere," Fernao agreed, doing his best to keep his voice steady. "We probably won't decide anything, not so it stays decided, but we should talk. Come back to my room with me after supper. Please."

The glance she turned on him was half alarm, half rueful amusement. "Every time you ask me to go to your room with you, something dreadful happens."

"I wouldn't call it that," Fernao said. The first time he'd asked her to his chamber, it had been to put rumors to rest. He hadn't intended to make love with her, or, he was sure, she with him. They'd surprised each other; Pekka had dismayed herself, and spent months afterwards doing her best to pretend it hadn't happened or, at most, to make it into a one-time accident.

"I know you wouldn't," she said now. "That doesn't necessarily mean you're right."

"It doesn't necessarily mean I'm wrong, either," Fernao answered. "Please." He didn't want to sound as if he were begging. That didn't necessarily mean he wasn't, though.

Before Pekka said anything, her supper arrived. Then she sent the serving girl back for a mug of ale like his. Only after she'd drunk from it did she nod. "All right, Fernao. You're right, I suppose: we should talk. But I don't know how much there is for us to say to each other."

"We'd better find out, then," he said, hoping neither his voice nor his face gave away the raw fear he felt. Pekka nodded as if she saw nothing wrong, so perhaps they didn't.

Fernao wanted to shovel food into his mouth, to be able

to leave the refectory as soon as he could. Pekka took her time. She seemed to Fernao to be deliberately dawdling, but he doubted she was. He was nervous enough to feel as if time were crawling on hands and knees—and that quite without sorcerous intervention. But at last Pekka set down her empty mug and got up. "Let's go," she said, as if they were heading into battle. Fernao hoped it wouldn't be anything so grim, but had to admit to himself that he wasn't sure.

He opened the door to his room, stood aside to let her go in ahead of him, then shut the door again and barred it. Pekka raised an eyebrow but didn't say anything. She sat on the chamber's one chair. Fernao limped over to the bed and eased himself down onto it. He leaned his cane against the mattress.

His face must have shown the pain he always felt going from standing to sitting or the other way round, for Pekka asked, "How's your leg?"

"About the same as usual," he answered. "The healers are a little surprised it's done as well as it has, but they don't expect it to get any better than this. I can use it, and it hurts." He shrugged. *Better than getting killed,* he almost said, but thought better of that before the words passed his lips.

"I'm glad it's no worse," Pekka said. "You did look like it was bothering you." She fidgeted, something he'd rarely seen her do. *This isn't easy for her, either,* Fernao reminded himself. She took a deep breath. "Go on, then. Say your say."

"Thank you." Fernao found he needed a deep breath, too. "I don't know what you would have done—what *we* would have done—if your husband had lived."

Pekka nodded shakily. "I don't, either," she said. "But things are different now. You must see that."

"I do," Fernao agreed. "But there's one thing that hasn't changed, and you need to know it. I still love you, and I'll still do anything I can for you, and I still want us to stay together for as long as you can put up with me." *And Leino is dead, and that might make things easier. Before he died, I never thought it might make things harder.*

"I do know that," Pekka said, and then, "I'm not sure you understand everything that goes with it. You want us to stay together, aye. How do you feel about raising up another man's son?"

In truth, Fernao hadn't thought much about Uto. Up till now a confirmed bachelor, he had a way of thinking about children in the abstract when he thought about them at all—which wasn't that often. But Uto was no abstraction, not to Pekka. He was flesh of her flesh, probably the most important thing in the world to her right now. *More important than I am?* Fernao asked himself. The answer formed in his mind almost as fast as the question. *He's much more important than you are, and you'd better remember it.*

"I don't know that much about children," Fernao said slowly, "but I'd do my best. I don't know what else to tell you."

She studied him, then nodded again, this time in measured approval. "One of the things you might have told me was that you didn't want to have anything to do with my son. That's what a lot of men tell women with children."

Fernao shrugged, more than a little uncomfortably. He understood that point of view. He would have taken it himself with a lot of women. With Pekka . . . If he wanted to stay with her, he had to take everything that was part of her. And . . . In musing tones, he said, "If we had a baby, I wonder what it would look like."

Pekka blinked. Her voice very low, she answered, "I've wondered the same thing a few times. I didn't know you had. Sometimes a woman thinks a man only cares about getting her into bed, not about what might happen afterwards."

"Sometimes that is all a man cares about." Remembering some of the things that had happened in his own past, Fernao didn't see how he could deny it. But he went on, "Sometimes, but not always."

"I see that," Pekka said. "Thank you. It's . . . a compliment, I suppose. It gives me more to think about."

"I love you. You'd better think about that, too," Fernao said.

"I know. I do think about it," Pekka answered. "I have to think about all the things it means. I have to think about all the things it might not mean, too. You've helped clear up some of that."

"Good," Fernao said. *You don't say you love me,* he thought. *I can see why you don't, but oh, I wish you would.*

What Pekka did say was, "You're a brave man—powers above know that's true. And you're a solid mage. Better than a solid mage, in fact; I've seen that working with you. There are times I think I never should have gone to bed with you in the first place, but you always made me happy when I did."

"We aim to please," Fernao said with a crooked smile.

"You aim well," Pekka said. "Does all that add up to love? It might. I thought it did before . . . before Leino died, and I didn't know what I was going to do. But that's turned everything upside down."

"I know." Fernao kept the smile on his face. It wasn't easy.

"I don't know what I'm going to do." Pekka smiled, too, ruefully. "Usually, the busier I am, the happier I am. When I'm doing things, I haven't got time to think. And I don't much want to think right now."

"That makes sense," Fernao agreed. He heaved himself to his feet without using the cane. That hurt, but he managed. He managed the couple of steps he needed to get over to the chair, too. Getting down beside it hurt more than standing up had, but he ignored the pain with the practice of a man who'd known much worse. "But there's happy and then there's happy, if you know what I mean." To make sure she knew what he meant, he kissed her.

It was, he knew, a gamble. If Pekka wasn't ready, or if she thought he cared about nothing but bedding her, he wouldn't do himself any good. At first, she just let the kiss happen, without really responding to it. But then, with what sounded like a small surprised noise down deep in her throat, she kissed him, too.

When their lips separated—Fernao didn't push the kiss as far as he might have, as far as he wanted to—Pekka said, "You don't make things easy, do you?"

"I try not to," Fernao answered.

"You've succeeded. And I'd better go." Pekka rose, then

stooped to help Fernao up and gave him his cane. He wasn't embarrassed for the aid; he needed it. Even as Pekka unbarred the door and left, Fernao nodded to himself with more hope than he'd known for some little while.

"What sort of delegation?" Hajjaj asked, thinking he'd misheard. His ears weren't all they'd once been, and he was unhappily aware of it.

But Qutuz repeated himself: "A delegation from the Kaunian refugees from Forthweg who have settled around Najran, your Excellency. Three of them are out in the corridor. Will you receive them, or shall I send them away?"

"I'll talk with them," the Zuwayzi foreign minister said. "I have no idea how much I'll be able to do for them—I can't do much for Zuwayzin these days—but I'll talk with them."

"Very well, your Excellency." Qutuz made an excellent secretary. He gave no sign of his own approval or disapproval. He got his master's instructions and acted on them—in this case by going out into the corridor and bringing the Kaunians back into the office with him.

"Good day, gentlemen," Hajjaj said in classical Kaunian when they came in. He read the language of scholarship and sorcery as readily as Zuwayzi, but was less fluent speaking it.

"Good day, your Excellency," the blonds chorused, bowing low. They all wore tunics and trousers; for men with their pale, easily sunburned skins, nudity was not an option in Zuwayza, even during her relatively mild winter.

"Two of you I have met before," Hajjaj said. "Nemunas, Vitols." He nodded to each of them in turn. Nemunas was older than Vitols, and had a scarred left hand. Before Forthweg fell to the Algarvians, they'd both been sergeants in King Penda's army—unusually high rank for Kaunians—which made them leaders among the blonds who'd fled across the Bay of Ajlun to keep from ending up in one of King Mezentio's special camps.

The third blond, the one Hajjaj didn't know, bowed again and said, "I am called Kaudavas, your Excellency."

"I am glad to meet you," Hajjaj said. As long as he stuck to stock phrases, he was fine.

Both Nemunas and Vitols stared at him. "It's been a while since we've seen each other, your Excellency," the older blond said. "Thanks very much for recalling our names."

"You are welcome," Hajjaj replied—another stock phrase. A good memory for names and faces came in handy for a diplomat. When he went beyond stock phrases, he had to think about what he said and speak slowly: "And you and your countrymen are welcome in my kingdom, and all three of you are welcome here. Would you care for tea and wine and cakes?"

All three Kaunians from Forthweg chuckled. "We'd sooner just get down to business, sir, if you don't mind," Nemunas said.

Hajjaj allowed himself a small smile. The blonds had learned how some Zuwayzi customs worked, sure enough. "As you wish," he said, and waved to the pillows piled here and there on the carpeted floor. "Sit down. Make yourselves comfortable. And then, please, tell me what I can do for you."

His guests had got used to making do with pillows instead of chairs and couches, too. They all made nests for themselves. Nemunas, who seemed to be their spokesman, said, "Sir, you know we've been sailing east out of Najran back to Forthweg, to hit the cursed redheads a lick or two."

"Officially, I do not know this," Hajjaj replied. "Had I known it officially"—he wondered if he'd correctly used the subjunctive there—"Zuwayza's former allies, the Algarvians you mentioned, would not have been pleased with me."

Kaudavas said, "We never did understand how anyone could ally with Mezentio's whoresons, if you don't mind my saying so." He was stamped from the same mold as his comrades; if anything, he was bigger and burlier than either of them, burly enough to make Hajjaj wonder if he had a little Forthwegian blood.

"Considering what the Algarvians did to you, I know why you say that," Hajjaj replied. "Still, we had our reasons."

"Now we've had something to do with the Unkerlanter navy men at Najran," Vitols said. "Maybe we can figure out what some of those reasons are."

"Ah?" Hajjaj leaned forward. "Dealing with Unkerlanters is often less than enjoyable. Does this have to do with your reasons for coming to Bishah to see me?"

"Aye," the Kaunians said as one, loudly and angrily enough to make Qutuz look in to see that the foreign minister was all right. Hajjaj waved him back. Nemunas went on, "The thing of it is, we want to keep right on sailing back to Forthweg. Swemmel's men haven't driven the redheads out of all of it yet. We can do some good there."

"And besides, we want revenge," Kaudavas added.

"Indeed," Hajjaj said. "Rest assured, I do understand this." Among the Zuwayzin, vengeance was a dish to be savored. No other Derlavaian folk thought of it in such artistic terms, though the Algarvians came close.

Vitols said, "But the Unkerlanter navy men won't let us go out. They say they'll sink us if we try, and they mean it, curse 'em."

"Can you do something about that, sir?" Nemunas asked. "That's why we came here, to find out if you could."

"I . . . see. I do not know." Hajjaj made a sour face. Najran was a Zuwayzi port, not one that belonged to King Swemmel. For the Zuwayzin not to be in full control of what happened there was galling. But Zuwayza, these days, kept only such sovereignty as Unkerlant chose to yield to her. Hajjaj drummed his fingers on his knee. "Let me ask a question. Are you loyal to this new king, this King Beornwulf, the Unkerlanters have named?" Forthweg, these days, kept even less sovereignty than Zuwayza did.

In almost perfect unison, the Kaunians from Forthweg shrugged. "Don't care about him one way or the other," Nemunas answered.

"He's just a Forthwegian," Vitols agreed.

This time, Hajjaj hid his smile. The blonds might be a persecuted minority, but they kept a haughty pride of their own. He said, "Let me ask it a different way: would you swear loyalty to King Beornwulf if that let you be loosed against the Algarvians still in Forthweg?"

Nemunas, Vitols, and Kaudavas looked at one another. They all shrugged again, more raggedly than before. "Why not?" Nemunas said at last. "When the war's finally over, we'll be living under him if we go back to Forthweg."

"He can't be much worse than that vain fool of a Penda," Kaudavas added.

His opinion of the former King of Forthweg closely matched Hajjaj's. The foreign minister also noted that some Kaunian refugees looked to be thinking about staying in Zuwayza. After the Six Years' War, the kingdom had taken in some Algarvian refugees. The blonds might also fit in.

None of that, though, had anything to do with the business at hand. "I shall speak to Minister Ansovald for you," Hajjaj promised. "I do not know what he will say, but I shall speak to him." The blonds were effusive in their thanks. They bowed themselves almost double as they left Hajjaj's office. No matter how much gratitude they showed, though, they had no idea of the size of the favor Hajjaj was doing for them.

Qutuz did. "I'm sorry, your Excellency," he said.

"So am I," Hajjaj answered bleakly. "Some things can't be helped, though." But he couldn't stay that calm, however much he tried. "Every time I talk to the Unkerlanter barbarian, I want to go take a bath right afterwards. And he has the whip hand now, powers below eat him."

Ansovald didn't deign to grant him an audience for three days. The Unkerlanter minister no doubt thought he was humiliating and angering Hajjaj. Hajjaj, however, was just as well pleased with delay here. At last, though, he had to don an Unkerlanter-style tunic and travel over to the ministry. He alighted from his carriage with a sigh. The Unkerlanter sentries looked through him as if he didn't exist.

By all the signs, Ansovald would also have loved to pretend Hajjaj didn't exist. He and the Zuwayzi foreign minister had never got on well. These days, Ansovald—a tough, beefy man with a permanent sour expression—not only had the whip hand, he enjoyed using it. "Well, what now?" he demanded in Algarvian when Hajjaj came before him.

"I have a petition to present to you," the Zuwayzi foreign minister replied, also in Algarvian. It was the only language they shared. Using it with the Unkerlanter had an ironic tang that usually appealed to Hajjaj. Today, though, he wondered at the omen.

"Go ahead," Ansovald rumbled, and fiddled with a fingernail as if more interested in that than in anything Hajjaj was likely to say. *No doubt he is,* Hajjaj thought unhappily. Nevertheless, he went on with the request the Kaunians from Forthweg had made. Ansovald did start to listen to him; he gave the Unkerlanter minister to Zuwayza that much. And, when he finished, Ansovald wasted no time coming to a decision. He looked Hajjaj straight in the eye and said, "No."

Hajjaj hadn't really expected anything else. Ansovald was here not least to thwart Zuwayza. But he asked, "Why not, your Excellency? Surely you cannot believe these Kaunians would prefer King Mezentio to King Swemmel? Why not loose them against the enemy you both hate?"

"I don't have to tell you a cursed thing," Ansovald answered. Hajjaj just inclined his head and waited. Ansovald glared at him. At last, patience won what anger—or anger openly revealed, at least—wouldn't have. "All right. All right," the Unkerlanter minister said. "I'll tell you why, curse it."

"Thank you," Hajjaj said, and wondered whether he was more pained to say those words or Ansovald to hear them.

Ansovald might have bitten into a lemon as he went on, "Because these Kaunians are a pack of cursed troublemakers, that's why."

"Don't you *want* Mezentio's men to have trouble?" Hajjaj asked.

"They've got trouble. We're giving it to them." Ansovald's glare settled on the Zuwayzi foreign minister. "If we weren't, I wouldn't be here yattering with you, would I?" Hajjaj spread his hands, yielding the point. Ansovald bulled ahead: "But that isn't the kind of troublemakers I meant. Aye, they'd give the redheads a hard time, as long as there are any redheads left in Forthweg. There won't be, though, not for very much longer. And after that—troublemakers make trouble, you know what I mean? Pretty soon, they'd start giving *us* trouble, just on account of we were there.

Why let 'em? You've got yourself some blonds, and you're welcome to them. My orders on this one come from Cottbus, and Cottbus knows what it's talking about."

Hajjaj considered. Ansovald's words did have a certain ruthless logic behind them—the sort King Swemmel came up with on one of his good days. Troublemakers *were* fond of making trouble, and against whom *didn't* always matter. Hajjaj had told the blonds he would try, and he'd tried. "Let it be as you say," he murmured.

"Of course it'll be as I say," Ansovald answered smugly. He thrust a thick finger out at Hajjaj. "Now, as long as you're here—when are you going to give this Tassi bitch back to Iskakis?"

"Good day, your Excellency," Hajjaj said with dignity, and rose to leave. "You may have a good deal to say about what goes on in my kingdom, but not, powers above be praised, in my household." But as he walked away, he hoped that wasn't more wishful thinking.

With nothing to do but lie on his back and eat and drink, Bembo should have been a happy man. The constable had often aspired to such laziness as an ideal, though a friendly woman or two had also played a part in his daydreams. A broken leg most emphatically had not.

It got me back to Tricarico, he thought. *Oraste was right—if I'd stayed in Eoforwic, if I'd stayed anywhere in fornicating Forthweg, I'd probably be dead now.* None of the news coming out of the west was good, even if the local news sheets did try to make it as palatable as they could.

What Oraste hadn't thought about was that, even back in his own home town in northeastern Algarve, Bembo still might get killed. Kuusaman and Lagoan dragons flew over the Bradano Mountains every night—and sometimes during the day—to drop their eggs on Tricarico. Bembo wondered how long it would be before enemy soldiers started coming over the mountains, too.

"However long it is, I can't do anything about it," he muttered. His leg remained splinted. It still hurt. It also itched maddeningly under the boards and bandages where he couldn't scratch.

A nurse came down the neat row of cots in the ward. The sanatorium was crowded, not just with men wounded in combat but with all the civilians hurt by falling eggs. Bembo had hoped to be something of a hero when he got back to Tricarico. Hardly anyone seemed to care, or even to notice.

"How are we today?" the nurse asked when she got to his cot.

"I'm fine." Bembo whipped his head around, as if to see if he were sharing the bed with other men he didn't know about. "Don't see anyone else, though."

He got a dutiful smile from the nurse. She looked tired. Everyone in Tricarico, or at least in the sanatorium, looked beat these days. She set a hand on his forehead. "No fever," she said, and scribbled something on the leaf of paper in her clipboard. "That's a good sign."

"How are *you,* sweetheart?" Bembo asked. He felt good enough to notice she was a woman, and not the homeliest one he'd ever seen.

She was pretty, in fact, when she smiled, which she did now—this one had nothing of duty in it. But her brightening had nothing to do with Bembo's charms, if any. "I got a letter from my husband last night," she answered. "He's in the west, but he's still all right, powers above be praised."

"Good," Bembo said, more or less sincerely. "Glad to hear it."

"Do you need to use the bedpan?" she asked.

"Well . . . aye," he said, and she tended to it, holding up the blanket on the cot as a minimal shield for his modesty. She handled him with efficiency King Swemmel might have envied, as if his piece of meat were nothing but a piece of meat. He sighed. You heard stories about nurses. . . . If he'd learned one thing as a constable, it was that you heard all sorts of stories that weren't true.

"Anything else?" she asked. Bembo shook his head. She went on to the fellow in the next cot.

One of the stories you heard was how bad sanatorium food was. That one, unfortunately, had turned out to be true. If anything, it had turned out to be an understatement. What Bembo got for supper was barley porridge and olives that had seen better days and wine well on the way to turning into vinegar. He didn't get much, either: certainly not enough wine to make him happy.

The fellow in the cot next to his was a civilian who'd got his leg broken here in Tricarico at about the same time as Bembo had over in Eoforwic. His name was Tibiano. By the way he talked, Bembo suspected he'd seen the inside of a constabulary station or two in his time. "I'll lay you three to two the fornicating islanders send dragons over again tonight," he said now.

"I wouldn't mind getting laid, but not by you, thanks," Bembo answered. Tibiano chuckled. Bembo went on, "I won't touch the bet, either. Those whoresons come over just about every night."

"Isn't that the sad and sorry truth?" Tibiano agreed. "Who would've thunk it? We started this war to kick everybody else's arse, not to get ours kicked. Those other bastards deserve it. What did we ever do to anybody?"

Having been in Forthweg, Bembo knew just what—or some of just what—his kingdom had done. He hadn't talked much about that since returning to Tricarico. For one thing, he hadn't thought anybody would believe him. For another, he would just as soon have forgotten. But he couldn't leave that unanswered. "There are some Kaunians who'd say we've done a thing or two to them." *And there would be a lot more, if they were still alive.*

"Blonds? Futter blonds," Tibiano said. "They've always tried to keep us Algarvians from being everything we ought to be. They're jealous, that's what they are. Like I say, they deserve it."

He spoke loudly and passionately, as people do when sure they're right. Several other men in the ward lifted their heads and agreed with him. So did the young woman who was taking away their supper tins. No one had a good word to say about any Kaunians. Bembo didn't argue. He didn't love the blonds, either. And the last thing he wanted was for anyone to say he did. Calling an Algarvian a Kaunian-lover had always been good for starting a fight. These days, though, calling him a Kaunian-lover was about the same as calling him a traitor.

Night came early, though not so early as it did farther south. Trapani endured hours more darkness each winter night than Tricarico did, and suffered because of it. But what Tricarico went through wasn't easy, either.

Bembo had just dropped into a fitful, uncomfortable sleep—he would have killed to be able to roll over onto his belly—when alarm bells started clanging. "Come on!" he shouted. "We're all supposed to run down to the cellar."

Curses and jeers answered him. Hardly any of the men in this ward could get out of their cots, let alone run. If an egg burst on the sanatorium, then it did, and that was all there was to it. Bembo cursed the bells. He'd heard them too often in Eoforwic. *And the last time you heard them there, you didn't get to a shelter, or even a hole in the ground, fast enough.*

In the dark ward, somebody asked, "Where are all the fancy spells the news sheets keep promising?"

"Up King Mezentio's arse," somebody else answered. Bembo probably wasn't the only one trying to figure out who'd said that. But the dark could cover all sorts of treason. At least for now, the disgruntled Algarvian had got away with speaking his mind.

Eggs didn't start falling right away. Algarvian dowsers were good at what they did. They'd probably picked up the enemy dragons' motion as soon as the beasts came over the Bradano Mountains. But how much good would that do without enough Algarvian dragons to go up there and knock the Kuusamans and Lagoans out of the sky? *Not much,* Bembo thought dismally.

As soon as eggs did begin to drop, beams from heavy sticks started probing up into the sky. But the air pirates had plenty of tricks. Along with eggs, they dropped fluttering strips of paper that drove dowsers mad: how to detect the motion of dragons when all that other motion distracted them? Because they couldn't tell the men at the heavy sticks exactly where the enemy dragons were, the beams from those sticks struck home only by luck.

And if an egg lands right on top of this stinking sanatorium, that'll be luck, too, Bembo thought—*bloody bad luck.* No one was supposed to try to drop eggs on buildings where healers worked, but accidents, mistakes, misfortunes happened.

When an egg burst close enough to rattle the shutters over the windows, someone in a ward down the hall started screaming. His shrill cries went on and on, then stopped very abruptly. Bembo didn't care to think about what had probably just gone on in that other ward.

Eggs kept falling through most of the night. Bembo got a little fitful sleep, but not much. The same, no doubt, would be true for everybody in Tricarico. Even people who weren't hurt wouldn't be worth much in the morning. Could metalworkers make proper shells for eggs when they had to pry their eyelids open? Could mages cast the proper spells to contain the sorcerous energy in those eggs? You didn't have to be Swemmel of Unkerlant to see how efficiency would go down.

"One more night," Tibiano said when the sun crawled up over the mountains to the east.

"Aye, one more night," Bembo agreed in tones as hollow as his wardmate's. He yawned till his jaw creaked. A serving woman brought a cart full of trays into the room. The yawn turned into a groan. "Now we have to live through one more breakfast."

After breakfast, a healer who looked even more exhausted than Bembo felt came thought the ward. He poked at Bembo's leg, muttered a quick charm or two, and nodded. "You'll do," he said, before racing on to Tibiano's cot. How many men's recoveries was he overseeing? Could he do any of them justice?

Bembo was dozing—if he couldn't sleep at night, he'd do it in the daytime—when a nurse said, "You've got a visitor."

He opened his eyes. He hadn't had many visitors since getting hurt, and this one . . . "Saffa!" he exclaimed.

"Hello, Bembo," the sketch artist said. "I thought I'd come by and see how you were." She didn't look good herself—not the way Bembo remembered her. She was pale and sallow and seemed weary unto death.

"I heard you had a baby," Bembo said. Only after he'd spoken did he stop and think that might be part of why she looked so tired.

"Aye, a little boy," she answered. "My sister is taking care of him right now."

"Wouldn't give *me* a tumble," he complained. Self-pity and self-aggrandizement were never far from the surface with him. "Who *is* the papa, anyway?"

"He was fighting down in the Duchy of Grelz last I heard from him," Saffa said. "A couple of months ago, letters stopped coming."

"That doesn't sound so good," Bembo said, and then, belatedly remembering himself, "I'm sorry."

"So am I. He was sweet." For a moment, Saffa managed the nasty grin that had always provoked Bembo—one way or another. She added, "Unlike some people I could name."

"Thank you, sweetheart. I love you, too," Bembo said. "If I could get up, I'd give you a swat on that round fanny of yours. Did you come see me just so you could try and drive me crazy?"

She shook her head. Coppery curls flew back and forth. "I came to see you because this stinking war has taken a bite out of both of us."

If the baby's father were still around, I wouldn't want anything to do with you. Bembo translated that without effort. But it didn't mean she was wrong. "This stinking war has taken a bite out of the whole stinking world." He hesitated. "When I'm back on my feet, I'll call on you, all right?"

"All right," Saffa said. "I'll tell you right now, though, I still may decide I'd sooner slap your face. Just so we understand each other."

Bembo snorted. "Some understanding." But he was nodding. Saffa without vinegar wasn't Saffa. "Take care of yourself. Stay safe."

"You, too," she said, and then she was gone, leaving Bembo half wondering if he'd dreamt her whole visit.

An egg flew in from the east and hit a house in the village Garivald's company had just taken away from the Algarvians. Chunks of the house flew out in all directions. A spinning board knocked down an Unkerlanter soldier standing only a couple of feet from Garivald. He started to get up, then clapped a hand to the small of his back and let out a yip of pain. The house fell in on itself and started to burn.

A Forthwegian couple in the middle of the street started howling. Garivald presumed it was their house. He couldn't make out much of what they were saying. To a Grelzer like him, this east-Forthwegian dialect made even less sense than the variety of the language people around Eoforwic spoke. Not only were the sounds a little different, a lot of the words sounded nothing at all like their Unkerlanter equivalents. He wondered if they were borrowed from Algarvian.

Another egg flew in. This one burst farther away. The crash that followed said somebody's home would never be the same. Shrieks rose immediately thereafter. Somebody's *life* would never be the same.

My life will never be the same, either, Garivald thought. *Powers below eat the Algarvians. It's their fault, curse them. I'd sooner be back in Zossen, drinking my way through the winter and waiting for spring.* Neither Zossen nor the family he'd had there existed any more. He turned to Lieutenant Andelot. "Sir, we ought to get rid of that miserable egg-tosser."

"I know, Sergeant Fariulf," Andelot answered. "But we've come so far so fast, we can't sweep up everything as neatly as we want to. On the scale of the war as a whole, that tosser doesn't mean much."

"No, sir," Garivald agreed. "But it's liable to take some nasty bites out of us." He thought for a moment. "I could probably sneak my squad through the redheads' lines and take it out. Things are all topsy-turvy—they won't have had the time to get proper trenches dug or anything like that."

What am I saying? he wondered. *Go after an egg-tosser behind the enemy's line? Have I lost all of my mind, or do I really want to kill myself?*

Andelot also studied him with a certain curiosity. "We don't see volunteers as often as we'd like," he remarked. "Aye, go on, Sergeant. Choose the men you'd like to have with you. I think you can do it, too." He pointed southeastward. "Most of the redheads in these parts are falling back on that town called Gromheort. They'll stand siege there, unless I miss my guess, and getting them out won't come easy or cheap." With a shrug, he went on, "Nothing but Algarve beyond, though. As I say, pick your men, Sergeant. Let's get on with it."

The men Garivald did pick looked imperfectly enamored of him. He understood that; he was giving them the chance to get killed. But he had an argument they couldn't top: "I'm going along with you. If I can do it, you can cursed well do it with me."

Behind his back, somebody said, "You're too ugly for me to want to do it with you, Sergeant." Garivald laughed along with the rest of the soldiers who heard. He couldn't help himself. But he didn't stop picking men.

Before they set out from the village, though, a couple of squadrons of dragons painted rock-gray flew over the place out of the west. "Hold up, Fariulf," Andelot said. "Maybe they'll do our job for us."

"They should have done it already," Garivald said. Even so, he wasn't sorry to raise his hand. None of the men he'd chosen tried to talk him out of waiting. He would have been astonished if anyone had.

That one Algarvian tosser hadn't had many eggs to fling. The distant thunder of the eggs the Unkerlanter dragons dropped brought smiles to all the men in rock-gray who heard it. "Don't know whether they'll flatten that egg-tosser or not," a soldier said. "Any which way, though, the redheads are catching it."

Only silence followed the edge of the thunder. No more eggs came down on the Forthwegian village. Andelot beamed. "That's pretty efficient," he said. "Maybe we'll be able to get a decent night's sleep here."

Not everybody would get a decent night's sleep. Andelot made sure he had plenty of sentries facing east. Had Garivald been the Algarvian commander, he wouldn't have tried a night attack. But the redheads were still dedicated counterpunchers. He'd seen that. Given even the slightest opening, they would hit back, and hit back hard.

Crickets were chirping not far from the campfire by

which Garivald sat when Andelot came up to him and asked, "Got a moment, Fariulf?"

"Aye, sir," Garivald answered. You couldn't tell a superior no. He hadn't needed more than one scorching from a furious sergeant to learn that lesson forever. And, in truth, he hadn't been doing anything more than marveling at hearing crickets in wintertime. There wouldn't have been any singing down around Zossen. He scrambled to his feet. "What do you need, sir?"

"Walk with me," Andelot said, and headed away from the fires and out into the darkness. Garivald grabbed his stick before following. Everything seemed quiet, but you never could tell. Andelot only nodded. If he'd discovered who Garivald was, he wouldn't have wanted him armed. So Garivald reasoned, at any rate. His company commander nodded again once they were out of earshot of the rest of the Unkerlanters. "Sergeant, you showed outstanding initiative there when you volunteered to go after the Algarvian egg-tosser. I'm very pleased."

"Oh, that." Garivald had already forgotten about it. "Thank you, sir."

"It's something we need more of," Andelot said. "It's something the whole kingdom needs more of. It would make us more efficient. Too many of us are happy doing nothing till someone gives them an order. That's not so good."

"I hadn't really thought about it, sir," Garivald said truthfully. If you didn't have to do something for yourself, and if nobody was making you do it for anyone else, why do it?

"Mezentio's men, curse them, have initiative," Andelot said. "They get themselves going without officers, without sergeants, without anything. They just see what needs doing and do it. That's one of the things that makes them so much trouble. We should be able to match them."

"We're beating them anyhow," Garivald said.

"But we should do better," Andelot insisted. "The price we're paying will cripple us for years. And it's something we should do for our own pride's sake. How does the song go?" He sang in a soft tenor:

"'Do anything to beat them back.
Don't hold off, don't go slack.'

Something like that, anyhow."

"Something like that," Garivald echoed raggedly. He was glad the darkness hid his expression from Andelot. He was sure his jaw had dropped when the officer started to sing. How not, considering that Andelot was singing one of his songs?

The company commander slapped him on the back. "So, as I say, Sergeant, that's why I'm so pleased. Anything you can do to encourage the men to show more initiative would also be very good."

"Why don't you just order them to . . . ?" Garivald's voice trailed away. He felt foolish. "Oh. Can't very well do that, can you?"

"No." Andelot chuckled. "Initiative imposed from above isn't exactly the genuine article, I'm afraid." He headed back toward the fires. So did Garivald. One of the nice things about being a sergeant was not having to go out and stand sentry in the middle of the night.

He woke the next morning before dawn, with Unkerlanter egg-tossers thunderously pounding the Algarvians farther east. Andelot's whistle shrilled. "Forward!" he shouted. Forward the Unkerlanters went, footsoldiers, behemoths, and dragons overhead all working together most efficiently. Garivald didn't worry, or even stop to think, that the Algarvians had devised the scheme his countrymen were using. It worked, and worked well. Nothing else mattered to him.

Artificers had laid bridges over the river that ran near Gromheort—nobody had bothered telling Garivald its name. Andelot clapped his hands when he thudded across one of those bridges. "Nothing between us and Algarve now but a few miles of flat land!" he shouted.

Garivald whooped. That there might be some large number of redheads with sticks between him and their kingdom was true, but hardly seemed to matter. If King Swemmel's men had surged forward from the Twegen and Eoforwic to here in a few short weeks, another surge would surely take them onto Algarvian soil. Garivald whooped again when he saw Unkerlanter behemoths on this side of the river. Foot-soldiers were a lot safer when they had plenty of the big beasts along for company.

But then one of those behemoths crumpled as if it had charged headlong into a boulder. A couple of the crewmen riding it were thrown clear; its fall crushed the rest. "Heavy stick!" someone close to the beast yelled. "Blazed right through its armor!"

Maybe that was just an enemy emplacement nearby. Or maybe . . . An alarmed shout rose: "Enemy behemoths!"

Even before the first egg from the Algarvian beasts' tossers burst, Garivald was digging himself a hole in the muddy ground. A footsoldier without a hole was like a tur-tle without a shell: naked, vulnerable, and ever so likely to be crushed.

Another Unkerlanter behemoth went down, this one from a well-aimed egg. The Algarvians knew what they were doing. They generally did, worse luck. Had there been more of them . . . Garivald didn't care to think about that. Beams from ordinary, hand-held sticks announced that Al-garvian footsoldiers were in the neighborhood, too.

"Crystallomancer!" Andelot bellowed. "Powers below eat you, where's a crystallomancer?" No one answered. He cursed, loudly and foully. "The fornicating *Algarvians* would have a crystallomancer handy."

Before he could embroider on that theme, Unkerlanter dragons dove on the enemy behemoths. Crystallomancer or not, someone back on the other side of the river knew what was going on. Under the cover of their aerial umbrella, the men in rock-gray moved forward again. Garivald ran past a couple of corpses in kilts, and past a redhead down and moaning. He blazed the Algarvian to make sure the fellow wouldn't get up again, then ran on.

But Mezentio's men hadn't given up. A crash from be-hind Garivald made him whirl. There was the bridge on which he'd crossed, smashed by an egg. A moment later, another one went up. A tall column of water rose into the air. "They're using those stinking sorcerously guided eggs again," somebody exclaimed.

"They did this to us back by the Twegen, too, and we managed fine then," Garivald said. But that bridgehead had been well established. This one was brand new. Could it stand against enemy counterattack? He'd find out.

Vanai hadn't known peace, hadn't known the absence of fear, since Algarvian footsoldiers and behemoths swept into, swept past, Oyngestun. Now Eoforwic was calm and quiet under the rule of King Beornwulf and the more obvious and emphatic rule of the Unkerlanters who propped him on his throne. She could go out without sorcerous disguise if she wanted to. Some Kaunians did. She hadn't had the nerve to try it herself, not after having had her nose rubbed in how little so many Forthwegians loved the blonds who lived among them.

But lack of love was one thing. The desire to kill her on sight was something else again. For the first time in more than four years, she didn't have to worry about that. Life could have been idyllic . . . if the Unkerlanters hadn't hijacked Ealstan into their army.

Fear for her husband swirled around her and choked her like nasty smoke. "It's not fair," she told Saxburh. The baby looked up at her out of big round eyes—eyes that, by now, were almost as dark as Ealstan's. Saxburh smiled enormously, showing a new front tooth. Now that it had come in, she was happy. She had no other worries. Vanai wished she could say the same herself.

"*Not* fair," she whispered fiercely. Saxburh laughed. Vanai didn't.

In a way—in a couple of ways, actually—this was worse than worrying about her grandfather when Major Spinello set out to work him to death. She'd agonized over Brivibas more from a sense of family duty than out of real affection. And she'd been able to do something to keep her grandfather safe, even if letting Spinello into her bed had been a nightmare of its own.

But all the love she had in the world that she didn't give to Saxburh was aimed at Ealstan. She knew he was going into dreadful danger; the Unkerlanters had beaten back Mezentio's men more by throwing bodies at them than through clever strategy. And one of the bodies was his—the only body she'd ever cared about in that particular way.

If bedding an Unkerlanter officer could have brought Ealstan back to Eoforwic, she would have done it in a heartbeat, and worried about everything else afterwards. But she knew better. The Unkerlanters didn't care what happened to one conscripted Forthwegian. And, for all their talk about efficiency, she wouldn't have bet they could even find him once he went into the enormous man-hungry monster that was their army.

So she had to live her life from day to day as best she could. Fortunately, Ealstan had managed to save up a good deal of silver. She didn't have to rush about looking for work—and who here, who anywhere, would take care of Saxburh even if she found it? One more worry, though a smaller one, to keep her awake at night. The silver, as she knew too well, wouldn't last forever, and what would she do when it ran out?

What she did after yet another night where she got less sleep than she wished she would have was take Saxburh, plop her into the little harness she'd made so she could carry the baby and keep both hands free, and go down to the market square to get enough barley and onions and olive oil and cheese and cheap wine to keep eating a while longer.

The market square was a more cheerful place than it had been for a long time. People went about their business without constantly looking around to see where they would hide if eggs started falling or if dragons suddenly appeared overhead. The Algarvians had struck at Eoforwic from the air a few times after losing the city, but not lately—and their closest dragon farms had to be far away by now.

New broadsheets sprouted like mushrooms on fences and walls. One showed a big, clean-shaven man labeled UNKERLANT and a smaller, bearded fellow called FORTHWEG advancing side by side against a mangy-looking dog with the face of King Mezentio. They both carried upraised clubs. The legend under the drawing said, NO MORE BITES.

Another had a drawing of King Beornwulf with the Forthwegian crown on his head but wearing a uniform tunic of a cut somewhere between those of Forthweg and Unkerlant. He had a stern expression on his face and a stick in his right hand. A KING WHO FIGHTS FOR HIS PEOPLE, this legend read.

Vanai wondered what sort of king he would end up making and how much freedom from the Unkerlanters he'd be able to get. She suspected—indeed, she was all but certain—she and Forthweg as a whole would find out. If King Penda didn't live out his life in exile, if he tried coming back to his native land, he wasn't likely to live long.

More food was in the market square and prices were lower than they had been for a couple of years. Vanai praised the powers above for that, especially since everything had been so dear during the doomed Forthwegian uprising against the redheads. She even bought a bit of sausage for a treat, and didn't ask what went into it. Saxburh fell asleep.

Over in one corner of the square, a band thumped away. They had a bowl in front of them, and every now and then some passerby would toss in a couple of coppers or even a small silver coin. Forthwegian-style music didn't appeal to Vanai; the Kaunians in Forthweg had their own tunes, much more rhythmically complex and, to her ear, much more interesting.

But the novelty of hearing any music in the market square drew her to listen for a while. Out here, in her sorcerous disguise, she wasn't just Vanai: she was also Thelberge. She thought of the Forthwegian appearance she wore almost as if it were another person. And Thelberge, she thought, would have liked these musicians. The drummer, who also sang, was particularly good.

He was so good, in fact, that she gave him a sharp look. Ethelhelm, the prominent musician for whom Ealstan had cast accounts for a while, had also been a drummer and singer. But she'd seen Ethelhelm play. He had Kaunian blood in him. Half? A quarter? She wasn't sure, but enough to make him tall and rangy and give him a long face. Enough to get him in trouble with the Algarvians, too. This fellow looked like any other Forthwegian in his late twenties or early thirties.

She couldn't applaud when the song ended, not with her hands full. Several people did, though. Coins clinked in the bowl. "Thank you kindly, folks," the drummer said; it was plainly his band. "Remember, the more you give us, the better we play." His grin showed a broken front tooth. He got a laugh, and a few more coppers to go with it. The band swung into a new tune.

And he was looking at her, too. She'd got used to men looking at her, both when she looked like herself and in her Forthwegian disguise. It was, more often than not, an annoyance rather than a compliment. She'd felt that way even before Spinello did so much to sour her on the male half of the human race.

But the drummer wasn't looking at her as if imagining how she was made under her tunic. He wore a slightly puzzled expression, one that might have said, *Haven't I seen you somewhere?* Vanai didn't think she'd ever seen him before.

The song ended. People clapped again. Vanai still couldn't, but she did set down some groceries and drop a coin in the bowl. One of the horn players lifted his instrument to his lips to start the next song, but the drummer said, "Wait a bit." The trumpeter shrugged, but lowered the horn once more. The drummer nodded to Vanai. "Your name's Thelberge, isn't it?"

"Aye," she said, and then wished she'd denied it. Too late for that, though. She countered as best she could: "I may know your name, too."

He had to be Ethelhelm, in the same sort of sorcerous disguise she wore. His voice was familiar, even if that false face wasn't. She *had* seen the disguise once before, but hadn't noticed it till it suddenly wore off and he turned into Ethelhelm on the street. Now he grinned again, showing that tooth. "Everybody knows Guthfrith," he said. "People have heard of me as far and wide as . . . the west bank of the Twegen River."

That got him another laugh from his little audience. Vanai smiled, too; the west bank of the Twegen couldn't have been more than three miles away. She said, "You play so well, you could be famous all over Forthweg."

"Thank you kindly," he said, "but that sounds to me like

more trouble than it's worth." As Ethelhelm, he'd been famous all over Forthweg. Before he disappeared, the Algarvians had squeezed him till his eyes popped—that was
what his Kaunian blood had got him. No doubt he spoke
from bitter experience. He went on, "I'm doing just fine
the way I am."

With the redheads driven out of Eoforwic, he could have
stopped being Guthfrith and gone back to his true name.
Or could he? Vanai wondered. Mezentio's men hadn't just
blackmailed him. They'd started putting words in his
mouth, too. When it was either obey or go to a special
camp, saying no wasn't easy. Still, some people might
reckon him a collaborator.

He pointed to Saxburh, asleep in the harness. "That'll be
Ealstan's baby, won't it?"

"That's right," Vanai answered.

"How's he doing?" asked Ethelhelm who was now Guthfrith—just as, in some ways, Vanai was, or could become,
Thelberge.

She'd told the truth once without intending to. She
wouldn't make the same mistake twice. Ethelhelm didn't
need to know Ealstan was far away, dragged off into the
Unkerlanter army. "He's fine," Vanai said firmly. "He's just
fine." *Powers above make it so. Powers above keep it so.*

"Glad to hear it," Ethelhelm said, and sounded as if he
meant it. But he and Ealstan hadn't parted on the best of
terms. Ealstan was one who thought he'd gone too far down
the ley line the Algarvians had given him. *I can't trust this
fellow,* Vanai thought. *I don't dare.*

A man said, "You going to gab all day, buddy, or can you
play, too?"

"Right." Ethelhelm's Guthfrith-smile was meant to be
engaging but looked a little tight. He nodded to the other
musicians. They swung into a quickstep that had been popular since the reign of King Plegmund—*not* the one,
though, that was known as "King Plegmund's Quickstep."
What with the Algarvian-created Plegmund's Brigade,
"King Plegmund's Quickstep" seemed likely to go into
eclipse for a while.

Vanai thought it a good time for her to go into eclipse,

too. She made her way out of the market square. As she went, she imagined she felt Ethelhelm's eyes on her back, though she didn't turn around to see if he was really watching her. One other thing she didn't do: she didn't leave the square by the way out leading most directly to her block of flats. That meant her arms were very tired by the time she got home, but it also meant Ethelhelm didn't find out in which direction she lived.

She wasn't sure that mattered. She hoped it didn't. But she didn't want to take chances, either. She ruffled Saxburh's fine, dark hair as she took her out of the harness. "No, I don't want to take chances," she said. "I've got more than just me to worry about."

Saxburh whimpered. She'd emerged from her nap crabby. Sure enough, she was wet. Changing her didn't take long. Changing her any one time didn't take long. Doing it half a dozen times a day and more . . .

"But everything's going to be all right. Everything will be just fine," Vanai said. If she said it often enough, it might come true.

"So this is Algarve," Ceorl said as the men of Plegmund's Brigade trudged into a farming village. He spat. The city wind that blew at his back, out of the west, carried the spittle a long way. "I thought Algarve was supposed to be rich. This doesn't look so fornicating fancy to me."

It didn't look so fancy to Sidroc, either. But he answered, "Algarve's just a place. Gromheort's right on our side of the border from it. You can see it from there. It doesn't look any different than Forthweg."

"You're a corporal now. You must know everything," Ceorl said.

"I know I'm a corporal, by the powers above," Sidroc said. Ceorl made a face at him. He ignored it. "I know this is a cursed miserable place, too. The part of Algarve you can see from Gromheort is a lot better country."

Down here in the south, the land was flat and damp, sometimes marshy. But some of the marshes froze in the winter. Unkerlanter behemoths had broken through a couple of places where the redheads hadn't thought they could go. And the men of Plegmund's Brigade had other things to worry about, too.

"If those whoresons in this village start blazing at us on account of they think we're Swemmel's buggers, I say we treat 'em just like we did the Yaninans who blazed Sergeant Werferth," Ceorl growled.

They'd already drawn a couple of blazes from panicky redheads. The Algarvians saw swarthy men in tunics and didn't stop to find out which swarthy men they were or whose side they were on. So far, the troopers of Plegmund's Brigade hadn't answered with massacre. "Looks like they're just running here," Sidroc said.

Sure enough, Algarvians—mostly women and children, with a few old men—fled the village on foot, on horseback, and in whatever carriages and wagons they could lay their hands on. Some of the redheads on foot carried bundles heavier than a soldier's pack. Others pulled light carts as if they were beasts of burden themselves. Still others took nothing at all with them, abandoning homes without a backward glance and relying on luck to keep them fed so long as they could escape the Unkerlanters.

"We're going to stand here," Lieutenant Puliano said, commanding the Forthwegians with as much aplomb as if he were a marshal. "I'll need two or three groups forward— that house there, that stand of trees, and that tumbledown barn. You know the drill. Let Swemmel's buggers come past you, then hit 'em from the sides and from behind. Questions? All right, then . . ."

One of the joys of being a corporal was that Sidroc got told off to lead one of Puliano's forward groups: the one in the stand of trees. "Dig in," he told the squad he headed. "This would have been a lot better cover if we were here in the summertime."

"What was that?" Sudaku asked in Algarvian. The blond from the Phalanx of Valmiera was picking up Forthwegian fast, but still had only so much. Sidroc translated his words into Algarvian. Sudaku nodded agreement.

With his short-handled shovel, Ceorl dug like a mole. He threw another shovelful of dirt on the mound in front of his deepening hole, then said, "Ain't a futtering one of us going to be here in the summertime." His Algarvian was as rough and laced with obscenities as his Forthwegian.

"No. We will have retreated by then," Sudaku said.

"That ain't what I meant, you stupid fornicating Kaunian," Ceorl said.

"If your dick were bigger—much, much bigger—you could bugger yourself," Sudaku replied. They both spoke without heat. Sudaku went on digging. So did Ceorl, who paused only to slice a thumb across his throat to show what he *had* meant.

A few eggs burst, perhaps a quarter of a mile in front of the grove where Sidroc and his double handful of men waited. "Feeling for us," Sidroc muttered, more than half to himself. Sure enough, the bursts crept closer, kicking up fountains of snow and dirt.

Only a couple of eggs burst among the trees. The rest marched into the village. Houses and shops crumbled into wreckage. Not all the Algarvian civilians were likely to have got clear. They'd be running around and screaming and getting in the way of the soldiers. As far as Sidroc was concerned, that was about all civilians were good for. But knocking a lot of buildings in the village to pieces wouldn't hurt the defense. If anything, it might help. Everybody in Plegmund's Brigade had had plenty of practice fighting in rubble.

"Heads up!" hissed somebody among the trees. "Here they come."

Sidroc's heart thuttered. His mouth went dry. He'd been through too many battles, skirmishes, clashes, fights. It never got easier. If anything, it got harder every time. At first, he hadn't believed he could die. He believed it now. He'd seen far too much to have any possible doubt.

Some of the oncoming Unkerlanters wore snow smocks over their rock-gray tunics. Some didn't bother. The men in white and those in Unkerlanter rock-gray were about equally hard to see. Winter hereabouts wasn't quite so harsh, quite so snowy, as it was farther west.

"Remember, let 'em by, like Lieutenant Puliano said," Sidroc reminded his men. "Then we give it to 'em up the arse."

He studied the way Swemmel's soldiers loped forward, then gave a soft grunt of satisfaction. Ceorl put that grunt into words: "They don't move like veteran troops. They ought to be easy meat."

"Aye—depending on how many of 'em there are," Sidroc answered.

"I see no behemoths," Sudaku remarked.

"Don't miss those fornicators," Sidroc said. He saw none of the great armored beasts, either. That was another sign the Unkerlanters moving on the village weren't first-rate men. Enemy doctrine assigned help first to the soldiers most likely to succeed.

"Ahh, the fools," Ceorl said as the enemy drew near. "The dick-sucking virgins. They aren't even sending anybody in here to see if we've got any little surprises waiting." His chuckle was pure evil. "They'll find out."

On toward the village trotted the Unkerlanters. "Wait," Sidroc said, over and over. "Just wait."

The men in and around the outlying house started blazing at Swemmel's soldiers first. Sidroc could hear the Unkerlanters' howls and curses, and even make sense of a few of those oaths. His men sat quietly in their holes, waiting and watching. They all expected the same thing. And they got it: the Unkerlanters wheeled toward the house, intent on flushing out their tormentors.

That that might expose their backs to another set of tormentors never seemed to cross their minds. "Now!" Sidroc shouted, and started blazing. One enemy soldier after another went down. For a couple of minutes, Swemmel's men couldn't even figure out where the beams wreaking such havoc among them were coming from. Sidroc laughed. "Easy!"

But then more Unkerlanters came forward, and they had some idea that danger lurked among the trees. Danger also lurked, though, by the tumbledown barn, and that hadn't occurred to them. The men from Plegmund's Brigade posted there worked the same kind of slaughter as Sidroc's squad had a few minutes earlier.

With that, the entire Unkerlanter advance came unglued. Swemmel's men had been hit from unexpected directions three times in a row. When they could follow orders exactly as they got them, they made fine soldiers. Having spent more than two years in the field against them, Sidroc knew exactly how good they could be. But when they got surprised, they sometimes panicked.

They did here. They streamed back toward the west, dragging some wounded men with them and leaving others, along with the dead, lying on the muddy snow. Sidroc let out a long sigh of relief. "Well, that wasn't so bad," he said. "I don't think we got even a scratch here."

"Only one trouble," Sudaku said. "They will come back."

"Which means we'd better move," Sidroc said. "They know where we are, so they'll be sure to give this place a good pounding." No sooner were the words out of his mouth than a messenger came up from Lieutenant Puliano, ordering the squad to shift to a new position in and around another outlying house. Sidroc preened. "Do I know what's what?"

"Let me kiss your boots," Ceorl said, "and you can kiss my—" The suggestion was not one a common soldier usually made to a corporal.

"If we're both still alive tonight, you're in trouble," Sidroc said. Ceorl gave him an obscene gesture, too. Sidroc laughed and shook his head. "You're not worth punishing, you son of a whore. That would just take you away from the front and make you safer than I am. I won't let you get away with it. Come on, let's move."

They'd just started digging new holes when a storm of eggs fell on the grove they'd abandoned. The house and barn where other squads had taken shelter also vanished in bursts of sorcerous energy. Sudaku spoke in his Valmieran-flavored Algarvian: "Now they think it will be easy."

"It would be easy—if they were fighting more Unkerlanters," Sidroc said. "But the redheads are smarter than they are." *If the redheads are so cursed smart, what are they doing with their backs to the wall here in their own kingdom? And if you're so fornicating smart, what are you doing here with them?*

But, in the short run, on the small scale, what he'd said turned out to be the exact truth. On came the Unkerlanters once more, plainly confident they'd put paid to the men who'd tormented them. On they came—and again got caught from the flank and rear and ignominiously fled before setting so much as a foot in the village they were supposed to take.

"This is fun," Ceorl said. "They can keep the whoresons coming. We'll kill 'em till everything turns blue."

A long pause followed. *We'd better move again, before they start pounding this place, too,* Sidroc thought. Before he could give the order, though, another runner from the village came up. "Lieutenant Puliano says to pull back," the man said.

"What? Why?" Sidroc asked irately. "Doesn't he think the blockheads in rock-gray will fall for it again? I sure do."

"But he gives the orders, and you sure don't," the messenger replied.

Since that was true, Sidroc had no choice but to obey. When he and his men—who still hadn't lost anybody, despite the slaughter they'd worked on the Unkerlanters—got back into the Algarvian village, he burst out, "Why are you bringing us back here? We can hold 'em a long time."

"Aye, we could hold 'em a long time here." Puliano didn't sound or look like a happy man. "But they've broken through farther north, and if we don't pull back a little ways they'll nip in behind us and cut us off."

"Oh," Sidroc said, and then, "Oh, shit." That was an unanswerable argument. But it also had its drawbacks: "If the army does keep pulling back, what is there left to fight for?" Puliano just scowled by way of reply, from which Sidroc concluded that that had no real answer, either. He wished it did.

Six

Drizzle on the island of Obuda was as natural and unremarkable as snow in Istvan's home valley. The sergeant stood to attention in his place in the captives' camp as the Kuusaman guards took the morning roll call and count. He stood in the same place every day, rain or shine. The guards made sure they got the numbers right; when anything went wrong with their count, everything stopped—including the captives' breakfasts—till they straightened things out.

Beside Istvan, Corporal Kun whispered, "This would go a lot smoother if the goat-eaters could count to twenty-one without playing with themselves."

That made Istvan laugh. A guard pointed at him and shouted, "To be quiet!" in bad Gyongyosian. He nodded to show he was sorry, then glared at Kun. It was just like his brief time in the village school: somebody else talked out of turn, and he got in trouble for it.

At last, the slanteyes seemed satisfied. Istvan waited for one of them to call out, "To queue up for feeding!" the way they usually did. Instead, though, the Kuusaman captain in charge of the guards said, "Sergeant Istvan! Corporal Kun! To stand out!"

Ice ran through Istvan. Out of the corner of his eye, he saw Kun start. But they had no choice. The two of them stepped away from their comrades, away from their countrymen. Istvan hadn't imagined how terribly lonely he could feel with so many eyes on him.

The captain nodded. "You two," he said, using the plural where he should have used the dual, "to come with me."

"Why, sir?" Istvan asked. "What have we done?"

"Not know," the Kuusaman answered with a shrug. "You to come for interrogation."

He pronounced the word so badly, Istvan almost failed to understand it. When he did, he wished he hadn't. Gyongyosian interrogations were nasty, brutal things. The Kuusamans were the enemy, so he couldn't imagine they would play the game by gentler rules.

But it was their game, not his. Under the sticks of the guards, he could obey or he could die. *I should have let Captain Frigyes cut my throat after all,* he thought. *It would have been over in a hurry then, and my life energy might have done something extra to the slanteyes. Now the stars are having their revenge on me.*

One of the guards gestured with his stick. Numbly, Istvan started forward, Kun at his side. Kun's face was a frozen mask. Istvan tried to wear the same look. If the Kuusamans thought he was afraid, it would only go worse for him. *And if they don't think I'm afraid, they're fools.*

But he would do his best to act like a man from a warrior race as long as he could. "You ought to give us breakfast before you question us," he told a guard as the fellow led him toward one of the gates in the stockade.

"To shut up," the guard answered.

Outside the gate, the Kuusamans separated him from Kun, leading him towards one tent on the yellow-brown grass and Kun to another. Istvan grimaced. That made telling lies harder.

He ducked his way into the tent. A couple of guards already stood in there. The Kuusamans didn't believe in taking chances. One of the men who'd led him out of the captives' camp walked in behind him. No, the slanteyes didn't believe in taking chances at all. A moment later, he realized why: the bright-looking Kuusaman sitting in a folding chair waiting for him was a woman. She wore spectacles amazingly like Kun's. It had barely occurred to him that the Kuusamans had to have women among them as well as men, or there wouldn't have been any more Kuusamans after a while. He wished there hadn't been.

"Hello. You are Sergeant Istvan, is it not so?" she said, speaking better Gyongyosian than any other slanteye he'd ever heard. She waited for him to nod, then went on, "I am called Lammi. May the stars shine on our meeting."

"May it be so," Istvan mumbled; he felt confused, out of his depth, but he'd be accursed if he would let a foreigner act more politely than he did.

"Sit down, if you care to," Lammi said, pointing to another folding chair. Warily, Istvan sat. The Kuusaman woman—she was, he guessed, somewhere around forty, for she had a handful of silver threads among the midnight of her hair, the first fine wrinkles around her eyes—went on, "You were taken before breakfast, eh?"

"Aye, Lady Lammi," Istvan answered, unconsciously giving her the title he would have given a domain-holder's wife back in his home valley.

She laughed. "I am no lady," she said. "I am a forensic sorcerer—do you know what that means?"

Forensic sounded as if it ought to be Gyongyosian—it wasn't the funny sort of noises Kuusamans used for a language—but it wasn't a word Istvan had heard before. He shrugged broad shoulders. "You're a mage. That's enough to know."

"All right." She turned to one of the guards and spoke in her own language. The man nodded. He left the tent. Lammi returned to Gyongyosian: "He is fetching you something to eat."

What Istvan got must have come from the guards' rations, not the captives': a big plate full of eggs and smoked salmon scrambled together, with fried turnips swimming in butter off to the side. He ate like a starving mountain ape. Kuusaman interrogations certainly didn't seem much like those his countrymen would have used.

While he shoveled food into his mouth, Lammi said, "What it means is, after something has happened, I investigate how and why it happened. You can probably guess what I am here to investigate."

Istvan's stomach did a slow lurch, as if he were aboard ship in a heavy sea. "Probably," he said, and let it go at that. The less he said, the less Lammi could use.

She gave him back a brisk nod. Behind the lenses of her spectacles, her eyes were very sharp indeed. "It means one thing more, Sergeant: if you lie, I will know it. You do not want that to happen. Please believe me—you do not."

Another lurch. Istvan almost regretted the enormous breakfast he was demolishing. Almost, but not quite. He'd eaten mush—and thin mush at that—for too long. Lammi waited for him to say something. Reluctantly, he did: "I understand."

"Good." The forensic mage waited till he'd chased down the last bit of fried turnip and given his plate to the guard who'd fetched it before beginning by asking, "You knew Captain Frigyes, did you not?"

"He was my company commander," Istvan replied. She had to have already learned that.

"And you also knew Borsos the dowser?" Lammi asked.

"Aye," Istvan said—why not answer that? "I fetched and carried for him here on Obuda, as a matter of fact, back when the war was young. And I saw him again when I was fighting in Unkerlant."

Lammi nodded once more. "All right. He never should have come to an ordinary captives' camp, but that was our error, not yours." She had a pad of paper in her lap, and drummed her fingers on it. "Tell me, Sergeant, what do you think of what your countrymen did here?"

"It was brave. They were warriors. They died like warriors," Istvan answered. Lammi sat there looking at him—looking through him—with those sharp, sharp eyes. Under that gaze, he felt he had to go on, and he did: "I thought they were stupid, though. They could not do you enough harm to make their deaths worthwhile."

"Ah." Lammi scribbled something in the notepad. "You are a man of more than a little sense, I see. Is that why you did not offer your throat to the knife?"

Istvan felt the ice under his feet getting thin. "I was ill that night," he said. "I was in the infirmary that night. I couldn't have done anything about it even if I'd thought it was a good idea."

"So you were, you and Corporal Kun," Lammi said. "And how did the two of you manage to be so, ah, conveniently ill?"

The ice crackled, as if he might fall through. And what

was Kun saying, over in the other tent? "I had the shits," Istvan said. Maybe the raw word would keep her from digging further.

He should have known better. He realized that even before her eyes blazed. "Did you think I was bluffing?" she asked quietly. "An evasion is also a lie, Sergeant. I will let you try again. How did you come to have the shits?" She spoke the word as calmly as a soldier might have. He supposed he should have guessed that, too.

But he evaded even so: "It must have been something I ate."

Lammi shook her head, as if she'd expected better of him. He braced himself for whatever the guards would do to him. He hoped it wouldn't be too bad. The slanteyes really were softer than his own folk. He saw Lammi raise her left hand and start to twist it—and then he suddenly stopped seeing. Everything went, not black, but no color at all. He stopped hearing. He stopped smelling and feeling and tasting. As far as he could prove, he stopped existing.

Have I died? he wondered. If he had, he knew none of the stars' light. *Or is it her wizardry?* Thinking straight didn't come easy, not when he was reduced to essential nothingness. His mind began to drift, whether he wanted it to or not. *How long before I go mad?* he wondered. But even time had no meaning, not when he couldn't gauge it.

After what might have been moments or years, he found himself back in his body, all senses intact. By the way Lammi eyed him, it hadn't been long. She said, "I can do worse than that. Do you want to see how much worse I can do?"

"I am your captive." Istvan tried to calm his pounding heart. "You will do as you do."

To his surprise, she gave him a nod of obvious approval. "Spoken like a warrior," she said, just as a Gyongyosian might have. She went on, "I have studied your people for many years. I admire your courage. But, with war the way it is these days, courage is not enough. Do you see that, Sergeant?"

Istvan shrugged. "It's all I have left."

"I know. I am sorry." Lammi gestured. The world disappeared for Istvan once more. He tried to get to his feet to spring at her, but his body would not obey his will. It was as if he had no body. After some endless while, his mind did drift free of the moorings of rationality. And when he heard a voice speaking to him, it might have been the voice of the stars themselves, leading his spirit toward them. He answered without the slightest hesitation.

The world returned. There sat Lammi, looking at him with real sympathy in her dark, narrow eyes. Realization smote. "It was you!" he exclaimed.

"Aye, it was me. I am sorry, but I did what was needful for my kingdom." She studied him. "So you and this Kun knew ahead of time. You knew, and you did nothing to warn us."

"I thought about it," Istvan said, and the admission made Lammi jerk in surprise. "I thought about it, but, no matter how stupid I thought the sacrifice was, I might have been wrong. And I could not bring myself to betray Ekrekek Arpad and Gyongyos. The stars would go dark for me forever."

Lammi scribbled notes. "That will do for now. I must compare your words to those of this other man, this Kun. I shall have more to ask you about another time." She spoke to the guards in Kuusaman. They took Istvan back to the camp. He wondered if the forensic mage would feed him so well the next time she asked him questions. He hoped so.

Marshal Rathar lay in a warm, soft Algarvian bed in an Algarvian house in the middle of an Algarvian town. He could have had a warm, soft Algarvian woman in the bed with him. Plenty of Unkerlanter soldiers were avenging themselves, indulging themselves, with rape or other, less brutal, arrangements. He understood that. A lot of revenge was owed. A lot would be taken. But, as marshal, he found rape beneath his dignity, and he hadn't seen a redheaded woman he really wanted, either.

Mangani—that was the name of the town. It lay not too far west of the Scamandro River, which was what the Algarvians called this reach of the Skamandros. The Scamandro flowed into the South Raffali. On the marshy ground between the South Raffali and the North Raffali lay Trapani. Mezentio's men had pushed almost as far as Cottbus. Now King Swemmel's soldiers were getting close to the Algarvian capital.

And we aren't the only ones, Rathar thought discontentedly as he got out of the warm, soft bed and went downstairs. General Vatran was already down there, eating porridge and drinking tea as he peered at a map through spectacles that magnified his eyes.

"Be careful," Rathar said. "King Mezentio is watching."

"Huh?" Vatran's bushy white eyebrows rose. "What are you talking about, sir?"

Rathar pointed to the far wall of the dining room, where a reproduction of a portrait of Mezentio hung at a distinctly cockeyed angle. Vatran eyed the image of the King of Algarve, then spat at it. His spittle fell short and splatted on the floor. Rathar laughed, saying, "May we get the chance to try that in person soon."

"That would be good," Vatran agreed. "But it won't be quite so soon as we'd like, curse it. The redheads have a pretty solid line set up on the east bank of the Scamandro. They're good with river lines, the buggers."

"They've had plenty of practice making them," Rathar said, "but we've smashed every one they've made. We'll smash this one, too . . . eventually."

"Eventually is right," Vatran said. "Maybe it's just as well they did slow us down for a while. We could use a little time to let our supplies catch up with our soldiers."

Marshal Rathar grunted. He knew how true that was. No other army could have come so far so fast as the Unkerlanters had, for no other army was so good at living off the countryside. But, while Unkerlanters could find more food than other forces and so needed to bring less with them, they couldn't find eggs growing on trees or in fields. They had indeed run short. Had the redheads had more themselves, they could have put in a nasty counterattack. But, while they remained brave and highly professional, they were far more desperately short of everything—men, behemoths, dragons, eggs, cinnabar—than their foes. And every mile King Swemmel's men advanced was a mile from which the Algarvians could no longer draw any of those essentials.

But King Swemmel's men weren't the only ones advancing in Algarve these days. Worry in his voice, Rathar asked, "How far west have the islanders come?"

"Just about all of the Marquisate of Rivaroli is in their hands, sir," Vatran answered. "That's what the crystallomancers say. The really bastardly part of it is, the fornicating Algarvians aren't putting up much of a fight against them."

"Of course they aren't. Whatever they have left, they're throwing it at us." Rathar understood why. The redheads knew to the copper how much Unkerlant owed them. They were doing everything they could to keep Unkerlant from paying.

"But if they fight us like madmen and if they don't hardly fight Kuusamo and Lagoas at all . . ." Vatran sounded worried, too. "If the islanders take Trapani and we don't, King Swemmel will boil both of us alive."

Rathar would have argued about that, if only he could. Since he couldn't, he went back to the kitchen and got a bowl of porridge and some tea for himself, too. He brought them out to the dining room and ate while he, like Vatran, studied the map. His army had no bridgeheads over the Scamandro. A couple of crossings had been beaten back. The redheads had learned, too. They knew how disastrous Unkerlanter bridgeheads could be.

Finishing his breakfast, he walked out onto the sidewalk and looked northeast toward Trapani. Mangani bustled with Unkerlanter soldiers. Some of them were marching east, toward the front. Their sergeants kept them moving in the profane way of sergeants all over Derlavai. Others, though, just milled about. Some were walking wounded who'd needed healing and weren't quite ready to return to the fighting line yet. Some were probably evading orders to move east. And some were queued up in front of a building with a chunk bitten out of its fancy façade: a soldiers' brothel. Rathar didn't know how the quartermasters had recruited the redheaded women in the brothel. Even the Marshal of Unkerlant was entitled to squeamishness about a few things.

A soldier came past Rathar carrying something or other. "What have you got there?" Rathar asked him.

The youngster stiffened to attention when he saw who'd spoken to him. He held up his prize. "It's a lamp, sir, one of those sorcerous lamps the redheads use."

Unkerlanters used them, too, in towns and cities. By his accent, though, this soldier, like so many of his countrymen, came from a peasant village. Gently, Rathar asked, "What are you going to do with it?"

"Well, lord Marshal, sir, I'm going to see if I can't take it on home with me," the young man answered. "The light it's got inside of it is an awful lot finer nor a torch nor a candle nor even an oil lantern."

Rathar sighed. A sorcerous lamp wouldn't work without a power point or a ley line close by. Those were dense in Algarve, much less so in Unkerlant. He started to tell the soldier as much, but then checked himself. What were the odds the fellow would live to go back to his village? What were the odds the lamp would stay unbroken even if he did? Slim and slimmer, no doubt about it. Rather reached out and clapped him on the shoulder. "Good luck to you, son."

"Thank you, lord Marshal!" Beaming, the soldier went on his way.

What will the world look like after this cursed war finally ends? Rathar wondered. *How can Unkerlant take its proper place among the kingdoms of the world if so many of our people are so ignorant? We're like a dragon, all strength and claws and fire and not a bit of brain.*

Shaking his head, Rathar watched a column of Algarvian captives trudging gloomily off into the west. Some were too young to make good soldiers, others too old. The Algarvians had all the brains in the world. *And if you don't believe it, just ask them,* Rathar thought, one corner of his mouth quirking up in a wry smile. Brains weren't enough all by themselves, either. Mezentio's men hadn't had quite the brawn they needed to do everything they wanted—for which the marshal gave the powers above fervent thanks.

Almost no Algarvian civilians showed themselves. How many huddled in their houses and how many had fled, Rathar didn't know. From everything he'd seen, the town

held next to no unwounded men between the ages of four-
teen and sixty-five. As for women . . . If he were an Algarvian woman, he wouldn't have wanted Unkerlanter soldiers
to know he was around, either.

He went back into the house he was using as a headquarters. In the few minutes he was outside, someone had taken
down the picture of King Mezentio and put up one of King
Swemmel. Rathar found his own sovereign's cold stare no
more pleasant to work under than that of the King of Algarve.

A crystallomancer came up to him and said, "Sir, the
redheads have taken out a couple of important bridges with
those steerable eggs of theirs."

"Those things are a stinking nuisance." Rathar felt like
kicking someone whenever he thought of them. For most of
the past year, Mezentio had been bellowing that Algarve's
superior sorcery would yet win the war. Most of the time,
those claims seemed nothing more than so much wind and
air. Things like steerable eggs, though, made the marshal
wonder what else Mezentio's mages might come up with,
and how dangerous it would prove. For now, he stuck to the
business at hand: "All we can do is all we can do. We need
to concentrate heavy sticks around bridges, and our dragons need to keep the Algarvians away from them."

"Aye, sir. Will you draft an order to that effect?" the crystallomancer asked.

"Pass it on orally for now. I'll assign it to some bright
young officer as soon as I get the chance," Rathar replied.
"There are other things going on right now, you know." The
crystallomancer saluted and hurried away.

Winter nights came early in southern Algarve, as they
did in the south of Unkerlant. It was cold here, too, though
southern Unkerlant got colder. Rathar felt a certain gloomy
pride in that. Unkerlant's appalling fall and winter weather
had played no small part in helping to hold the redheads out
of Cottbus.

The marshal had just gone up to bed—again, without a
redheaded girl to keep him company—when the eastern
horizon lit up. The glare was so bright, he wondered for a
moment if the sun hadn't hurried round behind the world to
rise again much sooner than it should have. He'd seen the

night sky brightened by bursting eggs more times than he could count. This wasn't like that. That was a flicker, a ripple, of light along a whole great stretch of the horizon. Here, all the light came from one place, and it really did seem almost bright enough for a sunrise.

It lasted about five minutes. Then, as abruptly as it had begun, it winked out. A sharp bellow of noise, as of an egg bursting not far away, rattled the window. Darkness and relative quiet returned.

For a moment. Someone dashed up the stairs and pounded on Rathar's door. "Lord Marshal, it's Brigadier Magneric, up by the Scamandro," a crystallomancer said.

"I'll come," Rathar answered, and did. When he sat down before the crystal, he asked the brigadier, "What in blazes was that just now?"

"In blazes is right, sir." Magneric, a solid officer, sounded like a man shaken to the core. "That was . . . a stick, I guess you'd call it. An Algarvian stick. But it was to the heaviest stick a floating fortress carries as the floating fortress' stick would be to a footsoldier's. A superstick, you might say. It blazed down, it blazed through, every fornicating thing it could reach. Men, behemoths, fieldworks—it went through them like a sword through a pat of lard. It *was* a sword, a sword of light. How can you fight something like that, lord Marshal?"

"I don't know. There's bound to be a way." Rathar sounded more confident than he felt. Then he said, "It stopped, you know."

"So it did, sir. Something must've gone wrong with it. But when will it start up again, and how bad will it be then?"

"I don't know." Rathar didn't relish admitting that, but he wouldn't lie to Brigadier Magneric. "Powers below eat the redheads. I hope they ate a good many of them just now." *What I really hope is that we can beat them before they get all their fancy new magecraft working the way it's supposed to. What if they'd started trying to do something like this two years sooner?* He shivered. Then a new thought occurred to him, a really horrible one. *If we ever fight another war after this, will anyone at all be left alive by the time it's done?* He had his doubts.

* * *

Marchioness Krasta got out of her pyjamas and stood naked in front of the mirror, examining herself. She shook her head in dismay. She'd always prided herself on her figure, and the way men responded to it told her she had every reason to do so (although she likely would have prided herself on it any which way, simply because it was hers). But now . . .

"I'm built like a tuber," she muttered. "Just like a fornicating tuber." She laughed, though it wasn't exactly funny. If not for fornicating, she wouldn't have been built this way.

Inside her belly, the baby kicked. She could see her skin stretch. Every so often, a hard, round protuberance would surface, as it were. That had to be the baby's head. She thought she'd identified knees and elbows, too.

Looking at herself in the reflecting glass, she saw something she hadn't noticed before. It had to have happened in the night, while she was sleeping—not that sleep came easy these days, not with the baby pressing half her insides down onto the saw blade of her spine.

"My navel!" she exclaimed in dismay. She'd always been vain about it. It was small and round and neat, as if someone with good taste and very nice fingers had poked one into the middle of her belly. No—it had been small and round and neat. Now . . . Now it stuck out, as if it were the stem of the tuber she seemed to be turning into.

She poked it with her own finger. While she held it, it went back to the way it had been, or something close to that. But when she let go, it popped right back out again. She tried several times, always with the same result.

"Bauska!" she shouted. "Where in blazes are you, Bauska?"

The maidservant came into the bedchamber at a run. "What is it, milady?" The question had started while she was still out in the hallway. When she saw Krasta, she let out a startled squeak: "Milady!"

Krasta took her own nudity in stride. Bauska was only a servant, after all. How could one be embarrassed in front of one's social inferiors? "Took you long enough to get here,"

Krasta grumbled, not bothering to put an arm in front of her breasts or her bush.

"What . . . do you need of me, milady?" Bauska asked carefully.

"Your belly button." Krasta tried without any luck to poke hers back in again and make it stay. "Once you had your little bastard, did it go back to the way it was supposed to be?"

"Oh," Bauska said. "Aye, milady, it did. And yours will, too, once you have yours. And now, if you will excuse me . . ." She strode out of the bedchamber.

By the time Krasta realized she'd got the glove, she was already dressed. She muttered something sulfurous under her breath. Bauska probably thought she wouldn't notice, or that she would forget if she did. The first had been a good bet, but one the servant hadn't won. The second was a miscalculation; Krasta had a long memory for slights.

She didn't indulge it on the instant; it wasn't as if she wouldn't see Bauska again some time soon. Going down to breakfast seemed more urgent. Now that she wasn't throwing up any more, she ate like a hog. Not all the weight she'd put on was directly connected to the baby.

Skarnu and Merkela were already sitting at the table. "Good morning," Krasta's brother said.

"Good morning," she replied, and sat down herself, well away from the two of them. That didn't keep Merkela from sending her a look as hot and burning as a beam from a heavy stick. Krasta glared back. *Cow,* she thought. *Sow. Bitch. Hen.* Amazing how many names from the farm fit the farm girl.

But she didn't say that. Merkela didn't just argue. Merkela was liable to come around the table and thump her. *Nasty peasant slut.*

Breakfast proceeded in poisonous silence. That was how breakfast usually proceeded when Krasta and her brother and his wench sat down together at table. The alternative was a screaming row, and those came along every so often, too.

The silence ended when Skarnu and Merkela rose after finishing ahead of Krasta. Merkela said, "I don't care if that is Valnu's baby. You were still an Algarvian's whore, and everybody knows it."

"Even the way you talk stinks of manure," Krasta retorted, imitating the country woman's accent. "And well it might—it's a wonder your eyes aren't brown."

Merkela started for her. Skarnu grabbed his fiancée. "Enough, the two of you!" he said. "Too much, in fact." Both women looked daggers at him. He rolled his eyes. "Sometimes I think the Algarvians fighting Unkerlant have it easier than I do—they don't get blazed at from two directions at once." He managed to get Merkela out of the dining room before she and Krasta lobbed any more eggs at each other.

My mansion, Krasta thought furiously. *What's the world coming to, when I can't even live at peace in my own mansion?* Peace anywhere around Krasta was contingent on people doing exactly as she said, but that never occurred to her.

She went into Priekule. If she couldn't get peace and quiet at home, she would go out and buy something. That always made her feel better. When the carriage stopped on the Boulevard of Horsemen to let her out, she was as cheerful as anyone built like a tuber and resenting it could be.

Some of the shops along the boulevard had new goods in them, imports from Lagoas and Kuusamo. Krasta window-shopped avidly. Just seeing something new after the dreary sameness of the occupation was a tonic. But a good many places remained closed; on a couple of doors, the scrawl of NIGHT AND FOG hadn't yet been painted over. Those shopkeepers would never come back from whatever the Algarvians had done with them.

She was looking at new jackets and feeling very large indeed when someone said, "Wasting money again, are you, sweetheart?"

There stood Viscount Valnu, his mocking grin wider than ever. Krasta drew herself up—which, with her bulging belly, made her back ache. "I'm not wasting money—I'm spending it," she said with dignity. "There's a difference."

"I'm sure there must be." Still grinning, Valnu came up, leaned forward over that belly, and kissed her on the cheek.

She was, to her surprise, thoroughly glad to get even

that little throwaway kiss. It was the first sign of affection she'd had from anyone for quite a while. Tears stung her eyes. She shook her head, angry and embarrassed at showing such emotion. *It's because you're pregnant,* she thought; this wasn't the first time she'd puddled up for no particular reason.

Polite as a cat, Valnu affected not to see. His voice still light and cheery, he said, "And what have you been doing lately besides wasting—excuse me, besides *spending*— money?" Also like a cat, he had claws.

"Not much." Krasta set a hand on her belly as a partial explanation for that. But it was only a partial explanation, as she knew. She didn't try—it never would have occurred to her to try—to hide her bitterness: "I don't get invited out much any more."

"Ah." Valnu nodded. "I am sorry about that, my sweet. I truly am. I've done my best to get people to be reasonable, but it doesn't seem to be a very reasonable time right now."

Those tears came back. To Krasta's dismay, one of them ran down her face. "It certainly isn't," she said. "Just because you didn't pretend the Algarvians had never come to Priekule, everyone who was so tiresomely virtuous during the occupation—or can pretend he was—gets up on his high horse and acts like you did all sorts of dreadful things." A woman with her hair just starting to grow back after a shaving walked down the other side of the street. Krasta did her best to convince herself she hadn't seen her.

"I said as much to your brother and his lady friend not so long ago," Valnu said.

"When was this?" Krasta asked sharply; he hadn't been by the mansion for some time. "*Where* was this?"

"At some boring party or other," he answered. "It was, in fact, one of the most boring parties I've ever had the bad luck to attend."

It was, in fact, one more party to which Krasta hadn't been invited. "It's not fair!" she wailed, and really did burst into tears.

Valnu put his arm around her. "There, there, my dear," he said, and kissed her again, this time without a trace of the smiling malice that was usually as inseparable from him as his skin. "Come on—I'll buy you some ale or some brandy or whatever you like, and you'll feel better."

Sniffling, trying to keep from blubbering, Krasta doubted she would ever feel better. But she let Valnu lead her to a tavern a few doors down. She didn't know anyone in there, for which she was duly grateful. She hadn't had much taste for spirits since she started carrying her child, any more than she'd had a taste for tea. But she'd been able to drink more tea lately. And, sure enough, a brandy not only felt good going down but also put up a thin glass wall between her and some of her misery.

"Thank you," she told Valnu, and her voice held none of the whine that so often filled it. If he'd shown any interest in taking her to bed just then, she would have given herself to him without the slightest hesitation, just from gratitude for his treating her like a human being. But he didn't. She looked down at her swollen front. Resentment returned. *Who would want to go to bed with somebody built like a tuber?*

"You don't look happy enough yet," Valnu said, and waved at the barmaid for another brandy for Krasta and another mug of ale for himself.

"I shouldn't," Krasta said, but she did. The glass wall got thicker. That felt good. She tried on a smile. It fit her face surprisingly well.

And then, when she was happier than she'd been in longer than she could remember without some thought, Valnu threw a rock through that glass wall and effortlessly smashed it: "Your brother threatened to send me an invitation to his wedding, and he finally went and made good on the threat."

"Wedding?" Krasta sat bolt upright, even if it did hurt her back. Skarnu had *said* he would marry the peasant wench who'd borne him a son, but it hadn't seemed real to Krasta. Now she couldn't avoid it. "When? Where?" she asked angrily. "He hasn't said a word to me about it."

"At the mansion," Valnu answered, and named the date.

"That's when, or just about when, the baby will come," she said in dudgeon very high indeed.

Valnu shrugged. "Even if it weren't, would you go?"

"Maybe to annoy them," Krasta said, but then she shook her head. "To see that nasty weed grafted on to my family tree? No. I wouldn't do it."

"Well, then," Valnu said.

Logically, that made perfect sense. Logic, though, had nothing to do with anything here. Krasta burst into tears all over again.

A straining team of unicorns hauled a dead dragon down the street in front of the block of flats where Talsu and his family were staying these days. The dragon was painted in Algarve's all too familiar green, red, and white. Looking down at the great dead beast slowly sliding by, Talsu remarked, "First time we've seen those cursed colors in Skrunda for a while."

"May it be the last," Traku said from the next window over. "I'm just glad it came down in the middle of the market square and didn't smash any more buildings when it hit." His father hawked, but in the end didn't spit down on the dragon.

The Jelgavans in the street showed less restraint. Small boys—and some men and women—ran out from the sidewalk to kick the dragon and pound on it with their fists. Some of them did spit, not so much on the dragon as on Algarve itself.

As the dragon went past, Talsu started to laugh. "Will you look at that?" he said, pointing. "Will you just *look* at that?" Behind the team of muscular unicorns dragging the dragon came a single donkey dragging the dead Algarvian dragonflier. People rushed forward to abuse his corpse, too. It already looked much the worse for wear.

Talsu's father said something incendiary about Algarvians in general and the dragonflier in particular. From the kitchen, Talsu's mother spoke in reproving tones: "That's no way to talk, dear."

"I'm sorry, Laitsina," Traku said at once. He turned to Talsu and went on more quietly: "I'm sorry it didn't happen to all the fornicating buggers, not just this one. They bloody well deserve it."

He wasn't quite quiet enough. "Traku!" Laitsina said.

"Aye. Aye. Aye." Talsu's father made a sour face and turned away from the window. "I may as well get back to work. Doesn't seem like I'm going to be allowed to do anything else around here."

"I heard that, too," Laitsina said indignantly. "If you can't say something without making the air around you smell like a latrine, you really should find a better way to express yourself."

"Express myself!" Traku's eyebrows pretty plainly said what he thought of his wife's opinion, but he didn't go against it, not out loud he didn't.

Instead, he sat down in front of a pair of trousers he'd been working on. All the pieces were cut out. He'd set thread along all the seams and done some small part of the sewing by hand. Now he muttered a charm taking advantage of the law of similarity. The thread he'd set out writhed as if it had suddenly come to life, becoming similar to the identical thread he'd already sewn by hand. In the wink of an eye, all the stitching on the trousers was done.

Traku held them up and inspected them. Talsu nodded approval. "That's very nice work, Father."

"Not bad, not bad." Traku looked pleased with himself. He was never sorry to hear himself praised.

And then, perhaps rashly, Talsu asked, "Wasn't the spell you used the one you got from that Algarvian officer? It's a lot easier on handwork than the ones we had before."

"As a matter of fact, it was." Traku paused, another expressive expression on his face. "All right, curse it. The redheads are smart bastards. I never said they weren't. It doesn't mean they're any less bastards, though."

"No, it doesn't," Talsu agreed.

Traku went on with his methodical, painstaking examination of the trousers. At last, he grudgingly nodded his satisfaction. "I suppose those will do." Having supposed, he tossed the trousers at Talsu. "They go to Krogzmu the olive-oil dealer, on the south side of town. He paid twenty down, and he still owes us twenty more. Don't let him keep the goods before you get the silver—in coins of King Donalitu, mind you."

"I wasn't born yesterday, or even day before yesterday."

Talsu neatly folded the trousers his father had thrown at him. "You don't have to treat me like I was three years old."

"No, eh?" Traku chuckled. "Since when?"

Talsu didn't dignify that with an answer. After he'd done such a nice job of folding them, he stuck the trousers under his arm, careless of the wrinkles he might cause—though they were wool, which didn't wrinkle easily. He strode—almost stormed—out of the flat. His father chuckled again just before he shut—almost slammed—the door. Had that chuckle come a beat sooner, he would have slammed it. As things were, he went downstairs and out onto the street with his nose in the air.

He went away from the dead dragon and dragonflier, not after them. He wouldn't have minded taking a kick at the Algarvian's corpse, but he was set on getting the trousers to Krogzmu, getting the money, and getting back to the flat as fast as he could. *I'll show him I know what I'm doing,* he thought. That something like that might have been what Traku had in mind never occurred to him, which was probably just as well.

Good intentions got sidetracked, as good intentions have a way of doing. A column of Kuusamans was tramping west through Skrunda. Till they passed, Talsu, like everybody else, had to wait. People took waiting no better than they usually did. Someone behind him in the crowd complained, "We might as well still be occupied by the Algarvians."

"Nonsense," somebody else said. Talsu thought he would tell the first speaker what a fool he was, but he didn't. Instead, he went on, "The Algarvians never wasted our time with this nonsense."

"That's right," a woman said, nothing but indignation in her voice. "My cat is getting hungrier every minute, and here I am, stuck in the road because of all these foreigners going by."

Talsu rolled his eyes. *Powers above!* he thought. *We don't deserve to be our own masters any more. We really don't.*

Behemoths lumbered along the street. Their armor seemed different from any that Talsu had seen on Algarvian behemoths or on the few the Jelgavans had put in the field, but he couldn't put his finger on the difference. The little, swarthy soldiers on the behemoths reminded him more of the redheads than of his own folk. They grinned and joked as they went forward; that was obvious though he knew not a word of Kuusaman. They were men with their peckers up. They felt like winners, which went a long way toward making them into winners. The Jelgavan army had always gone into a fight looking over its shoulder, wondering what might happen to it, not what it could do to the foe.

At last, the rear of the column went by—footsoldiers stepping carefully to avoid whatever the behemoths had left behind. The Jelgavans on both sides of the road who'd had to wait surged forward and made their own traffic jam. With a judicious elbow or two, Talsu got through it fairly fast. He wished he could have elbowed the woman with the hungry cat, but no such luck.

The Kuusamans heading west to fight the redheads weren't the only ones in town. A short, slant-eyed fellow who looked to have drunk too much wine lurched down the street with his arm around the waist of a giggling girl who wore a barmaid's low-cut tunic and tight trousers. A few months before, had she been giving the Algarvians her favors? Talsu wouldn't have bet more than a copper against it.

In a way, we are *still occupied,* he thought. Oh, the Kuusamans—and the Lagoans farther south—didn't treat the people of Jelgava the way the Algarvians had. But if they wanted something—as that drunken trooper had wanted what the barmaid had to give—they were probably going to get it. Talsu sighed. He didn't know what to do about that, except to hope Jelgava somehow could become strong enough to make foreigners take her seriously.

And how long will I have to wait for that? he wondered. *Can we ever do it while King Donalitu sits on the throne?* He had his doubts.

A new broadsheet he passed only made those doubts worse. CONCERNING TRAITORS, its big print declared, and it went on to define traitors as anyone who'd had anything at all to do with the Algarvians throughout the four years of occupation. By what it said, practically everyone in the kingdom was subject to arrest if his name happened to come to the notice of Donalitu's constabulary.

He'll have to leave a few people free, Talsu thought. *Otherwise, who would build the dungeons he'd need to hold the whole fornicating kingdom?* He laughed, but on second thought it wasn't very funny. Captives could probably build as well as free men, if enough guards stood over them with sticks.

"Ah, good," Krogzmu said when Talsu showed up with the trousers. "Let me just try them on. . . ." He disappeared. When he came back, he was beaming. Not only did he pay Talsu the silver he owed without being asked, he gave him a clay jar of olive oil to take home, adding, "This is some of what I squeeze for my own family. This is not what I sell."

Talsu's mouth watered. "Thank you very much. I know it'll be good." His own father did good tailoring for everyone, but better than good for his own household.

"Good?" He might have insulted Krogzmu. "Is that all you can say? Good! You wait here." The oil dealer disappeared back into his house. He returned a moment later with a chunk of bread and snatched the jar of oil out of Talsu's hands. Yanking out the stopper, he poured some oil on the bread, then thrust it at Talsu. "There! Taste that, and then you tell me if it's just good."

"You don't need to ask me twice." Talsu took a big bite. It was either that or get olive oil smeared all over his face. The next sound he made was wordless but appreciative. The oil was everything he could have hoped it would be and then some: sharp and fruity at the same time. It made him think of men on tall ladders in the autumn plucking olives from green-gray-leafed branches to fall on tarpaulins waiting below.

"What do you say to that?" Krogzmu demanded.

"What do I say? I say I wish you'd given me more," Talsu told him. Krogzmu beamed. That apparently satisfied him. To Talsu's disappointment, the praise didn't get him a second jar of that marvelous oil.

He headed home. Again, he had to wait in the middle of town. This time, though, the procession wasn't Kuusaman soldiers heading west to fight King Mezentio's men. It was hard-faced Jelgavans in the uniform of King Donalitu's elite constabulary leading along a motley collection of captives. The captives weren't Algarvians; they were every bit as blond as the constables, as blond as Talsu was himself.

A chill ran through him. Maybe Donalitu and his henchmen wouldn't have any trouble finding enough dungeons after all.

Ealstan had imagined a great many ways he might return to Gromheort. He might have come after the war ended, bringing Vanai and Saxburh to meet his mother and father and sister. He might have come back to make sure Elfryth and Hestan and Conberge were all right, and then returned to Eoforwic to bring his wife and little daughter to them. He might even have come as part of a triumphant Forthwegian army, driving the Algarvians before him.

Coming to Gromheort as part of a triumphant Unkerlanter army that cared little, if at all, for anything Forthwegian had never once crossed his mind. Nor had he thought the Algarvians would do anything but pull out of Gromheort once they faced overwhelming force. That they might pull back into his home town and stand siege there . . . No, he hadn't thought of that, not in his wildest nightmares.

But that was just what the redheads had done, and they'd thrown back several Unkerlanter efforts to break into Gromheort. By now, Mezentio's men trapped inside the city couldn't retreat into Algarve even if they'd wanted to. The Unkerlanter ring around Gromheort was twenty miles thick, maybe thirty. The Algarvians had only two choices: they could fight till they ran out of everything, or they could yield.

Unkerlanter officers under flag of truce had already gone into Gromheort twice, demanding a surrender. The Algarvians had sent them away both times, and so Ealstan sprawled in a field somewhere between Oyngestun and Gromheort, peering toward his home town.

Gromheort's wall had been more a formality than a defense for several generations. He knew that perfectly well. But seeing so many chunks of the wall bitten away by bursting eggs still hurt. What hurt worse was being unable to tell his comrades why it hurt. For one thing, they had trouble understanding him, and he them. Forthwegian and Unkerlanter were related languages, but they were a long way from identical. And, for another, they wouldn't have cared anyhow. Gromheort was nothing to them but one more foreign town they had to take.

Whistles shrilled. Officers along the line shouted, "Forward!" That word wasn't much different in Unkerlanter from its Forthwegian equivalent. Even if it had been, Ealstan would have been quick to figure out what it meant.

He didn't want to advance. He wanted to go back to Eoforwic, to Vanai and Saxburh. But one Unkerlanter word he had learned was the one for *efficiency*. In their own brutal way, Swemmel's men did their best to practice what they preached. Hard-faced fellows with sticks in their hands waited not far behind the line. Any soldier who tried to retreat without orders got blazed on the spot. Soldiers who went forward had at least a chance of coming through alive. The argument was crude, but it was also logical.

"Up!" a sergeant screamed. Sergeants didn't get whistles, but soldiers had to do as they said anyhow. Ealstan got up and trotted forward with the rest of the men in rock-gray.

Rock-gray dragons swooped low overhead, eggs slung under their bellies. The eggs burst in front of and inside Gromheort. Ealstan didn't know what to think about that. It made him more likely to live and his kinsfolk more likely to die. He wanted to give up thinking altogether.

"Behemoths!" That shout came in Unkerlanter. The word was nothing like its Forthwegian equivalent, which had been borrowed from Algarvian. Ealstan had had to learn it in a hurry. It meant either *Help is coming* or *We're in trouble*, depending on who owned the behemoths being shouted about.

These behemoths had Algarvians aboard them. They were sallying from Gromheort, doing their best to hold the Unkerlanters away from the town. Officers or no officers, sergeants or no sergeants, Ealstan threw himself down on the muddy ground. He'd seen behemoths in the desperate fighting in and around Eoforwic, and had a hearty respect

for what they could do. Most of the Unkerlanters close by
him dove for cover, too. Anyone who'd had more than the
tiniest taste of war knew better than to stay on his feet when
enemy behemoths were in the neighborhood.

Somewhere not far away, a crystallomancer shouted into
his glassy sphere. Before long, egg-tossers started aiming at
the Algarvian beasts. They did less than Ealstan would have
liked; only a direct hit, which took luck, would put paid to
the immense beasts in their chain-mail coats. But a barrage
of bursting eggs did keep Algarvian footsoldiers from going forward with the behemoths, and that left the animals
and their crews more vulnerable than they would have been
otherwise.

Ealstan swung his stick towards one of the redheads atop
a behemoth a couple of hundred yards away. He had to aim
carefully; behemoth crewmen wore armor, too. Why not?
They relied on the animals to take them where they needed
to go, and didn't get down on the ground themselves unless
something went wrong.

"There," Ealstan muttered, and let his finger slide into
the stick's blazing hole. The beam leaped forth. The Algarvian started to clutch at his face, but crumpled with the motion half complete. *He never knew what hit him,* Ealstan
thought. Instead of celebrating, he crawled toward a new
hiding place. If one of Mezentio's men had seen his beam,
staying where he was might get him killed.

More men fell from the Algarvian behemoths. The Unkerlanter footsoldiers, like Ealstan, had learned to pick off
crewmen whenever they got the chance. Had Algarvian
footsoldiers gone forward with the beasts, they could have
kept Swemmel's soldiers too busy to let them snipe at the
behemoth crews. But eggs bursting all around had held
back the unarmored footsoldiers.

Sullenly, the Algarvian behemoths drew back toward
Gromheort. Ealstan waited for the order to pursue. It didn't
come. The Unkerlanters around him seemed content to stay
where they were, even if they could have gained some
ground by showing initiative. There were also times when
the efficiency Swemmel's men talked so much about
proved only talk.

Night fell. That didn't keep the Unkerlanters from pounding Gromheort with eggs or the Algarvians in the town from answering back as best they could. Ealstan filled his mess tin with boiled barley and chunks of meat from a pot bubbling over a fire well shielded from sight by banks of dirt—Algarvian snipers sometimes sneaked out after dark to pick off whomever they could spot, and they were good at what they did. Poking one of the chunks with his spoon, Ealstan asked the cook, "What is this?"

"Unicorn tonight," the fellow answered. "Not too bad."

"Not, not too," Ealstan more or less agreed. Unicorn, horse, behemoth—he'd eaten all sorts of things he never would have touched before the war. Behemoth was very tough and very gamy. But when the choice lay between eating it and going hungry . . . Hard times had long since taught him that lesson.

He sat with his squadmates, going through the stew and talking. He couldn't always understand them, nor they him, but they and he kept repeating themselves and changing a word here, a word there, till they got it. They didn't hold his being Forthwegian against him. A couple of them still seemed to think he was just an Unkerlanter from a district where the dialect was very strange. They'd already seen he knew enough on the battlefield not to be a danger to them.

As for his method of joining King Swemmel's army, most of them had stories not a whole lot different. "Oh, aye," said a fellow named Curvenal, who, by his pimpled but almost beardless face, couldn't have been much above sixteen. "The impressers came into my village. They said I could go fight the Algarvians or I could get blazed. With that for a choice . . . The Algarvians might not blaze me, so here I am."

"Me, I'm from the far southwest," another soldier said. "I'd never even heard of Algarvians till the fornicating war started. All I want to do is go home."

Ealstan could have had something to say about Unkerlant's jumping on Forthweg's back after the Algarvians stormed into his kingdom. He could have, but he didn't. What point to it? None of these men had been in Swemmel's army then; Curvenal would have been about eleven years old. And most of his new comrades were peasants. He might be ignorant of their language, but they were ignorant of much more. How could one not have heard of Algarvians? Not have met any?—that, certainly; the far southwest of Unkerlant was far indeed. But not to know they existed? That astonished Ealstan. He'd never met any Gyongyosians, but he would have had no trouble finding Gyongyos on a map.

Under cover of darkness, more Unkerlanter soldiers came forward. As soon as it got light, dragons painted rock-gray started harrying Gromheort once more. Listening to the thud of bursting eggs, Ealstan wondered again how his family was faring. He hoped they were well. That was all he could do.

Behemoths lumbered toward the city wall. "Forward!" officers shouted. Forward Ealstan went, along with his squadmates, along with the fresh troops. The Algarvians fought like canny veterans. Some of the new Unkerlanter soldiers were very raw indeed, too raw to know to take cover when the enemy started blazing at them. They might as well have been grain before the reaper.

But they also took a toll on the redheads. Though it was a smaller toll, the Algarvians could afford less in the way of losses. And, seeing smoke rising all around Gromheort, Ealstan realized Swemmel's soldiers were coming at the city from every side. If they broke in anywhere, they would be ahead of the game.

No such luck. The Algarvians in Gromheort were trapped, but they hadn't given up—and they hadn't run out of food or supplies. They threw back this attack as they'd thrown back the others. They had courage and to spare—or maybe they didn't dare let themselves fall into Unkerlanter hands.

"Won't be anything left of that place before long," Curvenal said.

"I used to live there," Ealstan said in Forthwegian, and then had to struggle to get meaning across in Unkerlant, which formed past tenses differently.

"Is your family still there?" Curvenal asked.

Ealstan nodded. "I think so. I hope so."

The young Unkerlanter slapped him on the back. "That's hard. That's cursed hard. The redheads never got to my village, so I'm one of the lucky ones. But I know how many people have lost kin. I hope your folks come through all right."

Sympathy from one of Swemmel's men came as a surprise. "Thanks," Ealstan said roughly. "So do I." In ironic counterpoint, more eggs burst on Gromheort. He hoped his mother and father and sister were down in cellars where no harm could come to them. He also hoped they had enough to eat. The Algarvians would probably do their best to keep everything in the besieged town for themselves.

If any Forthwegians got food, he suspected his own family would. His father had both money and connections, and the Algarvians took bribes. Ealstan had seen that for himself, both in Gromheort and in Eoforwic. But even the redheads wouldn't give civilians food if they had none to spare.

All I can do is try to break into the city when we've worn Mezentio's men down enough to have a decent chance of doing it, Ealstan thought. *If I desert and try to sneak in on my own, the Unkerlanters will blaze me if they catch me and the Algarvians will if the Unkerlanters don't. And I couldn't do anything useful even if I did get in.*

Every bit of that made perfect logical sense, the sort of sense that should have calmed a bookkeeper's spirit. Somehow or other, it did nothing whatever to ease Ealstan's mind.

Hajjaj was glad Bishah's rainy season, never very long, was drawing to a close. That meant his roof wouldn't leak much longer—till next rainy season. Zuwayzi roofers were among the most inept workmen in the whole kingdom. They could get away with it, too, because they were so seldom tested.

"Frauds, the lot of them," he grumbled to his senior wife just after the latest set of bunglers packed up their tools and went down from the hills to Bishah.

"They certainly are," Kolthoum agreed. They'd been together for half a century now. It had been an arranged marriage, not a love match; leaders among Zuwayzi clans wed for reasons far removed from romance. But they'd grown very fond of each other. Hajjaj wondered if he'd ever spoken the word *love* to her. He didn't think so, but he couldn't imagine what he would do without her.

"As far as I'm concerned, they're just a pack of clumsy children playing with toys—and not playing very well," he went on.

"Odds are, we won't find out what sort of work they've done till the fall," Kolthoum said. "By then, they can expect we'll either have forgotten all the promises they've made or lost their bill or both."

"They can expect it, but they'll be disappointed," Hajjaj said. "They don't know how well you keep track of such things." His senior wife graciously inclined her head at the compliment. She'd never been a great beauty, and she'd got fat as the years went by, but she moved like a queen. From roofers, Hajjaj went on to other complications: "Speaking of toys . . ."

He needed no more than that for Kolthoum to understand exactly what he had in mind. "What's the latest trouble with Tassi?" she asked. "And why won't Iskakis dry up and blow away?"

"Because King Tsavellas of Yanina chose exactly the right moment to change sides and suck up to Unkerlant and we didn't," Hajjaj answered. "That means Swemmel's happier about the Yaninans than he is about us. And besides, Ansovald likes sticking pins in me to see if I'll jump. Barbarian." The last word was necessarily in Algarvian; Zuwayzi didn't have a satisfactory equivalent.

"Why doesn't Iskakis leave it alone, though?" Kolthoum asked fretfully. "It's not as if he wants her for herself. If she were a pretty boy instead of a pretty girl, he might. As things are?" She shook her head.

"Pride," Hajjaj said. "He has plenty of that; Yaninans are prickly folk. A Zuwayzi noble would want to get back a wife who'd run off, too."

"Aye, so he would, and something horrible would happen to her if he did, too," Kolthoum said. "Plenty of feuds have started that way. Tassi doesn't deserve to have anything like that happen to her. She can't help it if her husband would sooner have had a boy."

"I wish Marquis Balastro had taken her back to Algarve with him when he had to flee Zuwayza," Hajjaj said. "But he'd quarreled with her by then; that was what prompted her to come to me."

His senior wife gave him a sidelong glance. "You can't tell me you've been sorry, and you know it."

Since Hajjaj knew perfectly well that he couldn't, he didn't try. What he did say was, "The latest is, Ansovald had the gall to tell me Yanina might declare war on Zuwayza if I don't hand Tassi over."

"*Yanina* might," Kolthoum said. Hajjaj nodded. "But we don't border Yanina," she went on. Hajjaj nodded again. She asked, "Did he say *Unkerlant* might declare war on us on account of this?" Hajjaj shook his head. "Well, then," she told him, "we've got nothing to worry about. Enjoy yourself with her, and think of Iskakis every time you do."

"I wonder if she enjoys herself with me. I have my doubts," Hajjaj said, a thought he never would have aired to anyone in the world but Kolthoum.

"You've given her the pleasure of not having to live with Iskakis any more," his senior wife replied. "The least she can do is give you some pleasure in exchange."

Kolthoum's brisk practicality made a sensible answer. It did not, however, fill Hajjaj with delight. He had pride of his own, a man's pride. He wanted to think he pleased the pretty young woman who also pleased him. What he wanted to think and what was true were liable to be two different things, though.

"I take it you told Ansovald the Yaninans were welcome to invade us whenever they chose?" Kolthoum said.

"Actually, no. I'm afraid I lost my temper this time," Hajjaj said. Kolthoum waved for him to go on. With mingled pride and shame, he did: "I offered Iskakis a camel he could use as he planned on using Tassi."

"*Did* you?" His senior wife's eyebrows rose. After a moment's calculation—one almost too short for Hajjaj to notice, but not quite—she said, "Well, good for you. Unkerlant won't go to war against us because Iskakis doesn't get his wife back. King Swemmel's a madman, but he's a shrewd sort of madman."

"Most of the time," Hajjaj said.

"Most of the time," Kolthoum agreed.

"Iskakis is making himself troublesome, though," Hajjaj said. "I keep wondering if he'll hire some bravos to do me an injury."

Now Kolthoum's eyebrows flew upwards. "A Yaninan hire Zuwayzi bravos to do *you* an injury? I should hope not, by the powers above! I should hope no one in this kingdom would take his silver for such a thing. Zuwayza wouldn't *be* a kingdom if not for you."

That was, on the whole, true. Nevertheless, Hajjaj answered, "Men don't turn into bravos unless they love silver first and everything else afterwards. And young men don't remember—and probably don't care—how we got to be a kingdom again. It would be just another job as far as they're concerned, one that paid better than most."

"Disgraceful," Kolthoum said. "A hundred years ago, our ancestors never would have thought of such treason against their own kind."

Hajjaj shook his head. "I'm afraid you're wrong, my dear. I could say, ask Tewfik: he would remember. But he's not so old as *that,* and I don't need to ask him, because I already know. Unkerlant got hold of Zuwayza and held us as long as she did by playing our princes off against one another. These things have happened, and they can happen again."

"Well, they had better not, not to you, or whoever plays such games will answer to *me*." Kolthoum sounded as if she meant every word of that. From some Zuwayzi women, it would have been an idle threat. From Kolthoum . . . Hajjaj would not have wanted his senior wife angry at *him*. Kolthoum arose from the nest of cushions she'd made for herself and flounced away in considerable annoyance.

Why aren't I more upset at the idea? Hajjaj wondered. *Maybe because Iskakis is such a blunderer, any assassins he hires would likely make a hash of the job. Anyone who would let a woman as . . . entertaining as Tassi leave him can't be very bright.* Of course, Iskakis looked for entertainments of that sort elsewhere. *The more fool he,* Hajjaj thought.

Joints creaking, he got to his feet and went into the library. Surrounded by books in Zuwayzi, in Algarvian, in classical Kaunian, he didn't have to think about man's inhumanity to man . . . unless he pulled out a history in any of those languages. He didn't. A volume of love poetry from the days of the Kaunian Empire better suited his mood.

Motion in the doorway made him look up. There stood Tassi. Since becoming part of his household, she'd insisted on adopting Zuwayzi dress: which is to say, sandals and jewelry and, outdoors, a hat. To Hajjaj's eyes, she always looked much more naked than a woman of his own people. Maybe that was because he was used to the idea that people of her pale color were supposed to wear clothes. Or maybe her nipples and her bush stood out more than they did with dark-skinned Zuwayzin.

"Do I disturb you?" she asked in Algarvian, the only language they had in common.

Aye, he thought, but that wasn't how she meant the question. "No, of course not," he said, and closed the book of poems.

"Good." She came into the library and sat down on the carpeted floor beside him. "Do I hear rightly? Iskakis is being difficult again? Difficult still?"

That didn't take long, Hajjaj thought. Kolthoum didn't spread his business around the household, either. Servants going down the hall must have heard bits and pieces, and all the powers above put together couldn't keep servants from gossiping. "As a matter of fact, he is," Hajjaj replied. He wouldn't lie to her, not on matters touching her as well as him.

"Why not just"—she snapped her fingers—"send him away, tell King Tsavellas to pick a new minister? Then he will be gone, and so will the trouble."

"I can't do that," he said.

Tassi snapped her fingers again. "King Shazli can. And he will do as you say."

That did hold some truth. Hajjaj had hesitated to ask Shazli to declare Iskakis unwelcome in Zuwayza. He was a purist, and did not feel personal problems had any place in the affairs of his kingdom. If, however, Iskakis had killing him in mind, the Yaninan minister was the one mixing personal affairs and diplomacy. "I may ask him," Hajjaj said at last.

"Good. That is settled, then." Tassi took such logical leaps as easily, as naturally, as she breathed. "And I will stay here."

"Does that please you, staying here?" Hajjaj asked.

She looked at him sidelong. "I hope it pleases you, my staying here."

Aye, Tassi looked very naked indeed. He didn't think she let her legs fall open by accident just then, giving him a glimpse of the sweet slit between them. She used her naked flesh as a tool, a weapon, in ways that never would have occurred to a Zuwayzi woman who took nudity for granted.

Age gave Hajjaj a certain advantage, or at least a certain perspective, on such things. "You didn't answer what I asked," he remarked.

Tassi's lower lip pooched like an indignant child's, though that pouting lip was the only childlike part of her. Her lisping, throaty accent made even ordinary things she said sound provocative. When she asked, "Shall I show you I am pleased?" . . . Hajjaj didn't answer. Tassi got up and shut the door to the library.

Some time later, she said, "There. Are you pleased? Am I pleased?"

Hajjaj could scarcely deny he was pleased. He wanted to roll over and go to sleep. He wasn't so sure about Tassi, not in that same sense. "I hope you are," he said.

"Oh, aye." She dipped her head, as she often did instead of nodding. Her eyes sparkled. "And do you see? I do not ask for precious stones. They would be nice, but I do not ask for them. All I ask for is to stay here. You can do that for me. It is easy for you, in fact."

With a laugh, Hajjaj patted her round, smooth backside. On the surface, she spoke nothing but the truth. Below the surface . . . He'd never before heard anyone ask for jewels by not asking for them. She might even get some. And if she didn't, how could she complain?

Seven

Colonel Lurcanio was not happy to find himself back in Algarve. But for a few brief leaves, he'd been away from his home kingdom for almost five years. Had the war gone better, he would have remained in Priekule, too. Nothing would have pleased him more. Here he was, though, in southeastern Algarve, doing his best to hold back the Kuusamans and Lagoans who'd swarmed through the Marquisate of Rivaroli and were pushing farther west every day.

His own brigade left a good deal to be desired. It had lost far too many men and behemoths and egg-tossers in the failed counterattack against the islanders in western Valmiera. Lurcanio screamed to his superiors for replacements. Those superiors, when they didn't scream back, laughed in his face.

"Replacements?" a harried lieutenant general said. "We couldn't afford to give you what we gave you the last time. How do you think we're going to be able to make losses good now?"

"How do you think I can stop the enemy with what I've got left?" Lurcanio retorted. "I can't remember the last time I saw an Algarvian dragon overhead."

"Believe me, Colonel, you're not the only one with troubles," the lieutenant general replied. "Make do the best you can." His image in the crystal in front of Lurcanio looked down at some papers on his desk. "There are several regiments of Popular Assault soldiers not far from your position. Feel free to commandeer them and add them to your force."

"Thank you for nothing . . . sir," Lurcanio said. "I've already seen Popular Assault regiments. The men who aren't older than I am are too young to have hair on their balls—

some of them haven't even been circumcised yet. They can't stand up to real soldiers. They couldn't even if they had anything more than hunting sticks to blaze with."

He waited for the lieutenant general to call him insubordinate or to say the soldiers in question were better than he claimed. Back in Trapani, a lot of men still clung to illusions that had died at the front line. But the officer only sighed and said, "Do the best you can, Colonel. I don't know what else to tell you, except you're not the only one with troubles."

"I understand that, sir, but—" The crystal flared and then went blank before he could get his protest well begun. He said something sulfurous under his breath. He surely wasn't the only one with troubles. As best he could tell, the whole Kingdom of Algarve was falling to pieces before his eyes.

Things hadn't been this bleak even at the end of the Six Years' War. Then Algarve had asked for armistice while her armies still mostly stood on enemy soil. Now . . . He imagined asking Swemmel of Unkerlant for an armistice. Swemmel didn't want one. Swemmel wanted every Algarvian in the world dead. The way things were going, he was liable to get his wish, too. And the Lagoans and Kuusamans showed no sign of being in a dickering mood, either.

Of course they don't want to dicker with us, Lurcanio thought. *We came too close to beating them all this time. They don't want us getting another chance any time soon. They want to smash us flat instead.* Had he been a Kuusaman, he supposed he would have felt the same way. Had he been an Unkerlanter . . . Lurcanio shook his head. Some things were altogether too depressing to contemplate.

He strode out of the barn where his crystallomancer had set up shop. It was raining outside, a cold, driving rain on the edge of turning into sleet. Lurcanio pulled his hat down low to keep the rain out of his face. Eggs were bursting in the neighborhood, but not too many of them. The rain slowed down the enemy, too.

A sergeant came up to him, a plump little man in civilian

tunic and kilt at the underofficer's heels. "Sir, allow me to present Baron Oberto, who has the honor to be the mayor of the town of Carsoli," the sergeant said.

Carsoli was the town just west of the brigade's present position, the one Lurcanio was currently trying to hold. He bowed to Oberto. "Good day, your Excellency," he said. "And what can I do for you this afternoon?"

By the expression on Oberto's face, it wasn't a good day and was unlikely to become one. "Colonel," he said, surprising Lurcanio by correctly reading his rank badges, "I hope you will not find it necessary to fight inside my fair city. When the time comes, as we both know it must, I beseech you to pull back through Carsoli, so that the islanders can occupy it without doing it too much harm."

Lurcanio gave him a long, measuring stare. Oberto nervously looked back. "So you think the war is lost, do you?" Lurcanio said at last.

Oberto's head bobbed up and down, as if on a spring. "Of course I do," he said. "Any fool can see as much."

Any fool could have seen as much two years earlier, when the Unkerlanters drove the Algarvians back from Sulingen. Lurcanio bowed again, then backhanded Oberto across the face. The mayor of Carsoli cried out and staggered. "Be thankful I don't order you blazed on the spot. Get out of my sight. I have a war to fight, whether you've noticed it or not."

"You're a madman," Oberto said, bringing a hand up to his cheek.

"I'm a soldier," Lurcanio answered. In his own mind, he wasn't so sure the two were different, but he would never have admitted that to the luckless, cowardly mayor of Carsoli. Admitting it to Oberto might have meant admitting it to himself.

Hand still pressed to his face, Oberto staggered away. *I wonder if I ought to draft an order of the day reminding the men they are still obliged to do their duty,* Lurcanio thought. *If they give up, what hope have we?* A moment later, he grimaced and kicked at the muddy ground. *Even if they don't give up, what hope have we?*

He had been thinking about pulling back through Carsoli if enemy pressure grew too great. Now he resolved to fight in the place till not one brick remained atop another. *That's what you get, Oberto, curse you. You would have done better to keep your mouth shut, but what Algarvian could ever manage that?*

In a perfectly foul temper, he stormed off toward the farmhouse where he made what passed for his headquarters. Before he got there, though, another soldier called, "Colonel Lurcanio!"

"What is it?" he snarled.

"Er—" As the sergeant had done, this fellow had a civilian in his wake: no, not one civilian, but half a dozen or so. "These . . . people need to speak with you, sir."

"Oh, they do, do they?" Lurcanio snapped. "What in blazes do they want? And why do I need to say one fornicating word to them?" But then he got a good look at who came behind the soldier, and his fiery temper cooled. "Oh," he said, and, "Oh," again. He nodded. "Them. Aye, I'll talk to them."

The four men and two women who came up to Lurcanio wore tunics and kilts in the Algarvian style, but they were blonds, their hair soaked and falling down stringily over their faces. "You have to help us, Colonel!" the tallest man exclaimed, his Algarvian fluent enough but accented with the more guttural consonants and flat vowels of Valmieran. "By the powers above, you have to!"

Lurcanio had known him well enough back in Priekule. "I have to, eh? And why is that, Smetnu?" For a refugee without a kingdom to give him orders really was a bit much.

Smetnu had an answer for him, though: "I'll tell you why. Because I spent four years—more than four years—helping you, that's why. Didn't my news sheets sing King Mezentio's song all over Valmiera?"

"And my broadsheets!" another man added.

"And my plays," said a third.

"And our acting," one of the women and the fourth man said together.

The other woman, whose name was Sigulda and who was either married or at least thoroughly attached to

Smetnu, said, "If you don't help us, they'll catch up with us. And if they catch up with us . . ." She drew a thumb across her throat. Her nails were painted red as blood, which added to the effect of the gesture.

And the Valmierans were right. That was all there was to it. Lurcanio bowed. "Very well, my friends. I will do what I can. But I can do, perhaps, less than you think. You will have noticed, Algarve is falling deeper into ruin and disaster with each passing day."

They nodded. Their own kingdom—the Algarvian version of Valmiera they'd promoted and upheld—had already fallen into ruin. And now that Algarve was breaking under hammer blows from west and east, few of Mezentio's subjects could spare them any time or aid or effort. If anything, they were an embarrassment, a reminder of what might have been. They were, in spite of everything, Kaunians, and somehow not quite welcome even to watch Algarve's death throes. The destruction of a great kingdom was, or at least should have been, a private affair.

Unlike most of his countrymen, Lurcanio did feel a certain obligation toward them. He'd worked with them for a long time. Baldu, the playwright, had done some splendid work during the occupation. His dramas deserved to live— unless the Valmierans flung them all into the fire because he'd written them under Algarvian auspices and because some of his characters (not all, by any means) had friendly things to say about the men who'd occupied his kingdom.

Bowing again, Lurcanio asked, "Where would you go?"

"Any place where they won't hang us or burn us or blaze us!" The actor made as if to tear his hair, which struck Lurcanio as overacting.

"Very good," he said. "And where might that be, pray tell?"

Silence fell over the Valmierans—a gloomy, appalled silence. Not many places on the continent of Derlavai would be safe for them after Algarve finished losing the war, because all her neighbors would be eager for revenge against anyone and everyone who'd helped her.

"Siaulia?" Lurcanio suggested, and then shook his head. "No, if we lose here, what we hold on the tropical continent will be yielded to the victors. That's how these things work, I fear."

"Gyongyos?" Baldu suggested. "Can you get us there?"

It wasn't an impossible notion. Gyongyos was losing the war, too, but mountains shielded its heartland, and it was a long, long way from the greatest strength of its enemies. That same, unfortunately, didn't hold true for Lurcanio's own kingdom. He saw one other problem: "I can probably make sure you reach a port. But the ports in the south are mostly closed because of enemy dragons flying out of Sibiu, and in the north . . . It's a long, long way to Gyongyos. Not many of our ships—or those of the Gongs— get through. The enemy prowls the sea lanes, too. You might have a better chance of reaching some island in the Great Northern Sea. No one would come looking for you there, probably not for years."

The Valmieran collaborators looked even less happy than before. Lurcanio didn't suppose he could blame them. Those distant islands were ratholes, nothing else but. Then Smetnu asked, "Can you get us to Ortah?"

"I don't know," Lurcanio said thoughtfully. The neutral kingdom was much closer than Gyongyos. Even so . . . "I don't know what things are like in the west of Algarve right now. If you try to get to Ortah, you're liable to run right into the Unkerlanters' arms. You wouldn't like that."

"It's the best chance we have, I think," Smetnu said. The other Valmierans nodded. The news-sheet man went on, "*We* have a better chance with the Unkerlanters than with our own folk or the islanders."

He was probably—almost certainly—right. "Very well," Lurcanio said. He went into the farmhouse and wrote out a ley-line caravan pass for all six of them, explaining who they were and how they'd served Algarve. They took it and made for Carsoli's caravan depot. Lurcanio hoped it would do some good. His own honor, at least in this small matter, remained untarnished. His kingdom's honor? He resolutely refused to think about that.

Somewhere not far from Garivald, a wounded man moaned. Garivald wasn't sure whether he was an Unkerlanter or an Algarvian. Whoever he was, he'd been moaning for quite a while. Garivald wished he would shut up and get on with the business of dying. The noise he was making wore on everyone's nerves.

Dragons dropped eggs on the Algarvian town ahead, a place called Bonorva. It lay south and east of Gromheort. The plains of northern Algarve weren't much different from those of Forthweg. The Algarvians themselves had fought just as hard in Forthweg as they were here in their own kingdom. Indeed, they were still fighting in Forthweg: Gromheort stubbornly held out against everything King Swemmel's men could throw at it.

Lieutenant Andelot nodded to Garivald. "Well, Fariulf, even with their fancy steerable eggs, they weren't able to throw us back. Not enough men, not enough behemoths, not enough anything."

"Looks that way, sir," Garivald agreed. With ingrained peasant pessimism, he added, "We don't want it to rain right at harvest time, though. It'd be a shame to get killed with the war about won—or any other time, come to that."

Andelot nodded. "We can't get slack, though. The redheads are still fighting. It's good we're on their soil—they should know what they put us through, powers below eat them—but these are their homes. They won't want us to take them away, any more than we wanted them to take away our homes in Unkerlant."

He spoke like a man from Cottbus. Odds were, he hadn't lost his home to the Algarvians. He knew that would be bad, but he didn't know how bad it was. Garivald had watched the invaders storm into, storm past, his home village. He'd lived under their boot. He'd watched them hang a couple of irregulars in the market square. They might have hanged him there, when they found he was putting together patriotic songs. Instead, they'd hauled him off to Herborn to boil him alive, and the irregulars had rescued him before he got there.

"Better for everybody if this cursed war had never happened," he said.

"Aye, of course," Andelot replied. "But it's a little too late to wish for that now, wouldn't you say?"

Garivald only grunted. Andelot was right, no doubt about it. But Garivald could still wish, even if he knew what he wished for had no chance of coming true.

The next morning, he trudged past a column of Algarvian refugees Unkerlanter dragons had caught on the road. It wasn't pretty. It must have happened only the day before. The bodies didn't stink yet, but the almost cheerful odor of burnt meat lingered in the air. The dragonfliers had dropped eggs first, then come back so their beasts could flame the redheads the eggs hadn't knocked over—and, he was sure, some they had.

"Good riddance," was all Andelot said, and, "When the civilians run from us, they clog the roads. That makes it harder for Mezentio's soldiers to get where they need to go."

"Aye," Garivald answered. He'd hated the Algarvians ever since they broke into his kingdom. He'd killed his share of them—more than his share, very likely. He should have wanted all of them dead. A substantial part of him did want all of them dead, or thought it did. But . . . some of the scattered, twisted, charred corpses were very small. He thought of Syrivald and Leuba, his own son and daughter, no doubt as dead as these Algarvians. Thinking of them didn't make him want to see more redheads dead. It just made him wish no more children had to die, regardless of what color hair they had.

Somewhere not far away, a woman started screaming. Garivald had heard women scream on that particular note before. So had the men in the squad he led. Some of them, he was sure, had made Algarvian women scream on that note. They grinned and nudged one another.

"Keep moving," Garivald called to them. "We haven't got time to stop and have fun." They nodded and tramped on, but the grins stayed on their faces.

He'd thought his countrymen would run the Algarvians out of Bonorva that afternoon. So had Andelot, who'd said, "We'll be sleeping on real beds tonight, men." They all got a rude surprise. As they neared the outskirts of the city, Algarvian egg-tossers greeted them with a heavier pounding than any in which Garivald had been on the receiving end.

Unkerlanter egg-tossers quickly answered back; they

were more efficient now than they had been when Garivald got dragooned into King Swemmel's army. From what the handful of men who'd been in the fight a good deal longer than he said, they were much more efficient now than they had been in the early days of the war.

It didn't do them much good, not here. Alarmed cries rang out: "Behemoths! Algarvian behemoths!"

Hearing that was plenty to make Garivald throw himself down on his belly in the middle of a muddy field. Sure enough, a column of behemoths with redheads atop them came lumbering up out of the south. Footsoldiers in kilts loped along with the behemoths to keep the Unkerlanters from getting close enough to have an easy time harming the beasts.

Garivald looked around for Unkerlanter behemoths to blunt the head of that column. He didn't see very many. An Algarvian crew flung an egg that burst too close to him for comfort. The blast of sorcerous energy picked him up and slammed him to the ground. Clods of dirt rained down on him.

Orders were to stand your ground no matter what. Garivald looked around. If he and his men stood their ground here no matter what, they would all end up dead in short order. Lieutenant Andelot had praised his initiative before. He used it again, this time to shout, "Fall back!"

Some of the Unkerlanters had begun to retreat even without orders. The din of bursting eggs was loud off to the east, too, suggesting the Algarvians had another force of behemoths on the move there. King Swemmel's army had stormed across northeastern Unkerlant and Forthweg and into Algarve. Mezentio's men struck back when and as they could, but Garivald had never seen a counterattack like this before.

There was Andelot, trying to rally his men. Garivald shouted, "Sir, we're going to have to give back a little ground. They've got too many men and too many behemoths for us to hold them off right now."

He waited to see if Andelot would order him to try to hold at all hazards. He wondered if the company commander might have to suffer an unfortunate accident so someone with real sense could take over and do his best to lead the men to safety. But, biting his lip, Andelot nodded. "Aye, Sergeant, you're right, worse luck." He snapped his fingers. "I know what's gone wrong, curse it."

"Tell me," Garivald urged.

"There are some little cinnabar mines south of Bonorva," Andelot said. "You get quicksilver for dragonfire from cinnabar. The Algarvians haven't got much left. No wonder they're fighting like madmen to hold on to what they do have."

Garivald managed a haggard grin. "So much nicer to know why you're about to get killed."

"Isn't it, though?" Andelot replied. "Let's see what we can do about making the Algarvians do the dying instead."

What a company of footsoldiers could do on a battlefield swarming with behemoths was depressingly obvious: not much. More Unkerlanter behemoths did come down from out of the north to challenge the Algarvian beasts, but not enough. As if it were the early days of the war, the redheads had the bit between their teeth.

A week later, spring was in the air. Garivald was sure it would still be snowing down in the Duchy of Grelz, but northern Algarve was a long, long way from home. The wind blew warm from the sea. Birds started chirping in the trees. Fresh green grass sprang up; a few flowers bloomed. It would have been beautiful . . . if so much of the countryside hadn't been wrecked by war's fiery rake. And that rake had gone across the landscape first one way, then the other.

By that time, Garivald counted himself lucky to be alive. He'd never seen such a sustained Algarvian push before. It had driven his countrymen and him back a good thirty miles from the outskirts of Bonorva. He'd had to fight his way out of two encirclements, and sneak past Algarvian footsoldiers to escape a third. A lot of Unkerlanters hadn't made it.

"They're bastards, aren't they?" he said to Lieutenant Andelot as the two of them sprawled by the bank of a little stream. They were both filthy and unshaven and desperately in need of sleep.

"We knew that from the start," Andelot answered.

"They've pushed us back some, aye, but look at the price they've paid. And they're just about stopped now—we're hardly lost any ground today. When we start moving forward again, what will they use to stop us?"

"I don't know." Garivald didn't care about such things. *I'm no officer. I don't want to be an officer,* he thought. *Let them worry about where the fornicating war is going. I just want to stay alive till it finally gets there and stops, so I can get off.*

By all the signs, Andelot knew what he was talking about. Streams of Unkerlanter soldiers and behemoths were moving up toward the front. Rock-gray dragons swarmed overhead, with few in Algarvian colors in the air to hold them back. The redheads had done everything they could to drive back the men of Unkerlant, and it hadn't been enough.

More dragons flew by, all of them heading northeast to strike the enemy. Some had eggs slung under their bellies; others carried only dragonfliers. They protected the ones with the eggs, fought off the handful of Algarvian beasts that rose to oppose them, and swooped low to flame soldiers and civilians on the ground.

"They'll make Mezentio's men wish they were never born," Garivald said smugly.

But then, as he watched, the whole flight of Unkerlanter dragons tumbled out of the sky. It wasn't as if they'd been blazed down. It was more as if they'd run headlong into an invisible wall. Some of the eggs they carried burst while they were still in the air, others when they hit the ground.

"What in blazes—?" Garivald exclaimed.

Andelot took things more in stride. "Curse them, they made it work again," he said. Garivald's questioning noise held no words. Andelot went on, "The redheads keep coming up with new sorceries, powers below eat 'em. This one congeals the air some sort of way. Don't ask me how—I'm no mage. I don't think our mages know how this spell works, either, come to that. The one thing we do know is, for every ten times the Algarvians try it, they bring it off once, twice if they're lucky."

"That's too often," Garivald said.

"I know," Andelot said. "But it's only a toy. It won't

change the way the war turns out, not even a copper's worth. Most of the time, our dragons do get through."

Garivald nodded. Looked at from the perspective of the war as a whole, that did make perfect sense. Looked at from the perspective of the dragonfliers who'd just run into the Algarvian sorcery . . . He tried not to think about that. Before long, the regiment was moving forward again, so he didn't have to.

Ilmarinen stood in one of the passes that cut through the Bratanu Mountains. The air was as clear as mountain air was said to be. Finding a cliché that turned out to be true always amused him. Looking west—and looking down—he could see a long way into Algarve. There not too far away lay the town of Tricarico, with olive groves and almond orchards and rolling fields of wheat sweeping away till detail was lost even with this clear, clear air.

Beside Ilmarinen stood Grand General Nortamo, the commander of Kuusaman soldiers in Jelgava. He was, in fact, the overall commander of the Lagoans in Jelgava, too, however little they cared to acknowledge it. Grand general was not a usual rank in the Kuusaman army; it had been created especially for this campaign, to give Nortamo rank to match that of the Lagoan marshal who led King Vitor's men.

Nortamo was tall by Kuusaman standards; he might have had a little Lagoan blood in him. That would have helped explain his baldness, too. Most Kuusaman men, Ilmarinen among them, kept their hair. Nortamo hadn't. He wore hats a lot. Up here in the chilly mountains, nobody could smile at him because of it.

He was one of the blandest men Ilmarinen had ever met. *How did you get your job?* wondered the sardonic mage, who was a great many things, but none of them bland. *By making sure you never offended anybody? Seems more trouble than it's worth.*

"We took a little longer than we should have, getting through the mountains," Nortamo said. "But now, sorcerous sir, we are going to finish driving the Algarvians, and I don't see how they can stand in our way."

He also had a nearly infallible gift for stating the obvious. Ilmarinen sighed. *Is that what it takes to lead lots of men? A good smile and no surprises? Powers above be praised, all I ever wanted was to go off by myself and cast spells.*

"They probably won't stand in our way," he remarked now. "They'll probably hide behind things and blaze at us."

"Er—aye," Grand General Nortamo said. As befit a man with a gift for the obvious, he also owned a remorselessly literal mind. "Well, we've got the men and the behemoths and the dragons to root 'em out if they do. And we've got you wizardly types, too, eh?" He patted Ilmarinen on the back.

Ilmarinen had never been called a wizardly type in his entire life. He hoped with all his heart never to be called such again, either. "Right," he said tightly.

Oblivious to any offense he might have caused, Nortamo went on, "And you'll shield us from whatever funny sorceries Mezentio's men fling our way, won't you?"

"I do hope so," Ilmarinen answered. "It's my neck on the line, too."

"We'll do just fine." Nortamo spoke not so much in response to what he heard as to what he expected to hear. A lot of people were like that now and again. He had the disease worse than most.

He's brave, Ilmarinen reminded himself. *He's not particularly stupid. The men like him. They rush to do what he tells them. They think it's an honor.* He repeated that to himself several times. It kept him from trying to strangle Grand General Nortamo. Murdering the commanding general would get him talked about, however much satisfaction it might bring. And some people probably wouldn't understand at all.

In lieu of throttling Nortamo, Ilmarinen said, "As soon as I can, I'll want to talk with some captured Algarvian mages. The more I find out about what they're up to, the better the chance I have of stopping it."

"That makes sense," Nortamo said, though he didn't sound as if it had made enough sense to occur to him before

Ilmarinen mentioned it. "I'll do my best to arrange it for you, sorcerous sir." *I'll do my best to forget about it, and to make you nag,* was what that sounded like. Ilmarinen's hands twitched. *Could I strangle him before anyone noticed?* Tempting, tempting. Nortamo gave him a cheery little wave. "Now if you'll excuse me . . ." Off he went, unthrottled. Ilmarinen sighed.

Flashes of light in front of and then inside Tricarico showed where eggs were bursting—and where, Ilmarinen presumed, Kuusaman soldiers either were going forward or would be soon. He'd never been in Tricarico. He wondered how many Kuusamans had, back in more cheerful days. Not many, or he missed his guess. The provincial town didn't look to have much to recommend it.

No ley line ran through this pass. The road that did go through left a good deal to be desired. It might have been better before the war. In fact, it surely had been better. As Ilmarinen jounced along in a buggy, a second-rank mage gave him a happy wave and said, "Good to see you, sir. We're just about sure we've found all the eggs the Algarvians planted by now."

"That's nice," Ilmarinen answered. "If you turn out to be wrong, I'll write you a letter and let you know about it." The other wizard laughed. Occasional craters in the surface of the road said some of the Algarvian eggs had found Kuusaman soldiers before they were found. If one of them found him, he probably wouldn't be interested in writing letters for a while.

At some point in the descent, the driver paused to look back over his shoulder and remarked, "Well, we're in Algarve now."

Ilmarinen would argue with anybody at any time for any reason. "And how, precisely, do you know that?" he demanded. By way of reply, the driver jerked a thumb off to the right. Ilmarinen turned to look. An enormous dragon done in white, green, and red adorned a boulder. It was partly defaced; Kuusaman soldiers had added several rude scrawls to it. But it was unquestionably an Algarvian dragon. Ilmarinen nodded. "You're right. We're in Algarve."

A thin but steady stream of wounded soldiers came back

from the fighting. The ones who weren't too badly hurt still had plenty of spirit. "We'll get 'em," said a fellow with his hand wrapped in a bloody bandage. "They haven't got hardly any behemoths left. Pretty cursed hard to win a war without 'em."

That made sense to Ilmarinen. What made sense, though, wasn't necessarily true. By that afternoon, the Kuusamans were over the river both north and south of Tricarico, pushing hard to cut the city off and surround it. And then, just as the sun was setting on the broad Algarvian plain, the world suddenly seemed to hold its breath. Ilmarinen didn't know how else to put it. He'd felt the Algarvians' murderous magic so many time, he'd grown inured to it, as had most other mages. This . . . This was something else.

What are they doing? flashed through his mind when the sorcerous storm broke. A heartbeat later came another, perhaps even more urgent thought: *how are they doing it?* He'd heard that the Algarvians were pulling out all sorts of desperate spells, but hadn't really encountered one till now.

Their murderous magecraft had been bad. This was worse. That had used life energy in a straightforward way, even if Mezentio's men had no business stealing it as they'd done. This . . . Whoever the wizard essaying the spell was, he'd opened his spirit to the powers below. He didn't just aim to kill his foes. He aimed to torment them, to horrify them, to make death itself seem clean by comparison.

Ilmarinen felt Kuusaman sorcerers in the field try to throw up counterspells against the dark cantrip. He felt them fail, too, and felt the extinguishment of some of them. That was the only word he could find. They didn't die, at least not right away. They would have been better off if they had.

He essayed no counterspells. He had no idea whether that blackness *could* be countered, in any conventional sense of the word. He wasn't much interested in finding out, either. Instead, he hurled a bolt of sorcerous energy of the sort Pekka had discovered straight at the Algarvian attacking his countrymen.

The enemy mage hadn't expected that. His spell was so vicious, so dreadful, he might have assumed other wizards would attack it, not him. A lot of wizards would have. Ilmarinen didn't think like most of his professional colleagues. His own sorcerous stroke went home, a lightning bolt piercing the darkness. He felt the Algarvian sorcerer's outraged astonishment as the fellow died.

For a nasty moment, Ilmarinen feared that wouldn't be enough. The spell, once unleashed, seemed to want to go on by itself. It did crumble at last, but only slowly and reluctantly. Then the day seemed to brighten, though the sun was touching the western horizon.

Weary, shaken, disgusted as he was, Ilmarinen stormed off to Grand General Nortamo's headquarters, which he found in a farmhouse on this side of the river from Tricarico. A sentry tried to block his progress. He pushed past as if the man didn't exist. Nortamo was conferring with several of his officers. Ilmarinen ignored them, too. In a voice that brooked no contradiction, he said, "I need to talk to those captive mages, Nortamo. Now."

Nortamo looked at him. He was not a fool; he didn't argue. "Very well, sorcerous sir. You have my authorization. I will give it to you in writing, if you like."

"Never mind. We haven't time to waste." Ilmarinen hurried off to the small captives' camp where mages were housed and securely guarded by other mages. He had several of the highest-ranking captives brought before him. "How could any of you do . . . that?" he demanded in classical Kaunian. He spoke fluent Algarvian, but chose not to.

"How?" one of the Algarvians answered in the same tongue. "We are fighting to save our kingdom, that is how. What would you have us do, roll over and die?"

"Sooner than that?" Ilmarinen shuddered. "Aye, by the powers above."

"No," the mage said. "No one will enslave us, not while we still live to fight."

"Doing *that*, you enslave yourselves," Ilmarinen answered. "Better to be ruled by foreigners, don't you think, than by the powers below?"

"My wife and daughters are in the west," the Algarvian said. "I sent them word to flee. I do not know whether they could. If they did not, and the Unkerlanters have caught them . . . They are raping their way through my kingdom, you know."

"And what did you do to them?" Ilmarinen returned. "What did you do to the Kaunians in Forthweg?"

"This is a Kaunian war," the Algarvian mage declared. His comrades solemnly nodded. "Everyone picks on Algarve, and so of course we have to fight back in any way we can." The other wizards nodded again.

"War is bad enough. You made it worse," Ilmarinen said. "You made it much worse. Is it any wonder that every other kingdom has joined together to knock you down and make sure you can never do it again? By all you've done, you deserve it. You almost killed me when you loosed your attack on Yliharma."

"Too bad we failed, old man." The Algarvian didn't lack for nerve—but then, lacking for nerve had never been an Algarvian characteristic. "So long as we can fight back, we will, any way we can."

"Then you had better not complain about what happens to you afterwards," Ilmarinen said. Since he was on the side of the captors and not the captives, he took advantage of having the last word and walked out.

As soon as Bembo could get around with crutches and his splint, the healers in Tricarico threw him out of the sanatorium. He'd expected nothing else; wounded people kept flooding into the place. If the healers didn't need to keep an eye on him, they did need the cot he was filling.

He had no flat, of course, not any more. But finding a new one wasn't hard, not when he had silver to spend. And he did; he hadn't used much of his salary in all the time he'd been in Forthweg, and he'd done pretty well for himself shaking down the locals. He would have landed a place even sooner than he did if he hadn't insisted on living on the ground floor.

"Everybody wants those flats," a landlord with none to let told him. "Fast and easy to get to the cellar when the eggs start falling."

"I can't go *anywhere* fast and easy," Bembo said. Using crutches made it harder for him to gesture while he talked, and an Algarvian who couldn't talk with his hands was hardly alive. "You think I want to go up and down stairs with these things?"

The landlord shrugged. "Sorry, pal. I can't give you what I ain't got."

Bembo went off in a huff. He finally got a flat the next morning. Then he took a ley-line caravan over to his old constabulary station to find out where Saffa was staying these days. That took some doing; a lot of the constables there didn't remember him and didn't want to tell him anything. He finally got what he needed from Frontino, the warder at the gaol.

"Read any spicy romances lately?" Bembo asked him.

Frontino reached into his desk. "I've got a good one right here, matter of fact." The romance, called *Empress' Passion,* certainly *looked* good to Bembo. The cover showed a naked Kaunian woman, presumably the Empress in question, with her legs wrapped around an ancient Algarvic warrior with an improbable set of muscles. "The Kaunian Emperor, see, is going to sacrifice a bunch of Algarvian captives, till this guy"—Frontino tapped the warrior— "horns the Empress into talking him out of it. Then the captives get free and the blood really spills. I'm done—want to borrow it? The Empress, she screws up a storm." He held the book out to Bembo.

Almost to his own surprise, Bembo shook his head. "That whole business of sacrificing . . ." He looked around to make sure nobody but Frontino could hear him. "Everything they say about the Kaunians in Forthweg . . ."

"Pack of lies," the warder said. "Enemy dragons have been dropping little broadsheets about it, so it has to be a pack of lies. Stands to reason."

But Bembo shook his head again. "It's all true, Frontino. Everything everybody says is true, and nobody says even a quarter of what all really went on. I ought to know. I was fornicating *there,* remember."

Frontino didn't believe him. He could see as much. He thought about arguing. He thought about breaking one of his crutches over the warder's head, too, to let in a little sense. But that would have just landed him in the gaol. Muttering under his breath, he made his slow, hitching way out of the constabulary station and back to the ley-line caravan stop.

The block of flats next to Saffa's and one across the street were only piles of wreckage. Bembo had to go up three flights of stairs to get to her flat. He was puffing and sweating when he finally got there. A baby wailed behind the door he knocked on.

When Saffa opened it, she looked harried—maybe her brat had been crying for a while. "Oh," she said. "You."

He didn't quite know how to take that. "Hello, Saffa. I'm on my feet—sort of."

"Hello, Bembo." Her smile still had some of the sour tang he remembered. So did her words: "I'm glad to see you—sort of."

"Will you go to supper with me tomorrow night?" he asked, as if the whole Derlavaian War, including his broken leg, had never happened.

"No," she said. But she wasn't spitting in his eye, as she'd warned she might, for she went on, "I haven't got anyone to watch my son then. But three nights from now, my sister isn't working. I'll go then."

"All right," Bembo said. "Pick an eatery, and we'll go there. I've been away so long, I don't know what's good these days, or even what's standing." He'd got around by night in Gromheort and Eoforwic with no lights showing; he expected he could manage in his own home town.

But he turned out to be wrong. Tricarico fell to the Ku-usamans two days later.

He'd heard that the enemy was coming down out of the Bradano Mountains, of course. The news sheets couldn't very well deny that. But they did their best to claim the slanteyes would never cross the river, would never threaten the city. Bembo probably should have had more doubts than he did; he'd seen such optimistic twaddle in Forthweg, too. But the assault on Tricarico took him by surprise.

So did the feeble resistance his own countrymen put up inside the city. That left him half relieved—he had, after all, been in the middle of a city convulsed by fighting—and half ashamed. "Why aren't you giving them a battle?" he called to a squad of soldiers heading west, plainly intending to leave Tricarico.

"Why? I'll tell you why, porky," one of the men answered. Bembo squawked indignantly, and with some reason; he'd lost much of the paunch he'd once carried. Ignoring him, the trooper went on, "We're getting the blazes out on account of the slanteyes have already got men past this rotten place to north and south, and we don't want to get stuck here, that's why."

From a military point of view, that made good enough sense. Out in the west, fighting against the Unkerlanters, all too many garrisons had stayed in their towns too long, and got cut off and destroyed. Gromheort, where Bembo was stationed before transferring to Eoforwic, was going through such a death agony now. But even so . . . "What are we supposed to do?"

"Best you can, pal," the soldier answered. "That and thank the powers above it ain't the Unkerlanters coming into town." He trotted away, dodging craters in the street and jumping over or kicking aside bits of rubble nobody had bothered to clear away.

Had Bembo had two good legs, he would have kicked at rubble, too. As things were, he made his own slow way down the street. The trooper was right. The Kuusamans wouldn't rape or massacre everyone they saw just for the sport of it. At least, Bembo hoped they wouldn't. *I'm going to find out,* he realized.

He was back in his flat, with the shutters tightly drawn, when the Kuusamans did come into Tricarico. One of the windows in the flat had had glass in it when he rented the place; the landlord had tried to charge him more because of it. He'd laughed in the man's face, asking, "How long do you expect it to last?" And he'd proved a good prophet, for an egg bursting not far away soon shattered the pane into tinkling shards. He'd had a demon of a time cleaning up afterwards, too. Trying to handle crutches and broom and dustpan was more an exercise in frustration than anything else.

But Bembo couldn't stay in his flat forever, or even very long. He had to come out to look for something to eat. He'd never done much cooking for himself, even back when he'd been living in Tricarico. A constable with an eye for the main chance could get most of his meals from the eateries on his beat. In Forthweg, he'd done the same thing a lot of the time, and eaten in barracks like a soldier when he hadn't. And, with crutches, he would have been as awkward in the kitchen as he had been chasing slivers of glass around the floor. Of course, he was pretty awkward in the kitchen without crutches, too.

A few eggs were still bursting inside Tricarico when he emerged from his block of flats. At first, he thought that meant the Kuusamans hadn't yet come into the city after all. But then he saw several of them setting up sandbags so they could cover all sides of an intersection. They looked like runts; he was several inches taller than the biggest of them, and he wasn't exceptionally tall by Algarvian standards. But they had sticks and they had the same sort of urgent, disciplined wariness he'd seen in Algarvian soldiers in Forthweg. Any civilians who tried trifling with them would be very sorry very fast. He was sure of that.

More eggs burst. He realized his retreating countrymen were tossing them at his home town. They didn't care what happened to the people who lived in Tricarico as long as they killed or maimed a few Kuusamans. Bembo turned toward the west and scowled. *See if I do anything for you any time soon,* he thought, the *you* being either the departed soldiers or King Mezentio himself: even Bembo wasn't quite sure which. It amounted to the same thing either way.

"You!" someone said sharply, and for a moment Bembo thought the word remained in his own mind, not the world outside him. But then the fellow who'd spoken went on: "Aye, you—the chubby fellow with the crutches. Come here."

Bembo turned. There gesturing at him stood a skinny old Kuusaman with a few little wisps of white hair sprouting from his chin. He wore greenish-gray Kuusaman uniform, with a prominent badge that had to be a mage's emblem. "What do you want, uh, sir?" Bembo asked cautiously.

"I already told you what I wanted," the Kuusaman said in his almost unaccented Algarvian. "I want you to come here.

I have some questions for you, and I expect to get answers."
I'll turn you into a leech if I don't, lay behind his words.

"I'm coming," Bembo said, and made his slow way over
to the mage. Refusing didn't cross his mind, not because of
the implied threat but simply because one did as this man
said first and then wondered why afterwards, if at all. Still,
Bembo was not easily overawed, and had his own full measure of Algarvian cheekiness. He asked a question of his
own: "Who are you, old-timer?"

"Ilmarinen," the mage answered. "Now you know as
much as you did before." He eyed Bembo. Bembo didn't
like the way he did it; it seemed as if Ilmarinen were looking right into his soul. And maybe the mage was, for the
next thing he said, in tones of genuine curiosity, was, "How
could you?"

"Uh, how could I what, sir?" Bembo asked.

"Round up Kaunians and send them off to what you
knew was death and then go back to your bed and sleep at
night," the Kuusaman mage answered.

"How did you know that? I mean, I never—" But Bembo's denial faltered. Ilmarinen would know if he lied. He
was grimly certain of that. And so, instead of denying, he
evaded: "I saved some, too, by the powers above. Plenty of
my pals didn't."

Ilmarinen looked *into* him again. Grudgingly, the mage
nodded. "So you did—a handful, and usually for favors.
But you did, and I cannot deny it. A tiny weight in the other
pan of the scales. Now answer what I asked before—what
of all those you did not save?"

Bembo had spent years *not* thinking about that. He didn't
want to think about it now. Under Ilmarinen's eye, though,
he had no choice. At last, he mumbled, "The people set
over me told me what to do, and I went and did it. They
were the ones who were supposed to know what was going
on, not me. And what else could I have done?"

Ilmarinen started to spit into his face. Bembo was sure of
it. At the last instant, the mage checked himself. "A tiny
weight of truth there, too," he said, and spat at Bembo's feet
instead, then turned and walked away.

"Hey! You can't—" Bembo broke off as a sense of just

how narrow his escape had been flowed through him. The last thing in all the world he wanted was for that terrible old Kuusaman wizard to come back and look into his eyes again.

As soon as Istvan walked into the barracks, he knew he was in trouble. All eyes swung his way. Somebody got up and closed the barracks door behind him. "Well, well," somebody else said, "if it isn't the Kuusamans' little pet goat."

"Maaa! Maaa!" somebody else said shrilly. Several of his countrymen got off their cots and came toward him, hands bunching into fists.

Fear chilled him. Men occasionally got stomped or beaten to death here in the captives' camp on Obuda. Once in a while, the Kuusaman guards found out who did it and punished them. More often than not, though, they didn't. That sort of fate looked to be about to befall him.

He didn't turn and run. That wasn't so much because he came from a warrior race as because he felt sure more Gyongyosians were closing in behind him. Instead, he drew himself up very straight. "I have kept my honor," he said. "The stars shine on my spirit, and they know I have kept my honor."

"Liar," three men said together.

"Maaa! Maaa!" That hateful, mocking goat-bleat rang out again.

"I am no liar," Istvan declared. "Come on, all of you. I will fight you one at a time till I can fight no more. I will say nothing to the guards about what happened. By the stars, I swear it. Or show yourselves goat-eating cowards and mob me all at once."

They hesitated. He hadn't been sure he would get even that much. Then a burly man stepped out of the group and advanced on him, saying, "My fists and feet are better than you deserve."

Istvan didn't answer. He just waited. The other captive was bigger than he, and looked to know what he was doing. The fellow surged forward, head down, fists churning. Istvan blocked a blow with his arm, struck a stomach hard as oak, took a boot in the hip instead of in the crotch, and also lashed out with his foot. A buffet to the side of the head made him see stars that had nothing to do with the ones he reverenced. He grabbed his foe and threw him to the floor. The other captive tripped him on the way down.

But Istvan was the one who got up. He spat red on the floor. "Who's next?" he said, squinting a little because his left eye was half swollen shut.

Another Gyongyosian strode toward him. He won that fight, too, and waved for a third challenger. By then, every part of him hurt. He didn't think he would win the third fight, and he didn't. The other captive thumped his head against the floor, once, twice. . . . That was the last thing he remembered.

They could have killed him after he was out. When he woke up again, he rather wished they had. They'd kicked him around some. He could feel that. But it was almost lost in the thudding, nauseating pain in his head. He'd had his wits scrambled for him, sure as sure. He had trouble remembering where he was and even who he was. He did remember how three other captives in the barracks had got pretty good sets of lumps of their own, though. That gave him a certain small satisfaction, when he wasn't hoping his own head would fall off.

Corporal Kun walked into the barracks perhaps half an hour after Istvan came to. He took one look at Istvan and realized what must have happened to him. He had time for one horrified yelp before somebody said, "All right, squealer—your turn now." The captives fell on him and beat him bloody, but he was still breathing when they stopped. Maybe Istvan had won enough respect to keep them from wanting to kill his comrade any more.

At the roll call that evening, the Kuusaman guards stared at Istvan. "What you to do?" one of them asked.

"Nothing," he said stolidly. Where he had trouble recalling his name, he did remember the oath he'd sworn. The guards eyed Kun. He didn't look quite so bad as Istvan— and, somehow, he'd managed to keep his spectacles from shattering—but he was no beauty. Neither were the men who'd fought Istvan one after the next.

The guards shook their heads and shrugged. They'd seen

such things before. This time, at least, they weren't carrying corpses from the captives' camp.

A couple of days later, Istvan got summoned out of the camp for another interrogation with Lammi, the forensic sorcerer. By then, some of his bruises had turned truly spectacular colors. His ribs looked like a sunset. His face was no bargain, either. When he made his way into Lammi's tent—ducking through the flap hurt, too—the mage's jaw dropped. "By the stars!" she exclaimed in her good Gyongyosian. "What happened to you?"

No matter how well she spoke his language, Istvan didn't like to hear her use such oaths—what regard would the stars have for a foreigner like her? He answered as he'd answered the guard: "Nothing."

Lammi shook her head. "A little more nothing like that and they would lay you on a pyre. Now—tell me at once what happened to you."

"Nothing," Istvan repeated.

"You are a stubborn man. I have seen that," she said. "But you know I have ways to get answers from you."

"Nothing happened," Istvan said. As he'd expected, his command of his senses disappeared. Lammi might have miscalculated there. Taking away his senses took away his pain, too, the first relief he'd had from it since the fights. And she'd robbed him often enough, he was starting to get used to it. He didn't mistake her voice for that of the stars any more.

Presently, she brought him back to himself. "You are a very stubborn man," she said.

"Thank you," he answered, which made her blink.

She needed a moment to rally. "I think," she said, "we would do well not to send you back to your barracks." She picked up a crystal and spoke into it in Kuusaman, which Istvan didn't understand. Whoever was on the other end of the etheric connection answered in the same language. The crystal flared, then went inert. Lammi looked back to Istvan. "Corporal Kun, it seems, is also sporting bruises. How did that happen?"

"I don't know," he answered, and waited to go back to the unworld of no sight, no hearing, no smell, no taste, no touch. He looked forward to losing the sense of touch once more: indeed he did.

Lammi made an exasperated noise. "How can we find and punish the men who beat you if you will not tell us who they are?"

"What men?" Istvan said. The forensic sorcerer made another, louder, exasperated noise. With a shrug, Istvan went on, "I told you, nothing happened."

"Aye, that is what you told me," Lammi agreed. "And I am telling you once more, Sergeant, that, had a little more of such nothing happened, you would now be dead, and we would not be having this discussion." Istvan shrugged again. She was probably—no, certainly—right. She glowered at him. "We will be removing you from the captives' camp for your own protection. You do understand that?"

With one more shrug, Istvan answered, "You are the captors. I am the captive. You can do as you like with me. If you do too much, and word gets back to Gyongyos, your own captives will suffer."

The Kuusaman mage drummed her fingers on her notepad. She muttered something in her own tongue, then translated it into Gyongyosian: "Very difficult, too." Istvan inclined his head, as at another compliment. That made Lammi mutter again. When she returned to Gyongyosian once more, she said, "Very well, Sergeant. If you will not discuss this, you will not. Let us turn to something else, then."

"You are the captor," Istvan repeated.

"I do wonder," Lammi murmured. Istvan understood the words, but not everything behind them. She gathered herself and went on, "You have a scar on your left hand, Sergeant."

Istvan had been afraid in a physical sense of what the Kuusamans might do to him. Now, for the first time in the interrogation, he knew real terror. He had to force a one-word answer out through numb lips: "Aye."

"Sergeant Kun, your comrade, has an identical scar," Lammi continued.

"Does he?" Istvan said, shrugging yet again. "I hadn't noticed."

The world disappeared once more. Lammi, he remembered, knew when he lied. After some endless—but, happily, also painless—time, she allowed him to return to the sensible world. "I point out," she said, "that one of the men who was slain in the unfortunate incident, a certain,"—she checked her notes—"a certain Szonyi, aye, had an identical scar, duly noted on his identity documents. He too was a comrade of yours."

"He was," Istvan said. He couldn't very well deny it. Saying anything else—such as how much he missed his friend—would have just given Lammi another handle on him.

She waited for something more. When it didn't come, she shrugged and said, "How do you explain these three identical scars, Sergeant?"

"We all got them at the same time in Unkerlant," Istvan said. Again, he said no more. He fought against trembling. His heart pounded in his chest. He would sooner have gone through a dozen beatings than this.

Lammi peered at him through her spectacles. Try as he would to hide it, he feared she saw his agitation. "Why?" she asked softly.

She can tell when I lie. To Istvan, that was the most terrifying thought of all. Instead of lying, he said nothing at all. Whatever she chose to do to him would be better than a truthful answer to that question.

"Why?" Lammi asked once more. Istvan still did not answer. The inside of the tent was cool—the island of Obuda never got very warm, especially not in late winter—but sweat ran down his face. He could smell his own fear. He didn't know if Lammi could, but she could hardly miss the sweat. Still softly, she asked, "Is it a scar of expiation?"

"I don't know what that word means," Istvan said.

She could tell when he gave her the truth, too. That didn't do him much good, though. She simplified: "A scar, a wound, to wash away a sin?" Istvan still sat mute, which looked to be answer enough by itself. Lammi asked, "What sort of sin?"

"One I never meant to commit!" Istvan burst out. The Kuusaman mage just sat there, waiting. Again, he said no more. Again, it didn't seem to matter. Lammi looked at him, looked through him, looked into his heart. *She knows. By the stars, she knows,* he thought, and despair overwhelmed even terror. A Kuusaman, a foreigner, *knew* he'd eaten goat. She knew what it meant, too. She knew altogether too much about Gyongyos and its ways. *She owns me,* he thought hopelessly.

If Lammi did, she didn't seem anxious to take possession. "We will find you other housing, safer housing," she said, and spoke to the guards in Kuusaman. They led Istvan out of the tent.

Likely not by coincidence, Kun came out of the other interrogation tent at just the same time. He walked toward Istvan as Istvan headed toward him. The guards didn't interfere. Istvan looked at Kun's battered face, and at the devastated expression on it, the same expression he wore himself. The two men embraced and burst into tears. No matter how bright the night sky might be, Istvan didn't think the stars would ever shine on him again.

Very cautiously, Leudast stuck his head up from behind a shattered wall and peered across the Scamandro. He had reason for caution. The Algarvians had snipers on the east bank of the river, and they were very alert. A man who wasn't careful would have a beam go in one ear and out the other.

True, eggs were bursting over there, but that wouldn't make the redheads quit blazing. Leudast knew what sort of men he faced. They'd driven through Unkerlant to the outskirts of Cottbus. Had the war gone just a little differently . . .

"It's a good thing there weren't more of the whoresons," he muttered.

"What's that, Lieutenant?" asked Captain Dagaric, who'd taken over as regimental commander after Captain Drogden hadn't been careful enough while raping an Algarvian woman. Dagaric had efficiency written all over him. He was a good soldier, in a cold-blooded way. Nobody would love him, but he wouldn't throw men away out of stupidity, either. Given some of the things Leudast had seen, solid professionalism was nothing to sneeze at.

He repeated himself, adding, "Powers below eat 'em."

"They will." Dagaric spoke with assurance. "We are going to hammer them flat when we cross the river. That will be the last fight, because we *will* take Trapani once we get rolling."

"May it be so, sir," Leudast said. "This war . . . We had to win it. If we didn't, they'd've held us down forever."

"I only wish we could get rid of every last one of the buggers," Dagaric said. "If we treated them the way they treated the Kaunians up in Forthweg, we really wouldn't have to worry about Algarve for a long time to come."

Leudast nodded. He didn't think even King Swemmel *would* massacre all the redheads in the lands he was overrunning, but you never could tell with Swemmel. Any Unkerlanter would have said the same. And . . . "We've had to use our own people the way the Algarvians used the Kaunians from Forthweg. Mezentio's men deserve something extra to pay for that."

"You bet they do," Captain Dagaric said. "I expect they'll get it, too."

A weird wailing, laughing, gobbling noise came out of the east. Leudast grabbed for his stick. "What in blazes is that? Does it go with some new Algarvian magic?"

Dagaric pointed out to the Scamandro, where a big bird was swimming, its back checked in black and white, its beak a fish-catching spear. "No, it's just a loon—and you're another one, for letting the call spook you."

"They must be birds of the south," Leudast said. "They don't live on any streams up near the village I come from." More than half to himself, he added, "I wonder if anything's left of the place these days." Then he spoke to the regimental commander again: "And I don't see how you can blame me for being jumpy about the fornicating redheads and their magecraft, sir. With all the weird new spells they're throwing at us these days . . ."

With a dismissive gesture, Dagaric said, "A drowning man thrashes his arms and flails. Whoreson still drowns, though. The Algarvians send these stupid spells of theirs at us before they find out what the magic can do, or even if it works at all. No wonder most of it goes sour."

That made sense—up to a point. "Even the spells that maybe don't do everything they're supposed to can still hurt us," Leudast said. "We've seen it."

"They'd hurt us worse if the redheads really knew what they were doing," Dagaric said. That made Leudast blink. Like most Unkerlanters, he took it almost for granted that the Algarvians were cleverer than his own folk. They'd proved their wit in Unkerlant too often for him to think anything else. But Dagaric stubbornly plowed ahead: "Think how much trouble they could cause if all their fancy magic really *worked*. It mostly doesn't, though, and I'll tell you why. A couple-three years ago, the redheads figured they could lick us with what they already had, and they didn't worry about anything else. Then, when they started getting into trouble, that's when they decided to make the fire under their mages hotter. So they have all these spells that would do this, that, or the other thing—if only they worked right. But they cursed well don't, and we'll have licked Algarve before the redheads ever do get 'em right."

After Leudast thought that over, he slowly nodded. "The one thing Mezentio's men always foul up is, they always think they're smarter than they really are and they can do more than they can really do."

Dagaric nodded, too, most emphatically. "You've got it, Lieutenant. You've got it just right, matter of fact. And how fornicating smart does that make them? If they were anywhere near as smart as they want everybody else to think they are, would we be here halfway between the Yaninan border and Trapani? Would the stinking islanders be coming up the Algarvians' arse from the east?"

"No, sir," Leudast said. "They made everybody hate 'em and they made everybody afraid of 'em and now they've made everybody gang up on 'em, too. You look at it that way, maybe they really aren't so smart." He heard the wonder in his own voice. *We're winning the war. We're not only winning it, we've got it almost won. I can't quite see Trapani from here, but it won't be long.*

He wondered what would happen then. Maybe Swemmel would put everything he could into the war against Gyongyos. Leudast shook his head, marveling. He'd been fighting the Gongs when the Derlavaian War broke out. Maybe things would come full circle, and he'd fight them some more. If Unkerlant went after them now, he thought his kingdom would smash them.

But what then? Suppose Unkerlant didn't have an enemy left in the world. Suppose he got out of the army. *What would I do then? I've been fighting for a long time. I hardly know anything else any more.*

Go home. I suppose that's the first thing I have to do. See if anything is left of the village. See if I have any kin left alive. And then . . . There was that girl back in Grelz, that Alize. If I can find her again, that might turn into something. I wonder how much different farming is down there. I could find out.

He laughed at himself. A couple of minutes' thought, and he had the rest of his life neatly laid out. One thing the war had taught him was that plans mostly didn't work the way people thought they would ahead of time.

Dagaric slapped him on the shoulder, stopping his leyline caravan of thought. "Things look pretty quiet up here for now," the regimental commander said. "We can get back to our men."

"Aye, sir," Leudast said. They slipped away from the Scamandro's western bank. As they went off, the loon loosed its mad, laughing call once more. Leudast's shiver had nothing to do with the chilly weather. Nobody hearing that cry for the first time would think it came from a bird's throat. That it presaged some nasty Algarvian sorcery still struck him as much more likely.

Sentries challenged them twice on the way back to the Algarvian village in which the regiment was resting. The men weren't taking victory for granted, which struck Leudast as the best way to insure it. Another officer was heading up to the Scamandro for a look of his own at the enemy.

Another officer . . . Leudast stiffened to attention when he saw the big gold stars embroidered on the collar tabs of the oncoming man's cape. Only one soldier in all of Unkerlant wore those stars. Dagaric might all at once have turned to rigidly upright stone, too.

"Marshal Rathar, sir!" the two junior officers exclaimed together.

"As you were, gentlemen," Rathar said. "I always like to see officers doing their own reconnaissance. That's what I'm doing myself, as a matter of fact."

"There's what's left of a wall by the riverbank, sir." Leudast turned and pointed. "You have to be careful, though— the redheads have snipers on the far bank."

"Thanks." Rathar started to go on, then paused and gave him a quizzical look. "I know you, don't I?" Before Leudast could speak, Rathar answered his own question: "Aye, I do. You're the fellow who brought in Raniero, you and that other soldier."

"That's right, sir," Leudast said. "You made me a lieutenant and him a sergeant."

"What happened to him? Do you know?"

"Afraid I do, sir," Leudast answered. "An Algarvian sniper got him. Kiun never knew what happened. There are worse ways to go."

"You're right. We've all seen too many of them." Marshal Rathar grimaced. "So many good men gone. That's the worst thing about this stinking war. What will become of Unkerlant once it's finally over?"

Captain Dagaric presumed to speak: "Lord Marshal, sir, whatever it is, we'll be better off than these fornicating Algarvians."

"We'd better be, Captain." Rathar was polite enough, but didn't bother to ask Dagaric's name. With a nod to Leudast, he went on, "Good to see you again, Lieutenant. Stay safe." He went on toward the Scamandro.

"Thank you very much, sir," Leudast called after him. "You, too."

Rathar didn't answer. He just kept walking. Even so, Dagaric stared at Leudast as if he'd never seen him before. In accusing tones, he said, "You never told me the marshal knew you."

"No, sir," Leudast agreed.

"Why in blazes not?" the regimental commander burst out. "A connection like that—"

Leudast shrugged. "You wouldn't have believed me. Or if you did, you'd've thought I was bragging. So I just kept my mouth shut." For anybody raised in an Unkerlanter peasant village, keeping one's mouth shut almost always looked like a good idea. No telling who might be listening.

"A lieutenant in my regiment . . . knows the Marshal of Unkerlant." Dagaric still sounded dazed, disbelieving.

"No, sir. You had it right the first time," Leudast answered. "He knows me, some. I've met him a couple of times, that's all: once up in Zuwayza, in the first fight there, and then when Kiun and I got lucky with Raniero a little this side of Herborn."

Dagaric grunted. "I think you're too modest for your own good. If the Marshal of Unkerlant knows you, why are you only a lieutenant?"

"*Only* a lieutenant?" Leudast gaped. That wasn't how he looked at it—just the opposite, in fact. "Sir, you've got to remember—I come out of a peasant village. I didn't expect to be anything but a common soldier after the impressers got . . . uh, after I joined King Swemmel's army. I got to be a sergeant because I was lucky enough to stay alive when a lot of people didn't, and I got to be an officer because I was the fellow—well, one of the fellows—who nabbed the false King of Grelz when he was trying to get away."

"In *my* regiment," Dagaric muttered. Leudast stifled a sigh. His superior hadn't paid any attention to him. He didn't know why he was surprised. Superiors didn't have to listen to subordinates. Not having to listen was part of what made them what they were. Every so often, an exception came along. Leudast tried to be one himself, but knew he didn't always succeed.

He glanced east, toward the riverbank. Rathar squatted there behind what was left of the stone fence, just as he and Dagaric had done a few minutes before. The marshal showed both nerve and good sense in coming up to the front alone. The Algarvians had no idea he was there. He got the look he wanted and then came away. Leudast sighed with relief. He couldn't imagine the war without the marshal.

Eight

Colonel Sabrino led his wing—what was left of it—down to a landing on a makeshift dragon farm outside the little town of Pontremoli, a few miles east of the Scamandro. Some of the dragon-handlers on the ground knew what they were doing; others were boys and old men from a Popular Assault regiment, doing the best they could at jobs they'd never expected to have to handle.

Once Sabrino's dragon was chained to an iron spike driven deep into the muddy ground, he climbed down and wearily made his way toward the tents that had sprouted to await the wing's arrival. Captain Orosio's dragon had landed not far away. Orosio looked as worn as Sabrino, but managed a nod and a wave.

"Almost full circle," Sabrino said.

"Sir?" The squadron commander scratched his head. In the five and a half years he'd flown in Sabrino's wing, his hair had retreated a good deal at the temples. Sabrino wondered how much older he looked himself these days. He felt about ninety.

He waved to the east—not so very far to the east. "If we fall back any more, we'll be flying out of the dragon farm near Trapani, the one we left when we went to war against Forthweg."

"Oh." Orosio thought that over, then nodded. "By the powers above, you're right." He looked around. "Not fornicating many left who set out with us that day. You, me, two or three others—that's it. Sixty-four dragonfliers, and all the rest dead or maimed." He spat. "And how much longer d'you think *we'll* last?"

"As long as we do, that's all," Sabrino answered with a shrug that tried for typical Algarvian brio but didn't come up with much. "I have no fear any more, and I have no hope, either. We do what we do as long as we can keep doing it, and then . . ." He shrugged again. "After that, what difference would it make, anyhow?"

"Not much." Orosio pointed to the road that led east out of Pontremoli. "They don't think what we're doing now makes much difference, either."

Algarvians poured east in a steady stream, carrying whatever they could. In earlier days, in happier days, Sabrino had watched from the air as Unkerlanters fled west before King Mezentio's men, clogging the roads for King Swemmel's soldiers. Now the shoe—when the refugees had shoes—was on the other foot. His dragonfliers had flamed refugee columns in Unkerlant and dropped eggs on them. Now the men who flew dragons painted rock-gray had their turn with Sabrino's countrymen.

"Maybe some of them will get away," Sabrino said, fighting to keep despair from overwhelming him altogether. "Maybe they'll get to parts of the kingdom the Lagoans and Kuusamans are overrunning. That should keep them alive. The islanders don't kill for the sport of it, anyhow."

How many dead Kaunians? he wondered. How long would other kingdoms throw that in Algarve's face? Generations, probably. And who could blame them? *I tried to talk Mezentio out of it,* Sabrino thought. *As far as people in Algarve go, that gives me clean hands. Powers above help us all.*

Orosio said, "You think it's lost, then? You think we have no chance, no matter what King Mezentio says?"

"Aye, I think that," Sabrino answered. "Don't you?" Reluctantly, the squadron commander nodded. "All right, then," Sabrino said. "What do we do next?"

"Fight as hard as we can as long as we can," Orosio said. "What else is there?"

"Nothing I can see," Sabrino told him. "Not a single fornicating thing." As Orosio had, he spat into the muck. "And I'm not doing it for King Mezentio. This for King Mezentio." He spat again. "If it weren't for what Mezentio did back in the first autumn of the war with Unkerlant, we'd have a better chance now—and nobody would hate us quite so much."

Had Orosio taken that back to the ears of men who cared about such things—*to King Mezentio's equivalent of inspectors,* Sabrino thought scornfully—the wing commander would have found himself in trouble . . . as if trying to keep up the fight against the Unkerlanters weren't trouble enough. But Sabrino knew his squadron commander well enough to be sure Orosio would sooner be flamed out of the sky than betray him. What Orosio did say was, "Well, if it's not for the king and it's not for the kingdom, why not just pack it in?"

"Who says it's not for the kingdom?" Sabrino looked back toward that unending steam of Algarvians fleeing eastward. "The longer we keep going, the longer we hold back Swemmel's whoresons, the more people will have the chance to get away. That's worth doing, curse it."

"Ah." Orosio didn't need long to think it over this time. "You're right, sir. We've got to do what we can."

"However much that is—or however little." Sabrino raised his voice to call to the chief dragon-handler: "Sergeant! A word with you, if you please."

"Aye, sir?" The fellow hurried up to him. "What can I do for you, sir? We were just going to feed the beasts."

"That's what I wanted to ask you about," Sabrino said. "Did that shipment of cinnabar you were talking about ever get down here from the north? Without it, our dragons are only flaming half as far as the ones the Unkerlanters fly."

"Oh. That. Sorry, sir. No." The sergeant shook his head. "I don't think we can expect any more, either. I heard today Swemmel's men have overrun the mines south of Bonorva. That was about the last cinnabar we had left, sir, and we had to try and parcel it out amongst all the dragons we've still got in the air."

"The last of the cinnabar." Sabrino didn't know why it surprised him. He'd seen this day coming when the Algarvians were driven out of the cinnabar-rich austral continent—after their murderous magic went wrong there, as foreign magic had a way of doing, and wrecked their own army—and especially after they didn't swarm past Sulingen and into the cinnabar mines of the Mamming Hills in southern Unkerlant. He'd seen it coming, and seen it coming . . . and it was finally here.

Orosio put the best face on things he could: "Well, sir, our job just got a little harder, that's all."

Their job, for most of the past two years, had been impossible. Orosio surely knew that as well as Sabrino did. Sabrino let out another weary sigh. "Fishing without a net or a line, that's what we'll be doing. How many minnows can we grab out of the water with our bare hands?"

"Fish, sir?" The sergeant of dragon-handlers looked confused. A solid, capable man when doing what he knew how to do, he wouldn't have known a metaphor had one strolled up wagging its tail. Sabrino almost envied him. He wished he were more ignorant himself these days.

He ducked into his tent. A meal of sorts waited there: rye bread and a little crock of butter and a jug of spirits. Sabrino shook his head. Change the spirits to ale and his barbarous ancestors would have eaten like this in the days before they ever dreamt of challenging the might of the Kaunian Empire.

New barbarians at the gates now, Sabrino thought. He wondered whether he meant the Unkerlanters or his own people. He shrugged a fine, flamboyant Algarvian shrug. What difference did it make, really? He drank more of his supper than he ate, and went to bed with wits whirling.

When he woke up the next morning, his throbbing head seemed altogether in keeping with the general state of the world, or the Algarvian portion thereof. His head would eventually improve. He had his doubts about the Algarvian portion of the world.

Bread liberally smeared with butter did nothing to beat back his hangover. They did grease his stomach so the slug of spirits he poured down after them didn't hurt so much. When the spirits mounted to his head, he felt human again, in a melancholy way. How any Algarvian could feel anything but melancholy these days was beyond him.

The day was cool and cloudy, with a threat of rain in the air. Sabrino wouldn't have wanted to face bright sunshine just then. He started over to the crystallomancers' tent to

find out where along the tattered front his dozen or so dragons could do the most good. Before he got there, someone
called his name. He turned.

He knew he stared. He couldn't help it. The smiling
young fellow striding toward him might have come out of
the early days, the triumphant days, of the war. It wasn't so
much that his uniform tunic and kilt were clean and new
and well pressed, though at this stage of things that seemed
a minor prodigy to Sabrino of itself. But the stranger's expression and bearing seemed to say the past two years and
more had been nothing but a bad dream. Sabrino wished it
were so. Unfortunately, he knew better.

"Pleased to make your acquaintance, Colonel," the
younger man said, holding out his arm. As he and Sabrino
clasped wrists, he went on, "I have the honor to be called
Almonte, sir."

He wore a major's rank badges and, prominent on his left
breast, a mage's insigne. "Pleased to make your acquaintance," Sabrino echoed, though anything but sure he was
pleased. "What can I do for you?"

"No, Colonel, it's what I can do for you." Almonte was
excessively glib; he put Sabrino in mind of a commercial
traveler peddling silver spoons that would show the brass
beneath inside a month. He had plenty of brass himself; he
continued, "How would you like to lick the Unkerlanters all
the way back to their own kingdom?"

"If I could lick them back half a mile, I'd be tolerably
pleased," Sabrino answered. In Algarve's hour of desperation, all sorts of maniacs were getting their chances, for
how could they make things worse? "What have you got in
mind?"

"Riding with you to smite the enemy from the air with a
new, particularly potent sorcery I've devised," Almonte
answered.

"Have you tried it before?" Sabrino asked. "If you have,
how did it go?"

"I'm still here," Almonte answered.

"So are the Unkerlanters," Sabrino said dryly.

Almonte gave him a reproachful stare. "I am but one

man, Colonel. I do what I can for King Mezentio and Algarve. I hope you can say the same."

If he thought he would make Sabrino feel guilty, he erred. "Futter you, Major," the wing commander said, not bothering to raise his voice. "I fought on the ground in the Six Years' War, and I've been at the front in this one since the day it started. I don't owe Algarve any more than I've already given. Before I decide whether I want you on a dragon with me, suppose you tell me just what your precious spell is and what you think it can do to the Unkerlanters."

Biting his lip in anger, Almonte plunged into his explanation. He plainly didn't know how technical to be; sometimes he talked down to Sabrino, others his words went over the dragonflier's head. What he aimed to do was clear enough: loose horror and destruction on Swemmel's men from the air. How he proposed to go about it . . .

Sabrino didn't hit him. Afterwards, he wondered why. His stomach lurching as if his dragon had dived without warning, he said, "Get out of my sight this instant, or I'll blaze you where you stand. This makes killing Kaunians clean by comparison."

"Desperate times take desperate measures," the mage declared.

King Mezentio had said the same thing, just before the Algarvian wizards started butchering blonds. Sabrino hadn't been able to stop him. He was the king. This fellow . . . "If you want to try *that*, Major, I'd sooner see the Unkerlanters smash us down," Sabrino said.

"I shall return with orders from your superiors," Almonte snapped.

"Fine," Sabrino said. "You can go up on my dragon, or on any dragon in this wing, but there's no guarantee you'll come down." Almonte stalked off. He didn't come back. Sabrino hadn't thought he would.

In the blockhouse not far from the hostel in the Naantali district, Pekka spun a globe. Globes and maps were more than just pictures of the world; as even the sages of the Kaunian Empire had realized, they were also, in their own way, applications of and invitations to the law of similarity. Pekka looked from one of her colleagues to another. "This is our last great test," she said, and they all nodded. "If everything goes as it should, we can use this sorcery against any place in the world from here."

They all nodded: Raahe and Alkio, Piilis—and Fernao. Pekka did her best to treat him the same way she treated the other theoretical sorcerers. He didn't like that; his eyes, so like a Kuusaman's, showed as much. She hadn't been in his bed—she hadn't wanted to be in anyone's bed—since learning of Leino's death. But for a couple of trips back to Kajaani to see her son and her sister, she'd thrown herself into her sorcery, using work as an anodyne where someone else might have used spirits.

He couldn't very well complain, not here in front of everyone. What he did say was, "The blockhouse seems empty today, compared to so many of the things we've done. No secondary sorcerers here, for instance—just a crystallomancer."

"We don't need secondary sorcerers, not for this." Pekka waved at the bank of cages full of rats and rabbits. "We'll be sending the energy we release from the beasts so far away, we can safely keep the cages here."

I want to send the energy to Trapani, she thought savagely. *I want to lash the capital of Algarve with a whip of fire, till nothing there still stands.* But what good would that do? It wouldn't bring Leino back to life. Nothing could do that. A day at a time, she was realizing the finality of death.

"Shall we begin?" Raahe asked quietly. She was holding Alkio's hand. She and her husband were ten or fifteen years older than Pekka, but smiling like a couple of newlyweds.

"Aye," Pekka said: one harsh word. *Whom have I?* she wondered. Not Leino, not any more, not ever. *I did have Fernao. I could have him again. Is he what I really want, or was he just someone to keep me warm while Leino was far away?* She didn't know. She was afraid to find out.

I'm also too busy to find out. She recited the Kuusaman ritual words that preceded every spell save one cast in an emergency. Then she spun the globe again. This time, she purposely stopped it. Her fingernail tapped what looked like a fly speck in the eastern Bothnian Ocean. "Becsehely." She pronounced the Gyongyosian name as best she could. "Everyone is supposed to be off the island."

"Everyone had better be off the island," Fernao said. "Anyone who stayed behind would be very sorry."

"I begin," Pekka said, and started incanting. After so many runs through spells like this, she cast another one with almost as much confidence and aplomb as if she were a practical mage herself. *No, that's Leino,* she thought, and felt again the hole in her life. *That* was *Leino.* But she couldn't dwell on it, not now. The spell came first.

She felt the sorcerous energy building inside the blockhouse. The animals in the cages felt it, too. They scurried this way and that. Some tried to get out. Some tried to bury under the shavings and sawdust on the cage floors, to hide from what was happening. That wouldn't help them, but they didn't know it wouldn't.

Pekka chanted on. The passes that went with the incantation were second nature to her now. The other theoretical sorcerers stood by, lending strength and standing ready to rush to her aid if, in spite of everything, she faltered. That had happened before. She missed Master Siuntio—dead at the Algarvians' hands, too—and Master Ilmarinen. Fernao had saved her before. She didn't want to think about that, and, again, she didn't have to.

The animals were growing frantic now, the rats squeaking in fear and alarm. Pekka knew an abstract pity for them. *Better you than so many Kaunians or Unkerlanters or even Gyongyosians who are proud to volunteer their throats to the knife.* Glowing blue lines of sorcerous energy stretched between cages of young beasts and their grandparents. Those lines grew brighter by the moment, brighter and brighter and . . .

All at once, they flashed, intolerably brilliant. Pekka's eyes were closed against the glare by then, but that flash pierced her to the quick even so. When she opened her eyes afterwards, green-purple lines seemed printed across the world. Slowly, slowly, they faded.

Corruption's ripe reek filled the blockhouse, but only for a moment. The older rats and rabbits in the cages aged so catastrophically fast, they went past rotting to bare bones far quicker than the blink of an eye. The younger ones, by contrast, were propelled backwards chronologically, back to the days long before they were born. Had they ever truly existed, then? The mathematics there were indeterminate. But for sawdust and shavings, the cages that had held them were empty now.

"Divergent series," Pekka murmured. Sure enough, that was how to get the greatest release of sorcerous energy.

"We did everything as planned," Raahe said. "Now we find out if our calculations were right."

"That's the interesting part, or so Ilmarinen would say," Pekka replied. She hoped the cantankerous old master mage was all right. Losing him on top of all the other disasters of war would have been almost too much to bear. Deliberately forcing the thought from her mind, she turned to the crystallomancer. "Make the etheric connection to the *Searaven*."

"Aye, Mistress Pekka." The crystallomancer bent over her glassy sphere and murmured the charm that would link the blockhouse to the Kuusaman cruiser gliding along a ley line a few miles off the beaches of Becsehely. Her first attempt failed; the crystal refused to flare with light. She muttered something under her breath, then spoke aloud: "It *should* have worked. Let me try again."

"All right," Pekka said nervously. The amount of energy they'd released . . . If they'd miscalculated even by a little, it might have come down on the *Searaven* instead of the empty island at which they'd aimed.

But then the crystal did light up. After a moment, the flash faded and a naval officer's face appeared in the globe. "Here you are, Mistress Pekka," the crystallomancer said. "Here is Captain Waino."

"Powers above be praised," Pekka murmured as she hurried over to stand before the crystal. She raised her voice: "Hello, Captain. Please describe what—if anything—you and your crew observed on Becsehely."

"If anything?" Waino exclaimed. "Mistress, as far as that island's concerned, it's the end of the fornicating world—pardon my Valmieran."

Pekka smiled. "You're a naval man, and you talk like what you are."

"As you say, Mistress." Waino sounded like a man who'd just been through an earthquake. "Everything was normal as you please, and then lightning slammed down out of a clear sky and things blew up—it was as though every dragon in the world dropped a couple of eggs on Becsehely at the same time as the lightning hit it. But there weren't any dragons."

Behind Pekka, the other theoretical sorcerers cheered and applauded. Somebody gave her a glass of applejack. She didn't sip from it, but asked the officer, "What can you see of the island now?"

"Not forn . . ." Waino caught himself. "Not much. It's still covered in smoke and dust and steams. We will send men ashore for a further examination as things settle down."

"Very well, Captain. Thank you." Pekka nodded to the crystallomancer, who broke the etheric connection. After a pull at the apple brandy—now she'd earned it—Pekka said, "We *can* do this thing." The other theoretical sorcerers cheered again. They had glasses in their hands, too.

Trapani, Pekka thought again as they walked out to the sleighs to go back to the hostel. *Gyorvar, to teach Ekrekek Arpad a lesson he'll never forget. Cottbus, even, if King Swemmel ever needs the same kind of lesson.* She could feel the applejack, but the knowledge of power felt still more intoxicating.

As she always did, she rode with Fernao. The calendar said spring was here; the landscape wouldn't listen to the calendar for another month, maybe longer. Fresh snow had fallen the night before. By the low gray clouds overhead, more might come down any time. A reindeer-drawn sleigh remained the best way to get around.

Though blankets covered them and kept the driver from seeing what they did beneath, Fernao kept his hands to himself. He hadn't tried pushing things after Leino died. He knew Pekka well enough to understand that nothing would have been likelier to drive her away from him for good. And she'd stayed well apart from him on the trip out to the blockhouse. Now, for the first time time since that dreadful day she got the news, she let her head rest on his shoulder. *Maybe it's the applejack,* she thought. *Even if it isn't, I can blame it on the applejack.*

Fernao's narrow eyes widened. He put his arm around her. She discovered she was glad to have it there. She might not have been so glad had he tried to paw her, but he didn't. He didn't say anything, either. A Kuusaman would have. Most Lagoans, she thought, probably would. He was wise to keep quiet.

When they got to the hostel, they went upstairs together. Pekka's chamber was one floor higher than Fernao's, but she left the stairway with him. He still didn't speak, not till they stood inside his room. Then, at last, he said, "Thank you. I love you."

Do I really love him? Pekka wondered. *Do I love him in a way that might make my life whole again, or at least not ripped to pieces? Do I love him in a way that would make me want him to help raise Uto? Do I want to give Uto a half brother or half sister by him? I don't know, not for sure. But I think I'd better find out.*

"Before," she said, "our first times were accidents. This won't be. I mean it." Was she telling him or trying to convince herself? She wasn't sure of that, either.

Fernao just nodded. He said, "I've always meant it."

"I know," Pekka answered, and started to laugh. Men were supposed to be the ones who didn't want to get tied down. Women were supposed to look for loves that lasted. She and Fernao hadn't worked that way, though. *Maybe we will now,* she thought.

She stepped toward him at the same time as he was stepping toward her. When they embraced, the top of her head didn't come much past his shoulder. That sometimes bothered her. Today, it didn't seem to matter.

It mattered even less when they lay down together. Pekka wondered if she would, if she could, take any pleasure. She wouldn't have worried if she hadn't; sometimes having arms around her was enough. But Fernao took his time and paid what seemed like special attention to her. The only thing that could have kept her from eventually arching her back and moaning was . . . She couldn't imagine anything that could have. Certainly, nothing did.

As she lay with her legs entwined with his, she wondered how much that truly mattered. *Well,* she thought, lazy in the afterglow, *it can't hurt.*

All around Krasta, the servants at the mansion bustled like so many scurrying ants, getting the place ready for her brother's marriage to the horrible, bloodthirsty peasant wench with whom he'd unaccountably become infatuated. That was how Krasta looked at the match, at any rate, and nothing was going to make her change her mind. Hardly anything ever made her change her mind.

A wedding invitation wouldn't have done it. She was sure of that. It didn't matter, though; no invitation had been forthcoming. Skarnu and Merkela expected her to stay in her bedchamber by herself while they celebrated. They had their nerve, as far as she was concerned.

Worst of all was that they would probably get what they expected. Had she not been enormously pregnant, she might well have done her best to interrupt, to upstage, the ceremony she so despised. Being about the size of a behemoth, though, did put a crimp in such plans. All she wanted to do was have the baby and get it over with. She'd been feeling that way for most of the past month.

Even Bauska was pressed into the service of Skarnu and Merkela, which infuriated Krasta afresh. Her maidservant did show her a little sympathy when she had time to make an appearance, saying, "Oh, aye, milady, before I finally had Brindza, I would have paid anything to get her the blazes out of there."

"I should say so," Krasta exclaimed. She rested her hands on her enormous belly; her arms seemed too short to go round herself, though of course they weren't. And she had something else on her mind, too, something Bauska couldn't have dwelt upon: "And once this baby finally comes out, everyone will see it's a proper little blond, not some nasty Algarvian's bastard."

Bauska's mouth tightened. She left, even though Krasta hadn't told her she could. Krasta snarled something vile under her breath. To her way of thinking, having a normal, Valmieran-looking baby would automatically wash her clean of all the times she'd opened her legs for Colonel Lurcanio. Anyone would be able to look at the child and see at a glance that, when it really mattered, she'd lain with one of her own countrymen—and a nobleman to boot.

Her womb had been tightening every so often for some weeks. She'd got used to it, though she found it annoying— it squeezed on the baby, which was uncomfortable to her, and it evidently made the baby uncomfortable, too, for the little brat always did some extra thrashing and wiggling after things eased up. Krasta didn't like that, either; by now, the baby was big enough to kick and poke hard, and didn't care what tender parts of her it abused in the process.

Three days before her brother's wedding, the labor pains started in earnest. They were rhythmic, they were regular, and they were much more irksome than any pangs she'd known before. She cursed before calling for Bauska. She'd hoped the baby would wait till the middle of the marriage ceremony. If she'd started screaming for a midwife then, *that* would have taken everybody's mind off the catastrophe befalling her family.

But no such luck. When she became convinced these pains weren't going away, she shouted for Bauska. Her maidservant took her own sweet time getting there. When she did, Krasta demanded, "What was the name of that woman?"

"What woman, milady?" Bauska asked. Krasta had another pang then, and clenched her teeth against it. That told Bauska everything she needed to know. "Oh, the midwife," she said. "She's called Kudirka. Shall I have her summoned?"

"No, of course not," Krasta snapped. "I just wanted to know her name for no reason at all." And then, in case the maidservant was a fool or felt like pretending to be one, she made herself perfectly clear: "Aye, fetch her. This is going to be over, and I am going to show everybody what the truth is."

Bauska didn't answer that. She went away, which satisfied Krasta well enough. Presently, the carriage clattered down the walk and away from the mansion. After what was about an hour and seemed much longer, it came rattling back. By then, Krasta's labor pains had advanced to the point where she hardly noticed its return.

Kudirka walked into the bedchamber without bothering to knock. She was as broad-shouldered as an Unkerlanter and had a face like a frog, but something in her manner got through even to Krasta. "Take off your trousers, sweetie, and let's find out what's going on in there," the midwife said.

"All . . . right." Another pang seized Krasta before she could. Kudirka waited till it was over, then yanked the trousers off the marchioness herself. She proceeded to feel Krasta's belly and then to probe her a good deal more intimately than any lover ever had. Krasta yelped.

"Don't you worry about a thing," Kudirka told her. "Your hips are nice and wide. You won't have any trouble at all. A few hours of grunting, then some pushing, and then there's a baby in your arms. Easy as you please."

"Good," Krasta said. It all sounded simple and straightforward.

It didn't turn out to be that way, of course. It turned out to be boring and painful and exhausting. She discovered exactly why the process was called labor. Sweat plastered her hair to her forehead. It seemed to go on forever, and to hurt more and more as it continued.

At one point, Krasta started cursing every man she'd ever lain with, and cursing Kudirka, too. The midwife took it in stride. "It's a good sign, honey," she said. "It means you'll be ready to do your pushing pretty soon."

"There's more?" Krasta groaned. She'd been going through this for an eternity—it was getting dark outside, and she'd started in the morning. Kudirka only nodded. Then she went to the bedchamber and spoke to someone. Krasta paid little attention till Merkela came in. No matter how far gone she was, that registered. "Get out of here!" she squawked.

"No," the peasant woman answered. "I am going to see this baby before you have the chance to do anything with it or to it. If it's blond, it is. If it's not . . . I will know that, too."

Krasta cursed her as savagely as she knew how. She had no inhibitions left, none whatever. Merkela gave back as good as she got till Kudirka nudged her. Even she respected the midwife, and fell silent.

"I have to shit," Krasta said. "I have to shit more than I ever had to shit in my whole life."

"That's the baby," Kudirka said. "Go ahead and push it out."

Saying that was one thing; doing it turned out to be something else again. Krasta felt as if she were trying to pass a boulder, not a turd. And then, to her disgust, she *did* pass a turd. Without any fuss, Merkela disposed of the sheet on which it lay. *It must come of growing up on a farm,* Krasta thought. *She knows all about turds.*

Then she stopped thinking altogether, stopped everything except struggling to force the baby out of her. She hardly heard Kudirka's encouragement. The world, everything but her labor, seemed very far away. She took a deep breath, then let out an explosive noise somewhere between a grunt and a squeal.

"That's it!" the midwife said. "Do that twice more, three times at the most, and you'll have yourself a baby."

Krasta didn't know how many times she made that desperate effort. She was beyond caring by then. At last, though, just when she seemed certain to split in two, everything suddenly got easier. "The baby's head is out," Merkela said.

"A couple of more pushes and it's done," Kudirka added. "The head is the big part. Everything else will be easy."

For a miracle, she was right. She guided out the baby's shoulders and torso and legs. She and Merkela tied off the umbilical cord. Merkela cut it with a pair of shears. Krasta hardly noticed that. She was busy passing the afterbirth, a disgusting bit of business no one had told her about, and one that cost her the undersheet on her bed.

"You have a boy," Merkela said. She held the squalling baby in the crook of her arm with practiced ease. Not so long before, her son by Skarnu had been so tiny.

Through a haze of exhaustion, Krasta said, "I'll name him Valnu, for his father."

Kudirka said nothing at all. Merkela laughed and laughed. The wolfish quality in the peasant woman's mirth made Krasta shiver no matter how weary she was. Merkela held the baby under her nose, so close her eyes almost crossed. "You were an Algarvian's whore. I don't care who else you might have spread your legs for, but you were an Algarvian's whore, and by what comes out of your own twat you prove what went into it."

As newborns often are, Krasta's baby son was born almost bald. But the fine fuzz on his head was of a strawberry tinge no purely Valmieran baby's head would have had. It was, in fact, nearly identical in color to the hair of Bauska's bastard half-breed daughter, Brindza.

Laughing still, Merkela said, "If you're going to name it for its father, you stinking slut, you can call it Lurcanio."

The weariness Krasta knew then had nothing to do with the ordeal she'd just been through. She'd spent so much time and effort trying to convince everyone, including herself, that the child she was carrying was indeed Valnu's. She'd—mostly—made herself believe it. She'd made everyone else wonder. And now, to be betrayed by something as trivial as a few strands of hair on the baby's oddly cone-shaped head (she presumed that would change, even if the brat's wretched hair color never did) . . . It all seemed most unfair, as did anything that didn't go just the way she wished it would have.

"I—" she began.

"Shut up." Merkela's voice was flat and hard and vicious, the voice of a wildcat seeing prey it had long stalked at last helpless before it. She gave the baby to Kudirka, then grabbed the scissors she'd used to cut the cord. "I've waited too cursed long for this, by the powers above, but now you get what's coming to you." She grabbed a shock of Krasta's hair and hacked it off not a finger's breadth from her scalp.

"Powers below eat you, you can't—" Krasta said.

Merkela slapped her in the face. Only Lurcanio had ever dared do that to her before. "Shut up, I told you," Merkela snapped. She closed the shears and aimed them at one of Krasta's eyes. "What I'm doing is the least of what you deserve—the least, do you hear me? You can take it, or I'll give you plenty more. I'd love to, do you hear me? You don't know how much I'd love to." The shears jerked closer.

Krasta closed her eyes and flinched. She couldn't help herself. At any other time, she would have fought, regardless of whether she had a weapon of her own. Exhausted as she'd never been exhausted, sick in spirit as well, she kept her eyes closed and let Merkela do as she would. At last, though, the hateful *snip-snip* of the shears made her exclaim, "Futter you!"

"A Valmieran futters me," Merkela retorted. *Snip-snip.* "I didn't have a stinking redhead leave silver on the dresser every time he stuck it in." *Snip-snip.*

It wasn't like that. But Krasta didn't say it. What point? Merkela wouldn't have believed her, and wouldn't have cared even if she had believed her. At last, it was over. Kudirka set the baby—the half-Algarvian bastard, just like Bauska's—on Krasta's breast. It rooted and began to suck. Krasta didn't burst into tears. She was too worn for that. But, one after another, they trickled down her cheeks.

No one had ever formally released Skarnu from his service in the Valmieran army. And, unlike most of his countrymen, he'd never given up the fight against the Algarvians. And so, when he proposed to Merkela that he wed her while wearing a captain's uniform, she nodded. "That's how I first saw you, you know, coming toward the farmhouse with Raunu at your side," she said.

Remembering what he'd gone through during his kingdom's inglorious collapse almost five years before, he answered, "I hope I'll be cleaner at the ceremony than I was then."

Merkela laughed. Laughter came easy for her now that she'd finally proved right about Krasta. It was as if she'd won a brand-new victory against the Algarvians long after they'd left Priekule. And so, in a way, she had. Skarnu could have felt victorious about his own sister, too. He didn't. All he felt was sad. Krasta had made the wrong choice, and now she was paying for it. Hundreds, thousands, of women across Valmiera and Jelgava had paid as much. A good many men who'd collaborated with the red-heads had paid or would pay far more.

"Tomorrow," Merkela murmured. She laid a fond hand on Skarnu's arm. "It still hardly feels real. It feels like something out of one of the fairy tales my grandmother would tell me when I was a little girl."

"You had better get used to it, milady," Skarnu said solemnly, "for it's the truth." That he was marrying at all still struck him as surprising. That he was marrying a commoner would have seemed treason to his class before the war.

Little Gedominu, who was toddling around the bed-chamber they shared, fell down. The damage, obviously, was anywhere from minimal to imaginary, but he wailed, "Mama!" and started to cry anyway.

Merkela scooped him up. "It's all right," she said. After a moment or two in her arms, it *was* all right, too. Skarnu wished his own hurts were so easily fixed. That thought had hardly crossed his mind when Merkela flicked one of those hurts. She ruffled Gedominu's fine, golden hair and mur-mured, "You look the way you're supposed to. That's more than anybody can say about your nasty little cousin."

Skarnu sighed. He wished Krasta's baby had looked like a proper Valmieran. That would have taken the taint of scandal off the whole family. As things were, he sighed and said, "It's not the baby's fault."

"It certainly isn't," Merkela agreed. "It's *her* fault." She still didn't want to call Krasta Skarnu's sister. Ever since they'd first learned Krasta was keeping company with a redhead, they—and Merkela especially—had denied Skarnu even had a sister. That was harder now that they were living in the same house with Krasta, but Merkela managed. She went on, "She was going to name the baby Valnu."

"Too bad she couldn't," Skarnu said. "Sooner or later, these things have to come to an end."

"Not yet, by the powers above," Merkela declared. "When she had Lurcanio's bastard, I told her she should name it for him."

Skarnu sighed. "That doesn't help, you know. Krasta's

going to be your sister-in-law whether you like it or not."
He held up a hand. "You don't. You've told me. You don't
need to tell me again. Just remember, Valnu put in a good
word for her. He'd be dead if she'd opened her mouth at the
wrong time. Then there wouldn't have been any doubt who
the baby's father was."

"She opened her mouth at plenty of the wrong times,"
Merkela said. While Skarnu was still spluttering over that,
his fiancée added, "If she'd done it once more, she
wouldn't have had the little bastard in the first place." That
only made Skarnu splutter again.

In the end, he decided not to push the argument. He
wasn't going to change Merkela's mind. Part of him—not
half, but close to it—agreed with her, anyhow. What he
most wanted now was to get through the wedding ceremony
without any fresh scandal. Enlisting Merkela in that effort
was bound to be futile. Trying to enlist Krasta in it was
bound to be worse than futile. Skarnu had spent a lot of
time away from home, but not so much that he didn't know
what to do in such cases.

He approached Valmiru, who nodded wisely. "You are
holding the ceremony out of doors, is it not so?" the butler
said. When Skarnu agreed that he was—he could hardly
deny it, not with the pavilion already up behind the mansion—Valmiru nodded again. "Very well. I shall make a
point of allowing no physical disruption. I cannot necessarily promise there will be no commotion from within the
house, however."

"I understand that. Believe me, Valmiru, I'll be grateful
for anything you can do—and I'll make it worth your while,
too," Skarnu said. The butler's expression didn't change in
any way Skarnu could have defined, but he contrived to
look pleased nonetheless. They were indoors. Skarnu
looked up at the sky even so. "It had better not rain, that's
all I've got to say."

To his vast relief, it didn't. The wedding day dawned fine
and mild. It might have come from the end of springtime,
not the beginning. The ceremony was set for noon. Guests
started arriving a couple of hours early. Servants steered
them around the mansion to the pavilion in back of it. Giv-

ing the temporary structure that name could not disguise its origins: it was, in fact, an outsized tent borrowed from the Valmieran army. Being an officer who'd never been formally discharged had certain advantages when it came to laying one's hands on such things.

Every now and then, an alert listener—Skarnu, for instance—might have heard a newborn baby wailing inside the mansion. Most of the guests knew by then that the baby had hair of not quite the right color. A couple of people clapped Skarnu on the back in sympathy. Valnu gave him a comic shrug almost exaggerated enough to have come from an Algarvian, as if to say, *Well, it* could *have been mine.*

At one point, not long before the ceremony was to begin, a listener would not have needed to be alert in the least to hear Krasta trying to come outside and expressing her detailed opinions of the people who kept her from doing so. She waxed eloquent, in a vulgar way. Several people shrugged at Skarnu now.

White-mustached old Marstalu, the Duke of Klaipeda, conducted the ceremony. As far as Skarnu was concerned, conducting a wedding was about what he was good for. He'd commanded the Valmieran troops opposing Algarve in the early days of the war, and had had not a clue about beating back Mezentio's men. His nephew had been a collaborator, but that brush didn't tar him.

"He's splendid looking," Merkela whispered as she and Skarnu approached him. Skarnu thought she looked quite splendid herself, in tunic and trousers of glowing green silk, the color of fertility in Valmiera since the days of the Kaunian Empire. That it went well with his own darker green captain's uniform was a happy coincidence.

Marstalu looked like a kindly grandfather. He spoke classical Kaunian as if it were his birthspeech. He had enough years on him to make that seem almost plausible (his backward cast of mind during the fighting made it seem plausible, too, but Skarnu did his best not to dwell on that). Skarnu's own command of the old language left something to be desired; Merkela knew next to none. But they'd rehearsed. When the duke stopped and looked expectantly at them, that meant he'd just asked if they agreed to live together as man and wife. "Aye," Skarnu said loudly. Merkela echoed the agreement in a softer voice.

"It is accomplished," Duke Marstalu boomed, still in classical Kaunian. Then, the formal part of the ceremony concluded, he grinned and switched to ordinary, everyday Valmieran: "Kiss her, boy, before I beat you to it."

"Aye, sir." Skarnu saluted. "I've never had an order I was gladder to obey." He gathered Merkela in. All the guests cheered and whooped and clapped their hands. People pelted the newlyweds with flowers and nuts—more symbols of fertility. Some of the nuts flew back and forth in among the crowd, as if rival armies were tossing eggs at each other. Skarnu had seen that happen at other weddings, too.

After the ceremony, people ate and drank and danced and gossiped. If any more squawks came from the mansion, the noise the guests made drowned them out. Somebody slapped Viscount Valnu's face. Skarnu was at the far end of the pavilion then, and never did find out whether Valnu had offended a man or a woman.

And then, towards evening, the guests began to drift away. Valnu said, "I had a splendid time." Getting slapped hadn't bothered him in the least. He leered and added, "But not nearly so fine a time as the two of you are going to have—I'm sure of that." He kissed Merkela and then, for good measure, kissed Skarnu, too. After that, whistling and grinning, he took his leave.

"Impossible man," Merkela said, to which Skarnu could only nod. She glanced over to her new husband. "Are you *sure* he was on our side during the occupation?"

"Positive," Skarnu answered. His new bride sighed.

Servants had charge of little Gedominu for the evening. Skarnu held the door to the bedchamber open for Merkela. After she went in, he closed it and barred it behind them. She smiled. "No one's going to bother us tonight, and I won't try to get away."

"You'd better not." Skarnu took her in his arms. It wasn't as if they hadn't made love before; the son they weren't watching proved that. But the first time as man and wife still seemed special. "I love you," Skarnu told Merkela just before pleasure overwhelmed him.

He wasn't sure she heard him; she wasn't far from her own joy. But then, as their hearts both slowed, she reached up to stroke his cheek and said, "You must," in wondering tones. Some small part of her must have wondered if he would abandon her when he could. It being a wedding night, Skarnu got other chances to prove how wrong that was.

He and Merkela were both sodden with slumber when someone rapped on the bedchamber door much too early the next morning. His first coherent words were some of the harsher ones he'd picked up as a soldier. But then Valmiru's voice came through the door: "Your pardon, my lord, milady, but King Gainibu summons you to the palace at once. A carriage awaits."

That put a different light on things. "We'll be down directly," Skarnu said. He and Merkela dressed as fast as they could, dragged brushes through their hair, and hurried out to the front of the mansion, where a carriage did indeed wait. Half an hour later, they were bowing before the King of Valmiera.

"Congratulations to you both," Gainibu said. He still looked like a man who sometimes had too much to drink, but he didn't sound like a man who'd done it lately. Like his kingdom, he was recovering from the occupation. He went on, "I've been thinking about what sort of present to give you, and I believe I've found a good one."

"You're too kind, your Majesty," Skarnu murmured. Merkela kept silent. Speaking to the king had seemed even stranger to her than marrying a noble.

Gainibu said, "The estate formerly held by the late Count Enkuru and his son, the late Count Simanu, has been adjudged forfeit to the Crown because of their treason and collaboration with the foe." Skarnu nodded. That was the noble estate nearest Pavilosta. He'd had a good deal to do with Enkuru's demise; he and Merkela had both had a great deal to do with killing Simanu. The king continued, "I have it in mind to raise that estate from a county to a marquisate and to confer it on the two of you. That way, I know it will stay in loyal hands. What do you say to the notion?"

Skarnu glanced at Merkela. Her eyes glowed with astonished delight. She found words now: "We say, Thank you, your Majesty. Thank you from the bottom of our hearts."

With a chuckle, Gainibu remarked. "She's speaking for you already, is she? Well, I'm glad you're pleased. This will also let you get away from Krasta, and from her unfortunately irregular offspring. Oh, aye, I've heard about that. And may I make one suggestion?" He didn't wait for anyone's approval before giving it: "Take as many of your household staff as care to go."

Merkela laughed out loud at that. A little more reluctantly, so did Skarnu. He didn't think his sister would be very happy. He also didn't think King Gainibu cared.

For as long as he'd seen only soldiers, Sidroc had been able to hold on to his admiration for the Algarvians. Their fighting men knew what they were doing. Even with the odds against them, as they certainly were now, footsoldiers and behemoth crews and the men who served egg-tossers and dragonfliers went about their jobs with a matter-of-fact competence he'd never seen from his own people, from the Unkerlanters, or from the Yaninans (not that that last was saying much).

Now, though, Plegmund's Brigade was actually inside Algarve, fighting not to take the war to the Unkerlanters but to hold them out of Trapani. Sidroc and his comrades weren't just dealing with Algarvian soldiers any more. They had to deal with Algarvian civilians, too. And Algarvian civilians, to put it mildly, left him unimpressed.

"Get your crap out of the road, lady!" he shouted to a woman who seemed intent on taking everything she owned with her as she fled east—this though she had only a tiny handcart in which to carry it all. "Get it out of the way or we'll fornicating well kick it out of the way for you."

The woman in question was one of the plump, middle-aged sort who make a life out of running their towns—and their neighbors' affairs. Getting orders rather than giving them didn't sit well with her. "I don't know what the world is coming to," she said, "when we have barbarians loose in the streets of our cities."

"Futter you, lady," Sidroc said cheerfully. "You don't let us do what we're supposed to be doing, King Swemmel's boys'll get in here. You think we're barbarians? We're on your side, you stupid twat. The Unkerlanters take this place, about twenty of 'em'll line up, and they'll *all* futter you—if they don't decide you're too stinking ugly to waste cock on and bash in your stupid head instead."

His squad—Forthwegians and a couple of blonds from the Phalanx of Valmiera, which had fallen on even harder times than Plegmund's Brigade—laughed raucously. The Algarvian woman gaped as if she couldn't believe her ears. "I shall find a civilized man," she said, and flounced off.

She didn't have to flounce far before finding Lieutenant Puliano. He cut her off as she started to spin her tale of woe. "Shut up," he said. "I heard Corporal Sidroc, and I know bloody well he's right." He waved. "Go on through her stuff, boys. She doesn't need it, and it's just in the way."

Sidroc kicked a brass-wired bird cage as if it were a football on a pitch. The door flew open as it rolled. A couple of finches from Siaulia—brilliant little birds, all scarlet and gold and green—flew out of it and away. He hoped they'd do all right so far from home. The war wasn't their fault.

"Keep moving!" the lieutenant called. "You see more junk in the road, just go on through it."

Ceorl did just that, and seemed to take considerable pleasure in trampling the possessions the Algarvians in the town had spent a lifetime gathering. "You ask me, these whoresons don't deserve to win the war," he said. "If they can't figure out what in blazes is important and what they'd better leave behind, the powers below are welcome to 'em."

By all the signs, the powers below were going to get their hands on a lot of Algarvians regardless of whether they knew what to do with their goods. *And they'll probably get their hands on me, too,* Sidroc thought. He shrugged. He'd stuck with the redheads this far. He couldn't very well abandon them now.

He couldn't even strip off his uniform, find civilian clothes, and do his best to pretend he'd never been in the army. He looked about as unlike an Algarvian as it was possible for anyone this side of a black Zuwayzi to look. He would have had a better chance pretending to be an Unkerlanter.

Some few Algarvian soldiers, at least, were doing their best to slide out of the war. Maybe some of them got away with it. Not all of them did. As the men of Plegmund's Brigade tramped out of the town, they passed three redheaded corpses hanging from trees by the side of the road. The placards tied round their necks warned, THIS IS WHAT DESERTERS GET.

"They deserve it," Lieutenant Puliano said. "Anybody who gives up on his kingdom when it needs him the most deserves everything that happens to him, and more besides."

The Forthwegians in Algarvian service solemnly nodded. Unlike the redheads, they couldn't even try to go home again. The handful of blonds from Valmiera also nodded. They *really* couldn't go home again. They were far worse traitors in the eyes of their countrymen than the men of Plegmund's Brigade were to theirs.

But Sidroc had some gloomy thoughts of his own as he marched by the hanged deserters. *Even Mezentio's men are starting to see there's no hope left for them. If they can see it, I'd have to be a cursed fool to miss it myself.* He knew he wasn't the brightest fellow around. If he'd ever had any doubts on that score, spending years getting compared to his clever cousin Ealstan would have cured them.

He laughed, none too pleasantly. *If Ealstan was so fornicating smart, why did he fall in love with a Kaunian girl? I wonder if he ever found out he was getting that redheaded officer's sloppy seconds.* He laughed again. *I hope so.*

"Watch your step here, boys," Puliano called. "You don't want to go off the road, or you'd end up arse-deep in mud. This is swampy country."

"It doesn't look too bad," somebody said. And, indeed, it didn't. In fact, it looked greener than most of the firmer ground farther west. On dry land, spring was just starting to make itself known. Here, though, the swamp plants, or most of them, had kept their color through the winter. The road might almost have been passing through a meadow.

Sudaku stepped up alongside Sidroc. In his Valmieran-flavored Algarvian, he said, "This swamp is a sign we grow near to Trapani. I passed through the capital and through this country on the way west to join the Phalanx of Valmiera."

"Getting near Trapani, eh?" Sidroc said, and the blond's head bobbed up and down. Sidroc grunted. "That doesn't sound so good."

"No," the Kaunian said. "But, by now, what is left for us to do but die like heroes?"

Sidroc grunted again. "I didn't sign up to be a hero."

"But what else are we, fighting to the death for a cause surely lost?" Sudaku persisted.

"Who knows? Come to that, who cares?" Sidroc said. "Besides, if we lose—when we lose—who's going to call us heroes? Winners are heroes. They get the girls, and they don't get their uniforms mussed. In the stories, we're just the fellows who blaze at them and miss."

"Everyone is a hero in his own story," the Kaunian said. "The only trouble is, our stories, I fear, will be ending soon."

Before Sidroc could answer that—not that it needed much answering, for it seemed pretty obviously true—someone toward the rear of the weary, shambling column of men let out a frightened shout: "Dragons! Unkerlanter dragons!"

Looking back over his shoulder, Sidroc spied the great rock-gray shapes bearing down on his comrades—and on him. He wasn't ready for his story to end quite yet. "Into the mud!" he yelled, and dove for the side of the road.

It was the only hope the soldiers had, and they made the most of it they could. Like Sidroc, they floundered into the swamp as far as they could go. Some of them blazed. Others just tried to cover themselves in ooze. The dragons roared fiercely as they belched out fire. None of the flames came too close to Sidroc, but he felt the heat from them all the same. What happened to the men who'd stayed on the road wasn't pretty.

Survivors gathered themselves and trudged on. That was all they could do. Ceorl was as filthy as Sidroc. "You son of a whore, I thought they'd've got rid of you a long time ago," he said. "You're tougher than I gave you credit for."

"Thanks, I suppose," Sidroc said.

Up the road was a town called Laterza. It had taken as much damage as any other Algarvian town not far from Trapani. Standing in the middle of the main street, though, as if on a normal day, was a captain wearing a mage's emblem. "Ah, good," he said when he saw what sorts of soldiers Lieutenant Puliano led. "A band of mercenaries and auxiliaries." Sidroc didn't like his tone or the sneer on his face. *I've been through too much for him to have any business looking at me like that,* he thought. The mage went on, "You will furnish me all your Kaunians at once."

Sidroc didn't like the sound of that at all. Neither, evidently, did Puliano, who said, "Oh, I will, will I? And why is that?"

"Because it will aid the war, and because I, your superior, order it," the captain replied. *So I can kill them,* Sidroc translated in his own mind.

He wasn't the only one who made the same translation. Sudaku pushed his way forward. The man from the Phalanx of Valmiera stuck his stick in the mage's face. "Do you want anything to do with me or my countrymen?" he asked coldly.

"Arrest this man!" the mage gabbled.

"What for?" Lieutenant Puliano said with a smile. "Seems like a pretty good question to me. Maybe you'd better answer it."

"Do you want anything to do with me or mine?" Sudaku repeated.

The mage had nerve. Whatever Algarvians lacked, that was rarely it. He thought for a long time before finally shaking his head. And even after he did, he shook a fist at Lieutenant Puliano. "It's because of people like you that our kingdom's in the state it's in," he said bitterly.

"Because of people like me?" Puliano returned. "Have you looked in a mirror any time lately?"

"What's that supposed to mean?" the mage demanded. He really didn't know. Sidroc could see as much. That was as alarming as anything else that had happened to him lately— a pretty frightening thought, when you got down to it.

Sudaku said, "I think you had better disappear. I think that if you do not disappear, something bad will happen to you."

Again, even with a stick in his face, the Algarvian wizard seemed on the point of saying no. If he had, the blond from the Phalanx of Valmiera would have blazed his brains out. Sidroc was sure of that. The mage evidently came to the same conclusion. He turned on his heel and stalked away. His stiff back radiated outrage.

"Poor fellow," the Kaunian said. "He is angry at me because I do not propose to let him kill me. Well, too bad." He turned to Lieutenant Puliano. "Thank you, sir, for thinking I am worth more to Algarve alive."

"Mages are a pack of cursed fools," the redhead said. "If they were half as smart as they think they are, they'd be twice as smart as they really are. I know what a good soldier's worth. I haven't got any idea what that bastard's worth, and why should I waste time finding out?" He looked around at his ragtag followers. "Come on, boys. Let's get going. Wizards or no wizards, we've still got a war to fight."

How much longer can we keep fighting? Sidroc wondered. He had no idea. But the stick in his hand still held charges. The Unkerlanters hadn't nailed him yet. *They won't have an easy time doing it, either,* he told himself, and marched deeper into Algarve, on toward Trapani.

Marshal Rathar muttered something vile under his breath. His army had just tried to throw another bridgehead across the Scamandro, and the Algarvians had just crushed it. "Can't be helped," General Vatran said philosophically. "We still haven't built up enough men or supplies to do a proper job yet."

Logically, Rathar knew that was true. But logic had only so much to do with it. He glanced over at the portrait of King Swemmel on the wall. His imagination had to be running away with him, but he thought the king was glaring at him in particular. "It could have worked," he said. "It was worth a try."

"Oh, aye." Vatran nodded. "That's why we gave it a blaze. But it wasn't a sure thing, and it didn't pan out. Won't be long now before we can do it right."

"I know." But Rathar, still eyeing Swemmel's portrait, had a bad feeling there would be some unpleasant conversations with the king before that happened. He wondered if he could get away with telling the crystallomancers to tell Swemmel he was indisposed. Probably not, worse luck.

Vatran shuffled through leaves of paper. He pulled one out and handed it to Rathar. "Here, lord Marshal. You said you wanted to see these."

"I need to see them, if that's what I think it is. That's not the same thing as wanting to." Rathar took the paper and glanced through it. Sure enough, it was what he thought it was. He handed it back to Vatran. "Stinking werewolves."

Vatran made a sour face. "Trust the Algarvians to come up with a name like that."

"I don't care what you call them," Rathar said. "They're a pack of cursed nuisances, and no mistake."

He recognized the irony in his words. While Mezentio's men occupied great stretches of Unkerlant, his own countrymen had made their lives miserable, raiding their garrisons, sabotaging ley lines, and doing anything else they could to hurt the foe. Now, with Unkerlanter forces inside Algarve, the boot was on the other foot. The redheads behind his lines were doing their best to disrupt his operations. *Werewolves* was a fancier, more grandiose name than *irregulars,* but they did the same job.

With a shrug, Vatran said, "When we catch 'em, we hang 'em or we blaze 'em or we boil 'em. That way, they don't turn into anything worse than a nuisance."

A couple of years before, Algarvian generals had to have been saying the same thing about Unkerlanter irregulars. Rathar had the same response they must have had: "Once we win the war, the trouble will go away." Mezentio's men hadn't won the war. If he didn't win it now, he would deserve whatever Swemmel chose to do to him.

Vatran shuffled more papers. "There's still trouble with bandits back in the Duchy of Grelz, too."

Bandits, of course, was another name for irregulars and werewolves. Some of the Grelzers who'd aligned themselves with Mezentio and against Swemmel had been in grim earnest, and kept up their fight against Unkerlant even after the Algarvians were driven east and out of their duchy. But that problem had the same answer as the other one: "If we win here, the bandits will quiet down—and if they don't, we'll root 'em out one at a time if we have to."

"Aye—makes sense," Vatran agreed.

"Now, the next question, and the one where losing the bridgehead really hurts," Rathar said. "How far west have the islanders come, and how close to Trapani have they got?"

One of Vatran's white eyebrows twitched. "They're within about eighty miles, sir," he answered unhappily. "Still moving forward pretty fast, too, curse them."

"They're our allies," Rathar said. "We're not supposed to curse them. We're supposed to congratulate them." He looked east. "Congratulations—curse you."

Vatran laughed, though it really wasn't funny. "Of course, one reason they're moving so fast is that the redheads have all their best soldiers—all the best of whatever they've got left—pointed at us."

"That old, old song," Rathar said. "We're beating them anyhow, the bastards. And we're beating them in spite of all the funny magic they're throwing at us."

"Every time they try something new, our mages have fresh hysterics," Vatran said.

"They've been doing that ever since the redheads started killing Kaunians," Rathar replied. "Sometimes they find an answer, sometimes things just go wrong for the redheads, and sometimes we have so many men and behemoths, it doesn't matter anyway."

Vatran let out a long, heartfelt sigh. "I'll be glad when it's finally over, and that's the truth." He ran a hand through his curly white hair. "I'm too cursed old to go through what the Algarvians have put us through."

"Not obvious it'll be over even after we lick Mezentio," Rathar said. "King Swemmel hasn't said what he'll do about Gyongyos then. Maybe we'll all pack up and head west—a long way west."

"Maybe," Vatran agreed. "But do you know what, lord Marshal? Even if we do, I won't be nervous about it, the way I have been ever since we started fighting the redheads. Even if the Gongs should somehow lick us—and I don't think they can do it—it wouldn't be the end of the world. If the Algarvians had beaten us, our kingdom was dead. They'd've ruled us like we were some barbarian principality up in Siaulia, and they'd never have let us back up on our feet again."

Since Rathar thought the older general was right, he didn't argue with him. The war with Algarve was a war to the knife, no doubt about it. Mezentio's men might not have treated Unkerlant and its people quite so harshly as they had the Kaunians in Forthweg, but they wouldn't have made easy masters. They *hadn't* made easy masters in the parts of Unkerlant they'd held.

They're arrogant whoresons, and it cost them, Rathar thought. *If they'd pretended to come as liberators from Swemmel's hard rule, half the kingdom would have gone over to them. But they didn't think they needed to worry about what we thought. They gave Grelz an Algarvian for a king. They showed everybody they were even worse than Swemmel—and they paid for it. And now we'll be the masters in big chunks of Algarve, and we won't be sweet to the redheads, either.*

Someone hurried into the headquarters—an Unkerlanter major. "Marshal Rather!" he called. "I've got important news."

Rathar looked up from the map table. "I'm here," he said. "What's gone wrong now?" By the man's tone, something had. Vatran looked up, too, sharply. He picked up his mug of tea and started to sip from it.

"Here, lord Marshal," the newcomer said. "I'll have to show you." He took a couple of steps toward the map table—and then stopped and yanked his short officer's stick from his belt and swung it toward Rathar.

The Marshal of Unkerlant had half a heartbeat to know what a fool he'd been. *This is how General Gurmun died*, flashed through his mind. If the Algarvians could sorcerously disguise one of their own to look like an Unkerlanter up in Forthweg, why not on their own soil, too?

But the beam never bit into his flesh. Vatran flung his heavy earthenware mug at the false major's face. It caught him right in the teeth. He howled and clutched at himself, and his blaze went wild. Before his finger could find its way into the blazing hole again, Vatran and Rathar were both grappling with him. Rathar wrenched the stick out of his hands. The shouts and groans from the map chamber brought more soldiers rushing in. They seized the major and, after some fumbling, tied him up.

"He's gone mad, sir," a captain—a veritable Unkerlanter captain—exclaimed.

"No, I don't think so," Rathar answered. "I think if we leave him alone for a few hours, he'll start looking like one of Mezentio's majors, not like one of ours." He switched to Algarvian and addressed the would-be assassin: "Isn't that right, Major—or whatever your real rank happens to be?"

"I don't know what you're talking about," the fellow replied in Unkerlanter holding no trace of any accent save that of Cottbus—certainly no Algarvian trill. His mouth bled where the mug had caught him—and where the two Unkerlanter officers had hit him in the fight that followed.

"Aye, tell us King Mezentio didn't send you after the marshal," General Vatran jeered.

"He didn't," the man replied with a bloody grin. "King Swemmel did."

If he aimed to produce consternation in the headquarters, he succeeded. Horrified silence fell. Rathar himself broke it, saying, "You lie. If his Majesty wants me dead, he has no need to sneak in a murderer. He could simply arrest me, and his will would be done."

"You'd be too likely to rise against him, and the men are too likely to follow you," the fellow said.

All that had a certain ring of truth, regardless of whether

the failed assassin was what he claimed to be. All the more reason, then, for Marshal Rather to speak in ringing tones: "You lie. I am loyal, and his Majesty knows it." He turned to his men. "Take this lying wretch away. Do nothing to him for one day except keeping him under close guard. When his looks change and show him for the Algarvian he is, let me know."

They dragged the false major out of the headquarters. Rathar hoped with all his heart the man *would* show himself to be an Algarvian. If he didn't . . . The marshal didn't want to think about that. Being possessed of a disciplined mind, he didn't. Instead, he told Vatran, "Thank you," and asked, "How were you so ready there?"

Vatran shrugged. "Something about the way he looked, something about the way he sounded—it didn't feel quite right."

"He just seemed eager to me," Rathar said.

"Maybe that was it," Vatran said.

Rathar wondered if he was joking. After a moment, the marshal decided Vatran wasn't. After almost four grinding years of war against Algarve, how many Unkerlanter officers had any eagerness left? Algarvians, now . . . Algarvians went into everything with panache. This fellow hadn't looked or sounded like one, but he'd seemed enough like one to make Vatran at least wonder—and that, in turn, had ended up saving Rathar's neck.

"Thank you," the marshal said again.

"You're welcome," Vatran replied. He lowered his voice: "Now we just have to hope the lousy bugger really is a redhead."

"Indeed," Rathar said, and said no more. *Could* Swemmel have been so daft as to choose this moment to try to be rid of him? It didn't seem likely, but the same held true for a lot of things Swemmel did.

The crystallomancer's call came long after midnight. "He's an Algarvian," reported the officer charged with guarding important captives.

"Powers above be praised," Rathar said, and slept sound the rest of the night.

Nine

Every now and then, Talsu began seeing men in Jelgavan uniform in Skrunda. He didn't see many of them, not compared to the swarms of Kuusaman soldiers who kept going through his home town. The ones he did see roused mixed feelings in him. He was glad his kingdom showed signs of being able to defend itself again, at least with the help of its allies (he tried not to think of them as rescuers). For the Jelgavan soldiers, he felt nothing but pity. He'd been one himself. He knew what it was like.

For a while, he hoped things might have changed since the disaster that led to Jelgava's collapse four and a half years before. After all, King Donalitu had spent most of that time in exile in Lagoas. The Lagoans had a pretty good notion of what was what. Maybe Donalitu had learned something in Setubal—though the edicts he'd issued since his return argued against it.

But the first Jelgavan officer Talsu saw strutting through the streets of Skrunda smashed his hopes. The major was young and slim and handsome, not fat and homely like Colonel Dzirnavu, Talsu's old regimental commander. But the noble's badge on his chest and the way he shouted and screamed at the luckless men who had to follow him made memories Talsu would sooner have forgotten come flooding back.

He didn't say anything about the fellow to his father. Never having gone into the army, Traku didn't know what it was like. He idealized it in his mind, too. Even after the way Jelgava collapsed proved its army anything but ideal, Talsu's father didn't want to hear criticism and complaints.

In whispers—the only sort of talk that gave even a hope of privacy in the crowded flat—Talsu spilled out his worries to Gailisa when they both should have been asleep. "Nothing has changed," he said, despair in his voice. "*Nothing*. The same arrogant idiots still have charge of us. And if we ever have to do any fighting again—"

"Powers above keep it from happening," his wife broke in, also whispering.

"Aye, powers above keep it from happening indeed," Talsu agreed. "If we ever have to do any fighting again, whoever we go up against will roll over us, same as the Algarvians did. Our men will want their officers dead, and how can you fight like that?"

Instead of answering what was, Talsu was sure, an unanswerable argument, Gailisa twisted in the narrow bed they shared to kiss him. If she hoped to distract him, she succeeded. His arms went around her. Her breasts pressed against him through the thin fabric of their pyjama tunics. A moment later, she laughed very quietly. He was pressing against her somewhere, too.

He slid a hand under her tunic. She sighed, again softly, as he caressed her. His parents had the flat's only bedroom to themselves. His sister lay sleeping in her own cot only a few feet away. If he and Gailisa wanted to make love, they had to do it stealthily. Ausra was good about staying asleep—so good, Talsu wondered whether she sometimes knew what was going on and simply pretended not to—but he didn't want to bother her.

Gailisa stroked him, too. He kissed her and reached under her trousers. She rolled onto her back and let her legs slide open to make things easier for him. Then she slithered down the bed and unbuttoned his fly. Her mouth was warm and wet and sweet. Talsu set a hand on the back of her head, half stroking her hair, half urging her on. If she'd kept going till he exploded, he wouldn't have minded at all.

But, after a little while, she turned her back on him. Still lying on his side, he hiked her pyjama bottoms down just far enough. She stuck out her backside, and he went into her from behind. "Ah," she whispered.

He said her name as he began to move. She pushed back against him. The bed creaked, but less from the side-to-side motion than it would have with him atop her. And, when

Gailisa shuddered with pleasure a few minutes later, she put her face against the pillow so only a tiny sound escaped. Talsu tried to stay as quiet as he could, too. The joy that filled him, though, made him have trouble noticing how little or how much noise he made.

Ausra didn't stir in the other bed. Either he'd been quiet enough or she was more than polite enough. At the moment, Talsu didn't much care which. He leaned up on an elbow and kissed Gailisa, who twisted back toward him so their lips could meet. They both set their clothes to rights. Talsu happily fell asleep a few minutes later. Thoughts of Jelgavan soldiers and Jelgavan officers never entered his mind.

He wished he could have gone on not thinking about them, too. But, two days later, a sharp knock on the door to the flat made both him and his father look up from their work. "Sounds like business," Traku said hopefully.

"That would be nice," Talsu said. "I'll find out."

When he opened the door, there stood the Jelgavan major he'd seen before. The fellow was an inch or two shorter than Talsu, but contrived to looked down his nose at him just the same. "Am I correct in being given to understand that this is a tailor's establishment?" he asked in haughty tones.

"That's right . . . sir," Talsu answered. Regretfully, he added, "Won't you please come in?"

"Good morning, sir," Traku said when the major did stride into the flat. He sounded friendlier than Talsu had; he could hardly have sounded less friendly than his son. "What can we do for you today?"

"I require a rain cloak," the officer said. "I require it at once, as I shall soon be going into Algarve."

"I'll be happy to take care of you, sir," Traku said. "There will be a small extra charge for a rush job—I have some other business I'll have to put aside to take care of you right away, you understand."

"No," the major said.

Traku frowned. "I beg your pardon, sir?"

"No," the fellow repeated. "I will not pay extra, not a copper's worth. This is part of my uniform."

"Sir, I'm sure you already have a uniform-issue rain cloak, just like every other officer," Talsu said. "If you want something with a little extra style or quality, you do have to pay for it." He'd been through the army himself; he knew what the rules were.

The Jelgavan noble looked at him as if he'd just found him in his peach. "Who are you to tell me what I must do and must not do?" he demanded. "How dare you show such cheek?"

"Your Excellency, even officers have regulations," Talsu said.

"Do you want my business, or do you not?" the major said.

Talsu's father spoke reasonably: "Sir, if you want me to put your business in front of everybody else's, you're going to have to pay for that, because it'll mean other people's clothes won't get made as fast as they'd like." It probably wouldn't mean that. It would mean he and Talsu would have to work extra long hours to get the other orders done on time. Keeping things simple, though, seemed best.

"Other people?" The noble snorted. He plainly wasn't used to the idea of worrying about whether what he did bothered anyone else. "Do these 'other people' of yours have the high blood in their veins?"

"Aye, sir, a couple of 'em do," Traku said stolidly.

And that, to Talsu's amazement, turned the major reasonable in the blink of an eye. "Well, that's different," he said, still sounding gruff, but not as if he were about to accuse the two tailors of treason. "If it is a matter of inconveniencing folk of my own class . . ." He cared nothing about inconveniencing commoners. Bothering other nobles, though—that mattered to him. "How large a fee did you have in mind?"

Traku named one twice as high as he'd ever charged an Algarvian for a rush job. The Jelgavan noble accepted it without a blink. He didn't blink at the price Traku set for the rain cape, either. Maybe he had more money than he knew what to do with. Maybe—and more likely, Talsu judged—he just had no idea of what things were supposed to cost.

All he said on his departure was, "See that it's ready on time, my good men." And then he swept out, as if he'd been the king honoring a couple of peasants with the glory of his presence.

After the door closed, Traku said something under his breath. "I'm sorry, Father?" Talsu said. "I didn't catch that."

"I said, it's no wonder some of our own people went off and fought on the Algarvian side after King Donalitu came back. That overbred son of a whore and all the others like him don't make the redheads look like such a bad bargain."

"I've had that same thought a time or two—more than a time or two—myself," Talsu replied. "Aye, he's one over-bred son of a whore. But he's *our* overbred son of a whore, if you know what I mean. He won't haul us off by the hundreds to kill us for the sake of our life energy."

His father sighed. "You're right. No doubt about it, you're right. But if that's the best we can say for him—and it fornicating well is—it's pretty cold praise, wouldn't you say?"

"Of course it is," Talsu said. "But it's no surprise, or it shouldn't be one. Remember, you've just had nobles for customers. I've had them for commanders. I know what they're like." He almost said, *I know what's wrong with them.* Even if he didn't say it, it was what he meant.

"But the redheads have nobles, too," Traku said. "These Kuusamans have them. They must. But they don't act like their shit doesn't stink the way ours do. Why is that? Why are we stuck with a pack of bastards at the top?"

"I don't know," Talsu said. He didn't know any Jelgavans who did know, either. He grinned wryly. "Because we're lucky, I guess."

His father's fingers twisted in an evil-averting gesture that went back to the days of the Kaunian Empire. "That's the kind of luck I could do without. That's the kind of luck the whole kingdom could do without."

"Oh, aye," Talsu agreed. "But how do we change it?" He answered his own question: "We don't, not as long as Donalitu's our king. He's the worst of the lot." He sighed. "They don't have hardly any nobles in Unkerlant, people say."

"No, but that's on account of King Swemmel killed most of 'em," Traku said. "What the Unkerlanters have instead is, they have King Swemmel. Is he a better bargain?" Talsu didn't answer; by everything he'd heard, Swemmel was about as bad a bargain as anybody could make. His father rammed the point home: "Do you want to live in Unkerlant?"

"Powers above, no!" Talsu used that same ancient gesture. "But it's getting so I hardly want to live here any more, either."

"Where, then?" his father asked.

"I don't know." Talsu hadn't been altogether serious. After some thought, though, he said, "Kuusamo, maybe. The slanteyes are . . . looser than we are, if you know what I mean. I had some dealings with them when I was with the irregulars. They don't make a big fuss about rank and blood. They just do what needs doing. I liked that."

"How would you like a Kuusaman winter?" Traku asked with a sly smile.

Talsu shivered at the mere idea. "I don't suppose I would, not very much." He bent over the tunic he'd been working on when the major came in. If he and his father were going to get the rain cape done along with everything else, they could afford only so much chatter. And what was Kuusamo but moonshine, anyhow?

This time, the sleigh carrying Fernao and Pekka glided west, not east. Every stride of the harnessed reindeer took Fernao farther not only from the blockhouse but also from the hostel in the Naantali district. The hostel had deliberately been built a long way from a ley line. That made getting to it difficult and leaving inconvenient.

As if picking the thought—and some of the things behind it—from his mind, Pekka leaned toward him and said, "This feels very strange."

Fernao nodded. "For me, too," he said. "Going to see Kajaani will be . . . interesting."

Her laugh was nervous. "Bringing you there will be . . . interesting, too."

Seeing her home town wasn't what mattered, though.

Meeting her sister, meeting her son—those were what counted. "I wonder what they'll think of me," he said.

He waited for Pekka to say something like, *Of course they'll think you're wonderful.* A Lagoan woman would have. Pekka just answered, "That's why we're doing this: to find out, I mean."

"I know," Fernao said. As a moderately resolute bachelor, he hadn't gone through the ritual of meeting a woman's family before. And, in his younger days, he hadn't expected *family* to include a son.

Again halfway thinking along with him, Pekka said, "Uto will look up to you, I think." She smiled. "How can he help it, when you're so tall?" But the smile slipped. "I don't know about Elimaki. I'm sorry."

"It would be simpler if her husband hadn't run off with somebody else, wouldn't it?" Fernao said.

Pekka nodded. "It's too bad, too. I always liked Olavin," she said. "But these things do happen." *We ought to know,* Fernao thought. He kept that to himself; he didn't want to remind Pekka that she'd been carrying on with him before her husband got killed. And her thoughts hadn't gone in that direction, for she added a one-word parenthesis: "Men." Again, Fernao found it wiser to keep quiet.

The driver took them right up to the caravan depot at Joensuu, the little town closest to the hostel. As far as Fernao could see, Joensuu had no reason for existing except lying on a ley line. When the ley-line caravan glided into the depot, he was briefly startled to note it was northbound. Then Pekka said, "Remember? I warned you about this. We have to go around three sides of a rectangle to get to Kajaani."

He snapped his fingers in annoyance, no happier than any other mage at forgetting something. "Aye, you did tell me that, and it went clean out of my head." He put his arm around her. "Must be love."

From a Lagoan, that was an ordinary sort of compliment. As Fernao had seen, though, Kuusamans were more restrained in how they praised one another. Pekka still seemed flustered as they climbed up into the caravan car.

They had to switch caravans twice, once to a westbound line and then to the southbound one that would finally take them to Kajaani. Fernao hoped his baggage made the switches, too. Pekka was going home. She would have more clothes there. If his things didn't arrive, he'd wear what he had on his back till he could buy more—and he wasn't sure Kuusaman shops would have many garments for a man of his inches.

What with the delays in changing caravans, they traveled all through the night. Their seats reclined, as was true in most caravan cars, but still made only poor substitutes for real beds. Fernao dozed and woke, dozed and woke, the whole night long. When he was awake, he peered out the window at the snow-covered countryside. The night was moonless, but the southern lights glowed in shifting, curtainlike patterns of green and yellow. He'd seen them brighter on the austral continent, but the display here was far more impressive than it ever got up in Setubal.

The sun was just coming up over the horizon when the ley-line caravan topped the last forested rise north of Kajaani and glided down toward the port city. Even with the bright sun of early spring on it, the sea ahead looked cold. Maybe that was Fernao's imagination working overtime, and maybe it wasn't. That sea led southwest to the land of the Ice People.

Pekka yawned and stretched. She'd had a better night than Fernao. Seeing familiar landscape and then familiar buildings slide past the window, she smiled. "Oh, good! We're here."

"So we are." What Fernao saw didn't impress him. Kajaani, to him, looked like a Kuusaman provincial town, and nothing more. He knew he was spoiled; to him, any city save Setubal was likely to seem just a provincial town. He asked, "Can we see Kajaani City College from here?"

Shaking her head, Pekka pointed across the car, to the right. "It's on the western edge of town. If we get a chance, I'll take you over there. Having an illustrious Lagoan theoretical sorcerer along with me will make Professor Heikki unhappy, and I do what I can to keep her that way."

"Aye, you've told me about some of your squabbles,"

Fernao said. "What's your chairman's specialty? Veterinary magic? Is that what you said?"

"That's right," Pekka said. "And she's nobody of any consequence there. She'd make a splendid clerk, though. That's why she's been chairman so long, I suppose. But she inflicts herself on people who do real work, so nobody in the department can stand her."

"Kajaani!" the conductor called as the caravan, nearing the depot, slowed. "Everybody out for Kajaani, on account of this is the end of the line."

End of the world, Fernao thought. The ley-line caravan eased to a halt. The conductor opened the door at the front of the car. Pekka got to her feet. So did Fernao, leaning on his cane to help himself up. His leg and shoulder both complained. He'd known they would. *I'm lucky to have both legs,* he thought, and then, *if this is luck.*

Pekka got down ahead of him. She watched anxiously as he came down the little portable stairway. She was, he saw, ready to catch him if he stumbled. Being somewhere close to twice her size, he made sure he didn't, and reached the ground safely.

Someone—a woman on the platform—called Pekka's name. She turned. "Elimaki!" she exclaimed. A moment later, she added, "Uto!"

"Mother!" The boy swarmed toward her. He was, Fernao saw, nine or ten, with a good deal of Pekka in his face. When he sprang into her arms for a hug, the top of his head came past her shoulder. The woman who followed him also looked a good deal like Pekka. *Of course she does, you idiot,* Fernao thought. *She's her sister, by the powers above.* Elimaki was a couple of years younger, and a little stockier. She too hugged Pekka, but even as she did it she was eyeing Fernao with curiosity both undisguised and, he thought, more than a little hostile.

"I'm so glad to see both of you again," Pekka said, kissing first Uto and then Elimaki. She took a deep breath. "And I want you both to meet my . . . friend, Fernao of Lagoas."

Uto held out his hand. "Hello, sir," he said gravely. Sure enough, he added, "I didn't think you would be so tall." He was curiously studying Fernao, too.

Not a lot of Lagoans or other Algarvic folk got down here, Fernao suspected. He clasped Uto's hand, not his wrist, as he would have with one of his own countrymen. "I'm very pleased to meet you," he said. "I've heard a lot about you from your mother."

Pekka rolled her eyes. Even Elimaki had trouble holding her face straight. Uto looked more innocent than he had any hope of being. "I don't do that so much any more," he said, leaving *that* carefully unspecified.

"You do too, you scamp," Elimaki said. She nodded to Fernao. "And I have heard a lot about you."

"I probably don't do that so much any more, either," he answered, deadpan.

Pekka's sister gave him a sharp look, then smiled. "You'll have a carpetbag, won't you?" she said, looking back toward the caravan's baggage car.

"I do hope so," Fernao said. "I'd better find out."

"Why do you have that cane?" Uto asked as he limped toward the baggage car.

"Because I got hurt in the war, down in the land of the Ice People," he said.

"The Algarvians?" Uto asked, and Fernao nodded. The boy's face worked. "They killed my father, too, those—" He called the Algarvians a name nastier than any Fernao had known at the same age. Then he burst into tears.

While Pekka comforted him, Fernao reclaimed his carpetbag. It was there, which made him think kindly thoughts about the people who ran the Kuusaman ley-line caravans. He carried it back to Pekka and her son and her sister. Elimaki said to him, "I was thinking . . . The two of you might want to stay at my house tonight, not next door at Pekka's."

"I don't know." Fernao looked to Pekka. "What do you want to do? Either way is all right with me."

"Aye, let's do that," Pekka said at once, and shot her sister a grateful glance. "I don't want to go into my old house right now. It would tear me to pieces." Once she said it, it made good sense—indeed, perfect sense—to Fernao. With all those memories of past times with her dead husband there, he would seem nothing but an interloper.

"Let's go, then," Elimaki said. They caught a local caravan going east through the city, then walked up a hill past pines and firs to the street where Elimaki's house and Pekka's stood side by side. Seeing Fernao labor on the way up the hill, Pekka whispered to Uto. He took Fernao's carpetbag from him and carried it with pride.

Elimaki's house struck Fernao as enormous. In Setubal, the biggest city in the world, people were crowded too close together to let anyone but the very wealthy enjoy so much space. *An advantage to provincial towns I hadn't thought of.* "You'll want something to eat," Elimaki said, and disappeared into the kitchen. Pekka followed her. That left Fernao alone with Uto.

He didn't know what to say. He'd never had much to do with children. *If I want to stay with Pekka, though, I'll have to learn.* While he searched for words, Uto found some: "Aunt Eli says you're Mother's friend, her special friend."

As gravely as Uto had on meeting him, Fernao nodded. "That's true."

"Does that mean you're my special friend, too?"

"I don't know," Fernao said. "It's not just up to me, you know. It's up to you, too."

Pekka's son pondered that with the care his mother gave a new spell. At last, he nodded. "You're right. I guess I have to think about it some more." After another pause, he said, "I know I'm not supposed to ask you much about what you're doing, but you're helping Mother find magic to beat the Algarvians, aren't you?"

Fernao nodded again. "I can't tell you much about what I'm doing, either, but I can tell you that much. That's just what I'm doing."

A fierce light kindled in Uto's eyes. "In that case, I do want you to be my special friend. I'm still too little to pay them back for Father myself." However fierce he sounded, he started to cry again. Fernao held out his arms. He didn't know whether the boy would come to him, but Uto did. Awkwardly, he comforted him.

"Breakfast's ready," Elimaki called from the kitchen. Uto bounded away. He still had tears on his cheeks, but he was smiling again. Fernao followed more slowly. As he came into the kitchen, Elimaki saw Uto's tears. "Are you all right?" she asked.

"I'm fine," he answered carelessly, and turned to his mother, who was serving up plates of smoked salmon scrambled with eggs and cream. "I like your friend."

"Do you?" Pekka said, and Uto gave an emphatic nod. She tousled his hair. "I'm glad." Pekka looked toward her sister, as if to say, *I told you so.* Fernao pretended not to notice.

"I like him, too," Elimaki said, and then tempered that by adding, "More than I expected to," so Fernao wasn't sure how much credit he'd earned. Some, anyhow: by the relief in Pekka's eyes, perhaps even enough.

Vanai, these days, was a better housekeeper than she'd ever been, at least when it came to keeping the floor of her flat clean. She hadn't really sought such neatness; she'd had it forced on her. Saxburh crawled all over the flat. She could go surprisingly—sometimes alarmingly—fast. If she found anything she thought was interesting, it was liable to end up in her mouth before Vanai could take it away from her. The cleaner the floor was, the fewer the chances she had to eat anything disgusting or dangerous.

Saxburh didn't appreciate her mother's vigilance. As far as the baby was concerned, everything she could reach was supposed to go into her mouth. How could she tell what it was if she couldn't taste it? She fussed and squawked when Vanai took things away from her.

"Fuss all you like," Vanai told her after one rescue in the nick of time. "You can't eat a dead cockroach." By the way the baby wailed, she was liable to be stunted for life if she didn't get her fair share of dead bugs.

Keeping such things out of her hands and, more to the point, out of her mouth was Vanai's second-biggest worry. It was the biggest one about which she could do anything. Ealstan was and remained somewhere far away to the east. She wondered if she'd even know if anything—*powers above, forbid it!*—happened to him. She'd heard not a word since he got dragooned into King Swemmel's army. If he didn't come back after the war ended, that would tell her what she needed to know—or it might, for the Unkerlanters could simply have hauled him off to the other end of their vast kingdom.

How would I be able to find out, one way or the other? she wondered. The answer there was painfully obvious: *I wouldn't.* She pushed the worry to the back of her mind, as she did whenever she started fretting about what she couldn't help.

If only Ealstan were here . . . If Ealstan were here, he ·would find life in Eoforwic easier than it had been at any time since he and Vanai came to the Forthwegian capital. It had been weeks since Algarvian dragons appeared overhead. Gromheort still held out, but the rest of Forthweg belonged to Unkerlant these days—and, nominally, to King Beornwulf as well.

Beornwulf seemed to be doing what he could (and, perhaps, what the Unkerlanters would let him) to be a good king. Broadsheets outlawing price-gouging in the marketplace went up alongside sheets singing the praises of Swemmel's soldiers. Vanai looked out her kitchen window. A work crew was pasting up fresh broadsheets even now. *I wonder if I could put glass in the window again,* Vanai thought. *It wouldn't get broken right away, not any more.*

She couldn't afford to look out the window for long. She looked back toward Saxburh instead. It wasn't a dead cockroach this time—just a dust bunny. Vanai got it away from the baby. When Saxburh fussed, Vanai said, "Come on— let's go see what the new sheets say."

Scooping her daughter off the floor, she carried her down the stairs and out into the street. A few other people were looking at the new broadsheets, too, but only a few. There'd been too many broadsheets—from King Penda, from the Algarvians, and now from the Unkerlanters and their puppet king—for anybody to get very excited over one more. Vanai wasn't very excited, just curious and looking for an excuse to get out of the flat for a little while.

A Forthwegian man reading one of the new broadsheets pasted to a fence turned away with a disgusted gesture. Another one said, "Well, here's something else that won't fly." The first fellow said, "And what if it did? Doesn't hardly matter any more, does it? I ask you, is this a waste of time or what?" Shaking his head, he walked off.

Vanai went up to a broadsheet. "Oh," she said softly when she saw its title; the headline was CONCERNING KAUNIANS. She still wore her sorcerous disguise, and so still looked like a Forthwegian herself. Back before the war, Eoforwic had a name as the place where Forthwegians and Kaunians got on better than they did anywhere else in the kingdom. The reputation held some truth; Forthwegians and Kaunians here had rioted together on learning that the Algarvians were shipping blonds west to be murdered. But plenty of Forthwegians here despised Kaunians, too. Vanai had seen that along with the other.

And what would King Beornwulf have to say on the subject? She went up closer to the broadsheet so she could read the smaller print. The new edict came straight to the point, declaring, *All laws, orders, and regulations imposed by the Algarvian occupiers of the Kingdom of Forthweg concerning persons of Kaunian blood are henceforth and forevermore null and void. Persons of Kaunian blood legally residing in the Kingdom of Forthweg are and shall remain citizens of the said Kingdom, with full rights and privileges appertaining thereto, including the right to publish works in the Kaunian language (subject to the same limits of taste and decency as hold for works in the Forthwegian language). The status of persons of Kaunian blood residing in the Kingdom of Forthweg shall be and shall remain precisely what it was before the obscene and vicious Algarvian occupation, which in law shall be judged never to have occurred. Issued this day by order of King Beornwulf I of Forthweg, with the concurrence of his Unkerlanter allies.*

Unkerlanters didn't care much one way or the other about Kaunians. Only a handful of blonds lived in the far northeast of Unkerlant, not enough to make anyone in Swemmel's kingdom nervous about them. That was one of the few good things Kaunians from Forthweg had to say about Unkerlanters: they weren't Algarvians.

Vanai read aloud from the edict: ". . . the obscene and vicious Algarvian occupation, which in law shall be judged never to have occurred." She looked around at the wreckage and rubble of Eoforwic and laughed bitterly. And the wreckage of the city—the wreckage of the whole kingdom—wasn't the worst of it. People could rebuild ruined shops and houses and schools. How to go about rebuilding the lives the redheads had stolen, to say nothing of those they'd wrecked?

Publishing in Kaunian was legal again. But would anyone bother? Maybe some scholars would: people who wanted to be read by a wider audience, an audience in Kuusamo or Jelgava or even Algarve that had never learned Forthwegian. But how many writers now would turn their hands to romances or poetry or plays or new sheets in classical Kaunian? How many people were left alive to read them?

"Powers below eat King Mezentio," Vanai whispered. He hadn't killed off all the Kaunians in Forthweg. But he was liable to have killed Kaunianity here. That black thought had crossed Vanai's mind before. Having it come back after she read an edict favoring her people made tears sting her eyes.

Saxburh squirmed. She wanted Vanai to put her down and let her crawl around out here. It was a mild spring day. Birds chirped. A warm breeze blew down from the north. Vanai said, "No," to her daughter anyway, adding, "You're not going to get to eat any bugs out here."

She wished for a park with smoothly trimmed grass. She would take Saxburh there. The closest park she knew might not have had its grass trimmed since before the Derlavaian War. The ground there was bound to be cratered by bursting eggs. And every other park in and around Eoforwic was sure to be in the same state. So much rebuilding to do . . .

A woman came up and stood beside Vanai to read the broadsheet. She said, "I don't know why this new excuse for a king we've got even bothered with such a silly law. How many of these people are left, anyway? Not enough to waste anyone's time over, that's for sure."

What would she do if I told her I was a Kaunian? Vanai wondered. She didn't make the experiment. All she said was, "You may be right," and thought, *No, I won't give up my sorcerous disguise any time soon. I could make people hate my Thelberge self for what she does, but they don't hate her for what she is.*

And then a really nasty notion struck here. What if the other woman were a disguised Kaunian herself and, thinking Vanai a real Forthwegian, spoke out against blonds because she reckoned that expected of her? *How would I know? I wouldn't, any more than she knows what I am.*

She had no proof. By the nature of things, she wouldn't get any proof. But the thought, once lodged, wouldn't go away. If it were true, it wouldn't be Mezentio killing Kaunianity. No—Kaunianity would kill itself.

Vanai went back to her flat. Saxburh liked going upstairs; it felt different from walking on level ground. Vanai would have liked it better if she were carried instead of carrying, too.

"Judged never to have occurred," she said again when she got inside. Did that mean she'd never had to go to bed with Major Spinello? Did it mean she'd never had to wear this sorcerous disguise? Did it mean the redheads had never captured her and thrown her into the Kaunian quarter here in Eoforwic? Did it mean they hadn't killed tens, hundreds, thousands, tens of thousands, of blonds? She wished it did. Wishing meant nothing, or perhaps a little less.

"Dada," Saxburh said.

"No, I'm your mama," Vanai told her. The baby said *mama,* but less often. Vanai said, "Your dada will be home soon." *Powers above, I hope he will.*

"Dada," Saxburh said again. Vanai laughed. It was either that or start to cry. She'd done too much crying over the course of this war. *So long as I don't have to do any more.*

She went to the cupboard to see what she could make for supper. Barley, peas, turnips, beans, olives, cheese, olive oil—nothing very exciting, but enough to keep body and spirit together. Peasants in the countryside ate this kind of food their whole lives long. City people praised peasants for their healthy diet—and didn't try very hard to imitate it. The way things were these days, though, having enough of any kind of food, no matter how boring, was worth celebrating.

In a few days, she'd have to go down to the market square to get more. She wondered if Guthfrith who had been Ethelhelm would be there with his band. She'd seen the drummer and singer and songwriter several times. She didn't stop to listen to his music any more; he made her nervous. But he noticed her; she'd seen him follow her with his eyes more than once. That was not the least of the reasons he made her nervous. It wasn't the only one, though. He had a good notion that she was a Kaunian. With King Beornwulf's edict, it shouldn't have mattered. It shouldn't have, but it did. Kaunians in Forthweg rarely assumed edicts concerning them meant everything they said—unless the edicts were threats. With threats, whoever happened to be lording it over Forthweg was commonly sincere.

I have a weapon of my own, Vanai thought. Guthfrith was a fellow who played for coppers in the square. Ethelhelm, despite Kaunian blood, had been famous all over Forthweg. But, because of that Kaunian blood, Ethelhelm had decided it was wiser to collaborate with the Algarvians. If he tried to tar her, she could tar him.

She made a sour face. She hated to have to think that way. She hated to, but she would. If she had to keep her baby and herself safe, she'd do what needed doing and worry about everything else later. Like so many others across Derlavai, she'd learned ruthlessness in the war.

Marshal Rathar looked up at the night sky. Thick gray clouds covered it. He turned toward General Vatran—and accidentally bumped one of the bodyguards King Swemmel had ordered him to use after the Algarvians came altogether too close to assassinating him. "Sorry," he murmured.

"It's all right, sir," the bodyguard said. "Just think of us as furniture."

They were large, well-muscled pieces of furniture. Peering around them, Rathar said, "Everything's ready to go."

"It had better be," Vatran answered. "We've spent as much time building up toward things here as we did in the north last summer."

"We can't afford to have things go wrong," Rathar said. "Once we get over the Scamandro, we storm straight for Trapani. It's going to be *ours,* by the powers above. The islanders aren't going to take it. We've paid the biggest bills, and we deserve the biggest prize." That was what Swemmel said, and Rathar, here, emphatically agreed with him.

Vatran nodded, too. "With what all we've got here, sir, I don't see any way the redheads can stop us, or even slow us down much. How much longer till the dance starts?"

"A quarter of an hour," Rathar replied. "We get past the high ground on the east side of the river and everything should go fine from there."

"Here's hoping," Vatran said. "If they don't pull out any funny sorcery . . ."

That worried Rathar, too. What *did* King Mezentio have left, here in Algarve's last extremity? The mages who wore Unkerlant's rock-gray had grown ever more appalled at the spells the redheads tried. Not many of those spells had worked as well as the Algarvians wished, but what the enemy attempted kept getting wilder and darker.

"If we keep them busy enough fighting a regular war, they can't spend too much time or energy getting strange on us," the marshal said, and hoped he was right.

At the appointed hour, swarms of rock-gray dragons flew low over the Scamandro, pulverizing the Algarvians' works on the eastern bank with eggs and with flame. Hundreds, thousands, of egg-tossers flung more death across the river. At dozens of points along the front, artificers would be springing into action to bridge the Scamandro. *Let any one of those bridges stand, and we'll whip the redheads,* Rathar thought. He expected a great many more than one would stand. He expected most of them would, in fact. But one would do well enough. Any bridgehead on the eastern side of the Scamandro would give his kingdom the opening it needed.

Mages added something new to the attack: sorcerous lamps that seemed to shine bright as the sun. Their glare reflected off the underside of the clouds and helped light the way for the dragons and the men aiming the egg-tossers—to say nothing of distracting the foe. "We want Mezentio's men knocked flat before we cross," Rathar said.

"Looks like we're getting what we want, too," Vatran answered. Even as far from the front as Mangani was, he had to raise his voice to be heard over the din of bursting eggs.

A crystallomancer came up to Rathar. Saluting, he said,

"Lord Marshal, resistance on the far side of the river is lighter than expected. That's what the dragonfliers report."

"We've finally beaten them down," Vatran said.

"That would be good. That would be very good." Rathar wasn't sure he believed it, but in the opening minutes of an attack he was willing to be hopeful.

Another crystallomancer hurried up and saluted. "Sir, we have a bridgehead over the Scamandro and behemoths crossing in numbers to the east bank."

Vatran and Rathar both exclaimed in delight then, and clasped hands. The Algarvians had thrown back all their efforts to force earlier bridgeheads. *Let's see the whoresons throw this back,* Rathar thought. *I'd like to see any army in the world throw back this attack.*

More crystallomancers brought news of bridges crossing the river and behemoths and footsoldiers rushing across. All of them said the same thing as the dragonfliers had: resistance was less than expected. *Maybe we have knocked them flat,* Rathar thought. *If we have, we walk into Trapani instead of battering our way there. That would be nice.*

Aloud, he kept giving the same order over and over: "Keep moving! Try to take the high ground east of the Scamandro. Do everything you can to link up our crossings." The crystallomancers hurried away to take his words to the officers in the front line.

Dawn meant the sorcerers could douse the hideous lights they'd fashioned. It also meant he got some news he would rather not have had: on the far side of the Scamandro, the Algarvians had started fighting back fiercely. "How can they?" Vatran said when the crystallomancers reported that. "We should have squashed them flat as a bug."

"I think I know what they did," Rathar said. "I'm not sure, but I think so. I think they pulled back from their frontline positions before we hit them. They did that a few times back in Unkerlant. It would let them save a lot of their men and egg-tossers and behemoths, even if it did cost them land."

"They can't afford to lose anything right now," Vatran said.

"I know." Rathar nodded. "But if they'd lost the men, they surely would have lost the land, too. This way, they have a chance of counterattacking and driving us back—or they think they do, anyhow."

"We have to keep throwing men and behemoths at them," Vatran said.

"We're doing that. We haven't been building up here for nothing," Rathar said. "But it's going to be harder than we thought it would."

General Vatran made a sour face. "What isn't, with Algarvians?"

Rathar had no answer for that. The redheads had come horrifyingly close to conquering his kingdom. Now he was tantalizingly close to conquering theirs. But they hadn't made any of the fights easy, not a single one. They'd failed not because they weren't good soldiers, but because there weren't enough of them and because King Mezentio hadn't thought he would need to bother conciliating the Unkerlanters his men overran. Arrogance *was* an Algarvian vice.

It wasn't one that mattered here, though. *There still aren't enough of them to stop us,* Rathar thought. "Wherever we penetrate, send in reinforcements," he commanded. Again, crystallomancers relayed his words to the commanders at the front.

He hoped they wouldn't need the order. It was standard doctrine in Unkerlant. He gave it anyhow. In the heat of the moment, who could guess whether these front-line commanders bothered to remember doctrine?

More dragons flew east, to torment the Algarvians with eggs and with fire. Crystallomancers reported only a handful of enemy beasts rising to challenge them. There was no doubt whatsoever that the Unkerlanters had at last forced the line of the Scamandro. How much more they would be able to do, though, remained an open question.

"Powers below eat the redheads," Vatran growled as the day wore on with no sign of a breakthrough.

"They will," Rathar said. "We're feeding them."

"Not fast enough," Vatran grumbled. Rathar wished he could have argued with his general. Unfortunately, he agreed with him. The Algarvians had salvaged more than he'd thought they could, and they were fighting not only with their usual cleverness but also with the desperate courage of men who had nothing left to lose. They knew as well as Rathar that only they lay between his army and Trapani.

Another night and day of hammering produced only a little progress, and only a couple of lodgements on the high ground Mezentio's men were defending. Had everything gone according to plan, Rathar's behemoths would have been lumbering toward Trapani by then. But the Marshal of Unkerlant wasn't the only one who'd made plans for this moment, and those of the Algarvians looked to be working a little better than his.

"How long can this go on?" Vatran complained that evening.

"I don't know," Rathar answered. "I still think we're all right, though. We *have* made them fall back some, and we've still got reinforcements pouring in from the west. When they use up what they've mustered against us, it's gone, and gone for good."

But even he had trouble staying detached and optimistic when his men gained hardly any more ground on the third day of the attack than they had on the second. And *that* evening, Vatran wasn't the one doing the complaining. A crystallomancer came up to Rathar and said, "Sir, King Swemmel would speak to you at once."

Rathar had more than expected such a call. If anything, he was a little surprised the king had waited this long. "I'm coming," he said. Just for a moment, he imagined ordering the crystallomancer to tell Swemmel he couldn't come, that he was too busy. But no one had any business being too busy to talk to the King of Unkerlant.

Swemmel's image stared out of the crystal at Rathar. Not for the first time, the marshal thought his sovereign looked like an Algarvian. He had a long, pale face with a straight nose, though his hair and eyes were dark like a proper Unkerlanter's. Those eyes often had a febrile glow to them, and they positively blazed now. "We are not pleased, Marshal, not pleased at all," Swemmel said without preamble. "We had hoped and believed the news from the front would be better than what we have heard."

"I'd hoped so myself, your Majesty," Rathar replied. "For now, the Algarvians are fighting harder than I thought they could. But when springs come to the icebound rivers in the south, the ice *does* melt each year, and the water *does* flow down to the Narrow Sea. As the ice does, the Algarvians' lines *will* break up. The thaw is slow, but it *will* come."

"Very pretty," Swemmel said. "We did not know we had a poet commanding our armies. We want to be sure we *do* have a soldier commanding them."

Stiffly, Rathar said, "Your Majesty, the redheads thought I was doing well enough to make it worth their while to try to murder me. If you think someone else can do better, give me a stick and send me to the front line. I will fight for you in whatever way suits you best."

"We want Mezentio, Marshal," the king said. "Give us Mezentio, as you gave us Raniero. By the time Mezentio dies, he will have spent long and long envying his cousin."

Swemmel had boiled Raniero alive after his soldiers recaptured most of the Duchy of Grelz. Rathar didn't know what he could do to Mezentio that was worse, but his sovereign had had a year and a half to think about it. "I don't know if I can give you Mezentio, your Majesty," he said. "He will have somewhat to say about that himself, very likely. But I can give you Trapani, and I will."

"You should have done it already," Swemmel said peevishly.

"The day will come, your Majesty," Rathar promised. "And I think it will come soon. The Algarvians *have* lost ground here, and they can't afford to lose much more. This is the last obstacle in front of us. We *are* beating it down."

"Enemies everywhere," King Swemmel muttered. Rathar didn't think that was aimed at him. Had it been, Swemmel would have sacked him, or worse. The king gathered himself. "Break the Algarvians. Crush them beneath your heel—beneath *our* heel." That was the royal *we* again, proud and imperious.

"Your Majesty, it will be a pleasure," Rathar said. "And we *will* do it. It's only a matter of time." He hadn't finished before the crystal flared and Swemmel's image vanished. He'd told the king what he wanted to hear. Now he had to make it good. He hadn't lied. He didn't think it would take long.

Garivald had hated the Algarvians even before they overran his home village. But ever since he'd faced the redheads as an irregular—and especially since King Swemmel's impressers hauled him into the army and he'd fought Mezentio's men here in the north—he'd developed a sincere if grudging respect for them as soldiers. However outnumbered they were, they always fought cleverly, they always fought hard, and they always made Unkerlant pay more than it should have for every inch of land it took.

Always—until now. A couple of redheaded soldiers came out of a house with hands high over their heads and with fearful expressions on their faces. Garivald had been fearful, too, as in any fight. They might have killed him. He knew that all too well. But they'd given up instead. More and more now, Algarvians were throwing down their sticks and throwing up their hands. They knew, or some of them knew, they were beaten.

With a gesture from the business end of his stick, Garivald sent these redheads off to captivity. He didn't even bother rifling their belt pouches for whatever silver they carried. It was as if he were saying, *You fellows can go on. I'll catch some of your pals pretty soon and frisk them instead.*

Lieutenant Andelot called, "Well, Fariulf, they really are starting to go to pieces now. Even a few weeks ago, those whoresons would have made us pay the price of prying them out of there."

A few weeks before, the Unkerlanter army, or the part of it with which Garivald was most intimately concerned, had been falling back from Bonorva in the face of a fierce Algarvian counterattack. Mezentio's men couldn't sustain it, though. And, having used up so many men and behemoths, they hadn't been able to hold their ground against the Unkerlanters afterwards.

"I think you're right, sir," Garivald answered. By now, he

took his false name as much for granted as his real one. He pointed toward the southeast, the direction in which his regiment had been driving. "What's the name of the next town ahead?"

"I have to look." Andelot unfolded a map, then checked himself. "No. Here, Sergeant. You come see for yourself. If you've got your letters, you may as well use them."

"All right." Garivald trotted over to the company commander. "Whereabouts are we now?" Andelot showed him with a grimy-nailed finger. "And we're going this way, right?" Garivald asked. The young lieutenant nodded. Frowning in concentration, Garivald studied the map. "Then we're headed toward . . . Torgavi?" He wondered if he'd correctly pronounced the foreign name.

By the way Andelot beamed, he had. "That's good, Fariulf. Anybody would think you'd been reading for years." The lieutenant pointed to the blue line meandering past Torgavi. "And what's the name of this river here?"

Garivald squinted at the map again: the river's name was written in very small characters. "It's the Albi, sir," he said confidently; with a name that short, he was sure he hadn't made a hash of it.

And he hadn't. "Right again," Andelot said. "You do so well here. Why didn't you ever learn before?"

They'd been over this ground before. Shrugging broad shoulders, Garivald answered, "How could I have, sir? Our village had no school. Our firstman knew his letters, but I don't think anybody else who lived there did. I don't suppose any of the villages around ours were any different, either."

Andelot nodded. "I'm sure you're right, Sergeant. But things like that aren't good for the kingdom. We're less efficient than we ought to be. Just about all of these Algarvians can read and write. It makes them more flexible than we are, able to do more things. The same is true for the Kuusamans and Lagoans. They're our allies now, but who knows how long that will last once Mezentio gets what's coming to him? We need to start thinking about such things."

Garivald shrugged again. The men from the great island in the distant east hardly seemed real to him. Of course, it hadn't been so very long before that the Algarvians had hardly seemed real to him, either. He'd come to know them better than he'd ever imagined he would—and better than he'd ever wanted to, too. Would the same thing happen with the men of Kuusamo and Lagoas? He hoped not. Once the fight ended, all he wanted to do was find his way back to Obilot. He'd lost one family in the war. He hoped for the chance to start another.

Up ahead, somewhere near Torgavi, a few eggs burst. Less than a minute later, several more came down, these a lot closer to Garivald and Andelot. Garivald grimaced. "Not all the buggers have quit," he said.

"No, not yet," Lieutenant Andelot agreed. "That's why we're here—to take care of the ones too stubborn or too stupid to know they're licked." He blew a shrill blast on his whistle, loud enough to make Garivald's ears ring, and shouted, "Forward!"

"Forward!" Garivald echoed, and then, showing off what he'd learned, "Let's clear these bastards out of Torgavi."

All along the line, officers' whistles squealed. Officers and underofficers yelled, "Forward!" And forward the Unkerlanters went, trotting toward Torgavi across wheatfields and through olive groves. Garivald wondered why anyone wanted to cultivate olives. He didn't think much of the fruit, and the oil had a nasty flavor. He doubted olives would grow down in the Duchy of Grelz, and didn't miss them a bit.

Unkerlanter behemoths advanced with the footsoldiers, using their egg-tossers and heavy sticks to smash up the strongpoints the redheads were defending. Garivald took that cooperation for granted. Men who'd been in the army longer didn't. By what they said, the Algarvians had always been able to bring it off. King Swemmel's men had had to learn how, and a lot of the lessons had proved painful and expensive.

Dragons pounded Torgavi's defenders, too. Again, some of the Algarvians began coming out into the open and surrendering. But some of them kept fighting, too. *I don't want to die now,* Garivald thought as he flopped down near a house on the outskirts of Torgavi. *Why don't they all just give up, curse them? That would make things easier on them and easier on me, too.*

With a rumbling roar, a bridge across the Albi tumbled into the river. Mezentio's men must have wrecked it with eggs. Sure enough, some of them kept fighting as if the war still hung in the balance. *Fools,* Garivald thought. *Enough.*

A column of behemoths lumbered into Torgavi. Garivald waved as many men as he could forward; the behemoths protected footsoldiers, but the reverse also held true. That too was cooperation. Some Algarvian diehards in a house near the outskirts of the town blazed at the behemoths. The behemoth crews lobbed three or four eggs at the house. At such short range, the house crumbled as if made of pasteboard. No more blazes came from it.

"That's the way!" Garivald shouted. One of the crewmen on the closest behemoth waved to him. He waved back. That other soldier undoubtedly wanted to make it through the war and then go home, too.

After the Unkerlanters dealt with the diehards, the rest of the redheads in Torgavi decided they'd had enough. White flags and banners appeared in windows all over town. Kilted soldiers came out of the few strongholds they still held. They might have feared going into captivity, but they feared dying more. With brusque gestures, Garivald and the other Unkerlanters sent the captives to the rear.

Somewhere not far away, a woman started screaming. Garivald looked around for Lieutenant Andelot. When he caught the company commander's eye, Andelot just shrugged. Garivald nodded. The Algarvians had outraged plenty of women in Unkerlant; he'd seen that for himself in Zossen. Rough justice said his countrymen could pay them back in the same coin. The woman's screams went on. A moment later, more screams started, these rather shriller.

"Come on," Andelot called to the men within earshot. "Let's get down to the river and see if we can find a way to cross. Powers below eat the Algarvians for dropping the bridge in the water."

"Powers below eat the Algarvians." Garivald needed no qualifiers for that. Now Andelot was the one who nodded.

What remained of the bridge over the Albi were a couple of stone piers in the river that had supported it and a lot of twisted ironwork. On the far side of the stream, perhaps a hundred yards away, a couple of behemoths and a squad of footsoldiers approached the riverbank. Garivald started to dive for cover.

"Wait," Andelot said. The one word held such quiet excitement, it froze Garivald where he stood. Andelot went on, "Do you know, Fariulf, I don't think those are Algarvians at all."

"Who else would they be, sir?" Garivald shaded his eyes with the palm of his hand to see better. He didn't think the soldiers on the far bank wore kilts. They weren't blazing at his comrades and him. They were looking and pointing in much the same way as the Unkerlanters were. One of them trained a shiny brass spyglass on Garivald and the other soldiers here. Garivald could see the fellow jump when he got a good look. "Whoever he is, he just figured out *we* aren't redheads."

The fellow with the spyglass set it on the ground. Cupping his hands in front of his mouth, he shouted, "Unkerlant?"

"Aye, we're from Unkerlant," Lieutenant Andelot shouted back. "Who are you?"

Garivald couldn't make out all of the answer, but one word was very clear: "Kuusamo." Awe prickled through him. His countrymen and those fellows on the other bank of the Albi had fought their way across half of Derlavai to meet here.

That same realization went through the rest of Swemmel's soldiers, too. "By the powers above," someone said softly. "We've cut Algarve in half," somebody else added. Most of the men began to cheer. A couple began to weep. On the other bank, the Kuusamans were cheering, too.

"We've got to get across," Andelot said. He peered up and down the river.

So did Garivald. "There's a rowboat!" he exclaimed at the same time as Andelot started for it. Garivald hurried after his company commander. *If I ever have grandchildren, I can tell them about this,* he thought. Another soldier had the same idea. Garivald tapped the three bronze triangles that showed he was a sergeant. The other man bared his teeth in a disappointed grimace, but fell back.

Garivald was clumsy with the oars. He didn't care, and

Andelot didn't complain. They would have paddled with their sticks had the boat not held oars.

On the other bank, the Kuusamans greeted them with open arms. They gave the Unkerlanters smoked salmon and wine. Garivald had something stronger than wine in his water bottle. He gladly shared it. The swarthy little slant-eyed men smacked their lips and clapped him on the back.

None of them spoke Unkerlanter, and neither Garivald nor Andelot knew any of their tongue. A Kuusaman tried another language. "That's classical Kaunian," Andelot said. "I know of it, but I don't speak it." He had some Algarvian, and did his best with that. A couple of the Kuusamans proved to know some of the enemy's speech, too.

"What do they say, sir?" Garivald asked around a mouthful of salmon. The stuff tasted amazingly good.

"They say it won't be long now," Andelot answered. Garivald nodded vehemently, to show how much he hoped they were right.

As he had for weeks now, Ealstan peered longingly toward Gromheort. The Unkerlanter army, of which he was a small but unwilling part, hadn't pushed the attack against his home town so hard as it might have, seeming content to let time and hunger do some of their work for them. *The redheads in there are going hungry,* he thought. *That's fine, but my family is going hungry, too.*

He wondered if he had any family left alive. All he could do was hope. *Before long, I'll find out.* People said the Unkerlanter army down in the south had finally launched its great attack on Trapani. He didn't know whether that was true or just one more rumor. He suspected it held some truth, though, because the fight around Gromheort was heating up again, too.

Dragons dropped eggs on the city and swooped down to rooftop height to flame any enemy soldiers they could catch away from cover. Egg-tossers punished Gromheort still more. Behemoths came forward, assembling almost contemptuously outside the city to let the Algarvians know what would be heading their way.

An Unkerlanter officer went into Gromheort under flag

of truce to demand surrender one last time. The Algarvians sent him back. He happened to walk past Ealstan's regiment shaking his head. Somebody called to him, "We'll have to squash the whoresons, eh?"

"That's right," the envoy answered. Ealstan followed Unkerlanter fairly well these days. The officer added, "We can do it, too." Maybe he expected the soldiers to burst into cheers. If he did, he was disappointed. They'd seen too much fighting to be eager for more.

Before dawn the next morning, more dragons swooped down on Ealstan's poor, beleaguered city. Egg-tossers pummeled Gromheort anew. He grimaced at the chaos and destruction ahead. How could anyone, Algarvian soldier or Forthwegian civilian, have survived the pummeling the Unkerlanters had given the place?

As soon as the sunrise painted the sky with pink, whistles shrilled all around Gromheort. Officers and sergeants shouted, "Forward!" Clutching his stick, doing his best not to be afraid and not to let himself worry, forward Ealstan went.

Watching behemoths going forward, too, was reassuring. For one thing, they fought vastly better than individual footsoldiers could. For another, they drew blazes from the enemy, who knew how well they fought at least as well as Ealstan did. If the redheads were blazing at behemoths, they weren't blazing at him.

And redheads blazing there were. Regardless of whether Ealstan thought the Unkerlanter pounding should have killed them all, it hadn't. They plainly intended to make the attackers pay for every inch of the journey into Gromheort.

Perhaps fifty yards off to Ealstan's left, a behemoth's massive foot came down on an egg buried in the ground. The egg burst. An instant later, so did all the smaller eggs the behemoth was carrying. The blast of sorcerous energy knocked Ealstan off his feet and left him half stunned, his ears ringing. When he looked over there, he saw no sign the behemoth or its crew had ever existed except for a crater gouged in the earth.

"Forward!" The shout seemed to come from very far away now. But Ealstan knew what Swemmel's men would be yelling regardless of how well he heard them. And, again, he went forward. The Algarvians might blaze him if he did. The Unkerlanters would surely blaze him if he didn't.

An Algarvian—a filthy, scrawny fellow in the rags of a tunic and kilt—threw up his hands and came out of his hole as Ealstan and a couple of Unkerlanters drew near. "I surrender!" he shouted in his own language.

Ealstan's formal Algarvian was better than his formal Unkerlanter, in which he guessed at the meaning a lot of the time and sometimes guessed wrong. "Keep your hands high and go to the rear," he told the redhead. "If you are lucky, no one will blaze you." Mezentio's trooper knew how lucky he was not to have been blazed down on the spot. Babbling thanks, he hurried off toward whatever captivity might hold for him.

"You really speak some of their language," an Unkerlanter said admiringly. "It's not just 'Hands high!' and 'Drop your stick!' with you." He brought out the couple of phrases almost any Unkerlanter soldier could say.

Ealstan shrugged. "The Algarvians made me learn it in school."

"No, no, it's good you know it," the soldier in the rock-gray tunic said. "Maybe you can talk more of the whoresons into giving up." He didn't want to get blazed, either. The more of Mezentio's men who surrendered, the fewer who would fight to the end. That made good sense to Ealstan, too.

He didn't need long to see that this push was going to be different. Before, when the Unkerlanters probed at Gromheort, they'd eased off on running into stiff resistance. Not now. Now, the behemoths pounded Algarvian strongpoints outside the shattered walls. Footsoldiers pushed forward between those strongpoints. Mezentio's men were brave. Ealstan, who hated them as much as any man in Forthweg did, had seen that for himself, both during the dreadful fighting in Eoforwic and in his involuntary stay in King Swemmel's army. But courage wasn't going to do them any good, not this time. A starved cat forced to fight a mastiff might be brave, too. Its bravery wouldn't do it any good: the mastiff would kill it just the same.

As he ran toward a wrecked gate, he wondered how many times he'd come this way before. He knew the one he remembered best: walking back to Gromheort after the first time he'd made love with Vanai. He'd been dazed by joy then. He was dazed now, too, but that was because the buried egg and the load on the behemoth's back had burst too close to him. The oak grove where he'd lain with her was smashed to kindling; he'd been through it.

Redheads still fought, using the rubble of the wall and the gateway for cover. Beams scorched tracks of black through the grass near Ealstan's feet. Behemoths started tossing eggs at the gate. Ealstan saw pieces of a soldier fly through the air. A few more eggs bursting by the gateway meant far fewer blazes came back at the onrushing Unkerlanters.

With a whoop, Ealstan scrambled over the gray stones of the wall and into Gromheort. "Home!" he yelled. Then a beam flicked past his ear, so close he smelled lightning in the air. So much for exultation. He threw himself down behind another stone and blazed back.

Nothing was going to come easy. Mezentio's men had had weeks to fortify Gromheort, and they'd made the most of them. They'd probably used the luckless civilians as laborers. Every street seemed to have a barricade across it every block. Behemoths broke into the city and started knocking down barricades with their egg-tossers, but redheads in the buildings on either side of the street dropped eggs on them from rooftops and upper stories. Ealstan had seen in Eoforwic how expensive street fighting could be.

He'd thought—he'd hoped—he could simply head for the Avenue of Countess Hereswith, where his family lived. Things weren't so simple. The way Mezentio's men were fighting, his home might as well have been on the far side of the moon.

He was running from one barricade towards another when he got blazed. One second, everything was fine. Next thing he knew, his left leg didn't want to bear his weight any more. He landed hard, scraping both knees and one elbow. At first, those small injuries hurt more than his wound. Then they didn't, and he let out a raw-edged howl of pain.

He dragged himself into a doorway, leaving a trail of blood behind him like a slug's trail of slime. An Unkerlanter soldier crouched by him and started bandaging the wound, which was in the outside of his thigh. "Not too bad," the fellow said encouragingly.

"Easy for you to say," Ealstan answered. "It's not your fornicating leg." The Unkerlanter laughed, finished the job, and ran deeper into the city to fight some more.

Ealstan tried once to get up, but couldn't manage with the leg limp and useless. Having no other choice, then, he lay where he was and watched the bandage turn red. It didn't fill with blood too fast, which he found moderately encouraging; if it had, he might have bled to death. Some unknown stretch of time went by. The Unkerlanters drove ever deeper into Gromheort, and the din of battle washed past him.

Maybe he slept, or passed out. He was certainly surprised when an Unkerlanter soldier started to drag him out of the doorway by his feet. "I'm not dead, you stupid son of a whore," he snarled. He rather wished he were, for the sudden jerk on his wounded leg made it hurt like fire.

"Oh. Sorry, buddy," the soldier said. He called to a pal: "Hey, Joswe! Come give me a hand. I've got a live one here."

Between the two of them, they got Ealstan upright and lugged him back toward an infirmary Swemmel's men had set up near the edge of town. He almost wished they'd let him lie where he was; the howls of pain coming out of the place sounded anything but encouraging. But, when they helped him inside, he discovered a couple of Unkerlanter healers were there, working like men possessed along with a bearded Forthwegian they'd probably impressed into their service.

Ealstan didn't get a cot. He counted himself lucky not to have to lie on another wounded man: the place was packed, and getting more so by the minute. Healers and Forthwegian women with fresh bandages—also no doubt pressed into duty—had to walk carefully to keep from stepping on hands and feet.

After what seemed like forever, a healer got to Ealstan. He stripped off the field dressing and muttered a charm over the wound to keep it from going bad. A Forthwegian healer would have used a spell in classical Kaunian; the Unkerlanter spoke his own language. He said, "You'll do all right, soldier," shouted for one of the women to come give Ealstan a fresh bandage, and went on to the next hurt man.

The Forthwegian woman who stooped beside Ealstan was a couple of years older than he, on the skinny side, and looked weary unto death. She plainly had practice putting on bandages; maybe she'd done it for the Algarvians, too. "Thank you very much," Ealstan said in Forthwegian; he hadn't had many chances lately to use his own tongue.

"You're welcome," she replied, one eyebrow rising in surprise. Then she took another, longer, look at him. Her eyes widened; her mouth fell open. "Ealstan?" she whispered.

He recognized her voice where he hadn't known her face. "Conberge?" he said, and reached up to embrace his sister. They both burst into tears, careless of the staring Unkerlanters all around them. Ealstan asked, "Are Father and Mother all right? And"—he felt absurdly pleased with remembering—"your husband?" She hadn't been married when he fled Gromheort.

To his vast relief, she nodded. "They all were this morning, anyhow. We've spent a lot of time in the wine cellar, but most of the house is still standing. Well, it was, anyhow."

"Powers above be praised," Ealstan said, and let more tears fall. He added, "Mother and Father are grandparents. Vanai and I had a little girl, end of last spring."

Conberge set a hand on her own stomach. "They will be again, come wintertime." She added, "How did you turn into an Unkerlanter soldier? What will they do with you, now that you're hurt?"

"They caught me and gave me a stick. As for the other"—he shrugged—"we'll just have to find out."

Ten

Skarnu hadn't been back to Pavilosta since not long before escaping from Merkela's farm one jump ahead of the Algarvians. Whenever he'd gone into the village before, he'd played the role of a peasant. No, he'd done more than play the role: he'd lived it. He still had the calluses to prove it.

Now, though, he and Merkela and little Gedominu wouldn't be living at the farm. They would be moving into the castle where the traitor Count Enkuru and his son and successor, the traitor Count Simanu, had dwelt. First, though, there was the matter of formally installing Skarnu as the rightful overlord for the marquisate (newly elevated, by royal decree, from a county).

He asked Merkela, "Are you sure you don't mind having Raunu take over your farm?"

She shook her head. "I'm just surprised he wanted it. You city people don't usually have the first notion of what to do out in the country."

She hadn't had the first notion of what to do in the city, but Skarnu didn't press her about that. Instead, he said, "Well, you gave Raunu—and me—a good many lessons, and I think this woman he's sweet on will teach him a good deal more."

His old sergeant had found a farm widow, just as he had himself. Raunu's lady friend was a few years older and a good deal more placid than Merkela. She seemed to suit him well. *A lot of widows to choose from,* Skarnu thought. *Too many to choose from. Too many men dead.*

At the edge of Pavilosta's market square, an enterprising taverner had set up a table with mugs of ale and a selection of news sheets from bigger towns: the village couldn't support one itself. He waved to Skarnu, calling, "I always knew you were more than what you seemed."

And Skarnu dutifully waved back. That wasn't easy. He'd been drinking ale at that table and idly going through a news sheet when he saw that his sister was keeping company with an Algarvian. *And now I've got a bastard for a nephew,* he thought with a sigh. *And now it will be a long, long time before anybody will be able to look at Krasta without remembering that. How long does disgrace last?*

It had lasted long enough for most of her servants to have deserted her and come out to the countryside with Skarnu and Merkela. That suited Skarnu well. He didn't know the servitors who'd worked for his predecessors. Maybe they were all right. Maybe they'd collaborated as enthusiastically as Enkuru and Simanu had.

Of course, the servants from the mansion had had redheads there, too. And Bauska had a little girl with hair the same color as that of Krasta's baby boy. Not many people in Valmiera had completely clean hands these days.

I do, he thought. *Merkela does. The only trouble is, she doesn't want to yield even an inch to anyone who doesn't.* He sighed. He could see years of trouble ahead for the kingdom from quarrels like that.

But today wasn't a day to dwell on troubles. "Coming back to Pavilosta feels good," he said.

"I should hope so," Merkela answered. "I don't see how you stood living in Priekule for so long."

"All what you're used to," Skarnu said. But he'd had a couple of years to get used to living in this part of southern Valmiera. The thought of spending a good many years here didn't horrify him, as it would have before the war.

People from Pavilosta, the nearby village of Adutiskis, and the farms on the countryside in the area packed the market square. A good many of them waved to Skarnu as he and Merkela made their way through the crowd toward the traditional seat of installation. Every so often, he would spot someone he knew and wave back. Had he stayed in these parts as a peasant, the locals would have reckoned him *that fellow who's not from around here* till the day he died. They would probably say the same thing about him as a marquis—but they might not say it so loud.

A band struck up a thumping tune. Merkela drew herself straight with pride. "That's the count's air," she said, and then corrected herself: "No, I mean the marquis' air, don't I?" She squeezed Skarnu's hand.

He leaned over and gave her a quick kiss. "See what you get for taking in strange men who come stumbling out of the woods?"

"I never thought it would come to this," she said. Whether that meant marrying him or coming back to Pavilosta in such style, he didn't know and didn't ask. The two of them had finally made their way up to the seat, which was in fact two seats, one facing one way, one the other.

Skarnu sat down in the seat facing west, towards Algarve. That symbolized the feudal lord's duty to defend the peasantry against invasion. No doubt, in years gone by, it had been only one more formality in this ceremony. But, with the redheads only a few months gone from Valmiera, opposing them took on a new urgency. And people hereabouts knew Skarnu had been part of the underground. He really had done what he could to fight Mezentio's men. Murmurs of approval and even a few cheers rang out as he took his seat.

A peasant from just outside of Adutiskis sat in the other half of the ceremonial seat. Counts—and now a marquis—were traditionally installed in Pavilosta, so the other village provided the second actor in the drama. "Congratulations, your Excellency," the fellow said in a low voice.

"Thanks," Skarnu said. "Shall we get on with it?"

"Right you are," the peasant replied. "You do know how it's supposed to go?"

"Aye," Skarnu said, a little impatiently. "For one thing, we've rehearsed it a couple of times. And, for another, I was here in the square when Simanu, powers below eat him, made a hash of things." The collaborator had sat in the west-facing seat, but he'd had plenty of Algarvian officers and soldiers in the square to protect him from the folk whose overlord he was supposed to become.

"That whoreson," the peasant said. "He deserved every bit of what he got, and more besides. And now, your Excellency, if you'll excuse me . . ." He got to his feet and pushed through the crowd to the edge of the square.

Two cows waited there for him, one plump and sleek, the other distinctly on the scrawny side. He led them back to Skarnu, as another peasant—or perhaps this same fellow?—had led them back to Simanu.

The new overlord was supposed to choose the scrawny cow, showing that he reserved the best for the people living in his domain. Skarnu did. Simanu hadn't—he'd picked the fat one. Skarnu bent his head and let the peasant give him a light box on the ear, which meant he would attend to the concerns of those who lived under his lordship. Simanu, secure in the knowledge that the Algarvians backed him, hadn't worried about anything else, and had dealt the peasant a buffet that knocked him sprawling. The riot started immediately thereafter.

He made the redheads hate him, too, Skarnu thought. *They wanted peace and quiet in the Valmieran countryside, not trouble. But he was their tool, and they were stuck with him . . . till his untimely demise.* He'd blazed Simanu himself, which was not the way one noble usually acquired another's domain.

Loud cheers rang out when Skarnu accepted the lean cow and the buffet. This was the way the ceremony was supposed to go. Skarnu had lived as a farmer long enough to begin to understand how much people who worked the land for a living appreciated it when things went as they were supposed to go.

Now he had to make a speech. He didn't want to do that; he would sooner have had another box on the ear. But it was part of the ceremony, too, and so he couldn't escape it. He stood up on that west-facing seat. An expectant hush fell.

"People of Pavilosta, people of Adutiskis, people of the countryside, I am proud to become your marquis," he said. "I've lived among you. I know what sort of folk you are. I know how you never believed the redheads would rule here forever, and how you made their lives hard while they were here."

He got a nice round of applause. *And I know what a liar I am,* he thought. Aye, plenty of the locals had opposed Mezentio's men. But plenty hadn't. Several women in the crowd still had their hair shorter than most because they'd been shorn after the Algarvians withdrew. A good many men had done a good deal of business with the occupiers. But he didn't want to dwell on that part of the past.

"I fought the Algarvians, as you did," he said. "Whatever I can do to protect you from your enemies, I will do. Now you may know that King Gainibu appointed me to this place. But I will also tell you that I will do whatever I can to protect you from the king, should he ever act unjustly. That's a noble's duty to his people, and I'll do everything I can to meet it."

More cheering, this louder and more enthusiastic. In the old days, nobles really were a shield against royal power— not least because dukes and counts and such didn't care to give up any power of their own. Things weren't so easy for the nobility nowadays; kings were stronger than they had been. But the pledge was worth making.

He made another pledge: "I won't be a scourge on your womenfolk, however much I admire them. And I admire them so much, I married one of them."

He waved to Merkela, and kept waving till she finally waved back. That got him a different sort of applause, warmer and more sympathetic. What went through his mind was, *I'll take whatever I can get.* He hopped down from the high seat and gave the peasant who'd boxed his ear one goldpiece and three of silver. The amount was as traditional as everything else in the ceremony. He wondered how it had first been set, and how long ago. No one seemed to know.

People came up to clasp his hand, to congratulate him— and to start asking him for judgments on their problems and quarrels. Time after time, he said, "Let me find out more before I answer you." That seemed to satisfy most of the would-be petitioners, but not all.

Merkela said, "You did very well."

"Thanks," Skarnu answered. "Now in another twenty years I'll stand up there and make myself another speech. Till then, no thanks."

"But isn't that part of what being a marquis is about?" Merkela asked. "Even a son of a whore like Enkuru would do it every so often. 'My people,' he would call us, as if he owned us. But we liked to come into Priekule to listen to him. It gave us a break from what we did every day."

Skarnu thought about that. Back in Priekule, nobles were common as dirt. Remembering some of the people in the capital, Skarnu knew the resemblance didn't end there. And, with King Gainibu at the apex of the social hierarchy, one count or marquis more or less didn't matter much.

Here in the countryside, things were different. *People here won't ever meet the king, or even see him. So who's at the top of the column, then? I am, by the powers above. I'm the one everybody's going to be looking at.*

Slowly, he nodded. "You're right," he told Merkela. "I'm going to have to get out there and show myself, even if I don't much want to do it."

"It needs doing," she said seriously.

"All right," Skarnu said. "But that means you're going to have to get out and show yourself a lot, too. After all, you're the main connection I've got to this part of the kingdom. You're the one who's lived here all her life. You'll have to help me."

Merkela had been smiling when she told Skarnu he'd need to face the people. The smile slipped when he suggested she needed to do it, too. The shoe pinched differently on her foot. Even if she needed a moment to gather herself, though, she nodded, too. Skarnu had expected that she would. He put his arm around her. Of one thing he was abundantly certain: she didn't run away from anything.

Sabrino's mother had died while he was fighting in the Six Years' War. He'd got compassionate leave to go home and see her laid on her pyre, but he hadn't been there during her last illness. His father had lived another fifteen years before passing away from a slow, painful wasting disease. He remembered going into the sickroom one day and realizing what he saw on the old man's face was death.

He looked at Algarve now. What he saw on his kingdom's face was death.

Not far west of his wing's dragon farm, the last Algarvian army holding the Unkerlanter hordes back from Trapani was breaking up. That it was breaking up didn't surprise him. If anything, the surprise lay in how long it had held together and how badly it had hurt Swemmel's soldiers. His wing, with a paper strength of sixty-four dragons, had eight ready to fly right now. They'd flown and flown and flown. They'd done everything they could, despite exhaustion, despite being without cinnabar. Every Algarvian in uniform had done everything he could.

The kingdom was dying anyhow. Not enough Algarvians remained in uniform to matter.

"Maybe we ought to stand aside, surrender, let the Unkerlanters and the cursed islanders finish overrunning us," Sabrino told Captain Orosio as they ate black bread and drank spirits in a miserable little tent that some pen-pushing idiot back in Trapani had surely recorded on a map as the headquarters of a full-strength wing. "Everything would be done then, and the kingdom wouldn't get trampled like a naked man trying to stand up to a herd of behemoths."

Orosio looked up from his mug. "Colonel, you'd better be careful what you say, and who you say it to," he answered. "Even now—maybe especially now—you can't talk about giving up. They'll grab you for treason and blaze you."

Sabrino's laugh held all the bitterness in the world. "And much difference that would make, to me or to Algarve. I don't think it'll happen, anyhow. Mezentio was going to raise us to the powers above. Instead, he's dropped us down to the powers below, and he won't quit till they've eaten every fornicating one of us." He took a swig. The spirits held out, if nothing else did. "Won't be long now."

"You *can't* talk that way, sir." Orosio sounded worried. "It really *is* treason."

"Go ahead and report me, then. You'll make yourself a hero, a hero of Algarve!" Sabrino said. "The king'll pin the medal on you himself, and give you your very own wing. You too can command eight dragons, you poor, sorry sod. That's half as many as a squadron is supposed to have, but who's counting?"

"Sir, I think you'd better go to bed," Orosio said stiffly. He would never report Sabrino, but the wing commander realized he'd pushed further than even his longtime comrade could go. With a sigh, Orosio asked, "What's left for us now?"

"What?" Sabrino waved his hand. "Nothing."

"No, sir." The younger man sounded very sure. "We have to go on till we can't go on any more. No point to quitting now, is there? We've come too far for that."

"You're right," Sabrino said with a sigh. Orosio looked relieved. But the two of them didn't mean the same thing, even if they said the same words. Orosio would go on fighting because fighting was all he had left. Sabrino would go on because he had nothing whatsoever left.

Maybe we aren't so different after all, he thought, and drained his mug.

Off to the west, the sound of bursting eggs was a continuous low rumble, and it had been getting closer. It might have been an approaching thunderstorm. *It's a storm, all right. It will blow away the whole kingdom.* But, when Sabrino cocked his head the other way, he heard bursting eggs off to the east, too: Unkerlanter dragons, tormenting Trapani. Before long, he'd be in the air again, doing his best to knock some of them out of the sky. *And I will. And it won't change a thing.*

"Sir . . ." Orosio hesitated, then went on, "That mage who wanted to fly with you? Maybe you should have let him."

"That filthy bastard? No." Even without the spirits he'd poured down, Sabrino's voice would have held no doubts. "He wouldn't have thrown back Swemmel's army, and you know it as well as I do. He'd have just given all our enemies one more reason to hate us and punish us. Don't you think they've got enough already?"

"I don't know, sir." Orosio yawned enormously. "I don't know anything, except I'm bloody tired."

"Let's both go to sleep, then," Sabrino said, "and see how long till somebody kicks us out of bed."

It wasn't nearly long enough. Some time in the middle of the night, a crystallomancer shook Sabrino awake and said, "I'm sorry, sir, but they're screaming for dragonfliers up at the front."

"When aren't they?" Sabrino answered around a yawn. He climbed out of his cot and yawned again. His head hurt, but not too bad. "All right. We'll do what we can."

Popular Assault men and a few real dragon-handlers were loading eggs under the bellies of the wing's surviving beasts as Sabrino and the handful of dragonfliers he still led strode out toward their mounts. "Northwest," the crystallomancer told him. "That's where the most trouble is."

Sabrino shook his head. "The most trouble is everywhere. But if they want us to fly northwest tonight, northwest we shall fly."

He didn't like flying by night, either. Telling where he was going and what he was supposed to be doing was much harder then. No one had asked his opinion. If some officer thought things were desperate enough to need dragons in the darkness . . . Well, with the war in its present state, the poor whoreson was all too likely to be right.

As the dragonfliers scrambled aboard their mounts, Sabrino said, "Try not to get killed, gentlemen. Algarve will need you again later." If they wanted to think he meant, *Algarve will need you to fly more missions,* that was all right with him. If they wanted to think he meant, *Algarve will still need you after the war is over and lost,* that was all right, too, and closer to the truth.

He whacked his dragon with the goad. The beast screamed with fury as it flung itself into the air; it liked flying at night no better than he. But it obeyed. As dragons went, it was a tractable mount—not that dragons went very far in that direction.

A bright moon, nearly full, spilled pale, buttery light over the landscape. Fires and bursting eggs and the flashes from blazing sticks of all weights added more. For night flying, this was pretty easy work.

Sabrino had no trouble finding the fighting front. For that

matter, he could have found it with his eyes closed, just from the din of bursting eggs. Every time he took his forlorn little wing into the air, the front lay farther east. Unkerlanter armies were lapping around the defenders despite all the Algarvians could do to hold them back. Before long, Trapani would be caught in a ring of iron, a ring of fire.

I hope my wife had the sense to flee, the wing commander thought. *The city is going to fall, and it won't be pretty.* The collapse of the Kaunian Empire more than a thousand years before came to mind. Then, though, Algarvic folk had been doing the sacking. Soon, they would be on the receiving end.

I don't see anything we can do to stop that. Maybe we can still push the day back a bit. The image of a harried-looking Algarvian crystallomancer down on the ground appeared in the crystal Sabrino carried. "Powers above be praised!" the fellow said. "They've bridged the stream in front of us, and they're pouring men and behemoths across. Can your wing take it out?"

"We can try," Sabrino answered, thinking again of symbols on maps. "You should know, though, that my wing consists of eight dragons, no more."

"Eight dragons? Eight?" The crystallomancer made a horrible face. "That isn't what I was given to understand."

"I don't care what you were given to understand," Sabrino said harshly. "Everything we've been given to understand about this whole fornicating war is a pack of lies. Now where's this Unkerlanter bridge?"

The crystallomancer told him. He soon discovered he could have found it without help. The Unkerlanters had torches at both ends and along the bridge itself to guide their men and beasts to and across it. *Arrogant bastards,* Sabrino thought. *They don't even believe we're still in the game. Time to show them they've made a mistake.*

He ordered his dragon down in an attack run as perfect as any he'd ever made. He released the eggs it carried at exactly the right moment. They both burst in the center of the bridge, sending Unkerlanter soldiers and behemoths splashing into the stream. One after another, the men in his wing followed him down. By the time they were done, not much remained of the bridge.

"Nice job, boys," Sabrino said into his crystal. "Now let's go home and go back to bed."

He'd just turned toward the dragon farm from which he'd come when the Unkerlanter dragons struck his wing. There were only a couple of squadrons of them—but that meant they outnumbered his comrades and him three or four to one. And their dragons were fresh, not worn out, and were full of cinnabar. They flamed twice as far as the Algarvian beasts could.

For all that, Sabrino's men were wise in the ways of dragonflying, and quickly took out a couple of the enemy beasts—one with flame from behind, the other by a canny blaze that killed the Unkerlanter dragonflier and let the dragon fly wild. Sabrino thought they might yet break free and win their way back to the dragon farm once more.

He saw the dragon that got him and his own mount as nothing but a blur in the moonlight, and then a tongue of flame licking toward him. An instant later, he screamed, but his shriek was lost, drowned, in the great bellow of agony from his dragon. Wind beat in his face as the dragon lurched toward the ground, but he hardly noticed. His left leg felt on fire.

When he looked down, he saw his left leg *was* on fire. So was the dragon. He beat at the flames with his fist. The dragon could still fly, though, after a fashion—the Unkerlanter beast had flamed at long range, not wanting to close. Had its dragonflier come closer, he would be dead now, and so would his mount. Things were bad enough as they were. Sabrino wanted to pass out, but the torment in his leg wouldn't let him. He pounded the dragon with the goad, steering it back toward the southeast.

It didn't make it all the way to the dragon farm. It came down in the middle of a field of beets. The shock of the landing made Sabrino scream again. The stench of the dragon's burnt flesh, and of his own, filled his nostrils.

He loosened the harness and fell to the ground. If the dragon crushed him or flamed him in its own agonies, everything would be over, and he wouldn't have minded at all. But it rampaged away, leaving him lying there and hoping for death.

Before it found him, Algarvian soldiers did. They'd come to deal with the wounded dragon, but they took Sabrino back to a healer's tent. The healer took one look at what was left of his leg and said, "I'm sorry, Colonel, but that will have to come off."

"Oh, please!" Sabrino groaned. The healer blinked in surprise, then nodded. A couple of stalwart helpers lifted Sabrino and set him down in what looked like an oversized rest crate. His awareness of the world was interrupted.

When it returned, so did pain. The healer gave Sabrino a bottle of thick, sweet, nasty stuff. He drained it dry. After what seemed forever but couldn't have been above a quarter of an hour, the pain retreated. The healer said, "You'll live, I think. With a cane and a peg, you may even walk again. But for you, Colonel, the war is over."

Under the drug, that hardly seemed to matter. Under the drug, nothing much seemed to matter. *Maybe I should have started taking this stuff, whatever it is, a long time ago,* he thought vaguely. He smiled at the healer. "So what?" he said.

Up till the Derlavaian War broke out, Ilmarinen hadn't known many Unkerlanters. The vast kingdom had its share of talented mages, but they published less often than their colleagues farther east—either that or they published in their own language rather than in classical Kaunian. And Unkerlanter, in Ilmarinen's biased opinion, was a language fit only for Unkerlanters. Mages from Unkerlant didn't come to colloquia as often as their counterparts in the kingdoms of eastern Derlavai. Maybe they were afraid of revealing secrets. Maybe King Swemmel feared they would, and didn't let them out.

Now Ilmarinen had all the chances he wanted to see Unkerlanters up close. A regular ferry service ran across the Albi River, which separated Kuusaman occupiers of Algarve on the east bank from Swemmel's soldiers on the west. Ilmarinen found the idea of a ferry interesting, too. In Kuusamo, where the rivers froze up in wintertime, they were used less often than here in the mild north of Derlavai.

Ilmarinen, of course, found almost everything interesting. Whenever he got the chance, he stuck his mage's badge in the pocket of his tunic and crossed over to the west side of the Albi to learn what he could about the Unkerlanters. The ferry, a stout rowboat, had a crew half Kuusaman, half Unkerlanter. When a man from one land needed to talk to one from the other, he was more likely to use Algarvian than any other tongue. For the master mage, that was one more irony to savor.

On the west bank of the Albi, the Unkerlanters looked less than delighted about having visitors from the east. But the Kuusamans were their allies, so they couldn't very well point sticks at them and keep them out. Ilmarinen wondered what Swemmel's men made of him. Without his mage's badge, what was he? A colonel with too many years on him and too much curiosity for his own good.

As far as he was concerned, there was no such thing as too much curiosity for his own good. He walked here and there, peered at this and that, and asked questions whenever he found someone who would admit to speaking a civilized language—which didn't happen very often; a lot of Unkerlanters seemed to go out of their way to deny knowing anything.

For a while, that not only perplexed Ilmarinen but also annoyed him. But he had a mind quick to see patterns. If Swemmel was apt to make someone disappear for saying or doing the wrong thing, what could be safer than saying and doing nothing? But Swemmel's people couldn't very well have beaten the Algarvians by doing nothing. It was a puzzlement. Ilmarinen loved being puzzled.

He did find a young lieutenant named Andelot who spoke some Algarvian and didn't seem afraid to speak it to him. The fellow said, "Aye, is true. We have not so much initiative. Is a word, initiative?"

"It's a word, sure enough," Ilmarinen answered. "How in blazes did you win without it?" He had a good many shortcomings of his own. Lack of initiative had never been one of them. Too much initiative? That was a different story.

"By doing what our commanders order us to do," Andelot replied. "This is most efficient way we find." When he spoke Algarvian, he seemed stuck in the present indicative.

"But what happens when your commanders make a mistake?" Ilmarinen asked. Obeying without question struck him as inhuman. He had a certain amount of trouble—perhaps more than a certain amount—obeying at all. "What happens when a lieutenant like you or a sergeant, say, needs to fix a mistake? How do you do that when you have no initiative?"

"We have some. We have less than Algarvians, maybe, but we have some. I admit, if we have more, we do better." Lieutenant Andelot turned and called in Algarvian to another, older, man, who came over and saluted. Returning to a language Ilmarinen could follow, Andelot said, "Here is Sergeant Fariulf. I am sorry, but he speaks Algarvian not. He has initiative. He shows over and over."

"Well, good for him," Ilmarinen said. At first glance, Fariulf was just another peasant in uniform, one badly in need of a shave and a bath. First glances, though, showed only so much. "Ask him how he decides to use it, then."

Andelot spoke again in Unkerlanter. Fariulf replied in the same tongue. His eyes were guarded as they flicked first to his superior officer, then to Ilmarinen. Andelot said, "He says, if I do it not, who does? When I need to do, I do."

Ilmarinen hardly heard the answer. He was staring at Fariulf. Sometimes—not always—a mage could feel power. Ilmarinen felt it here. It wasn't sorcerous power, or not exactly sorcerous power, but it radiated out from the man like heat from a fire. Finding such in an Unkerlanter peasant was the last thing Ilmarinen had expected. He was so startled, he almost remarked on it.

A second look at Fariulf convinced him that wouldn't be a good idea. The sergeant would have hidden that power if he could; Ilmarinen sensed as much. Whatever was inside Fariulf—if that was even the man's true name, which Ilmarinen suddenly doubted—he didn't want anyone else to know it was there. Andelot didn't know; Ilmarinen was sure of that.

The lieutenant had said something. Lost in his own thoughts, Ilmarinen had no idea what it was. "I'm sorry?" he said.

"I say, how you give better answer about initiative?" Andelot repeated.

"I doubt you could." But Ilmarinen was still eyeing the sergeant. And Fariulf, or whatever his real name was, was eyeing him, too. Something like shock showed itself in the Unkerlanter's eyes. He knew Ilmarinen knew what he was—or some of what he was, anyhow. That alarmed him.

Little by little, Ilmarinen realized the fellow might be dangerous if he stayed frightened. This was, after all, the Unkerlanter side of the river. *If I have an accident, how hard would anyone try to find out whether it was really accidental? Not very, unless I miss my guess.*

Picking his words with care, the Kuusaman mage said, "I believe the more initiative a man shows, the more he does for himself, the better off he's likely to be, and the better off the world is likely to be."

Andelot translated for Fariulf. Ilmarinen smiled and nodded. He hadn't even been lying. Now, would the Unkerlanter see as much? Andelot said, "Maybe that so in your kingdom. Believe me, sir, not always so in Unkerlant."

Ilmarinen did believe him. In Unkerlant, from everything he'd heard, everything he'd seen, a man who stuck his neck out was asking the axe to come down. The mage wanted to talk more with Sergeant Fariulf, to see if he could learn just what sort of power burned behind the stocky man's eyes. He would have to be careful. He saw as much. Andelot plainly had no idea what a wonder he had for an underofficer.

But Fariulf—an Unkerlanter, sure enough—was wary about giving up whatever secrets he possessed. He spoke in his own language. Andelot translated: "Colonel, he asks if you done with him, if he can go back to duties."

What Ilmarinen felt like doing was kidnapping Fariulf and dragging him over to the eastern bank of the Albi so he could wring knowledge from him like a man wringing water from a towel. He reluctantly recognized he couldn't do that. And Fariulf, alerted now, would yield him very little. Ilmarinen gave up, something he didn't like to do. "I'm done with him, aye. Tell him thanks, and tell him good luck."

The sergeant got to his feet and took off. His power, his secrets, went with him. Ilmarinen could feel them leaving.

He sighed. Andelot asked, "Is anything else with me, Colonel? I too have duties."

Get out of my hair, old man. That was what he meant, even if he was too polite to say so. "No, nothing else, Lieutenant," Ilmarinen answered. *Except for your sergeant, you haven't got anything very interesting.* "I thank you for your time, and for your translating."

As Ilmarinen returned and started back toward the ferry, another officer came by. This one, Ilmarinen saw, wore a chest badge along with the rank badges on his collar tabs. Ilmarinen figured out what the badge meant as soon as the fellow looked at him. He felt himself recognized for what he was, just as he'd recognized Fariulf for something out of the ordinary. The newcomer spoke rapidly in Unkerlanter. Andelot exclaimed in surprise, then returned to Algarvian: "This mage say—*says*—you too are mage. Is so?"

He couldn't even lie. The other wizard would know he was doing it. "Aye, I'm a mage," he replied. "So what?"

More back-and-forth in Unkerlanter. After a bit, Andelot said, "This other mage says you are no ordinary mage. He says you are strong mage, mighty mage. Is so?"

Powers below eat you, Ilmarinen thought at the Unkerlanter wizard. It wasn't so much because the fellow was right, but because, by being right, he'd made sure Ilmarinen couldn't casually visit this side of the river any more. Getting escorted to things he was supposed to see didn't strike him as much fun.

"Is so?" Andelot persisted.

"Aye, it's so," Ilmarinen said with a sigh.

"You are spy?" the young lieutenant asked—a very Unkerlanter question.

"I'm an ally," Ilmarinen answered. "Spies are enemies. How can I possibly be a spy?"

"How can you be spy?" Andelot echoed. "Easy." The other mage, who didn't speak Algarvian, had a good deal to say in Unkerlanter. Andelot didn't sound very happy about hearing any of it. When Swemmel's sorcerer finished, the lieutenant said, "You go back to your side of river now. You stay on your side of river now. You not welcome on this side of river now."

"And is that how one ally treats another?" Ilmarinen demanded, doing his best to show more indignation than he felt.

"Do you show us all your secrets?" Andelot returned. Because Unkerlanters had to keep so many secrets so inspectors and impressers wouldn't drag them away and do something dreadful to them, they were convinced everyone had secrets and guarded them and tried to spy out other people's.

"Plenty of your officers on our bank of the Albi, too," Ilmarinen said. *And, odds are, they're spies, or some of them are,* he thought.

"That is that bank of river. This is this bank of river," Andelot said, as if that made all the difference in the world. Maybe, to him, it did. He pointed east, toward the riverbank. "You have to go now."

Ilmarinen went, protesting all the while. To go quietly would have been out of character for him. Andelot and the mage walked with him. He wondered what the Unkerlanters didn't want him to see. He wondered if there really was something he shouldn't see. *Curse Swemmel's whoresons,* he thought. *When you start dealing with them, you have to start thinking like them.*

Lieutenant and wizard stood watching till he boarded the ferry, till it began to move, till it reached the other side of the river. *What don't they want me to see? Is anything at all there? Can I find out?* He was planning ways and means when he realized he'd given himself a new challenge.

Spring in Skrunda was an enjoyable time most years: warm without being too hot, with just enough rain to keep things green and growing. Talsu enjoyed this spring even more than the past few. Not only were the Algarvian occupiers gone from Jelgava, but the news sheets shouted of the triumphs of allied armies deep inside Algarve itself. A few Jelgavan regiments were in the fight, too. By the way the news sheets trumpeted what they did, they might have been whipping King Mezentio's men all by themselves.

Some people—people who hadn't seen action themselves—doubtless believed the news sheets. Talsu knew better. He knew what sorts of armies the Kuusamans and Lagoans had. He had a pretty fair notion of what sort of army the Unkerlanters had. In amongst all those fighters, a few regiments of Jelgavans would have been like a fingernail: nice to have, but hardly essential to the body as a whole.

When he remarked on that to his father, Traku said, "Well, we've got to start somewhere, I expect."

"I suppose so," Talsu admitted, "but do we have to cackle so much about it?" He made a noise that might have come from a chicken after it laid an egg.

Traku laughed and then tossed him a pair of linen trousers. "Here—these are ready to go to Mindaugu for summer wear. He's got himself too much silver to sweat in wool."

"I'll take them," Talsu said. "I'll be glad to, in fact—his house is near the grocery where Gailisa's working."

"Don't dawdle away the whole day there," his father said. "I would like to get a little more work out of you."

"Foosh," Talsu said. His father laughed. Talsu grabbed the trousers and headed across town with them. When he got to Mindaugu's, the wealthy wine merchant took them, ducked away to try them on, and came out beaming. He gave Talsu his silver. Talsu looked the coins over, as he'd got into the habit of doing. "Wait a bit. This one's got Mainardo's ugly mug on it."

Mindaugu made a sour face. "I thought I'd made a clean sweep of those." He suddenly looked hopeful. "The silver's still good, you know." Talsu just clicked his tongue between his teeth. He had right on his side, and he knew it. Muttering, Mindaugu replaced Mainardo's coin with one that had King Donalitu's image. Talsu stuck it and the others in his pocket and headed off to the grocery store.

I won't spend too much time there, he thought, *but a fellow is entitled to see his wife every once in a while, isn't he?* He'd been married for more than a year, but still felt like a man on his honeymoon.

As he left the wine merchant's, a couple of utterly ordinary middle-aged men in clothes even more ordinary (a tailor's son, he noticed such things) who'd been leaning

against a wall stepped out into the middle of the sidewalk—
and into his path. "You Talsu son of Traku?" one of them
asked, his voice mildly friendly.

"That's right," Talsu answered; only afterwards did he
wonder what would have happened had he lied. As things
were, he just said, "Do I know you?"

"You know us well enough," replied the man who hadn't
asked his name. He reached into a trouser pocket and
pulled out a short stick such as a constable might use. "You
know us well enough to come along quietly, don't you?"

Ice ran through Talsu. When he first saw the stick, he
thought the men were a couple of robbers. He would have
given up the silver he'd just got—it wasn't worth his life.
But they knew his name. And they wanted *him,* not his
money. That could only make them King Donalitu's men.
As he bleated, "But I haven't done anything!" he thought he
would rather have dealt with robbers.

"Quietly, I said." That was the fellow with the stick.

"Charge is treason against the Kingdom of Jelgava,"
added the other one, the one who'd asked his name.

"Come along," they said again, this time together. The
one who didn't have his stick out took Talsu's arm. The
other one fell in behind them so he could blaze Talsu at the
first sign of anything untoward.

Numbly, Talsu went where they took him. If he'd done
anything else, something dreadful would have happened to
him. He was sure of that. Donalitu's men had no reputation
for restraint. They didn't lead him in the direction of the
constabulary station, which surprised him enough to make
him ask, "Where are we going?" He added, "I really
haven't done anything," not that he thought it would do him
any good.

And it didn't. "Shut up," one of them said.

"You'll find out where," the other told him.

He did, too, when they marched him into the ley-line
caravan depot. He wondered how they would keep things
quiet and discreet in an ordinary caravan car. But, being
servitors of the king, they didn't have to worry about ordinary cars. They had a special laid on just for them—and
him. He would gladly have done without the honor.

"What about my family?" he howled as the car—which had bars across the windows and sorcerous locks on the door—rolled out of Skrunda, heading southeast.

"Can't pin anything on 'em yet," one of the men who'd seized him said. That wasn't what Talsu meant, nor anything close to it, but he didn't try to make himself any clearer. He'd caught the unmistakable regret in the fellow's voice.

The other man said, "You want to confess now and make it easy on everybody?"

Everybody but me, Talsu thought. Of course, they didn't care about him. He said, "How can I confess when I haven't done anything?"

"Happens all the time," the fellow answered.

Talsu believed that. He'd spent time in a dungeon before. "How can you arrest me for treason when the cursed redheads arrested me for treason?" he demanded.

"Happens all the time," Donalitu's bully boy said again. "Some people have treason in their blood." While Talsu was still spluttering over that, he went on, "Turn out your pockets. Everything that's in 'em. You leave anything at all behind, you'll be sorry—you can bet your arse on that." He shoved a tray at Talsu.

Having no choice, Talsu obeyed. King Donalitu's men examined everything with great care, especially the coins he set on the tray. Talsu let out a silent sigh of relief that he'd got Mindaugu to take back the silverpiece with Mainardo's Algarvian visage on it. These whoresons could have made a treason case from it without any other evidence. *What difference does it make, though?* he thought bitterly. *They can make a treason case from no evidence at all.*

Late in the afternoon, the ley-line caravan car glided to a halt. "Come on," one of Talsu's captors said. The other one murmured the charm that opened the door. The dungeon lay right by the ley line, out in the middle of nowhere. Talsu hadn't expected anything else. These whoresons wouldn't want to walk very far once they got out of the car.

Guards searched Talsu as soon as he got into the dungeon. They found nothing; the fellows who'd seized him had got it all. But they had their jobs, too, and did them.

Then they threw him in a cramped little cell that held nothing but a bucket and a straw pallet. He sighed. It wasn't as if he hadn't been through this before.

I have to be ready for the first interrogation, he thought. *They'll let me get hungry first*—he was hungry already—*and they'll probably wake me up so I'll be all muzzy. But I have to be ready. They'll want to break me right then and there. If I break, I'm theirs. I can't give in.*

He made himself as comfortable as he could, and waited. A cart rattled down the corridors. *Suppers,* Talsu thought; he knew the sound of that cart. It didn't stop at his cell. He sighed, disappointed but not surprised.

After darkness fell, he stretched out on the musty pallet. His growling belly kept him awake for a while, but not for too long. His dreams were nasty and confused.

The door flew open with a crash. A bright light blazed into his eyes. Two guards grabbed him and hauled him to his feet. "Come on, you!" one of them shouted. Talsu went. Had he not gone, the guards would have beaten him and then dragged him where they wanted him to go. They might—they probably would—beat him later. He was willing to put off the evil moment as long as he could.

But when they took him into the interrogation chamber, he let out a cry of horror and dismay even before they slammed him down onto a hard, backless stool. The Jelgavan major on the other side of the desk greeted him with a smile. "Hello, Talsu son of Traku," he said. "You remember me, I see."

Talsu shuddered. "I'm not likely to forget you," he said. The Jelgavan major had interrogated him during his last stretch in the dungeons. Then, he'd been asking questions for King Mainardo and the Algarvians. Now he served Donalitu, as he had before the redheads invaded. Then he'd been a mere captain. Bitterly, Talsu remarked, "I see you got promoted."

"I'm good at what I do," the interrogator said placidly. He wagged a finger at Talsu. "Didn't I tell you I would still be here, still doing my job, under whoever happened to be ruling the kingdom?"

"You served the Algarvians with all your heart," Talsu said. "If that's not treason, what in blazes do you call it?"

"Following orders," the major replied. "I am a useful man, and known to be loyal to the king. Neither of those applies to you." His tone sharpened. "You are charged with associating with Kugu the silversmith, a known Algarvian agent and collaborator, during the late occupation. What have you got to say for yourself?"

"You idiot!" Talsu howled, too outraged to remember where he was. "I went to Kugu trying to join the underground *against* the fornicating Algarvians. You know that's true. You have to—he's the son of a whore who betrayed me to the redheads."

"I'm not referring to that association," the interrogator told him. "I'm referring to the association you continued to have with him after you were released from your last period of confinement. That's plainly treason against King Donalitu."

"Are you out of your mind?" Talsu said. "I *had* to associate with Kugu then. If I didn't, you people would have thrown me back into a cell." He'd also arranged for the silversmith's untimely demise, but he didn't even bother bringing that up. He couldn't prove it, as he'd done it by stealth and sorcery.

"That is no excuse," the interrogator said. "You also provided the occupying authorities with the names of certain people you believed to be loyal to King Donalitu. Arrests were made as a result of your actions. Punishments were inflicted. I will have you know, this is a very serious charge."

"Occupying authorities?" Talsu started to get up to throttle the fellow. The guards slammed him down onto the stool again. They didn't try to keep him from talking: "What occupying authorities? *You* were the bastard who tormented me—and tormented my wife, too—till I gave you names. I *did* get into the underground, and I fought the Algarvians while you were probably still torturing people for them."

"Subject does not deny the charges," the major murmured, jotting a note on the pad in front of him. Talsu

howled again, a wordless cry of fury. The interrogator gestured to the bully boys. They went to work on Talsu. Before
long, he had plenty more reasons to howl.

Over the years, Bembo had grown used to giving orders. It
wasn't just that he'd been a constable in occupied Forthweg. He'd been a constable long before that, here in Tricarico. People jumped when he told them to jump. They did
him favors to stay on his good side. He'd had no trouble
getting all sorts of bribes and other sweeteners.

   That was over now, and his broken leg had nothing to do
with it. The leg was healing as well as it could, though it
looked thin as a twig under the splints that protected it. But
Algarvians didn't give orders in Tricarico any more. The
city belonged to the Kuusamans now, and they made who
was in charge very plain.

   Bembo and Saffa sat at a table in a sidewalk café, drinking wine he would have turned up his nose at before the war
and eating olives and salted almonds. Saffa's nose—much
cuter than Bembo's—wrinkled. "What's that stink?" she
asked.

   Taking everything into account, Tricarico had been
lucky during the war. Devastation had mostly left it alone,
and, when the town fell, it fell fast. Having been in Eoforwic, Bembo knew things didn't have to be that way. The
grinding fight there had also left him intimately acquainted with the stench in question. "That's dead bodies,"
he answered, and surprised even himself with how casually the words came out.

   "Oh." Saffa grimaced. "That's right. Those three in the
town square. I'd forgotten."

   "Naughty." Bembo waggled a forefinger at her. "The Kuusamans don't want you to forget. They don't want any of
us to forget. That's why they hanged those three stupid bastards right in the middle of the square four days ago, and
it's why they haven't taken 'em down, too."

   "Stupid bastards?" The constabulary sketch artist let out
an indignant squawk. "They were patriots, heroes, martyrs."

   "They were cursed fools," Bembo said. "If you aren't in
the army and you blaze at the people who've taken your

town and they catch you, this is one of the things that're liable to happen." He remembered some of the things that had happened in Eoforwic. Compared to those, hanging was a mercy. Saffa didn't know about things like that, and didn't know how lucky she was not to.

"But the Kuusamans are the enemy," she protested.

"That's why we have an army—or had an army," Bembo answered. "Civilians who try to fight against soldiers are what you call free-blazers. If the soldiers catch 'em, they're what you call fair game."

"They were brave," Saffa said.

"They were bloody dumb," Bembo told her. "They didn't do themselves any good, and they didn't do Algarve any good, either. We don't have any soldiers in the field anywhere within a hundred miles of here, not any more we don't." He threw his hands in the air in a gesture of extravagant despair. "Powers below eat everything, we've *lost*."

Saffa stared at him. The truth there was obvious. The little slant-eyed soldiers in the streets made it so. Maybe she somehow hadn't realized everything it meant, though, till he all but shouted in her face. She bit her lip, blinked a couple of times, and quietly began to cry.

"Don't do that!" Bembo exclaimed. He fumbled for a handkerchief, didn't find one, and gave her a café napkin instead. "Come on, sweetheart. Please don't do that." He had a soft spot for weeping women. Most Algarvian men did.

"I can't help it," she said, dabbing her eyes. "I don't think Salamone is ever coming home, not from fighting the horrible Unkerlanters." Her tears came faster, harder.

Bembo muttered something more or less polite. Salamone was the fellow who'd fathered her son. She still hadn't let Bembo into her bed, or come into his. He wondered why he bothered with her; he wasn't usually so patient with women. Maybe it was because he'd known her before things got bad, and she was a line back to those better days. He took a pull at his wine to disguise a snort. That was an alarming thing to think about somebody all over prickles like Saffa.

She gave him a look holding a good deal of her old vinegar. "I know what *you're* thinking. You hope those savages have him for supper, and without any salt, too."

"No such thing!" Bembo said with an indignation all the louder for being less than sincere. But then he followed it with the truth: "I wouldn't wish getting caught by the Unkerlanters on anybody at all."

Saffa eyed him, then slowly nodded. "You may even mean that."

"I do!" Bembo exclaimed. "Remember, darling, I was in Eoforwic when all the Unkerlanters in the world came rolling east across Forthweg straight at me." Being who he was, of course he saw the battles of the summer before, so disastrous for Algarve, in that light. He ate an almond, then went on, "And the cursed Forthwegians rose up and stabbed us in the back, too. Fat lot of good it did them—now they've got Swemmel sitting on 'em instead of us, and may they have joy of that."

"It's all a mess," Saffa said, which summed things up as well as any four words Bembo might have found.

"That it is," he said dolefully, and then, when a plump woman with a pitted complexion almost stumbled over his splinted leg—which had to stick out from the table a bit—his gloom turned to spleen: "Watch it, lady!"

She glared at him. "If you were any kind of a man, you'd have let yourself get killed before all *this* happened." Her wave encompassed the whole of Tricarico and, by extension, the whole of Algarve. She might have held Bembo personally responsible for the lost war.

He wouldn't have taken that from Saffa, and he certainly wasn't about to take it from a stranger he didn't find attractive. "If I had anything to do with you, I certainly would have let myself get killed before I came home," he said, and bit his thumb at her, a fine Algarvian insult.

The plump woman screeched like a wounded trumpet. She drew back a foot to kick Bembo's bad leg. He grabbed a crutch by the wrong end and got ready to swing it like a club. Algarvians were normally the most chivalrous of men, but he wasn't about to let anybody do that leg any more harm.

Saffa snatched up the bowl of olives and made as if to throw it at the woman. The olives glistened with oil; they would have ruined the plump woman's kilt and frock. Bembo wondered if she didn't find that a more dangerous threat than his makeshift bludgeon. Mumbling curses under her breath, she stalked off with her nose in the air.

"Thanks," Bembo told Saffa.

"You're welcome," she said. "That stupid sow had no business coming down on you so. You did everything for the kingdom you could. What did *she* do? Sit around and eat cakes the whole war long, by the look of her."

Everything I could do for the kingdom? Bembo wondered. He really had fought, and he really had kept order in foreign towns. *And you sent powers above only know how many Kaunians off on their last rides.* Had that helped Algarve or hurt it? Hurt it, probably, for such things made all her neighbors more certain they couldn't afford to lose. But his superiors had ordered it, and so he'd done it.

He wished he hadn't had that thought. He saw in his mind's eye that horrible old Kuusaman mage who'd looked through him as if the ocean of his soul were no more than ankle-deep. What that fellow thought of him . . . No, better not to imagine what that fellow thought of him. And the Kuusaman had given him the benefit of the doubt, too. Bembo shivered even though the day was warm, almost hot. He gulped down the rest of his wine and waved for more.

Before it got there, Saffa's eyes narrowed with anger. "Oh, that's too much," she said. "That really is too much."

Bembo wondered what he'd done now, but her rage wasn't aimed at him. She pointed. He twisted in his chair. Up the street came a couple of Jelgavan officers in tunics and trousers, looking around at Tricarico as if they'd conquered it themselves.

"Those stinking Kaunians have their nerve," Saffa said savagely. "They shouldn't show their faces here. It's not like *they* beat us."

"No, it isn't," Bembo agreed. "Even so . . ." His voice trailed off. As far as he could see, Algarvians were going to have a hard time saying anything bad about Kaunian folk, even if it was true (maybe especially if it was true), for generations to come. He saw no way to say that to Saffa, precisely because she didn't know all the things he did. *She's the lucky one,* he thought again.

She stared at the trousered blonds, looking daggers into their backs, till they went round a corner. Then she turned back to Bembo and said, "Your flat is only a couple of blocks from here, isn't it?"

"That's right," he answered.

"Let's go back there," she said. "We'll see what happens." She cocked her head to one side, laughing at his flabbergasted expression. "Don't get your hopes up too far. You don't move very fast. I have plenty of time to change my mind."

He knew that was true, but couldn't hurry on his crutches no matter how much he wanted to. He spent most of the time on the way trying to remember how messy the flat was. If Saffa laughed at him for being a slob, she might not want to do anything but laugh.

She raised an eyebrow at the state of the front room when he opened the door, but said only, "I expected worse." And she did go into the bedchamber with him, and, he being hampered by the splint, she rode him as if he were a racing unicorn. But that was a race they both could win—and, by the way she threw back her head and cried out at the end, they both did.

Then she sprawled down onto him, her breasts soft and firm against his chest. "Ask you something?" he said, running his hand along the sweet curves of her back down toward her bottom.

One of Saffa's eyebrows quirked upward. The smile she smiled down at him was lopsided, too. "It can't be that one, and I didn't know you knew any other questions."

His hand paused on her backside and pinched, not too hard. She squeaked. Bembo said, "I didn't even need to ask that one. You asked me instead, remember?"

"Well, maybe I did," she said, and bent down to kiss the end of his nose. He'd wondered if she would bite instead, but she didn't. "All right, Bembo—what's your other question?"

"I was just wondering why," he answered. "Not that I'm

not not happy you did"—he kissed her this time—"but how come? You'd been telling me no for so long, I'd kind of got used to it."

"Maybe that's why you hadn't been pestering me so much lately," Saffa said. But it was a serious question, and after a small pause she gave it a serious answer: "We've really lost. There's nothing we can do about it. Seeing those cursed Jelgavans walking along like they owned the town gave me a kick in the teeth. Salamone isn't coming home. I've got to start over somewhere."

"And I'm it?" Bembo said. It might have been a serious answer, but it was a long way from flattering.

But Saffa nodded. "And you're it." This time, her smile held fewer barbs. "Better than I thought you'd be, too."

"Thanks—I suppose," he said. She laughed. He hadn't slipped out of her, and felt himself growing hard once more. He began to move, slowly and carefully. "Shall we try again, then?"

"So soon?" Saffa sounded surprised.

"Why not?" Bembo answered grandly. The only reason why, of course, was that he'd been so very long without. He didn't have to tell her that, though. And she didn't seem displeased. After a while, she seemed very pleased indeed. Bembo knew he was.

Colonel Lurcanio sat beneath an oak tree just coming into full leaf and contemplated the death and ruination of his kingdom and its army. He didn't think the Unkerlanters were in Trapani yet, but he didn't know how much longer his countrymen could hold them away from the capital. The last few reports coming by crystal from Algarve's greatest city had held a note of frantic desperation under their defiance. The past couple of days, no reports at all had come from Trapani: enemy mages were blocking the emanations. That didn't strike him as a good omen.

"It wouldn't have mattered," he muttered. Even if King Mezentio had personally appealed to him to come to the capital's rescue, he couldn't have obeyed his sovereign. A good-sized Algarvian army remained in the field here in the southeastern part of the kingdom, but it was cut off from the rest of Algarve by the Lagoans and Kuusamans. Having bypassed it, the islanders seemed content to leave it alone so long as it didn't make a nuisance of itself.

Captain Santerno came up to Lurcanio. The combat veteran didn't bother saluting. Lurcanio didn't bother reproving him. Without preamble, the captain said, "Sir, how in blazes are we going to get out of this mess?"

"That's a good question, Captain," Lurcanio replied. "As best I can see, there's no way. If you want to tell me I'm wrong, I'd be delighted to hear the whys and wherefores, believe me."

Santerno cursed with soldierly fluency. When he ran out of curses—which took a while—he said, "I don't see any way, either. I was hoping you did."

"Me?" Lurcanio said. "What do I know? After all, I spent the war shuffling papers in Priekule and laying Valmieran women." Santerno hadn't thrown his previous duty in his face, but his scorn for Lurcanio because of it had never been far from the surface.

Now the captain had the grace to cough and shuffle his feet and show a certain amount of embarrassment. "Turned out you knew what you were doing in the field after all, sir," he said. "I stopped doubting it after the way you led the brigade down toward the sea this past winter during our last big attack in Valmiera."

"We might have gone farther if those Kuusamans holed up in that one town hadn't cramped the whole attack." Lurcanio sighed. "But it probably wouldn't have made any difference in the long run."

"Maybe not." Santerno drew himself up with a certain melancholy pride. "We scared the buggers out of a year's growth, though."

"I suppose we did," Lurcanio replied. "And how many men and behemoths and dragons did we throw away doing it? We could have used them against the Unkerlanters instead, don't you think, and got more with them."

His adjutant shrugged. "I don't give orders like that, sir. I just follow the ones I get."

"We all just followed the ones we got, Captain." Lurcanio waved, as if to show this last bypassed army trapped in its pocket. "And look what we got for following them."

Before Santerno could answer that, a soldier came up to Lurcanio and said, "Sir, there's an enemy soldier coming up under flag of truce."

"Is there?" Lurcanio heaved himself to his feet, however much his weary bones protested. "I'll see him." The soldier nodded and trotted off to bring back the foe.

"He's going to ask for our surrender," Santerno said.

"Probably," Lurcanio agreed. "I can't give it to him, of course." *I would if I could,* he thought, but kept that to himself. Aloud, he went on, "All I can do is pass him along to General Prusione, and I expect I will."

But his resolve wavered when he saw the fellow who came in under the white flag. Not that the major in the greenish brown tunic and trousers was ugly, but he was, unquestionably, a Valmieran. "Do you speak classical Kaunian, Colonel?" he asked in that tongue. "I regret to tell you, I have no Algarvian."

"I know Valmieran, Major," Lurcanio replied in that language. "What can I do for you this afternoon?"

"My name is Vizgantu, Colonel," the Valmieran said, plainly relieved to be able to use his own speech. "Please take me to your commander. I have been sent to request the surrender of the Algarvian army in this pocket, further resistance on your part plainly being hopeless. Why spill more blood to no purpose?"

Lurcanio took a deep breath. "Major Vizgantu, I am going to send you back to your own superiors instead. I mean no personal offense to you, sir, but having a Valmieran demand our surrender is an insult, nothing less. We may have lost this war, but we did not lose it to your kingdom. I spent more than four very pleasant years in Priekule. I should have a child there now, as a matter of fact."

Captain Santerno laughed out loud. Major Vizgantu turned red. Doing his best to choke back rage, he said, "You are in a poor position to tell the armies opposing you what to do, Colonel. By the powers above, I hope you pay for your insolence."

My whole kingdom is paying, Lurcanio thought. What

Algarve had made her neighbors pay never entered his mind—that was their worry, not his. He turned to the soldier who'd brought the Valmieran to him. "You may take this gentleman to the front once more. His flag of truce will be honored as he returns to his own side, of course."

"You bastard!" Vizgantu snarled.

"My bastard, as I told you, is back in Priekule," Lurcanio answered calmly. *Unless it's Valnu's bastard.* He shrugged. He would gladly claim paternity here, just to watch the Valmieran steam. He wondered how many times Krasta had been unfaithful to him, and with whom. Another shrug. *As many as she thought she could get away with, or I miss my guess.* It wasn't as if he'd spent all his nights in her bed.

Off went the Valmieran, still furious and not trying very hard to hide it any more. Santerno came over and slapped Lurcanio on the shoulder. "Well done, your Excellency, well done! Your occupation duty turned out to be good for something after all. You put that fellow in his place as neatly as you please."

"And now we find out how much we'll pay for my pleasure," Lurcanio replied. "If the islanders are annoyed enough, they'll plague us with their egg-tossers for the rest of the day."

And the Lagoans and Kuusamans did exactly that. The egg-tossers the Algarvians had left did their best to reply. Huddling in a hole in the ground, Lurcanio was glumly certain their best would not be good enough.

The next morning, Major Vizgantu returned, white flag and all. A different soldier brought him to Lurcanio, saying, "Sir, this cursed Kaunian says he is ordered to report to you, if you're still alive."

"I think I may qualify," Lurcanio answered, which made the soldier chuckle. Lurcanio bowed to the Valmieran. "And a good day to you, Major. We meet again."

"So we do," Vizgantu said coldly. He took from his pocket a folded leaf of paper, which he held out to Lurcanio. "This is for you."

"Thank you so much." Lurcanio unfolded the paper. It

was written in classical Kaunian. *To Colonel Lurcanio of the Algarvian army, greetings,* he read. *Major Vizgantu is my chosen representative in requesting a surrender of the Algarvian forces currently surrounded in this area. If you do not permit him to proceed to your commander, no other representative will be proffered, and no other request for surrender will be made. The fate of your army will be left, in that case, to the chances of the battlefield. The choice, sir, is yours. Your humble servant, Marshal Araujo, commanding allied armies in southern Algarve.*

"Have you read this?" Lurcanio asked the Valmieran. A slight smirk was all the answer he needed. He let out a long sigh. The enemy commander had had his revenge, and had taken more than he'd expected. Was Araujo bluffing? Lurcanio studied the note again. He didn't think so, and he knew the army of which he was a part had no hope of stopping any serious push the Lagoans and Kuusamans—aye, and the Valmierans—chose to make.

"What is your answer, Colonel?" Vizgantu demanded.

Lurcanio contemplated his choice: give up his pride or give up any hope for the soldiers in the pocket with him. He knew more than a few of his countrymen who would have sacrificed the army for the sake of pride. Had he been younger, he might have done the same himself. As things were . . .

He thought of salvaging what he could by insulting the Valmieran again, by saying that if Marshal Araujo, a distinguished soldier, chose to use a man who was anything but as his emissary, that had to be respected, but he himself deplored it. He thought of it, then shook his head. It would have come out as childish petulance, no more. All he said was, "I shall send you forward, Major."

"Thank you," Vizgantu said. "You might have done this yesterday and saved everyone a good deal of difficulty."

"So I might have, but I did not," Lurcanio replied. "And I doubt everything was perfectly smooth in Valmiera almost five years ago, when you folk found yourselves on the other end of victory."

Vizgantu gave back a proverb in classical Kaunian:

"The last victory counts for more than all the others before it."

Since Lurcanio knew that to be true, he didn't try to argue it. He just sent the Valmieran major deeper into the pocket the Algarvians still held. If the Algarvian commander chose to surrender, that was, or at least might have been, his privilege. And if he chose to fight on . . .

If he chooses to fight on, he's a madman, Lurcanio thought. That, of course, had little to do with anything. If the Algarvian commander chose to fight on, his men would keep fighting for as long as they could. Lurcanio didn't know what good it would do, but he hadn't known what good further fighting would do for quite a while. He didn't want to die at this stage of the war—his goal was to be blazed by an outraged husband at the age of 103—but he knew he would go forward if ordered, or hold in place as long as he could.

The order didn't come. Instead, that afternoon a runner announced, "General Prusione will yield up this army at sunrise tomorrow."

"It's over, then," Lurcanio said dully, and the runner nodded. He looked not far from tears.

It wasn't quite over, of course. Around Trapani and here and there in the north, the Algarvians still fought on. Surrendering to Unkerlant was different from yielding to Lagoas and Kuusamo—different and much more frightening. The Algarvians had plenty of reason to worry about how their enemy in the west would treat them once they gave up, and even about whether King Swemmel would let them give up.

But that wasn't Lurcanio's concern. He took a certain pride in knowing he'd made a tolerably good combat soldier. It hadn't mattered, though. However well he'd fought, Algarve still lay prostrate.

When the sun rose, he led his men out of their holes. Lagoan soldiers relieved them of their weapons and whatever small valuables they had. Lurcanio strode into captivity with his head up.

Eleven

ᖇᖇᗰᎧᏇᎮ

News-sheet vendors in Eoforwic shouted that Gromheort had fallen. Vanai cared very little about that. The
vendors also shouted about the hard fighting Forthweg's
Unkerlanter allies had done. Vanai cared very little about
that, either. But she did fear hard fighting in Gromheort
would have taken a toll on the civilians there. She hoped
Ealstan's family had come through as well as possible.

News-sheet vendors said never a word about Oyngestun.
Vanai would have been astonished if they had. Her home
village, a few miles west of Gromheort, wasn't important
enough to talk about unless you lived there. She didn't
worry about her own family; her grandfather was all she'd
had left, and Brivibas was dead. Vanai wasn't particularly
sorry, either. Tamulis the apothecary was the only person in
the village she cared about even a little. He'd been kind to
her after her grandfather took up with Major Spinello, and
even after she'd had to take up with Spinello herself. But
Tamulis was as much a Kaunian as she was, which meant
the odds he'd come through weren't good.

Saxburh pulled herself upright with the help of the sofa
in the flat and cruised from one end to the other, holding on.
As soon as she let go, she fell down. She laughed. It hadn't
hurt her a bit. Of course, she didn't have very far to fall.
She looked over at Vanai. "Mama!" she said in an imperious tone that couldn't mean anything but, *Pick me up!*

"I'm your mama," Vanai agreed, and did pick her up.
Saxburh called her *mama* much more often than *dada* these
days. She said a couple of other words, too—*hat* most often, after a cheap linen cap she loved to jam down onto her
head—and a lot of things that sounded as if they ought to
be words but weren't. She was getting close to her first

birthday. Vanai found that preposterously unlikely, but
knew it was true.

Saxburh tried to eat her nose. That was the baby's way of
giving kisses. Vanai gave her a kiss, too, which made her
squeal and giggle—and, a moment later, screw up her face
and grunt. Vanai sniffed. Aye: what she thought had happened had happened.

"You're a stinker," she said, and set about cleaning up the
mess. Saxburh didn't like that so well. And, being more
mobile than before, she kept doing her best to escape. Vanai
had to hold her with one hand and wipe her bottom and put
a fresh rag on her with the other. Battle won, she kissed
Saxburh again and asked, "How would you like to go down
to the market square with me?"

It wasn't really a question, for Saxburh had no choice.
Vanai scooped her up and stuffed her in her harness. She
also scooped up some silver, grimacing as she did so. The
money wouldn't last a whole lot longer, and she didn't know
what she would do when it looked like running out. *Whatever I have to do,* she thought, and made another sour face.

Whatever I have to do reminded her of something else.
She renewed the spell that let her look like a Forthwegian.
She did that whenever she went outside these days. She
couldn't see the effect of the magic on herself, and didn't
want it wearing out where other people could see her. It was
again legal to be a Kaunian, but that didn't mean it was
easy.

She chanted a third-person version of the disguising
spell over Saxburh, too. With her daughter, she could see it
work. Thanks to Ealstan, Saxburh already had dark hair and
eyes, but her skin was too fair and her face too long for her
to look quite like a full-blooded Forthwegian. A little sorcery, though, mended that for hours at a time.

Vanai clicked her tongue between her teeth as she carried
the baby down to the street. "I *am* going to teach you Kaunian," she said softly. "If I have to teach you when to speak it
and when not to, I'll do that, too." Maybe Kaunianity
wouldn't be extinguished in Forthweg. Maybe it would just
go into hiding. Considering what the Algarvians had tried
to do to her people, that would be something of a triumph.

Little by little, Eoforwic showed signs of coming back to life. A postman nodded to Vanai as she lugged Saxburh toward the market square. "Good morning," he said, and tipped his hat. She nodded back. No one had sent her or Ealstan anything for a long time, but she'd started checking the brass box in the lobby to her block of flats again. These days, the idea of finding something there wasn't an absurdity.

Maybe Ealstan will post me a letter, the way he did when I was still living in Oyngestun, she thought. If he had sent her any, they hadn't got to her. She wondered whether Unkerlanter soldiers were even allowed to write letters. For that matter, she wondered how many Unkerlanters even knew how to write. Her opinion of Forthweg's western neighbors was no higher than the view Forthwegians had of their more numerous cousins.

Guthfrith's band thumped and blared away in a corner of the market square. Vanai stayed away from that corner of the square, and hoped Guthfrith—who, when not sorcerously disguised himself, was also the much more famous Ethelhelm—hadn't noted her arrival.

She bought black olives and raisins and smoked almonds. She fed raisins to Saxburh as they went back to the block of flats. Only when she was halfway there did she realize she'd taken no pains to keep Ethelhelm from seeing which way she went. She shrugged. She didn't think he'd given her any special notice. She hoped not. He made her nervous.

When she looked back over her shoulder, she saw no one following her. She cocked her head to one side and listened. The band was still playing, which meant Ethelhelm was still where he belonged. Vanai sighed with relief and went on. She let Saxburh walk beside her for a few paces holding her hand. The baby seemed to think she was a very large person indeed after that, and didn't want to go back into her harness again.

In the lobby of the block of flats, Vanai tried the mailbox. To her astonishment, it held an envelope with an image of King Beornwulf in one corner—a rather smeary image, plainly turned out in a hurry to avoid having to use frankings from Algarve or from King Penda's day. The envelope was addressed to her as Thelberge and to Saxburh.

"It's your father!" she exclaimed to Saxburh. Who else would know the baby's name? But that wasn't Ealstan's script, which she knew as well as her own. With her daughter and the food on her hands, opening the envelope was impractical down here. She thrust it into her handbag and raced up the stairs to her flat faster than she'd ever gone before.

She took the baby out of the harness and set her on the floor. As always after going to and from the market square, Saxburh was glad to escape and crawl around. Vanai tore the envelope open, and had to be careful not to tear the letter inside it, too. She unfolded the leaf of paper and began to read.

To her surprise, the letter inside was in accurate classical Kaunian, not Forthwegian. *To my daughter-in-law and granddaughter: greetings,* Vanai read. *I hope that this finds both of you well, and that it reaches you safely. Now that Gromheort and Eoforwic are once more under the same administration, I have some hope that this may be so, and send it in that hope.*

She smiled; that was an opening as formal as any in the surviving letters from the glory days of the Kaunian Empire. But the smile fell from her face as she read on: *I must tell you that Ealstan was wounded in the leg during the final Unkerlanter attack on Gromheort. He discovered we had come through the siege by one of those coincidences that would embarrass a writer of romances: he was nursed at a station for the wounded by his sister Conberge.*

The wound is healing. It threatens neither life nor the limb, though he may have something of a limp even after the healing is complete. I am doing everything I can to have him formally released from Unkerlanter service. Not only has he shed his blood for King Swemmel, but he is unlikely to be on his feet before the war against Algarve ends. If I were dealing with the redheaded barbarians, the matter would be easy. With those from the west, it is less so, but I hope I can manage it.

He sends you his love, as should not surprise you. Writing letters home is actively discouraged among the Unkerlanter soldiery, but I shall do my best to smuggle out a note if he manages to produce one. In the meantime, let me say that I very much look forward to meeting both you and your daughter, and that both of you will be welcome in this house in whatever guise you wear. Your father-in-law, Hestan.

That should have ended it. That was enough, and more than enough. But Ealstan's father also wrote, *You should know that my brother, Hengist, yet lives, and that he and I are as completely estranged as two men can be. When last I heard, Hengist's son, Sidroc, survived, too. Since he remains in Plegmund's Brigade, perhaps this state of affairs will not continue indefinitely.*

Vanai looked over at Saxburh, who'd just pulled herself up and fallen down again. Her own tears blurred the little girl in her sight. "Your father is . . . still alive," Vanai said. That he was wounded was less than she'd hoped, but ever so much better than it could have been. "He'll be all right, or pretty much all right. He may even get out of the Unkerlanter army before too long. Powers above, make it so."

Saxburh paid no attention. When Ealstan came home, his daughter would have to get to know him all over again. Vanai slowly nodded. That was all right. Saxburh would have the chance to do it. Having the chance was all that really mattered.

"He'll be all right," Vanai said again. She went through the letter for a second time, then nodded once more. Reading Hestan's words, she saw, or thought she saw, a good deal about how Ealstan had come to be the way he was. She was always glad to be reminded not all Forthwegians despised the Kaunians who dwelt in their kingdom beside them.

Ealstan is . . . going to be all right. Even that much sang within her. She began to think about what things would be like once the war finally ended and Forthweg started pulling itself together. *I won't have to stay in this miserable flat the rest of my life. Saxburh and I could go to Gromheort. I could find out if the Thelberge face I wear really does look like Conberge, the way Ealstan's been saying it does.*

I could meet other people who care whether I live or die. After everything she'd been through, that thought struck her as strange. Then she shook her head. The Algarvians had cared whether she lived or died, too. The trouble was, they'd wanted her dead. Hestan and his wife—Elfryth, that was her name—wouldn't. Presumably, Conberge wouldn't, either. The same might even hold true for her husband, whose name Vanai couldn't have remembered had her life depended on it.

She went over and picked up Saxburh and gave her a big, loud, smacking kiss. Saxburh thought that was the funniest thing in the world. Vanai carried the baby to the window. She needed all the sunshine she could find.

A moment later, she pulled back again. If that wasn't Guthfrith coming up the street . . . But it was, and she didn't want him seeing her up here. *Why aren't you playing music?* she thought angrily. If he walked into this block of flats, her anger was going to turn to fear.

To her relief, he walked past instead. But under the relief, unease remained. She went looking for a leaf of paper with which to answer Hestan. Before too long, civilian ley-line caravans would again be running between Eoforwic and Gromheort. Maybe she would do well to go east just as soon as she could.

Ahead of Leudast, Trapani burned. He could see the capital of Algarve now, see the tall buildings that marked the heart of the great city. Some of them were plainly shorter than they had been before dragons started dropping eggs on them. If they all fell over, Leudast didn't care.

He just wanted to be there at the end of the fight, when— if—that finally came. The Unkerlanters had fought their way into the suburbs of Trapani. They'd surrounded the city. But the last couple of rings of defenses still lay ahead. So did whatever nasty magecraft the redheads had left.

A storm of eggs fell on the Algarvian positions in front of Leudast's men. A couple of behemoths lumbered toward them and flung more eggs at whatever the tossers behind the lines hadn't flattened. Leudast blew a blast from his officer's whistle. "Forward!" he yelled.

Not all the Algarvians were dead, however much he wished they would have been. They knew everything there was to know about taking shelter. As soon as the Unkerlanters broke cover to rush toward them, they popped up and started blazing. Men in rock-gray tunics fell, some hit, some diving for cover.

"Hands high!" Leudast shouted in Algarvian. "Sticks down!"

An Algarvian emerged from behind a wall. He did have his hands high. Leudast gestured with the business end of his stick. The redhead hurried away. Leudast doubted he was more than fifteen years old. King Mezentio was scraping the bottom of the barrel.

Of course, so was King Swemmel. Some of the men Leudast led had no more years on them than the new captive. Had the Algarvians been strong enough to keep the war going another couple of years, neither they nor the Unkerlanters would have had any men at all left alive.

Seeing that the first redhead who surrendered didn't get killed out of hand, more of Mezentio's men—or rather, Mezentio's boys—came out of hiding with their hands above their heads. Leudast and his countrymen sent them off to the rear, too. But then beams from closer to the center of Trapani knocked down several of the kilted soldiers who were trying to get out of the fight. Leudast dove for cover again, but the diehards up there seemed more interested in blazing Algarvians who yielded than the Unkerlanters who made them give up.

In Swemmel, such men would have served as behind-the-lines inspectors whose job was to get rid of any man seeking to retreat without orders. Leudast had always despised them—despised them and feared them, too. He wasn't sorry to see the other side also had them. If nothing else, it proved his kingdom wasn't the only one where such whoresons grew.

Behemoths tossed eggs at the buildings and piles of rubble from which the diehards were blazing. As the Unkerlanter footsoldiers rushed toward the strongpoints, the surviving redheads popped out of their holes and blazed away at them, shouting, "Algarve!" and "Mezentio!"

The fight didn't last long. Not all that many Algarvians were stubborn enough to fight so fiercely for a cause now hopeless, and Swemmel's men were there in large numbers. But the Algarvians who did fight refused to take a step back, dying in place instead. And they made the Unkerlanters pay full price—pay more than full price—for digging them out.

More Algarvian soldiers did give up once the knot of diehards was gone: fear of them had kept others fighting. But Mezentio's soldiers had turned a park and a few nearby houses into a strongpoint. They had some egg-tossers there, and a behemoth mounting a heavy stick that took advantage of the rubble to blaze from cover again and again, knocking over several Unkerlanter beasts.

Might as well be Sulingen, Leudast thought. He'd been through the block-by-block fighting there, perhaps the worst of the whole war. A moment later, he wished the comparison hadn't occurred to him. He'd been wounded in Sulingen, too. He didn't want that to happen again. He'd picked up another wound later on, in the Duchy of Grelz. As far as he was concerned, two pale, puckered scars for the sake of his kingdom were quite enough.

Clearing the redheads from their little redoubt took all day. Not till dragons swooped down from above and killed that behemoth did the job get done. Things were easier in that regard here than in Sulingen. The Algarvians had hardly any dragons left now. Back then, Leudast had spent plenty of time cowering in holes in the ground as Algarvian beasts flamed and dropped eggs from above.

Not that holes in the ground were any too pleasant now. Leudast dragged a dead Algarvian out of a good one in the middle of the park and settled down for the night. He'd just gone to sleep when he had to come out of the hole and fight again: using darkness as their cloak, Mezentio's men made a ferocious counterattack, and almost drove the Unkerlanters from the ground they'd taken. More dragons and behemoths finally threw the redheads back.

"These buggers don't know how to quit, do they, sir?" asked a young soldier named Noyt. His voice broke in the middle of the question; he didn't need to scrape a razor across his cheeks to keep them smooth. He'd been a little boy when the war started.

"They're like snakes," Leudast agreed. "They'll fight you till you cut the head off—and if you pick up the head a couple of hours later, it'll twist around and bite you even though it's dead."

He rolled himself in his blanket and fell asleep—and woke again in short order when a mosquito bit him on the end of the nose. The Algarvians might not have many dragons left in the air, but Trapani lay in the middle of a marsh. Plenty of things with wings came forth to attack the Unkerlanters.

When morning came, Leudast woke again, this time with the feeling something was badly wrong somewhere, even though he couldn't put his finger on what. He was an officer these days, and entitled to sniff around and try to find out (he'd done the same thing as a sergeant, and as a common soldier, too, but fewer people could squelch him now). He walked up to Captain Dagaric and asked, "What's going on, sir? Something is, sure as sure, and I don't think it's anything good."

"You think so, too, eh?" the regimental commander answered. "I hadn't noticed anything myself, but I saw a couple of mages putting their heads together and muttering a few minutes ago."

"That doesn't sound good," Leudast said. "What are the fornicating Algarvians going to throw at us now?"

"Who knows?" Dagaric said with weary cynicism. "We'll have to find out the hard way, I expect. That's what we're for, after all."

"Huh," Leudast said. "I've had to find out too cursed many things the hard way. Once in a while, I'd like to know ahead of time."

He went off in search of the mages his superior had seen, and found them under an oak whose trunk was badly scarred with beams. As Dagaric had said, they were talking in low voices, and both looked worried. Leudast stood around waiting for them to notice him. He waited more ostentatiously with each passing minute. At last, one of the sorcerers said, "You want something, Lieutenant?"

"I want to know what the redheads are brewing up," Leudast answered. "They've got something ready to pop, sure as blazes." Both wizards wore captain's rank badges, but he didn't waste much military courtesy on them. They were only mages, after all, not *real* officers.

They looked at each other. One of them asked, "Have you wizardly talent?"

"Not that I know of," Leudast said. "Just a bad feeling in the air."

"Very bad," the mage agreed. "Something is coming, and we don't know what. All we can do is wait and see."

"Can we send dragons to drop eggs on the heads of the whoresons cooking up whatever it is?" Leudast asked. "If they're trying not to get smashed into strawberry jam, they can't very well cast spells."

The wizards brightened. "Do you know, Lieutenant, that isn't the worst idea anyone has ever had," said the one who did the talking.

"You boys are the ones to take care of it," Leudast said, hiding a smile. "You're the ones who deal with crystals and such." The mages might outrank him, but he could see what needed doing. They sometimes put him in mind of bright children: they could come up with all sorts of clever schemes, but a good many of those had nothing to do with the real world.

Whistles shrilled again. Leudast trotted away from the mages without a backwards glance. If the attack was heating up again, he needed to be with his men as they pushed on toward the heart of Trapani. But, as he moved forward, he suddenly discovered that he wasn't going forward at all: his feet were moving up and down, but each new step left him in the same place as had the one before it.

Cries of alarm said he wasn't the only Unkerlanter soldier thus afflicted. He didn't know how the Algarvian mages were doing this, but they plainly were. A glance told him the behemoths were similarly frozen in place. Unkerlanter soldiers started falling as hidden redheads blazed them.

They could still run away from the heart of Trapani. Some of them did. Leudast discovered he could move sideways and, more important, that he could duck. "Get down!" he called to the men closest to danger. "Get into cover! You can do it." Some people wouldn't have figured it out for themselves, but would manage to do it once told they could.

Scuttling behind a boulder, Leudast wondered if the entire Unkerlanter assault on Trapani, all the way around the Algarvian capital, had been frozen in its tracks. He wouldn't have been surprised. Algarvian mages didn't think small. They never had, not since they started killing Kaunians—and, very likely, not before then, either. Algarvians were flamboyant folk.

Eggs kept on bursting deeper inside Trapani. "They can't stop everything!" Leudast exclaimed. He'd had the right of it while talking with his own wizards. It was up to the fellows who served the egg-tossers now. If they killed or wounded or at least distracted the sorcerers who made the spell work, the attack could resume again. If not . . .

Leudast looked up. A couple of dragons painted Unkerlanter rock-gray hovered like oversized kestrels, unable to go forward no matter how powerfully they beat their great wings. Even as he watched, a beam from an Algarvian heavy stick tumbled one of them from the sky.

He waited, every now and then blazing from behind that boulder. Maybe the eggs the Unkerlanters hurtled into Trapani finally did what they were supposed to. Maybe Mezentio's mages could hold their spell for only so long. Maybe—though he wouldn't have bet much on it—their Unkerlanter counterparts at last beat down their wizardry. Whatever the reason, shouts of, "Urra!" rang out when Swemmel's soldiers discovered they could go forward again.

Why are we cheering? Leudast wondered as he ran towards a house from which a couple of diehards were blazing. *Now we've got another chance to get killed.*

One of the diehards showed himself at a window—only for a moment, but long enough for Leudast's beam to cut him down. "Urra!" Leudast yelled. "King Swemmel! Revenge!" Maybe that one word said everything that needed saying. *Aye, we might get killed, but we'll do a lot of killing first.* Before long, Trapani was going to fall. He intended to be one of those who helped bring it down. "Urra!" he cried again, and ran on.

* * *

Not a lot of mail came to the hostel in the Naantali district. As far as most of the world was concerned, that hostel didn't exist. Pekka and the other mages who labored there might as well have dropped off the face of the earth. Even relatives who knew the sorcerers were working somewhere didn't usually know where, and relied on the post office to get letters where they needed to go.

One envelope that got to Pekka did not, at first, look as if it had come to the right place. The printed design on the corner that showed postage fees had been paid was not Kuusaman. After a bit of puzzling, she figured out the letter was from Jelgava. *I don't know anyone in Jelgava,* she thought. *I certainly don't know anyone in Jelgava who knows I'm here.*

Even the script challenged her. Printed Jelgavan used the same characters as Kuusaman, but the two kingdoms' handwritings were quite different. Her name wasn't on the envelope. A chill ran through her when she realized Leino's was.

She turned the envelope over. There on the back, in red, was a stamp in her own language: MILITARY POST—DECEASED. FORWARD TO NEXT OF KIN.

Pekka's lips skinned back from her teeth. That explained how she'd got the letter—explained it in more detail than she'd wanted. She opened the envelope. The letter inside was in Jelgavan, too. She had only a few words of the language, and could make out next to nothing of what it said.

She found Fernao in the refectory at suppertime. He was demolishing a plate of corned venison and red cabbage. "Do you read Jelgavan?" she asked, sitting down beside him. Pointing to his supper, she added, "That looks good."

"It is," he said, and then asked, "Why do you need me to read Jelgavan? I can probably make sense of it—it's as close to Valmieran as Sibian is to Algarvian, maybe closer, and I don't have much trouble with Valmieran."

"Here. I got this today." Pekka gave him the letter. "I knew you were good with languages. Can you tell me what it says?" A serving girl came up. Pekka ordered the venison and cabbage for herself, too.

"Let me see." Fernao started to read, then looked up sharply. "This is to your husband."

"I know." Pekka had destroyed the envelope with that hateful rubber stamp. "It got sent to me. What does it say?" She wondered, not for the first time, if Leino had had a Jelgavan lover. She could hardly be angry at him now if he had; it would go some way toward salving her own conscience.

Even so, she started when Fernao said, "It's from a woman." He continued, "She's writing about her husband."

Was the fellow angry at Leino? Pekka didn't care to come right out and ask that. Instead, she said, "What does she say about him?"

"Says he helped your husband when he was with the ir-regulars, but now he's disappeared, and she's afraid he's been thrown into a dungeon," Fernao replied. "She asks if Leino can do anything to get him out."

"A Jelgavan dungeon." Pekka winced. Jelgavan dun-geons had an evil reputation. Leino, she remembered, had met King Donalitu aboard the *Habakkuk*, met him and de-spised him. Helping anyone who'd fallen foul of his men seemed worth doing. She asked, "Who is this fellow?"

"His name is Talsu. He's from a town called Skrunda—whereabouts in Jelgava that is, powers above only know. I know I don't, not without a book of maps," Fernao said. "His wife's called Gailisa."

That name meant nothing to Pekka. Talsu, on the other hand . . . "Aye, Leino said something about him in a letter. He helped our men slip through the Algarvian lines in front of this Skrunda place."

"You probably ought to see what you can do for him, then," Fernao said. Pekka smiled and nodded, glad he was thinking along with her. Leino had done a lot of that; if Fer-nao could, too—and if she could with him—that struck her as promising. Fernao's next question was thoroughly prac-tical: "Do you think you *can* do anything?"

"By myself? No. Why should any Jelgavan want to listen to me? But I've got connections, and what good are they if I don't use them?" Listening to herself, Pekka had to laugh. She sounded very much like a woman of the world, not a

theoretical sorcerer from a town that looked southwest toward the land of the Ice People. She'd seen Fernao smile a
couple of amused and tolerant smiles in Kajaani, though
he'd done his best to hide them.

He nodded vigorously now. "Good for you. At least half
the time, knowing people counts for more than knowing
things does."

Pekka's supper arrived then. She ate quickly, for she
wanted to get to the crystallomancers' chamber as soon as
she could. When she walked in, she said, "Put me through
to Prince Juhainen, if he's not too busy to talk."

"Aye, Mistress Pekka," said a crystallomancer: the same
woman who'd summoned her to this chamber to hear
Juhainen tell her Leino was dead. Pekka tried not to think
of that now. The crystallomancer went about her business
with unhurried precision. After a couple of minutes, she
looked up from the crystal, in which the prince's image had
appeared. "Go ahead."

"Hello, your Highness," Pekka said. "I have a favor to
ask of you, if you'd be so kind."

"That depends, Mistress Pekka," Juhainen answered.
"One of the things I've learned the past couple of years is
not to make promises till I know what I'm promising."

"I'm sure that's wise," Pekka said, and went on to explain what Talsu's wife had asked of her.

"A Jelgavan dungeon, eh?" Prince Juhainen's mouth
twisted, as if he'd just smelled something nasty. "I don't believe I would wish my worst enemy into a Jelgavan dungeon. And you say this Talsu fellow actually helped our
men?"

"That's right, your Highness." Pekka nodded.

"And they've flung him into one of these miserable
places anyhow?" Juhainen said. Pekka nodded again. The
prince scowled. "That is not good," he declared, which,
from a Kuusaman, carried more weight than screamed
curses from an excitable Algarvian. He continued, "Thank
you for bringing it to my notice. I shall see what I can do."

"Will the Jelgavans heed you, sir?" Pekka asked.

"If gratitude means anything, they will," Juhainen answered. But his smile was wry. "As often as not, gratitude

means nothing at all between kingdoms. Truth to tell, Mistress Pekka, I don't know what will happen. I don't know whether anything will happen. But I do mean to find out." He turned and nodded to someone: to his own crystallomancer, for the sphere in front of Pekka flared and then, to the eye, became once more nothing but glass.

The crystallomancer on duty at the hostel said not a word. Of course she'd heard everything that passed between Pekka and Juhainen, but the secrecy inherent in her craft kept her silent, as it should have done.

When Pekka went upstairs, she went to Fernao's room, not to her own. "Well?" the Lagoan mage asked.

"Pretty well," Pekka told him. "Prince Juhainen says he'll see what he can do."

"Good," Fernao said. "If Donalitu and his flunkies will listen to anybody, they'll listen to one of the Seven Princes of Kuusamo." His smile, though, had the same wry edge as Juhainen's had. "Of course, they're Jelgavans. There's no guarantee they will listen to anybody."

"Ordinary Jelgavans aren't bad. They're just—people," Pekka said. "I was up on the beaches of the north there once, on . . . on holiday." The holiday had been her honeymoon with Leino. She felt an odd constraint—or maybe it wasn't so odd—about talking too much with Fernao about her life with her husband.

"Their nobles, though . . ." Fernao's chuckle held little mirth. "Most hidebound people in the world, bar none. They make Valmieran nobles look like levelers, and that's not easy."

"I hope Prince Juhainen can do something for that poor fellow," Pekka said. "How terrible, to help his kingdom and end up in a dungeon anyhow."

"Donalitu and his bully boys root out treason wherever they think they see it," Fernao replied. "My guess is, they root it out whether it's really there or not. Sooner or later, they'll end up breeding real treason that way, whether it would have sprung up without them or not."

"That makes more sense than what Donalitu's doing," Pekka said. "Leino wrote that some Jelgavans were fighting on King Mezentio's side in spite of what Mezentio's men were doing to Kaunians. Now that I hear what happened to this Talsu, that makes a little more sense to me."

"Donalitu is a bad bargain, and nobody could possibly make him better," Fernao said. "The only thing I would give him is that he's better than Mezentio." He sighed. "I'm not altogether sure I'd give King Swemmel even that much. He's a son of a whore, no doubt about it—but he's a son of a whore who's on our side."

"Any war that puts us on the same side as the Unkerlanters . . ." Pekka shook her head. "But the Algarvians really have done worse."

"So they have." Fernao didn't sound any happier about it than Pekka had. "Worse than the Unkerlanters—if that's not bad, I don't know what is." He changed the subject: "Are we going to go ahead with the demonstration out in the Bothnian Ocean?"

"We certainly are," Pekka said, also relieved to talk about something else. "That needs doing, wouldn't you say?"

"If it works, certainly. If it doesn't . . ." Fernao shrugged. "Well, it's certainly worth trying, the same as getting this what's-his-name—"

"Talsu," Pekka said.

"Talsu," the Lagoan mage echoed. "Getting him out of the dungeon. The demonstration's a little more important, though."

"I should hope so," Pekka exclaimed. "If the demonstration does what we want it to, it might even end this war." The very words tasted strange to her. The Derlavaian War had gone on for almost six years (though Kuusamo had been in the fight for only a little more than half that time): long enough for death and devastation and disaster to seem normal, and everything else an aberration. It had cost Pekka as much as she'd feared in her worst nightmares, and, a couple of times, all but cost her life.

"When the war is over . . ." Fernao didn't sound as if he really believed in the possibility, either. "May it be soon, that's all—and may we never have another one."

"Powers above, make that so!" Pekka said. "Another war, starting from the beginning with everything we've learned during this one? With whatever else we learn afterwards, too? I don't think there'd be anything left of the world once we got through."

"You're probably right," Fernao said. "And do you know what else? If we're stupid enough to fight another war after everything we've seen these past few years, we don't deserve to live: the whole human race, I mean."

"I don't know that I'd go quite so far." But then Pekka thought about it for a little while. Deliberately inflict these horrors again, with the example of the Derlavaian War still green in memory? She sighed. "On the other hand, I don't know that I wouldn't, either."

Hajjaj stepped into the crystallomancers' chamber down the hall from the foreign ministry offices in the royal palace. The crystallomancer on duty sprang to his feet and bowed. "Good day, your Excellency," he said.

"Good day, Kawar," Hajjaj replied. The crystallomancer beamed. Hajjaj had long since learned how important knowing and recalling the names of underlings could be. He went on, "What is the latest word from the south?"

"That depends on whose emanations you're listening to, your Excellency," Kawar said.

"I wouldn't have expected anything else," the Zuwayzi foreign minister said. "Give me both sides, if you'd be so kind, and I expect I'll be able to sort them out for myself."

Bowing, Kawar said, "Just as you require, sir, so shall it be. By what the Unkerlanters say, Trapani is surrounded, cut off from the outside world, and sure to fall in the next few days. Fighting in the rest of Algarve is dying down as the redheads realize resistance is suicide, and useless suicide at that."

"And the Algarvian response to this is?"

"Your Excellency, by what the Algarvians put out over the ether, they still think they've got the war as good as won—although none of their reports comes from inside Trapani any more," Kawar answered. "They say their capital will stay Algarvian. They say Gromheort and the Marquisate of Rivaroli will be Algarvian again, and they say their secret sorceries will smash Swemmel's savages. That's what they *say*, sir."

By that, Kawar no doubt meant he didn't believe a word of it. Hajjaj understood such skepticism. He didn't believe a word of it, either. The Algarvians' claims reminded him of the last ravings of a man about to die of fever. They had no connection to reality that he could find. He sighed. Mezentio's men had been Zuwayza's cobelligerents against Unkerlant—though the redheads, with some reason, would have taken that the other way round.

None of those reflections was anything a crystallomancer needed to hear. Hajjaj said, "Thank you, Kawar. It sounds as though things will be over there before too long."

Kawar nodded. With another word of thanks, Hajjaj left the crystallomancers' chamber. What might happen after the fighting finally stopped worried him a good deal. King Swemmel had given Zuwayza relatively lenient terms for getting out of the Derlavaian War—he'd been shrewd enough not to provoke Hajjaj's kingdom to desperate resistance while the bigger battle with Algarve still blazed. But would he keep the terms of the peace he'd made after he didn't have to worry about Algarve any more? Swemmel was not notorious for keeping promises.

That raised the next interesting question: if Swemmel tried to take a firmer grip on Zuwayza, what should—what could—the Zuwayzin do about it? *Not much* was the answer that immediately occurred to Hajjaj. He didn't think King Shazli would like it. He didn't like it himself. But liking it and being able to do anything about it were liable to be two different things.

When he walked back to his own offices, his secretary greeted him with, "And the latest is?"

"About what you'd expect, Qutuz," Hajjaj replied. "The death throes of Algarve, except the Algarvians refuse to admit they're any such thing."

Qutuz grunted. "What will it take, do you suppose? The very last of them dead, and their last house knocked flat?"

"It may take something not far from that," Hajjaj said sourly. "No one would ever claim the Algarvians are not a stubborn folk."

"No one would ever claim they're not a *stupid* folk, for

fighting on when all it does is get more of them killed," Qutuz said.

"There's some truth in that, I shouldn't wonder," the Zuwayzi foreign minister admitted. "But I think rather more of it comes from a bad conscience. They know what they've done in this war. They know what all their neighbors, and especially the Unkerlanters, might to do them once they surrender. Compared to that, dying in battle may not look so bad."

"Hmm." Qutuz bowed. "I daresay you're right, your Excellency. If Swemmel wanted to stick his hooks in me, I might think hard about taking a long walk off the roof of a tall building."

"Even so," Hajjaj said. "Aye, even so."

He sat down on the carpet behind his low desk and got to work. Reestablishing ties to kingdoms that had been Algarve's foes—and to kingdoms the Algarvians had occupied for years—produced a flood of paperwork. King Beornwulf of Forthweg had just formally accepted the envoy King Shazli had sent to him, and had named a certain Earl Trumwine as Forthwegian minister to Zuwayza. Hajjaj had never heard of Trumwine, and didn't know anyone who had. What would he be like? The Zuwayzi foreign minister shrugged, thinking, *He can't be worse than Ansovald.* King Swemmel's minister to Zuwayzi set a standard for irksomeness by which all envoys from other kingdoms were judged.

After writing a brief letter of welcome for Trumwine— *I'll see soon enough how big a hypocrite I am*—Hajjaj tended to a couple of other matters even more trivial. He was just sanding a memorandum dry when Qutuz came in from his outer office and said, "Excuse me, your Excellency, but an officer from the army high command is here. He'd like to speak with you for a moment."

"From the army high command?" Hajjaj said in surprise. Since Zuwayza yielded to the Unkerlanters, the army high command hadn't had a great deal to do. Hajjaj nodded. "Send him in, by all means."

The officer was a generation younger than Hajjaj. He had

a colonel's emblem on his hat, and also painted on the bare skin of his upper arms. "Good day, your Excellency," he said. "My name is Mundhir."

"Pleased to make your acquaintance, Colonel," Hajjaj said. "Would you care for tea and wine and cakes?"

"If you're generous enough to give me the choice, sir, I'll decline," Mundhir said with a slightly sardonic smile. Hajjaj smiled, too. The ritual of tea and wine and cakes could easily chew up half an hour or an hour with small talk. Mundhir wanted to get straight to business. He continued, "If you'd be so kind as to accompany me back to headquarters, General Ikhshid would be most grateful."

"Would he?" Hajjaj murmured, and Colonel Mundhir nodded. Hajjaj clicked his tongue between his teeth. "I know what that means: Ikhshid's got something he doesn't want to talk about on a crystal. Do you know what it is?"

Mundhir shook his head. "No, your Excellency. I'm sorry, but General Ikhshid didn't tell me."

"I'll come, then." Hajjaj's joints clicked and crackled as he got to his feet. Mundhir looked capable and reliable. If Ikhshid didn't want to tell such a man what was going on, it had to be important.

Colonel Mundhir escorted Hajjaj through the palace to army headquarters. The foreign minister could have found his way without help, but didn't begrudge it. The sentries outside the headquarters stiffened to attention as he came up. Not having any military rank, he nodded back at them.

Ikhshid was a round, white-haired fellow—a man of nearly Hajjaj's age. Normally good-natured, he greeted Hajjaj with the rise of a snowy eyebrow (before going off to study in colder, more southerly, lands, Hajjaj would have thought of it as a salty eyebrow) and said, "Good to see you, your Excellency. We have a bit of a problem, and we'd like your views on it before we try to straighten it out."

"We as in Zuwayza, we as in the army, or have you assumed the royal we like King Swemmel?" Hajjaj asked.

"We as in Zuwayza," Ikhshid answered, ignoring the raillery. That was unlike him; Hajjaj decided the problem had to be more serious than he'd first thought. Ikhshid gestured toward the doorway to his own office. "We can talk in there, if you like." Hajjaj didn't say no. Once they'd gone inside, Ikhshid shut the door behind them and barred it.

"Melodramatic," Hajjaj remarked. Again, Ikhshid didn't rise to the bait. He hadn't so much as offered tea and wine and cakes, either. The Zuwayzi foreign minister took that as another sign something important had happened. He said, "You'd better tell me."

Without preamble, Ikhshid did: "We had a sailboat come ashore not too far from Najran, but far enough so the Unkerlanters at the port don't know anything about it—I hope. Because it's a sailboat, mages wouldn't have spotted it when it crossed a ley line or three. Marquis Balastro is aboard the fornicating thing, and so are a dozen or so other Algarvians with fancy ranks, and their wives—or maybe girlfriends—and brats. They're all screaming for asylum at the top of their lungs. What do we do about 'em?"

"Oh, dear," Hajjaj said, in lieu of something stronger and more pungent.

"Do we get rid of 'em on the sly?" Ikhshid asked. "Do we hand 'em over to Swemmel's men to show what good boys we are? Or do we let 'em stay?"

"The first thing you'd better do is get them away from Najran," Hajjaj replied. "If the Kaunians settled there find out they've landed, we won't have to worry about this set of exiles for long."

"Mm, you're right about that," General Ikhshid agreed. "But you still haven't answered my question. What *do* we do with 'em, or to 'em?"

"I don't know," Hajjaj said distractedly. "By the powers above, I really don't. If Ansovald finds out they're in the kingdom, he'll spit rivets, and so will King Swemmel. From their point of view, it would be hard to blame them."

"I understand," Ikhshid said. "That's why I called you here." He suddenly looked worried. "Or should I have gone straight to the king instead?"

"I'll talk things over with him," Hajjaj promised. "We won't do anything final till he approves it."

"I should hope not," Ikhshid said. "But what do *you* think we ought to do?"

"I don't like handing over fugitives. It goes against every clan tradition. I don't like killing them, either," Hajjaj said.

"Neither do I, but I also don't like getting caught with them here," Ikhshid said. "And we're liable to. You know it as well as I do. They don't speak our language, they aren't brown, they *are* circumcised, they've got red hair, and they wrap themselves in cloth all the time."

"Details, details," Hajjaj said dryly, and startled a laugh out of the army commander. The Zuwayzi foreign minister went on, "My recommendation is to take them to some inland village—Harran, say—and do our best to keep word of them from blowing back here to Bishah. If we can stash them off to one side for a while, things may calm down before they're discovered."

"If." Ikhshid freighted the little word with a great weight of meaning.

"General, if you have a better idea, I should be delighted to hear it," Hajjaj said.

"I don't," Ikhshid replied at once. "I just wondered if you had the nerve to try and get away with that. We'll be in a ton of trouble if the Unkerlanters find out about it."

He wasn't joking. If anything, he was understating what might happen. Even so, Hajjaj answered, "We're still a free kingdom—after a fashion. Let me take this to the king. As I said, he'll have the final decision." Shazli seldom overruled him. This once, he might.

"Good luck," Ikhshid said.

"Thanks. I fear I'll need it." Hajjaj hoped he could talk Shazli around. No matter what the circumstances, he had trouble with the idea of giving anyone over to the Unkerlanters.

Krasta adjusted the wig on her head. As far as she was concerned, the hair in the wig wasn't nearly so fine or so golden as her own. The miserable thing was also cursedly hot. But she wore it from the moment she got up in the morning till she went to bed. It hid the shame of the shearing Merkela had given her, and let her go out into Priekule without reminding the world she'd bedded an Algarvian during the occupation. Being able to hold her head up counted for more than comfort.

Her son—her sandy-haired son, her bastard son, the proof of exactly what she'd been doing—started yowling in the room next to her bedchamber. She'd hired a wet nurse and a governess to look after the little brat, whom she'd named Gainibu in the hope that the King of Valmiera would hear of it and understand it as an apology of sorts. As a matter of fact, thus far she'd hired two governesses and three wet nurses. For some reason, they had trouble getting along with her.

After a little while, the racket stopped. Krasta didn't go in to check on the baby. She supposed the wet nurse was giving him her breast. But she was doing her best to pretend, even to herself, that she'd never had him. His wails didn't make that easy, but she'd always been good at deceiving herself.

She had money in her pockets. She had a new driver, one who didn't drink. She could escape the mansion, escape the baby she didn't want to acknowledge, go into Priekule, and come back with *things*. What they were hardly mattered. While she was buying them, she didn't have to think about anything else.

But, just as she left the bedchamber and headed for the stairs, the butler—the new butler—came up them toward her. (She was offended that so many of her servants had chosen to go south with Skarnu and his peasant slut of a new wife, but she'd never dwelt on why they might have decided to leave her service.)

"Milady, Viscount Valnu is here to see you," the new butler said.

"I certainly am," Valnu himself agreed from the hallway below. "Come down here, sweetheart, so I *can* see you."

Krasta hurried past the butler. Valnu seemed to be the only person in all of Priekule who didn't blame her for the way she'd lived during the occupation. Of course, he'd slept with a lot more Algarvian officers than she had; she was sure of that. But he'd done it in the line of duty, so to speak. And he didn't run the risk of proving it to the world nine months after the fact.

He swept her into his arms and gave her a kiss. "How have you been?" he asked.

"Tired," Krasta answered. Up in his bedroom, little Gainibu started to cry again. Krasta could hardly ignore him then, however much she wanted to. She jerked a thumb at the stairway down which the noise was wafting. "That's why."

"Ah, too bad," Valnu said with sympathy that at least sounded sincere. "Have you got anything to drink, darling? I'm dry as the Zuwayzi desert."

It was early in the day, but that worried Krasta no more than it did Valnu. "Come along with me," she purred. "We'll find something that suits you—and me, too."

Something turned out to be apricot brandy. Valnu knocked back a shot of it. So did Krasta. The sweet warmth in her mouth, and in her belly, felt good. Valnu poured his glass full again, then raised a questioning eyebrow at her. She nodded eagerly. He poured for her, too. "What shall we drink to?" he asked. "That first time, we were just drinking to drinking."

"That's good enough for me," Krasta said. She let more brandy slide down her throat. This time, she gave herself a refill, and, a moment later, Valnu as well. "Curse me if I know why I don't stay drunk all the time. Then I wouldn't have to think about . . . things."

"Cheer up, my dear," Valnu told her. "However bad it looks, it could be worse."

"How?" Krasta demanded. As far as she could see, nothing could be worse than her being unhappy.

But Valnu answered, "Well, you could be an Algarvian, for instance: say, somebody inside Trapani. The fighting there can't last much longer, or so the news sheets say. And the Unkerlanters don't like redheads at all."

That, no doubt, was true. But it was also far away. Krasta's concerns were much more immediate. She glared at him. "Powers below eat you, why couldn't you have had stronger seed?" she snarled. "Then I'd have a proper blond baby, and people wouldn't want to spit at me all the time." Her hand started to go to the wig, but she pulled it down. She didn't want to draw that to anyone's notice.

"I could ask you something like, why didn't you give me more chances?" Valnu answered. "Dear Lurcanio had a lot more than I did."

"You weren't living here," Krasta said. "And you couldn't send me off and do horrible things to me if I didn't do what you wanted." She didn't mention that, at the time, she'd enjoyed quite a few of the things Lurcanio had done and had had her do. That was only one more inconvenient fact to be forgotten.

"You shouldn't complain too much, my love." Valnu patted her hand. "After all, you didn't have the unfortunate accident you could have." Now he pointed up toward the nursery. "You had a different sort of unfortunate accident."

"Unfortunate? I should say so." Krasta drank her third brandy as quickly as the first two. "That miserable little bastard ruins everything—everything, I tell you. And the servants you can get nowadays! It's scandalous!" Few of the newcomers were as deferential as the ones who'd been at the mansion for a long time. Like those in charge of Gainibu, a couple had quit already, but *their* replacements seemed no better.

"I am sorry," Valnu said. "I'm afraid I don't know what I can do about any of that."

"At least you've tried to do something," Krasta said. "And when you come to visit, I know you're not coming to laugh at me or to curse me."

"I wouldn't do that." Valnu sounded unusually serious—maybe it was the brandy talking. "You could have betrayed me to the Algarvians whenever you chose, except you didn't choose."

"No. Of course not." Krasta shook her head. "How could I do that to someone I know socially?"

Valnu laughed, sprang to his feet, and bowed. "You are a true noblewoman, milady." Krasta would have taken that as a pretty compliment, but he went on, "And you show you're every bit as useless as most of the members of our class—myself included, whenever I get the chance to be useless, anyhow."

"I'm not either useless. Don't you dare say I am," Krasta snapped. "You're as mean to me as that horrible bitch my brother married." Tears stung her eyes. She still cried much more easily than she had before getting pregnant.

"I didn't say you were anything I'm not," Valnu answered. "Every kingdom needs a few truly useless people, to show the rest how to enjoy life. Look at the Unkerlanters. Efficiency, efficiency, efficiency, every bloody minute of the day and night. Would you want to live like that?"

"I should hope not." The idea of doing anything as the Unkerlanters did it was deeply repugnant to Krasta.

"Well, there you are." Valnu sounded as if everything made perfect sense. He raised his glass. "Here's to uselessness!" He drank.

So did Krasta, though she'd bristled when he called her useless only moments before. She eyed him, then said, "I can never be sure when you're making fun of me and when you're not."

"Good," Valnu told her. "I don't want to be too obvious. If I were, I would lose my precious air of mystery." The pose he struck looked more absurd than mysterious.

Krasta laughed. She couldn't help herself. She could feel the apricot brandy, too. It helped build a wall between her and the unpleasant world all around. She giggled and said, "If it were any other time, I'd seduce you right now. But . . ." She shook her head. The baby had come out through there, and she didn't want anything else going in for a while yet.

"If you were really bound and determined to, there are plenty of things we might try that haven't got anything to do with *that*," Valnu remarked. "Just speaking theoretically, of course."

"Of course," Krasta echoed. "You'd know all about those, wouldn't you?"

That such words might wound never occurred to her. If they did, Valnu didn't show it. Instead, he bared his teeth in a grin of sorts. "How many times have I told you, my dear?—variety is the life of spice."

Krasta sent him an owlish stare and poured herself more brandy. "You came over here to have your way with me, didn't you?"

"I came over to say hello." Valnu gave her one of his bright, bony smiles and waved. "'Hello!'" The smile got wider. "Anything else would be a bonus. You know, I didn't intend to go to bed with you back ten months ago now, either."

"We didn't go to bed." Krasta giggled again. "I ought to know. The rug rubbed my backside raw."

"Now I was speaking metaphorically," Valnu said in lofty tones.

"How is that different from theoretically?" Krasta asked.

"It's different, that's how." Valnu's words slurred, ever so slightly. The brandy was working in him, too.

When Krasta got to her feet, the room swirled around her. "Come on," she told Valnu, as loftily as if she were ordering one of her servants about.

Valnu didn't get up right away. Had Krasta had a little less to drink, or drunk it a little more slowly, she would have realized he was thinking it over, and she would have got angry. As things were, she just stood there, swaying a little, waiting for him to do as she said. And he did, too. All he said when he rose was, "Well, why not?"

The butler blinked when Krasta and Valnu went past him on the stairway. He didn't know Krasta very well. None of the new servants did. She thought that was funny, too.

Valnu proved to know some very pleasant alternatives. After Krasta bucked against his tongue, after her breathing and her pulse slowed toward normal, she ran her hands through his hair and said, "You didn't learn *that* from any Algarvian officers."

"My sweet, doing anything over and over without change, no matter how enjoyable, grows boring in the end," Valnu said.

She wasn't in the mood to argue. "Here, lie on your side," she said, and slid down. Just before she started, she made as if to push him out of bed.

He looked surprised for a moment, then laughed, no doubt remembering the carriage ride on the dark streets of Priekule, as she did. "You'd better not do that now," he said, mock-fierce.

"What should I do, then?" Krasta asked. Before Valnu

could answer, she did it. He seemed at least as appreciative as she had when their positions were more or less reversed.

She gulped and choked a little at the end. She almost asked him how she compared to some of those Algarvian officers, but kept quiet instead. It wasn't that she lacked the brass: much more that she worried he might tell her the unvarnished truth.

"Well," Valnu said brightly, "maybe I ought to come over and say hello more often."

"If you're sure you wouldn't be bored," Krasta said.

"Oh, not for a while, anyhow," he replied. She glared. Valnu laughed and said, "You deserved that." Krasta shook her head. As far as she was concerned, she never deserved anything but the very best.

"Will we be ready for the demonstration?" Fernao asked Pekka. "After all, it's only a week away."

"Everything went fine the last time we tried it," she answered. "The only difference is, this time a few more people will be watching. Why are you so worried about it?"

"I always want everything to go as well as it can," the Lagoan mage said. "You know that's true." Pekka nodded. If she hadn't, he would have been highly affronted. He went on, "Besides, the war is almost over. The faster we can make all the pieces end, the better for everybody."

"I'm not so sure about that," Pekka said grimly. "If we could use Trapani for the demonstration, I wouldn't mind a bit. And you know *that's* true."

Fernao nodded. He knew it very well. But he said, "The Unkerlanters seem to be doing a pretty fair job of taking care of Trapani all by themselves. They're already in the city, fighting their way toward the palace."

"I know. But I wish I had the revenge myself, not at second hand," Pekka said.

"You sound more like a Lagoan than a Kuusaman," Fernao remarked. His people, like other Algarvic folk, took vengeance seriously. Kuusamans usually didn't. They claimed they were too civilized for such things. *But I can see how getting your husband killed would make you change your mind.* Fernao didn't say that. The less he said about Leino, he was convinced, the better off things between Pekka and him would be.

"Do I?" Pekka said. "Well, by the powers above, I've earned the right." Her thoughts must have been going down the same ley line as his.

"I know," he said. When she brought her past out into the open, he couldn't very well ignore it. And that past had helped shape what she was now. Had it been different, she would have been different, too, perhaps so different that he wouldn't have loved her. That thought by itself was plenty to make him nervous.

She turned the subject, at least to some degree, saying, "Uto likes you."

"I'm glad." Fernao meant it, which surprised him more than a little. He went on, "I like him, too," which was also true. "He'll be quite something when he grows up."

"So he will, unless somebody strangles him some time between now and then," Pekka said. "I'd be lying if I said I hadn't been tempted a couple of times myself. Uto will be . . . how should I put it? A long time learning discipline, that's what he'll be."

Fernao could hardly disagree. But, since the talk had swung to Pekka's family, he asked, "What about your sister? She didn't say more than a few words to me while we were in Kajaani."

"You know why Elimaki was wary of you, too. She wouldn't have been, or not so much"—Fernao could have done without that little bit of honesty from Pekka, however characteristic of her it was—"if Olavin hadn't started cavorting with his secretary or clerk or whoever she is. If we hadn't done anything till after Leino got killed, Elimaki would have been easier in her mind. But I think it will turn out all right in the end."

"Do you?" Fernao wasn't so sure.

But Pekka nodded. "I really do. She didn't like the idea of what we'd been up to, but she liked you better than she thought she would. She told me so when we were down there, and she hasn't said anything different in her letters since. And Elimaki has always been one to speak her mind."

I'm not surprised, not when she's your sister, Fernao

thought. He didn't say that, not when he wasn't quite sure how Pekka would take it. What he did say was, "What are we going to do when the war is done?"

"I want to go back to Kajaani City College," Pekka said. "If I can keep *dear* Professor Heikki out of my hair, it's a good place to do research." She cocked her head to one side and studied him. "And I *thought* you might be interested in coming down to Kajaani, too."

"Oh, I am," he said hastily—and truthfully. He didn't want her getting the wrong idea about that. But he went on, "Not what I meant, not exactly. We've spent so much time working on this new sorcery. We'll be out of our kingdoms' service and ahead of everybody else in the world. Put those together and they likely add up to a good-sized pile of silver."

"Ah." Now Pekka nodded. "I see. Some might be nice, I suppose. But I think I'd sooner do what I want to do than do what someone else wants me to, no matter how much money I might make."

"Theoretical sorcerers can use money just as much as anybody else can," Fernao said.

"I know," she answered. "The questions are, how much do I need? and, how much do I care to change to get it?"

By the way she spoke, the answers to those questions were *not very much* and *not very much,* respectively. To some degree, Fernao felt the same way—but only to some degree. He said, "If I can do work I'd enjoy anyhow, I wouldn't mind being paid well for it."

"Neither would I," Pekka admitted. "*If.* If somebody wants to push me in directions I'd sooner not go, though, that's a different story. And when you start trying to turn magecraft into money, that sort of thing happens a lot of the time." She sent him a challenging glance. "Or will you tell me I'm wrong?"

If he tried to tell her she was wrong, she would have some sharp things to tell him. He could see that. And he didn't think she was wrong. It was a question of . . . *Of degree,* he thought. "We would have to be careful—no doubt about that," he said, "But sorcery and business do mix, or they can. Otherwise, the world wouldn't have changed the way it has the past hundred and fifty years. A lot of the people who were in the right place at the right time were mages. And if you want to know what I think, when there's a choice between having money and not having it, having it is better."

"With everything else equal, aye," Pekka agreed. "But things aren't always equal, not when it comes to money. And you don't always have money. Sometimes money ends up having you. I don't want that to happen to me."

Fernao knew more than a few people who would do anything for money. He didn't care to go down that ley line, either. He said, "You of all people wouldn't have to worry, I don't think."

"For which I thank you," Pekka said seriously. "Some of the things we've done here *shouldn't* be turned into charms anyone could buy, if you want to know what I think."

"Which ones do you have in mind?" Fernao asked.

"For starters, the ones that could let old people borrow years from their young descendants—or maybe, once the techniques are improved, from anybody young," Pekka answered. "Can you imagine the chaos? Can you imagine the crimes?"

Fernao hadn't tried to imagine such things. Now he did, and cringed. "That could be very bad," he said. "I can't argue with you. You've got a twistier mind than I do, to come up with such an idea."

"I didn't," Pekka said. "Ilmarinen did, after one of our early experiments. That was before you joined us. He saw just how things might work."

"Why am I not surprised?" Fernao said. "But nobody's talked much about that kind of possibility since I've been here."

"I don't think anybody wants to talk about it," Pekka said. "The more people who know about it, the more people who think about it, the likelier it is to happen, and to happen soon."

"Soon." Fernao tasted the word, and found he didn't care for its flavor. "We aren't ready to do anything like that."

"No, and we won't be, not for years and years—if we ever are," Pekka said. "But whether we're ready for it and whether it happens are two different questions, don't you see? And that's probably the biggest reason why I'm not very interested in getting rich quick."

Fernao's laugh was at least half rueful. He said, "Well, one thing: you make it easier for me to support you in the style to which you've been accustomed."

"You don't need to worry about supporting me—not with silver, anyhow," Pekka said. "I've always been able to do that. It's the other things we need to worry about: getting along with each other, bringing up Uto the best we can."

"Seeing about a child or two of our own, too," Fernao added.

"Aye, and that, too," Pekka agreed. Fernao fought down bemusement. For his whole life, his interest in children had been theoretical at best. At worst . . . He'd had one lady friend who'd thought he made her pregnant. He hadn't; an illness had thrown her monthly courses out of kilter. What he'd felt then was alarm bordering on panic. Now . . . Now he smiled as Pekka went on, "I've spent some time wondering what our children would look like. Haven't you?"

"Now that you mention it, aye," Fernao answered, adding, "If we have a little girl, I hope she's lucky enough to look like you."

That flustered Pekka. He'd seen that a lot of his compliments did. Partly, he supposed, it was because she was so stubbornly independent. The rest came from a fundamental difference between his folk and hers. Among Lagoans, as with Algarvians, flowery compliments were part of the small change of conversation. Nobody took them too seriously. Kuusamans were more literal-minded. They rarely said things unless they meant them—and they assumed everyone else behaved the same way. His pleasantries gained a weight, a force, here that they wouldn't have had back in Setubal.

"You're sweet," Pekka said at last, and Fernao was confident she meant it. He was also very glad she meant it.

"What I am," he said, "is happy. I love you, you know."

"I do know that," she agreed. "I love you, too. And . . ." She sighed and let it rest there. When Fernao didn't ask her to go on, she looked relieved.

He didn't ask her because he already had a good notion of what she wasn't saying: something like, *And now it's all right*. With Leino still living, she'd been torn. Fernao knew that; he could hardly help knowing it.

If Leino had lived, she would have chosen him, he thought. *He was familiar. He was a Kuusaman. And he was the father of her son, and that counted for a lot with her.*

Pekka looked at him and turned his thoughts away from such reflections, which was just as well. Otherwise, he would have come back to remembering that he owed his happiness to another man's death, and to the despised Algarvians. He hated himself whenever such ideas scurried over the ley lines of his mind, but he could hardly drive them away once for all. They held too much truth, and so kept coming back.

"We'll do the best we can," she said. "I don't know what else we can do. If we work hard, it should be good enough."

"I hope so," Fernao said. "I think so, too." He knew little more about getting along with one special person for years and years than he did about raising a child. But Pekka knew both those things well. *As long as I've got a good teacher,* Fernao thought, *I can learn anything.*

Twelve

All the regular news sheets in Trapani were dead. But the Algarvians still turned out something they called *The Armored Wolf*. Printed on small leaves of cheap, sour-smelling paper, it kept right on screaming shrill defiance at all of King Mezentio's enemies and declaring that victory lay just around the corner.

Crouched behind a barricade only a couple of hundred yards in front of the royal palace, with Unkerlanter eggs bursting all around him, Sidroc was certain the only thing lying around the next corner was a swarm of Unkerlanter footsoldiers and behemoths. He folded his copy of *The Armored Wolf* and stuffed it into his belt pouch.

Ceorl asked, "Why are you wasting time with that horrible rag? Seeing it once is bad enough. Nobody'd want to look at it twice."

"I'm not going to look at it twice," Sidroc said. "I'm almost out of arsewipes, though, and it'll do well enough for that."

"Ah. All right." Ceorl's big head bobbed up and down. "You're not as dumb as I thought you were when you came into the Brigade. If you were, you'd've been dead a long time ago."

Sidroc shrugged and spat. "Dumb doesn't matter—*you're* still breathing, for instance." Ceorl's fingers twisted in an obscene gesture. Laughing, Sidroc gave it back. He went on, "You're still here, and I'm still here, and Sergeant Werferth, who made a better soldier than both of us put together, what happened to him? He stopped a beam in Yanina, that's what. Bad futtering luck, nothing else to it."

Before Ceorl could answer, smoke on the breeze set him coughing. Whole great stretches of Trapani burned, with no one doing much to try to put out the fires. The Algarvians couldn't, and the Unkerlanters didn't care.

Slowly, the smoke cleared. Ceorl's face was as black with soot as his beard. Sidroc doubted his own was any cleaner. Ceorl said, "Not fornicating likely we're going to end up any different."

"No," Sidroc agreed. "This stretch around the palace is about what's left. Maybe a few other little patches, but they don't do anybody any good. Everything else, Swemmel's buggers have got it."

"And they want Mezentio," Ceorl said. "They want that whoreson bad."

Being a corporal, Sidroc could—should—have reproved him. Instead, he nodded. The Unkerlanters *did* want Mezentio. Their dragons dropped leaflets promising not just safety but enormous rewards for any Algarvians who gave them the king. Sidroc supposed the same applied to the men of Plegmund's Brigade. He didn't care. It wasn't that he didn't trust the Unkerlanters, though he didn't. But, after spending the past two and a half years battling them, he didn't want to have anything to do with them except over the business end of a stick.

A couple of men in rock-gray tunics darted out from a doorway and dashed toward rubble in front of the barricade. Using the business end of his stick, Sidroc blazed one of them. The other made it and started blazing back.

Sidroc scuttled along the barricade to find a new place from which to blaze at the foe. Stay anywhere very long and you asked for a sniper's beam through the head. Behind him, an Algarvian declared, "*I* will deal with these cursed savages."

That was interesting enough to make Sidroc turn his head. "Who in blazes are *you*?" he asked the redhead standing there—standing there, Sidroc noted, with no regard whatsoever for his own safety. Considering what was going on all around—considering that Trapani was, not to put too fine a point on it, falling—that took even Algarvian arrogance a bit far.

"I am Major Almonte," the fellow replied. With his left hand, he brushed the mage's badge he wore on his left breast. "I have the power to hurl the Unkerlanters back in dismay."

"Oh, you do, do you?" Sidroc grunted. Almonte nodded. He believed what he was saying. Sidroc didn't, not for a minute. "If you're such hot stuff, pal, what are Swemmel's buggers doing within blaze of the royal palace here?"

"It's not my fault," Almonte said. "My superiors would not listen to me, would not let me show the full reach of my genius."

From not far away, Ceorl said, "Another fornicating crackpot." Sidroc laughed. Almonte might be an Algarvian and an officer by courtesy, but what difference did that make here and now?

The redhead glared at both Forthwegians. "You are nothing but mercenaries," he said. "You have no business criticizing me."

"Talk is cheap, pal," Sidroc said.

"Futter yourself," Almonte said crisply. "By the powers

above, I will show you—I will show the world—what I can do." He scrambled over the barricade and faced the Unkerlanters without the least shred of cover.

When they didn't blaze Almonte down in the first instant, Sidroc knew he had some—more than a little—power. Beams flew toward him, but none bit. It was as if they were beneath the redhead's notice. He raised both hands above his head and began a spell. It was, Sidroc noted, not in Algarvian but in classical Kaunian: he'd learned enough in school to recognize the language. He snickered. Hearing it now, of all times, and in the heart of Trapani, of all places, was pretty funny.

But then the laughter curdled in his mouth. The hair on his arms and at the back of his neck tried to prickle up in fear. Almonte's magecraft seemed to draw darkness from beneath the flagstones on which he stood and cast it at the Unkerlanters. Sidroc briefly heard them cry out in alarm before that darkness—did he really see it, or sense it with something older and even more primitive than sight?—washed over them. Then they fell silent. Sidroc was somehow certain none of them would ever cry out again.

Major Almonte did, in pride and triumph. Sidroc leaned over and threw up. Ceorl looked green, too. "I'd sooner lose than use a magic like that," he muttered. Sidroc nodded.

Almonte shook his fist at the sudden silence in front of the palace. "Die, swine!" he cried. "If the stinking dragonfliers had let me take my spells aloft, I'd have done more and worse to you. But even now . . ." He resumed the incantation. That cold, dark, deadly silence spread farther. Unkerlanter lives went out liked snuffed candle flames.

Swemmel's men might not have known exactly what was happening to them, but they knew something was, and they knew whence the trouble came. They hurled eggs at Almonte from tossers beyond the reach of his sorcery. Sidroc threw himself flat. Eggs bursting all around Almonte burst too close to him.

The Algarvian mage had had a spell for turning aside beams. When Sidroc lifted his head again, he discovered Almonte had owned no such warding against bursts of sorcerous energy and the metal from egg shells they flung about. The mage was down and screaming and bleeding. He looked more like a piece of butchery than a man.

Sidroc could have blazed him to put him out of his misery. What with the sort of magic Almonte had been using, he was more than glad to let him suffer.

"They'll come after us as soon as they realize he can't do anything to them any more," he warned Ceorl.

"I know," the ruffian said.

Come the Unkerlanters did, behind a fresh barrage of eggs. "Urra!" they shouted, more in relief, Sidroc thought, than anything else. "Urra! Swemmel! Urra!" Despite good blazing from the barricades and from the palace itself, they gained lodgements here and there and began blazing down the Algarvians and the men from Plegmund's Brigade and the Phalanx of Valmiera who still stood against them.

"Fall back!" Sidroc yelled. "We'll be cut off if we don't!" He'd done enough in this fight—he'd done enough in his whole term of service in Plegmund's Brigade—that no one could accuse him of cowardice. He ran back toward the royal palace, his men—those still on their feet—with him.

As he ran, he hoped the redheads inside wouldn't take the soldiers of Plegmund's Brigade for Unkerlanters and blaze them down. That would have been the ultimate indignity. In the end, though, how much did it matter? He didn't think he would last very long any which way.

He made it into the palace unblazed, and took up a new position at a window that had offered a magnificent view but was really too long, too open, to give good cover. To his right knelt Ceorl and a blond Valmieran from the Phalanx, to his left a redhead from the Popular Assault who couldn't have been above fifteen and an older Algarvian, a bald fellow with a beaky nose.

The old man could handle a stick. "There's another one down," he said, stretching an Unkerlanter lifeless in front of the palace. "But it won't last. It can't last, powers below eat them all."

Sidroc shuddered. Major Almonte, he thought, had dealt much too intimately with the powers below. "We'll hold on a while longer," he said, and then took another look at the man crouching there beside him. His voice rose to a startled squeak: "Your, uh, Majesty."

King Mezentio nodded briskly. "I will ask the same favor of you, Corporal, that I've asked of a good many men already: when you see this place falling, have the courtesy to blaze me down. I do not care to fall into Swemmel's hands alive."

"Uh, aye, sir." Sidroc nodded. He wouldn't have wanted the King of Unkerlant to get his hands on him, either.

"Meanwhile . . ." Mezentio blazed again. He nodded, but then grimaced. "I should have won Algarve should have won. This kingdom proved itself weak. It doesn't deserve to live."

And who led it to where it is? Sidroc thought. But he didn't see how he could say such a thing to the King of Algarve. Even as he cast about for ways that wouldn't sound too blunt, the moment passed. A great racket of bursting eggs and crumpling masonry and shouting men arose from the rear of the palace. A redhead dashed up to Mezentio, crying, "Your Majesty! Your Majesty! The whoresons are inside! We have some barricades in the corridors, but powers above only know how long they'll hold." Crashes and more screams said one of them had just gone down.

"All over," Mezentio said, his voice soft and sad. "We came so close, but it's all over. We weren't strong enough. We all deserve to go into the fire." He bowed to Sidroc. "Will you do the honors?" As Sidroc numbly nodded, the king spoke to the messenger: "Know that this man slays me at my request. Let him be rewarded for it, and in no way punished. Do you understand?"

"Aye, your Majesty." Tears ran down the redhead's face.

Mezentio bowed to Sidroc again. "Do what needs doing. Try to blaze true, to make it as quick as you can." He closed his eyes and waited.

Sidroc did it. He'd done it for wounded comrades more than once before. Seeing King Mezentio slump over dead raised no special horror in him. It was as if he had nothing at all left inside. Ceorl set a hand on his shoulder. "Powers above," the ruffian whispered.

Fresh shouts came from the back of the palace, these

much closer. Sidroc got to his feet. "Come on," he said savagely. "There's still some fighting left." As he and the men he led ran forward, panic-stricken Algarvians ran back toward them. "Cowards!" he shouted, and ran on. With nothing left inside him, what did he have to lose?

A beam took him in the side as he came round a corner. He went down, but kept blazing. Another beam bit, this one deep. He tasted blood in his mouth as his stick slipped from fingers that would not hold it. He was still moving a little when an Unkerlanter lieutenant paused, saw he wasn't quite dead, and put a beam through his temple before charging on.

Though he got better food and better lodging in his new quarters outside the main captives' camp on Obuda, Sergeant Istvan missed the company of his fellow Gyongyosians. When he grumbled about that to Lammi, the Kuusaman forensic mage raised a thin black eyebrow. "But they beat you," she said. "And they would do it again if they had the chance."

Istvan's broad shoulders went up and down in a shrug. "I know. But they're my own folk even so. You Kuusamans"—he shrugged again—"I don't think the stars shine on you."

One of his own people would have been furious at such an insult. Lammi only shrugged in her turn, which proved how foreign and alien she was. She knew Gyongyosian customs well, but they didn't bind her. That made her more alarming to him, not less. She said, "I am willing to take my chances on it."

Few, if any, Gyongyosians would have been so willing. Lammi didn't talk about the scar on Istvan's left hand, or about what it meant. Had his fellow captives known what it meant, they would have done worse to him than they would have for mere suspected treason. What could make treason *mere*? Goat-eating could, and Istvan knew it all too well.

His captors let him see Kun now and then. Each of them was wary with the other, for each knew the other had, however unwillingly, confessed to the abomination they'd both committed. Kun seemed more content away from his countrymen than Istvan did. "They're a pack of fools, most of them," he said loftily.

"Oh, and you're not?" Istvan said.

"Not that kind, anyhow," the former mage's apprentice replied. "I got sick of men from mountain valleys long before those louts set on me."

"*I'm* a man from a mountain valley," Istvan reminded him, his big hands balling into fists.

"Proves my point, wouldn't you say?" Kun grinned at Istvan's flabbergasted expression. "And you, my dear fellow, you put up with me far better than most."

Istvan thought about that for a little while. He said, "We've been through too much together. If the two of us don't put up with each other, no one ever will."

Kun grimaced. "And if that isn't a judgment on both of us, stars go dark if I know what would be."

A couple of days after that, Lammi summoned both of them. That surprised Istvan. They'd never been questioned together. Nor were they this time. The Kuusaman mage spoke briskly: "How would the two of you like to be free to return to your own land?"

"Don't play with us," Istvan said roughly. "That isn't going to happen, and you know it. We're here till the war is over." *And who knows for how long after that?*

But Lammi shook her head. "Not necessarily. And I ask no treason of you. By the stars, I do not. All I ask is that you go on board ship, go back to the waters off Becsehely, watch a certain something, and then, when you are released, tell your own superiors exactly what you saw." She held up a hand to forestall questions. "You would not be the only men doing this—far from it."

"Why us?" Kun asked.

"Because you are in a certain amount of difficulty here," Lammi answered, "and because you have shown more than a certain amount of wit. We feel confident you would tell those set above you the truth."

"Why shouldn't we just keep quiet?" Istvan asked. "And what's off Becsehely?" They both knew the miserable little island east of Obuda better than they wanted to; they'd been captured there.

Lammi said, "You will see what is off, and on, Becsehely. And you will, I think, find good reason for telling the truth as you see it. Of course, if you would rather stay here on Obuda . . ."

"I'll go," Istvan said. Kun hesitated, but only briefly.

Lammi smiled. "I thought that might prove persuasive. Pack whatever gear you have. The ley-line cruiser will be here tomorrow at first light."

Istvan had a duffel bag ready in good time. No captive had much in the way of belongings. Kun's duffel was heavier, but Kun cared more about books than Istvan ever had. A carriage took both of them to the harbor, which had been repaired since Captain Frigyes' bloodthirsty magic did its work. The cruiser was long and sleek and deadly, somehow more dangerous-looking than a Gyongyosian ship. When they boarded the vessel, a Kuusaman military clerk checked their names off a list. A fellow in greenish Kuusaman naval uniform escorted them to a cabin.

"You two stay here," the Kuusaman said in Gyongyosian. Like most of his countrymen who spoke the language, he used the plural rather than the dual.

The cabin was big enough to boast two cots side by side. Istvan and Kun wouldn't even have to quarrel over who got the top bunk. Istvan said, "If this is what the slanteyes do for captives, they must live mighty soft themselves."

"They do," Kun said. "They're richer than we are. They've had modern magecraft longer than we have, and they do more with it than we do."

"But we are the warrior race," Kun said with pride in his countrymen still diminished only a little from what he'd felt when summoned into Ekrekek Arpad's service.

Kun sighed. "I suppose I'd waste my time asking you how much good that's done us or who's winning the war, and so I won't."

By "not asking" in that particular way, of course, he put the question all the more effectively. Istvan chewed on it for some little while. He liked the flavors of none of the answers he found. To keep from showing how little he liked them, he peered out the porthole. To his surprise, Obuda was already receding in the distance. "We're moving!" he exclaimed.

"Well, what if we are?" Kun seemed determined to stay

contrary. "Stars above, this is a ley-line ship. Did you expect to hear sails flutter and the wind howl in the rigging? Use your head before you use your mouth."

"Oh, go bugger a goat," Istvan said. Coming from a valley far back in the mountains, he knew little about ships, ley-line or otherwise. The only times he'd been aboard them were on journeys across the Bothnian Ocean during the war. He'd never been in a two-man cabin then, but down in the hold with a lot of other soldiers, most of whom were just as ignorant of the sea and its ways as he was.

He did remember the meal gong. Either the Kuusamans had the same signal or they'd got a gong so they could use something with which their Gyongyosian passengers were familiar. Armed Kuusamans directed Istvan and Kun and the other Gyongyosians who emerged from cabins along the corridor to the iron chamber where they would eat. A large sign on the wall declared, WE DO NOT SERVE GOAT ABOARD THIS SHIP. YOU MAY EAT FREELY, WITH NO FEAR OF POLLUTION. Istvan hoped the slanteyes were telling the truth. If they weren't . . . The scar on his hand throbbed. He'd already learned more about ritual pollution and the way it ate at a man than he'd ever wanted to know.

Perhaps three dozen Gyongyosians queued up to take trays and utensils and bowls of the stew a couple of bored-looking Kuusaman cooks served up. The food was better than he'd got in the captives' camp, but not so good as the guards' rations he'd eaten since being extracted from among the rest of the captured Gyongyosians. The cooks gave each man one mug of ale and as much tea as he wanted.

Most of the other captives aboard the ley-line cruiser were officers. Istvan saw one man in a brigadier's uniform, a couple of colonels, and a lot of majors and captains. One of those captains turned to him and asked, "Well, Sergeant, why did they pick you for this charade?"

"I have no real idea, sir," Istvan answered cautiously. "Maybe because I fought on Becsehely."

With a laugh, the officer said, "Well, that makes some sense. I don't know why they chose me, I'll tell you that.

My guess is, the slanteyes drew my name out of a hat or a pot or whatever they use for such things."

Corporal Kun asked, "Sir, do you have any idea what they're going to show us when we get there?"

"Not the slightest clue." The captain shook his head. "I speak some Kuusaman, and I've asked, but the slanteyes won't say. They haven't talked out of turn where I could hear 'em, either, worse luck. Stars above be dark for them forever, they're keeping their mouths shut tight."

The ley-line cruiser stopped at another island east of Obuda and picked up four men from a captives' camp there. Istvan wondered just how many Gyongyosian captives the Kuusamans held. *Too many* was the first answer that occurred to him.

When the cruiser stopped a couple of miles off the beaches of Becsehely, the Kuusamans summoned all their Gyongyosian passengers to the deck. The island looked as flat and unlovely as Istvan remembered it. It also looked extraordinarily battered, as if it had been fought over only the other day, not some months before. A Kuusaman officer spoke in Istvan's language: "Watch what we do here. When we give you back to your own people, tell the truth about it."

Back on Obuda, Lammi had said almost exactly the same thing. By the looks on the faces of the men who hadn't come from Obuda, they'd heard the speech before, too. Kun raised an eyebrow and murmured, "The same old song."

But then the Kuusaman added a new verse: "Remember, this could be Gyorvar, or any other place we choose."

As if his words were a cue, a lash of fire fell on Becsehely from a clear blue sky. It wasn't lightning; it was flame, as if from a dragon a mile long. But there was no dragon, nothing at all in the sky over Becsehely but air. The lash fell again and again and again. Even across a broad stretch of sea, it was too brilliant to look at directly; Istvan had to squint and hold a hand up to his face to protect his eyes. Even across that stretch of sea, he could feel the heat, too. And, where the flame slid off the battered land and into the Bothnian Ocean, great clouds of steam rose up.

"Stars preserve us," muttered the captain with whom he'd spoken at supper. "That *could* be Gyorvar." Despite the heat coming from the tormented island, a chill seized Istvan and wouldn't let him go.

As if for variety, the flames eased and bursts of sorcerous energy, as if from great eggs, pounded Becsehely. Istvan marveled that the island didn't sink beneath the sea. At last, as abruptly as it had begun, the magecraft ended. Shimmering waves of heat still rose from Becsehely.

"We will set you free now," the Gyongyosian-speaking officer said. "Tell your people the truth. Tell them what could happen to them if they go on with the war. Tell them it has gone on too long. It *will* end soon."

The ley-line cruiser glided east, away from Becsehely and toward the few islands in the Bothnian Ocean Gyongyos still held. Down in the bowels of the ship, a crystallomancer would, Istvan supposed, try to arrange a truce to hand over the captives. *I might go back to Kunhegyes, to my own valley,* he thought. Then he looked down at the scar on his hand. *As long as I bear this, do I want to go home at all?*

Marshal Rathar had always liked to have his headquarters as far forward as he could. With his army battering its way into the very heart of Trapani, he'd set up shop in a large house in the northern suburbs of the city, just out of reach of the last few Algarvian egg-tossers. He and General Vatran pored over a map of the city looted from a book dealer's, stabbing pins with rock-gray heads into one landmark after another.

"They can't hold on much longer," Vatran said.

"They've already held out longer than they had any business doing," Rathar said. He knew how many of his brigades the redheads had bled white. If they had to do much more fighting after this, they would have a hard time of it. But this was—this had to be—the end.

No sooner had that thought crossed his mind than a crystallomancer rushed into the dining hall that was doing duty as a map room. "Marshal Rathar!" he shouted. "Marshal Rathar!"

"Aye, that is my name," Rathar agreed mildly. Vatran snorted.

But the crystallomancer was too full of himself, too full of his news, to pay any attention to a feeble joke. "Marshal Rathar, sir, an Algarvian general's come out from what the redheads hold of the palace, sir, and he wants to yield up the soldiers the redheads still have fighting!" He leaped in the air with glee.

"Oh, by the powers above," General Vatran whispered.

Back in the village where he'd grown up, Rathar had thought no moment in his life could surpass lying down with a woman—actually, she'd been a girl, a couple of summers younger than he—for the first time. Now, all these years later, he discovered he'd been wrong. "It may be over," he murmured, and that sounded sweeter than *I love you* had back then.

"Aye, sir," the crystallomancer said, and then, "Shall I have the redhead brought here, sir? And he's asking for a truce while you dicker. Shall I say we grant him that?"

Fussing over details spoiled some of the glory, but it needed doing. "Aye, have him brought here," Rathar replied. "And aye, he can have a truce till he returns to his own lines." The marshal's right hand folded into a fist. "That shouldn't take long. He hasn't got much to bargain with. Send out the necessary orders."

Saluting, the crystallomancer hurried away. General Vatran straightened up over the map table. He too saluted. "Congratulations, sir."

"Thank you." Rathar felt as if he'd gulped a bottle of spirits: half numb, half exalted. Over the next quarter of an hour, he listened to the egg-tossers falling silent, one battery at a time. Quiet seemed eerie, unnatural. He hadn't heard much of it, not these past four years. Somewhere not far away, a cuckoo began to sing. Maybe it had been singing before, but he hadn't been able to hear it then.

There was a small commotion outside his headquarters when the Algarvian general got there. Rathar's sentries tried to remove the redhead's sword before allowing him into the marshal's presence. The officer proved to speak good Unkerlanter, and hesitated not at all about making his view clear: "Are you uncivilized, uncultured? You do not take the weapon of a brave foe who is still negotiating his army's surrender!"

"Let him keep the blade for now," Rathar called. The sentries brought the Algarvian into the map room. The fellow wore a grimy, wrinkled uniform and looked as if he hadn't slept for a couple of days. He came to attention and gave Rathar a salute. Returning it, Rathar named himself and introduced General Vatran.

"I am General Oldrade," the Algarvian replied. "I have the honor to command my kingdom's forces in and around Trapani. I must tell you, Marshal, that we can no longer offer resistance against your armies." He looked about to burst into tears.

"Has King Mezentio sent you forth with this word?" Rathar asked. "You must understand, General, that my sovereign will require Mezentio's personal surrender. King Swemmel has left me no discretion whatsoever in this matter."

Oldrade shrugged. "I cannot give you what I do not have, sir. After defending the royal palace to his last breath, his Majesty perished yesterday. I have seen the king's body with my own eyes, and know this to be true."

"Lucky bastard," Vatran muttered. Oldrade didn't react, so perhaps Vatran had been quiet enough to keep him from hearing.

Rathar was inclined to agree with his general. Compared to what Swemmel had wanted to do to Mezentio, dying in battle was the quick, easy way out. "You understand, General, that we shall have to be fully satisfied on this point." Swemmel wasn't going to be fully satisfied no matter what. He'd wanted his sport with, his vengeance on, Mezentio.

"You may examine the king's body," Oldrade said.

"My understanding is that Mainardo, having abdicated as King of Jelgava, now succeeds his older brother as King of Algarve," General Oldrade answered. "King Mainardo is now arranging the surrender of Algarvian forces in the northeast to the Kuusaman army."

Swemmel won't get his hands on Mainardo, was what that meant. The Kuusamans were unlikely to boil the new

King of Algarve alive or give him any of the other interesting and lingering ends he might deserve. *Too bad,* Rathar thought, but he didn't see what he or Unkerlant could do about it. *Maybe the Jelgavans will take care of it for us. They have almost as many reasons to hate Mainardo as we do—we did—to hate Mezentio.*

"What terms are you prepared to give us, Marshal?" Oldrade asked.

"Assuming that what you say about Mezentio is true, will will grant your soldiers' lives," Rathar said. "We offer no more than that."

Oldrade drew himself up, the picture of affronted dignity. "This is mean-spirited in the extreme!" he said indignantly.

"Too bad," Rathar said. "If you like, I will send you back to your lines, and we can take up the fight again. See how many of your men come away with their lives then."

"You are a hard, cruel man," Oldrade said. "And your king—"

"Say what you like about me," Rathar broke in. "You insult King Swemmel at your peril. Now, then—do you accept these terms, or not?"

"For the sake of my men, I must accept them." Tears ran down Oldrade's face. Rage? Humiliation? Sorrow? Rathar couldn't say. All he knew was, no Unkerlanter would have thus bared himself before a foe. Vatran turned away, embarrassed to look at the Algarvian.

"I will have a secretary write out the terms, in Unkerlanter and Algarvian," Rathar said. Oldrade, still weeping, nodded. The Marshal of Unkerlant went on, "I will also send out men with flags of truce and mages to magnify voices, letting everyone know the fighting here is over. When you pass back into your own lines, you do the same." Oldrade nodded again. Rathar guessed the battle wouldn't end at once, but would sputter out over several days. People would die for no reason whatever. He shrugged, hoping he was wrong but knowing he wouldn't be able to stop such things.

"You have given us harsh terms," Oldrade said. "I hope that, as tempers cool, you will be more generous in your triumph."

The Algarvian general was three or four inches taller than Rathar. The marshal had to tilt his head back to look down his nose at Oldrade, and he did. "What sort of terms would you have offered if you had taken Cottbus?" he asked. General Oldrade flushed and did not answer. He didn't have to; they both knew the truth there.

Vatran said, "We ought to send a mage to check Mezentio's body, make sure it's not somebody else wearing a sorcerous disguise."

"A good point," Rathar said. "I will have the secretary put that in the surrender document."

"You are the conquerors." Oldrade didn't try to hide his bitterness. "You may do as you please."

"That's right," Rathar said, and called his secretary. He told the young lieutenant what he wanted. The secretary was fluent in both his own language and Algarvian, which Rathar also spoke and read. He skimmed through both texts, then passed them to Oldrade.

After reading them, the redhead nodded. He pulled a pen from a tunic pocket. Rathar pushed a bottle of ink toward him. The pen scratched across both instruments of surrender. Oldrade said, "Would you please have your mages make copies for me to take back to . . . what is left of my command?"

"Of course, General." In small matters, Rathar could afford courtesy. "With the fall of Trapani, this war is as near over as makes no difference. May we never fight another one."

"May it be so," Oldrade agreed. With a sigh, he unbuckled his sword and held it out to Rathar. "Now it is yours, sir, the negotiations being complete."

"I accept it in the name of my king," Rathar said. "Go now, and make the surrender known to your men. Your escort will take you back through the lines." General Oldrade bowed, spun on his heel, and left the headquarters.

"Congratulations, lord Marshal," Vatran said again. "We've done it."

Rathar returned the general's salute. "So we have," he said. "And now to let his Majesty know we've done it." He went off to the crystallomancers' room. Arranging an etheric connection back to Cottbus didn't take long. He hadn't thought it would; the crystallomancers had to have been waiting for this moment. As soon as King Swemmel's image appeared in the crystal before the marshal, he said, "Your Majesty, the Algarvians in Trapani have yielded, the surrender to spare their lives but nothing more. The enemy's capital is yours."

"And what of the enemy's king?" Swemmel demanded. "We want Mezentio."

"He is said to have died in the fighting, your Majesty," Rathar answered. "I am sending a sorcerer to make sure the corpse is his."

King Swemmel snorted contemptuously. "Mark our words—he turned coward at the end. He dared not face what we would have done to him for all that he did to our kingdom." Rathar thought his sovereign likely to be right. In Mezentio's place, he wouldn't have cared to endure Swemmel's wrath, either. The king went on, "Who now claims the throne of Algarve, if Mezentio is truly dead?"

"His brother Mainardo, your Majesty," Rathar said. "He is said to have yielded himself up to the Kuusamans in the northeast."

"They will not kill him, as he deserves. No." Swemmel sounded worried, almost frightened. His eyes flicked back and forth, back and forth, as if watching demons only he could see. "No. They will leave him alive, leave him on what they call the throne of Algarve. The stinking whoresons, they will use him for a cat's paw, a stalking horse, against *us*."

"They want Algarve beaten as much as we do, your Majesty," Rathar said.

"Algarve *is* beaten," the king said. "Now they want us crushed as well. They think they can loose their sorceries in the middle of the Bothnian Ocean without our knowing it, but they are wrong—wrong, we tell you!" Swemmel's voice rose to something close to a scream.

Rathar knew nothing about sorceries in the middle of the Bothnian Ocean. He wondered if Swemmel did, or if the king were only imagining them. "We've won here," he said. King Swemmel nodded, but with none of the joy Rathar had hoped he'd show. And Rathar's own joy, in turn, died before being fully born. He wondered if he would ever find a way to forgive Swemmel for that.

Gyorvar, the capital of Gyongyos, lay where four rivers came together near the coast to form a single stream. A ley line went up that stream from the sea to Gyorvar, so the cruiser *Csikos*, after skirting the Balaton Islands, could take the men it had received from its Kuusaman counterpart straight to the city.

"Home," Kun murmured as the tall buildings came into sight.

It wasn't home to Istvan. So many houses and shops and enormous structures whose use he didn't know all jammed together were as alien to him as the forests of western Unkerlant or the low, flat expanse of Becsehely—Becsehely as it had been when he'd served there, not the scarred and burnt and ruined place the island had become.

"My own people," Istvan said, as close as he could come to agreeing with the former mage's apprentice.

Behind the lenses of his spectacles, Kun's eyes gleamed. "You're going to see more of your own people than you want to for a while, unless I miss my guess."

"Huh," Istvan said. "I never would have imagined."

As soon as the *Csikos* tied up at a quay, swarms of men in clean uniforms with the badges of Eyes and Ears of the Ekrekek swarmed aboard. "Istvan, Sergeant!" one of them shouted, reading from a list.

"Here!" Istvan waved his hand.

"You come with me," the fellow said, and checked off his name. "Petofi, Captain!"

"Here!" The officer waved as Istvan had. He was tall and gaunt, with a nasty scar on his left cheek that stopped just short of his eye.

"Good. You two are mine." The Eye and Ear of the Ekrekek checked off Petofi's name, too. "Come along with me, both of you. We've got carriages waiting to take you to interrogation headquarters."

Istvan wasn't sure he liked the sound of that. In fact, he was sure he didn't like the sound of it. But he was only a sergeant. What could he do but obey? Captain Petofi had some ideas on that score. "One moment," he said dryly. "A long time ago, I learned never to go anywhere with a stranger."

"I am not a stranger." The Eye and Ear tapped his badge to show what he meant. Captain Petofi just stood where he was. With a grimace, Ekrekek Arpad's man said, "You may call me Balazs, if it makes you happy."

"After what we have seen, it will take a good deal more than that to make us happy, Balazs," Petofi said. "Is it not so, Sergeant?"

"Uh, aye, sir, it is." Istvan stammered a little, surprised the scarred officer had bothered speaking to him.

"Well, part of my job is finding out about all that," Balazs said easily. "Now that you know who I am, you come along with me, and we'll see what you think you know."

Captain Petofi bristled anew at that. Istvan didn't rise to it; he was watching another Eye and Ear leading Kun away. Now he was alone, all the comrades with whom he'd gone through so much stripped away. He was back among his countrymen, true, but how could the smooth, slick, smug Balazs or the dour Petofi understand what had happened to him these past six years? Petofi might, some: he'd seen war and he'd been a Kuusaman captive, too. But he was an officer and, no doubt, a nobleman, and thus a breed apart from a man who'd come out of a village in a mountain valley.

"Come along, come along," Balazs repeated: it seemed to be his favorite phrase. Istvan and Petofi followed him down the gangplank and over to one from among the swarm of carriages waiting at the base of the pier. The Eye and Ear held the door open for the two returning captives. When he shut it, it clicked as if locking. There were no handles on the inside, and the windows were too small to crawl through. Balazs got up with the driver. The carriage began to move.

Petofi's face twisted into what Istvan belatedly recognized as a wry smile; the officer's scar made his expressions hard to read. "Here we are, captives again," Petofi said. "The fools think they will sit on what we know, as a duck sits on an egg, and the egg will never hatch—or burst.

A billy goat's cock up their arses couldn't make them pay heed to what needs doing."

"Aye, sir," Istvan answered, but he'd only half heard the captain. The carriage's windows might be small, but they let him see more of Gyorvar than he ever had before. Individual houses looked familiar: gray stone buildings, mostly of two stories, all vertical lines, with steep slate roofs to help keep snow from sticking. But he'd never seen so many—never seen a tenth so many—all together. And there were so many buildings that, though done in the same style, dwarfed those houses. How many households could inhabit a building eight stories high and half a block wide? How did they keep from feuding with one another? From things Kun had said, he knew clan ties were looser here in the city than they were back in his valley, but he had no feel for what that meant. He also couldn't imagine why Gyorvar needed so many shops, and so many different kinds of shops. They sold more things than readily came to mind.

Captain Petofi's chuckle brought him back to himself. "Your first time in Gyorvar, Sergeant?" the officer asked.

"I've been through before, sir," Istvan answered, "but this is the first chance I've ever had to look around a little. It's . . . not like my home valley."

"Come from up in the mountains, do you?" Petofi said, and Istvan nodded. Petofi smiled his twisted smile. "I was just a little boy when my father moved the family here— Ekrekek Arpad's father had summoned him to the city. I'd lived in the mountains myself till then. It's a different world, sure as sure."

"Aye, sir, it certainly is," Istvan agreed.

After an hour or so, though, they came to a part of the world that looked thoroughly familiar. A barracks was a barracks, here or on Obuda. A barracks was a barracks, in fact, whether Gyongyosians or accursed foreigners like Kuusamans ran it. So Istvan had discovered, at any rate.

The carriage stopped. Balazs jumped down and opened the door that couldn't be opened from the inside. "Come with me," the Eye and Ear said again. "That hall right there, and we'll find out what you know."

Istvan felt a certain amount of relief on discovering the

hall didn't contain a torture chamber. Interrogation, among Gyongyosians, could be a serious business indeed. Balazs even gave Petofi and him food and ale. Coriander and pepper and caraway in the sausage reminded Istvan he was back in his own kingdom, though the pork wasn't nearly so rich with fat as it would have been back in Kunhegyes.

"Now," Balazs said once the two returned captives had refreshed themselves, "tell me what the stars-denying slanteyes claim to have shown you."

"Fire and destruction, sent from afar," Istvan answered.

"Even so," Captain Petofi agreed. "Sorcery we cannot hope to match. They chose a worthless island, and made it more worthless still. But they can do the same to Gyorvar, and I see no way we could stop them. My spirit aches to say it, but I do not see how we can hope to win the war against them."

"They told you they would visit this horror on our stars-beloved capital, did they?" Balazs inquired.

"They did," Petofi said. "But they hardly needed to. A blind man can see that, if they did it to Becsehely, out in the middle of the Bothnian Ocean, they can do it wherever they choose."

Balazs' smile was far smoother than that of the wounded captain. "How do you know this?" he asked. "Again, did they tell you? Did they, perhaps, make a point of telling you?"

"How else could it have been?" Istvan said. "There was just the island, and us watching what happened to it." He shuddered at the memory of the fire, and of the clouds of steam rising from the tormented sea.

"They could have had mages in the bowels of the very ship you rode, casting these fearsome spells," the Eye and Ear said. "Or, for that matter, what they said was destruction could have been nothing but illusion. Either of those is easier to believe than that they really have these powers they claim."

He doesn't believe because he doesn't want to believe, and because he didn't see with his own eyes, Istvan thought. He said, "Sir, anybody who's fought the slanteyes—or who's been in one of their captives' camps—knows they're stronger mages than we are. By the stars, they really did this thing."

"So speaks a sergeant from back in the Ilszung Mountains," Balazs said. "Do you claim to know everything of what is possible and what is not when it comes to sorcery?"

"No, sir," Istvan answered. "All I claim is, I know what happened right in front of my own eyes. If you don't believe me—if none of you people believe the captives the Kuusamans set free—our land will be sorry on account of it."

"You should know, Sergeant," Balazs said, his voice growing cold, "that the laws against treasonous talk and defeatism have been tightened up lately, as they should have been. You would be wise to have a care in what you say."

Captain Petofi spoke up: "And you, wretch, you would be wise to listen to the underofficer. He spoke with a warrior's courage, telling nothing but the truth, and you mock him and scorn him and answer him with threats. By the stars, with goatheads like you set over us, it's no wonder we're losing the war."

Like most Gyongyosian men, Balazs let his shaggy, tawny beard grow high on his cheeks. It didn't grow high enough to hide his flush of anger, though. "You have no business talking to me that way, Captain. I tell you what Ekrekek Arpad has told the land: we shall win this fight against the stars-detested savages of Kuusamo. If the Ekrekek of Gyongyos says a thing is so, how can a couple of ragged captives say otherwise?"

Istvan gulped. If Arpad said something was so, then it was bound to be so. Everything he'd ever learned proclaimed the truth of that. The stars spoke to Arpad, and Arpad spoke to Gyongyos. So it had ever been; so it would ever be.

But Petofi said, "If Ekrekek Arpad had been on that Kuusaman cruiser, he would have known the truth, the same as we did. And if we're winning the war, how did the slanteyes ravage an island that used to belong to us?"

"I give you one last warning, Captain," the Ekrekek's Eye and Ear said. "We have places where we send defeatists, to keep them out of the way so their cowardice can't infect the true warriors of Gyongyos."

Petofi bowed. "By all means, send me to one of those places. The company and the wit are bound to be better there than here."

"You'll get your wish," Balazs promised. He rounded on Istvan. "What about you, Sergeant? I trust you have better sense?"

That could only mean, *Say what I want you to say, and things will go easy for you.* Istvan gulped again. *I just got out of a captives' camp,* he thought with something not far from despair. Petofi eyed him without saying a word. *Sell yourself, wretch,* his eyes seemed to say. Sighing, Istvan said, "How can you ask me to lie when the stars looking down on me know I tell the truth?"

"Another fool, eh?" Balazs scribbled a note on a leaf of paper in front of him. "Well, I already told you—we have places for fools."

Ilmarinen was not a hunter. He had no qualms about eating game or meat. He just saw no sport in killing beasts. Men were supposed to be smarter than animals, so where was the contest? (The way men had behaved during the Derlavaian War did make him wonder about his assumption, but he'd still never heard of a deer or a wolf picking up a stick and blazing back at a hunter.) Still and all, though, one hunting phrase he'd heard stuck in his mind: *in at the death.* With Trapani fallen, he wanted to be in at the death of Algarve.

If that meant leaving Torgavi, he wasn't altogether sorry to go. He hadn't had much fun there anyhow, not since the Unkerlanters figured out he was a mage and ordered him to stay on his own kingdom's side of the Albi. He went instead to Scansano, where Mainardo, once King of Jelgava and now King of Algarve, headed what passed for his kingdom's government these days.

Kuusaman and Lagoan soldiers—and a few Jelgavans— patrolled the streets of Scansano these days. Mainardo had ordered the Algarvian soldiers fighting in the northeast of his kingdom to lay down their sticks even before his brother, King Mezentio, died in the fall of Trapani. All that was left now was for Mainardo to order all the Algarvians still fighting to do the same.

Mainardo reigned not from a palace, not even from the local count's mansion, but from a hostel, as if to underscore how temporary his power was likely to prove. Ilmarinen managed to arrange a room in the very same hostel for himself.

"How did you do that?" a Kuusaman news-sheet writer asked him at a tavern across the street. "They told me they were full up."

"It wasn't hard," the mage answered. "I bribed them."

"That really worked?" The writer's narrow eyes widened. "I know they say Algarvians are like that, but I didn't believe it."

"Believe it," Ilmarinen said. "It's true." He laughed at the look on the news-sheet writer's face. Kuusamans were straightforward in their dealings with one another. When they said aye or nay, they commonly meant it. Offer one of Ilmarinen's countrymen a little money on the side to change his mind about something, and he was much more likely to shout for a constable. Algarvians weren't like that. They used bribes the same way mechanics used grease.

"Will the surrender come today?" the writer asked. "That's what everybody is saying, anyhow."

"I'll tell you how you'll know," Ilmarinen answered. The writer leaned toward him. He said, "When there's a ley-line caravan from out of the west, then you'll know it's really over."

"Out of the west?" Now the young news-sheet writer looked confused.

Ilmarinen wondered how the fellow was allowed to run around without a nursemaid. As gently as he could, he spelled things out: "Mainardo has to surrender to the Unkerlanters, too, you know."

"Oh. Aye." The writer thought. "Do you suppose they'll send Marshal What's-his-name to the ceremony?"

"Marshal Rathar," Ilmarinen said, holding on to his patience with both hands. The news-sheet scribbler gave him a bright nod. The name meant hardly more to him than that of some half-forgotten Kaunian Emperor. Unkerlant might have been—much of Unkerlant *was*—on the other side of the world as far as most Kuusamans were concerned. "He does have business here," Ilmarinen pointed out.

"I suppose so." The writer sounded magnanimous in agreeing to that much. With further magnanimity, he said, "They did do some of the fighting, too."

"Some?" Ilmarinen choked on his wine. He had a notion of what Swemmel's kingdom had paid first to halt the Algarvians short of Cottbus and then to drive them back—a small notion, a foreigner's notion, a notion he was sure was ludicrously inadequate. Unkerlant had beaten the Algarvians, aye. How many years—how many generations— would she take to recover from her triumph? "Son, they did more of it than the Lagoans and us put together. Three times as much, easily."

The writer stared at him. "You're joking."

Ilmarinen's patience dropped and broke. "And you're an idiot," he snapped. "Do they really let you run loose without diapers? How do you keep from making messes on the floor?"

"Who do you think you are?" the news-sheet writer said indignantly.

"Someone who knows what he's talking about," Ilmarinen answered. "Obviously something you've never had to worry about." He finished his wine and stalked out.

As he'd predicted, Marshal Rathar's ley-line caravan came in the next morning. The caravan had had to pass through a few regions where the Algarvians were still supposed to be fighting. It wasn't scratched. That, to Ilmarinen, was a telling sign that the war, at least here in the east of Derlavai, had almost come to an end.

When Rathar descended from the caravan car, Ilmarinen contrived to be in the first rank of those waiting to greet him. He would, he thought, have used sorcery if he'd had to, but it hadn't proved necessary. His colonel's emblems, his mage's badge, and a few judicious elbows did the trick.

Rathar turned out to be younger than he'd expected. And, also to his surprise, the Marshal of Unkerlant paused and pointed to him. "You are the mage Ilmarinen, is it not so?" Rathar asked in Algarvian. Classical Kaunian wasn't widely taught in his kingdom, and he must have known Ilmarinen wouldn't speak his language.

"That's right," Ilmarinen answered in the same language as officers and dignitaries stared at him. "What can I do for you, sir?"

"What does Kuusamo do in the Bothnian Ocean?" Rathar asked.

"Fight the Gongs," Ilmarinen answered. "Fish. Things like that. What anyone else does in an ocean."

Rathar shook his head. He looked like a dissatisfied bear. "That is not what I meant. What magic does Kuusamo do in the Bothnian Ocean?"

"None that anyone's told me about," Ilmarinen said, which had the virtue of being technically true. He had some ideas about the sorts of things his colleagues back in the Naantali district of Kuusamo might be doing, but he couldn't prove them. He hadn't heard much from those colleagues since leaving to fight—which made sense, for if captured he couldn't tell what he didn't know.

"I do not believe you," the Unkerlanter marshal said. Ilmarinen shrugged. So did Rathar. His shoulders were twice as wide as Ilmarinen's. One of the junior officers accompanying him, a man with *bodyguard* written all over him, tapped Rathar on the shoulder. Rathar nodded impatiently. Flanked by his entourage, he walked on.

The surrender ceremony took place that afternoon in the hostel's dining room, the only chamber big enough to hold even a respectable fraction of all the people who wanted to be there. King Mainardo sat behind a table at one end of the room. A couple of Algarvian officers stood at his right and left hands, both of them looking extraordinarily glum. Grand General Nortamo of Kuusamo, Marshal Araujo of Lagoas, and Marshal Rathar of Unkerlant faced him. Their entourages crowded behind them. Ilmarinen stood among Nortamo's followers, and had to go up on tiptoe to see over some of them.

Along with the soldiers of the three kingdoms that had done the bulk of the work in beating Algarve were smaller contingents from Valmiera and Jelgava and Sibiu. And Rathar had a man in Forthwegian uniform in his party. Ilmarinen looked to see if he also had a Yaninan in tow. He didn't.

Nortamo spoke in Algarvian: "The Derlavaian War has gone on too long and cost too much. The allied kingdoms have prepared the instrument of surrender I hold for Algarve. Having caused so much torment for all surrounding kingdoms, having lost her own king in the fight, Algarve now acknowledges defeat and accepts responsibility for the consequences of her own dark deeds." He walked over to Mainardo and set the surrender document in front of him.

"May I speak before I sign this paper?" the new King of Algarve asked.

"Say what you will," Nortamo replied. "You must know, though, that it will not change the terms, which are no less than your complete and unconditional surrender."

"Oh, aye, I know that," Mainardo answered. Mezentio had been a fiery leader. His younger brother only seemed tired. With a nod, Mainardo said, "I cannot help but recognize that we are beaten. It is a truth. It is plain to all. But I say to you all that our courage, our sacrifice, our suffering, shall not be in vain. You may defeat us, but we shall rise again one day." He inked a pen, signed the surrender, and handed it back to the Kuusaman commander.

Nortamo also signed it. He gave it to Marshal Araujo. After the Lagoan leader affixed his signature, he ceremoniously carried it to the table at which Marshal Rathar was sitting.

"I thank you," Rathar said. "On behalf of my sovereign, I too have a word to say. Algarve did its best to murder Unkerlant. It is not sorry it fought this war. It is only sorry it lost." In that, Ilmarinen judged, he was absolutely right. Rathar continued, "We intend to make Algarve sorry for a long, long time."

He wrote his name, then called up the Forthwegian officer with him to add another signature. That done, he passed the document on to the minor kingdoms of the east—not that Valmiera would have reckoned itself such before the war began. At last, everyone had signed the surrender.

Nortamo spoke to the Algarvian officers: "You gentlemen will be so kind as to give up your swords. You are now war captives."

Looking daggers at him, the officers obeyed. King Mainardo said, "What of me?"

"For the moment, you are king of however much of Algarve we decide to let you rule," the Kuusaman commander replied. "You would be wise to hope you continue in this role, even if you reckon it less than exalted. King Donalitu has already submitted a request for your extradition to Jelgava."

Ilmarinen happened to know that Donalitu had demanded—loudly demanded—Mainardo's extradition to Jelgava. As far as Ilmarinen could tell, Donalitu had never in all his days done anything so demeaning as submitting a request.

Marshal Rathar said, "King Swemmel also has a claim on your person, you to represent King Mezentio and receive punishment for all Algarve did to Unkerlant."

Now there's an interesting choice, Ilmarinen thought. *If I had to go to either Donalitu or Swemmel, whom would I pick?* The Kuusaman mage shook his head. Choices like that made suicide look downright attractive.

Mainardo might have had more complaints or protests. If he did, hearing he was sought as a guest—in a manner of speaking—by both Jelgava and Unkerlant shut him up in a hurry. Marshal Araujo of Lagoas held up the instrument of surrender and said, "Let us all, on both sides, praise the powers above. The war in the east of Derlavai is over."

Ilmarinen would have praised the powers above more if they'd never let the Derlavaian War start in the first place. But no one had asked his opinion there, and he had to admit that a finished war was better than one still going on. *Well, a half-finished war, anyhow,* he thought, and looked east, in the direction of Gyongyos. Then he looked west. The Gongs were closer in that direction, even if it wasn't the one by which Kuusamo got at them.

Talsu was amazed at how readily he adjusted to a new round of life as a captive. Bad food and not enough of it, occasional beatings, interrogations that went nowhere—indeed, that seemed pointless—he'd been through them all before. He didn't enjoy any of them. But they didn't come as a shock this time, the way they had during his first stretch of time in a dungeon. The questions were somewhat different. The answers the interrogators—including his old unfriend, the major—wanted from him weren't the same, either. All the principles behind them remained identical.

He had just been out in the yard—the most precious hour of a captive's day, when he was reminded that fresh air and sunshine and birds and trees still existed—and was then, as usual, marched back to his cell. The gloom and the stink and the cold hard stone all around were doubly hard to bear after blue sky and bright sun and the scent of something growing. Talsu lay down on his pallet. Something was growing in the straw, too: mildew. As a tailor's son would, he knew the musty odor only too well. He also knew better than to complain. If he did, he would sleep on stone.

With a squeal of hinges, the door flew open. Alarm blazed through him. Whenever guards came in when they weren't supposed to, trouble was on the way. He'd learned that lesson when he'd been locked away at Algarvian orders. Having King Donalitu in charge hadn't changed things a bit.

"Come with us," one of the guards growled. Two others pointed sticks at Talsu, to make sure he wouldn't suddenly leap on them and pound them all into the ground. Being thought more dangerous than he really was had seemed flattering the first time it happened. Now it just struck him as absurd.

If he didn't get up, they would beat him and drag him. He knew that. As he rose, he couldn't help asking, "What is it this time?" Sometimes they gave him a hint about which way the questioning would go.

Sometimes—but not today. "Shut up," one of them told him. "Come along," a second added. "You *stinking* son of a whore," the third one said.

Had they let him bathe, he wouldn't have stunk. He didn't say anything of the sort. They seemed in an evil temper, even for guards in a dungeon. He hoped that didn't mean another beating was coming. The bruises from his last one were only just starting to go from purple to yellow.

They frogmarched him down the corridor, up a flight of

stairs, and into an interrogation chamber. There waiting for
him sat the major who'd been a captain when in Algarvian
service. The major was a professional. He did his job without mercy, but also without malice: Talsu had seen as
much. That made the look of fury on his face all the more
frightening.

"You *stinking* son of a whore," he said, and Talsu's testi-
cles tried to crawl up into his belly. Whatever was coming,
for whatever reason it was coming, would be very bad. He
didn't know why, but he did know that *why* often didn't matter. They had him. They could do as they pleased with him.

"Sir, do we really have to do this?" a guard asked, and all
hope within Talsu died. If it worried the guards, it would be
dreadful indeed.

"Aye, we do, powers below eat him," the major replied.
He yanked open a desk drawer and pulled out the clothes
Talsu had been wearing when he was arrested and the con-
tents of his pockets. Glaring at Talsu, he demanded, "Are
these goods yours? Is this everything you had in your possession when you were taken into the custody of King Donalitu's security personnel?"

"I . . . think so," Talsu answered. Now thoroughly confused, he dared ask, "What's going on?"

"I'll tell you what," the interrogator snarled. "You must
have kissed some Kuusaman's arse, because the miserable
slanteyes want you out of here. And so you're going out of
here—way out of here. Get into your clothes. You'll be
their problem from now on, and they're fornicating well
welcome to you."

Things were happening too fast for Talsu to follow. He
wondered if they were going to kill him and give his body
to the Kuusamans. Then he decided they wouldn't do
that—the major wouldn't have been so angry about dispos-
ing of his corpse.

He dressed in a hurry. The only Kuusamans with whom
he'd had much to do were the mage near Skrunda and the
soldiers he'd led past his home town. How could one of
them have heard he'd been tossed in a dungeon? How
would one of them have had the clout to get him out? He
had no idea. He didn't much care, either.

"Sign this." The major shoved a leaf of paper at him.

"What is it?" Talsu asked. As he picked up a pen, he looked at the paper. "A certificate of good treatment? Are you out of your mind? Why should I sign it? It's a bloody lie."

"Why should you sign it?" The major looked at him. "Because we won't turn you loose if you don't, that's why." He folded his arms across his chest and waited.

Talsu started to bend over the certificate, then stopped, weighing the odds. He wouldn't have been here if the Kuusamans hadn't leaned on King Donalitu's government, that was plain. But, since they had . . . Who owned the power here? Talsu straightened up and set down the pen. "Futter you," he said evenly.

Behind him, the guards growled. He tensed and started to shrink in on himself, fearing he'd misjudged and earned another beating. But the major of interrogators just gave him a sour stare. "We're well rid of you," he declared, "and the Kuusamans are welcome to you."

What did that mean? Before Talsu could even ask, the major gestured to the guards. They grabbed Talsu and hustled him out of the interrogation chamber. He went out through the exercise yard—blinking at the bright sun, as he always did when he first saw it—and out through the gate. He blinked again, this time at not having walls around him. Was this where . . . ?

It was. A ley-line caravan glided up. A couple of nondescript men, men who looked amazingly like the fellows who'd arrested him, got down from a caravan car. One of them jerked a thumb at Talsu. "This the bastard?" he asked.

"It's him, all right," a guard agreed. The fellows from the caravan car and the guards signed some papers. Then the guards gave Talsu a shove. He climbed up into the caravan car. So did his new keepers. The ley-line caravan slid off toward the southeast.

"Where are we going?" Talsu asked.

"Balvi," one of the men said. "Shut up," the other one added. He would have had no trouble working in a dungeon.

"Balvi!" Talsu exclaimed. He'd never been to the capital of Jelgava. Before his days in the army, he'd never been far from Skrunda. The mountains he'd seen and fought in then hadn't endeared him to the idea of travel. Neither had his couple of trips to King Donalitu's dungeons. "Why Balvi?"

"Shut up." This time, both keepers spoke together. In casual, conversational tones more frightening than fierce menace would have been, one of them went on, "You'd be amazed how much we can make you hurt without leaving a mark on you."

"That's true," the other one agreed. Talsu was willing to believe them. He sat quietly in the compartment—save for one brief trip to ease himself, during which both keepers went with him—till the ley-line caravan glided into the depot at Balvi late that afternoon. A carriage waited for them there. Talsu craned his neck for glimpses of the capital's famous buildings. Even the royal palace was worth seeing, no matter what he thought of King Donalitu.

Once inside the carriage, Talsu risked a question: "Where are we going?"

"Kuusaman ministry," answered one of the men with him.

"You're their worry now," the other one said, "and good riddance to you."

"What do you mean?" Talsu said. "You sound like you're throwing me out of the kingdom."

"That's just what we're doing," a keeper said. "If the slanteyes want you so bad, they're welcome to you, as far as Jelgava is concerned."

Talsu was still chewing on that when the carriage stopped in front of a larger, more impressive building than any Skrunda boasted. The Kuusaman banner, sky blue and sea green, flew in front of it and atop it. "Out," the other keeper said. Talsu got out. So did his shepherds.

A couple of Kuusamans took charge of them just inside the ministry. They spoke classical Kaunian—spoke it better than Talsu or his keepers, though it was the grandfather of Jelgavan but unrelated to the islanders' tongue. That left Talsu obscurely embarrassed. The keepers signed several leaves of paper. Talsu began to feel as if he were no more than a sack of lentils passed from one dealer to another.

With a last glower, King Donalitu's men left the ministry.

One of the Kuusamans told Talsu, "Come with me. I shall take you to Minister Tukiainen."

"I thank you," Talsu said in his halting classical Kaunian. "But may I not wash myself first?" *Middle voice,* he thought. He was increasingly conscious that he hadn't had the chance to bathe any time lately.

After putting their heads together and talking in their own language, the Kuusamans both nodded. "Let it be as you say," one of them replied. "But you would do well— please believe me when I say this—to bathe quickly."

A quick bath didn't get rid of all the grime clinging to Talsu, but did leave him smelling less like something just off the midden. The Kuusamans escorted him to Minister Tukiainen's office. He almost didn't notice the minister, though, for Gailisa was sitting in the office. They flew into each other's arms. "What are you doing here?" he asked her.

"It is her doing that you are both here." Minister Tukiainen spoke good Jelgavan. By speaking, he reminded Talsu of his existence. He went on, "She wrote a letter that brought your plight to the notice of the Seven Princes. We requested your release . . . and so, here you are."

"Thank you, sir." Reluctantly untangling himself from Gailisa, Talsu bowed. He asked, "Uh, sir, why am I *here*? Why didn't they just let me go back to Skrunda?"

"Because your government has decided you and your wife are both troublemakers," Tukiainen answered. "You are not welcome in Jelgava any more. King Donalitu has said that, since Kuusamo is interested in you, you should be Kuusamo's responsibility. And so"—he smiled—"we shall take care of that. As soon as may be, we shall send you to Yliharma and help you set up in business there. You are a tailor, your wife tells me. A skilled tailor should do well in Kuusamo."

Things were moving too fast for Talsu. That morning, he'd been in the dungeon, with no particular hope of ever getting out again. Now he was not only out of the dungeon but also, evidently, on his way out of his own kingdom. He tried to make himself sorry or angry or anything of the sort. He couldn't. All he felt was joy. "Thank you, sir," he said, and bowed again. "I feel like—like I'm escaping."

"And so you are," Master Tukiainen said. "To us, this whole kingdom is like a dungeon. In my opinion, you are well out of it."

"I'll have to learn Kuusaman," Talsu said. That, at the moment, was the least of his worries.

Thirteen

L eudast marveled that he could walk through the streets of Trapani without being ready to dive into a hole at any moment. The Algarvians' formal surrender in the city hadn't quite ended the fighting. Diehards and soldiers who hadn't got the word kept blazing at the Unkerlanters for several days more. Even King Mainardo's announcement of a general Algarvian surrender hadn't quite done the job. By now, though, all the redheads had either laid down their sticks or were lying down themselves—lying down and not about to get up again.

A skinny Algarvian woman came out of a battered house. "Sleeping with me?" she called in bad Unkerlanter, and twitched her hips in case Leudast hadn't been able to understand her.

He shook his head and walked on. He hadn't turned the corner before she called the same invitation to another Unkerlanter soldier. Leudast got propositioned a couple of times a day. Some of his countrymen said it proved all Algarvian women were whores. Leudast didn't know whether it proved they were whores or just that they were hungry.

Everybody—everybody Algarvian, anyhow—in Trapani was hungry these days. Leudast couldn't see that the Unkerlanter authorities were working very hard to keep the redheads fed. He lost no sleep over it. When Mezentio's men held big stretches of Unkerlant, they hadn't done much to keep the peasants and townsfolk there fed, either. *Let 'em get a taste of empty,* he thought. *Let 'em get more than a taste, by the powers above.*

He had to stop then. A column of captives came shambling by: glum, hollow-cheeked men in filthy, tattered Algarvian uniforms, the stubble on their faces almost but not
quite grown out into beards. Most of them were redheads,
but he spotted a knot of men who looked like Unkerlanters,
though they wore tan tunics and kilts like the Algarvians.
Their dark beards were thick and full.

"Who are those whoresons?" he called to a guard. "Traitors from the Duchy of Grelz?" He was a lieutenant nowadays because he'd captured the Algarvian calling himself
King of Grelz. Some of the men from the duchy in the
southeast of Unkerlant kept fighting against King Swemmel even after that.

But the guard shook his head. "No, sir," he answered.
"These bastards are Forthwegians: the outfit that called itself Plegmund's Brigade. And see? They've got a couple of
Valmieran swine with 'em. The Algarvians picked up
garbage all over the place." He laughed at his own wit.

"Plegmund's Brigade, eh?" Leudast nodded. "Aye, I ran
up against them a time or two." He hadn't cared for the experience; the Forthwegians had been tough and nasty.

One of them, a fellow who looked as if he'd been a robber before joining Plegmund's Brigade, must have understood him, for he spoke in his own language: "Too futtering
bad we didn't get you, too."

Having come from northeastern Unkerlant, not far from
the Forthwegian border, Leudast followed Forthwegian better than most of his countrymen would have. He also heard
another captive say, "Powers below eat you, shut up, Ceorl!
You want to make it worse than it is already?"

"Where are these men going?" Leudast asked the guard.

"Sir, I don't know for certain, but I think they're off for
the Mamming Hills," the fellow replied.

"Ah," Leudast said, and said no more. Ceorl's comrade
had been wasting his time worrying. If these captives were
bound for the Mamming Hills, it was already about as bad
as it could be. He didn't need to fret about making it worse.

More captives cleared debris from a broad square in
front of the royal palace. Leudast scowled at the burnt and
shattered wreckage of King Mezentio's residence. He'd

been in on some of the fighting there, and the Algarvians had battled room by room, corridor by corridor. And then, when his own side had finally cleared them out, they'd found Mezentio already dead. If that wasn't a cheat, what was? Capturing Mezentio's cousin Raniero had made Leudast an officer. What would capturing Mezentio himself have gained some lucky Unkerlanter? Colonel's rank? A duchy? Anything this side of the sky itself seemed possible.

But Mezentio, curse him, had taken the easy way out. What would King Swemmel have done to him, had he fallen alive into Unkerlanter hands? Mezentio hadn't wanted to find out. Leudast didn't think he would have wanted to find out, either, not in Mezentio's shoes. He remembered how bravely Raniero had gone into the boiling water—and how he'd shrieked afterwards, for as long as he still kept life in him. And Mezentio, without a doubt, would have ended up envying Raniero his easy fate.

Several Unkerlanters came out of the palace, along with one Algarvian who towered half a head over them. The group walked toward Leudast without even noticing he was there: all the Unkerlanters were officers of age and rank exalted enough to make a young lieutenant seem no more important than any other chunk of rubble littering the ground.

One of the officers—a brigadier—was speaking to the redhead: "You had better understand, you will keep the job as long as you do as his Majesty commands. Disobey, and all you will be is very, very sorry."

"I'm not likely to make a mistake about that, am I?" The Algarvian spoke fluent, almost unaccented Unkerlanter. His wave encompassed the whole of the capital, the whole of the kingdom. "Considering the example I have before me, I would have to be a madman to step out of line."

"This does not always stop Algarvians," the brigadier replied. "We have seen as much. I hope I am plain: if you are not pliable, you are dead . . . slowly."

"I told you once, I understand," replied the redheaded— noble? Leudast supposed he had to be.

"You had better, that's all," the brigadier said. He and the other officers swept past Leudast. *I won't stare after them,* Leudast thought. *They might notice me, and I don't want to be noticed now.*

What sort of job did they have in mind for the Algarvian? By the way they were talking, it might almost have been king. But, with Mainardo, Algarve already had a king. Of course, if Swemmel decided not to recognize Mezentio's brother and raised up a candidate of his own, who would, who could, stop him? He'd already done that in Forthweg. Why not here, too? The only drawback Leudast could see was that any redhead was likely to betray Unkerlant the instant he thought he could get away with it.

That wasn't his worry. If the candidate looked like giving trouble, he expected King Swemmel would spot it before it got bad enough to be dangerous. Swemmel looked for trouble the way fussy old women looked for weeds in their garden plots—and when he found it, he yanked it up by the roots.

Not far beyond the royal palace stood a building so solidly made, it had come through the fierce fighting in Trapani almost undamaged. Men were carrying sacks—sacks obviously heavy for their size—out the front door and loading them into wagons. What looked like a regiment's worth of guards surrounded the wagons.

"What's going on here?" Leudast asked one of the guards.

"Sir, this is the treasury of the Kingdom of Algarve," the man answered. His eyes were hard and alert, warning that Leudast would do well not to seem *too* interested.

Despite that warning look, Leudast couldn't help letting out a low whistle. "Oh," he said. "And it's about to become part of the treasury of the Kingdom of Unkerlant?"

"You might say something like that, sir," the guard replied.

"Good," Leudast said. "The fornicating redheads cost us plenty. Only fair they should pay us back. I just wish gold and silver could really pay for all the lives they robbed us of."

"Aye, sir." Something of the guard's humanity showed through the hard mask of his face. "I lost a brother last year, and my home village isn't far from Durrwangen, so powers above only know if any of my kin are left alive."

"I hope so," Leudast answered. It was all he could say; some of the biggest and most important battles of the war had been fought around the southern city of Durrwangen a couple of summers before. Leudast had been there, on the eastern side of the bulge the Algarvians were trying to pinch off. He still marveled that he'd come through in one piece.

"So do I." The guard's stick twitched, just a little. Leudast took the hint. Anyone who spent too long watching the plundering of the Algarvian treasury might be suspected of wanting some of the plunder for himself. As a matter of fact, Leudast did want some of the plunder for himself, but not enough to get blazed for it. He left in a hurry.

When he got back to his regiment's encampment in a park not too far from the palace, it was boiling like an anthill stirred by a stick. "What's going on?" he asked a soldier from his company.

"Orders, sir," the man replied.

That told Leudast less than he wanted to know. "What kind of orders?" he demanded, but the soldier had already hurried off. In a way, Leudast got the answer to his question: the orders were of the urgent kind.

"Oh, there you are, Leudast," Captain Dagaric said. "I've been looking for you."

"I'm here, sir," Leudast answered, saluting. "What in blazes is going on?"

"We're moving out of Trapani, that's what," the regimental commander told him. "Moving out by tonight, as a matter of fact."

"Powers above!" Leudast exclaimed. "Moving out where?" His first, automatic, glance was toward the east. "Are we going to start the war up again, and take on the Kuusamans and Lagoans?"

"No, no, no!" Dagaric shook his head. "We're not going east. We're going west. We're going a long way west, as a matter of fact. A long, long way west."

"About as far west as we can go?" Leudast asked.

Dagaric nodded. "That's right. We've got some unfinished business with the Gongs, you know. . . . What's so funny?"

"Nothing, sir, or not really funny, anyhow—but strange, all the same," Leudast said. "Back a million years ago, or that's what it seems like now—back before the big Derlavaian War started, anyway—I was fighting in the Elsung Mountains, in one of those little no-account skirmishes that don't matter at all unless you happen to get killed in them. I've been through all this, and now I'm going back."

He wondered how many other Unkerlanters who'd fought in the halfhearted border war against Gyongyos were left alive today. Not many—he was sure of that. Once more, he counted himself lucky only to have been wounded twice. *Well, now the cursed Gongs will get another chance,* he thought, and wished he hadn't.

More than his regiment was leaving Trapani: much more than his regiment. Once his men got to the ley-line caravan depot, they had a long wait before they filed onto the cars that would take them across most of the length of Derlavai. "Why did we have to hurry so much, if we're just standing around here?" somebody grumbled.

"That's the way the army works," Leudast said. "And believe me, standing around is a lot better than getting blazed at. Besides, it'll take us ten days, maybe more, to get where we're going. You might as well get used to doing nothing."

He remembered his last passage out to the borders of Gyongyos as far and away the longest, most boring journey he'd ever made, with nothing to do but watch endless miles of flat countryside slip past. But battle, once he got to the uttermost west, hadn't been boring, however much he wished it were. He didn't expect it would be this time, either. As he finally filed aboard the ley-line caravan car, he hoped against hope he would prove wrong.

Ceorl had known for a long time that he would get it in the neck. If he hadn't signed up for Plegmund's Brigade, a Forthwegian magistrate would have given it to him. The second time they caught you for robbery with violence, they didn't bother locking you up; they just got rid of you. The judge had been in what passed for a kindly mood for him: he'd been willing to let the Unkerlanters do the job instead of taking care of it himself with a signature.

And so Ceorl had gone to fight in the south. For a while—all the way up through the battles in the Durrwangen bulge—he'd hoped he'd managed to cheat the judge, because Algarve had still had a chance to win the war. After that . . . He shook his head. After that, it had been almost two years of hard, grinding retreat. He'd started out somewhere between Durrwangen and Sulingen, and ended up one of the last holdouts in the ruins of King Mezentio's palace in Trapani.

Even then, the Unkerlanters hadn't been able to kill him. Along with the other survivors from Plegmund's Brigade, the blonds from the Phalanx of Valmiera sprinkled in among them, and the Algarvians who'd been stubborn enough to stick it out to the very end, he'd come forth with his hands high, sure enough, but also with his head high.

He turned to Sudaku. Aye, Sudaku was a stinking Kaunian, but he'd fought as well as anybody else this past year. In Algarvian—Sudaku had picked up some Forthwegian, but not a lot—Ceorl said, "The one thing I didn't figure on was that Swemmel's whoresons'd go right on having chances to do us in even after we surrendered."

"Powers below eat me if I know why not," Sudaku replied. "Did you think they would pat us on the bottom and tell us to go home and to be good little boys from here on out? Not likely."

"Ah, futter you." Ceorl spoke altogether without malice. He cursed as automatically as he breathed, and thought no more of one than of the other. He was a brick of a man, stocky even by Forthwegian standards, with bushy eyebrows, a big hooked nose, and a smile that usually looked like a sneer.

"The Unkerlanters are going to futter us all," Sudaku said. "They can take their time about it now, but they're going to do it."

He was right, of course. Ceorl knew it. If *he'd* been on top of the world, he would have paid back everybody who'd ever done him dirt. He had a long list. But his list, he had to admit, paled beside the one King Swemmel must have been keeping all these years. What Swemmel's list amounted to was, *the whole Kingdom of Algarve and anybody who ever helped it in any way.* That was a list worth having, a list worth admiring.

And Swemmel was getting his money's worth from it, too. Once upon a time, this captives' camp outside of Trapani had been a barracks complex holding perhaps a brigade's worth of men. Six or eight times that many soldiers—or rather, ex-soldiers—were crammed into it now. They got just enough food to keep them from starving in a hurry. It was as if the Unkerlanters wanted to savor their suffering.

"Pretty soon," Sudaku said, "a plague will start, and they will need to bring in a ley-line caravan to carry out the corpses by carloads."

"You're a cheery bastard, aren't you?" Ceorl answered. "I almost hope a plague *does* start. The stinking Unkerlanters'd catch it, too, and it'd fornicating well serve 'em right."

With a shrug, the man from the Phalanx of Valmiera said, "You should want to live. If you get out of this place, if you go back to your own kingdom, you can hope to do what you did before the war. I am not so lucky. For a Valmieran who has fought for Algarve, there is nothing left."

"Oh, my arse," Ceorl said. "You ever get back to your own kingdom, pick a new name and pick a new town and start telling lies like a fornicating madman. Tell 'em about how the redheads, powers below eat 'em, did you all kinds of dirt. Your people would buy it. Most people are nothing but a pack of fornicating fools."

Sudaku laughed out loud. "Maybe you are right. It might be worth a try. What a reason to live: to spend the rest of my life telling lies."

Ceorl poked him in the chest with a forefinger. "Listen, pal, after *this* war, folks'll be telling lies for the next fifty years. Anybody who ever had anything to do with the redheads is going to say, 'No, no, not me. I tried to kick those bastards right in the nuts.' And all the Algarvians who were the meanest whoresons, they'll go, 'No, I didn't have any idea what was going on. That was those other fornicators, and they're already dead.' You think I'm kidding? Just wait and see."

"No, I do not think you are kidding," the blond said. "It will happen. Maybe I could do that . . . if I ever got back to Valmiera. But I do not think I am going to."

He was likely right for himself, but Ceorl had some hope of escaping. But for his beard, he looked like an Unkerlanter, and he could make a stab at the language of King Swemmel's soldiers. If he could murder a guard and get into the fellow's uniform tunic, he might sneak out of the captives' camp. And if he could do that, anything might happen.

He was still contemplating ways and means two days later, when the Unkerlanters emptied out the captives' camp by marching half the men in it—including the survivors of Plegmund's Brigade—out of the place and through the streets of Trapani.

"Who are those whoresons?" an Unkerlanter lieutenant asked a guard as the captives trudged along. "Traitors from the Duchy of Grelz?"

"No, sir," the guard answered. "These bastards are Forthwegians: the outfit that called itself Plegmund's Brigade. And see? They've got a couple of Valmieran swine with 'em. The Algarvians picked up garbage all over the place." Ceorl followed his words well enough.

"Plegmund's Brigade, eh?" The officer nodded. "Aye, I ran up against them a time or two."

"Too futtering bad we didn't get you, too," Ceorl muttered.

"Powers below eat you, shut up, Ceorl!" another Forthwegian captive said as they went on their way. "You want to make it worse than it is already?"

"How?" Ceorl asked as they shambled on. The other fellow had no answer for him.

They stopped by the ruins of the central ley-line caravan depot. The queue of captives snaked toward the platforms. Ceorl thought of a way in which things might be worse, and spoke to the other men from Plegmund's Brigade in Forthwegian: "We better stick together, whatever happens. Otherwise, the fornicating redheads're liable to come down on us hard, on account of we're odd men out." His eyes flicked toward Sudaku. "You catch that?" he asked the blond from the Phalanx of Valmiera, also in his own language.

"Bet your arse I did," the Kaunian replied in the same tongue. He'd been with the men of Plegmund's Brigade long enough to have learned to curse in Forthwegian, and had picked up other bits and pieces as well. Ceorl slapped him on the back. The ruffian despised blonds on general principles, but didn't dislike the handful beside whom he'd fought.

To his surprise, the caravan car to which the Unkerlanter guards steered his lot of captives was one made for carrying passengers. He'd expected to go aboard one that had borne freight, or perhaps animals. To be able to sit down in an actual compartment and watch the landscape go by . . . That didn't sound so bad.

It also wasn't what happened. A compartment was made to hold four people. The Unkerlanters shoehorned a couple of dozen into that space. "You fit!" one of them shouted in bad Algarvian. "You make selfs fit! You no do, we do."

Men squeezed onto the seats, onto the floor, and up onto the baggage racks above the barred windows. Ceorl saw at once that those racks offered more room to stretch out than anywhere else in the compartment. He swarmed up onto one. An Algarvian had the same idea at almost the same time. Ceorl's elbow got him in the pit of the stomach. He dropped back into the seething crowd below.

Ceorl hauled Sudaku out of the crowd and up onto the rack with him. "Thanks," the blond said in Algarvian. "Why did you do that?"

Before Ceorl could answer, the redhead he'd elbowed and a pal rose again like a couple of spouting leviathans and tried to haul him down. Ceorl's boot got one of them in the face. "Oh no you don't, you son of a whore!" he said. Meanwhile, Sudaku had driven off the other Algarvian. "*That's* why," Ceorl said. "Everybody's got to have somebody to watch his back for him."

"Ah." The Kaunian nodded. "I see it. We are like too many wolves in too small a cage."

"I don't know anything about wolves," Ceorl said. "All I know about is gaols, but I know them good. Either you eat meat or you *are* meat. Powers below eat all those other bastards. Nobody's going to eat me."

He leaned down from the baggage rack to kick an Algarvian who was wrestling with a man from Plegmund's Brigade for a space on one of the seats. The Algarvian crumpled. The Forthwegian shoved him aside and waved to Ceorl. Ceorl grinned back. He'd had plenty of practice at this kind of dirty fighting. It was different from soldiering. Here, everyone except a few chums was an enemy. *Have to remind the chums who they are,* he thought.

By the time things in the compartment sorted themselves out, he had a good line on who was strong and who was weak. The weak, the friendless, and the stupid were jammed into the space on the floor between the seats. Some of them were nothing more than footrests for the stronger captives.

Yells from the compartment down the corridor said the Unkerlanters were filling it the same way. Once the car was full, a door slammed. The ley-line caravan still didn't move. Plenty of other cars remained to be filled.

Up in his aerie, Ceorl was comfortable enough. He didn't want to think about what the poor whoresons folded in on themselves down below were going through. He didn't want to, and so he didn't. They hadn't had the brains or the ballocks to take care of themselves. Nobody else would do it for them.

After what seemed like forever, the ley-line caravan glided out of the depot. From where he was, Ceorl couldn't see a great deal, but he did know they were heading west. He shrugged. He'd already got the upper hand on things, and expected he'd be able to keep it no matter where he ended up.

Rations were hard bread and salted fish that set up a raging thirst in whoever ate them. He got a good-sized chunk of bread and one of the biggest fish. He also got first pull at the cup from the water bucket the Unkerlanters grudgingly allowed their captives.

When he and his comrades were herded into the compartment, he hadn't expected to stay there for three days. One man died on the trip. No one noticed till he wouldn't take his piece of bread. Even after the captives shoved his corpse out into the corridor, the compartment seemed just as crowded as it had before.

On the morning of the third day, the ley-line caravan finally stopped. "Out!" the guards shouted in Unkerlanter and Algarvian. "Out!"

A lot of the captives had trouble moving. Not Ceorl, whose fettle was about as fine as it could be. He sprang down from the caravan car and looked around. Not far away stood ramshackle wooden barracks. Low, rolling hills dotted the countryside. The air smelled of wood smoke and something else, something with a harsh, mineral tang to it.

"Where in blazes are we?" he said.

"These are the Mamming Hills." A guard pointed to a black hole. "Cinnabar mine. We'll work you till you die, you whoreson." He threw back his head and laughed. "It won't take long."

Count Sabrino lay on his cot. He'd been on his feet—no, on his foot—a few times by now, but moving around while upright still left him not only exhausted but in more pain than he'd known when dragonfire set his leg alight. The healers talked about fitting him with a jointed artificial leg one day, but he didn't take that seriously—not yet. The only thing he took seriously these days was the decoction of poppy juice that pushed aside the worst of the pain.

He knew he'd started craving the drug for its own sake as well as for the relief it brought. *One of these days, I'll worry about that, too,* he thought. *If the pain ever goes away, I expect I'll find a way to wean myself from the decoction.*

What he hadn't expected was that the missing leg still hurt, even though it wasn't there any more. The healers told him such things were normal, that most people who lost limbs kept a sort of phantom memory and perception of what they'd once had. He didn't argue with them: he was hardly in a position to do so. But that phantom presence struck him as the strangest thing about being mutilated.

Or so it did till the afternoon when a healer came up to him and said, "You have a visitor, Count Sabrino."

"A visitor?" Sabrino said in surprise. No one had come to see him since he was injured. He could think of only a couple of people who might. "Is it Captain Orosio? Or my wife, perhaps?" He didn't know if either of them was alive. *If they aren't, they won't come,* he thought, and laughed under his breath.

"Uh, no, your Excellency," the healer replied. "No and no, respectively." The fellow coughed a couple of times, as if to say Sabrino was very wrong indeed.

"Well, who in blazes is it, then?" the colonel of dragonfliers demanded. As he got more used to the decoction of poppy juice, more of his own temper pierced the haze it gave his wits.

Instead of answering straight out, the healer said, "I'll bring in the gentleman. Excuse me, your Excellency." He hurried away. When he came back, he had with him a white-haired Unkerlanter officer with a chestful of medals. "Your Excellency, I have the honor to present to you General Vatran. General, Count Sabrino."

"You speak Unkerlanter?" Vatran asked in Algarvian.

Sabrino shook his head. "Sorry, but no." He started at the Unkerlanter. "What are you doing here? You're Marshal Rathar's right-hand man."

"That is why I am here," Vatran went on in Algarvian. He wasn't fluent, but he could make himself understood. Catching the healer's eye, he jerked a thumb at the door. "You. Get lost." That got through, sure enough. The healer fled.

"What . . . do you want with me?" Sabrino asked. He still had trouble believing he wasn't imagining this.

Vatran walked over and shut the door the healer had just used. That bit of melodrama done, he came back to Sabrino's bedside and said, "How you like to be King of Algarve?"

"I'm sorry." Sabrino burst out laughing. "You know I'm hurt. You know I'm taking a pretty strong decoction for the pain." Vatran nodded curtly. Sabrino went on, "It does some strange things sometimes. I thought you just asked me if I wanted to be King of Algarve."

"I do say that," General Vatran replied. "You want to be King of Algarve, you be King of Algarve. So say King Swemmel."

"But Algarve already has a king," Sabrino said. "King Mainardo." He'd almost said *Mezentio,* but remembered hearing Mezentio was dead.

In his own guttural language, Vatran said something pungent about Mainardo. Sabrino followed part of it. He didn't speak Unkerlanter, not really, but years in the west had taught him something about swearing in that language. Vatran was plainly a master of the art. In Algarvian, the general continued, "Powers below eat Mainardo. He is trouble. King Swemmel want a man he can trust for king. We ask one redhead already, but he play games with us. No games here." He drew a thumb across his throat to show exactly what he meant.

He meant the invitation. Sabrino wasn't so drugged that he didn't understand that. Slowly, with as much caution as the poppy juice left in him, he asked, "Why does King Swemmel think I am the right man for this job?"

"You are Algarvian. You are noble." General Vatran ticked off points on his fingertips, as if he were trying to sell Sabrino a jug of olive oil. "You are brave fighter, so men respect you. And we know you quarrel with King Mezentio."

"Ah," Sabrino said. Now things grew clearer. "And so you think I would make a proper traitor?" With the drug in him, he couldn't be very cautious.

Vatran shook his head. "Not a traitor. How can Algarve hurt us now, no matter who is king? Other bastard, he not see that." He made the throat-cutting gesture again.

And he had a point, or a sort of a point. Sabrino wagged a forefinger at him. "If you didn't care who was king, why would you mind having Mainardo keep the crown?"

"Mainardo is Mezentio's brother." Vatran went back to counting on his fingers. "And he is puppet of Lagoas and Kuusamo. This not good, not for Unkerlant."

He had a certain brutal honesty to him, even when he played the game of intrigue. Algarvians were suaver, smoother. . . . *And much good that did us,* Sabrino thought. "You would want me to be a puppet of Unkerlant's, eh?"

"Why, of course," General Vatran answered. "I tell you about this other bastard—he stupid. You think we let your kingdom get big and strong so you kick us in the balls again, you crazy."

Brutal honesty, indeed, went through Sabrino's mind. He shook his head. "To my way of thinking, I would have to be a traitor to do the job as you want it done."

The Unkerlanter shook his head again. "No, no, no. You can ward your subjects, can shield them. This much, I think King Swemmel let you have."

Can shield them from Unkerlanter soldiers, was what he had to mean. Even so, Sabrino said, "I thank you, sir—and I mean that, for you offer me an honor I never dreamt would come my way. Even so, I must decline."

"Why?" When General Vatran frowned, his bushy white eyebrows came down and together, so that they formed a bar over his eyes. "His Majesty not be happy. You are right man for job. Algarvian. Noble. You don't like Mezentio."

"I think you misunderstand something," Sabrino said. "Shall I be very plain?" With the decoction of poppy juice in him, he could hardly be anything else.

"Say on," Vatran rumbled ominously.

"You know I disagreed with King Mezentio," Sabrino said, and the Unkerlanter officer's big, heavy-featured head went up and down. "And because of that, you think I would be able to work well with your king."

General Vatran nodded once more. "Aye. It is so."

But Sabrino shook his head. "No. It is not so. And, sir, I will tell you why it is not so." He wagged that forefinger at Vatran again. "It is not so because I wanted my kingdom to beat yours every bit as much as King Mezentio did. Believe me: I wanted to march through Cottbus in triumph every bit as much as Mezentio did." He glanced down at the asymmetrical shape under the sheet on the cot. "But we didn't march through Cottbus, and I won't be doing any marching now."

"Why you quarrel with your king, then?" Vatran demanded. His voice held a certain amount of respectful wonder. Sabrino thought he understood that. From everything he'd heard, quarreling with Swemmel was something an Unkerlanter did at most once.

"Why? Purely over means, not over the end," Sabrino said. By Vatran's new frown, he saw the Unkerlanter didn't follow that. He spelled it out: "I didn't think killing Kaunians was a good idea. I never thought it was a good idea. I thought it would make all our enemies hate us and fear us and fight us harder than ever."

"You right," Vatran said.

And much good that did me, Sabrino thought. *I never imagined you Unkerlanters would slaughter your own to strike back at us. None of the eastern kingdoms would have done such a thing. You knew this fight was to the death, too.* Aloud, he said, "I suppose I was. I thought we would have beaten you without doing any such thing. Maybe I was right about that, and maybe I was wrong. But that was my quarrel with my king, the long and the short of it." *Mezentio didn't dispose of me for arguing with him, the way Swemmel would have. But he never forgave me, either.*

Vatran grunted. "This why you a colonel when war starts and you still a colonel when war stops? I wonder some on that. Make more sense now."

"Aye, that's why," Sabrino agreed. "And so, you see, you cannot rely on me to make a puppet King of Algarve, either. I am no man's puppet, not even my own sovereign's."

"You brave to say this," Vatran observed. "You maybe stupid to say this, too. You likely stupid to say this."

"Why? Will Swemmel blaze me for it?" Sabrino asked.

"Don't know," Vatran replied. "Wouldn't be surprised."

Sabrino shrugged. "Well, if he does, he does. I've been through too much to worry about it. Let him do what he will do."

"This is your last word?" Vatran asked. Sabrino nodded. The Unkerlanter general sighed. "All right. I take it away with me. You are brave man. You are also fool." There, for the first time, he almost tempted Sabrino to change his mind. If being a fool qualified a man for the kingship, he reckoned himself the best qualified sovereign Algarve had ever had.

After General Vatran left, the healer came back into Sabrino's chamber. Curious—nosy—as any Algarvian, he asked, "What did the barbarian want?"

"He wanted to proclaim me King of Algarve," Sabrino answered.

He waited to see what the healer would make of that. For a moment, the fellow just gaped, not sure how to take it. Then he started to laugh. "Well, I asked for that, didn't I?" he said. "All right, your Majesty, I'll be careful around you from now on."

"I'm not anyone's Majesty," Sabrino said. "I turned him down."

That only made the healer laugh harder. "I can see why you would have. A chap like you, you have to hold out for a *really* good position, eh?"

No wonder Mezentio got so testy, Sabrino thought. *He ruled a whole kingdom full of people like this. I suppose I was just another little nuisance to him.* Till Vatran's offer, he'd never tried to imagine what the world looked like from the perspective of a king. *Powers above! Why would any-body want the job?*

Still laughing, the healer said, "Why didn't you ask him if you could be King of Unkerlant instead? There's a place that could really use a civilized man running things."

"I don't want to be King of Unkerlant." Sabrino wondered if an Unkerlanter mage was somehow listening to every word he said. Given some of the things he'd heard about King Swemmel, he wouldn't have been surprised. He didn't want that mage hearing anything untoward. "I don't want to be king at all, not any place."

"Well, all right." The healer plucked at his mustachios, which he'd managed to keep perfectly waxed throughout Algarve's collapse, conquest, and occupation. "If it were me, though, I'd grab anything I could get." He plucked some more. "Maybe we ought to switch you to a decoction that's not quite so potent."

He thinks I imagined the whole thing, Sabrino realized.

"I suppose you're going to tell me I made up the Unker-lanter general, too," he said.

With a shrug, the healer answered, "Who knows what's real these days?" Sabrino laughed, but it wasn't as if the fellow didn't have a point.

"Another letter!" Vanai said to Saxburh as she fished it out of the brass letterbox in the lobby of her block of flats. The envelope bore no return address, and was addressed to her as Thelberge. Her heart leaped when she recognized the script. "And it's from your father!"

"Mama," Saxburh said. She didn't say *dada* so much these days. Had Ealstan been here, had she had someone to say it to, that would have been different. Vanai was sure of it.

She picked up her daughter and the jug of olive oil she'd bought. "Come on. Let's go upstairs, and we'll find out what he says." She longed for the days when Saxburh would be able to walk up those stairs by herself; the baby wasn't a lightweight any more. She wasn't so much of a baby any more, either. She'd started taking her first few toddling steps without holding on to anything, and her first birthday was only a few days away.

Of course, she didn't care anything about the letter. "Hat!" she said, as soon as she got back to the flat. She found her special little hat and jammed it down onto her head. "Hat!"

"That's a hat," Vanai agreed. She almost tore Ealstan's letter in her eagerness to get it out of the envelope. *Hello, sweetheart!* Ealstan wrote. *That you're seeing this proves I'm not an Unkerlanter soldier any more. They kept me long enough to use me up, then decided they didn't want me with a hole in my leg.*

I would like you and Saxburh to come back here to Gromheort to live. I wouldn't have said that before everything that happened. Eoforwic used to be the easiest place in the kingdom for your people and for mixed couples to get along. Now . . . Now I don't know how easy it will be anywhere. I wish I didn't have to say something like that, but I'm afraid it's true.

Vanai feared it was true, too. As he usually did, Ealstan made hard, solid sense. That was one of the things that had interested her in him from the beginning. Now that she'd seen a letter from his father, she had a better notion of how he came by it.

I don't know how your money is holding out, he wrote: a bookkeeper's son and a bookkeeper himself, he thought of such things. *If you need more, let me know. If you don't, buy passage on the first ley-line caravan car you can and come east. Don't wait to write us which caravan you'll be on. You know where we live. Take a cab from the depot. This old town went through a lot in the siege, but the rubble is out of the streets and you can get from there to here.*

All my kin here can't wait to meet you and see you and find out what you look like—both ways—and to see our little girl. Conberge is going to have a baby, too, so Saxburh will have a cousin to grow up with. And I miss you more than I can tell you, and I can't wait to hug you and kiss you and do whatever else I can talk you into. With all the love there is—your husband, Ealstan.

Pack up everything she could carry? Wait not a minute? Vanai started to shake her head, then paused. She'd done that before, when she came here to Eoforwic with Ealstan. How glad she'd been to get out of Oyngestun, too! And how likely it was that getting out of Oyngestun had saved her life.

No Algarvians lurked these days, waiting to throw her into a special camp. But she'd spent too much of her time here in Eoforwic in hiding. She had no friends here, and she didn't really want to make any. She'd been through too much. Things might be better in Gromheort. They could hardly be worse.

Ealstan was right. Before the Derlavaian War, the capital had been the best place in Forthweg for Kaunians, mixed couples, and half-breeds. Nowadays, Vanai doubted any place in the kingdom would be very good.

I can go on looking like Thelberge when I show my face outside the house, she thought. *Inside? Inside, I don't think it will matter. Now that I've seen Hestan's letter, I really don't think it will.* She glanced over to Saxburh, who was standing by herself in the middle of the floor and looking enormously proud. *And you* will *learn Kaunian, too, along with Forthwegian.*

"Come here," Vanai called. "Come here—you can do it." Saxburh toddled about halfway to her, then fell down and crawled the rest of the way. "Good girl," Vanai said, scooping her up. "How would you like to go to Gromheort and meet your grandfather and grandmother?"

Saxburh didn't say no. *No* wasn't a word she'd discovered yet. From things Vanai had heard, that would change when her daughter turned two or so. Vanai checked her dwindling store of silver. She didn't know what caravan fares were like these days, but, unless they'd gone altogether mad—which most prices hadn't—she still had plenty to get to Gromheort.

She took the money. She packed a couple of tunics for herself and clothes and cloths for the baby. She made sure she had a length of golden yarn and one of black so she could renew their sorcerous disguises. And she packed some food for herself and her daughter, though she was glad Saxburh was still nursing. That made travel much more convenient.

The silver went into her handbag. Everything else filled a duffel bag. She put Saxburh back into the harness that let her carry the baby without using her hands, then went downstairs. When the first of the month came, the landlord would come knocking on the door for the rent, and he'd get a surprise. Till then, who would know—who would care?—whether she was there or not?

She headed for the street corner to get a cab to the caravan depot. She knew she might be there for a while, and hoped Saxburh wouldn't decide to fuss.

"Hello, Thelberge," someone said, pausing on the corner along with her. "You look like you're going somewhere."

"Oh . . . Hello, Guthfrith," Vanai said. The drummer and singer was about the last person she wanted to see. As she was, he was wearing a purely Forthwegian sorcerous disguise. That made her ask, "Or should I call you Ethelhelm?" She wanted him to remember she knew who and what he was.

He grimaced. "Ethelhelm's dead. He's never coming back to life. Too many people, uh, don't understand what happened during the war."

Don't understand how you got too friendly with the redheads, you mean, Vanai thought. Ethelhelm had started out as a bold foe of the Algarvians. But his Kaunian blood let them put pressure on him that they couldn't use against an ordinary Forthwegian. And he'd buckled under it, cozying up to them to help keep the comforts he'd earned as a leading musician in Forthweg.

He went on, "I don't suppose I'm the only one these days who's going by more than one name."

"I don't know what you're talking about," Vanai answered, though she did perfectly well.

"Oh, I doubt that," he said—in classical Kaunian.

Vanai made herself shrug. "Sorry—I never learned that language. What did you say?" She didn't want to give him any kind of hold on her. Spinello had taught her what men did with such things. She didn't know what Ethelhelm wanted from her, and she didn't care to find out. She looked down the street for a cab, but didn't see one. Where were they when you needed them?

"Hat!" Saxburh said—in Forthwegian. Vanai hadn't taught her any Kaunian yet, for fear she would blurt it out at the wrong time. This, Vanai thought, would have been exactly the wrong time.

Ethelhelm took no notice of what the baby said, though. He just nodded to Vanai and said, "Why are *you* worrying? It's not illegal to be Kaunian any more."

"If you don't leave me alone, I'm going to shout for a constable," Vanai said. "I don't want anything to do with you."

"You wouldn't have shouted for a constable when they had red hair," Ethelhelm said. "I know what you are."

"You don't know anything at all," Vanai told him. "And I know what you are, too: somebody who sucked up to the Algarvians when it looked like a good idea. Now you can't even wear your own face, because too many people know what you did."

The face Ethelhelm was wearing turned red. "You stinking Kaunian bitch!" he exclaimed. "I ought to—"

"You ought to dry up and blow away." Vanai saw a cab and waved frantically. She let out a sigh of relief when the hackman waved back and steered his carriage through the traffic toward her. Eyeing Ethelhelm, she added, "And if you try bothering me any more, I'll put a curse on you the likes of which nobody's seen since the days of the Kaunian Empire. If you don't think I can, you're wrong." She set down the duffel bag, slung her handbag to the crook of her elbow, and pointed at him with both index fingers at once.

That was a bluff, nothing else but. So was her threat. Even the most ordinary modern mage could counter any ancient curse. She'd studied the subject; she knew as much. Forthwegians who hadn't studied it reckoned the Kaunians of imperial days very wise and very dangerous. Here, despite his mixed blood, Ethelhelm counted as a Forthwegian.

He went from red to pale in a heartbeat. His own fingers twisted in a sign to turn aside sorcery—not an effective sign, if the knowledge Vanai's grandfather had drilled into her was true. "Powers below eat you," he said. His right hand folded into a fist.

I'll kick him right in the crotch, Vanai thought. *That's where it'll do the most good.* A wagon in front of the cab had stopped for no apparent reason. She glared at it. *Get out of the way, you miserable whoreson!*

Ethelhelm drew back his fist. Before he could swing, someone with a loud voice said, "You don't want to do that, pal."

"Thank you, Constable!" Vanai said fervently. "This man's been bothering me, and he won't go away."

"Oh, I think he will." The constable spun his truncheon on its leather loop. "Either that or he'll get his face mashed. We don't put up with hitting people on the streets." He stepped toward Ethelhelm. "Which way's it gonna be, buddy?"

"I'm leaving," Ethelhelm said, and he did.

"Thank you!" Vanai said again. She'd never been so grateful to any Forthwegian except Ealstan in her life.

"Part of the job, lady," the constable said. "Is that cab stopping for you?"

"Aye, it is," she answered, and turned toward the driver. "The central ley-line caravan depot, please."

"Sure thing." He climbed down to hold the door open for her. "Climb on in—careful of your baby. Here, let me have that bag."

He closed the door behind her. The constable walked off. *Would he have helped me like that if he'd known I'm a Kaunian?* Vanai wondered as the cab started to move. She shrugged. No way to know, though she had her doubts. One thing she could do now, in the near-privacy of the cab: renew the spells that kept her and Saxburh looking like Forthwegians. With luck and a decent caravan schedule, she wouldn't have to do it again till they got to Gromheort.

"Supper soon," Elfryth told Ealstan, as if he couldn't have figured it out himself from the savory smell of chicken stewing with onions and mushrooms. His mother smiled at him. "It feels good, having one of our babies back in the house with us for a while."

"Babies?" Ealstan said. "Just because I'm toddling around . . ." He could walk, but was glad to have a cane in each hand to help bear his weight. Then he smiled, too. "I wonder if my daughter's toddling yet."

"She's what? About a year old?" Elfryth asked. Ealstan nodded. His mother sighed. "I wish I could see her. I hope Vanai paid attention to your letter."

"You're not the only one." Ealstan's tone of voice made his mother laugh. His ears got hot. "I mean . . ."

"I know what you meant," Elfryth said. "If anything goes to show you're not a baby any more, that does. That and your beard."

"I was already wearing a beard when I, uh, left," Ealstan said. *Ran away because I was afraid I'd killed Sidroc,* was what he'd meant there. He grimaced. *I wish I had killed him. Then he wouldn't have killed Leofsig, and Leofsig was worth a hundred of him. A thousand.*

Thoughts like those were probably going through his mother's mind, too. She'd been there when he and Sidroc fought. She'd been there when Sidroc smashed Leofsig with a dining-room chair, too. *She's been through a lot,* Ealstan realized—not the sort of idea he was used to having about his mother.

She said, "It's a lot thicker now, though. It was a boy's beard then. It isn't any more." She hesitated, then added, "It reminds me a lot of your brother's, there just before—" She broke off. She'd been thinking of Leofsig, too, then.

Ealstan limped over to her and leaned one of his canes against his hip so he could set a hand on her shoulder. He'd gone off to Eoforwic and Conberge had got married, but his older brother would never come to the house again. Elfryth smiled up at him, but unshed tears made her eyes brighter than they should have been.

Someone knocked at the door. "Who's that?" Ealstan and his mother said together. She went on, "I'll find out. I can move faster than you can these days. Stir the chicken, if you please."

"All right," he said to Elfryth's back. She was hurrying toward the entry hall. Ealstan plied the big iron spoon.

"Aye?" his mother said at the door, in the polite but distant tone she used for commercial travelers and other strangers.

"Is . . . is this the house of Hestan the bookkeeper?"

Chicken utterly forgotten, Ealstan hobbled toward the entry hall at the best speed he could manage. He was halfway there before he realized he was still holding the stirring spoon, not his other cane. That had fallen over. He hadn't noticed.

"Aye, it is," his mother said doubtfully as he rounded the corner. "And you are—?"

"Vanai!" Ealstan said.

"Ealstan!"

Somehow, his mother got out of the way as they rushed to embrace each other. Ealstan couldn't squeeze her so tight as he wanted; she had Saxburh in a harness in front of her. For a glorious forever that couldn't have lasted more than a minute and a half in the real world, Ealstan forgot everything but his wife. Then the baby started to cry and his mother said, "Well, I don't suppose I need an introduction now."

"Oh!" Ealstan didn't want to let go of Vanai; the arm whose hand still held that serving spoon stayed around her shoulder. But he made himself turn back to Elfryth. "Mother, the quiet one is Vanai, and the noisy one is Saxburh. Sweetheart, this is my mother, Elfryth."

Before Vanai could say anything, Elfryth did: "Powers above, Ealstan, don't leave her standing out in the street like a peddler." She darted forward and took the duffel bag Vanai was carrying away from her. "Come in, my dear, come in. My husband and my son told you you were welcome here, and they both have a habit of meaning what they say. Do come in."

"Thank you." Vanai took Saxburh out of the harness and set her on the ground. The baby stood easily. She hadn't been able to do that when the Unkerlanters hauled Ealstan into the army. "She wants to run around," Vanai said. "She didn't have much of a chance while we were on the caravan car or in the cab." And, sure enough, Saxburh's wails stopped. She looked up· at Ealstan with big, dark eyes shaped like his own.

"She's beautiful," Elfryth said.

That made Vanai smile, but only for a moment. "This isn't her true seeming, you know—or mine, either, for that matter." She sounded a little—more than a little—anxious about reminding Elfryth she was a Kaunian.

But Ealstan's mother only shrugged. "Aye, I know you don't really look like my daughter—"

"Ha!" Ealstan broke in, and pointed at Vanai. "I told you so." She stuck out her tongue at him. They both laughed.

Gamely, Elfryth went on, "But I'm sure you're beautiful in your own way, too, and so is your daughter." She crouched down. "Hello, little one!"

Saxburh stared at her, and then at Ealstan. Pointing to him, Vanai said, "That's your dada. We've got your dada back."

"Dada?" Saxburh didn't sound as if she believed it. She turned to Vanai and spoke imperiously: "Hat!" Vanai reached into her handbag and took out a little hat Ealstan had never seen before. She set it on Saxburh's head.

Saxburh jammed it down till it almost covered her eyes. "Hat!" she squealed.

"You're still standing in the street," Elfryth told Vanai. "Please come in. You must be tired. I'll get you some wine and cheese and olives, and supper will be ready pretty soon." She noticed Ealstan was still holding the serving spoon, took it away from him, and went back into the house.

"Come on," Ealstan said.

"All right." Vanai looked anxiously at him. "How are you?"

"I'm getting better," he answered. "It still hurts, and I still have some trouble getting around—I left my other cane back in the kitchen when I heard you out here—but I'm getting better. And I'm a *lot* better, seeing you here."

"I like your mother." Vanai sounded relieved. She also did sound tired. "Come on, sweetie—we're going in there," she told Saxburh. Holding her hand, the baby walked into the entry hall.

"She couldn't do that when the Unkerlanters grabbed me," Ealstan said.

"She does all kinds of things she couldn't do then," Vanai answered as he closed and barred the door behind them. "A few months don't matter much to us, but they're a big part of Saxburh's life."

Ealstan reached out and lightly patted her on the backside. "Who says a few months don't matter?" he said. She smiled back over her shoulder at him.

"Come in here," Elfryth called from the kitchen. "I've poured the wine—and your cane is by the doorway there, Ealstan."

"Thanks, Mother," he said. "I don't know if I ought to drink any wine. I'm so happy, I feel drunk already."

"*I'm* going to," Vanai declared. "After I've come halfway across the kingdom with a baby in tow, I've *earned* some wine, by the powers above! This kitchen is wonderful," she said to Ealstan's mother. "It's three times the size of the one in our flat in Eoforwic. It's bigger than the one I had back in Oyngestun, too, and laid out better."

"I'll show you around the house in a little while, if you like," Elfryth said. "First, though, I thought you'd want to relax for a bit."

"That would be nice." Vanai shook her head. "No, that would be more than nice. That would be wonderful!" She picked up a mug of wine. "What shall we drink to?"

"To being able to drink together!" Ealstan said. Vanai nodded. So did his mother. They all drank.

"I'll have to dig out your old high chair and your old cradle," Elfryth said.

"You still have them?" Ealstan said in astonishment.

"Of course we do," his mother answered. "We knew we would have grandchildren one day, and we thought they would come in handy. They're down in the cellar—I remember seeing them when we spent so much time there during the siege." Seeing the mugs had emptied in a hurry, she poured them full again.

They drank more slowly the second time through. Ealstan could feel the wine. By the way her expression grew slack, it hit Vanai hard. When the next knock on the door came, they all jumped. "That'll be Father," Ealstan said. He was closest to the door. He didn't move as fast as he had when he heard Vanai's voice, but he got there soon enough. He threw open the door and announced, "They're here!"

"Who's here?" Hestan asked, but then he went on, "No—don't tell me. By the idiot grin on your face, I've got a pretty good idea." He pushed past Ealstan and went into the kitchen, where he spoke in classical Kaunian: "Vanai? I am your father-in-law, and I am very glad to meet you at last."

"Thank you, sir," she said in the same language. "I'm very glad to meet you, too. This is your granddaughter."

"I suspected as much," Hestan said gravely. "Who else in this house would be sitting there banging the lid of a pot on the floor? Well, perhaps Ealstan, but he is larger."

"Slander," Ealstan said from behind him.

Vanai looked from one of them to the other and back again. "Now I understand some things about you that I didn't before," she told Ealstan.

"I come by absurdity honestly," he agreed.

"Supper's just about ready," his mother said. "I know I can find that high chair." She did, too, and triumphantly brought it into the dining room. Saxburh ate little bits of torn-up chicken and bread, and drank well-watered wine from a cup whose lid had three little holes. She made a mess. Elfryth smiled at Ealstan in a way that said she remembered him doing the same thing.

Halfway through supper, the sorcerous disguises Vanai had given herself and the baby wore off. All Hestan said to Ealstan was, "You married a pretty girl either which way." Ealstan nodded. He hadn't seen much of Vanai's true Kaunian features for a long time.

Vanai couldn't see her own features change, of course, but she noticed it on Saxburh and understood what Hestan's comment had to mean. "I can put the spell back on," she said hastily.

"Only if you want to," Ealstan's father said. "Myself, I don't think there's any need to, not when you're among friends."

"Among friends," Vanai echoed. She shook her head in wonder, her gray-blue eyes wide. "You don't know how strange that sounds to me. Be thankful you don't know."

Hestan didn't try to argue. All he said was, "Strange or not, it's true here."

"It certainly is," Elfryth agreed. Vanai brushed at her eyes with the back of her hand. She didn't quite cry, but Ealstan thought she came close.

After supper, Saxburh fell asleep in Vanai's lap. Maybe the wine helped, but the baby had had a long, hard day, too. Ealstan's mother brought out the cradle. "It was right by the high chair," she said. Vanai laid Saxburh in it.

Before too much longer, Vanai started yawning herself. Ealstan and his father moved a bed from a guestroom into the one he was using. That crowded the chamber, but he didn't care. Yawning still, Vanai went off to bed.

"I see what you see in her," Ealstan's father said after the door closed.

"She's very sweet," his mother added, nodding. "And I want to eat your daughter up."

"We're all back together again," Ealstan said. "That

counts for more than anything." His wounded leg twinged. He ignored it. In spite of it, what he'd said remained true.

He waited till he thought Vanai would surely be asleep, then tiptoed back to the bedroom, careful not to tap with his canes. Opening the door as quietly as he could, he stepped inside, then closed it behind him.

From the new bed, Vanai whispered, "I thought you'd never get here. If you'd waited much longer, I really would have fallen asleep." She flipped back the bedclothes. Under them, she was bare. "I've missed you," she said.

"Oh, darling," was all Ealstan answered—with words, anyhow.

Prince Juhainen's image stared out of the crystal. "Aye, Mistress Pekka," he said. "The demonstration was everything we could possibly have wanted it to be. The Gongs who saw it with their own eyes were horrified. The crew aboard the ley-line cruiser all agree on that."

"But the Gyongyosians in Gyorvar won't believe them," Pekka said. "Is that where the problem lies?"

"That seems to be it, aye," the prince answered. "They have made it plain they intend to keep fighting."

Pekka scowled. "We could have brought the lash down on Gyorvar straightaway. Don't they see that? We try to warn them, we try to show them mercy, and they refuse to take it? Are they mad?"

"Just stubborn, I think," Juhainen said. "If they insist on paying the price, you can make them pay it?"

"Aye, your Highness," Pekka said, "though I don't like to think about doing that to a place with people in it."

"If they'll heed nothing else, we do have to gain their attention," Juhainen said.

"I suppose so, sir," Pekka said. "In fact, I know you're right. But doing something like . . . that to Gyorvar or to one of the Gongs' other towns still comes hard. I'd sooner have done it to Algarve."

"I know you would, and I understand your reasons," Juhainen said. "In your turn, though, you have to understand those are not reasons of state."

"Revenge isn't the only reason I said that, your Highness," Pekka replied. "It plays a part; I'd be lying if I told you anything else. Taken all in all, though, the Gongs have fought a pretty clean war. They're just enemies, people who want the same islands we do and won't take no for an answer. The few times they've used the murderous sorcery the Algarvians came up with, the men they killed to fuel it were all volunteers—real volunteers, by everything we could learn. With what Mezentio's men did, they deserved being on the receiving end of this more than Gyongyos does."

"Very well. I see your point," Prince Juhainen said. "But if we can't convince them to give up the fighting any other way, we shall have to hit them over the head with a rock. Better that than all the Kuusaman soldiers' lives we would have to spend invading their homeland. Or do you think I'm wrong?"

Even if I did think you were wrong, you and the rest of the Seven would go right on down the ley line you've chosen. Pekka knew that perfectly well. But, in fact, she agreed with the prince. "No, your Highness. If this lets us win the war quickly, then we should do it. I hope the Gongs give up before we loose the magic on them, though."

"Well, so do I—but if not, not," Juhainen said. "Is there anything else, Mistress Pekka?" When Pekka shook her head, the prince gestured to his crystallomancer, who broke the etheric connection. Light flared in the crystal in front of Pekka, and then it went dark and inert.

She walked back to her chamber. Fernao sat at the desk there, filling leaves of foolscap with calculations. He set down the pen and levered himself upright with the help of his cane. "Hello," he said. "I love you."

"I love you, too," Pekka said, smiling. It was true. Things being as they were, she didn't even have to feel guilty when she said it. But that thought by itself was enough to raise guilt in her. When Fernao held out his arms to hug her, she slipped into his embrace as if it could shield her from all the complications of the world. She wished it were so. Unfortunately, she knew better.

After kissing her, Fernao asked, "What did the prince say?"

That brought another piece of the outside world into the chamber—not that it hadn't already been there on the leaves of foolscap. "About what we thought," Pekka said. "The Gongs don't seem to believe that we can do this to them, in spite of the demonstration at Becsehely."

"They're fools," Fernao said.

"They're a stubborn folk. They always have been," Pekka said. "If they weren't, they wouldn't have been able to keep so much of their own way of life while they added on modern, eastern Derlavaian–style sorcerous techniques. They're strange and they're hard, and we're going to have to break them."

"Right now, I'd do almost anything to end the Derlavaian War." Fernao pointed to the papers on Pekka's desk. "We *can* do this. Gyorvar's farther away than that Becsehely place, but not enough to change the spell much. There's no sign the Gyongyosians have any counterspells in place."

"I'm not sure there are any counterspells for this magecraft," Pekka said.

"I'm not sure there are, either, but we're just starting to explore it, so there may be," Fernao said. Pekka nodded; he had a point. He went on, "Whether there are or not, there certainly aren't any up for Gyorvar. If we want to . . ." He snapped his fingers. "We can."

"I know." Pekka clicked her tongue between her teeth. "I don't like to think about being able to wreck a city from halfway around the world."

"Neither do I," Fernao said. "But I'll tell you this: I'd rather be able to do it than to know someone else could do it to me and I couldn't answer back."

Pekka thought about that, too, then slowly nodded. "If we have to do this to Gyorvar, I wonder how King Swemmel will take it," she said. "Actually, I don't wonder. I've got a pretty good idea: Swemmel will have fawns."

" 'Have kittens,' we'd say in Lagoan," Fernao told her. "Amounts to about the same thing either way, I suppose. I wonder how long the Unkerlanters will take to figure out what we've done and how we've done it."

"Years," Pekka said confidently. "They're brave and

they're very tough and they're very big, but they're very backward, too."

"I wonder. I really do," Fernao said. "The Algarvians thought the same thing about them, I suppose, and look at the surprise they got."

"They deserved the surprise they got," Pekka said. "They should have got more and worse, as a matter of fact."

"That's not what I meant." Fernao wagged a finger at her in an Algarvic gesture. "What's more, you know it's not what I meant. Unkerlanter mages turned out to know their business pretty well. If they matched what Mezentio's men did, why shouldn't they match us, too?"

"It doesn't seem likely to me," Pekka said. "What will Swemmel do to push them forward? Kill the sorcerers who tell him it can't be done as fast as he wants?"

She'd meant it for a joke, but Fernao nodded. "He might. Nothing concentrates the mind like the prospect of being boiled alive in the morning."

Pekka made a horrible face. "That's disgusting."

"I know," Fernao answered. "That doesn't mean it won't work."

"There are times I wish I'd never performed my experiments," Pekka said.

"If you hadn't, someone else would have," Fernao said. "It might have been an Algarvian or an Unkerlanter. If anyone can do this, better Kuusamo and Lagoas than most other places I could name."

"I think you're right," she said. "If you were to ask an Algarvian or an Unkerlanter, though, he would tell you different."

"Oh, no doubt," Fernao agreed. "That doesn't mean they'd know what they were talking about, though." He laughed. "After all, what are they but a bunch of ignorant foreigners?"

"You're impossible," Pekka told him. "And"—she jabbed a finger his way—"as far as I'm concerned, you're an ignorant foreigner, too, even if you do speak Kuusaman with a south-coast accent."

"Whose fault is that?" Fernao said. "Besides, if I settle

down with you in Kajaani, will I still be a foreigner?" He
held up a hand. "I know I'll still be ignorant. You don't need
to remind me of that."

"No, eh?" Pekka was a trifle annoyed that he'd seen her
next gibe coming before she could make it. She thought
about the question he'd put her. "I don't know if you'd be a
foreigner or not. A lot of that would depend on you,
wouldn't you say, and on how much you'd want to fit in?"

Fernao bent down and kissed the top of her head. That
reminded her how much taller he was than the average Kuusaman, woman or man. He said, "I'll never look like one
of your countrymen."

"You do have the eyes," she answered, and he nodded.
She went on, "And there are a fair number of Kuusamans—
people who speak Kuusaman, who think of themselves as
Kuusamans—with red hair and with legs longer than they
need to be, especially in the western part of the land, the
part close to Lagoas. You have some short, dark, slant-eyed
folk who think of themselves as Lagoans, too."

"We have people who look like everything under the sun
who think of themselves as Lagoans," Fernao said. "For the
past hundred years, people have been coming to Setubal to
get away from wherever they were living. They think of
themselves as exiles, but their children learn Lagoan. And
we're a mongrel lot, anyhow—we mostly look Algarvic,
but you said it: we've got Kuusaman blood in us, too, and
some Kaunian blood besides, from the days of the Empire's
province in the northwest of the island."

Pekka snapped her fingers. "That reminds me," she said.
"Kuusamo is going to get some new Kaunian blood of its
own. Remember the poor fellow from Jelgava whose wife
wrote to Leino when he got thrown in a dungeon?"

"I translated the letter for you. I'd better remember," he
answered. "So you know what happened to him, do you?"

"Aye." Pekka nodded. "The Seven Princes complained to
King Donalitu. Donalitu let him out of the dungeon, all
right, but he kicked him and his wife out of Jelgava altogether. They've just come to Yliharma. He's a tailor, I
think."

"He'll have to get used to doing some new things," Fernao said with a chuckle. "Kaunians wear trousers, Algarvic folk wear kilts, and Unkerlanters and Forthwegians wear long tunics, but you Kuusamans throw on whatever you please."

"We aren't Kaunian. We aren't Algarvic," Pekka said. "And we don't need our clothes to tell us who and what we are."

Fernao reached out and patted her on the bottom. "I should hope not. Sometimes it's more fun finding out things like that with no clothes at all."

"That's not what I meant, and you know it," Pekka said severely, but the corners of her mouth couldn't help curling up. "If you move to Kajaani, will you stay in kilts all the time, or will you wear leggings and trousers now and again, too?"

"I don't know," Fernao answered. "I hadn't really thought about it."

"Well, maybe you should, if you're talking about turning into a Kuusaman," Pekka said. He did, quite visibly. After a bit, to her relief, he nodded.

Fourteen

───────── ༄ ─────────

Hajjaj had been going on about his business and doing his best to forget that a good many high-ranking Algarvian refugees had taken up residence in Zuwayza. He'd always known how much trouble that might cause. Till it did, though, he'd kept hoping it wouldn't.

As so many of his hopes had been since Unkerlant attacked his kingdom more than five years before, that one was wasted. Without warning, a blocky Unkerlanter strode into the outer office of the foreign ministry. Hajjaj heard him arguing with Qutuz. That wasn't hard; everyone along the whole corridor surely heard the Unkerlanter's shouts in accented Zuwayzi.

Getting to his feet, the foreign minister went out to the outer office, where he found his secretary nose to nose with the irate Unkerlanter. "What's going on here?" Hajjaj asked mildly.

"This . . . gentleman"—plainly *not* the description Qutuz had in mind—"desires to speak with you, your Excellency."

"I do not desire. I demand," the Unkerlanter said. "And I demand that you come to the Unkerlanter ministry at once. At once, do you understand me?" The man snorted like a bull. Either he was a better actor than any of his countrymen Hajjaj had seen, Minister Ansovald included, or he was genuinely furious.

If he was really that angry, Hajjaj knew what was likeliest to make him so. Alarm ran through the Zuwayzi foreign minister. *This is too soon for them to have found out,* he thought. *Much too soon, in fact.* He did his best to sound calmer than he felt: "A man does not make demands of another kingdom's minister in his own office, sir."

"That's what I told him, your Excellency," Qutuz said. "That's just what I told him, curse me if it isn't."

"Shut up, both of you!" the Unkerlanter shouted. "You, old man, you can come with me right now, or we can have another war right now. There's your choice, powers below eat you."

"This is an outrage!" Qutuz exclaimed.

"Too bad," the Unkerlanter said. He scowled at Hajjaj. "Are you coming or not? You say no, you watch what happens to this pisspot of a kingdom."

They know, Hajjaj thought gloomily. *They must know.* With a sigh, he replied, "I will come with you—under protest. May I dress first, to match your custom?"

"Don't waste the time. It's inefficient," the Unkerlanter said. "Get your scrawny old carcass moving, that's all."

"Very well. I am at your service," Hajjaj said. He nodded to Qutuz. "I'll see you later." *I hope I will. I hope they let me leave the ministry.* He took a broad-brimmed hat from the hat rack in the outer office and set it on his head. "Let us go."

At this season of the year, even Zuwayzin went out as little as they could in the middle of the day. The sun smote down from as close to the zenith as made no difference. The palace's thick walls of mud brick shielded against the worst of the heat. Out in the streets, the air might have come from a bake oven. Hajjaj's shadow puddled at his feet, as if even it were looking for someplace to hide.

The Unkerlanter ignored the heat. He had a carriage waiting outside. The driver—also hatless, and a bald man to boot—sat steaming under that merciless sun. Hajjaj hoped he wouldn't keel over halfway to the Unkerlanter ministry. The fellow who'd stormed into his office spoke to the driver in their own language, then held the carriage door open for Hajjaj—one of the few formal courtesies he'd ever had from an Unkerlanter. By the way the man slammed it shut after getting in behind the Zuwayzi foreign minister, that courtesy hadn't come easy.

They got to the ministry unscathed. The driver kept right on sitting out in the open. "You really should let him come inside and cool off," Hajjaj remarked. "This weather can kill, you know."

"You worry about your business," the Unkerlanter told him. "We will tend to ours."

"Zuwayza has been saying that very thing to Unkerlant for centuries," Hajjaj said. "Somehow, you never seem to listen."

The fellow escorting him didn't seem willing to listen. Unkerlanters, as Hajjaj had said, never did listen to their northern neighbors. Being badly outweighed, Zuwayzin had to listen to Unkerlanters, no matter how little they cared to. This particular Unkerlanter took Hajjaj straight to Minister Ansovald, and spoke two words in his own tongue: "He's here." Hajjaj was far from fluent in Unkerlanter, but had no trouble understanding that.

Ansovald glared at Hajjaj. Hajjaj had met the Unkerlanter minister's glares before, and bore up under this one. When he didn't immediately crumple and admit guilt, Ansovald shouted, "You treacherous son of a whore!"—in Algarvian, because Hajjaj didn't have enough Unkerlanter to carry on diplomacy—if such this was—in that language.

"Good day, your Excellency," Hajjaj said now. "As always, I am delighted to see you, too."

Irony was wasted on Ansovald. Like so many of his countrymen, he seemed immune to both shame and embarrassment. *To serve King Swemmel, he needs to be,* Hajjaj thought. But Unkerlanter boorishness was far older than the reign of the current King of Unkerlant.

"We're going to hang all those Algarvian bastards," Ansovald shouted now. "And when we're done with that, we're liable to hang you, too. How far will that scrawny neck of yours stretch?"

"I don't know what you're talking about," Hajjaj said.

"Liar," Ansovald said. What would have been an ugly truth from another man sounded like a compliment from him. "You're hiding Balastro and a whole raft of other redheads in a stinking little town called Harran. We want 'em. We're going to get 'em, too—or you'll be sorry, and so will everybody else in this tinpot kingdom."

"Even if I were to admit their presence, which I do not, on what grounds could you want them?" Hajjaj asked.

"Conspiracy to violate the Treaty of Tortusso by annexing Rivaroli. Conspiracy to wage war against Forthweg, Valmiera, Jelgava, Sibiu, Lagoas, Kuusamo, *and* Unkerlant. Conspiracy to murder Kaunians from Forthweg," Ansovald answered. "Those will do for starters. We can find plenty more. Don't you worry about a thing. We'll try 'em before we hang 'em, so everything looks pretty."

Hajjaj winced. He hadn't expected Ansovald to come up with such a detailed, and damning, indictment. No doubt a good many of the Algarvian refugees were guilty of those things. Still, he said, "If they had won the war, they could charge you with as many enormities as you blame them for now."

Ansovald didn't even waste time denying it. All he said was, "So what? The bastards lost. You can turn 'em over to us, or we can bring in soldiers to come and get 'em. That's the only choice you've got, Hajjaj. King Swemmel isn't playing games here, believe you me he isn't."

The last thing Hajjaj wanted was Unkerlanter soldiers in Zuwayza. If they came, would they ever leave? *Not likely,* he thought. But he said, "There is no law between kingdoms governing whether one may make war on another or how to fight such wars."

"Maybe there isn't, but there's going to be," the Unkerlanter minister to Zuwayza replied.

"Where is the justice in hanging a man for breaking a law that was not a law when he did what he did?" Hajjaj asked.

"Futter justice," Ansovald said. "We're not going to let those buggers get away, and that's flat. You have three days, Hajjaj. Give 'em up or we'll come get 'em."

"I cannot guarantee your soldiers' reception if you do," Hajjaj said.

"Try and stop 'em." Ansovald relished being on top.

"We shall do what we have to do," Hajjaj said coldly. "Your master will not thank you for starting a war here when he plainly has plans farther west."

"Only goes to show you don't know King Swemmel," Ansovald said.

"Are we quite through here? Have you made all your demands?" Hajjaj asked. "If so, I shall take your words to King Shazli."

"Go on. Get out." Ansovald gestured contemptuously. Biting his lip, Hajjaj turned and left the minister's chamber. The hard-faced young Unkerlanter waited outside, and escorted him to the carriage in stony silence. The carriage, he saw, had a new driver. He didn't remark on it. He wanted nothing more than to get away from the Unkerlanter ministry.

Back at the palace, he hurried to King Shazli's private audience chamber. He had to wait there, for the king was greeting the new minister from Sibiu. Shazli came in rolling his eyes. "I'm glad to be out of those clothes," he said. "Would you care for tea and wine and cakes, your Excellency?"

"No, thank you, your Majesty," Hajjaj answered. "Your Majesty, we have a problem." He summed up what Ansovald had told him, leaving out only the coarse language and the shouts.

When he'd finished, Shazli frowned. "Do you think he means these threats?"

"Aye, your Majesty, I fear I do. I fear he does."

"I was afraid of that." Shazli let out a long, sad sigh. "When we took in these Algarvians, I made up my mind I would not let the kingdom suffer on account of them. I still hold to that. If Swemmel wants them so badly, I shall give them to him."

That took Hajjaj by surprise. "Your Majesty!" he exclaimed. "Will you turn over men who helped in our revenge, who fought side by side with us for as long as they could? Where is the loyalty a man must show his friends?"

"I am willing to be loyal to my friends, in their place," the king answered. "But their place is behind that of my own people. I will not go to war with Unkerlant to save these Algarvians. I will not even risk war with Unkerlant to protect them."

"I don't think Swemmel could fight much of a war to get these redheads," Hajjaj said. "From everything we've been able to learn, he's shipping soldiers west as fast as he can, to drive the Gyongyosians out of his kingdom." In an aside, he added, "I have warned Minister Horthy of this—discreetly, of course." He returned to the main topic: "While the Unkerlanters are busy in the west, they can't bother us too badly."

"I am sorry, your Excellency, but I dare not take the chance," King Shazli said. "The Algarvians *will* be surrendered."

Shazli had rarely overruled Hajjaj. Having it happen now hurt more than all the other times put together. "I must protest, your Majesty," Hajjaj said stiffly.

"I'm sorry," Shazli told him. "In this matter, my mind is made up."

Hajjaj took a deep breath. "That being so, you leave me no choice but to offer my resignation." He'd done that a handful of times in his long tenure; it had always persuaded the king to change his mind.

King Shazli sighed. "You have served this kingdom long and well, your Excellency. Without you, there might well be no Kingdom of Zuwayza today. But I shall do what I think I must do. I hope you will consult with me on my choice of your successor."

"Of course, your Majesty." Hajjaj bowed his head. He'd tried. He'd failed. Now it was time to go. So he tried to tell himself. But the blood pounded in his ears. He suddenly felt very old, very shaky. Just as he'd been a part of Zuwayza for so very long, so Zuwayza was also a part of him. Had been a part of him. *It's over,* he told himself. *It's all over.*

Colonel Lurcanio sat across the table from a young Lagoan major who spoke Algarvian with such a thick accent, he would sooner have conversed with the fellow in classical Kaunian: he swallowed vowels and case and verb endings, as if he were still speaking his own tongue. "There's . . . some difficulty about your release, your Excellency," the Lagoan said.

"Thank you so much, Major Simao, for informing me of this," Lurcanio said, acid in his voice. "Without your telling me, I never should have noticed."

Simao turned almost as red as his hair. "Your attitude, Colonel, is not helpful," he said reproachfully.

Pride and annoyance rang in Lurcanio's voice: "Why should I be helpful? I see the men I commanded being freed from this captives' camp, and I see myself still confined. What I fail to see is the reason for it. I should like to return to Albenga as quickly as possible. My county is under Unkerlanter occupation, and I want to do everything I can to protect the people from King Swemmel's savages."

"You are speaking of my kingdom's allies," Simao said, more stiffly than ever.

"The more shame to you," Lurcanio retorted.

"You are most uncooperative," the Lagoan said.

Lurcanio threw his arms wide. "I have surrendered. I will not go back to war if you turn me loose. What more do you want? Do you ask me to love you? There, I fear, you ask for too much."

"That is not the issue," Simao said. "You spoke of your county under Unkerlanter occupation. My kingdom has a request from Valmiera to return you to Priekule to answer for what you did there while Algarve was the occupying power."

"How thoroughly barbarous," Lurcanio said, using scorn

to hide the unease prickling through him. "The war is over. Will you blame me for fighting on my kingdom's side?"

Major Simao shook his head. "No, Colonel. We have investigated that. When you were in the field, you fought as a soldier should fight. When you were on occupation duty, however . . . Does the phrase 'Night and Fog' mean anything to you?"

That unease curdled into outright fear. How much did Simao know of the quiet, vicious war between occupiers and occupied? How much of it had been war, and how much murder? Lurcanio didn't precisely know himself. He wondered if anyone else did.

"You do not answer my question, Colonel," Simao said sharply.

"I've heard the phrase," Lurcanio said. If he denied even that much, he was too likely to be proved a liar. "One heard all sorts of things during the war—don't forget, I spent four years in Priekule. I fathered a child there, and not, I assure you, in a rape. That may be one reason for the Valmierans' malice."

Simao shrugged. "Then you object to being returned to Priekule?"

"Of course I object!" Lurcanio said. "You Lagoans and the Kuusamans—aye, and the Unkerlanters—beat us in battle. You earned the right to dictate to us. But the Valmierans?" He made a horrible face.

"Or is it that Algarve thought she would never have to answer for what she did there?" Simao asked. Before Lurcanio could answer, the Lagoan went on, "And, of course, there were the massacres of Kaunians from Forthweg—and other Kaunians from Valmiera and Jelgava—when you aimed your sorcery across the Strait of Valmiera at my island."

"I know nothing of any of that," Lurcanio said, which was a lie he thought he could get away with. He really didn't know much about such things. He also hadn't gone out of his way to find out. Better not to ask where groups of people pulled out of gaols were going.

Major Simao scribbled something on a leaf of paper. "I have noted your objection," he said. "You will be notified as to whether it is heeded."

"How?" Lurcanio asked. "Will you drag me out of here and haul me off to Valmiera?"

"Probably," the Lagoan answered. "You are dismissed."

As Lurcanio left the makeshift office in the captives' camp, another worried-looking Algarvian officer went in. *I wonder what he did during the war,* Lurcanio thought. *I wonder how much he'll have to pay for it. We had our revenge on our enemies—and now they're having theirs on us.*

He mooched around the camp. More often than not, time hung heavy here. Even the interview, however unpleasant, had broken routine. He could look up to the sky of his kingdom, but more than a palisade separated him and his fellow captives from the rest of Algarve. Outside the camp, his countrymen had begun to rebuild. Here . . .

Lurcanio shook his head. Rebuilding would come here last. Memory and misery reigned here, nothing else. Algarvian soldiers walked as aimlessly as Lurcanio did himself. For close to six years, they'd done everything they could do, and what had it got them? Nothing. Less than nothing. They'd had a thriving kingdom before the war. Now Algarve lay in ruins, and all her neighbors despised her.

". . . So we made the feint from the front, and when the Unkerlanters bit on it, we hit 'em from behind," one scrawny captive was telling another. "We cleaned 'em out of that village neat as you please."

His pal nodded. "Aye, that's good. Those whoresons never did pay enough attention to anything that wasn't right under their noses."

One of them had two bars under his wound badge, the other three. They went on hashing over the fights they'd been through as if those battles still meant something, as if other Algarvian soldiers remained in the field to take advantage of what they'd so painfully learned. Lurcanio wondered how long the war would stay uppermost in their thoughts. He wondered if it would ever be anything but uppermost.

I'm lucky, he thought. *I was only in the field for the early campaigns, and then at the end. In between, I had those four civilized years in Priekule.* It wasn't so much that his body had come through unscarred, though he was anything but sorry to have escaped the enormous grinding battles in the west: a great many men had gone from Valmiera to fight in Unkerlant, and precious few ever came back again. But Lurcanio hadn't had the war branded on his spirit to the same degree as most of his fellow captives.

He shrugged an elaborate, Algarvian shrug. *I don't think I have, anyway.* He'd spent most of his nights in Priekule in his own bed or, more pleasantly, in Krasta's. Instead of warring with a stick, he'd fought his battles against the Valmieran irregulars with a pen.

And I won most of them, he thought. The kingdom had stayed quiet, or quiet enough, under Algarve's heel till the situation in the west and in Jelgava grew too desperate to let the occupiers stay. For a moment, he took pride in that. But then he shrugged again. What difference did it make? No matter how well he'd done his job, his kingdom had lost the war. That mattered. The other didn't.

Two days later, he was summoned from the ranks of the captives at morning roll call. His wasn't the only name the Lagoan guard called out. About a dozen men, most of them officers but with two or three sergeants among them, stepped forward.

Major Simao came out of the administrative center. "You men have been ordered remanded to Valmieran custody for investigation of murders and other acts of cruelty and barbarism inflicted on the said kingdom during its occupation by Algarve," Simao droned, his mumbling, nasal Lagoan accent making the bureaucratic announcement even harder to follow.

But Lurcanio understood what it was all too likely to mean. "I protest!" he said. "How can we hope to get a fair investigation from the Valmierans? They want to kill us under form of law."

"How many of them did you kill without bothering with form of law?" Simao said coldly. "Your protest is denied."

Lurcanio hadn't expected much else. But the speed—and the relish—with which Simao rejected his appeal were illuminating. He'd known the kingdoms allied against his own hated Algarvians. Seeing that hatred in action, though, showed him how deep it ran.

As the Lagoans marched the captives out of the camp and toward wagons that would, Lurcanio supposed, take them to a ley-line caravan depot, one of the sergeants said, "Well, we're futtered royal and proper. Only question is whether they blaze us or hang us or drop us in the stewpot."

"Valmierans don't do that," Lurcanio said. But then he added, "Of course, by the look of things, they might make an exception for us."

"That's right." The sergeant nodded. "But I'll tell you something else, sir: they can only get me once, and I got a lot more'n one o' those stinking blond bastards."

"Good for you," Lurcanio said. Algarvian bravado ran deep. He hoped he would be able to keep it up himself when he needed it most.

Sure enough, the wagon ride—with as many Lagoan soldiers as captives: a compliment of sorts—took them to a small depot. The soldiers stood watch over them till an eastbound ley-line caravan came up and stopped. One of the cars had bars across the windows. A Lagoan guard favored the captives with a nasty smile. "Like the ones you used for Kaunians you killed, eh?" he said in Algarvian, a comparison Lurcanio could have done without.

After Lurcanio and the other captives and most of the guards boarded the caravan car, it glided away. The bars didn't keep Lurcanio from peering avidly out the windows. As the caravan drew near the border with Valmiera, he saw long columns of redheaded, kilted men and women and children trudging westward, some pushing handcarts, some with duffels slung over their shoulders, a lucky handful with a horse or a donkey to bear their burdens.

That Algarvian-speaking guard said, "The Valmierans throw you whoresons out of the Marquisate of Rivaroli. No more trouble there. No more treason there, either."

Algarvians had lived in Rivaroli for more than a thousand years. Even when Valmiera annexed the marquisate after the Six Years' War, no one had talked of expelling them. But a generation and more had gone by since then. These were new times—hard times, too.

At a stop by the border, the Lagoan guards left the caravan car. Blonds in trousers took their place. "Now you get what is coming to you," one of them said, proving he too spoke Algarvian. His laugh was loud and unpleasant.

"Go ahead. Have your joke," the irrepressible sergeant said. "I bet you ran away from the fighting, too, just like all your pals." The Valmieran spoke in a low voice to his comrades. Four of them beat the sergeant bloody while the rest held sticks on the other Algarvian captives to make sure they didn't interfere.

"Any other funny men?" the guard asked. No one said a word.

On through Valmiera glided the ley-line caravan. In the early afternoon, the landscape started looking familiar to Lurcanio. Before long, he saw the famous skyline of Priekule. *I enjoyed myself here, aye,* he thought. *All the same, I'd sooner have kept the memories.*

Krasta paid as little attention to news-sheet hawkers as she could. When she came to the Boulevard of Horsemen, she came to spend money, to get away from her bastard son, and to show herself off. She had her wig all done up in curls, in the style of the glory days of the Kaunian Empire. A lot of Valmieran women wore their hair that way these days, perhaps to affirm their Kaunianity after the Algarvian occupation. The wig was hot and uncomfortable, but her own hair hadn't grown out far enough for her to appear in public without its help. Better—far better—discomfort than humiliation.

Hawkers who worked the Boulevard of Horsemen were supposed to be discreet and quiet, so as not to disturb the well-heeled women and men who shopped there. Such rules had gone downhill since the Algarvians pulled out, though. These days, the men who waved the sheets on street corners were about as raucous here as anywhere else in Priekule.

"Redheads coming back for justice!" one of them yelled as Krasta came out of a clothier's. During the war, the dummies in the window had worn some of the shortest kilts in town. These days, of course, they were all patriotically trousered. The vendor thrust a sheet in Krasta's face. "It's our turn now!"

She started to wave him away in annoyance, but then checked herself. "Let me have one." She couldn't remember the last time she'd bought, or even looked at, a news sheet, and had to ask, "How much?"

"Five coppers, lady," the fellow answered apologetically, adding, "Everything's up since the war."

"Is it?" Krasta paid as little attention to prices as she could. She gave him a small silver coin, took the news sheet and her change, and sat down on a local ley-line caravan bench to read the story.

It was what the hawker had said it was: an account of how a dozen Algarvians who'd helped rule Valmiera for King Mezentio were being brought back to Priekule to stand before Valmieran judges and answer for their brutality and atrocities. *It is to be hoped,* the reporter wrote, *that the vicious brutes will get no more mercy than they gave.*

"That's right." Krasta nodded vigorously.

She had to turn to an inside page to find out what she really wanted to know: the names of the Algarvians coming back to Priekule. Those didn't seem to matter to the fellow writing the story: as far as he was concerned, one Algarvian was as good—or rather, as bad—as another. At last, though, the reporter came to the point. Krasta shook her head when he called an Algarvian brigadier *a fiend and a known pervert, a man who took pleasure in killing.* She'd met the officer in question at several feasts and dances. Maybe he liked boys, but he liked women, too; he'd pinched her behind and rubbed himself against her like a dog in heat.

"What do reporters know?" she muttered.

But then she saw the next name, the name she'd wondered if she would find. *With the previously mentioned officer is his henchman, the vile and lecherous Colonel Lurcanio, who made our capital a place of terror for four long years. Lurcanio openly boasts of the child he sired on Marchioness Krasta, from whose mansion at the edge of the capital he leaped out like a wolf on honest citizens.*

Krasta read that twice, then furiously crumpled up the

news sheet and flung it in a trash bin. "Powers below eat him!" she snarled. Had Lurcanio stood before her and not a panel of judges, he wouldn't have lasted long. She'd thought him a gentleman, and one of the things a gentleman didn't do was tell.

He hadn't just told—he'd told the news sheets. People who knew her of course knew her baby had hair the wrong color. Some of them had cut her—including some who'd been at least as cordial to the occupiers as she had. But this . . . in the news sheets . . . Every tradesman she'd ever dealt with would know she'd had an Algarvian's bastard.

Heels clicking on the slates of the sidewalk, she hurried down the Boulevard of Horsemen to the cross street where her carriage waited. When she got there, she found her new driver reading the news sheet. She wished she still had the one who drank to while away the time. "Put down that horrible rag," she snapped.

"Aye, milady," the driver said, but he carefully folded the sheet so he could go on reading it later. "Shall I take you home now?" He spoke as if certain of the answer.

But Krasta shook her head. "No. Drive me to the central gaol."

"To the central gaol, milady?" The driver sounded as if he couldn't believe his ears.

"You heard me," Krasta said. "Now get moving!" She sprang into the carriage, slamming the door behind her.

He took her where she wanted to go. If he hadn't, she would have fired him on the spot and either engaged a new driver or tried to take the carriage back to the mansion herself. She was convinced she could do it: drivers certainly weren't very bright, and they had no trouble, so how hard could it be?

Luckily for her—she'd never driven a carriage in her life—she didn't have to find out. "Here you are, milady," the driver said, stopping in front of a fortresslike building not far from the royal palace.

Krasta descended from the carriage and swarmed toward the gaol, an invading army of one. "What do you want?" asked one of the men at the entrance.

Were they constables? Soldiers? She didn't know and

she didn't care. "I am the Marchioness Krasta," she declared. "I must see one of the nasty Algarvians you have locked up here."

Both the guards bowed. Neither of them opened the formidably stout door, though. "Uh, sorry, milady," said the fellow who'd spoken before. "Nobody can do that without the warder's permission."

"Then fetch the warder here at once." Krasta's voice rose to a shout: "At once, do you hear me?"

If they'd read the news sheet, if they'd paid attention to her name, they might not have been so willing to do as she said. But Valmierans were used to yielding to their nobles. One of them left. He returned a few minutes later with a fellow in a fancier uniform. "May I help you, milady?" the warder asked.

"I must see Colonel Lurcanio, one of your Algarvian captives," Krasta said, as she had before.

"For what purpose?" the warder asked.

"To ask him how he dares have the nerve to tell so many nasty, lying stories about me," Krasta said. That the stories might be nasty but weren't lies had entirely slipped out of her memory.

"What was your name again?" the warder inquired. Fuming, Krasta told him. "Marchioness Krasta . . ." the man repeated. "Oh, you're the one who . . ." By the way his expression sharpened, Krasta could tell he'd read the day's news sheet himself. "You say these are lies?" he asked.

"I certainly do say that," Krasta answered. Saying it, of course, didn't mean it had to be true. She dimly remembered that distinction.

The warder didn't note it. He bowed to her and said, "All right. You come with me."

She came. The place was grimier and smellier than she'd imagined. The warder led her to a room with two chairs separated by a fine but strong wire mesh. To her annoyance, he not only made her leave her handbag outside but also turn out her pockets and put whatever she had in them on a tray. "I'm not going to give this Algarvian anything except a piece of my mind," she said.

With a shrug, the warder said, "These are the rules."

Against the rules, plainly, the powers above themselves contended in vain. Even Krasta, who was anything but shy about arguing regardless of whether or not she had a case, forbore to do so here. The warder said, "You wait. Someone will bring him."

Krasta waited longer than she cared to. Staring at the wire mesh made her feel imprisoned herself. She drummed her fingers on her trouser leg, trying to fight down her annoyance. After about a quarter of an hour—it seemed much longer to Krasta—two guards brought in Lurcanio. They shoved him toward the chair on the far side of the mesh. "Here's the whoreson," one of them said as the other slammed the door.

Instead of sitting down on the hard chair, Lurcanio bowed to Krasta. "Good day, milady," he said in his musically accented Valmieran. "Have you come to gloat, or perhaps to throw nuts to the monkey in the cage? I could use the nuts. They do not feed me very well—which, considering how you Valmierans stuff yourselves, is doubly a crime."

"How dare you tell the news sheets you fathered my boy?" Krasta demanded. "How *dare* you?"

"Well, did I not?" Lurcanio asked. "I surely had more chance than anybody else. But did Valnu or whoever get there at the right time?"

"That has nothing to do with anything," Krasta said, suddenly recalling little Gainibu's unfortunate hair color. Lurcanio laughed out loud, which only infuriated her further. "How dare you *say* it?"

Lurcanio gave back a serious answer, perhaps the most annoying thing he might have done: "Well, for one thing, it is—or it appears to be—the truth."

"What has *that* got to do with anything?" Krasta yelped, very conscious of the difference between what was said and what was.

"And, for another"—Lurcanio went on as if she hadn't spoken—"I can still strike a blow of sorts by telling the truth here. You Valmierans are going to be as hard on me as you know how; I doubt that not at all. Why shouldn't I make things as difficult as I can for you?" Malicious amusement sparked in his cat-green eyes.

Revenge Krasta understood. She didn't care to have it aimed at her. "It's not gentlemanly!" she exclaimed.

"I am not in a gentlemanly predicament, you stupid little twat," Lurcanio snapped. "You were pleasant in bed, but you haven't the brains the powers above gave a hedgehog. I fought a war here in Priekule, and they intend to murder me under form of law on account of the way I fought it. I cannot do much to stop them, either. Now, have you got that through your thick skull?"

"Futter you!" Krasta said shrilly.

"I would tell you to go right ahead, my former dear, but the mesh is too narrow to make it practical," Lurcanio replied.

"Powers below eat you, you put my name in the news sheets," Krasta said.

"And when have you ever complained about that?" Lurcanio asked.

"Futter you!" Krasta said again. This time, she didn't wait for an answer, but flounced out of the visiting chamber. When she slammed the door behind her, an earthquake might have hit the building. The warder, who was waiting in the anteroom, jumped. "Get me out of this horrible place," Krasta snarled, snatching up her chattels.

The warder started to say something, looked at her, and thought better of it. He led her back to the entrance. He did dare a, "Goodbye," then.

Krasta ignored him. She stalked back to her driver. "Take me home this instant—this instant, do you hear me?" she said. The driver, sensibly, obeyed without a word.

Bembo threw away his cane and stood up on his own two legs in the middle of his flat. Actually, judging by what his kilt displayed, he stood up on about a leg and a half. The one that had been broken in Eoforwic was still only a little more than half as thick as the other. But he *did* stand, and he didn't fall over.

"How about that, sweetheart?" he said to Saffa.

She looked up from her baby, who was nursing, to clap her hands. Seeing the baby at her breast never failed to make Bembo jealous, even though he knew how foolish that was: the baby wasn't interested for the same reasons as his. "That's good," she said. "Pretty soon, you'll be able to run like the wind."

"Well . . ." Bembo looked down at his portly form. He'd lost a good deal of weight since getting hurt, and he was still portly. *I might be able to run like a slow breeze one of these days,* he thought. That was about as much speed as he had in him. He said, "Maybe I will be able to start walking a beat before too long. Having some money coming in again would be good."

"Aye." Saffa nodded. Her little boy was falling asleep; her nipple slipped out of his mouth. She raised the baby to her shoulder to burp him, then set her tunic to rights. As she patted the baby's back, she went on, "You know something?"

"I know all kinds of things," Bembo said. "What have you got in mind?"

Saffa made a face at him. "I was going to say, you're nowhere near as big a bastard as I thought you were before I let you get lucky. Maybe I ought to keep my mouth shut."

"Maybe you should," Bembo agreed. She made another face. He laughed. "You asked for that."

"If you got everything you asked for, you wouldn't think that was so cursed funny," Saffa said hotly. Her temper would kindle on the instant, and then calm down again just as fast. Even when she was angry, she noticed people around her, which Bembo wouldn't have done. When he gnawed on his lower lip instead of giving her a snippy answer, she asked, "What's the matter?"

"Nothing," he said, and limped over to a chair. He was glad to sit down; standing hadn't been easy, and walking without a cane made him feel as if he'd fall over at every step he took with his bad leg.

Saffa knew a lie when she heard one. How many lies had she heard, from how many men? Bembo didn't want to think about that. She gave him an exasperated look and said, "I didn't mean to bite you there. I didn't think I *had* bitten you. Why do you think I did?"

"You don't want to know," Bembo answered. "Believe me, you don't."

Before Saffa said anything, she eased her son, who'd fallen asleep, down off her shoulder and held him in the crook of her arm. Then, with her free hand, she shook a finger at Bembo. "Why don't I? What do you think I am, a baby myself?"

"Curse it, Saffa, I don't want to think about this stuff myself, let alone talk about it with anybody else," Bembo said.

"*What* stuff?" she said.

If I got everything I asked for . . . Bembo shuddered. He remembered too well the old Kuusaman mage's eyes piercing him like swords, looking at the memories he concealed from everyone—including, as best he could, from himself. "I told you, you don't want to know. And I don't want to talk about it."

Saffa got up from the couch, using her free hand to help her rise. She went into the flat's cramped kitchen. Bembo listened to her opening cupboards in there. When she came back, she was carrying a mug of spirits, which she set on the wooden arm of Bembo's chair. "Drink," she said. "Then talk."

Bembo picked up the mug willingly enough. He rarely needed a second invitation to drink. "You poured that quick," he said. "You're good at doing things with one hand."

"I'd better be," she answered. "It's like he's *attached* to me all the time." She joggled the baby, who never stirred. "Powers above only know what I'm going to do when he gets too big to carry in one arm, though. But never mind that." She pointed imperiously to the mug.

He drank. "Do you really want to know?" he said. The spirits weren't what made him ask. It was much more that he hoped to perform an exorcism, or perhaps to lance a festering wound. "If you really want to know, I'll tell you."

Saffa leaned forward. "Go on, then."

"You know all the things the islanders and the blonds say we did?" he asked.

Her lip curled. "I'm sick of the lies they tell."

"Those aren't lies," Bembo said. Saffa's jaw fell. He

went on, "As a matter of fact, they don't know the half of it." And he told her of clearing Kaunians out of the villages near Gromheort, of sending them off in packed ley-line caravans to the west (and occasionally to the east), of forcing them into their guarded districts in Gromheort and later in Eoforwic, and of hauling them out of those districts and loading them into caravans, too. He told of their desperation, of the bribes he'd taken and the bribes he'd turned down. By the time he got done, the mug of spirits was finished, too.

He'd fallen into the days gone by while he was talking. He'd hardly paid any attention to Saffa through most of that torrent; he'd been peering back into his time in Forthweg, not at her. Now, at last, he did. She was white, her face set. "We really did those things?" she said in a small voice. "*You* really did those things? You've hinted before, every once in a while, but—"

"No buts," Bembo said harshly. "Don't press me about this again, or I'll make you sorry for it, do you hear me?"

"I'm sorry for it already," Saffa said. "I don't want to believe it."

"Neither do I, and I was there," Bembo said. "If I'm lucky, by the time I'm an old man I won't have nightmares about it any more. If I'm very lucky, I mean."

Saffa eyed him as if she'd never seen him before. "You were always a softy, Bembo. How could you do . . . things like that?"

"They told me what to do, so I did it," Bembo answered with a shrug. But it hadn't been quite that simple, and he knew it. He remembered Evodio, who'd begged off pulling blonds out of houses, and who'd regularly drunk himself into a stupor because he couldn't stand what the Algarvians were doing in Forthweg. He said, "It's like a lot of things: after a while, you don't think about it, and it gets easier."

"Maybe." Saffa didn't sound convinced. She got to her feet and went back into the kitchen. When she returned, she had another mug in hand. She set this on the little table in front of the sofa, saying, "I could use some spirits myself after that. Do you want some more while I'm still up?"

"Please," Bembo said. "If I drink enough, maybe I'll forget for a while." He didn't believe that. He wouldn't forget till they laid him on his pyre. But his memories might at least get a little blurry around the edges.

Saffa sipped spirits before saying, "Hearing about things like that makes me ashamed to be an Algarvian."

"Doing things like that . . ." But Bembo's voice trailed away. "It was better than going farther west and fighting the Unkerlanters."

Only after he'd spoken did he remember what had happened to the fellow who'd sired Saffa's son. The sketch artist's face worked. She looked down at the baby. "I suppose so," she whispered.

"Well, it was safer than going to fight the Unkerlanters," Bembo amended. "Better?" He shrugged again. "I saw some real war of my own, you know, when the Forthwegians rose up in Eoforwic. That was a pretty filthy business, too. The only difference was, both sides were blazing then. You did what needed doing, that's all."

He thought about Oraste, who'd cursed him for getting wounded and escaping Eoforwic before the Unkerlanters could overrun it. He thought about fat Sergeant Pesaro, who'd stayed behind in Gromheort when he and Oraste got transferred to Eoforwic. He wondered if either one of them still lived. Not likely, he supposed, not after what had happened to the two Forthwegian cities. And even if they did, would the Unkerlanters ever let them come home again? Even less likely, he feared.

Saffa said, "I don't think I know you at all. I was always sure what to expect from you: you'd make your bad jokes, you'd try to get your hand up under my kilt, you'd strut and swagger like a rooster in a henyard, and every once in a while you'd show you were a little smarter than you looked, the way you did when you figured out that the Kaunians here were dyeing their hair to look like proper Algarvians. But I never dreamt you had—that—underneath."

"Before Captain Sasso ordered me west, I didn't," Bembo answered. "Saffa, don't you see? Everybody who comes back alive from the west is going to have stories like mine—oh, maybe not just like mine, but the same kind of stories. Fighting that war did something horrible to Algarve, and the whole kingdom's going to be a long time getting over it."

"We're going to be a long time getting over everything," Saffa said. "What with this new king the Unkerlanters have put on the throne in the west, we're not even one kingdom any more."

"I know. I don't like that, either," Bembo said. "For powers above only know how long, there were all these little kingdoms and principalities and grand duchies and plain duchies and marquisates and baronies and counties and whatnot here instead of a real kingdom of Algarve, and our neighbors would play them off against each other so we fought amongst ourselves. I'd hate to see that day come again, but what can we do about it?"

"Nothing. Not a single thing." Saffa sipped at her spirits. She still studied Bembo with a wary—indeed, a frightened—curiosity he'd never seen from her before. "But, since I can't do anything about it, I don't see much point to worrying over it, either. You, though . . . Do I want to have anything to do with you any more when you've—done all these things?"

Bembo pointed to the baby sleeping in her arms. "If the kid's father was here, he'd give you the same kind of stories I did. Us constables didn't do clean things, but neither did the army, and you can take that to the bank. Would you tell his father what you just told me?"

"I hope so," Saffa said.

"Aye, you probably would," Bembo admitted. "You've got a way of saying what's on your mind." He sighed. "Sweetheart, I want you to stay. You know that."

Saffa nodded. "Of course I do. And I know why, too." She made as if to spread her legs. "Men," she added scornfully.

"Women," Bembo said in a different tone, but also one old as time. They both laughed cautious laughs. He went on, "I'm not going to lie and say I don't like bedding you. If I didn't, would I care whether you went or not? Curse it, though, Saffa, it's not the only reason. Would I have chased you so hard when you weren't giving me anything if that was all I cared about?"

"I don't know. Would you? Depends on what you had going on the side, I suppose."

"You're making this as hard as you can, aren't you?" Bembo said. Saffa's answering shrug was unmistakably smug. He stuck out his tongue at her. "Powers above, you stupid bitch, don't you know I really like you?"

"Oh, Bembo," she crooned, "you say the sweetest things." He grimaced again, in a different way; he could have put that better. But she didn't up and walk out on him, either, so maybe things weren't so bad after all.

Skarnu liked his move to the provinces much better than he'd thought he would. He stayed busy learning what needed doing in his new marquisate and in setting to rights whatever he could. The Algarvian occupation had made endless squabbles flare up—and some had been smoldering for years. The more recent ones were usually straightforward. Some of the long-standing disputes, though, proved maddeningly complicated. They gave him a certain small sympathy for the collaborationist counts who'd preceded him as local lords.

"How am I supposed to know how to rule on a property dispute that's been going on so long, everybody who first started quarreling about it's been dead for twenty years?" he asked Merkela at breakfast one morning.

"That's how things are here," she answered. "There are quarrels older than that, too."

"Why haven't I seen them?" he said, sipping tea.

"People are still making up their minds about you," Merkela told him. "They don't want to stick their heads up too soon and be sorry for it later."

Skarnu grunted. He'd seen that sort of country caution when he'd lived on the farm with Merkela. He didn't care to have it aimed at him, but could understand how it might be. To a lot of people in the marquisate, people who hadn't heard about him till he came here as local lord, what was he? Just a stranger from Priekule. He wouldn't have understood that before the war. He did now.

When he remarked on it, Merkela said, "Oh, you'll always be that stranger from Priekule to a lot of people. After a while, though, they'll know you're honest even if you aren't from here, and then you'll hear from them."

"All right." He set down his cup. "Pass me the inside of the news sheet, would you? People complain about me because I'm new, do they? Well, I complain about the news sheets we get, too. By the time I see them, they're old news."

"Old back in Priekule, maybe," she said. "Nobody else around here sees them any sooner than you do."

She had a point, even if it wasn't one he would have thought of. He was used to getting news as soon as it happened. He hadn't been able to do that hereabouts during the war, but the war had thrown everything out of kilter. Not being able to do it for the rest of his days depressed him.

But why should it? he wondered. *Merkela's right—no one else in these parts will know more about what's going on than I do.*

His wife passed him the part of the news sheet she'd been reading. He went through it greedily; if he couldn't get the news on time, at least he could seize all of it the news sheet offered. "Ha!" he said. "So we're going to get some revenge from the redheads who ran the occupation? Just what they deserve, too."

"We can't take full revenge from them unless we go through their countryside and start grabbing people and killing them," Merkela said. "I wouldn't mind a bit."

"I know," Skarnu answered. The war itself had done that to a good deal of the Algarvian countryside, but he didn't say so. Whatever had happened to Algarve, Merkela wouldn't think it was enough. Skarnu had no love for the Algarvians, either, but. . . . He stiffened. "Well, well."

"What is it?" his wife asked.

"One of the redheads they've hauled in is my nephew's father," Skarnu answered. Merkela needed a moment to work out who that was, but bared her teeth in a fierce grin when she did. Skarnu nodded. "Aye, they've got their hands on Lurcanio, sure enough."

"I hope they hang him," Merkela said. "What he'd have done if he ever got his hands on you—"

"We met once, you know, under flag of truce, and he honored that," Skarnu said. Merkela waved his words away, as being of no account. Maybe she was right, too; by that time, the Valmieran underground had become a power in the land, and the Algarvians had troubles enough in other places to want to keep things here as quiet as they could. He added, "I really don't think my sister blabbed anything special that had to do with me."

Tartly, Merkela answered, "I suppose the next thing you'll tell me is that she doesn't have a sandy-haired little bastard, too."

Skarnu coughed and reached for the teapot to pour himself another cup. He couldn't tell her anything of the sort, and they both knew it. He sipped his tea and concentrated on reading the news sheet. "They're charging him with brutality during the occupation, and with sending Valmierans off to be sacrificed."

"They *will* hang him, then, and a good thing, too," Merkela declared, "for he did do those things. If he'd caught you, Mezentio's men would have used your life energy, and they would have been glad to do it."

In fact, Skarnu doubted that. He suspected the redheads would have killed him right away if they'd got hold of him. In their shoes, that was what he would have done with a dangerous captive, and he knew he'd proved himself dangerous. But he didn't argue with his wife. Even if she was wrong as to details, she was right about the bigger picture.

She asked, "Do you suppose they'll call you back to the city to testify against him?"

"I don't know. I hadn't thought of that." He read on, then clicked his tongue between his teeth in annoyance. "Curse him, he's bragging in the news sheet about fathering Krasta's baby. That'll do the family name a lot of good."

"You see?" Merkela said with something like triumph. "You and Valnu had doubts about who did what, but the redhead hasn't got any."

"He hasn't got any he's admitting, anyhow," Skarnu said. "In his place, I'd likely be trying to embarrass us as much as I could. I wouldn't be surprised if that's why he claims the baby for his own."

"Whatever reasons he's got, he's right," Merkela said.

Since Skarnu couldn't very well argue with that, he buried his nose in the news sheet again. Glancing up over the top of it, he saw the triumphant look on Merkela's face. He let out a silent sigh. His wife despised his sister, and nothing in the world looked like changing that. He'd hoped at first that time might, but thought himself likely to be disappointed there. That might eventually matter very much—but even if it did, he failed to see what he could do about it.

Instead of bringing it up and starting an argument, he found another story in the news sheet to talk about: "The last little Algarvian army in Siaulia has finally surrendered."

That made Merkela raise her eyebrows. "I didn't even notice," she said. "What took the whoresons so long?"

Laughing, Skarnu wagged a finger at her. "That's not how a marchioness talks."

"It's how I talk," Merkela said. "And you didn't answer my question."

"They stayed in the field a long time and caused a lot of trouble," Skarnu said. "Not a lot of real redheads in the army there, of course—most of the soldiers are natives from the Siaulian colonies. And they lost their last crystal a while ago, so nobody here on Derlavai could let them know Algarve'd given up. The Lagoan general up there let the Algarvian brigadier in charge keep his sword."

"I know where I'd have let him keep it—right up his . . ." Merkela's voice trailed off as she realized that wasn't fitting language for a marchioness, either.

"By everything the news sheets said, the Algarvians fought a clean war up there," Skarnu said.

"I don't care," his wife replied. "They're still Algarvians." To her, that was the long and short of it.

Servants cleared away the breakfast dishes. Skarnu went out to the reception hall. "Good morning, your Excellency," Valmiru said. The butler bowed low.

"Good morning to you, Valmiru," Skarnu said. "What's on the list for today?" The servitor was doing duty for a majordomo, and handling the job well.

"Let me see, sir," Valmiru said now, taking a list from a tunic pocket and donning spectacles to read it. "Your first appointment is with a certain Povilu, who accuses one of his neighbors, a certain Zemglu, of complicity with the Algarvians."

"Another one of those, eh?" Skarnu said with a sigh.

"Aye, your Excellency," Valmiru replied, "although perhaps not quite of the ordinary sort, for Zemglu has also lodged a charge of collaboration against Povilu."

"Oh, dear," Skarnu said. "One of *those*? How many generations have these two families hated each other?"

"I don't precisely know, sir—one of the disadvantages of coming here from the capital," Valmiru replied. "I had hoped you might be familiar with the gentlemen from your, ah, earlier stay in this part of the kingdom."

"No such luck," Skarnu said. "Are they from over by Adutiskis?" At Valmiru's nod, he nodded, too. "Merkela's farm was close to Pavilosta. I know those people better." He sighed again. "But I'm everybody's marquis, so I have to get to the bottom of it if I can."

He sat in the seat of judgment in the reception hall and looked out at Povilu and Zemglu and their supporters. Povilu was squat and Zemglu was tall and skinny. They'd each brought not only kinsfolk but, by the packed hall, all their friends as well. The two sides plainly despised each other. Skarnu wonder if they would riot.

Not if I can help it, he thought. "All right, gentlemen. I will hear you," he said. "Master Povilu, you may speak first."

"Thank you, your Excellency," Povilu rumbled. He was a man of no breeding, but he'd obviously practiced his speech for a long time, and brought it out well. He accused his neighbor of betraying men from the underground to the redheads. Zemglu tried to shout objections.

"Wait," Skarnu told him. "You'll have your turn."

At last, Povilu bowed and said, "That proves it, your Excellency."

Skarnu waved to the other peasant. "Now, Master Zemglu, say what you will."

"Now you'll hear truth, sir, after this bugger's lies," Zemglu said. Povilu howled. Skarnu silenced him. Zemglu went on to accuse his neighbor of having left one daughter behind so he wouldn't have to show Skarnu her bastard child.

"That was rape!" Povilu yelled.

"You say so now," Zemglu retorted, and went on with his accusations. His followers and those of Povilu pushed and shoved at one another.

"Enough," Skarnu shouted, hoping they would listen to him. Eventually, they did. Still at the top of his lungs, he went on, "Now you'll listen to me." Povilu and Zemglu both leaned forward, tense anticipation on their faces. Skarnu said, "I doubt either of you has clean hands in this business. I *don't* doubt you were enemies before the Algarvians came, and that you're trying to use the cursed redheads to score points off each other. Will you tell me I'm wrong?"

Both peasants loudly denied it. Skarnu studied their followers. Those abashed expressions told him he'd hit the mark. He waited for Povilu and Zemglu to fall silent again—it took a while—then held up his hand.

"Hear my judgment," he declared, and something close to silence fell. Into it, he said, "I charge the two of you to live at peace with each other for the next year, neither of you to do anything—*anything,* do you hear me?—by word or deed to trouble the other. If you care to pursue these claims at the end of that time, you may, either to me or to his Majesty the king. But be warned: justice may fall on both of you alike. For now, go back to your lands and think on what happens when you aim sticks at each other from a distance of a yard."

Still glaring at each other, the peasants and their followers filed out of the reception hall. Skarnu hoped he'd bought a year. If he hadn't, he promised himself both sides in the quarrel would regret it.

Grandmaster Pinhiero looked out of the crystal at Fernao. Fernao had made the etheric connection with the head of the Lagoan Guild of Mages himself; no Kuusaman crystal-lomancers were in the room with him. Pekka, fortunately, understood he sometimes had to talk with his countrymen without anyone's overhearing him. "This thing can be done?" Pinhiero said.

"Aye, sir, it can be done," Fernao answered. "I don't doubt it for a moment."

"And it will be done if the Gongs are too stubborn to see sense?" the grandmaster persisted.

"I don't doubt that, either," Fernao said. He didn't go into details about just what sort of sorcery might be used. Gyongyosian mages were probably trying to spy on these emanations. So were Unkerlanter mages. He wouldn't have been surprised if the Valmierans and Jelgavans were doing their best to listen in as well. But if the Gongs were looking for evidence that what their captives had seen at Becsehely was faked, they would be disappointed.

Pinhiero nodded. "And you know, of course, the workings of the sorcery. You can bring them back to Setubal?"

"I know the workings," Fernao agreed. He took a deep breath. "As for the other, though, sir, I'm not so sure. I don't know if I'll be coming back to Setubal. The way things look now, I would doubt it."

He waited for the storm to burst. He didn't have to wait long. Rage filled Pinhiero's foxy face. "You got her drawers off, so now you love her kingdom better than your own, too, eh?" he growled. "I was afraid this would happen, but I thought you had better sense. Shows what I know, doesn't it?"

"I have done our kingdom no harm, nor would I ever," Fernao said stiffly. "But I am allowed to please myself now and again as well."

"Is that what you call it?" the grandmaster said. "I'd tell you what I call it, though I don't suppose you care to hear."

"You're right, sir—I don't," Fernao said. "I will send you what I can by courier. I will answer any questions you may have. But I don't think I'll come back to Setubal any time soon. I'll have to arrange to have my books and instruments shipped here."

"Kajaani," Grandmaster Pinhiero said scornfully. "How well will you love it when the first blizzards roll in? It's a town with ten months of winter and two months of bad snowshoeing."

Shrugging, Fernao answered, "Lagoas didn't worry about that when I got sent to the land of the Ice People."

"You had to go there," Pinhiero said. "But to *want* to go to Kajaani? A man would have to be mad."

"It's not that bad—a pleasant little place, really," Fernao said: about as much praise as he could find it in himself to give. Pointedly, he added, "And I am fond of the company I'd be keeping."

"You must be, to think of leaving Setubal behind." Pinhiero spoke with the automatic certainty that his city was, and had every right to be, the center of the universe. Not so very long before, Fernao had known that same certainty. The grandmaster went on, "What do they have in the theaters there? Do they even have theaters there?"

"I'm sure they do," answered Fernao, who didn't know. But he added, "Since I haven't gone to the theater since before I left for the austral continent, though, I won't lose much sleep over it."

"Well, whatever you saw then in Setubal should be coming to Kajaani any day now," Pinhiero said, soothing and sarcastic at the same time. Fernao glared. The grandmaster added, "Are you sure she didn't ensorcel you?"

That did it. Fernao growled, "Just because nobody's ever been daft enough to fall in love with you, you old serpent, you don't think it can happen to anyone else, either."

"I thought you had better sense," Pinhiero said. "I thought you'd be sitting in my seat one of these years. I hoped so, in fact."

"Me? Grandmaster?" Fernao said in surprise. Pinhiero nodded. The younger mage shook his head. "No, thanks. I like the laboratory too well. I'm not cut out for politics, and I don't care to be."

"That's why you have someone like Brinco," Pinhiero said. "What's a secretary for?"

"Doing work I don't feel like doing myself? Is that what you're saying?"

Pinhiero nodded. "That's exactly what I'm saying, my

dear young fellow. A chap like Brinco does the work that
needs doing, but that you don't care to do. That gives me
time to go out and chat with people, keep myself abreast of
what's on their minds. If you'd sooner spend your odd moments in the laboratory, no one would hold it against you."

"Very kind of you." Fernao meant it. He knew a grandmaster should be a man like Pinhiero, a man who enjoyed
backslapping and politicking. Pinhiero had to know it, too.
If he was willing to bend the unwritten rules for a theoretical sorcerer like Fernao, he badly wanted him back. Fernao
sighed. "You do tempt me, sir. But the point is, I'd sooner
spend my odd moments—just about all my moments—in
Kajaani."

"I'm going to be blunt with you," Pinhiero said. "Your
kingdom needs what you know. It needs every scrap of
what you know, for you know more about this business than
any other Lagoan mage." He paused, frowning. "You do
still reckon yourself a Lagoan, I trust?"

That hurt. Fernao didn't try to pretend otherwise. He
said, "You'd better know that I do, or I'd break this etheric
connection and walk away from you . . . sir. I've already
told you, if you want to send a man to me, I will tell him
and write down for him everything I know. Lagoas and Kuusamo are allies; I don't see how the Seven could possibly
object to that, and King Vitor would have every right to
scream if they did."

Pinhiero still looked unhappy. "Better than nothing," he
admitted, "but still less than I'd like. You surely know how
the cleanest-seeming written instructions for a spell don't
help a mage as much as having another mage, a knowledgeable fellow, take him through the conjuration."

"I'm sorry. I'm doing the best I can." What Fernao didn't
say was that he feared he wouldn't be allowed to come back
to Kuusamo if he went to Lagoas. As Grandmaster Pinhiero
had pointed out, he knew too much.

"When the time comes, then, I will make the necessary
arrangements with you," Pinhiero said sourly. "I suppose I
should congratulate you on finding love. I must say, though,
that your timing and your target could have been better."

"As for timing, you may possibly be right," Fernao admitted. "As for whom I fell in love with—for one thing, that's none of your business, and, for another, you couldn't be more wrong if you tried for a year. And now I think we've said about everything we have to say to each other."

Grandmaster Pinhiero bridled. He wasn't used to having Fernao—he wasn't used to having anybody—speak to him that way. But he wasn't King Swemmel. He couldn't punish Fernao for speaking his mind, especially if Fernao no longer cared about advancing through the Lagoan sorcerous hierarchy. All he could do was glare as he said, "Good day," and cut the etheric connection.

The crystal flared, then became no more than a sphere of glass. Fernao let out another sigh, a long, heartfelt one, as he rose from the chair in front of it. Nervous sweat ran from his armpits and made the back of his tunic stick to his skin. Defying the grandmaster—essentially, declaring he was abandoning allegiance to his kingdom—didn't, couldn't, come easy.

When he left the chamber, he found the Kuusaman crystallomancer outside, her nose in a romance. "I'm finished," he told her in his own language, and then wondered how he'd meant that.

He walked up to his room. A couple of mosquitoes whined in the stairwell. Outside the hostel, they swarmed in millions, so that going out for long was asking to be eaten alive. When all the ice and snow melted, they made puddles uncountable, as they did in spring and summer on the austral continent. And oh, how the mosquitoes and gnats and flies reveled in those spawning grounds!

Fernao swatted one of the buzzing bugs when it lit on the back of his wrist. The other—if there was only one other—didn't land on him, which meant it survived. He heard more buzzes in the hall. Something there bit him. He slapped at it, but didn't think he got it.

He was muttering to himself when he went into his chamber. Pekka sat studying a grimoire there, as engrossed as the crystallomancer had been in her book. She looked up from it with a smile, which faded when she saw how grim

Fernao looked. "You didn't have a happy time with your grandmaster, did you?" she said.

"Worse than I thought I would," Fernao answered. "I told him he could send someone to learn what I know once I get settled in Kajaani. I think I would be foolish to go back to Setubal any time soon. For all practical purposes, I've walked away from my kingdom."

Pekka put down the sorcerous text without bothering to mark her page. "You had better be quite sure you want to do that."

He limped over to her and let his free hand, the one without the cane, rest on her shoulder. She set her hand on top of his. "I'm sure," he answered. "It follows everything else that's been on this ley line we've traveled."

"Will it be all right? Truly?" she asked. "Can you live in Kajaani after Setubal?"

"The company's better," he said, which made her smile. He went on, "Besides, once Pinhiero's man squeezes everything I know about this business out of me, the Lagoan Guild of Mages will forget I was ever born. You wait and see whether I'm right. You won't do any such thing."

"I should hope not!" Pekka squeezed his hand.

Fernao hoped not, too. He was betting his happiness on it. "In the end," he said, "people matter more than kingdoms do. The kings who would say different aren't the sort of rulers I care to live under." He thought of Mezentio, of Swemmel, of Ekrekek Arpad, and shook his head. "We have one more job to do—if we must do it—and then two of them won't trouble us any more."

Pekka nodded. "And one will hold more of Derlavai in his sway than any one sovereign ever did before."

"So he will," Fernao agreed. "But he'll be more afraid of us than we are of him, and he'll have reason to be, too."

"That's true," she admitted.

"When this war's finally over, spending some quiet years in Kajaani will look very good to me," Fernao said. "Very, very good." Pekka squeezed his hand again.

Fifteen

⌒⌒⌒⌒⌒

Garivald's company stood at attention in the town square of Torgavi, not far from the Albi River, the river dividing the part of Algarve occupied by Unkerlant from the part the Kuusamans had overrun. Lieutenant Andelot strode along in front of the soldiers in their rock-gray tunics. "All men who have volunteered for further service in King Swemmel's army, one step forward!" he commanded.

About half the soldiers took that step. Here, for once, they were genuine volunteers. Along with the rest of the men who wanted nothing more than to go home, Garivald stayed where he was. Andelot dismissed the men who wanted to go on soldiering. He dismissed the common soldiers who'd chosen to leave the army. He talked briefly to one corporal who also wanted to leave, then sent him away, too. That left him alone in the square with Garivald.

"At ease, Sergeant Fariulf," he said, and Garivald relaxed from the stiff brace he'd been holding. Andelot eyed him. "I wish I could talk you into changing your mind."

"Sir, I've done enough," Garivald answered. "I've done more than enough. Only thing I want is to get back to my farm and get back to my woman." Obilot would have clouted him in the ear for talking about her like that, but she was far, far away, which was such a big part of what was wrong.

"You can't possibly hope to match a sergeant's pay and prospects with some little plot of ground down in the Duchy of Grelz," Andelot said.

"Maybe not, sir," Garivald said, "but it's *my* little plot of ground." And that was true, now. Whoever had owned that farmhouse before Garivald and Obilot took it for their own was most unlikely to come back after it. The house that had been his own—the village that had been his own—no longer existed.

"I ought to order you to stay in," Andelot said. "You're far and away the best underofficer I've ever had."

"Thank you, sir," Garivald said. "If you gave me an order like that, though, I probably wouldn't stay the best underofficer you ever had for long."

"You'd end up sorrier about that than I would," Andelot said, which was bound to be true. But the young officer didn't go on with his threat. Instead, he threw his hands in the air. "I still wish I could talk you into changing your mind."

"Sir, I want to go home," Garivald said, stubborn as only an Unkerlanter peasant knew how to be.

"Curse it, you even learned to read and write here in the army," Andelot exclaimed.

"And I thank you for teaching me, sir," Garivald said. "I still want to go home."

"All right," Andelot said. "All *right*. I could keep you here regardless of what you want. I expect you know that." He waited for Garivald to nod, then continued, "But you did serve me, and serve the kingdom, well enough to deserve better than that. If you hadn't spotted that sorcerously disguised redhead, who knows how much mischief would have come to our bridgehead by Eoforwic? Go home, then, and good luck to you."

"Thank you, sir," Garivald said. Andelot was at bottom a decent fellow, which made him unusual among the officers Garivald had seen—and which put him at a disadvantage when trying to deal with peasant stubbornness.

"I'll give you your mustering-out papers tomorrow, and passage on westbound ley-line caravans to . . . what's the name of the closest town to your farm?"

"Linnich, sir," Garivald answered. "Thank you very much."

"I'm not at all sure you're welcome," Andelot told him. "Go on. Get out of my sight. I tell you frankly, I wish I had some good reason to change my mind. If this regiment had been sent west to fight the Gyongyosians . . . But we weren't, and so you get what you want."

Garivald hurried away. Algarvians on the streets of Tor-gavi hurried to step aside. A couple of bold redheaded women—sluttish redheaded women, in the reckoning of someone from a Grelzer peasant village—made eyes at him. He ignored them; he knew they wanted money or food from him, and cared nothing about himself. He'd visited a brothel a couple of times. There, at least, the bargain was open.

An Algarvian man in a filthy, threadbare uniform tunic and kilt stared at Garivald, too, and then turned away. Some surrendered soldiers were starting to come back to their home towns. Garivald knew he would have a hard time put-ting his life together once he got back to the farm. How much harder would it be for the redheads, with their king-dom under Unkerlant's heel?

He didn't waste much sympathy on them. They'd done their best to conquer his kingdom and to kill him. They'd come much too close to managing both, too. That fellow on the street looked as if the war hadn't ended in his eyes.

When morning came, Andelot asked, "Have you by any chance changed your mind?"

"No, sir," Garivald replied without hesitation.

"Very well. Here are your orders." Andelot handed him a folded leaf of paper. "This includes your travel authoriza-tion. A westbound caravan leaves from the depot in about an hour. Good luck to you, Sergeant."

"Thank you very much, sir," Garivald said once more. As soon as Andelot left, he unfolded the orders to make sure they were what the company commander had said. He didn't want to get off the caravan car to find that the orders told whoever checked his papers there to arrest him on sight. But everything was as it should have been. The only mention of his destination was as the place where he was to receive his mustering-out bonus. He wondered if he really would get the money. Getting his back pay would have been plenty to satisfy him.

Soldiers with duffel bags slung over their shoulders crowded the depot. Most of them made way for him: the sergeant's emblems he wore on the collar tabs of his tunic still carried weight. He got a seat without trouble, too, and no one presumed to take the space next to his. He put his own duffel there. This wouldn't be such a bad trip: nothing to do but look out the window till he got home.

Later than it should have, the caravan left the depot. *So much for efficiency,* Garivald thought. Unkerlanters spent a lot of time talking about it and not very much practicing it. He shrugged resignedly. That was nothing he didn't already know.

Looking out the window proved poor sport. The landscape was battered and cratered. Every time the ley-line caravan glided through an Algarvian town, the place was in ruins. The redheads had done everything they could to hold back his countrymen. They hadn't been able to do enough.

Mile after mile of wreckage and devastation and ruin went by. Here and there, in the countryside, Algarvians tended to their crops. Most of the people in the fields were women. Garivald wondered how many men of fighting age the redheads had left. *Too many if they've got any at all,* he thought.

Then he wondered how many men of fighting age his own kingdom had left. One of the soldiers in the compartment with him was close to fifty; the other looked at most seventeen. Unkerlant had won a great victory, and had paid a great price.

For a moment, he wondered if the price had been too great. Only for a moment—then he shook his head. Whatever his kingdom had paid to beat Algarve, it would have paid more had Mezentio's men overrun all of Unkerlant. He'd seen how the Algarvians had ruled the stretches they'd occupied. Imagining that kind of rule going on and on, year after year, across the whole kingdom made him shiver even though the caravan car was stuffy and warm, almost hot.

Then he shivered again. No matter how brutally the Algarvians had ruled in Unkerlant, more than a few Grelzers—and, he supposed, more than a few men from other parts of the kingdom as well—had chosen to fight on their side and against King Swemmel. He'd had no love for Swemmel himself, not till the redheads showed him the difference between bad and worse. That anyone could have chosen Mezentio over Swemmel only proved how much better things might have been in his homeland.

For that matter, things were better in Algarve than they were in his homeland. He wondered why the redheads had tried to conquer Unkerlant. What did they want with it? Their farmers were richer than Unkerlanter peasants dreamt of being. And their townsfolk . . . To his eyes, their townsfolk all lived like nobles, and rich nobles at that.

How can they have lived the way they did when we live the way we do? He wondered about that, too. If the redheads managed such prosperity, why couldn't his own kingdom? Unkerlant was far bigger than Algarve, and had more in the way of natural riches—he knew how many problems the Algarvians had had because their dragons ran out of quicksilver. But it didn't seem to matter, not in the way people lived.

Maybe we'll live like that, too, once the war is done. We won't have it hanging over us like a thundercloud at harvest time. He could hope that might be so. He could hope, but he had trouble believing it. Mezentio's subjects had lived better than Swemmel's before the war, too. Of course, Unkerlant had gone through the Twinkings War while Garivald was a boy. That might have had something to do with it. Or it might not have, too—Algarve, after all, had fought and lost the Six Years' War.

Garivald shrugged again, yawned, and gave it up. Here, he knew all too well how little he knew. He was a peasant who'd had his letters for less than a year. Who was he to try to figure out why his kingdom had a harder time than the Algarvians at doing so many different things? He could see it was true. Why remained beyond him.

He fell asleep not long after the sun went down. By then, the ley-line caravan had left Algarve and gone into Forthweg. The Forthwegians were better off than his own countrymen, too, but to a lesser degree. He didn't know why that was so, either, and he refused to dwell on it. Sleep was better. After some of the places he'd slept during the war, a ley-line caravan car might have been a fancy hostel.

When he woke, he was in Unkerlant once more. It wasn't the Duchy of Grelz, but it was his kingdom. And it had taken a worse battering than either Forthweg or Algarve. The Algarvians had wrecked things coming west, then the

Unkerlanters pushing back toward the east. Counterattacks from both sides meant war had touched many places not once, not twice, but three or four times or even more.

As in Algarve, most of the people in the fields were women. Here, though, great stretches of land seemed to have no one cultivating them. What sort of crop would the kingdom have this year? Would it bring in any crop?

Garivald had plenty of time to wonder. He had to change ley-line caravans twice, and didn't get in to Linnich for another day and a half. A couple of inspectors met the departing soldiers. Garivald didn't think much of it; someone had to pay the men their mustering-out bonuses. "How long in Algarve?" one of the men asked him.

"Since the minute our soldiers got there," Garivald said proudly.

"Uh-*huh*," the fellow said, and scribbled a note. "You have your letters, Sergeant?"

He'd asked other men that question; Garivald had heard them answer no. More proudly still, he nodded. "Aye, sir, I do."

"Uh-*huh*," the inspector said again. "Come along with me, then." He led Garivald toward a back room in the depot.

"Is this where you'll pay me off?" Garivald asked.

Instead of answering, the inspector opened the door. Two more inspectors waited inside, and three unhappy-looking soldiers. One of the inspectors aimed a stick at Garivald's face. "You're under arrest. Charge is treason of the kingdom."

The other sergeant tore the brass squares of rank from Garivald's collar tabs. "You're not a sergeant any more—just another traitor. We'll see how you like ten years in the mines—or maybe twenty-five."

Hajjaj had never felt so free in his life. Even before he'd gone off to the university at Trapani, he'd had nothing but public service ahead of him—in those long-ago days before the Six Years' War, service to Unkerlant, and service to his own revived kingdom in the years since. He'd worked hard. He'd been influential. Without false modesty, he knew he'd served Zuwayza well.

And then King Shazli had chosen to go his own way, not Hajjaj's. Now a new, more pliant, foreign minister served the king. Hajjaj wished them both well. He wasn't used to not worrying about things outside his own household. Now, though, affairs of state were passing him by. *I could get used to that,* he thought. *I could get used to it very soon.*

He had wondered if Shazli would also order him to give Tassi back to Iskakis of Yanina. That hadn't happened. It didn't look like happening, either. Propitiating Unkerlant was one thing. Propitiating Yanina was something else again, something over which not even defeated Zuwayza needed to lose much sleep.

"You ought to write your memoirs," Kolthoum told Hajjaj one blazing summer day when they both stayed within the house's thick mud-brick walls to have as little as they could to do with the furnace heat outside.

"You flatter me," he told his senior wife. "Ministers from great kingdoms write their memoirs. Ministers from small kingdoms read them to find out how little other people remember of what they said."

"You don't give yourself enough credit," Kolthoum said.

"There are more problems than you think," Hajjaj said. "What language should I use, for instance? If I write in Zuwayzi, no one outside this kingdom will ever see the book. If I use Algarvian . . . Well, Algarvian is a stench in everyone's nostrils except in Algarve, and people there have more urgent things to worry about than what an old black man who wears no clothes has to say. And I'm so slow composing in classical Kaunian, the book would probably never get finished. I *can* write it, certainly—one has to—but it's less natural to me than either of the other tongues."

"I notice you don't mention Unkerlanter," Kolthoum remarked.

Hajjaj answered that with a grunt. Like anyone else who'd grown up back in the days when Zuwayza was part of Unkerlant, he'd learned some of the tongue of his kingdom's enormous southern neighbor. He'd taken patriotic pride in forgetting as much of it as he could since. He still spoke a bit, but he wouldn't have cared to try to write it.

And even if he had, hardly anyone east of Swemmel's kingdom understood its tongue.

But none of that was to the point. The point was that he wouldn't have used Unkerlanter to save his life. Kolthoum knew as much, too.

Tewfik walked into the chamber where Hajjaj and his senior wife were talking. With a short, stiff bow, the ancient majordomo said, "Your Excellency, you have a visitor: Minister Horthy of Gyongyos has come up from Bishah to speak with you—if you'd be so kind as to give him a few minutes, he says."

Horthy didn't speak Zuwayzi. Tewfik didn't speak Gyongyosian—or a lot of classical Kaunian, either. The Gyongyosian minister to Zuwayza must have had some work to do, getting his message across. But that was beside the point. Hajjaj said, "Why would he want to speak to me? I'm in retirement."

"You may leave affairs behind, young fellow, but affairs will take longer to leave you behind," Tewfik said. That *young fellow* never failed to amuse Hajjaj; only to Tewfik did he seem young these days. The majordomo went on, "Or shall I send him back down to the city?"

"No, no—that would be frightfully rude." Hajjaj's knees creaked as he got to his feet. "I'll see him in the library. Let me find a robe or some such thing to throw on so I don't offend him. Bring him tea and wine and cakes—let him refresh himself while he's waiting for me."

Unlike most Zuwayzin, Hajjaj kept clothes in his house. He dealt with too many foreigners to be able to avoid it. He threw on a light linen robe and went to the library to greet his guest. Gyongyos was far enough away for the political implications of kilt or trousers not to matter much.

When Hajjaj entered the library, Horthy was leafing through a volume of poetry from the days of the Kaunian Empire. He was a big, burly man, his tawny beard and long hair streaked with gray. He closed the book and bowed to Hajjaj. "A pleasure to see you, your Excellency," he said in musically accented classical Kaunian. "May the stars shine upon your spirit."

"Er, thank you," Hajjaj replied in the same language. The

Gyongyosians had strange notions about the power of the stars. "How may I serve you, sir?"

Horthy shook his head, which made him look like a puzzled lion. "You do not serve me. I come to beg the boon of your conversation, of your wisdom." He sipped at the wine Tewfik had given him. "Already you have gone to too much trouble. The wine is of grapes, not of the—dates, is that the word?—you would usually use, and you have taken the time to garb yourself. This is your home, your Excellency; if I come here, I understand your continuing your own usages."

"I am also fond of grape wine, and the robe is light." Hajjaj waved to the cushions piled on the carpeted floor. "Sit. Drink as much as you care to, of wine or tea. Eat of my cakes. When you are refreshed, I will do for you whatever I can."

"You are generous to a foreigner," Horthy said. Hajjaj sat and used pillows to make himself comfortable. Rather awkwardly, Horthy imitated him. The Gyongyosian minister ate several cakes and drank a good deal of wine.

Only after Horthy paused did Hajjaj ask, "And now, your Excellency, what brings you up into the hills on such a hot day?" As host, he was the one with the right to choose when to get down to business.

"I wish to speak to you concerning the course of this war, and concerning possible endings for it," Horthy said.

"Are you sure I am the man with whom you should be discussing these things?" Hajjaj asked. "I am retired, and have no interest in emerging from retirement. My successor would be able to serve you better, if you need his help in any official capacity."

"No." Horthy's voice was sharp. "For one thing, my being here is in no way official. For another, with due respect to your successor, you are the man who knows things."

"You honor me beyond my deserts," Hajjaj said, though what he felt was a certain amount—perhaps more than a certain amount—of vindication.

"No," Horthy repeated. "I know why you resigned. It does you honor. A man should not abandon his friends, but should stand by them even in adversity—especially in adversity."

Hajjaj shrugged. "I did what I thought right. My king did what he thought right."

"You did what you thought right. Your king did what he thought expedient," Horthy said. "I know which I prefer. Therefore, I come to you. The Kuusamans have threatened us with some new and titanically destructive sorcery. Unkerlant masses men against us. How may we escape with honor?"

"Do you believe the threat?" Hajjaj asked.

"Ekrekek Arpad does not, so Gyongyos does not," Horthy replied. "But there has been so much dreadful magic in this war, more would not surprise me. I speak unofficially, of course."

"Of course," Hajjaj echoed.

"Do you know—have you heard—anything that would lead you to believe the Kuusamans either lie or speak the truth?" the Gyongyosian minister asked.

"No, your Excellency. Whatever this magic may be—if, in fact, it is anything at all—I cannot tell you."

"What of Unkerlant?"

"You already know that. You are the last foe still in the field against King Swemmel. He loves you not. He will punish you if he can. The time has come that he thinks he can."

Horthy's broad, heavy-featured face soured into a frown. "If he should think that, he may find himself surprised."

"So he may," Hajjaj agreed politely. "Still, your Excellency, if you thought your own kingdom's victory certain, you would not have come here to me, would you?"

He wondered if he'd phrased that carefully enough. Gyongyosians were not only touchy—which bothered Hajjaj not at all, coming as he did from a touchy folk himself—but touchy in ways Zuwayzin found odd and unpredictable. Horthy muttered something in his own language, down deep in his chest. Then he returned to classical Kaunian: "There is, I fear, too much truth in what you say. Can Gyongyos rely on your kingdom's good offices in negotiating a peace with our enemies?"

"You understand, sir, that I cannot answer in any official

sense," Hajjaj said. "Were I still part of his Majesty's government, I would do everything I could toward that end: of that you may be certain. You might have done better to consult with my successor, who can speak for King Shazli. I cannot."

"Your successor would have asked me about what Gyongyos proposes to yield," Horthy growled. "Gyongyos does not propose to yield anything."

"My dear sir!" Hajjaj said. "If you will yield nothing, how do you propose to negotiate a peace?"

"We might discover that we had previously misunderstood treaties pertaining to borders and such," the Gyongyosian minister replied. "But we are, we have always been, a warrior race. Warriors do not yield."

"I . . . see," Hajjaj said slowly. And part of him did. Every man, every kingdom, needed to salve pride now and again. The Gongs found odd ways to do it, though. Professing a misunderstanding was one way not to have to admit they were beaten. Whether it would do to end the Derlavaian War . . . "Would Kuusamo and Lagoas and Unkerlant—especially Unkerlant—understand your meaning?"

"Your own excellent officials might help to make them understand," Horthy said.

"I see," Hajjaj said again. "Well, obviously, I can promise nothing. But you are welcome to tell anyone still in the government that I believe finding a ley line to peace is desirable. Anyone who wishes may ask me on this score."

Horthy inclined his leonine head. "I thank you, your Excellency. This is the reassurance I have been seeking."

He left not much later. As the sun sank in the west and the day's scorching heat at last began to ease, Hajjaj's crystallomancer told him General Ikhshid wished to speak with him. Perhaps because they were much of an age, Ikhshid had stayed in closer touch with Hajjaj than had anyone else down in Bishah. Now the white-haired officer peered out of the crystal at him and said, "It won't work."

"What won't?" Hajjaj inquired.

"Horthy's scheme," Ikhshid replied. "It won't fly. The Gongs aren't going to be able to get away with saying,

'Sorry, it was all a mistake.' They're going to have to say, 'You've beaten us. We give up.'"

"And if they won't?" Hajjaj said.

Ikhshid's face was plump, and most of the time jolly. Now he looked thoroughly grim. "If they won't, my best guess is they're going to be very, very sorry."

Because Ceorl was a war captive, he'd expected to be treated worse than the Unkerlanters who also had to labor in the cinnabar mines of the Mamming Hills. He didn't need long to realize he'd made a mistake there. The guards in the mines and the barracks treated all their victims—Unkerlanters, Forthwegians, Algarvians, Kaunians, Gyongyosians, Zuwayzin—the same way: badly. They were all small, eminently replaceable parts, to be used till used up, and then discarded.

I'm going to die here, and die pretty soon unless I do something about it, the ruffian thought as he queued up for supper. He had a mess tin not much different from the one he'd carried in Plegmund's Brigade. The only real difference was that he'd eaten pretty well as a soldier. The Unkerlanters fed the men in the mines horrible slop. He counted himself lucky when he found bits of turnip in the stew. As often as not, what he got were nettle leaves. He could have done more work with better food, but Swemmel's men didn't seem to care about that. And why should they have? They had plenty of people to take his place.

Behind him, an Algarvian said, "I'm too bloody worn to eat."

He won't last long, Ceorl thought. Men who gave up, who didn't shovel every bit of food they could into themselves no matter how vile it was, quickly turned up their toes and died. Sooner or later, Ceorl was convinced, everyone in the mines would die; the Unkerlanters had set up the system with extermination in mind. But he wouldn't give them the satisfaction of making it easy.

The queue snaked forward. Ceorl thrust his tin toward the cooks behind their vats of stew. They were also captives. They had it soft, as far as anyone here did. At the very least, they were unlikely to starve to death. They'd probably had to sell their souls—and, for all Ceorl knew, their bodies, too—to get where they were. He didn't care. He wanted the same chance.

"Fill it up," he said, a phrase similar in Unkerlanter and Forthwegian. And the cook did, digging his ladle deep down into the big pot to give Ceorl the best of what there was. Ceorl hadn't been here long, but he'd already got a name for himself as a man who wouldn't tamely yield up his life.

The luckless Algarvian behind him got mostly water in his mess tin. He didn't even complain. He just went off to find a spot where he could spoon it up. He would probably leave it unfinished, too. Someone else would get what he left. Before long, he would leave, feet first.

In the refectory, Sudaku was holding a space for Ceorl. "Thanks," the ruffian said, and sat down beside the blond from Valmiera. Sudaku had a good thick bowl of stew, too; people knew he was Ceorl's right-hand man.

"Another happy day, eh?" Sudaku said.

"Bugger happy. We got through it." Ceorl shoveled stew into himself the same way he'd shoveled ore for so long. "It'll be better tomorrow," he went on. "The supervisor who's on then doesn't know anything. Powers above, he doesn't even suspect anything. We won't have to work so hard."

"Quota," Sudaku said doubtfully.

Scorn filled Ceorl's laugh. "The Unkerlanters talk about efficiency, but they fornicating lie. They don't keep quota, either. I know they lie about that."

"Something to what you say," Sudaku admitted. Ceorl wanted to laugh again, this time at the blond. Sudaku was a trusting soul, an honest man or something close to it—not far from a fool, the way Ceorl reckoned things. But he was strong and brave, and he'd had his eyes opened for him in the desperate fighting of the last few months of the war. Anyone who came through that without learning from it would have deserved whatever happened to him.

"Come on," Ceorl said. "Let's get back to the barracks. We've got to keep watch on things, or else we're in trouble."

"Right." Sudaku didn't doubt that. Nobody in his right mind could doubt it. Only the strong had any hope of lasting here. If you didn't show your strength, you often couldn't keep it.

Bunks in the barracks were in tiers that went up four high. In the warmth of the brief southern summer, where a man slept didn't matter so much. But Ceorl had been through Unkerlanter winters. He and the gang from Plegmund's Brigade he headed had taken bunks close by the coal stove in the middle of the hall. They'd taken them and defended them with fists and boots and improvised knives. When they settled down for the night now, nobody troubled them.

On the other side of the stove, a group of Algarvian captives had carved out a similar niche for themselves. Their leader was a burly fellow whose faded, tattered uniform didn't quite match those of the soldiers alongside whom Ceorl had fought. That didn't mean the ruffian was ignorant of what sort of uniform it was.

"Ha, Oraste!" he called. "Throw anybody in gaol lately?"

"Futter you, Ceorl," the redhead replied without rancor. "You'd have done better if somebody *had* jugged you. Sooner or later, they'd've let you out. But let's see you get out of this."

Ceorl gave back an obscene gesture. Oraste laughed at him, though the Algarvian's eyes never lit up. Like any redhead, Oraste was indeed here for good. Even if he escaped the mines, he'd be hunted down in short order, for he stood out among the Unkerlanters like a crow among sea gulls. Because he couldn't get away, he naturally thought nobody else could.

You're not as smart as you think you are, Ceorl thought. Thinking themselves more clever than they really were—and than anybody else was—had always been the Algarvians' besetting vice. But Ceorl looked like anybody else around these parts. Forthwegian wasn't impossibly far removed from Unkerlanter. If he managed to escape, he thought he could stay free.

A couple of Unkerlanter thieves swaggered into the barracks, each with some of his followers in train. They waved to Ceorl and to Oraste as equals. Their gangs held the other bunks close by the stove. They'd made as much of their captivity as they could. Even the guards treated them with respect.

They and their henchmen took their places. Beyond, back toward the walls, came Algarvian captives and Unkerlanters who didn't belong to any of the principal gangs in the barracks. They were the luckless ones, the spiritless ones, who would soon lose the battle for survival. And as they died off, new men, just as lost, would pour in to take their places. Ceorl knew a sort of abstract admiration for King Swemmel. He made sure he was never short of captives.

Between supper and lights-out, men gossiped, told stories—told lies—about what they'd done in the war (except for who was talking about whom, and in which language, those of Algarvians and Unkerlanters sounded very much alike, and nobody cared who'd been on which side—here in the Mamming Hills, they were all losers), gambled, and passed around jars of clandestinely brewed spirits. Some of them, especially those beginning to fail, fell asleep as soon as they could and stayed asleep in spite of all the noise the others made.

Ceorl had learned better than to roll dice with Oraste. He couldn't prove the redhead's dice were crooked, but he'd lost to him too often to believe it nothing but chance. He didn't say anything as Oraste started fleecing a young Unkerlanter too new here to know better than to accept such invitations. Ceorl didn't care what happened to the Unkerlanter, and he was curious about how Oraste cheated so smoothly.

He didn't find out that night, any more than he had when the redhead had taken his money. After a while, even though the sky remained pale—which it would do through most of the night—a guard came in and shouted, "Lights out!"

That meant shuttering the windows, too, so that something approaching real darkness filled the barracks. Ceorl lay down on his bottom bunk, which boasted one of the thickest mattresses in the building. He'd made himself as comfortable, as well off, as one of Swemmel's captives could be. Things could have been a lot worse—he even knew that. He also knew it wasn't remotely close to being enough. He would break out if he ever found the chance.

As usual, he slept hard. The next thing he knew, the guards were screaming at the captives to get out of their bunks and line up for roll call. Routine there hadn't changed since the captives' camp outside of Trapani. Ceorl took his place, waited to sing out when his name was called, and wondered if the Unkerlanters would make a hash of the count, which they did about one day in three. *Efficiency,* he thought, and laughed a mocking laugh.

To complicate things, a ley-line caravan full of new captives chose that moment to arrive in the barracks. The guards bringing in the new fish and those trying to keep track of the ones already there started screaming at one another, each group blaming the other for its troubles. Ceorl spent his time eyeing the newcomers.

Most of them looked to be Unkerlanter soldiers—or rather, former Unkerlanter soldiers. No, Swemmel wasn't shy about jugging his own people, any more than he'd been shy about murdering his own people when the Algarvians started killing Kaunians. Swemmel wanted results, and he got them.

No one cared about roll call for a while. The captives just stood there. Had it been winter, they would have stood there till they froze. Nobody dared ask permission to go to breakfast. Eating before roll call and the count were done was unimaginable. In fact, they didn't have breakfast at all. The delay just meant they went straight to the mines. If they had nothing in their bellies, too bad.

Ceorl shoveled cinnabar ore into a handbarrow. When it was full, another captive lugged it away. Shoveling wasn't so bad as chipping cinnabar out of the vein with picks and crowbars. It also wasn't so bad as working in the refinery where quicksilver was extracted from some of the cinnabar. Despite sorcery, quicksilver fumes killed the men who worked there long before their time.

Before too long, some of the new fish started coming down into the mine. They would have needed a while to get processed, to have their names recorded and to get assigned to a barracks and a work gang. That was efficiency, too, at least as the Unkerlanters understood it. To Ceorl, it often seemed like wheels spinning uselessly on an ice-slick road. But Swemmel's men had won the war, and didn't have to worry about what he thought.

One of the new men spoke with such a strong Grelzer accent, Ceorl could hardly understand him. "Powers below eat you," the ruffian said, doing his best to make his Forthwegian sound like Unkerlanter. "I spent a good part of the war hunting whoresons like you."

The Unkerlanter followed him. "I was in the woods west of Herborn," he answered. "A lot of the bastards who hunted me didn't go home again."

"Is that so?" Ceorl threw back his head and laughed. "I hunted through those woods, and you stinking irregulars paid for it when I did."

"Murderer," the Unkerlanter said.

"Bushwhacker," Ceorl retorted. He laughed some more. "Fat fornicating lot of good our fight back then did either one of us, eh? We're both buggered now."

He had to repeat himself to get the Unkerlanter to understand that. When the fellow finally did, he nodded. "Fair enough. We both lost this war, no matter what happened to our kingdoms." He stuck out his hand. "I'm Fariulf."

"Well, futter you, Fariulf." Ceorl clasped it. "I'm Ceorl."

"Futter you, too, Ceorl," Fariulf said, squeezing. Ceorl squeezed back. The trial of strength proved as near a draw as made no difference.

"Work!" a guard shouted. Sure enough, no matter which of them was the stronger, they'd both lost the war.

Everything in Yliharma was different from anything Talsu had ever known. The air itself tasted wrong: cool and damp and salty. Even on the brightest days, the blue of the sky had a misty feel to it. And, even in summer, fog and rain could come without warning and stay for a couple of days. That would have been unimaginable in Skrunda.

The Kuusamans themselves seemed at least as strange to him as their weather did. Even Gailisa was taller than most of their men. Children eyed both Talsu and his wife in the streets, not being used to fair blue-eyed blonds. Adults did the same thing, but less blatantly. To Talsu, little swarthy slant-eyed folk with coarse black hair were the strange ones, but this was their kingdom, not his.

It wasn't even a kingdom, or not exactly—somehow, the Seven Princes held it together. The Kuusamans drank ale, not wine. They cooked with butter, not olive oil, and even put it on their bread. They wore all sorts of odd clothes, which, to a tailor, seemed even more peculiar. Their language sounded funny in his ears. Its grammar, which he and Gailisa tried to learn in thrice-weekly lessons, struck him as stranger yet. And its vocabulary, except for a few words plainly borrowed from classical Kaunian, was nothing like that of Jelgavan.

But none of that marked the biggest difference between his homeland and this place to which he and Gailisa had been exiled. He needed a while to realize what that big difference was. It came to him one afternoon as he was walking back to the flat the Kuusamans had given Gailisa and him: a bigger, finer flat than the one his whole family had used back in his home town.

"I know!" he said after giving his wife a kiss. "I've got it!"

"That's nice," Gailisa said agreeably. "What have you got?"

"Now I know why, up in Balvi, the Kuusaman minister told us living in Jelgava was like living in a dungeon," Talsu answered. "Everybody always went around watching what he said all the time."

She nodded. "Well, of course. Something bad would happen to you if you didn't, or sometimes even if you did." Her mouth twisted. "We know all about that, don't we?"

"Aye, we do," Talsu agreed. "And *that's* the difference. *We* know all about it. The Kuusamans don't. They say whatever they please whenever they feel like it, and they don't have to look over their shoulders while they're doing it. They're *free*. We weren't. We aren't, we Jelgavans. And we don't even know it."

"Some do," Gailisa answered. "Otherwise, why would the dungeons be so full?"

"That's not funny," Talsu said.

"I didn't mean it for a joke," she told him. "How could I, after everything that happened to you?"

Having had no ready comeback for that, he changed the subject: "What smells good?"

"A reindeer roast," Gailisa replied. Talsu chuckled. She rolled her eyes. There might have been a few reindeer in Jelgavan zoological parks, but surely nowhere else in the kingdom. She went on, "All the butcher shops here have as much reindeer meat as beef or mutton. It's cheaper, too."

"I'm not complaining," Talsu said. "You've picked it up before, and it tastes fine." He kissed her again to show her he meant it—and he did. He went on, "I wish the language were easier. I can't get started in business till I can talk to my customers at least a little."

"I know," Gailisa said. "When I buy things, I either read what I want off the signs—and I know I make a mess of that, too, because some of the characters don't sound the same here as they do in Jelgavan—or else I just point. It makes me feel stupid, but what else can I do?"

"Nothing else I can think of," Talsu said. "I do the same thing."

The next day, though, Talsu and Gailisa found a parcel in front of their door when they came back from their language lesson. Unwrapping it, he pulled out a Jelgavan-Kuusaman phrasebook. It looked to have been made for Kuusaman travelers in Jelgava, but it would help the other way round, too. Gailisa unfolded a note stuck in the little book. "Oh," she said. "It's in classical Kaunian." She knew next to none of the old language, so she handed Talsu the note.

His own classical Kaunian was far from perfect, too, but he did his best. " 'I hope this book will help you,' " he read. " 'It helped me when I visited your kingdom. I am Pekka, wife to Leino, whom you helped, Talsu. I am glad I could help you leave your kingdom. My husband was killed in the fighting. I was pleased to do anything I could for his friends.' "

"He's the one I wrote to," Gailisa said.

"I know," Talsu answered. "I didn't know he'd got killed, though. She must have been the one who helped me get out

of the dungeon, too, then." He blinked. "It's something—
that they paid attention to a woman, I mean."

"Maybe she's important in her own right," Gailisa said.
"She must be, in fact. The Kuusamans seem to let their
women do just about anything their men can. I like that, if
you want to know the truth."

"I'm not sure it's natural," Talsu said.

"Why not?" his wife demanded. "It's what you were
talking about before, isn't it? It's freedom."

"That's different," Talsu said.

"How?" Gailisa asked.

In his own mind, Talsu knew how. The kind of freedom
he had in mind was no more than the freedom to say what
you wanted without fear of ending up in a dungeon because
the wrong person heard you. Surely that was different from
the freedom to do what you wanted regardless of whether
you were a man or a woman. Surely it was . . . and yet, for
the life of him, he found no way to put the difference into
words.

"It just is," he said at last. Gailisa made a face at him. He
tickled her. She squealed. They weren't equal there: she
was ticklish, and he wasn't. He took unfair advantage of it.

After the next language lesson a couple of days later, the
instructor—a woman named Ryti, whose standing went
some distance toward proving Gailisa's point—asked Talsu
and his wife to stay while the other students were leaving.
In slow, careful Jelgavan, she said, "We have found a tailor
who is looking for an assistant and who speaks classical
Kaunian. Would you like to work for him?"

"I'd like to work for anyone," Talsu answered in his own
tongue. "I'd like to work for myself most, but I know I don't
speak enough Kuusaman yet. I couldn't understand the
people who'd be my customers."

"How much will this fellow pay?" Gailisa asked the
practical question.

When Ryti answered, she did so, of course, in terms of
Kuusaman money. That still didn't feel quite real to Talsu.
"What would it be in Jelgavan coins?" he asked. Ryti
thought for a moment, then told him. He blinked. "You
must be wrong," he said. "That's much too much."

After a little more thought, the language instructor shook her head. "No, I do not believe so. One of ours is about three and a half of yours, is it not so?"

It was so. To Talsu, Kuusaman silver coins were big and heavy, but not impossibly big and heavy. Things cost more in Yliharma than they had back in Skrunda, but not a great deal more. The money this fellow offered a tailor's assistant would have made an independent Jelgavan tailor prosperous. "How much does this man make for himself?" Talsu asked.

"I cannot answer that," Ryti answered. "But he does make enough to be able to pay you what he says he will. We have looked into that. We do not want people going into bad situations."

"Tell me his name. Tell me where his shop is," Talsu said. "Tell me when I need to be there, and I'll be there at that time tomorrow."

"Good." The instructor smiled. "I told him I thought you were diligent. I see I am right. His name is Valamo. His shop is near the center of town, not far from the hostel called the Principality. Here—let me draw you a map." She did, quickly and competently. "Where are you staying now?" she asked. When Talsu told her, she nodded. "I thought you dwelt in that district. There is a ley-line route that will take you close to the shop. Valamo says he would like you to be there by an hour after sunrise."

This far south, the sun rose very early in the summertime: one more thing Talsu was getting used to. Even so, he nodded. "I will."

And he did, though he missed the caravan stop closest to the tailor's shop and had to get out at the next one and then go running back up the street. People stared at him. He didn't care. He didn't want to be late, not on his first day.

"Greetings. You must be Talsu," Valamo said in classical Kaunian when he came in out of breath and sweaty. The tailor wasn't young. Past that, Talsu had trouble guessing. Kuusamans seemed to show their years less than his own countrymen did.

"Aye, sir," Talsu answered in the same tongue. "Thank you for taking me in. I shall work hard for you. I promise it."

"Good. Glad to hear it." Despite a Kuusaman accent, Valamo was more fluent in the old language than Talsu was himself. Talsu found that distressing, as he had with other Kuusamans who knew more classical Kaunian than he did. Valamo said, "Come here behind the counter, and I will show you what wants doing."

The first jobs he gave Talsu were simple repairs. Talsu handled some of them with no more than needle and thread, others with the craft tricks that were sorcery but hardly seemed like it. Before long, he was done. "Here you are," he told Valamo.

"Thank you." His new boss was polite enough, but inspected the work with a knowing eye before nodding. "Good. You have some notion of what you are doing. One can never tell beforehand, you understand. I speak without intending to cause offense."

"Of course," Talsu said. "What else have you for me to do?"

"I have the pieces of an outfit here," Valamo said. "Join them together, if you would be so kind."

"Of course," Talsu said again. He examined the pieces, got needle and thread to sew small parts of them together, and then used the sorcery an Algarvian mage had taught his father to finish the joining. All told, it took about an hour. He brought Valamo the finished garment.

This time, the Kuusaman tailor gave him a very odd look. "How did you get done so fast?" he asked. "Did you use one of those basting spells that will not last?"

"No," Talsu answered. "Judge for yourself."

Valamo poked and prodded at the tunic and leggings. He examined the stitchery, not only with his bare eyes but with a jeweler's loupe and with spells. At last, he said, "This looks to be good work. But how did you do it so well so quickly?"

Talsu explained, finishing, "I shall be glad to teach you the charm."

"You have earned your pay, by the powers above," Valamo exclaimed. "You have more than earned it. Please do teach me that spell. Before long, I am sure you will use it in a place of your own."

"A place of my own," Talsu echoed dreamily. Could he ever find such a thing in this foreign land? Slowly, he nodded to himself. *Maybe I can.*

Ealstan looked at his father. "Aye, of course I'll help you with this business," he said. "I have my doubts you really need any help from me, though."

"Well, that depends," Hestan answered. "Two can often do a job quicker than one. I suppose I could manage it myself, but I know for a fact it would take me longer. And the town officials have said they'd pay for an assistant. I'm hoping you recall that nine comes after eight and not the other way round."

"I still have some notion of how to cast accounts," Ealstan agreed. "I made a living at it in Eoforwic. You taught me well, Father—I knew more than most of the men who'd been bookkeepers for years."

That teased out one of his father's rare, slow smiles. "You make me proud of myself," Hestan said, "and that's a dangerous thing in any man."

"Why is being proud of what you're good at dangerous?" Ealstan asked. "Most ways, Eoforwic makes Gromheort look like a provincial town, and—"

"It is," his father broke in.

"But you would have made any of the bookkeepers there ashamed to call himself by the name," Ealstan went on, as if the older man hadn't spoken. "You could have gone there and got rich, Father. It makes me wonder why you stayed here."

"Don't forget, up till about the time I was your age, Gromheort was in Algarve and Eoforwic was in Unkerlant," Hestan replied. "Forthweg didn't get its freedom back till after the Six Years' War. And then, not much later, I married your mother and settled down. And I never truly wanted to be what you'd call rich. Enough is enough. Too much?" He made a face. "If you go after money for the sake of money instead of for the sake of being comfortable, it has you—you don't have it any more."

"I'm not so sure I believe that," Ealstan said.

Hestan smiled again, at least with half his mouth. "I'm

sure I didn't, not at your age. And you asked why being proud of what you're good at is dangerous? I'll tell you why: it can make you proud of yourself in general, and it can make you think you're good at things you're not."

Ealstan considered, then nodded. If that wasn't his careful, cautious father, he didn't know what was. Using a cane, Ealstan got to his feet. "Well, I already told you: if you want me to come along, I will. And if our city fathers want to know where every last copper in the rebuilding of Gromheort is going, I'll help you tell them."

"Good," Hestan said. "Truth to tell, I don't think the city fathers care so much. Baron Brorda never did, back before the war, and things haven't changed a great deal since. But the Unkerlanters want to know what everything is worth. Efficiency, you know." In a different tone of voice, that would have been praise.

As Ealstan and his father walked toward the door, Saxburh toddled down the hall toward them. "Dada!" she said. She called Ealstan that with much more conviction these days than she'd shown when she first came to Gromheort. He picked her up, gave her a kiss, and then jerked his head back in a hurry so she couldn't grab a couple of handfuls of beard and yank. She looked over at Hestan. She had a name for him too now: "Pop!"

"Hello, sweetheart." Ealstan's father kissed her, too. This time, Hestan's smile was broad and rather sappy. He took to being a grandfather with great relish.

When Vanai came around the corner, Ealstan was glad enough to put Saxburh down. Handling her and the cane was awkward, and her weight put extra strain on his bad leg. "Mama!" Saxburh squealed, and dashed for Vanai as fast as her legs would take her. As far as the baby was concerned, Vanai was the center of the universe, and everyone and everything else—Ealstan included—only details.

"Out and about?" Vanai asked as she bent to scoop up Saxburh.

"Bookkeeping," Ealstan answered.

"Ah," she said. "Good. We can use the money. Your parents are wonderfully generous, but . . ." She didn't know what to make of generous parents—or of any parents, come to that. Ealstan didn't care to think about what being raised by Brivibas would have been like.

Hestan switched to classical Kaunian: "You make it sound as if you were a burden. How long will it be before you understand that is not so?"

"You are very kind, sir," Vanai replied in the same language, which meant she didn't believe him for a moment.

Ealstan's father understood the meaning behind the meaning, too. He let out a slightly exasperated snort. "Come on, son," he said. "Maybe you can talk some sense into her when we get home."

"Oh, I doubt it," Ealstan answered. "After all, she married me, so how much sense is she likely to have?"

Now Vanai snorted. "A point," Hestan said. "A distinct point. That speaks well for your sense, but not for hers."

Although Ealstan laughed at that, Vanai didn't. "How can you say such a thing?" she demanded. "If he wasn't mad to marry a Kaunian in the middle of the war, what would you call madness?"

"I knew what I was doing," Ealstan insisted.

"You can argue about that later, too," his father said. "Come on."

Gromheort still looked like a city that had undergone a siege and a sack. Streets were largely free of rubble, but blocks had houses missing and practically every house still standing had a chunk bitten out of it. People on the street were still thinner than they should have been, too, though not so thin as when Ealstan fought his way into the city.

Some of the men weren't undernourished at all: Unkerlanter soldiers doing constable's duty, as Algarvian soldiers had before them. "When do we get to be our own kingdom again?" Ealstan asked, after walking past a couple of them.

"Things could be worse," his father answered. "As I told you back at the house, when I grew up we weren't our own kingdom. Swemmel could have annexed us instead of giving us a puppet king like Beornwulf. I feared he would."

"Penda's still my king," Ealstan said, but he pitched his voice so no one but Hestan could hear him.

"Penda was no great bargain, either," Hestan said, also

softly. "He led us into a losing war, remember, and more than five years of occupation."

"But he was *ours*," Ealstan said.

Hestan's laugh held both amusement and pain. "Spoken like a Forthwegian, son."

A labor gang trudged past, its men carrying shouldered shovels and picks and crowbars as if they were sticks. They had reason to walk like soldiers: most of them were Algarvians in tattered uniforms. The men herding them along had smooth faces and wore rock-gray tunics, which meant they came from Unkerlant.

Ealstan eyed the few Forthwegians in the labor gang. "I keep wondering if I'll see Sidroc one of these days," he said.

His father's face hardened. "I hope not. I hope he's dead. If he happens not to be dead and I do see him, I'll do my best to make sure he gets that way."

Each word might have been carved from stone. Ealstan needed a heartbeat to remember why his father sounded as he did. He'd already fled to Eoforwic himself when Sidroc killed Leofsig. He knew it had happened, but it didn't seem real to him. His memories of his cousin went back further, to school days and squabbles no more serious than those between a couple of puppies. Hestan, though, had watched Leofsig die. Recalling that, Ealstan understood every bit of his father's fury.

The gang went by. On the sidewalk coming toward Ealstan and his father was Hestan's brother, Hengist. He saw the two of them and deliberately turned away. Ealstan's father muttered something under his breath. "Him, too?" Ealstan asked in dismay—he hadn't seen, or looked for, Uncle Hengist since returning to Gromheort.

"Him, too," Hestan said gravely. "When he finally found out from dear Sidroc some of the reasons why you'd run away, he tried to turn me in to the Algarvians."

"Powers below eat him!" Ealstan exclaimed, and then, "*Tried* to turn you in to the redheads?"

His father chuckled, a noise full of cynicism. "One thing my dear, unloving brother forgot was how much the Algarvians enjoy taking bribes. I paid my way out of it, the same as I paid Mezentio's men to look the other way when Leofsig broke out of their captives' camp and came home. Saving my own neck cost me less, because I only had to pay off a couple of constables. Still, it's the thought that counts, eh?"

"The thought that counts?" Ealstan echoed. "He wanted you dead!" His father nodded. After a couple of angry steps, Ealstan said, "You ought to denounce him to the Unkerlanters. That would pay him back in his own coin."

"First you talk like a Forthwegian, and then you talk like a bookkeeper," Hestan said. "Anyone would think you were my own son." He stooped, picked up a quarter of a brick, and tossed it up and down, up and down. "Don't think I haven't thought about it. I remember everything he did to me, and everything Sidroc did to the whole family, and I want vengeance so much I can taste it. But then I remember he's my brother, too, in spite of everything. I don't need revenge that badly."

"*I'd* take it." Ealstan's voice was fierce and hot.

"For my sake, let it go," his father said. "If Hengist ever causes us more trouble, then aye, go ahead. But I don't think he will. He knows we could tell the Unkerlanters about Sidroc. That would make Hengist a traitor, too, if I rightly read some of these new laws King Beornwulf has put forth. How's your leg holding up?"

"Not bad," Ealstan answered. He didn't push his father any more about Sidroc or Uncle Hengist; Hestan wouldn't have changed the subject like that unless he didn't want to talk about them at all.

A couple of minutes later, Hestan said, "Here we are. If I remember rightly, the Algarvians used this place for one of their field hospitals. The Unkerlanters did try not to toss eggs at those on purpose, which is probably why it's still standing."

Ealstan recognized a couple of the men waiting for them inside the red brick building. The place kept the smell of a field hospital, even now: pus and ordure warring with strong soap and the tingling scents of various decoctions. It must have soaked into the bricks.

One of the men he didn't know spoke to Hestan: "So this is your boy, eh? Chip off the old block. If he's as good with numbers as you are, or even half as good, we'll be well served."

"He manages just fine," Hestan answered. He introduced Ealstan to the men, saying, "If it weren't for this crowd, a lot less of Gromheort would be standing today."

"Pleased to meet you all," Ealstan said. "I spent a good deal of the time outside of town, trying to knock things flat."

"Boy does a good job at everything he sets his hand to, doesn't he?" Hestan said. Several of the powerful men in Gromheort laughed.

"Let's see what the two of you can do when you set a hand to our books here," said the one who'd spoken before—his name was Osferth. He pointed to the two ledgers, which sat side by side on a table at the back of the hall. "Got to keep King Swemmel's inspectors happy, you know, if such a thing is possible."

Ealstan's father sat down in front of one, Ealstan himself in front of the other. He sighed with relief as the weight came off his wounded leg. The two bookkeepers bent over the ledgers and got to work.

As far as Colonel Lurcanio could tell, the Valmierans didn't know much about interrogation and were doing their level best to forget everything they could about what had happened to their kingdom while the Algarvians occupied it. The officer posturing at him now was a case in point.

"No," Lurcanio said with such patience as he could muster. "I did not rape Marchioness Krasta. I had no need to rape her. She gave herself to me of her own free will."

"Suppose I tell you the marchioness herself has given you the lie?" the officer thundered, as if trying to impress a panel of judges.

"Suppose you do?" Lurcanio said mildly. "I would say— I do say—she is lying."

"And why should we prefer your word to hers?" the Valmieran demanded. "You have more to gain by lying than she does."

"If you care about the truth there, you might really try to find it," Lurcanio said. "You could ask Viscount Valnu what he knows, for instance."

As he'd hoped it would, that knocked the interrogator back on his heels. Valnu was a hero of the underground, so his word carried weight. And Lurcanio's guess was that he, unlike Krasta, wouldn't lie for the fun of it. Also, interrogating someone else meant the Algarvians might not try to question Lurcanio himself under torture or under sorcery. He hadn't raped Krasta, but they might find plenty of other things for which to put a rope around his neck.

The officer said, "Viscount Valnu cannot *know* the truth."

"Indeed," Lurcanio agreed. "Only Krasta and I can *know* the truth. But Valnu will know what Krasta said to him about what we did, and I have no doubt she said a great deal: getting her to stop talking has always been much harder than getting her to start."

"When will you give over your slanders of the decent citizens of Valmiera?" the officer demanded indignantly.

"For one thing, truth is always a defense against a charge of slander," replied Lurcanio, who feared other charges awaited against which he had no defense. But he intended to make his captors squirm as long as he could, and so went on, "As for dear Krasta, considering some of the things we did, I am not altogether sure she is one of your precious 'decent citizens of Valmiera.' Still, I will tell you she enjoyed them all, whether decent or not."

"How dare you say such things?" the Valmieran officer gabbled.

Lurcanio hid a smile. He didn't play by the rules the victors thought they'd set up. He didn't act afraid, and he wasn't apologetic. That confused the blonds. As long as they were confused, as long as they had trouble deciding what to do about—and to—him, he wasn't too bad off. If they did decide . . . "How dare she say such things about me?" he returned, sounding as indignant as he could. "I, at least, am telling the truth, which she certainly is not."

"You were her lover at the same time as you were trying to hunt down and kill her brother, the illustrious Marquis Skarnu," the officer said, as if he'd scored a point.

"Well, what if I was?" Lurcanio answered. "That may have been in poor taste, but you will have precious few men left in a kingdom if you set about killing everyone guilty of poor taste. And Skarnu was in arms against my kingdom, as he himself would be the first to tell you. He was, in fact, in arms against my kingdom after King Gainibu surrendered. What do you people do to Algarvians captured in arms against your occupying armies? Nothing pretty, and you know it as well as I."

"That has nothing to do with what you tried to do to Skarnu," the Valmieran said.

"Of course it does, you foolish little man," Lurcanio said. "If you are too dense to see it, I hope they take you away and give me an interrogator with the sense to understand plain speech in his own language." That was the last thing he wanted, but the officer didn't need to know it.

"If you insult me here, it will only go harder for you," the blond warned, flushing with anger.

"Ah. Splendid!" Lurcanio gave him a seated bow. "I thank you for admitting that what I did and did not do during the late war has in fact nothing to do with what will happen to me."

"I said nothing of the sort!" The Valmieran turned redder still.

"I beg your pardon." Lurcanio bobbed his head once more. "That was what it sounded like to me."

"Guards!" the officer said, and several Valmieran soldiers took one step forward from the places against the wall where they'd stood. The interrogator pointed to Lurcanio. "Back to his cell with this one. He's not ready to tell the truth yet."

A Valmieran sergeant pointed his stick at Lurcanio's belly. "Get moving," he said. Him Lurcanio obeyed without backtalk and without hesitation. A confused or frightened ordinary soldier was liable to get rid of his confusion and fear by blazing. Games that tied the earnest and rather stupid interrogator in knots would be useless or worse against a man for whom simple brutality solved so many problems.

We thought simple brutality could solve the problem of the underground, Lurcanio thought as he marched along in front of the guards. *Were we any more clever than a simple sergeant?* Valmieran captives snarled curses at him when he went past their cells. He strode by as if they didn't exist. They threw things less often then. They weren't supposed to have anything to throw, but he knew those rules could bend when authorities wanted something unfortunate but also unofficial to happen to a captive.

Today, he reached his own cell unscathed. The door slammed behind him. A bar outside the cell thudded down. The sergeant muttered a charm to keep anyone from magically tampering with the bar. Lurcanio wished he were a mage. He shrugged. Had he been, he would have gone to a more sorcerously secure prison than this one.

As cells went, he supposed his wasn't so bad. It was certainly better than the ones his own folk had given Valmieran captives during the war. His cot was severely plain, but it was a cot, not a moldy straw pallet or bare stone. His window had bars, but it was a window. He had a privy, not a stinking slop bucket. He would have fired any cook who gave him food like the stuff he got here, but he did get enough to hold hunger at bay.

But what did this mild treatment mean? Did he have some chance of getting back to Algarve because the Valmierans weren't sure of exactly what he'd done? Or were they keeping him comfortable now because they knew how harsh they would soon be with him? He didn't know. By the nature of things, he couldn't know. Brooding over it would have gone a long way toward driving him mad, and so he did his best not to brood. His best wasn't always good enough.

Presently, they fed him again. Light leaked out of the sky. He had no lamp in the cell. The hallways had lamps, but not much light came through the small window in the door. He lay down and went to sleep. This was an animal sort of life, and he tried to store up rest against a time when he might badly need it.

Somewhere in the middle of the night, the door flew open. Guards hauled him out of bed. "Come on, you son of a whore!" one of them growled. Another gave him a round-house slap in the face that snapped his head back.

Ah, he thought as they hustled him along the corridors to a room where he'd never gone before. *At last, the gloves come off.* He was afraid—he would have been an imbecile not to be afraid—but he was oddly relieved, too. He'd been waiting for a moment like this. Now it was here.

The guards slammed him down onto a hard stool. A bright light blazed into his face. When he involuntarily looked away, he got slapped again. "Face forward!" a guard shouted.

From behind that blazing lamp, a Valmieran rasped, "You were the one who sent some hundreds of folk of Kaunian blood south to the Strait of Valmiera to be slain for your kingdom's foul sorceries."

"I do not know anything about—" Lurcanio began.

Yet another slap almost knocked him off the stool. "Don't waste my time with lies," warned the blond behind the lamp. "You'll be sorry if you do. Now answer my questions, you stinking, worthless sack of shit. You were the one who sent those people to die."

It wasn't a question. That didn't matter. What mattered was that the Valmierans knew how to play the game of interrogation after all. His head ringing, the taste of his own blood in his mouth, Lurcanio fought to gather himself. If he admitted the charge, he was a dead man. That much he could see. "No," he said through bruised and cut lips. "I was not the one."

"Liar!" the interrogator shouted. One of the guards punched Lurcanio in the belly. He groaned. For one thing, he couldn't help himself. For another, he wanted them to think him hurt worse than he was. "So you weren't the one, eh?" the Valmieran sneered. "A likely story! Well, if you say you weren't, who was? *Talk,* powers below eat you!"

That question had as many eggs buried in it as a field on the western front. Another slap encouraged Lurcanio not to take too long answering. He didn't know how much the Valmierans knew. He didn't want to betray his own countrymen, but he didn't want the charge sticking to him alone, either. He'd had something to do with sending blonds south, but he was a long way from the only one.

"Our orders came from Trapani," he said. "We only followed—"

This time, the slap did knock him off the stool. He thudded down onto stone. The guards kicked him a few times before they picked him up. The interrogator, still unseen, said, "That won't work, Algarvian. Aye, those whoresons in Trapani'll get the axe for what they did. But you don't get off for following orders. You know the difference between war and murder. You're a big boy."

"You are the victors," Lurcanio said. "You can do with me as you please."

"You bet your balls we can, redhead. You just bet," the Valmieran gloated. "But weren't you listening? You've got a chance—a skinny chance, but a chance—of saving your lousy neck. Name names, and we just might be happy enough with you to keep you breathing."

Is he lying? He probably is, but do I dare take the chance? Lurcanio thought, as well as he could think with pain pouring through him. *And if I name the names of others—or even if I don't—who will be naming me?* One more thing he didn't care to dwell on.

"Talk, you fornicating bastard," the interrogator snarled. "We know all about your fornicating, too. She'll get hers— wait and see if she doesn't. You have this one chance, pal. Talk now or else don't . . . and see what happens to you then."

Would all his captive countrymen keep quiet? A bitter smile twisted Lurcanio's lips. Algarvians were no less fond of saving their own skins than the folk of any other kingdom. Somebody would name him—and even if someone didn't, how many documents had the Valmierans captured? There'd been no time to destroy them all.

"Last chance, Algarvian; very, very last," the fellow behind the lamp said. "We know what *you* did. Who did it with you?"

Lurcanio felt old. He felt tired. He hurt all over. Had they been toying with him up till now, to make this seem harsher when it came? He had no answers, save that he didn't want to die. That, he knew. "Well," he said, "to begin with, there was . . ."

Sixteen

$\sim$

Cottbus had changed. Marshal Rathar hadn't seen the capital of Unkerlant this gay since . . . Now that he thought about it, he'd never seen Cottbus so gay. Gaiety and Unkerlanters seldom went together.

He'd seen the capital gray and frightened before the Derlavaian War, when nobody knew whom King Swemmel's inspectors would seize next, or on what imagined charge. And he'd seen Cottbus past frightened the first autumn of the war against Algarve: he'd seen it on the ragged edge of panic then, with functionaries burning papers and looking to flee west any way they could, expecting the city to fall to the redheads any day. But Cottbus hadn't fallen, and he'd also seen it grimly determined to do to King Mezentio what he'd come so close to doing here.

With Algarve beaten, the city itself seemed on holiday. People in the streets smiled. They stopped to chat with one another. Before, they would have reckoned that dangerous. Who could say for certain whether a friend was only a friend, or also an informer? No one, and few took the chance.

Unkerlant remained at war with Gyongyos, of course, but who took the Gongs seriously? Aye, they were enemies, no doubt of that, but so what? They were a long way off. They'd never had a chance to get anywhere near Cottbus, no matter how successful they were in the field. They could have been nuisances, but no more. As far as Rathar was concerned, that made them almost the ideal foes.

What made them even more perfect as enemies was the war they were fighting against Kuusamo through the islands of the Bothnian Ocean. They'd been losing that war for some time, and pulling men out of western Unkerlant to try, without much luck, to tip the balance back their way.

They'd got away with that, because Unkerlant had been busy elsewhere. Now . . .

Now Rathar walked across the great plaza surrounding the palace at the heart of Cottbus. The square was more crowded than he ever remembered seeing it. Women's long, bright tunics put him in mind of flowers swaying in the breeze. He laughed at himself. *You'll be writing poetry next.*

Even inside the palace, courtiers and flunkies went about their business with their heads up. A lot of them were smiling, too. They didn't look as if they were sneaking from one place to another, as they so often did. "Come with me, lord Marshal," one of them said, nodding to Rathar. "I know his Majesty will be glad to see you."

What Rathar knew was that King Swemmel was never glad to see anybody. And when he got to the anteroom outside the king's private audience chamber, age-old Unkerlanter routine reasserted itself. He unbelted his ceremonial sword and gave it to the guards there. They hung it on the wall, then thoroughly and intimately searched him to make sure he bore no other weapons. Once they were satisfied, they passed him in to the audience chamber.

Routine persisted there, too. Swemmel sat in his high seat. Rathar sank down on his knees and his belly before his sovereign, knocking his forehead against the carpet as he sang the king's praises. Only when Swemmel said, "We give you leave to rise," did he get to his feet. Sitting in Swemmel's presence was unimaginable. The king leaned forward, peering at him. In his high, thin voice, he asked, "Shall we serve Gyongyos as we served Algarve?"

"Well, your Majesty, I doubt our men will march into Gyorvar any time soon," Rathar replied. "But we ought to be able to drive the Gongs out of our kingdom, and I think we should take a bite out of them, too."

"Many men hereabouts have told us that Gyongyos will be utterly cast down and overthrown," the king said. "Why don't you, who command our armies, promise the like or even more?"

Courtiers, Rathar thought contemptuously. *Of course they can promise everything: they don't have to deliver. But I do.* "Your Majesty," he said, "I can tell you what you want to hear, or else I can tell you the truth. Which would you rather?"

With King Swemmel, the question had no obvious answer. Swemmel had punished plenty of men who'd tried to tell him the truth. Whatever fantasies went on in his mind must often have seemed more real to him than the world as it was. He wasn't stupid. People who thought he was commonly paid for that mistake in short order. But he was . . . strange. He muttered to himself before coming out with something that astonished Rathar: "Well, we don't want Gyorvar anyhow."

"Your Majesty?" The marshal wasn't sure he'd heard straight. Grabbing with both hands had always been Swemmel's way. To say he wasn't interested in seizing the capital of Gyongyos was . . . more than strange.

But he repeated himself: "We don't want Gyorvar. There won't be anything left of the place before long, anyhow."

"What do you mean, your Majesty?" Rathar asked cautiously. He could usually tell when the king drifted into delusion. He couldn't do anything about it, of course, but he could tell. Today, King Swemmel was as matter-of-fact as if talking about the weather. He was, if anything, more matter-of-fact than if talking about the weather, for he rarely had anything to do with it. He was a creature of the palace, and came forth from it as seldom as he could. His journey to Herborn to watch false King Raniero of Grelz die had been out of the ordinary, and showed how important he thought that was. *If I'd captured Mezentio, he would have come to Trapani, too,* Rathar thought.

"We mean what we say," Swemmel told him. "What else would we mean?"

"Of course, your Majesty. But please forgive me, for I don't understand what you're saying."

King Swemmel made an exasperated noise. "Did we not tell you the cursed islanders, powers below eat them, can keep nothing secret from us, no, not even if they work their mischief in the middle of the Bothnian Ocean?"

Rathar nodded; the king had said something like that in one of their conversations by crystal. But the marshal still failed to see how the pieces fit together. "I'm sorry. What does whatever the Kuusamans and Lagoans may be up to out in the Bothnian Ocean have to do with Gyorvar?"

"They will do it there next," Swemmel replied, "and when they do . . ." He made a fist and brought it down on the gem-encrusted arm of his high seat. "No point to spending Unkerlanter lives on Gyorvar. The Gongs will spend lives, by the powers above. Oh, aye, how they will spend them!" Sudden gloating anticipation filled his voice.

Sudden alarm filled Marshal Rathar. "Your Majesty, do you mean the islanders have some strong new sorcery they can work against Gyorvar?"

"Of course. What did you think we meant?"

"Till now, I didn't know." Rathar wished he'd learned a great deal sooner. Swemmel clutched secrets like a miser clutching silver. "If they can do that to Gyorvar, can they also do it to Cottbus?"

As soon as the words were out of his mouth, he wondered if he should have kept quiet. Swemmel was sure everyone around him was out to get him and every kingdom around Unkerlant out to destroy it: and that in good times. In bad, the king's fear could be like a choking cloud. But now Swemmel only nodded grimly. "They can. We know they can. We are not safe, not until we learn how to do the like to them."

"How long will that be?" Rathar asked. Kuusamo and Lagoas were not enemies to Unkerlant—not now. If they could badly harm this kingdom while Unkerlant couldn't strike back, that limited how far Swemmel—and Rathar— dared go in antagonizing them.

Swemmel half snorted, half spat in disgust. "That fool of an Addanz does not know. He spent the war chasing after Algarvian mageries, and now, when we ask him—when we order him—to switch ley lines, we find he cannot do it quickly. He calls himself archmage. We call him archidiot."

Rathar knew a certain amount of sympathy for Addanz. He'd done what he'd needed to do for the kingdom's survival. Doing much of it had horrified him; he wasn't a man who took naturally to murder. But he and his fellow wizards had to learn new things. Without a doubt, Swemmel was right about that.

"Has he any idea how long this will take? Any idea at all?" Rathar tried again. He might have to try to head off Swemmel himself at some time in the future. One more war might be—probably would be—one more than Unkerlant could stand.

"He speaks of years," the king said. "Years! Why were the blunderers he leads not doing more before?"

That was so breathtakingly unfair, Rathar didn't bother responding to it. He stuck to what he could handle: "Will having the islanders know what they know, whatever it is, hurt our campaign against the Gongs?"

"It should not." Swemmel glowered down at Rathar. "It had better not, or you will answer for it."

"Of course, your Majesty," Rathar said wearily. He tried to look on the bright side of things: "Kuusamo and Lagoas want Gyongyos beaten, too. And then the war—all of the war—will be over. Then we can go on about the business of putting the kingdom back on its feet again."

As far as he was concerned, that was the most important thing ahead for Unkerlant. King Swemmel gave an indifferent sniff. "We have enemies everywhere, Marshal," he said. "We must make sure they cannot harm us." Did he mean *we* as the people of Unkerlant or in the royal sense? Rathar couldn't tell, not here. He wondered if Swemmel recognized the distinction. The king went on, "Everyone who stands in our way shall be cast down and destroyed. Enemies and traitors deserve destruction. If only Mezentio had lived!"

If Mezentio had lived, he might still be alive, alive and wishing for death. Thinking about what Swemmel would have done to the King of Algarve made Rathar shiver, though the audience chamber was warm and stuffy. To keep from thinking of such things, he said, "We'll soon be in position to begin the attack against Gyongyos."

"We know." But Swemmel didn't sound happy, even at the prospect of beating the last of his foes still in the field. A moment later, he explained why: "We spend our blood, as usual, and the cursed islanders reap the benefit. D'you think they could have invaded the Derlavaian mainland unless our soldiers were keeping the bulk of the Algarvian army busy in the west? Not likely!"

"No, your Majesty, not likely," Marshal Rathar agreed, "unless, that is, they used this new strong sorcery of theirs, whatever it is, against Mezentio's men."

He did want to keep King Swemmel as closely connected to reality as he could. If Kuusamo and Lagoas had this dangerous new magical weapon, Swemmel needed to remember that, or he—and Unkerlant—would fall into danger. But the king's muttering and eye-rolling alarmed Rathar. "They're all against us, every cursed one of them," Swemmel hissed. "But they'll pay, too. Oh, how they'll pay."

"We have to be careful, your Majesty," Rathar said. "While they have it and we don't, we're vulnerable."

"We know we do, and so we shall," King Swemmel replied. "We shall pay the butcher's bill in Gyongyos on account of it. But the day of reckoning shall come. Never forget it for a moment, Marshal. Even against those who play at aiding us, we shall be avenged."

Rathar nodded. Only later did he wonder whether that warning was aimed at Kuusamo and Lagoas . . . or at him.

Bembo knew he wouldn't win a footrace any time soon. If a robber tried to run away from him, odds were the whoreson would get away. On the other hand, that had been true throughout his career as a constable. Long before he'd got a broken leg, he'd had a big belly.

By the middle of summer, though, the leg had healed to the point where he could get around without canes. "I'm ready to go back to work," he told Saffa.

The sketch artist snorted. "Tell that to somebody who doesn't know you," she said. "You're never ready to work, even when you're there. Come on, Bembo—make me believe you're not the laziest man who ever wore a constable's uniform."

That stung, not least because it held so much truth. Bembo put the best face on it he could: "Other people look busier than I do because I get it right the first time and they have to run around chasing after themselves."

"Captain Sasso might believe that," Saffa said. "A lot of times, officers will believe anything. Me, I know better."

Since Bembo knew better, too, he contented himself with sticking out his tongue at her. "Well, any which way, I'm going to find out. I never used to think I'd be glad to walk a beat in Tricarico. After everything that went on in the west, though, this will be a treat." He wouldn't have to worry about rounding up Kaunians here, or about a Forthwegian uprising, or about the Unkerlanters rolling east like a flood tide about to drown the world. Criminals? Wife-beaters? After all he'd been through in Gromheort and Eoforwic, he would take them in his still-limping stride.

At the constabulary station, the sergeant at the front desk—a man only about half as wide as Sergeant Pesaro, who'd sat in that seat for years—nodded and said, "Aye, go on upstairs to Captain Sasso. He's the one who makes you jump through the hoops."

"What hoops are there?" Bembo asked. "I got my leg broken fighting for my kingdom—not constabulary duty, *fighting*—and now I've got to jump through hoops?"

"Go on." The sergeant jerked a thumb at the stairway. He was no more disposed to argue than any other sergeant Bembo had ever known.

"Ah, Bembo," Sasso said when Bembo was admitted to his august presence. "How good to see you back healthy again."

"Thank you, sir," Bembo replied, though he felt none too healthy. Climbing the stairs had been hard on his leg. He wasn't about to admit that, though. Nodding to the officer, he went on, "I'm ready to get back to it."

Captain Sasso nodded. He wasn't much older than Bembo; well-founded rumor said he'd gained his fancy rank by knowing to whom to say aye at any given moment. "I'm sure you are," he replied. "But there are certain . . . formalities you have to go through first."

The sergeant had spoken of jumping through hoops. Now Sasso talked about formalities. "Like what, sir?" Bembo asked cautiously.

"You went west," Sasso said.

"Aye, sir, of course I did," Bembo replied. Sasso was the one who'd sent him west, along with Pesaro and Oraste and several other constables.

"We have orders from the occupying powers that no man who went west is to serve as a constable before he goes through an interrogation by one of their mages," Captain Sasso said. "The penalties for going against that particular order are nastier than I really want to think about."

"What kind of interrogation? What for?" Bembo was honestly confused.

Captain Sasso made a steeple of his fingertips and spelled things out for him: "The occupying powers don't want anyone who was involved with whatever may have happened in the west with the Kaunians to do any kind of work that entails the trust of the kingdom. You have to understand, Bembo—it's not up to me. I didn't give the order. I'm only following it."

Bembo grunted. He'd only followed orders in the west. Were they going to punish him for it now? And how nasty would this interrogation prove? Every time he thought about that dreadful old Kuusaman wizard, his heart stuttered in his chest. That whoreson had been able to look all the way down to the bottom of his soul. *He didn't spit in my face,* Bembo reminded himself. *Quite.*

He steadied himself. "Bring on the cursed wizards. I'm ready for 'em."

Sasso blinked. "Are you sure?"

"Of course I'm sure," Bembo answered. "Either they'll let me back in or they won't. If they don't, how am I worse off than I would be if I didn't try at all?"

"A point," the constabulary captain admitted. "You have nerve, don't you?"

"Sir, I have the balls of a burglar." Bembo grinned at Sasso. "I nailed 'em to the wall of my flat, and the burglar's talked like this"—he raised his voice to a high falsetto squeak—"ever since."

Captain Sasso laughed. "All right. You'll get the chance to prove it. Come along with me. I'll take you to the mage. Do you know any classical Kaunian?"

"Only a little," Bembo said. "I'm like most people—they tried to thrash it into me at school, and I forgot it as soon as I escaped."

"Escaped?" Sasso got up from his desk. "You've got a way with words, too. Thinking back, I remember that. How many of the reports you filed before the war were nothing but wind and air?" Before Bembo could answer, the captain shook his head. "Don't tell me. I don't want to know. Just come on."

"Where are we going?" Bembo asked. "If the stinking Kuusamans want to deal with constables, don't they have a wizard here?"

"Powers above, no!" Captain Sasso said. "We go to them. They don't come to us—they won the fornicating war. But I don't dare *not* go to them, powers below eat 'em all. Like I said, if they find out I've hired anybody who isn't checked . . ." He let out a hiss to show what was likely to happen to him.

"Ah," Bembo said. "All right." *If we have to go somewhere else for this, that explains why Saffa didn't know about it and warn me.*

The Kuusaman garrison—to which a few Jelgavan soldiers and officials were also attached—was headquartered not far from Tricarico's central plaza. The Jelgavans acted as if Bembo and Sasso were beneath their notice. The Kuusamans simply dealt with them. Jelgava had lost its share of the war; Kuusamo had won its. Bembo wondered what that said about the two kingdoms. Actually, he didn't wonder. He had a pretty good idea what it said—nothing good about King Donalitu's realm.

To his relief, the Kuusaman mage who questioned him turned out to speak fluent Algarvian. "So," the fellow said. "You used to be a constable, and you want to be a constable again? And in between times you were . . . where? Answer truthfully." He made a couple of passes at Bembo. "I will know if you lie—and if you do, you will not be a constable again."

Bembo wondered whether to believe him. An Algarvian would not have phrased the warning so baldly. But Bembo had seen that Kuusamans didn't indulge in flights of fancy, as his own countrymen delighted in doing. Besides which, he saw no point in lying here. "I was in Gromheort, and later in Eoforwic. I fought against the Forthwegian uprising there, and I was wounded when the Unkerlanters flung eggs into the place at the start of their big attack."

"I see," the slant-eyed mage said neutrally. "This is all very interesting, but not very important."

"It is to me," Bembo said. "It was my leg."

"Not very important to what we are talking about here," the Kuusaman said. "What we are talking about here is your dealings with the Kaunians in these two cities and thereabouts. You had dealings with Kaunians in these two cities and thereabouts, did you not?"

"Aye," Bembo answered. He'd been a constable in the west. How could he have helped dealing with blonds?

"All right, then." The Kuusaman grudged him a nod. "Now we come down to it. Did you ever *kill* any Kaunians while you were on duty in these two cities and thereabouts?"

"Aye," Bembo said again.

"Then what are you doing here wasting my time and yours?" the Kuusaman demanded, showing annoyance for the first time. "I shall have to speak to your captain. He knows the regulations, and knows them well."

"Will you listen to me?" Bembo said. "Let me tell you how it was, and powers below and your miserable spell both eat me if I lie." He told the mage the tale of how he and Oraste had met the drunken ruin of a Kaunian mage sleeping in an overgrown park in Gromheort, and how the Kaunian hadn't survived the encounter. "He was out after curfew, and he would have done something to us—he tried to do something to us, which is why we blazed the old bugger. And what does your precious magecraft have to say about that?"

"At first glance, it seems the truth. But I shall probe deeper." The Kuusaman made more passes. He muttered in his own language. By the time he got done, he looked dissatisfied. "This is the truth—the truth as you remember it, at least."

If he asked a question like, *Is that the only time you killed a Kaunian?*—if he asked a question like that, Bembo would never be a constable again. To keep him from asking it, Bembo went on, "I don't suppose you want to hear about the time I pulled two Kaunians right out of the old noble's castle in Gromheort and let 'em get away."

"Say on," the Kuusaman mage told him. "Remember, though: if you lie, you will be permanently disqualified."

"Who said anything about lying?" Bembo said with what he hoped was a suitable show of indignation. He told the mage about spiriting Doldasai's parents out of the castle the Algarvians used as their headquarters in Gromheort and uniting them with their daughter, finishing, "Go ahead and use your fancy spell. *I'm* not lying." He struck a pose, as well as he could while sitting down.

The Kuusaman mage made his passes. He muttered his charm. His eyebrows rose slightly. He made more passes. He muttered another charm, this one, Bembo thought, in classical Kaunian. Those black eyebrows rose again. "How interesting," he said at last. "This *does* seem to be the truth. Will you now tell me you did it from the goodness of your heart?"

"No," Bembo said. "I did it on account of I thought I'd get a terrific piece if I managed it, and I did, too." He'd never mentioned Doldasai to Saffa, not even when he was spilling his guts to her, and he never intended to, either.

To his surprise, the Kuusaman turned red under his golden skin. *Prissy whoreson,* Bembo thought. "You are venal," the mage said. "I suspect you took bribes in the form of money, too." He might have accused Bembo of picking his nose and then sticking his finger in his mouth.

But Bembo only nodded. "Of course I did." Fearing the spell wasn't what made him tell the truth there. To him—to most Algarvians—bribes were nothing more than grease to help make wheels turn smoothly and quietly.

The mage looked almost as if he were about to be sick. "Disgustingly venal," he muttered. "But that is not what I am searching for. Very well. I pronounce you fit to resume service as a constable." He filled out forms as fast as he could. Plainly, he wanted Bembo out of his sight as fast as he could arrange it. He was too embarrassed, or perhaps too revolted, to probe much deeper.

Bembo hadn't thought things would work out just like that, but he had thought they would work out. He usually did. And, more often than not, he turned out to be right.

* * *

Little by little, Vanai got used to living in Gromheort. Little by little, she got used to not living in fear. She needed a while to believe in her belly that no one would come through the streets shouting, "Kaunians, come forth!" The Algarvians were gone. They wouldn't be back. A lot of them were dead. And the Forthwegians who'd bawled for Kaunian blood along with the redheads during the occupation were for the time being pretending they'd never done any such thing.

Living in the same house with Ealstan's mother and father helped Vanai get over the terror she'd known. It proved to her, day after quiet day, that Forthwegians could like her and treat her as a person regardless of her blood. Ealstan did, of course, but that was different. That was special. Elfryth and Hestan hadn't fallen in love with her, though they certainly had with her daughter.

Conberge often visited the house. The first time Vanai met Ealstan's older sister, she stared intently at her, then asked, "Do I really look like that when I wear my Forthwegian mask?"

"I should say you do," Conberge answered, eyeing her with just as much curiosity. "We could be twins, I think."

"Oh, good!" Vanai exclaimed. "I'm so lucky, then!" That raised a blush from Conberge despite her swarthy Forthwegian complexion. Vanai meant it, too. She thought Conberge an outstandingly good-looking woman in the dark, buxom, strong-featured way of her people.

"I'm prettier with her face than I am with my own," she told Ealstan that night.

"No, you're not," he answered, and kissed her. "You're beautiful both ways." He spoke with great conviction. He didn't quite make Vanai believe him, but he did prove he loved her. She already knew that, of course, but more proofs were always welcome. She did her best to show Ealstan it went both ways, too.

As summer advanced, she and Conberge stopped looking just alike when she wore her sorcerous disguise, for her sister-in-law's belly began to bulge, as her own had not so very long before. Conberge also grew even bustier than she had been, which Vanai thought almost too much of a good thing. She doubted whether Grimbald, Conberge's husband, agreed.

The two of them walked to the market square together one blistering afternoon. Vanai had Saxburh along. Conberge watched her niece. "I ought to carry around a little notebook," she said, "so I'll know, 'All right, she does *this* when she's *that* old, and then when she gets a little older she'll do *that* instead.' "

Vanai rolled her eyes. "What she's doing now is being a nuisance." She'd brought along a carriage, but Saxburh pitched a fit every time she tried to put her into it. She'd just learned to walk, and walking was what she wanted to do. That meant her mother and her aunt had to match her pace, which annoyed Vanai but didn't bother Saxburh at all.

"It's all right," Conberge said. "I'm in no hurry." She set a hand on her belly. "I feel so big and slow already, but I know I'm going to get a lot bigger. I'll be the size of a behemoth by the time I finally have the baby, won't I?"

"No, not quite. But you're right—you'll think you are," Vanai answered.

A squad of Unkerlanter soldiers patrolled the market square. Vanai was finally used to men who shaved their faces, though the smooth-faced Unkerlanters had startled her the first few times she saw them. They didn't give her cold chills, the way Algarvian troopers would have. For one thing, they didn't despise her people in particular. For another, they didn't leer the way the redheads did. When they stared around, it seemed much more like wonder at being in a big city. She couldn't know, but she would have guessed they all came from villages far smaller than Oyngestun had ever been. And they all looked so young: she doubted any of them could have been above seventeen.

When she remarked on that, Conberge nodded. "Unkerlant had to give sticks to boys," she answered. "The Algarvians killed most of their men." Vanai blinked. In its bleak clarity, that sounded like something Hestan might have said.

They bought olive oil and raisins and dried mushrooms—summer wasn't a good season for fresh ones, except for some that growers raised. When they put parcels in the carriage, Saxburh started to fuss. "What's the matter with you?" Vanai asked. "You don't want to use it, but you don't want anyone else using it, either? That's not fair." Saxburh didn't care whether it was fair or not. She didn't like it.

Vanai picked her up. That solved the baby's problem, and gave Vanai one of her own. "Are you going to carry her all the way home?" Conberge asked.

"I hope not," Vanai answered. Her sister-in-law laughed, though she hadn't been joking.

"Do we need anything else, or are we finished?" Conberge said.

"If we can get a bargain on wine, that might be nice," Vanai said.

Conberge shrugged. "Hard to tell what a bargain is right now, at least without a set of scales." Vanai nodded. A bewildering variety of coins passed current in Forthweg these days. King Beornwulf had started issuing his own money, but it hadn't driven out King Penda's older Forthwegian currency. And, along with that, both Algarvian and Unkerlanter coins circulated. Keeping track of which coins were worth what kept everybody on his toes.

Conberge coped better than most. "I'm jealous of how well you handle it," Vanai told her.

"My father taught me bookkeeping, too," Conberge answered. "I'm not afraid of numbers."

"I'm not afraid of them, either," Vanai said, remembering some painful lessons with Brivibas. "But you don't seem to have any trouble at all."

"He gave me his trade," Conberge replied with another shrug. "He didn't stop to think there might not be anyone who'd hire me at it."

"That's not right," Vanai said.

"Maybe not, but it's the way the world works." Conberge lowered her voice. "Going after Kaunians isn't right, either, but that doesn't mean it doesn't happen. I wish it did."

"Now that you mention it, so do I," Vanai said. She pointed across the market square. "Look—there's someone else with dried mushrooms. Shall we go over and see what he's got?"

"Why not?" Conberge seemed content, perhaps even eager, to change the subject, too. "I'm not going to go in the

other direction when someone has mushrooms for sale."
Forthwegians and Kaunians in Forthweg shared the passion
for them.

"I wonder what he'll have," Vanai said eagerly. "And I
wonder what he'll charge. Some dealers seem to think
they're selling gold, because there aren't so many fresh
ones to be had." She would have hurried to the new dealer's
stall, but no one with a toddler in tow had much luck hurrying. Halfway across the square, she started to notice people
staring at her. "What's wrong?" she asked Conberge. "Has
my tunic split a seam?"

Her sister-in-law shook her head. "No, dear," she answered. "But you don't look like me any more."

"Oh!" Taking Saxburh off her shoulder, Vanai saw the
baby looked like herself, too, and not like a full-blooded
Forthwegian child any more. *I forgot to renew the spell before we went out,* she thought. *I never used to do that. I must
be feeling safer.*

Now, though, she was going to find out if she had any
business feeling safer. How long had it been since these
people had seen a Kaunian who looked like a Kaunian?
Years, surely, for a lot of them. How many of them had
been hoping they would never see another Kaunian again?
More than a few, no doubt.

Vanai thought about ducking into a building and putting
the spell on again. She thought about it, but then shook her
head. For one thing, too many people had seen her both
ways by now, and seen her change from one appearance to
the other. For another . . .

Her back straightened. *All right, by the powers above, I
am a Kaunian. My people were living in Forthweg long before the Forthwegians wandered up out of the southwest. I
have a right to be here. If they don't like it, too bad.*

Conberge walked along at her side as naturally as if
nothing out of the ordinary had happened. That steadied
Vanai. Her sister-in-law wasn't ashamed to be seen in public with her, no matter what she looked like. *But how many
people are going to wonder whether Conberge's a Kaunian
in disguise now?* she wondered, and hoped Ealstan's sister
wouldn't think of that.

Nobody shouted for a constable. Being a Kaunian wasn't against the law in Forthweg any more. But laws had only so much to do with the way the world worked. Vanai feared people would start shouting curses or throwing things. If they did, would the Unkerlanter soldiers on patrol try to stop them? She supposed so. Even if the soldiers did, though, the damage would still be done. She would never again be able to show her face as a blond in Gromheort, and maybe not in Forthwegian disguise, either.

No one threw anything. No one said anything. No one, as far as Vanai could tell, so much as moved as she came up to the Forthwegian who was selling dried mushrooms: a plump fellow somewhere in his middle years. Into that frozen silence—it might have sprung from a wizard's spell rather than from one wearing off—she spoke not in Forthwegian but in classical Kaunian: "Hello. Let me see what you have, if you please?"

Even Conberge inhaled. Vanai wondered if she'd gone too far. Using her birthspeech wasn't illegal any more, either, but when had anyone last done it in public here? Would the mushroom-seller try to shame her by denying that he understood? Or would he prove to be one of those Forthwegians who'd either never learned or who'd forgotten his classical Kaunian?

Neither, as it happened. Not only did he understand the language she'd used, he even replied in it: "Of course. You'll find some good things here." He pushed baskets toward her.

"Thank you," she said, a beat slower than she should have—hearing her own tongue took her by surprise. Around her, the market square came back to life. If the dealer took her for granted, other folk would do the same. *Now I have to buy something from him,* she thought. *No matter how much he charges, I have to buy. I owe it to him.*

But the fellow's prices turned out to be better than the ones Vanai and Conberge had got from the man on the other side of the square. He wrapped up the mushrooms she bought in paper torn from an old news sheet and tied it with a bit of string. "Enjoy them," he told her.

"Thank you very much," she said again, not just for the mushrooms.

"You're welcome," he answered, and then leaned toward her and lowered his voice: "I'm glad to see you safe, Vanai."

Her jaw dropped. Suddenly, she too spoke in a whisper: "You're someone from Oyngestun, aren't you? One of us, I mean. Who?"

"Tamulis," he said.

"Oh, powers above be praised!" she exclaimed. The apothecary had always been kind to her. She asked, "Is anyone else from the village left?"

"I don't know," he replied. "You're the first one I've seen with nerve enough to show your true face. More than I've got, believe you me."

It hadn't been nerve. It had been a mistake. *But I got by with it,* Vanai thought. *If I want to, I can do it again. Maybe I can do it again, anyway.* Somehow, that *maybe* felt like victory.

Garivald had thought he would forever hate all Algarvians and the men who'd fought for the redheads. Now he found himself swinging a pick beside one of Mezentio's men while a former soldier from Plegmund's Brigade shoveled the cinnabar ore they'd loosened into a car another Unkerlanter had charge of. "Being careful," the Algarvian said in bad Unkerlanter. "Almost dropping pick on my toes."

"Sorry," Garivald answered, and found himself meaning it. He'd worked beside this particular redhead before, and didn't think he was a bad fellow. Here in the mines in the Mamming Hills, the captives, whatever they looked like, weren't one another's worst foes. That honor, without question, went to the guards.

All the captives—Unkerlanters, Forthwegians, Gyongyosians, Algarvians, black Zuwayzin—hated the guards with a passion far surpassing anything else they felt. They worked alongside their fellows in misery well enough. The guards were the men who made life a misery.

"Come on, you lazy whoresons!" one of them shouted now. "You don't work harder, we'll just knock you over the head and get somebody who will. Don't think we can't do it, on account of we cursed well can."

Maybe some of the foreigners in the mine were naive enough to believe the guards wouldn't kill any man they felt like killing. Garivald wasn't. He doubted whether any Unkerlanter was. Inspectors and impressers had always meant that life in Unkerlant was lived watchfully. Anyone who spoke his mind to someone he didn't know quite well enough would pay for it.

The work went on. Here in the summertime, it would still be light when the men in the mines came up after their shift ended, as it had been light when they came down to their places at the ends of the tunnels. Come winter, it would be dark and freezing—worse than freezing—above ground at each end of the shift. Down here in the mine, winter and summer, day and night, didn't matter. To a farmer like Garivald, a man who'd lived his life by the rhythm of the seasons, that felt strange.

Of course, his being here at all felt strange. No one thought he was Garivald, the fellow who'd been a leader in the underground and come up with patriotic songs. As Garivald, he *was* a fugitive. Anyone who'd presumed to resist the Algarvians without getting orders from King Swemmel's soldiers was automatically an object of suspicion. After all, he might resist Unkerlant next. Plenty of Grelzers had. Some of them were in the mines, too.

But no. Garivald was here because of what he'd done, what he'd seen, while using the name of Fariulf, which he still kept. *What did I see?* he wondered. Much of what he'd seen in battle, he wanted only to forget. But that wasn't what had made the inspectors seize him when he got off the ley-line caravan. By now, thanks to a good deal of thought and some cautious talk with other captives, he had a pretty good notion of why he was here.

What did I see? I saw the Algarvians were a lot richer than we are. I saw they took for granted things we haven't got. I saw their towns were clean and well run. I saw their farms grew more grain and had more livestock than ours do. I saw water in pipes and lamps that run on sorcerous energy and paved roads and a thick ley-line network. I saw people who weren't hungry half the time, and who weren't nearly so afraid of their king as we are of ours.

Being an Unkerlanter, he even understood why his countrymen had yanked him out of freedom—or what passed for it hereabouts—and sent him to the mines. If he'd gone back to his farm, to his life with Obilot, he would have come into the town of Linnich every so often, to sell his produce and buy what the farm couldn't turn out. And he might have talked about what he'd seen in Algarve. That, in turn, might have made other people wonder why they couldn't have so much their enemies took for granted. *Oh, aye, I'm a dangerous character, I am,* Garivald thought. *I could have started a rebellion, a conspiracy.*

A lot of the men in the mines were no more truly dangerous than he was. But he knew some who were. That fellow from Plegmund's Brigade who'd once tried to comb his band out of the forest west of Herborn sprang to mind. No one would ever make Ceorl out to be a hero. He didn't pretend to be one, either. He was a born bandit, a son of a whore if ever there was one.

And he flourished here in the mines. He led a band of Forthwegians and a couple of Kaunians. They hung together and got good food and good bunks for themselves. When other gangs challenged them, they fought back with a viciousness that made sure they didn't get challenged often.

And Ceorl seemed to like Garivald, as much as he liked anyone. That puzzled the Unkerlanter. At last, he decided being old enemies counted almost as much as being old friends would have. Out in the wider world, the notion would have struck him as absurd. Here in the mines, it made a twisted kind of sense. Even seeing someone who'd tried to kill you reminded you of what lay beyond tunnels and barracks.

"We've got to get out of here," Ceorl kept saying to whoever would listen. His Unkerlanter was foul; listening took effort. But he spoke his mind—spoke it without the least hesitation. "We've got to get out. This place is a manufactory for dying."

"A man at the head of a gang can live soft," Garivald told him. "Why do you care what happens to anybody else?"

"I spent too fornicating much time in gaol," Ceorl answered; Forthwegian obscenities weren't too different from their Unkerlanter equivalents. "This is another one." He spat. "Besides, this cinnabar stuff's poison. Look at the quicksilver refineries. And even the raw stuff's bad. I was talking with somebody from a dragon groundcrew. It'll kill you—not fast, but it will."

Garivald shrugged. He didn't know whether that was true, but he wouldn't have been surprised. The mines weren't run as health resorts for miners. "What can you do about it?" he asked reasonably. "Run away?"

"No, of course not," Ceorl said. "I wasn't thinking of anything like that. Not me, pal. I know better, by the powers above."

He spoke louder than he had been, louder than he needed to. Looking over his shoulder, Garivald saw a grim-faced guard within earshot. He doubted Ceorl had fooled the guard; of course any captive in his right mind wanted to get away. But the Forthwegian couldn't very well say he wanted to break out of the captives' camp and mine complex. Escape was punishable, too.

A couple of days later, at the end of a blind corridor, Ceorl picked up the thread as if the guard had never interrupted it: "How about you, buddy? You want to get out of here?"

"If I could," Garivald said. "Who wouldn't? But what are the odds? They've got it shut up tight."

The Forthwegian laughed in his face. "You may be tough, but you ain't what anybody'd call smart."

Garivald marveled that the ruffian found him tough, but he let that go. "What do you mean?" he asked.

"There's ways," Ceorl answered. "That's all I'm gonna tell you—there's ways. Maybe not if you're a redhead or a blond, but if you're the right kind of ugly, there's ways. Speaking the lingo helps, too."

As far as Garivald was concerned, Ceorl didn't really speak it. But his own Grelzer dialect made a lot of his countrymen automatically assume he'd been a traitor. Unkerlanter came in a lot of flavors. Maybe people somewhere in the kingdom talked the way Ceorl did.

Garivald rubbed his chin. "You aren't the right kind of ugly if you keep that beard."

Ceorl grinned. "Aye, I know it. I'll get rid of the fornicating thing when the time comes. Till then, though . . ." He eyed Garivald. "If you don't feel like staying here till you croak, wanna come along?"

"If they catch us, they're liable to kill us."

"And so?" Ceorl shrugged. "What difference does it make? I ain't gonna live the rest of my days in a fornicating cage. They think I am, they can kiss my arse."

For Garivald, it wasn't the rest of his life. His official sentence was twenty-five years. But he'd be a long way from young if they ever let him out—and if he lived to the end of the sentence. How likely was that? He didn't know, not for certain, but he didn't like the odds.

Informing on Ceorl might be one way to get his sentence cut. He realized as much, but never thought of actually doing it. He hated informers even more than he hated inspectors and impressers. The latter groups, at least, were open about what they did. Informers . . . As far as he was concerned, informers were worms inside apples.

"What would you do if you got out?" he asked Ceorl.

"Who knows? Who cares? Whatever I futtering well please," the ruffian replied. "That's the idea. When you're out, you do what you futtering well please."

He didn't know Unkerlant so well as he thought he did. Nobody in the kingdom, save only King Swemmel, did what he pleased. Eyes were on a man wherever he went. He might not know they were there, but they would be.

Well, if a fornicating Forthwegian doesn't know how things work, if he gets caught again, what do I care? Garivald thought. *If I can get out of here, I know how to fit back into things. All I'd have to do is separate from him.*

Would he have thought like that before the war? He didn't know. He hoped not. The past four years had gone a long way toward turning him into a wolf. He wasn't the only one, either. He was sure of that. He stuck out his hand. "Aye, I'm with you."

"Good." He'd already known how strong Ceorl's grip

was. By all the signs, the Forthwegian had been born a wolf. "We'll be able to use each other. I know how, and you can do most of the talking."

"Fair enough," Garivald said. *And if we do get out, which of us will try to kill the other one first?* As long as one of them knew about the other, they were both vulnerable. If he could see that, Ceorl could surely see it, too. He studied the ruffian. Ceorl smiled back, the picture of honest sincerity. That made Garivald certain he couldn't trust the Forthwegians very far.

"What are you whoresons doing down there?" a guard called. "Whatever it is, come do it where I can keep an eye on you."

"You wanna watch me piss?" Ceorl said, tugging at his tunic as if he'd been doing just that. The tunnel stank of urine; he'd made a good choice for cover. The guard pulled a horrible face and waved him and Garivald back to work.

He's got nerve, Garivald thought. *He isn't stupid, even if he doesn't understand Unkerlant. If he has a plan for getting out of here, it may work.*

As Ceorl walked back toward the mouth of the tunnel, he muttered, "This whole fornicating kingdom's nothing but a fornicating captives' camp." Garivald blinked. Maybe the man from Plegmund's Brigade understood Unkerlant better than he'd thought.

Garivald started swinging his pick with a vim he hadn't shown before. He wondered why. Could hope, however forlorn, do so much? Maybe it could.

Since Sabrino had declined to become King of Algarve, or of a part of Algarve, he'd got better treatment in the sanatorium. He'd expected worse. After all, he'd warned General Vatran he wouldn't make a reliable puppet. He had no reason to think the Unkerlanter general disbelieved him. Maybe Vatran had more courtesy for an honest, and crippled, enemy than he'd expected.

Little by little, Sabrino learned to get around on one leg. He stumped up and down corridors at the sanatorium. Eventually, he even got to go outside, to test his crutches and his surviving leg on real dirt. He remained in pain. Decoctions of poppy juice helped hold it at bay. He knew he'd come to crave the decoctions, but he couldn't do anything about that. If the pain ever went away, he would think about weaning himself from them. Not now. Not soon, either, he didn't think.

"You're doing very well," his chief healer said one day, when he came back worn and sweaty from a journey of a few hundred yards. "You're doing much better than we thought you would, in fact. When you first came in here, plenty of people doubted you would live more than a few days."

"I was one of them," Sabrino answered. "And I would be lying if I said I were sure you did me a favor by saving me."

"Now, what sort of attitude is that?" The healer spoke in reproving tones.

"Mine," Sabrino told him. "This is my carcass, or what's left of it. I'm the one who's got to live in it, and that's not a whole lot of fun."

The healer tried cajolery. "We'd hate to see everything we did go to waste after we worked so hard to keep you going."

"Huzzah," Sabrino said sourly. "I'm not a fool, and I'm not a child. I know what you did. I know you worked hard. What I still don't know is whether you should have bothered."

"Algarve is mutilated, too," the healer said. "We need all the men we have left, wouldn't you say?"

To that, Sabrino had no good answers. He sat down on his cot and let the crutches fall. "I never thought I would hope for calluses under my arms," he said, "but these cursed things rub me raw." Before the healer could speak, Sabrino wagged a finger at him. "If you tell me I've got the rest of my life to get used to them, I'll pick up one of those crutches and brain you with it."

"I didn't say a thing," the healer replied. "And if you kill a man for what he's thinking, how many men would be left alive today?"

"About as many as *are* left alive today, if you're thinking about Algarvians," Sabrino said. He lay down and fell asleep almost at once. Part of that was the decoctions—though sometimes they also cost him sleep—and part of it was the exhaustion that came with being on his feet, if only for a little while.

When he woke, the healer was hovering above his cot. In his long white tunic, he reminded Sabrino of a sea bird. He said, "You have a visitor."

"What now?" Sabrino asked. "Are they going to try to make me King of Yanina? I couldn't be worse than Tsavellas, that's certain."

"No, indeed, your Excellency." The healer turned toward the doorway and made a beckoning motion. "You may come in now."

"Thank you." To Sabrino's astonishment, his wife walked into the room.

"Gismonda!" he exclaimed. "By the powers above, what are you doing here? I sent a message to tell you to get to the east if you could, and I thought you had. The Kuusamans and Lagoans beat us, but the Unkerlanters. . . ." His gesture was broad, expansive, Algarvian. "They're Unkerlanters."

"I know," Gismonda said. "By the time I made up my mind to get out of Trapani, it was too late. I couldn't. And so"—she shrugged—"I stayed."

The healer shook a warning finger as he walked to the door. "I'll be back in half an hour or so," he said. "He is not to be overtired. And," he added pointedly, "I am leaving this door open."

With the decoction in him, Sabrino didn't much care what came out of his mouth. Leering at the healer, he said, "You don't know how shameless I can be, do you?" The fellow left in a hurry.

"Now, really!" Gismonda said, sounding a little amused but much more scandalized. "You may be dead to shame, my dear, but what makes you think I am?"

She'd been a beauty when they wed. She was still a handsome woman, but one who showed she had iron underneath. She'd rarely warmed up to Sabrino in the marriage bed. She gave him what he wanted when he wanted it with her, and, like a lot of Algarvian wives, she'd looked the other way when he took a mistress. But she'd always been fiercely loyal, and Sabrino had never embarrassed her, as some husbands enjoyed doing to their wives.

Now, instead of answering her, he asked the question uppermost in his mind: "Are you all right?"

"Oh, aye." She nodded. "All things considered, the place isn't too badly damaged. And as for the Unkerlanters . . ." Another shrug. "One of them had some ideas along those lines, but I persuaded him they were altogether inappropriate, and they've given me no trouble since."

"Good for you." Sabrino wondered if Gismonda's "persuasion" had been something swift and lethal in a cup of wine or spirits, or whether a show of sternness had convinced the Unkerlanter to take his attentions elsewhere. That wouldn't have been beyond her, but Swemmel's men, by all Sabrino had heard and seen, weren't always willing to take no for an answer. He said, "I hope you didn't take too much of a chance."

"I didn't think so," Gismonda replied, "and I turned out to be right. I have had some practice at judging these things, you know. Men *are* men, regardless of which kingdom they come from."

She spoke with what sounded like perfect detachment. *And if that's not a judgment on half the human race, powers below eat me if I know what would be,* Sabrino thought. He knew what his own countrymen had done in Unkerlant. It didn't go very far toward making him think she was wrong. "Well, any which way, I'm glad you came through safe, and I'm very glad to see you," he said.

"I would have come sooner," she said, "but the first word I got was that you were dead." She angrily tossed her head. "It wasn't anything official—by then, the official ley lines had all broken down. But one of the officers from your wing—a captain of no particular breeding—came to the house to give me the news that he had seen you flamed out of the sky."

"That would have been Orosio," Sabrino said. "Breeding or not, he's a good fellow. I wonder if he came through alive."

"I don't know. That was the name, though," Gismonda said. "If he came to tell me such a story, he might at least have had the courtesy to get it right. It must have been kindly meant—I can't doubt that—but. . . ."

"I'm lucky to be alive," Sabrino answered. *If this is luck,* he added, but only to himself. Aloud, he went on, "I can't blame him for thinking I was dead. If your dragon goes down, you usually are. Mine didn't smash into the ground, and didn't crush me after I got out of the harness. Luck—except for my leg." He couldn't pretend that hadn't happened, no matter how much he wanted to.

His wife nodded. "I'm very sorry."

It was more than polite, less than loving: exactly what he might have expected from Gismonda. "How did you finally find out Orosio had it wrong?"

"A mad rumor went through Trapani a couple of weeks ago—a rumor that the Unkerlanters had offered to make some wounded dragonflier King of Algarve, or of what they held of Algarve, and that he'd turned them down flat." Gismonda's green eyes glinted. "I know you, my dear. It sounded so much like something you would do, I started asking questions. And here I am."

"Here you are," Sabrino agreed. "I'm glad you are." He held out his hands to her. They still hadn't touched. That was very much like Gismonda, too. But she did take his hands now. She even bent down by the side of the bed and brushed her lips across his. He laughed. "You *are* a wanton today."

"Oh, hush," she told him. "You're as foolish as that healer of yours."

He patted her backside—not the sort of liberty he usually took with her. "If you wanted to shut the door . . ."

"I wasn't supposed to make you tired," Gismonda said primly.

Sabrino grinned. "You just told me the fellow was a fool. So why pay attention to him now?"

"Men," Gismonda said again, maybe fondly, maybe not. "You'd sooner have lost your leg than *that*."

"No." The grin fell from Sabrino's face. "I'd sooner not have lost anything. This hasn't been easy, and it hasn't been fun, and I'll thank you not to joke about it."

"I'm sorry," his wife said at once. "You're right, of course. That was thoughtless of me. When do they think you'll be able to leave here?"

She was clever. Not only did she change the subject, she reminded him what he would be able to do when he healed, not of what he'd lost. "It shouldn't be too much longer," he answered. "I am on my feet—on my foot, I should say. I'd just gone out and about not long before you got here. They're talking about fitting a made leg to the stump, but that won't be for a while longer. It needs to heal more."

"I understand," Gismonda said. "When you do get out, I'll take the best care of you I can—and I'll do what I can for *that,* too, once we're someplace where no one is likely to walk in on us."

"I appreciate it." Sabrino's tone was sardonic. As soon as the words were out of his mouth, he realized that was a mistake. If he was to get any pleasure from a woman from now on, from whom would it be but Gismonda? Who else would be interested in a mutilated old man? No one he could think of.

Half a lifetime earlier, such a reflection would have cast him into despair. Now ... At just this side of sixty, he burned less feverishly than he had when he was younger. The decoctions he drank to hold pain at bay helped dampen his fire, too, and the brute fact of the injury he'd taken also reduced his vitality.

He sighed. "Even if you had shut the door there, I wonder if anything would have happened."

"One way or another, I expect we'll manage when you're well enough to come home," Gismonda said. "In your own way, Sabrino, you are reliable."

"For which I thank you indeed," he replied. "It may be flattery—in my present state of decrepitude, it's bound to be flattery—but you mustn't think I'm not grateful to you for keeping up the illusion."

"Isn't that part of what marriage is about? Keeping up illusions, I mean. On both sides, mind you, so husband and wife can go on living with each other. Or maybe you'd sooner just call it politeness and tact."

"I don't know." Sabrino groped for a reply, found none, and let out a small, embarrassed laugh. "I don't know what to say to that. But I can use the distillate of poppy juice as an excuse, and count on you to be polite enough not to let me see you don't believe a single, solitary word of it."

Gismonda smiled. "Of course, my dear."

The healer bustled in. "Well, well, how are we doing?" he asked in a loud, hearty voice.

"No *we,* my dear fellow. I turned the kingship down," Sabrino said grandly. The healer laughed. Gismonda smiled again. Sabrino was gladder for that; he knew she made a more discriminating audience.

In the refectory, Pekka raised her mug of ale in salute. "Powers above be praised that we aren't teaching teams of mages any more!" she said, and took a long pull at the mug.

"I'll certainly drink to that." Fernao did. Setting his mug on the table, he gave her a quizzical look. "But I'm surprised to hear you say such a thing. How will you go back to Kajaani City College if you feel that way?"

Pekka cut a bite from her reindeer chop. Chewing and swallowing gave her time to think. "It's not the same," she said at last. "That won't be an emergency. And"—she looked around the refectory before she went on, making sure none of the mages they'd worked with was in earshot—"and I won't be trying to get through to so many stubborn dunderheads. Some of the people we tried to teach must still be sure the world is flat."

"I ran into that, too," Fernao said. "You wouldn't expect it from mages—"

"I thought the same thing at first," Pekka broke in, "but now I'm not so sure. Mages know the world is full of sorcerous laws. When we showed them the ones they thought they knew weren't really at the bottom of things, some of them didn't want to hear that at all."

"They certainly didn't," Fernao agreed. "Some of them didn't want to believe the spells I was casting actually worked, even though they saw them with their own eyes. But even so, the ones we did manage to train went out and stopped the Algarvians as if they'd run into a wall."

That was true. Pekka couldn't deny it, and was glad she couldn't. "Have you read the interrogation reports from some of the captured Algarvian mages?" she asked.

"Aye." Fernao nodded. His smile might have belonged on the face of a shark: it was all teeth and no mercy. "They still haven't figured out how we did what we did. They know we did something they couldn't match, but there are about as many guesses as to what it is as there are mages."

"And not very many of them are even close to what we really did," Pekka said. "That makes me happier, too, because it's likely to mean the Unkerlanters aren't close to figuring it out, either. I hope they're not."

"So do I," Fernao said. "As long as they don't figure it out, we still hold the whip hand. The longer we can keep it, the better." He took another sip from his mug, then asked, "Anything new from Gyongyos?"

"Not that I've heard," Pekka answered with a mournful shake of the head. "If they don't decide we meant that warning demonstration, we'll have to show them it was real. I don't want to do that. So many people . . ."

"It will end the war," Fernao said. "It had better, anyhow."

That made Pekka drain the rest of her ale in a hurry. The notion that the Gongs might try to keep fighting even after having horror visited on them had never crossed her mind. No one rational would do such a thing. But, were the Gyongyosians rational, wouldn't they have quit already? They'd surely seen by now that they couldn't hope to win . . . hadn't they?

"What would we do if they didn't quit?" she muttered.

"Smash another city of theirs, I suppose," Fernao answered. "Better that than invading—or do you think I'm wrong?"

"No." Pekka waved to one of the serving women and ordered more ale. "I don't want to have to cast this spell once, though. Twice?" She shuddered. When the new mug of ale got there, she gulped it down fast, too.

Her head started to spin. Fernao wagged a finger at her. "Am I going to have to carry you up to your bedchamber?"

She laughed. It sounded like the laugh of someone who'd had a little too much to drink. "Ha!" she said, feeling very witty—and slightly tongue-tied. "You just want me defenseless"—she had to try twice before she could get the word out—"so you can work your evil will on me."

"Evil?" Fernao raised a gingery eyebrow. "You thought it was pretty good the last time we tried anything."

As best she could remember—none too clearly, not at the

moment—he was right. "That hasn't got anything to do with anything," she declared.

"No, eh?" Fernao said. "I—"

A commotion at the entrance to the refectory interrupted him. "What's that?" Pekka said. Kuusamans didn't commonly cause commotions. She got to her feet to see what was going on.

So did Fernao. Since he was a good deal taller, he could see more. When he exclaimed, Pekka couldn't tell whether he was delighted or horrified. A moment later, he spoke two words that explained why perfectly well: "Ilmarinen's back."

"*Is* he?" Pekka said, in tones identical to his.

Back Ilmarinen was. He somehow contrived to look raffish even in the uniform of a Kuusaman colonel. Catching sight of Fernao, who stood out not only on account of his inches but also for his red hair, the elderly theoretical sorcerer waved and made his way toward him, shaking off the mages and servants clustering round. A few steps later, Ilmarinen caught sight of Pekka, too, and waved again.

Pekka waved back, trying to show more enthusiasm than she felt. *What's he going to say, seeing the two of us together?* she wondered. It was a question whose answer she could have done without.

What Ilmarinen did say was, "I was very sorry to hear about Leino. He was a good man. I'd hoped to see him in Jelgava, but I got up to the front just too late."

"Thank you," Pekka answered. She couldn't find anything exceptionable in that.

"Aye." Ilmarinen spoke almost absently. He looked from her to Fernao and back again. Glowering up at the Jelgavan, he said, "You'd better take good care of her."

"I can take care of myself, Master Ilmarinen," Pekka said sharply.

Ilmarinen waved that aside, as being of no account. He waited for Fernao to speak. "I'm doing my best," Fernao said.

"You'll have to do better than that," Ilmarinen said with a dismissive snort. He waved a forefinger under Fernao's nose. "If you make her unhappy, I'll tear your arm off and beat you to death with it, do you understand me? I'm not kidding."

"Master Ilmarinen—" Pekka felt herself flush.

"I didn't think you were, Master," Fernao said seriously, almost as if he were speaking to Pekka's father.

But Ilmarinen wasn't feeling fatherly: old, perhaps, but not fatherly. "By the powers above, if I were twenty years younger—ten years younger, even—I'd give you a run for your money, you overgrown galoot, see if I wouldn't."

"Master Ilmarinen!" Pekka hadn't thought her cheeks could get any hotter. Now she discovered she'd been wrong.

She wondered if Fernao would laugh in Ilmarinen's face. That wouldn't have been a good idea. To her relief, Fernao saw as much for himself. Nodding soberly, he said, "I believe you." Pekka believed him, too. Master Siuntio would have tempted her more. Ilmarinen? She just didn't know about Ilmarinen, and she never had. In a land of steady, reliable people, he was hair-raisingly erratic. About three days out of four, she found that a bad bargain. The fourth, it seemed oddly attractive.

"You'd better believe me, you redheaded—" Ilmarinen began.

Before he could get any further, though, he found himself upstaged. Pekka wondered if that had ever happened before; Ilmarinen usually did the upstaging. But now Linna the serving woman whooped, "Illy! Sweetie!" and threw herself into the theoretical sorcerer's arms.

"Illy?" Pekka echoed, deliciously dazed. She couldn't imagine anyone calling Ilmarinen that. When she thought about it, she also had trouble imagining anyone calling him *sweetie*.

As Linna kissed Ilmarinen—and as he responded with an enthusiasm that said he wasn't so very old after all—Fernao said, "Obviously, Master, you have a prior commitment here."

When Ilmarinen wasn't otherwise distracted, he said, "A man should be able to keep track of more than one bit of business at the same time."

Bit of business, eh? Pekka thought, amused and indignant at the same time. He sounded almost like an Algarvian. But then her amusement evaporated. While Leino lived, she'd had to keep track of more than one bit of business at the same time herself. How would that have turned out in the end? She shook her head. She would never know now.

Ilmarinen kissed Linna again, patted her, gave her a silver bracelet, and told her, "I'll see you in a little while, all right? I've got some business to talk with these people." She nodded and went off. Ilmarinen hadn't been talking business before, but Pekka didn't contradict him.

As Ilmarinen pulled up a chair, another serving woman—the one who'd been taking care of the table— came up and asked him what he wanted. He ordered salmon and ale. She went back to the kitchen. Pekka asked, "What brings you back here, Master? You went off to see what the war was like."

"So I did, but now the war in the east is over," Ilmarinen answered. "Pity anything in Algarve is still standing, but it can't be helped. Nothing that happened to those bastards was half what they deserved. But what am I doing here? You're going to drop a rock on the Gongs some time soon, aren't you?"

"How do you know that?" Pekka demanded. "Who told you?" That whole sorcerous project was supposed to be as closely held a secret as Kuusamo had.

Ilmarinen only laughed. "I don't need people to tell me things, sweetheart. I can figure them out for myself. I know what you were up to here, and I can see where it was going. I want to be here when it arrives. I want to help it arrive, as a matter of fact."

"The magecraft has come a long way since you left us," Fernao said. "How quickly can you prepare?"

"I've been doing some thinking on my own." Ilmarinen took a few bedraggled leaves of paper from his beltpouch and spread them on the table. "My guess is, you're headed in this direction."

Pekka leaned forward to study the calculations. After a minute or so, she looked up at Ilmarinen, awe on her face. "You're not just even with us," she said quietly. "I think you're ahead of us." Slowly, Fernao nodded.

With a shrug, Ilmarinen said, "It was something to keep me busy in my spare time. I didn't have much, or I'd've done more."

Something to keep me busy in my spare time, Pekka thought dazedly. She and Fernao and the rest of the mages here in the Naantali district were clever and talented. She knew that. But Ilmarinen had just reminded her of the difference between talent and raw genius. She shook her head, trying to clear it. All she could find to say was, "I'm glad you're back."

Seventeen

⌘

After Ilmarinen got down from his carriage, he gave the blockhouse in the Naantali district a salute half affectionate, half ironic. "Congratulations," he told Pekka and Fernao, who alighted just after him. "You never did quite manage to kill yourselves here, or to blast this place off the face of the earth."

Fernao's smile showed fangs. "You were the one who came closest to that, you know, when you told Linna goodbye and came out here with your miscalculations."

Ilmarinen scowled; he didn't like being reminded of that. "I still say there's more to that side of the equation than you're willing to admit. You don't want to see the possibilities."

"You don't want to see the paradoxes," Fernao retorted. "You ignored such a big one when you came out here, you could have taken half the district with you."

That was also true, and Ilmarinen liked it no better. Before he could snap back at Fernao again, Pekka said, "It's so good to have you back, Master. The bickering got dull after you went away."

"Did it?" Ilmarinen's smile was sour. "Well, I can't say I'm surprised."

Raahe and Alkio and Piilis got out of their carriages. So did the secondary sorcerers, who would transmit the spell to the animals that would power it: an enormous bank of cages, larger than any Ilmarinen had seen. No one approached the blockhouse with any great eagerness. Except for Ilmarinen, all the mages here had already seen that this spell worked as advertised, so they weren't out to discover anything new. That might have accounted for part of their reluctance. The rest . . .

"You remind me of so many hangmen on execution day," Ilmarinen said.

"That's about what I feel like," Pekka said. "We've tried everything we could to make the Gongs heed us, but they wouldn't. If they had, we wouldn't need to do this. I wish we didn't."

"They're proud and they're brave and they still don't believe they're overmatched," Ilmarinen said. "When you run into someone like that, you usually have to hit him in the face to get his attention."

"We are. I understand the need," Pekka said. Ilmarinen found himself nodding. When he first got to know her, he'd made the mistake of thinking her soft; he'd had to change his mind about that in short order. She went on, "I understand it, but I still don't like it."

"It will end the war," Fernao said. "It had better end the war."

"Aye. It had better." Pekka's tone was bleak. "If it doesn't . . . I don't want to think about doing this twice, or more than twice, not to cities."

"That's one of the reasons we have some hope of getting away with this and keeping our spirits clean," Ilmarinen said. "Believe me, if the Algarvians had known what we do, they wouldn't have thought twice about using it. The deeper in trouble they got, the nastier the wizardry they tried and the less they counted the cost. They *deserved* having the Unkerlanters overrun them, and if that's not a judgment I don't know what is."

"Let's go do what needs doing," Pekka said. "We have a crystal in the blockhouse—I ordered one moved there. If the Gyongyosians decide to be sensible at the last moment, we can abort the spell."

She's grasping at straws, Ilmarinen thought. *She has to know she's grasping at straws, but she's doing it anyhow. Can't blame her for that. Blame? Powers above, I admire her for it. But it won't do any good. If the Gongs were going to quit, they'd have quit by now. Beating them on the field hasn't been enough to make them change their minds. Maybe this will be. If it is, it'll be worthwhile.*

One after another, the mages marched into the block-house. It was as cramped as Ilmarinen remembered. With his bad leg, Fernao was the last one through the door. He slammed it shut and let the heavy bar fall into place. The blockhouse might have been sealed away from the rest of the world.

"No need for that, not any more," Ilmarinen said.

"Maybe not," Fernao said, "but by now it's become part of our ritual." Ilmarinen nodded. Routine did have a way of crystallizing into ritual. And Fernao was a good deal more fluent in Kuusaman these days than he had been before Ilmarinen left the Naantali district. The Lagoan wizard hardly ever needed to fall back into classical Kaunian now. His south-coast accent was also stronger than it had been. Ilmarinen glanced toward Pekka. He had no doubt where Fernao had picked up his style of speaking.

Pekka might have felt his eye on her. If she had, she didn't know why he'd looked her way, for she said, "Master Ilmarinen, are you sure you're comfortable here? In spite of your work, you're a latecomer to this sorcery."

"I'll pull my weight," Ilmarinen answered. "This is the end, the very end. I want to be a part of that."

"All right." She nodded. "You're entitled to it. So much of the work we've done is based on your calculations. If it weren't for you, we wouldn't be here today. I will say, though, I hope you don't plan on standing on your head, the way you did in the hallway outside my office."

"No," Ilmarinen said. "What we're here for today is standing Gyongyos on its head. That's a different business."

Piilis said, "So it is, Master, but one day you must tell us why you chose to stand on your head in the hallway outside Mistress Pekka's office."

"I was demonstrating an inverse relationship," Ilmarinen replied. Piilis blinked but didn't smile. He was bright enough—more than bright enough—but had only a vestigial sense of humor. He might have gone further had he had more. Or he might not have, too. Ilmarinen had his own opinion about such things, but recognized it was no more than an opinion.

"Are we ready?" Pekka asked. No one denied it. She took a deep breath and intoned, "Before the Kaunians came, we of Kuusamo were here. Before the Lagoans came, we of Kuusamo were here. After the Kaunians departed, we of Kuusamo were here. We of Kuusamo are here. After the Lagoans depart, we of Kuusamo shall be here."

Ilmarinen repeated the ritual words with her. So did the rest of the Kuusaman mages crowding the blockhouse. And so, he noted, did Fernao. That was interesting. Before Ilmarinen left, the Lagoan mage had always hung back from the stylized phrases with which Kuusamans began any sorcerous endeavor. No more, though. Was he starting to think of himself as a Kuusaman, then?

Even if Fernao did think of himself as belonging to the land of the Seven Princes, Ilmarinen didn't and wouldn't. *And neither would the Lagoan, if he weren't sleeping with a Kuusaman woman,* the master mage thought. But then he shrugged. Plenty of men—and women, too—had changed their allegiance over the years for reasons like that.

"I ask you once more, Master," Pekka said: "Are you ready to take your place in this spell along with the rest of us?"

"And I tell you once more: I am," Ilmarinen replied. "I think I can keep up with you. Do you doubt it?"

He found himself flattered by how quickly she shook her head. "By no means," she told him, and looked to the other mages. "Are we all ready?" When no one denied it, Pekka took a deep breath, let it out, and said, "Pursuant to the orders conveyed to me by the Seven Princes of Kuusamo, I begin."

Whenever she incanted up till now, it was always just, "I begin," Ilmarinen thought. *Does she want to have it on the record that she's following orders? A lot of Algarvians tried to do that. Or is her conscience bothering her a little, so she wants to lay the blame on the Seven and not on herself?*

He had little time to wonder about such things. His own spell along these lines would have required only one operator: he'd designed it for himself. The charm the mages here had come up with was a good deal more complex. *And when did you ever know a committee to do anything that wasn't clumsy and cumbersome?* Ilmarinen asked himself.

But that wasn't altogether fair, and he was honest enough to admit it to himself. His spell was a bare-bones affair. A good sorcerer needed arrogance, and he had it in full measure. He'd simply assumed nothing would go wrong as he loosed the cantrip on the world. If anything did go wrong—if, by some mischance, he made a mistake—the spell would ruin him in short order.

This version, if more complicated, was also a good deal safer. Raahe and Alkio and Piilis not only helped draw and aim the sorcerous energy: they also stood ready to turn it aside in case Pekka or Fernao or Ilmarinen himself stumbled.

I don't intend to stumble, he thought, as Pekka pointed to him and he took up the chant. The passes he used were a good deal more elegant—and more difficult—than those the mages here had worked out. He accepted the revised words they'd come up with. Safety for elegance was a reasonable trade. But he thought their passes ugly. He felt sure he could manage these, and so he used them.

No mage intends *to stumble,* went through his mind. By then, though, he'd finished that portion of the spell. He pointed to Fernao and poised himself to deflect any trouble if the Lagoan slipped. Fernao still irked Ilmarinen, but no denying he'd come a long way in a short time.

He got through his portion of the spell without difficulty, even if Ilmarinen reckoned his passes graceless. Then Pekka took over once more, and brought the charm up to its first plateau. Ilmarinen could feel the power already gathered, and could also sense the shape and size of the power still to be drawn. As he sensed it, awe washed over him. *Could I have managed this by myself? I thought I could, but maybe I was wrong. Arrogance brings down as many mages as clumsiness.*

Pekka pointed to him. He nodded, stopped thinking, and started incanting once more. They'd given him the task of getting the cantrip past that first plateau, up to the point where the power, the sorcerous energy, having all been gathered, could be launched against any target the mages chose.

Ilmarinen felt as if he were pushing a boulder up a hill. For a bad moment, he wondered if the boulder would roll down over him and crush him. Then, without any fuss, he felt added strength from Pekka and from Fernao. The Lagoan mage nodded to him, as if to say, *We can do it.* And, with his help, they could. That boulder of power went up the metaphorical hill again—and, somehow, began to move up it faster and faster, which just proved metaphor was not only slippery but also dangerous.

"Now!" Ilmarinen grunted hoarsely. Pekka pointed to Raahe, Alkio, and Piilis, Fernao to the secondary sorcerers. The power didn't belong *here*. It needed to be on the far side of the world, where a new day would soon be dawning.

With the other mages in the blockhouse, Ilmarinen felt the sorcerous energy fly east. They cried out in triumph. And then, some tiny fraction of a heartbeat later, Ilmarinen and the others felt it strike home against Gyorvar.

He cried out again, almost before the echoes of his first shout had faded. But what he felt this time was a long way from triumph.

When Istvan went back to Gyongyos, he hadn't expected merely to exchange one captives' camp for another. By now, though, he'd concluded he wouldn't be getting out of this center near Gyorvar any time soon. All the guards spoke his language. The food was what he was used to. But for those details, he might as well have been back on Obuda.

"You have a simple way to go free," Balazs told him. The interrogator spoke in calm, reasonable tones: "All you need do, Sergeant, is say you are convinced the accursed Ku-usamans, may the stars never shine on them, tried to trick and terrorize you with their show on Becsehely."

"All I have to do is lie, you mean," Istvan said sourly. "All I have to do is turn my back on the stars."

"Your attitude is most uncooperative," Balazs said.

"I am trying to tell you the truth," Istvan said in something not far from despair. "If you don't listen, what will happen to Gyongyos?"

"Nothing much, I expect," the interrogator answered. "Nothing much has happened to our stars-beloved land up till now. Why should that change?"

"Because the slanteyes have given us a little time to make up our minds," Istvan said. "Pretty soon, they'll go ahead and do this to us."

"If they can, which I do not believe—which everyone with a dram of sense, from Ekrekek Arpad on down, does not believe," Balazs said. "Most of your comrades have also seen sense and been released. You know what you have to do to join them. Why make an avalanche of a snowflake?"

"You would say the same thing if you were trying to talk me into eating goat," Istvan said. The scar on his left hand throbbed. He ignored it. And, where nothing else had, that remark succeeded in insulting Balazs. He stalked away, his nose in the air, and bothered neither Istvan nor Captain Petofi the rest of the day.

Petofi noticed the interrogator's absence. At supper, he asked why Balazs had gone missing. Istvan explained. The officer, normally a dour man, laughed out loud. But then he sobered. "He probably went into Gyorvar to denounce you," he warned. "You may have got satisfaction now, but for how long will you keep it?"

Istvan shrugged. "They already have me in what might as well be another captives' camp. What can they do to me that's so much worse?"

"Those are the sorts of questions you would do better not to ask," Petofi replied. "All too often, they turn out to have answers, and you generally end up wishing they didn't."

"Too late to worry about it now, sir," Istvan said with another shrug. "I already opened my big mouth. Today was mine, and I'll enjoy it. If he makes me sorry after he gets back here from Gyorvar, then he does, that's all, and I'll have to see if I can find some other way to get my own back."

Sadly, the captain shook his head. "Those whoresons are armored against attack by virtue of their office. Being the ekrekek's Eyes and Ears, they think they can do as they please, and they are commonly right."

"Balazs isn't Arpad's Eye and Ear," Istvan said. "He's the ekrekek's . . ." He named an altogether different portion of his sovereign's anatomy, one as necessary as an eye or an ear but much less highly esteemed.

"No doubt you're right," Petofi said, this time favoring him with no more than a wintry smile. "Being right, of course, will get you what being right usually does: the blame, and nothing else."

On that cheerful note, the captain nodded to Istvan almost as if they were equals and then left the dining hall for his own private room—he was an officer, after all. Istvan didn't linger long himself. He felt oppressed, and he didn't think it was at the prospect of Balazs' coming revenge. The very air felt heavy with menace. He tried to tell himself it was his imagination. Sometimes he succeeded for several minutes at a stretch.

Balazs had told one truth, anyhow: the barracks hall where Istvan slept held only a handful of other stubborn underofficers besides himself. He didn't care much, save that he missed Corporal Kun. Kun must have thought telling a few lies a small enough price for going home to Gyorvar. Istvan hardly blamed him. He knew mulishness was all that kept him here.

With Kun gone, he was in no mood for company anyhow. Lamps-out came as more than a little relief. Gyorvar's distant lights came in through the south-facing windows, casting a pale, grayish illumination on the northern wall of the barracks. It was less than moonlight, more than starlight—not enough to disturb Istvan in the least when he fell asleep.

Having fallen asleep, he promptly began to wish he'd stayed awake. He kept starting up from a series of the ghastliest nightmares he'd ever had the misfortune to suffer. In one of them, Captain Tivadar cut his throat instead of his hand on finding out he'd eaten goat. That was one of the gentler dreams, too. Most of the others were worse, far worse: full of red slaughter. He couldn't always remember the details when he woke, but his pounding heart and the terrified gasps with which he breathed told him more than he wanted to know.

And then, some time toward morning, he woke to bright sunlight streaming in through the window. But it wasn't morning, not yet, and the window didn't face east. And the light into the barracks might have been as bright as sunlight, but it wasn't sunlight. It rippled and shifted like waves—or flames.

With a cry of horror and despair, Istvan sprang to his feet and rushed to the window. He knew what he would see, and he saw it: the same destruction poured down onto Gyorvar as had descended upon Becsehely. He'd been closer to the disaster in the Kuusaman ley-line cruiser than he was now, but he wasn't so far away as to have any doubt about what was happening.

Even through the window, even across the miles separating him from the capital of Gyongyos, savage heat beat on his face. For a moment, that was the only thought in his mind. Then he wondered what it was like in Gyorvar itself, and then, sickly, he wished he hadn't.

Well, he thought, *if that accursed Balazs went into the capital, he isn't coming back. May the stars not shine on his spirit.*

He faced that loss with equanimity. But then one of the other men in the hall whispered, "If Ekrekek Arpad's there, he couldn't live through . . . *that.* If his kin are there, they couldn't, either."

That was horror of a different sort. The Ekrekek of Gyongyos was the only man alive who communed with the stars as an equal. That was what made him what he was. If he died, if all his kin died in the same searing instant—who would rule Gyongyos then? Istvan had no idea. He doubted anyone had ever imagined such a nightmare could befall the land.

"What do we do?" another soldier—or was he another captive?—moaned. "What *can* we do?"

The flames pouring out of the sky onto Gyorvar abruptly ceased, though they remained printed on Istvan's vision when he blinked. Gyorvar without the ekrekek, without the ekrekek's whole family? Arpad's house had reigned in Gyongyos since the stars made the world. That was what people said, at any rate.

And so? Istvan wondered. *If Arpad had the brains of a carrot, he would have realized Kuusamo was trying to warn us, not trying to bluff us. Now he's paid for being wrong—along with the stars only know how many people who never did anyone any harm. If there's any justice, the stars will refuse to shine on* his *spirit.*

"Other lands just have kings," Istvan said. "Maybe we can get along with nothing more than a king, too."

"But—" Three shocked-sounding men began an automatic protest.

Istvan cut them off with a sharp chopping motion of his right hand. "We'd better be able to get along with nothing more than a king. How much good did Ekrekek Arpad do us? We lost the war, we lost Gyorvar—stars above, we might as well have had a goat-eating savage on the throne."

Two of the soldiers at the window with him backed away, as if afraid he had some deadly, highly contagious disease. The third one, a corporal, said, "You're right, by the stars."

"I wonder what we'll do now, and who the new Ekrekek or King or whatever he is of Gyongyos will be," Istvan said, and then, with a shrug, "It probably won't matter, not to the likes of us."

"No," said the underofficer who'd nodded—his name was Diosgyor. "Only thing that matters to us is whether they let us out."

Captain Petofi strode into the barracks hall in time to hear that. "We'll need to be very lucky to get away," he said.

"Why?" Istvan said in dismay. "We were right. Everything we told them was true—and everything we warned them about came true."

Petofi nodded. "All the more reason for locking us up and

losing the key, wouldn't you say, Sergeant? Few offenses more dangerous than proving right when your superiors say you must be wrong. Of course"—he grimaced—"most of our superiors, or the ones immediately concerned with us, are dead."

"Uh—of course." Istvan's stomach lurched. He hadn't even tried to think about how many people might have died in Gyorvar. Thinking about the ekrekek and his kinsfolk was bad enough. Add in all the ordinary men and women and children . . . "By the stars, sir, this wasn't war. This was murder!"

"You're half right," Petofi said. "In a way, looked at from the Kuusaman point of view, this *was* murder. But the slanteyes did their best not to commit it. They could have loosed this magic on Gyorvar as soon as they found it. Instead, they let us watch when they threw Becsehely on the pyre. They let us watch and take back word of what we'd seen. Arpad wouldn't hear it, though." He sighed. "Wouldn't you say he helped kill himself, and all of Gyorvar with himself?"

Slowly, Istvan nodded. Corporal Diosgyor said, "Can we still go on fighting the war now?"

"By the stars, I hope not!" Istvan and Captain Petofi exclaimed at the same time. It was impossible to say which of them sounded more horrified. And then Istvan let out a different cry of horror and despair.

"What's wrong?" This time, Petofi and Diosgyor spoke together.

"My comrade, Corporal Kun," Istvan said. "He gave the Eyes and Ears what they wanted . . . and he lives—lived—in Gyorvar. We fought together on Obuda, in the forests of Unkerlant, and on Becsehely. He was the cleverest man I ever knew." He would never have praised Kun so where the ex–mage's apprentice could hear him. Now, though, Kun would never hear anything again. "If either of us died, I thought I'd surely be the one."

"May the stars shine on his spirit forevermore," Petofi said. "If he was in Gyorvar, that is the most any man can hope for."

"I know," Istvan said heavily. He was a warrior from a

warrior race. Tears were for women, or so he'd heard from boyhood. He'd never come so close to shedding them as he did now, not since he'd grown out of childish things. "He was . . . a brother to me, a brother in arms."

"Many of us have lost brothers," Petofi said. "With Gyorvar gone, Gyongyos has had its heart torn from it. And what can we do? I have no answers."

Istvan had no answers, either. No one left alive did. He was sure of that. And the answers Ekrekek Arpad and the other dead had come up with were wrong. He'd been sure of that even before fire enfolded Gyorvar in its dreadful embrace. Now the whole world knew it was true.

Leudast knew he'd passed through the enormous forests of western Unkerlant on his way to fight the Gongs in the Elsung Mountains. He hadn't imagined how huge they really were. Back in those distant days, that halfhearted border war and Gyongyos' skirmishes with Kuusamo among the islands of the Bothnian Ocean had been the only flareups in an otherwise peaceful world. The rest of Derlavai had gone through six years of darkness—and the Gongs were still fighting Unkerlant here in the uttermost west and the slanteyes in the Bothnian Ocean.

"Let's see how much longer the whoresons last," Leudast muttered under his breath. If it turned out to be much longer, he would own himself surprised. Even as he muttered, Unkerlanter egg-tossers pounded the Gyongyosian positions near the western edge of the woods. He didn't quite know how his countrymen had managed it, but they'd moved a *lot* of egg-tossers through the trees till they bore on the lines the Gongs still held.

Hardly any Gyongyosian egg-tossers answered back. The Algarvians had fought hard for as long as they could. Whenever King Swemmel's men started flinging eggs at them, they'd responded sharply. That remained true up to the day they surrendered. They'd gone down, but they'd gone down swinging.

The Gyongyosians, by contrast, hardly seemed to believe what was hitting them. Things had been quiet here in the distant west for the past couple of years. Unkerlant had thrown as much as possible into the fight against Algarve, while the Gongs had taken their men farther west still to fight the Kuusamans in a watery sort of war Leudast didn't pretend to understand.

He understood perfectly well the task lying ahead of him. Seizing his shiny bronze officer's whistle, he blew till the shrill note made his ears ring. "Forward!" he shouted. "Now we take the land away from them!"

Forward his company went—one company among hundreds, more likely thousands. Forward went behemoths, down game tracks and sometimes down no tracks at all. Overhead, dragons dropped more eggs on the Gongs skulking in the forest and swooped low to incinerate whatever they found in clearings. No brightly painted Gyongyosian beasts rose to challenge them. They had the sky to themselves.

The terrain here was as rugged as any in which Leudast had fought on the other side of his kingdom. The woods west of Herborn weren't a patch on these. They could have been swallowed up as if they never were, in fact. Leudast and his men had to pick their way forward past great tree trunks scattered and tumbled like so many jackstraws.

But the country in which they were fighting did more to hold them back than did the Gyongyosians. Here and there, a few tawny, shaggy-bearded men in leggings did keep blazing at them, but they overran those pockets of resistance like men beating boys. "Nothing's going to slow us down now!" Leudast shouted exultantly. "It's not like it was when we were fighting the fornicating Algarvians—it'll be easy!"

Powers above, am I really saying things like that? he wondered. But he was. Even at the end of the war against the redheads, they'd been dangerous whenever they managed to scrape together enough men and beasts and eggs to make a stand or to counterattack, and they'd always looked for chances to hit back. The Gongs, by contrast, seemed stunned at the attack rolling over them.

For the first couple of days of that attack, Leudast knew it reminded him of something he'd been through before, but couldn't put his finger on what. Then, encamped for the night in a clearing, he snapped his fingers in sudden realization. "What is it, sir?" one of his men asked.

He still had trouble getting used to being called *sir.* But that wasn't the reason he answered, "Oh, nothing important." All at once, he understood why the Gongs were acting as they were. The Unkerlanter army had behaved exactly the same way when the Algarvians swarmed over the border more than four years earlier. They'd been hit by a force not just stronger than they were but also almost beyond their comprehension. Gyongyos had never expected a blow like this.

Unkerlant, thanks to its vast spaces and dreadful winters, had managed to ride out the Algarvian storm. Leudast didn't think the Gongs would be able to do the same. They didn't have so much land to yield, and they did have another war to worry about: the fight on the Bothnian Ocean came closer to the offshore Balaton Islands, closer to Gyorvar itself, every day.

And so, while the Unkerlanters swarmed forward, a lot of Gyongyosian soldiers simply threw up their hands, threw down their sticks, and went off into captivity. Some of them looked relieved, some looked resigned. One, who spoke a little Unkerlanter, asked, "What you do, move here so fast?"

He got no answer. The guards leading him and his countrymen back toward the camps that would house them kept them moving. Even if someone had sat him down and explained exactly what the Unkerlanters were doing, he might not have understood it. Leudast wouldn't have understood exactly what the redheads were doing just after they started doing it. All he would have known—all he had known at the time—was that something dreadful had happened to his countrymen.

Less than a week after the great attack began, the Unkerlanters burst out of the vast forest and into the more open country that led to the foothills of the Elsung Mountains. Behind them, Leudast knew, pockets of Gongs still held out. *So what?* he thought. Pockets of Unkerlanters had still held out as the Algarvians swarmed west, too. The redheads had mopped them up at their leisure.

Peering ahead at the mountains, Leudast wondered how close he was to where he'd been when the Derlavaian War—what everybody but Unkerlant reckoned the Derlavaian War—broke out. He shrugged. He couldn't tell. One set of peaks looked much like another to a man raised on the broad plains of northeastern Unkerlant.

He was settling his company for the night when Captain Dagaric called him and the other company commanders together. Dagaric took them out onto the meadow, well away from the common soldiers' campfires. "What's gone wrong, sir?" Leudast asked. Obviously, something had, or Dagaric wouldn't have acted as he was doing.

He said, "I just got word from the regimental crystallo-mancer—Gyorvar's been destroyed. Gone. Vanished. Off the map. Disappeared." He snapped his fingers to show how thoroughly wrecked the capital of Gyongyos was.

"Well, that's good, isn't it, sir?" another lieutenant asked. "If we smashed the place up, that'll hurt the Gongs, won't it?"

"Oh, the Gongs are hurting, all right," Dagaric said. "Ekrekek Arpad's dead, and so is everybody in his clan, as far as anyone can tell. The whoresons who're left are all running around like chickens after the axe."

"Then what's wrong, sir?" the other junior officer repeated. "If we got rid of Gyorvar, of Arpad—"

"*That's* what's wrong," Dagaric broke in. "*We* didn't do it. We didn't have anything to do with it. The Kuusamans smashed Gyorvar, with some newfangled sorcery they came up with."

"Powers below eat them," Leudast said softly. He remembered how lucky he'd been to come through alive after the Algarvians started murdering Kaunians the first autumn of their war with Unkerlant. The only answer his kingdom had found was killing its own people—a solution, he thought, no one but Swemmel would have imagined.

Another company commander, a sergeant, asked, "Can we match this magic?"

Dagaric shook his head. "No. The slanteyes know how to do it, and we don't."

"That's not good." Leudast thought he was the first to

speak, but three or four company commanders said the same thing at more or less the same time.

"Of course it's not," Dagaric said. "Those whoresons'll hold it over our head like a club, you see if they don't. But that hasn't got anything to do with our job here. Our job here is kicking the stuffing out of the Gongs, and it's more important than ever that we do it up good and proper."

"How come, sir?" somebody asked.

The regimental commander made an exasperated noise. "The more we grab now, the better off we'll be. For now, we're still officially friends with Kuusamo. How long will that last, though? Anybody's guess. So we grab with both hands while the grabbing's good."

"Makes sense," Leudast said. "And the Gyongyosians were falling to pieces against us even before this happened. Now that it has, they ought to turn to mush."

"I hope they do," Dagaric said. "Other chance is that they might decide to make us pay as much as they can from here on out because everything's lost. I hope they don't try to do that, but we've got to be alert for it. I want you to let your men know it could happen. Don't tell them about Gyorvar, not yet. I haven't got any orders on how we're supposed to present that to them."

Leudast felt foolish warning his troopers the Gongs might turn desperate without telling them why. Nobody asked questions, though; curiosity was not encouraged in the Unkerlanter army. He did say, "We'll know better when we see how things go in the morning."

Lying there wrapped in a blanket, listening to eggs burst not so far away—but almost all of them off to the west, falling amongst the Gyongyosians—he realized that might not be so. Dagaric had ordered him to keep the news of the destruction of Gyorvar from his men. Would officers on the other side also keep it from the shaggy soldiers they led? He wouldn't have been surprised.

"Forward!" he shouted when first light came. Forward the men went. The Gongs continued to crumble. Their disintegration was so quick and thorough, in fact, that Leudast couldn't tell whether they knew some dreadful sorcery had claimed their capital. Unkerlant had been hammering their armies before the news came, and went right on hammering them now.

Three days later, Dagaric's regiment was well up into the foothills of the Elsung Mountains. Looking east, back in the direction from which he'd come, Leudast saw nothing but a sea of dark green, a sea that stretched out to the horizon and far beyond. Ahead towered the mountain peaks. Even in the summertime, they remained shrouded in snow and mist. He didn't look forward to climbing higher in them. He'd done that once, all those years before, and found mountain warfare harder work for fewer rewards than any other kind he'd met since.

No help for it, though, he thought, and ordered the men forward once more. But then, as the sun set ahead of him, a Gyongyosian with a white flag came out from behind a lichen-covered boulder. He waited to be recognized for what he was, then called out in musically accented Unkerlanter: "It is over. You and the slanteyes have beaten us. We can fight no more. We admit it, and we surrender."

"By the powers above," Leudast whispered. "I lived through it." Those four words seemed to say everything that needed saying.

Krasta looked from the ornate parchment to the Valmieran official who'd given it to her. "What *is* this?" she asked in distaste; those seals and stamps meant little to her.

"It is what it says it is, milady," the flunky replied. "It summons you to appear before his Majesty's court day after tomorrow to testify as to your dealings during the time of occupation with a certain accused Algarvian, namely one Captain Lurcanio."

"Why on earth would I want to do that?" Krasta demanded. She *didn't* want to do it; she couldn't think of anything she wanted to do less.

But the official said, "By the laws of the kingdom, your desires here are irrelevant and immaterial. Having been served with this summons, you are required to appear. Failure to do so will—not may, milady, but assuredly will—result in your being fined or imprisoned or both. Good day."

He turned and strode down the walk, away from Krasta's

mansion. She started to shout an obscenity after him, but ended up whispering it instead. She still hoped for something like a pardon from King Gainibu. Insulting one of his servants wouldn't help her get it.

She glared down at the summons. She wanted to tear it to pieces. As if it knew what she wanted and were mocking her, a couple of sentences in amongst the legalese leaped out. *This document must be presented at your court appearance,* she read. *It will be counterstamped to document the said appearance.* As she'd whispered curses at the man who'd brought the summons, so she aimed more at the document itself.

No help for it, though. She put on the most demure outfit she could find—the trousers were so baggy, they might have done duty for a Forthwegian-style long tunic (or so she imagined, anyhow). Again, her wig was a confection of piled blond curls: it shouted her Kaunianity to the world. The hair underneath that was still growing out shouted something else altogether, but she refused to pay any attention to that.

The last thing she expected when she got to the royal courthouse was a pack of news-sheet scribblers standing outside. They shouted rude questions at her: "How good was the redhead, Marchioness?" "That's really his baby, isn't it?" "Will you tell the judges you fell in love with him?"

Nose in the air, she stalked past them as if they didn't exist. A bailiff led her to the courtroom and had her sit in a row of chairs reserved for witnesses. Lurcanio himself sat not far away. He grinned and blew her a kiss. Her nose went up higher. He laughed, outwardly as brash as ever. To her dismay, more reporters in the courtroom scribbled notes about the byplay.

A panel of judges came in. Two of them wore black tunics and trousers of a cut even baggier than the ones she had on. They were supposed to be dressed as ancient Kaunian judges, she thought. The third was a soldier. His uniform glittered. He had two rows of medals on his chest. He sat in the middle, between the other two.

Everyone rose and bowed when the judges took their

places. Krasta was a beat behind most people, because she didn't know she was supposed to. "Be seated," the soldier said in a voice that sounded as if he'd used it on the battle-field.

To Krasta's indignation, she wasn't the first witness sum-moned to the box. A weedy little commoner stood there and droned on and on about captured documents. It would have had to be more exciting to rise to dullness. Krasta yawned, buffed her nails, and yawned again. The judges kept on questioning the fellow for what seemed like forever. Then, when they finished, Lurcanio started in on him. She didn't like that. If he could ask her questions, too . . .

At last, the military judge dismissed the boring com-moner. "Marchioness Krasta, you will come forward," he said. "The clerk will administer the oath."

Forward Krasta came. The clerk took away her summons and stamped it. Then, in a monotone, he said, "Do you swear the testimony you give here today and in any subse-quent appearances will be the truth and nothing but the truth, knowing you may be sorcerously monitored and you are subject to the kingdom's statutes pertaining to perjury?"

"Aye," Krasta said.

People tittered. One of the judges in old-fashioned black said, "The customary response, milady, is, 'I do.' "

"I do, then," Krasta said with a toss of her head.

"Having sworn, the witness may enter the box," the mili-tary judge intoned. When Krasta had taken her place, he went on, "You are the Marchioness Krasta, sister to Mar-quis Skarnu?"

"That's right," she answered.

"And, during the late war, you were mistress to the Colo-nel Lurcanio, the defendant here?"

However much Krasta wished she could deny it, she had to nod and say, "Aye, I was." Lurcanio could give her the lie if she did say no, and doubtless would take malicious glee in doing just that. She scowled at him. She'd been so *sure* Algarve had won the Derlavaian War. Mezentio's men had beaten Valmiera, hadn't they? What else was there? Five years ago, she hadn't thought there was anything else. She'd learned differently since.

After rustling a couple of leaves of paper to find the name, the chief judge asked, "And Colonel Lurcanio is the father of your son, Gainibu?"

If Krasta had wished she could deny the one, she wished even more that she could deny the other. But it wasn't Lurcanio who would give her the lie if she did: it was her own son's sandy, all too un-Valmieran hair. As venomously as she could, she said, "Aye," again.

"I note, milady, you are not on trial here," the judge said. "We seek information against the Algarvian. Now, to resume: being Lurcanio's mistress, you yielded yourself to him of your own free will?"

"Not always," Krasta exclaimed. "Why, there was this one time when he—"

Lurcanio burst out laughing, a coarse, rude, raucous laugh. "You deserved that, you miserable bitch," he said. "I caught you rubbing up against Valnu. He must have been tired of boys that day, but I wanted to remind you he liked them at least as well as he liked you."

All three judges rapped furiously with their gavels. All three of them were red-faced. One of the civilians said, "The recorder will expunge that from the transcript of this proceeding."

"For the most part," the military judge resumed, "you did yield yourself of your own free will to Colonel Lurcanio? Is that correct, Marchioness?"

"I suppose so," Krasta said, most unwillingly.

"Very well, then," the judge said. "You being his willing mistress, do you believe you were in his confidence? Did he trust you enough to talk to you of his affairs?"

"If he'd had affairs and I found out about them, I wouldn't have let him touch me, the miserable whoreson." Krasta tossed her head again. Did they think she had no pride at all?

Several people laughed, which puzzled and angered her. The judges gaveled them to silence. The senior man, the one in uniform, said, "That is not what I meant. What I meant was, did he talk to you about his duties during the occupation?"

"To *her*? Powers above, sir, do I look so foolish?" Lurcanio said. "I am affronted that you should ask such a thing."

His tone told Krasta she should have been angry at him again, but she couldn't see why. He'd told the truth. "No, he didn't talk to me about anything like that," she answered. "Why would he have? I can't imagine anything more boring."

The judges put their heads together. Krasta leaned toward them, as she would have tried to eavesdrop on any conversation near which she found herself. Here, she had no luck. One of the civilian judges asked, "Did this Algarvian ever mention to you his work in transporting Kaunians to the south coast of this kingdom for the purpose of slaying them and utilizing their life energy?"

"Oh. *That!*" Krasta said. *If I tell them he talked about it, I can hurt him.* She saw that very clearly. "Aye, he told me all about that. He bragged about it, in fact, over and over again."

"That is not the truth," said a nondescript little man in the front row.

"Marchioness Krasta, you swore an oath of truthfulness and were informed of the penalties involved in violating the said oath," the military judge said. "The mage has informed us that response was untruthful. Perhaps your error was accidental. I shall give you one—and only one—chance to revise your testimony, if you care to do so."

"What was the question again?" Krasta asked. The judge repeated it. Resentfully, Krasta said, "I suppose I was wrong. I suppose he didn't talk about it." The boring little man nodded.

With almost simultaneous sighs, the judges put their heads together again. The man in uniform asked, "Did Colonel Lurcanio ever speak to you about the Algarvian edict called Night and Fog?"

"No," Krasta said after giving the mage a dirty look.

"Did he ever speak to you about the way Algarve treated captives from the underground it captured?"

"No," Krasta said. "But he wouldn't do anything to save the Kaunian Column of Victory when the redheads knocked it over."

"That is also a crime against Kaunianity," one of the civilian judges said. "Still, evidence suggests he was not a primary perpetrator."

"We had hoped the Algarvian might have been more forthcoming with you," the other judge in black said.

"I was forthcoming in her, not with her," Lurcanio said with a nasty grin.

"And you weren't half as good as you think you were, either!" Krasta squealed furiously, while the judges banged their gavels again and again. That little mage in the first row stirred, but Krasta fixed him with such a glare, he kept his mouth shut.

"That will be quite enough of that," the military judge declared. "Very well, Marchioness Krasta, you may stand down from the witness box. As my colleague said, we hoped you might have more to offer."

"Oh, I have plenty to offer," Krasta said. "I hope you blaze him. He has his nerve, dragging my name through the dirt."

"Marchioness, when you chose to sleep beside him for four years, you dragged your own name through the dirt to a degree greater than anyone else could have done. You are dismissed."

Outside the courtroom, Krasta expected another swarm of vicious news-sheet scribblers. But they had vanished, as if a wind had risen and blown away a pile of rubbish. Instead, news-sheet hawkers were out in force, all screaming out the identical headline: "Gyongyos surrenders! Derlavaian War ends!"

"Isn't it splendid, milady?" Krasta's driver said as he handed her up into the carriage. "The war's finally over!"

"Aye, splendid," she said. Part of her really meant it. The rest was irked: the end of the war had forced her out of public notice. True, the notice would have been unflattering. But if no one noticed her at all, how could she be sure she really existed?

Fernao peered down from his perch behind the dragonflier. Once this journey was done, he hoped with all his heart never to travel on dragonback again. He'd set out from Kihlanki in easternmost Kuusamo six days before, and had island-hopped his way east across the Bothnian Ocean. He wasn't quite saddlesore, but he wasn't far from it, either. The dragons and dragonfliers had changed several times a day. He lacked that luxury, and remained his weary self.

They'd flown over the Balaton Islands earlier in the day. Now, at last, they passed above the narrow sea separating the Balatons from the Gyongyosian mainland. Gyorvar lay not far ahead.

A Gyongyosian dragon rose to meet the newcomer. Seeing the beast, gaudy in red and yellow and blue and black, relieved Fernao and alarmed him at the same time. The Gongs were supposed to send up a dragon to meet him and guide him to a working dragon farm outside shattered Gyorvar. They were supposed to, aye. But what if this weren't the appointed beast, but a lone-wolf dragonflier intent on whatever revenge he could get from a Kuusaman dragon and a Lagoan mage? Because the Gyongyosians were a warrior race, such worries went through Fernao's mind as the other dragon neared. They'd surrendered, but did they really mean it?

Then the Gong on the dragon's back waved and pointed southeast. Fernao and his dragonflier waved back. The dragonflier whacked his mount with a goad. After a couple of bad-tempered screeches, it followed the Gyongyosian beast.

Tawny-bearded dragon handlers secured the Kuusaman beast to a spike: dragon farms the world around operated on similar principles. Fernao slid down from his perch on the dragon's back and looked around. The grass under his feet was . . . grass. Some of the bushes a little farther away looked unfamiliar to him, but he would have had to be an herbalist to recognize the differences. The buildings on the edge of the dragon farm . . .

They had steeply pitched roofs. In that, they resembled buildings in Kuusamo and Lagoas and Unkerlant, which also saw a lot of snow. But they didn't look like houses or hostels. They looked like gray stone fortresses. They were spaced well apart from one another, too, as if the Gyongyosians didn't think it safe to have them too close together. When the Gongs weren't warring with their neighbors, they often fought among themselves. Their architecture showed it, too.

A man emerged from the nearest of those fortresslike buildings and walked toward Fernao. He wore a sheepskin jacket over wool leggings. Gray streaked his beard and hair. "You are the mage from Kuusamo?" he called in slow, oddly accented, but understandable classical Kaunian.

"I am Fernao, a mage of the first rank, aye. Actually, I represent both Lagoas, my own kingdom, and Kuusamo," Fernao replied. "And you are, sir . . . ?"

"I am called Vorosmarty, a mage of five stars," the Gyongyosian said. "It is a rank more or less equal to your own. How can you be trusted to represent two kingdoms?"

"I am from Lagoas, as I said. And I am engaged to be married to a Kuusaman mage. Neither kingdom feels I would betray its interests," Fernao said. That wasn't strictly true. Grandmaster Pinhiero was less than delighted to have him representing Lagoas. But he was the best bargain Pinhiero could get, and so the grandmaster had had to make the best of it.

Vorosmarty shrugged. "Very well. This is not truly my concern. I am ordered to show you Gyorvar, to show you what your magecraft has done. I obey my orders. Come with me. A carriage waits for us."

He didn't, he couldn't, know that Fernao was one of the mages who'd unleashed that sorcery. His *your* had to mean *your kingdoms'*. Fernao didn't intend to enlighten him, either. He said, "You are ordered? Who gives orders in Gyongyos these days?" With Ekrekek Arpad and his whole family dead, how were the Gyongyosians running their affairs?

"Marshal Szinyei, who ordered our surrender, has announced that the stars commune with his spirit, and has declared himself our new ekrekek." Vorosmarty's voice was studiously neutral. Fernao judged he would be unwise to ask the Gyongyosian wizard how he felt about Szinyei's elevation.

As he got into the carriage, he did ask, "How far to Gyorvar?"

"Perhaps six miles," Vorosmarty replied. "No dragon farm closer than this one survived in working order." His gray eyes flicked over to Fernao. "In the name of the stars, what did your wizards do?"

"What we had to," Fernao said.

"That is no answer," the Gyongyosian said.

"Did you expect one?" Fernao replied. "Even if I knew how this wizardry was made"—no, he wouldn't admit it—"I could not tell you."

Vorosmarty grunted. "I am sorry. I do not know how to act like a defeated man. No such disaster as this has ever befallen my kingdom."

"Lagoas and Kuusamo tried to warn your sovereign," Fernao said. "He would not believe the warnings, but we were telling the truth." Vorosmarty only grunted again. Had he been one of the advisors telling Ekrekek Arpad the islanders couldn't do as they claimed? If he had, he wouldn't want to admit that.

Gyongyosian farmhouses also looked like strongpoints, designed as much for defense as for comfort. Since they were of stone, their exteriors showed little damage. But the fence rails were wood. Before the carriage had got even halfway to Gyorvar, Fernao saw that the sides of the rails facing the city were scorched. Vorosmarty noticed his gaze and nodded. "Aye, your spell did that, even this far away."

Before long, fruit trees showed leaves sere and brown, as if autumn had come early. But something worse than autumn had come to Gyorvar. After another half mile or so, even stone farmhouses looked as if they had been through the fire. And the trees weren't just scorched—they were burnt black on the side facing the Gyongyosian capital, and then, a little later, burnt black altogether.

The air stank of stale smoke. Here and there, smoke still rose from one place or another. A different stench also rode the breeze: the stench of death. "You threw this whole city on a pyre," Vorosmarty said as they passed a party of workers taking bodies out of a block of flats.

"You would not yield," Fernao said. "This was the way we saw to make you know you were beaten."

Vorosmarty shuddered. "When you raise your children, do you spank them with swords?"

"No, but our children are not trying to kill us," Fernao replied. "When our children grow up to be murderers, we do hang them." The Gyongyosian mage sent him a resentful look. He pretended not to see.

As they got closer to the heart of Gyorvar, devastation grew worse. Only a few upthrusting charred sticks showed where wooden buildings had stood. Stone structures were more common. They went from looking burnt to looking slagged, as if the stone blocks from which they were built had begun to melt. A little later on, there was no doubt of what had happened to them: they looked like butter sculptures starting to sag on a hot day. The death stink got stronger.

"This was a great city once," Vorosmarty said. "How long shall we be rebuilding it?" The carriage rattled over something in the middle of the road. Wreckage? A burnt body? Fernao didn't want to know.

He said, "You should have thought of the risks you were taking when you went into this war. You should have had the sense to yield when you saw yourselves losing it."

"Risks?" the Gyongyosian rumbled. "War has risks, aye. But this?" He shook his head. His beard seemed to bristle with indignation.

"For the past century and more, the thaumaturgical revolution has made war more horrid at the same time as it has made life better during times of peace," Fernao said. "You Gyongyosians should have realized that. Yours was the only kingdom not of eastern Derlavai that kept its freedom and learned these arts itself."

"We never imagined the stars had written . . . this for us," Vorosmarty said. The carriage stopped. Vorosmarty opened the door. "Here we are in the heart of the city. Come out, representative of Kuusamo and Lagoas. Come see what your sorcery has wrought."

Fernao got out and looked around. He wished he didn't have to breathe. The smell was so thick, he was sure it would soak into the fabric of his tunic and kilt. Here where the sorcery had been strongest, the flames hottest and thickest, next to nothing remained standing. Buildings had melted and puddled. The sun sparkled off curves of resolidified stone as smooth as glass.

Perhaps a quarter of a mile away, something had been massive enough to stay partly upright despite everything the spell had done. Pointing toward those ruins, Fernao asked, "What was that?"

The look Vorosmarty gave him was so savage, he took an involuntary half step back. "What *was* that?" the Gyongyosian echoed. "Nothing much, outlander—no, nothing much. Only the palace of the ekrekeks since time out of mind and the central communing place of the stars." He scowled again, this time at himself. "This language does not let me say how much that means, or even the thousandth part of it."

"May I go there?" Fernao asked.

"You are the conqueror. You may go where you please," Vorosmarty replied. When Fernao started straight toward the ruined palace, though, his guide said, "You would be wise to stay on the streets, as best you can. Some of the melted stone is but a crust. Your foot may go through, as with thin ice, and you would cut yourself badly."

"Thank you," Fernao said, and then, "I did not suppose that would make you unhappy."

"It would not," Vorosmarty said frankly. "But you might blame me for not having warned you, and, since you are the conqueror, who knows what you might order done to me and to this land?"

Fernao hadn't thought of that. *You don't make the best conqueror, do you?* he thought. He hadn't had much practice for the role. Picking his way with care, he started toward what remained of the very heart of Gyorvar. When he got to the palace, he found people going in and out through an opening—a doorway, he supposed, though no sign of a door remained—in a wall. Vorosmarty said something in Gyongyosian. One of the men nearby answered back. "What does he say?" Fernao asked.

"This sergeant says he saw what you did to Becsehely," Vorosmarty replied. "He says he wishes everyone would have heeded the warning." The sergeant added something else. Again, Vorosmarty translated: "He says it is even worse close up than it was from the Kuusaman ship."

Fernao ducked into the palace. Though the walls had held out the worst of the sorcerous fire, not much inside remained intact. Maybe the Gongs had already carried out what they could salvage. Maybe there hadn't been much worth salvaging.

Vorosmarty said, "You did this to us, Lagoan, your folk and the Kuusamans. Now a new starless darkness walks the earth. One day, maybe, it will stop at Setubal."

"I hope not," Fernao said. "I hope we are coming out of the darkness of these years just past." Vorosmarty held his peace, but he did not look convinced. *Well, he wouldn't,* Fernao thought. Somehow, that left him less happy, less secure, than he would have liked after such a triumph.

From the crenelated battlements of his castle, Skarnu looked out over his new marquisate. The castle, on high ground, was admirably sited for defense; the traitorous Simanu and Enkuru's ancestors had known what they were doing when they built here. Not till egg-tossers came along would anyone have had much chance of taking this place.

Merkela came up beside him and pointed to where fields ended and forest began, a mile or two away. "That was where we settled Simanu," she said. "Good riddance to him, too."

"Aye." Skarnu put his arm around her. "It's over now. We've won. Nobody's at war with anybody, anywhere in the world." He shook his head, half in sorrow, half in wonder. "And how long has it been since the last time that was so?"

His wife shrugged. She didn't worry much about the world at large. Her worries, as usual, lay closer to home. "There are still collaborators loose. We have to smoke them out."

"Aye," Skarnu repeated. It *did* need doing, but fewer people, these days, still shared Merkela's zeal. A lot of them wanted nothing more than to go back to living their lives as if the Derlavaian War had never happened. As day followed day, Skarnu found it harder and harder to blame them.

Merkela said, "Did you see the news sheet that came yesterday? They put that woman in the witness box against Lurcanio." She still refused to call Krasta Skarnu's sister. When she hated, she did a thorough job.

"I saw it," Skarnu answered with a sigh. "At least the news of peace pushed it to the back pages. Every time I think we've had all the embarrassment we're going to get from that, I turn out to be wrong."

"It doesn't look like they'll summon you," Merkela said.

"No, it doesn't," Skarnu agreed. "I'm not really surprised. The only dealings I ever had with the redhead were the kind the people on opposite sides in a war usually have. He played by the rules then."

"I hope they call Vatsyunas and Pernavai," his wife said. "They can tell the judges what the Algarvians did to Kaunians in Forthweg."

The married couple had been aboard the ley-line caravan Skarnu and Merkela helped sabotage as it went past her farm. If that caravan hadn't been sabotaged, all the captives aboard it would have been sacrificed for their life energy. As things were, a good many of them had scattered over the Valmieran countryside. Vatsyunas and Pernavai had worked on Merkela's farm for a while, and had both worked with the underground, too.

"What I remember about Vatsyunas is the way he spoke Valmieran," Skarnu said. That got a smile and a nod from Merkela. Stern as she was, she couldn't deny Vatsyunas had sounded pretty funny. His birthspeech, of course, was classical Kaunian. He'd known not a word of Valmieran, one of the old tongue's daughters, when he found himself here. In learning, he'd seemed like a man stuck in time halfway between the days of the Kaunian Empire and the modern world.

"He'd make himself understood," Merkela said, "and he would be able to testify from the other side about what the redheads did to folk of Kaunian blood."

"Aye, but would he be able to testify that Lurcanio had anything to do with the caravan he was on?" Skarnu asked.

"I don't know," Merkela replied, "and I don't much care, either. All I care about is that all the redheads get what's coming to them. I hope the soldiers in Algarve are taking plenty of hostages, and I hope they're blazing them, too."

She'd lost her first husband when Mezentio's men took him hostage and blazed him. If they hadn't seized Gedominu (after whom she'd named her son), she wouldn't be wed to Skarnu now, and wouldn't be a marchioness. Skarnu wondered if she ever thought about that. After a moment, he also wondered if it was true. He and Merkela had been drawn to each other before the redheads took Gedominu. What would have happened if they hadn't?

No way to know. Would they have kept on holding back? Or would they have lain together even with Gedominu still there? What would he have done if they had? Looked the other way? Maybe—he'd been twice Merkela's age. But maybe not, too. He might have come after both of them with a hatchet . . . or with a stick.

Skarnu shrugged. It hadn't happened. It belonged in the vague, ghostly forest of might-have-beens, along with such things as Valmiera holding her own against Algarve and magic being impossible. They might be interesting to think about, but they weren't real and never would be.

Merkela said, "I'm going down to tend to the herb garden."

"All right," Skarnu answered, "but don't you think the cook's helper could handle the job well enough?"

"Maybe, but maybe not, too," his wife said. "I'm sure I know at least as much about it as she does, and I don't care to sit around twiddling my thumbs all day. I was taking care of an herb garden as soon as I was big enough to know how. Why should I stop doing it now?"

Because noblewomen don't do such things. Because it makes the servitors nervous when they do. Skarnu might have thought that, but he didn't say it. It made sense to him. He knew it would have made perfect sense to Krasta. But he also knew it would have been meaningless to Merkela. As she'd said, she'd worked since she got big enough to do it. Stopping because her social class had changed was beyond her mental horizon.

Come to that, Skarnu himself had been more useless back in Priekule before the war than he was here and now. He looked out over his domain. Everything he could see, near enough, was his to administer. True, that would have meant more a few centuries earlier, when being a marquis was like being a king in small. King Gainibu held the ultimate authority here these days, and Skarnu was no rebellious vassal.

But he still had low justice in this domain—subject to an appeal to the king's courts, but such appeals were rare. And he was doing his best to get to the bottom of real cases of collaboration, and to make sure people didn't launch false accusations to pay back old enemies. He'd fined a couple of people for doing exactly that, and dared hope the rest would get the message.

High overhead, a goshawk called out: *"Kye-kye-kye!"* The hawk had a better view than Skarnu did, and better eyes, too. *In the old days,* Skarnu thought, *I might have flown a bird like that at game.* Falconry, though, was one thing of which he knew nothing. He laughed softly. *I have enough trouble keeping Merkela's feathers unruffled.*

That was a joke, but it also held no small amount of truth. His wife was as she was, and nothing he could do would change her very much. He'd taken a while to realize that, but was convinced he'd touched truth there. So far as he could tell, Merkela hadn't tried very hard to make him over. Maybe that showed good sense. Maybe it just showed she'd been married once before.

He waved up toward the goshawk. The bird, of course, paid him no attention. It rode the breeze that ruffled his hair. The air was its element, as the ground was his. "Good hunting," he called to it, and he went down the spiral stair to his own proper place.

They made them turn this way so attackers would have the wall hampering their right arms, while defenders could freely swing their swords, he thought. *Even in the long-gone days, they worried about tactics.*

When he came down into the main hall, Valmiru the butler said, "I'm glad to see you, your Excellency." His tone implied, *I'd have come to get you if you'd stayed up there much longer.*

"Are you?" Skarnu asked suspiciously. Any time a servitor used a tone like that, it made him doubt he was glad to see the said servitor. "What's gone wrong now?"

Valmiru gave him an appreciative nod. "A gentleman—

a country gentleman—requests a few moments of your time." He coughed. "His request was, ah, rather urgent, your Excellency."

A junior servant piped up: "He said he'd whale the stuffing out of anybody who got in his way. He's drunk as a lord, he is." Then, realizing he hadn't picked the best simile, he gulped. "Begging your pardon, your Excellency."

"It's all right." Skarnu turned to the butler. "And what is this . . . country gentleman's name, and why does he want to see me so badly?"

"He called himself Zemaitu, sir," Valmiru answered. "He would not tell me precisely what he wants. Whatever it is, though, he is most emphatic in wanting it. And he is indeed somewhat elevated by spirits."

"Well, I'll listen to him," Skarnu said. "If he's too greatly elevated, we'll just throw him out." After his time in the army and the underground, dealing with one drunken peasant didn't worry him.

But when he saw Zemaitu, he had second thoughts. Here stood a bear of a man, taller than Skarnu and broad as an Unkerlanter through the shoulders. By the aroma that hovered around him, he might have come straight from a distillery. He gave Skarnu a clumsy bow. "You've got to help me, your Excellency," he said. His voice was surprisingly high and light for a man of his bulk.

"I will if I can," Skarnu answered. "What am I supposed to help you about, though? Till I know that, I don't know what I can do."

"I want to marry my sweetheart," Zemaitu said. "I want to, but her old man won't let me, even though we made our promises back before the war." A tear ran down his stubbly cheek; he was very drunk indeed.

"Why won't he?" Skarnu asked. He thought he could guess the answer: one of them, would-be groom or prospective father-in-law, was accusing the other of getting too cozy with the redheads.

And that turned out to be close, though not quite on the mark. "I was in the army," Zemaitu said, "and I got captured when Mezentio's whoresons broke through in the north. I spent a while in a captives' camp in Algarve, and then they put me to work on a farm there, growing things so their men could go off and fight. And now Draska's pa, he says I sucked up to the Algarvians, and he don't want me in the family no more. You got to help me, your Excellency, sir! What in blazes could I have done but work where they told me to?"

"That's all you did? You worked on a farm?" Skarnu asked sternly.

"By the powers above, sir, I swear it!" Zemaitu said. "You got a mage, sir, he can see for hisself. I ain't no liar, not me!"

A truth spell was a simple thing. Skarnu set a hand on the peasant's shoulder. "We'll do that," he said. "Not because I don't believe you, but to convince your sweetheart's father. When you were in their power, they could set you to work where they pleased. You're lucky they didn't do worse to you."

"I know that, sir," Zemaitu said. "I know that now."

"All right, then. I'll settle it," Skarnu said. Zemaitu started sniffling again. Skarnu clapped him on the back. Sometimes, his post was worth having.

Eighteen

"Good day to you," Valamo said in classical Kaunian as Talsu walked into the Kuusaman tailor's shop.

"Good day to you, sir," Talsu answered in Kuusaman. A word, a phrase, a conjugation at a time, he was picking up the language of the land that had taken him in. The flat vowels, some short, some long, still felt strange in his mouth, but people understood him when he spoke. Unless they slowed down for him, though, he had trouble understanding them.

"How are you today?" Valamo asked, switching to Kuusaman himself.

"I am well, thank you." Talsu came out with another stock phrase. Then he had to fall back on classical Kaunian: "What is there for me to do today?"

"Some leggings, a cape to finish, a few other things," Valamo said, also in the old tongue. He smiled at Talsu. "Since you taught me that wonderful charm, we get more done in less time."

Talsu smiled back, and managed a dutiful nod. He still had mixed feelings about that charm. It was everything the Algarvian who'd taught it to his father and him said it would be. If only he hadn't learned it from a redhead! The spell itself was surely clean, but hadn't it grown in tainted soil?

"Well, to work," he said, pushing down his qualms as he did almost every day. He had that bit of Kuusaman down solid; Valamo said it at any excuse or none. Talsu's new boss was a sunnier man than his own father, but no less dedicated to doing what needed doing and making sure everyone else did, too. Talsu asked, "What do you want me to do first?" He could never go wrong there, either, even if he did have to say it in classical Kaunian.

"Do the cape," Valamo told him. "Once you get done with that, tell me, and I will see what wants doing next."

That was also in classical Kaunian; Talsu could answer in Kuusaman, and did: "All right."

He was busy working on the cape—a much heavier garment than anyone in Jelgava would have worn, and one more like those he'd made for Algarvian soldiers bound for Unkerlant—when the bell above the door to Valamo's shop chimed. When Talsu looked up, he started in alarm, for he thought the man walking into the shop was himself an Algarvian. The fellow was a tall redhead, and wore a tunic and kilt.

But he also had narrow eyes set on a slant, and wore his hair gathered in a neat ponytail at the nape of his neck. *A Lagoan,* Talsu realized, and let out a sigh of relief.

If he was a Lagoan, though, he spoke excellent Kuusaman—spoke it too fast for Talsu to follow, in fact. He blinked when Valamo turned to him and said, "He does not want to talk to me. He wants to talk to you."

"To me?" Talsu said, startled into Jelgavan. Switching to classical Kaunian, he nodded to the newcomer. "What do you want, sir?"

"Can you follow my Valmieran?" the fellow asked. Talsu nodded; his own tongue and that of the other Kaunian kingdom in the east were close kin. "Good," the redheaded man said. "I want you to make me a wedding suit."

"A wedding suit?" Talsu echoed, still taken aback. Then his wits started to work. "Why me? You seem to know who I am."

"Aye, I do," the Lagoan answered. "You see, the woman I am marrying is named Pekka." He waited to see if that would get a reaction from Talsu.

"Oh!" Talsu exclaimed. "Please make her happy . . . ah?"

"My name is Fernao," the Lagoan said.

"Thank you, Master Fernao," Talsu said. "Please make her happy. I owe her so much. If it weren't for her, I would still be sitting in a Jelgavan dungeon."

"I translated your wife's letter," Fernao told him. "She had a little something to do with this, too."

"Then I thank you, too, sir," Talsu said. "If I had my own shop, I would be proud to make you your suit for nothing. As things are . . ." He glanced over toward Valamo.

"I did not come in here for that," Fernao said. "I can afford to pay you, and to pay your boss."

Talsu's boss took advantage of the pause to ask, "What is going on? I see the two of you know each other, but I cannot follow the language you use."

He spoke in classical Kaunian. Fernao started to reply in the same language—he used it more fluently than Valamo, much more fluently than Talsu—but then switched to Kuusaman, in which he was also very quick and smooth. *How many languages does he know?* Talsu wondered. He wished Fernao hadn't switched to Kuusaman; it gave him no chance to follow what was going on.

Valamo went back to classical Kaunian: "This is your friend, then?"

"I would like to think so, aye," Talsu answered in the same tongue. "I would be honored to think so."

"I would like to think so, too," Fernao said. With Algarvic courtesy, he bowed. Talsu nodded in return. *He's not an Algarvian,* he reminded himself. *All the redheaded kingdoms have some of the same customs, and Lagoans helped free Jelgava.* After seeing so much of Mezentio's men in Skrunda, he needed the reminder.

"Good." Valamo beamed. "Very good. A wedding suit, is it? That is very good, too. I am sure Talsu will do a splendid job. He is a clever fellow. As soon as he learns our tongue and saves up a stake, he will do very well in a shop of his own. A wedding suit." His narrow eyes narrowed further. "Shall we speak of price now?"

"Take the price from my pay," Talsu said. "I want to do this."

"No, no, no." Fernao shook his head. "I will go somewhere else before I let that happen. I want to bring you business, not to cost you money."

"Seeing what I owe the lady you are marrying—" Talsu began.

"Hush," Valamo said sharply. "He has said he will pay. Good enough—he will pay." Sure enough, the tailor was all business. But just when that thought went through Talsu's mind, Valamo went on, "I will offer some discount—say, one part in four."

Now Fernao bowed to him. "That is very generous, sir."

"We have several styles," Valamo said. "While the gentleman is here, I will show him some of the possibilities." He took a big book off a shelf and opened it on the counter. "Sir, if you would . . . Aye, and you, too, Talsu. You should get a notion of what you will be doing."

With a sheepish smile, Talsu said, "I certainly should. I have to find out what a Kuusaman wedding suit looks like. I do not make—*have not made*—a Kuusaman wedding suit before now."

To Fernao, Valamo added, "Understand, these are only for guidance. If what you see does not please you, or if you want to combine two styles you do see, we can do that, too."

Fernao studied the illustrations. So did Talsu. To him, the clothes Kuusamans wore to get married were ridiculously gaudy, but nobody wanted his opinion. Fernao pointed to one and said, "This ought to suit me."

"You are a man of taste," Valamo said. "That is a very fine style for a man who is tall and slim, as you are."

"Except for my eyes, I am never going to look like most Kuusamans," Fernao said. "But this should do well enough."

"Not all of us look like me," Valamo said generously. "Most, aye, but not all. You have that Lagoan accent, and I do not suppose you will lose it, but how did you come to speak Kuusaman like a man from the south coast? Most foreigners try to talk like folk from Yliharma."

Fernao laughed. "That is because of the company I keep. My fiancée is from Kajaani."

"I see. I see." Valamo laughed, too. "Aye, that makes sense." To Talsu, he said, "You see, here is another foreigner who has learned our tongue. You can do it, too."

"I hope so," Talsu said. He asked Fernao, "How long did it take you to feel comfortable speaking Kuusaman every day?"

"Somewhere between one year and two," Fernao answered. "At first, I would have to use classical Kaunian for words I did not know in Kuusaman. And I should warn you that you may not learn as fast as I did, for I am good with languages."

"But he is also a younger man than you," Valamo said. "He has time to learn."

"I am no scholar," Talsu said, "but I am doing my best."

"What more can a man do?" the Kuusaman tailor responded. "Now, do your best to measure the gentleman."

"One moment," Fernao said. "First, a part in four off a price of . . . ?"

The haggle quickly went from classical Kaunian into Kuusaman. Talsu knew his numbers, so he could follow pieces of it. He did his best to pick up other words from context. He thought he learned the term for *swindler*, which struck him as a useful thing to know. But the Kuusaman tailor and the Lagoan didn't start screaming at each other, even if they did throw insults around. As Talsu had seen,

Algarvians got—or at least acted—much more excited in a dicker.

"Bargain," Valamo said at last, and stuck out a hand. Fernao took it. To Talsu, Valamo said, "What are you standing there for? Get to work!" He bared his teeth in a smile to show he meant it for a joke, or at least some of a joke.

Talsu took out the tape measure. "Now I will measure you. If you put your tunic on this hanger, sir, so I can get the most accurate measurements . . ."

In Valmieran, Fernao said, "I am not used to having people as tall as I am around me here in Kuusamo."

"I understand that," Talsu answered in Jelgavan. "Children here often think I am something very strange."

"I have had that happen, too," Fernao said. "At least they would not suspect you of being an Algarvian."

"Well, no," Talsu said. "Raise your arm, if you please, sir. I need another measurement." When he was through, he nodded to the Lagoan. "That will be all for now. I expect I can have your suit ready for you in a week or so."

"Good enough," Fernao said. "Thank you very much." He reclaimed his tunic, donned it again, and left the shop.

"That was a nice bit of business he just brought us, even with the discount," Valamo said.

"So it was," Talsu said. "Doing it will be a pleasure."

"A man should enjoy his work," the Kuusaman tailor agreed. "A man should also make money at his work. The Lagoan gentleman understood that. You should, too."

"If I have to choose between money and friendship, I know what my choice will be," Talsu said. "If he is going to wed the woman who helped me escape from that dungeon, I owe him everything I can give him."

"You owe him your best work. He owes you a fair price," Valamo said. "He will pay one. Now you have to do your best for him."

"I intend to," Talsu said.

"Good. Before long, you will be working for yourself, in your own shop. Your labor is all you have. Make it as good as you know how, but do not give very much of it away, or you will not eat."

"Good advice," Talsu said. "Let me see the patterns for

the style he picked out, please." Valamo passed him the book. He'd never tried anything so complicated, not on his own, but he thought he could do it. He went into the back of the shop to see exactly what fabric he had available, then settled down and got to work.

Bembo hadn't wanted to come back to duty on night patrol, but he didn't dare complain. From Captain Sasso's point of view, he supposed putting him here on the schedule made sense. Sasso already had a solid rotation of constables. Nobody much cared to go out at night, so why not give the newcomer that shift?

I'll tell you why not, Bembo thought. *If I trip over a high cobblestone I didn't see in the dark and break my leg again, I'll be very annoyed.* But he couldn't say that to Sasso, for fear the captain would tell him he couldn't do the job.

Six years had gone by, near enough, since he'd had the night shift when the war was new. Things had been pretty quiet then, and were pretty quiet now, for the same reason: a curfew was in force. Kuusaman patrols also tramped the streets. Bembo had had to show them his badge once already tonight. He didn't care for that, but liked the idea of getting blazed even less.

Tricarico wasn't black now, as it had been when the Derlavaian War was new. No enemy dragons flew overhead, ready to drop eggs on the city. But more than a few enemy dragons now ate their stupid heads off on Algarvian territory. If Bembo's people ever thought of rising up against their occupiers . . . He shuddered. The idea of suicide had never appealed to him.

He strode up the street toward the stump of the old Kaunian column in the center of town. The column itself had come down while he was in Forthweg—razed by the Algarvians, not by enemy action. Not much from the Kaunian past survived in Tricarico these days: not much in all of Algarve, from what he'd heard. The stump was bare, plain marble, about as tall as a man. The reliefs above it? Gone.

Beyond the remains of the column, somebody moved. Bembo's stick was in his hand on the instant. "Who goes?" he said sharply.

"It's only me," a woman's voice answered. "You wouldn't do anything to bother me, now would you?"

"Who the blazes—?" Bembo burst out. But the voice was familiar. "Fiametta, is that you?"

"Well, who else would it be, sweetheart?" she said as she came around what was left of the column. Her tunic might have been painted on; her kilt barely covered her shapely backside. "Bembo?" she asked, stopping short in surprise when she recognized him. "I thought you were dead!"

"Not quite," Bembo said. "What are you doing out after curfew? You ought to know better than that."

"What do you think I was doing?" Fiametta twitched her hips. "I was working, that's what. I'll go along home like a good little girl, I promise."

Bembo barked laughter. "You haven't been a good little girl since you got too big to make messes in your drawers. I caught you out right about here back when the war started, remember? I ought to run you in."

"You wouldn't do that!" the courtesan exclaimed in dismay.

"Why wouldn't I?" Bembo said. "You know what time it is. You're out late. You can't very well say I beat your door down and dragged you out of bed."

"Have a heart, Bembo!" Fiametta said. Bembo just stood there, looking official. The woman muttered something under her breath. He couldn't make out what, which was probably just as well. She sighed. "Look, suppose I give you some, too? Will you leave me alone then? It wouldn't be the first time, you know."

He didn't even think about Saffa. Constables and courtesans made bargains like this all the time. "Now you're talking," he said.

They found an alley where the street lights didn't reach. When Bembo came out a few minutes later, he was whistling. Fiametta, he supposed, headed to her home, or maybe just to another paying job. He wondered what she would do if she ran into a Kuusaman patrol. From everything he'd seen, the Kuusamans didn't make deals like that.

The rest of his shift passed less enjoyably, but he didn't have to do much. That suited him fine. The sun climbed up over the Bradano Mountains. He met his relief on the streets, then made his way back to the constabulary station to check out. As he neared the stairs, a skinny old man came up the street from the other direction. The fellow called his name.

"Aye, that's me," Bembo answered. "Who are you? Curfew doesn't end for another hour or so." If this fellow had no good explanation for being out and about, he'd grab him and haul him in. That would show people what a diligent fellow he was.

"You don't know me?" The skinny man looked down at himself. "Well, I can't say I'm surprised. There was more of me when we saw each other last."

Bembo's jaw dropped. "Sergeant Pesaro? Powers above! If this isn't old home week, I don't know what. But you were in Gromheort. How did you get out alive?"

Pesaro shrugged. "I hadn't quite starved to death when the Unkerlanters took the place—advantage to being fat, you know—and the fellow I surrendered to let me do it instead of blazing me. I got lucky there, I know. They didn't feed me much in the captives' camp, but they finally let most of us go—easier than hanging on to us, I expect. I've walked across most of Algarve to get here, on account of an awful lot of the ley lines still aren't working the way they're supposed to."

"You *were* lucky," Bembo said.

"If you want to call it that," Pesaro answered. "How about you? You were in Eoforwic when the Unkerlanters took it, so I didn't think I'd ever see your ugly mug again."

"I got wounded—broken leg—when the Unkerlanter attack opened up," Bembo said. "We still had a line of retreat open from the town, so they shipped me out. I don't think Oraste got away."

"Well, he always was a tough bastard," Pesaro said. "If Swemmel's men caught him, he'll have the chance to prove it. And if they didn't catch him, he's bound to be dead."

Bembo climbed the stairs and held the door open. "Come on, Sergeant. Show 'em you still know what's what."

"All I know is, I'm cursed glad I'm still breathing," Pesaro said as he wearily joined Bembo at the top of the stairs. "There were plenty of times when I didn't think I would be."

"Who you jawing with, Bembo?" the desk sergeant asked. "You arrest somebody?"

"No, Sergeant," Bembo answered. "Look, here's Sergeant Pesaro, back from the west. If he can make it back, maybe more people will."

"Sergeant Pesaro?" The desk sergeant sounded as if he couldn't believe his ears. He got up and stared at Pesaro. "Why, by the powers above, it is. Welcome home, Sergeant. Always good news when another one comes back." He glanced over at Bembo. "Well, almost always."

"And I love you, too, Sergeant," Bembo said sweetly.

Hearing Pesaro's name brought constables and clerks out from the back rooms of the constabulary station. They pounded the newcomer's back, clasped his wrist, and congratulated him on coming home again. *They never paid that much attention to me,* Bembo thought resentfully. But then he smiled to himself. *Let them fuss as much as they want. I've got Saffa warming my bed, and Pesaro won't be able to match that—or he'd better not, anyhow.*

Even Captain Sasso, who was in early, came down from his lofty office to greet Pesaro. "Good to see you, too, Captain," Pesaro said. "I wondered if I ever would, after you sent me west."

That brought a moment of silence. Bembo hadn't dared say any such thing to Sasso. The constabulary captain licked his lips. Everyone waited to hear how he would answer. At last, he said, "Well, Sergeant, back then none of us thought things would turn out the way they did."

Now it was Pesaro's turn to think things over. Grudgingly, he nodded. "All right, Captain, that's fair enough, I guess."

When Bembo went back to his flat, he found Saffa getting ready to go in to work. She burst into tears when he told her Pesaro had come back to Tricarico. She seemed so delighted, Bembo wondered if she *had* slept with the sergeant before he went west. But then Saffa said, "If he can come home . . ." She didn't finish the sentence, but she didn't have to. *If he can come home, my little bastard's daddy can come home, too, and then the powers below eat you, Bembo.* That was what she meant, that or something enough like it not to matter.

Bembo almost said something sharp in return, but at the last minute he decided to keep his mouth shut—something that came close to constituting an unnatural act for an Algarvian. He kissed her, patted her on the backside, yawned, and headed for the bedroom. He *was* tired. Saffa, he thought, gave him a grateful look for not picking a fight. Just before he fell asleep, he heard the door close as she went off to the constabulary station.

He got a rather different welcome when he came back to his flat a couple of mornings later. Saffa stood just inside the doorway. "You *son* of a whore!" she shouted, and slapped him in the face hard enough to rock him back on his heels. "You stick it into that cheap slut, and then you want to touch me? Not futtering likely!" She belted him again, backhand this time.

Though his ears rang, he did ask the right question: "What in blazes are you talking about?" He'd nearly said, *How did you know?* That would have lost the game before it even started.

But asking the right question didn't do him a bit of good, for Saffa ground out, "Fiametta told Adonio what you did, and Adonio brought the lovely news back to the station, and now everybody there must know it. And if you think you'll *ever* lay a finger on me again, let alone anything else—" She swung at him again.

He caught her by the wrist. When he didn't let go right away, she tried to bite his hand. "Stop that, powers below eat you!" he said. "I can expl—"

"I don't want to hear it," Saffa said. "I never want to hear it. You're not even wasting time telling me it's all a lie." She tried to twist away. He didn't let go. She snarled, "You'd better turn me loose, Bembo, or I'll *really* start screaming."

"All right, bitch," he said, "but if you try and take my

head off again I promise you'll lose teeth. Got it?" Saffa nodded warily. Even more warily, Bembo let go of her arm.

She took a quick step back. "I spent most of the night getting my stuff out of this place," she said. "I have to see you at the station, but that's *all* I have to do. As far as I'm concerned, you're dead. *Dead,* do you hear me?"

"Curse it, Saffa, all I did was—"

"Screw a tart the first chance you got. No thanks, pal. You don't play those games with me. Nobody plays those games with me."

"But, sweetheart," Bembo whined, "I really love you." Did he? He doubted it, but knew he had to sound as if he did. "It was just one of those things." He even made the ultimate sacrifice: "Darling, I'm sorry."

"Sorry till the next time you think you can get it wet on the side. Goodbye!" Saffa hyphenated the two syllables by slamming the door so hard, the frame quivered. Bembo stood staring at it for several heartbeats. Then he walked into the flat's little kitchen, poured himself a glass of spirits, and drank it down, all alone.

Ceorl scratched at his cheeks. He'd been doing that for days now, and cursing and fuming every time he did it. "This fornicating itch is driving me out of my mind," he said. "I don't know what I'm going to do about it."

One of the Unkerlanter gang bosses—one of the few captives who ranked as Ceorl's equal in the cinnabar mine—said, "Why don't you cut your throat? Then we won't have to listen to you any more." But even he smiled when he said it. He didn't want trouble from Ceorl. Nobody, not captives, not guards, wanted trouble from Ceorl.

Another Unkerlanter, one less prominent in the camp hierarchy, said, "Why don't you cut off that ugly beard? Maybe that would do some good. It sure looks like you've got the mange."

"It does not," Ceorl said indignantly. He was right, too; he had a fine, thick, curly beard. But he could have kissed that Unkerlanter—he'd been waiting for days for somebody to suggest shaving to him. He scratched again, then cursed again. "Powers above, maybe I will cut it off. Anything would be better than what I'm going through now. Who's got a razor he can lend me?"

The gang boss said, "You'll need a scissors first, to get that mess short enough so a razor will cut it."

"If you say so," Ceorl answered. "I don't know anything about this shaving business. I really may cut my throat."

He didn't get the chance to find out for another couple of days. He carefully spent all that time grumbling about how his face itched. When he got a scissors and a broken piece of mirror to guide his hand, he snipped away at the whiskers he'd never done more than trim before. By the time he set down the scissors, he was shaking his head. "I really do look mangy now."

The Unkerlanter called Fariulf handed him a straight razor and a cup of water to wet down what was left of his whiskers. "You won't once you're done here," he said.

Ceorl rapidly discovered he despised shaving. He cut himself several times. The razor scraped over his face. Had he really had an itchy skin, he was sure what he was doing would only have made things worse. His hide, in fact, did itch and sting by the time he got done. He shook his head again. "People have to be out of their cursed minds to want to do this every day." Reaching for the scrap of mirror, he added, "How do I look?"

His Unkerlanter was still foul. He knew that. People mostly understood him now, though. Somebody—somebody behind him, whom he couldn't note—said, "You're still ugly, but not the same way."

Looking into the mirror, Ceorl had to admit that wasn't far wrong. A stranger stared back at him: a man with a thrusting chin with a cleft in it, hollows below his cheekbones, and a scar above his upper lip he'd never seen before. He hadn't shown the world his bare face since he was a boy. He looked as if he'd suddenly got five years younger. He also looked like an Unkerlanter, not a Forthwegian.

"How does it feel?" Fariulf asked.

Lousy, Ceorl thought. But that was the wrong answer. He splashed a little water from the cup onto his abused face and ran the palm of his hand over his cheeks and chin. His skin felt as strange to him as it looked. Making himself smile, he said, "I think it's better. I'm going to have to keep doing this."

Acquiring a razor of his own didn't take long. Unkerlanter miners died all the time. Survivors split what little they had. They weren't supposed to have razors, but the guards usually winked at that—picks and shovels and crowbars made weapons at least as dangerous. One of those razors ended up in Ceorl's hands. Little by little, he learned to shave without turning his face into a mass of raw meat.

One afternoon, he took Sudaku aside and said, "When I give you the word, I'm going to want you and the boys to screw up the count."

"Ah." The blond from the Phalanx of Valmiera nodded, unsurprised. "Going to disappear, are you?"

"I don't know what you're talking about," Ceorl answered. He slapped Sudaku on the back. "I wish you could come along. But it wouldn't work, you know." He wasn't even lying; Kaunian or not, Sudaku made a pretty good right-hand man.

But Sudaku *was* a Kaunian, a blond. If he escaped from this mine, from this captives' camp, he couldn't possibly pretend to be an Unkerlanter. Ceorl could. "Good luck," Sudaku told him, and sounded as if he meant it.

"Thanks," Ceorl said. "I'll let you know when." Sudaku nodded. Ceorl knew he was taking a chance by saying even this much, but judged he could trust Sudaku so far. And the longer the head start he and Fariulf got when they broke out of this mining compound, the better the chance they had of getting away clean. If Ceorl hadn't believed in taking risks, he never would have become a robber or joined Plegmund's Brigade.

Then he had to get as ready as he could. Saving food wasn't easy, not when the captives got barely enough to keep them alive. Still and all, he managed to accumulate a good many little bricks of black bread. They would be stale and hard by the time he made his move, but he would still be able to eat them. He hoped Fariulf was making similar preparations. He hoped so, but he didn't try to find out. If Fariulf *wasn't* ready once they broke out, too bad for him.

Ceorl bided his time. When he did make the move, he

knew it would have to succeed. If it didn't, he would never see a second chance. Fariulf kept asking, "When? When?"

"I'll tell you when," Ceorl answered. "Don't hop out of your tunic."

Waiting paid off. A couple of weeks after he started shaving, the runs went through the camp. Most of the time, men needed leave to visit the latrine trenches. When they were liable to foul themselves if they waited, the guards waived the rule. It wasn't for the sake of the miners; Ceorl knew as much. It was so the guards wouldn't have to smell the stink or watch where they put their feet. Why mattered little to him. The waiver did.

He sidled up to Fariulf in the mine and said, "Tonight, a couple of hours after midnight." The Unkerlanter nodded without looking up; he'd learned such lessons as a captive's life could teach him. Later that day, Ceorl managed to whisper a couple of words in Sudaku's ear: "Tomorrow morning." The blond didn't even nod. He just gave Ceorl the sort of wave he would have used in the field to show he'd understood an order. *This may work*, Ceorl thought, and then, *It had better work.*

Even in the middle of the night, he wasn't the only one heading for the latrine trenches. He didn't want to think about what easing himself would be like in the middle of winter. He didn't intend to be here to find out.

He didn't hurry to the stinking trenches. Before long, Fariulf caught up with him. "What now?" the Unkerlanter asked.

"Now you get a guard to pay attention to you," Ceorl answered. "I don't care how you go about it—just do it. Once you manage it, we go from there."

"Right," Fariulf said. Then he added the same thought Ceorl had had earlier in the day: "This had better work."

"You aren't taking any chances I ain't," Ceorl said. Fariulf nodded.

Out beyond the slit trenches, guards paced beyond a deadline marked off by a rail fence. Any captive who crossed the deadline got blazed. So camp rules said. Ceorl had other ideas.

Fariulf squatted over a trench and started moaning and

grunting in such a good simulation of agony that even Ceorl, who knew better, wanted to do something for him. When a guard drew near, Fariulf moaned, "I want to go to the infirmary! I've got to go to the infirmary!"

"Shut up," the guard said, but his steps slowed. Fariulf didn't shut up. He kept on giving a splendid impression of a man in distress. The guard never noticed Ceorl sliding under the fence. Ceorl had had practice killing men silently before joining Plegmund's Brigade, and much more practice since. He slid up behind the Unkerlanter, clapped a hand over his mouth, and drew the razor across his throat. Even he had trouble hearing the whimpering gurgle that was the only sound the fellow made. He eased the body to the ground, picked up the guard's stick, and started walking his beat.

Fariulf rose and hurried over to him. "Stay down," Ceorl hissed. "Don't draw eyes." Fariulf flattened out on the ground. Ceorl gave him a kick in the ribs to remind him to keep low. "Get going. I'll be along."

He marched along till he saw another guard coming out of the darkness and made sure the other fellow saw him. Then he turned, as if going back along the beat. He almost went past the spot where he'd killed the guard; Fariulf had dragged the corpse somewhere out of the way. "Efficiency," Ceorl muttered: nearly too much efficiency.

He hurried out, and soon caught up with the Unkerlanter. The trenches and fences around the mine were designed to keep captives in. Before the war, they probably would have done a good enough job. They weren't adequate for confining men who'd faced worse barricades, and better manned ones, in Unkerlant and Forthweg and Yanina and Algarve. Ceorl killed another guard on the way out, again without a sound.

"We're leaving a trail," Fariulf said.

"Did you want him to nab us?" Ceorl snarled, and the Unkerlanter shook his head.

For all of King Swemmel's preaching about efficiency, the guards took a long time to realize anything was amiss. Ceorl and Fariulf were out of the enclosure around the cinnabar mine by then, looking around for somewhere to lie up during the approaching day. "I didn't think it would be this easy," Fariulf said. "Why doesn't everybody escape?"

"Most people are sheep," Ceorl said scornfully. "Would *you* have tried breaking out if I hadn't pushed you?" A troubled look on his face, Fariulf shook his head.

But the search, once it started, was not to be despised. No matter how Sudaku muddled the count, two dead guards got noticed. Dragons circled low overhead. Teams of guards swept through the hills. Had Ceorl and Fariulf not learned their trade in a harder school than this, they might have been taken that first day. As things were, they stayed hidden in scrubby bushes, and pushed north after nightfall. Fariulf did have food of his own, which was as well, for Ceorl had no intention of giving him any of his.

To Ceorl's amazement, Fariulf had no idea where in his own kingdom the Mamming Hills lay. "Once we get over the Wolter, we'll be back in regular country, without all these bastards snooping around," Ceorl said.

"Inspectors are everywhere," Fariulf told him sadly.

The warning made Ceorl fight shy of approaching the few herdsmen he saw in the hills. Perhaps it didn't make him wary enough, though. He and Fariulf were nearing the Wolter when dogs started baying close behind them. A moment later, men shouted, their voices harsh as crows' caws. "They've seen us!" Fariulf said, panic in his voice.

Ceorl shoved the Unkerlanter away. "Split up!" he said. "It'll be harder for them to catch us both." What he expected was that the pursuer would go after Fariulf, for the other man wasn't so good in open country as he was himself. Maybe Fariulf had been an irregular, but he hadn't learned enough.

So Ceorl thought. But the men in rock-gray came after him instead. Some of them were veterans, too. He could tell by the way they spread out and came forward in waves, making him keep his head down.

He blazed one at close range anyhow, then whirled and blazed another. When he whirled again, a beam caught him in the chest. As he crumpled, he thought, *Maybe living in a cage wouldn't have been so bad after all.* But, as he'd given no second chances, he got none. Darkness swallowed him.

* * *

Garivald stared at the Wolter. He'd never imagined a river could be so wide—he hadn't been able to see out when the ley-line caravan car took him over it to the mine in the Mamming Hills. He wasn't a bad swimmer, but knew he would drown if he tried to cross it. If he stayed here on the south bank, the guards would hunt him down. He was sure of that, too, even if they hadn't pursued him after he left Ceorl.

I need a boat, he thought. He saw none, though at night that proved little: a big one might have been tied up a quarter of a mile away, and he would never have known it. He doubted one was; Swemmel's men knew more about efficiency than to make things easy for their captives. *A raft,* he thought. *A tree trunk. Anything to keep me afloat.*

He wondered what he would do even if he got to the far bank of the Wolter. He had no money. He had nothing, in fact, except his boots, the ragged tunic on his back, and a rapidly dwindling store of bread. Before long, he would have to start stealing food from the local peasants and herders. If he did that, he knew he wouldn't last long.

He wrapped brush around himself—a miserable bed, but better than bare ground—and went to sleep. *When I wake up, maybe everything will be all right,* he thought. He had no idea why he'd come up with such a preposterous unlikelihood, but if he hadn't believed it would he have tried to escape with the Forthwegian?

A shout, thin in the distance, threw him out of sleep a little before sunrise the next day. He sprang up, ready to flee. Had they found his trail after all?

But the shout came from the river, not the land: Garivald realized as much when he heard it again, this time fully conscious. He stared out toward the Wolter. His jaw dropped. He began giggling, as if suddenly stricken mad.

Maybe I was, he thought giddily. *Maybe I'm not really seeing this.* He'd hoped for a tree trunk, to help him cross the river. Never in all the days of the world, he told himself, had such a hope been so extravagantly fulfilled.

Thousands, tens of thousands, hundreds of thousands— for all Garivald knew, millions—of felled trees floated on the Wolter, drifting downstream toward . . . what? Sawmills, he supposed. He wondered why anyone would have cared to build sawmills on a river sure to freeze up in winter. Maybe those sawmills were like the mines: a scheme to get some use out of captives instead of just killing them outright. Or maybe King Swemmel had simply pointed at a map and said, "Build sawmills here." If he had, the sawmills would have gone up, regardless of whether the Wolter froze.

Here and there, tiny in the distance, insignificant among the countless trunks of the floating forest, men with poles rode logs, somehow staying upright. Now and again, they would use the poles to keep the tree trunks from jamming together. It was one of their shouts that Garivald had heard.

He didn't waste more than a couple of minutes gawping. How long would that seemingly endless stream of trees endure? If it passed without his taking advantage of it, how long would he have to wait till another one came down the Wolter? Too long—he was sure of that.

When he got down to the riverbank, he shed his boots, pulled his tunic off over his head, and plunged into the Wolter. Although it flowed from down out of the warmer north, its waters still chilled him. He struck out toward the immense swarm of logs.

Before long, Garivald wondered if he'd made a dreadful mistake. Going from log to log across the river hadn't seemed so hard till he tried it. Not getting crushed by all that floating, drifting timber was a lot harder than he'd imagined.

He'd made it perhaps halfway through the logs when one of the men riding herd on them spotted him. "What in blazes are you doing here, you son of a whore?" the fellow bawled.

"Getting away from the mines," Garivald shouted back. If the log-rider came over to try to seize him, he'd do his best to drown the man.

But the fellow with the pole only waved when he heard that. "Good luck, pal," he said. "Me, I never saw you. My brother went into the mines almost ten years ago, and he never came out."

Powers above, there are some decent people in this kingdom after all, Garivald thought as he went on toward the far bank of the Wolter. After the way he'd got dragged into the army—and after the way he'd been seized coming out of it—he'd had his doubts. He couldn't dwell on that, though, for he had to scramble to keep an oncoming log from crushing him to jelly against the one he was riding.

He went from one log to another. And then, quite suddenly, no more logs remained between him and the far bank, which was now the near bank. He swam till his feet hit bottom. Then he waded ashore and redonned his sodden tunic and even soggier boots. His belly growled; the bread hadn't survived the trip across the Wolter. He trudged away from the stream, hoping to find a road or a village.

When he saw a man working in a field, he waved and called, "I'll do whatever you need for a supper and a chance to sleep in a barn."

The farmer looked him over. He still wasn't dry, nor anywhere close to it. "What happened to you?" the fellow asked. "Looks like you fell in a creek."

"Oh, you might say so," Garivald agreed dryly—his words made the grade, even if he didn't.

Or so he thought, till the farmer screwed up his face and said, "You're not from around these parts, I don't reckon."

"No." Garivald admitted what he could hardly deny—he did sound like a Grelzer. He came out with the best excuse he could: "I'm just another soldier who got dumped in the wrong place trying to get back to my own farm and my own woman."

"Huh." The local looked toward the Wolter. There was, Garivald realized, bound to be a reward for men who turned in escaped captives. But the farmer said, "So you've got a place of your own, eh? Well, prove it."

After grubbing cinnabar out of a vein with pick and crowbar, farm work wasn't so bad. When the sun swung to the west, Garivald followed the farmer back to his hut. He got a big bowl of barley porridge with onions and dill and sausage, and a mug of ale to wash it down. Set beside the little bricks of bread and famine stews in the mines, it seemed the best meal he'd ever eaten.

He did sleep in an outbuilding, next to a couple of cows. He didn't care. When morning came, the farmer gave him another bowl of porridge, a length of sausage to take with him, and a couple of coins. Tears came to Garivald's eyes. "I can't pay this back," he said.

"Pay it forward," the local told him. "Someday you'll run into another poor bastard down on his luck. Now go on, before somebody gets a good look at you."

Day by day, Garivald worked his way north and east, toward the Duchy of Grelz. Most people, he thought, took him for an escapee, but no one turned him in to Swemmel's inspectors. He got meals. He got money. He got shelter. And he got a good look at what the war had done to this part of Unkerlant. What he'd seen in Grelz suddenly didn't seem so dreadful.

The city of Durrwangen was still in ruins. Plenty of labor gangs were slowly putting the place back together again. Captives didn't man all of them. Garivald got the idea that King Swemmel didn't have enough captives to do all the things he wanted to do. He joined a gang that paid a little—not much, but a little. He'd had plenty of practice in Zossen at making a little stretch. Before too long, he'd saved enough silver for a ley-line caravan fare to Linnich.

And then, when he went to the depot in Durrwangen to buy the fare, he bought it for Tegeler, the next town northwest of Linnich—he remembered the name from his journey back from Algarve. Someone in Linnich might be looking for him. No one in Tegeler would be. The price went up a little, but he reckoned it silver well spent.

When he climbed down from the caravan car in Tegeler, he saw a lounger keeping an eye on people descending. But the lounger had never seen him before, and had no reason to suspect him of anything. Aye, he was ragged and none too clean, but a lot of men on the ley-line caravan could have used a bath and new clothes.

He started for Linnich on foot. He didn't know exactly how far it was: if he'd had to guess, he would have said about twenty miles. It proved farther than that, for he needed a day and a half to get there. He had no trouble cadging a couple of meals along the way. For one thing, there were no works with lots of captives anywhere close by. For another, his Grelzer accent sounded just like everyone else's hereabouts.

Garivald didn't go into Linnich, but skirted the town. Maybe Dagulf hadn't told the impressers where he was working a farm. Maybe. But he didn't want his former friend—or anyone else—to have another chance at betraying him.

He worried about going back to the farm, too. Did an inspector have an eye on it, wondering if he'd return? How many inspectors did King Swemmel have? Garivald had no idea. Of one thing he was sure, though: Obilot was all he had left in the world. Without her, he might as well have stayed in the mines.

The track leading to the farm was as overgrown as it had been the last time he'd walked it, more than a year before, between the impressers who'd hauled him into the army. What did that mean? He couldn't know till he got where he was going, which didn't stop him from worrying. His heart pounded in his chest as he came round the last bend and saw the farm at last.

Crops are getting ripe, he thought. And then he spied Obilot, weeding in the vegetable patch by the farmhouse. He didn't see anyone else. That had been another worry. He'd been gone a long time, including some little while after the end of the war. How could anyone blame her for thinking he was dead?

She looked up and saw him coming through the fields toward the house. The first thing she did was reach for something beside her—*a stick,* Garivald thought. Then she checked the motion and got to her feet. Garivald waved. So did Obilot. She ran to him.

She almost knocked him off his feet when she took him in her arms, but her embrace helped keep him upright. "I knew you would come back," she said. "I don't know why, but I did."

"Where else would I come?" Garivald said, and kissed her for a long time. That dizzied him; it felt stronger than spirits. But he couldn't afford to get drunk on anything, even sensuality, now. He asked, "Do they watch this place?"

Obilot's eyes narrowed. "It's like that?" she said. He nodded. "I haven't seen anybody," she told him. "Not since Dagulf . . . died, and that was a while ago now."

"Oh?" Garivald said. "How did that happen?"

"Nobody seems to know," Obilot answered, not quite innocently enough. "Are we going to have to find another abandoned place and learn new names for ourselves all over again?"

Garivald looked around. She'd done an astonishing job of keeping this farm going. All the same, he nodded. "I'm afraid so. A couple of men ended up dead when I got out of the mines."

"Mines? Oh." Obilot nodded, too, briskly and without regret. "All right, we do, then. We can manage. I'm sure of it."

"We'll have a chance," Garivald said, ingrained peasant pessimism in his voice. But then he shrugged. In Unkerlant, a chance was all you could hope for, and more than you usually got.

Istvan climbed down from the wagon near the mouth of the valley that held Kunhegyes and the neighboring villages. "Thank you kindly for the lift, sir," he told the driver, a gray-bearded man with stooped shoulders.

"Glad to help, young fellow," the other Gyongyosian replied. "Nothing's too good for our fighters, by the stars. You'd best believe it."

"Uh, the war is over," Istvan said—maybe the wagon driver hadn't heard. "We lost." He brought the words out painfully. They hurt, aye, but they were true. No one who'd seen Gyorvar could doubt it even for a moment. He wished he hadn't seen Gyorvar himself. He wished he hadn't seen a great many things he'd had to see.

But the driver waved his words away, as if they were of no account. "Sooner or later, we'll lick 'em," he declared. Istvan doubted he had a particular 'em in mind—any enemy of Gyongyos would do. He wished things still looked so simple to him. They never would again. The driver flicked his whip and said, "Stars shine bright on you, Sergeant."

"And on you," Istvan called as the wagon rattled away.

Shouldering the duffel that held his few belongings, he trudged toward Kunhegyes. He wasn't sure he'd been formally discharged from the army. Back in the coastal lowlands, government had been a matter of opinion since the death of Ekrekek Arpad and the destruction of Gyorvar. No one in all his long journey east had asked to see his papers. He didn't expect anyone here would, either.

He looked around his home valley with wonder on his face. He'd been back only once since the war began. The place had seemed smaller then than when he'd gone forth to fight for Gyongyos. It seemed smaller still now, the mountains looming over the narrow bit of land trapped between them. *Mountain apes up there,* Istvan thought. He'd seen one of those, too. *I've seen too much.* He looked down at the scar on his left hand, the scar that had expiated his goat-eating, and shuddered. *Aye, I've seen much too much.*

Somewhere back on Obuda—or, more likely, back in Kuusamo by now—a little slant-eyed mage knew what he'd done. That made him shudder, too. Not that she would ever come to Kunhegyes—Istvan knew better than that. But he knew she knew, and the knowledge ate at him. He might as well have been naked before the world.

He tramped up to Kunhegyes' battered old palisade. He had a much keener eye for field fortifications than he'd owned when he left the village. A couple of egg-tossers could have knocked it down in nothing flat. Rocks and bushes within stick range might give marauders cover. *I'll have to talk to somebody,* he thought. *Never can tell what those whoresons from the next valley over—or even from Szombathely down the valley from us—might try and do.*

A sentry did pace the palisade. That was something. Istvan wondered how much, though. Had the fellow been more alert, he would have already spotted him. That thought had hardly gone through Istvan's mind before the lookout stiffened, peered out toward him, and called, "Who comes to Kunhegyes?"

Istvan recognized his voice. "Hail, Korosi," he called back. The villager had made his life difficult before he'd gone into Ekrekek Arpad's army, but he'd been mild enough when Istvan visited on leave. Easier to overawe a youth than a veteran on leave, Istvan supposed.

"Is that you, Istvan?" Korosi said now. "Have you got another leave?"

"Another leave?" Istvan gaped. "Have the stars addled your wits? The war's over. Haven't you heard?" He'd known his home village was backward, but this struck him as excessive. Kun would have laughed and laughed. But Kun was dead, struck down by the sorcery that had slain Gyorvar.

Korosi said, "Some commercial traveler tried to tell us that a couple of days ago, but we figured it was a pack of lies. He spouted all sorts of nonsense—the ekrekek, stars love him, slain; Gyorvar gone in a flash of light; the goat-eating Unkerlanters licking us in the east; us surrendering, if you can believe it. Some of us wanted to pitch him in the creek for that pack of crap, but we didn't."

"A good thing, too, because it isn't crap," Istvan said, and watched the village bruiser's jaw drop. Istvan qualified that: "Well, I don't know about Swemmel's bastards, not so I can take oath about it, but the rest is true. I was stationed near Gyorvar, I saw the city die, and I've been in it since. The ekrekek's dead, and so is his whole family. And we *have* yielded—it was either that or get another dose of this wizardry. I saw a Lagoan going through what's left of Gyorvar, looking to see just what the magic did. One of our mages was with him, and acting mild as milk."

"You're making that up," Korosi said. In a different tone, it could have been an insult, even a challenge. But Istvan had heard men cry, "No!" when they knew they were wounded but didn't want to believe it. Korosi's protest was of that sort.

"By the stars, Korosi, it's true," Istvan said. "Let me in. The whole village needs to know."

"Aye." Korosi still sounded shaken to the core. He descended from the palisade and unbarred the gate. It creaked open. Istvan walked through. Korosi shut it behind him. He looked around. *I probably won't go far from this place for the rest of my life.* Part of him rejoiced at the realization.

The rest saw how small and cramped Kunhegyes seemed, as if crouching behind its palisade. True, the houses and shops stood well apart from one another—a precaution against ambushes—but they themselves were nothing beside those of Gyorvar. Istvan shook his head. *No, beside what once was in Gyorvar. Only rocks and houses alike melted to slag there now.*

Korosi's booted feet thumped on the wooden stairs as he went up to the walkway once more. People came out into Kunhegyes' narrow main street. Istvan found himself the center of a circle of staring eyes, some green, some blue, some brown. "Did I hear you right?" somebody asked. "Did you tell Korosi it's over? We lost?"

"That's right, Maleter," Istvan said to the middle-aged man. "It is over. We did lose." He repeated what had happened to Gyorvar, and to Ekrekek Arpad and his kin.

Quietly, women began to weep. Tears didn't suit the men of a warrior race, but several of them turned away so no one would have to see them shed any. The sounds of mourning drew more folk into the street. One of them was the younger of Istvan's two sisters. She shrieked his name and threw herself into his arms. "Are you all right?" she demanded.

He stroked her curly, tawny hair. "I'm fine, Ilona," he said. "That's not what people are upset about. I told them the war was lost."

"Is *that* all?" she said. "What difference does that make, as long as you're safe?"

Istvan's first thought was that that was no attitude for a woman from a warrior race to have. His second thought was that maybe she owned better sense than a lot of other people in Gyongyos. Remembering what had happened to Gyorvar, he decided there was no *maybe* to it. "What's happened here?" he asked. "That's what's really important, isn't it?" *It is if I stay here the rest of my days, that's certain sure.*

"Of course it is." Ilona had no doubts; she'd never been out of the valley. "Well, for one thing, Saria"—Istvan's other sister—"is betrothed to Gul, the baker's son."

"That weedy little worm?" Istvan exclaimed. But he

checked himself; Gul might have been weedy when he went off to war, but probably wasn't any more. And his father had, or had had, more money than Istvan's own. "What else?" he asked.

"Great-uncle Batthyany died last spring," his sister told him.

"Stars shine bright on his spirit," Istvan said. Ilona nodded. Istvan went on, "He was full of years. Did he pass on peacefully?"

"Aye," Ilona said. "He went to sleep one night, and he wouldn't wake the next morning."

"Can't ask for better than that," Istvan agreed, trying not to think of all the worse deaths he'd seen.

His sister took him by the hand and started dragging him toward the family house—*my house again, at least for a while,* he thought. She said, "But what happened to *you*? By the stars, Istvan, we all feared you were dead. You never wrote very often, but when your letters just plain stopped coming. . . ."

"I couldn't write," he said. "I got sent from the woods of Unkerlant out to this island in the Bothnian Ocean—"

"We know that," Ilona said. "That was when your letters stopped."

"They stopped because I got captured," Istvan said. "I was in a Kuusaman captives' camp on Obuda for a long time, but then the slanteyes sent me to Gyorvar."

"Why did they send you there?"

"Because of something I'd seen. I wasn't the only one. They wanted us to warn the ekrekek they'd do the same to Gyorvar if he didn't yield to them. He didn't, and so they did. I wish he would have. We'd all be better off if he would have—him included."

By that time, they'd come to his front door. Alpri, his father, was nailing the heel of a boot to the sole. The cobbler looked up from his work. "May I help—?" he began, as he would have when anyone walked into the shop that was also a house. Then he recognized Istvan. He let out a roar like a tiger's, rushed around the cobbler's bench, and squeezed the breath from his son. "I knew the stars would bring you home!" he shouted, planting a kiss on each of Istvan's cheeks. "I *knew* it!" He let out another roar, this one with words in it: "Gizella! Saria! Istvan's home!"

Istvan's mother and his other sister came running up from the back of the house. They smothered him in kisses and exclamations. Someone—he never did see who— pressed a beaker of mead into his hand.

"You're home!" his mother said, over and over again.

"Aye, I'm home," Istvan agreed. "I don't think I'm ever going to leave this valley again."

"Stars grant it be so," Gizella said. Istvan's father and his sisters all nodded vigorously. Somehow, they held beakers of mead, too.

Had Istvan got out of the army not long after going in, he would have had no qualms about staying close to Kunhegyes the rest of his days, either. But he'd seen so much of the wider world the past six years, the valley still felt too small to suit him as well as it might have. *I'll get used to it again,* he thought. *I have to get used to it again.*

A pull at the sweet, strong mead went a long way toward reconciling him to being home. "With the war lost, with the ekrekek dead, where would I go?" he said, as much to himself as to his family. Alpri and Gizella and Saria all exclaimed again, this time in shocked dismay, so he had to tell his news once more.

"What will we do?" his father asked. "What can we do? Have the stars abandoned us forever?"

Istvan thought about that. "I don't know," he said at last. "I'm not even sure it matters. We have to go on living our lives as best we can any which way, don't you think?" Was that heresy or simply common sense? He had the feeling Kun would have approved. The scar on his left hand didn't throb, as it often did when he found himself in doubt or dismay. And, that evening, the stars shone down brilliantly on the celebrating village of Kunhegyes. Maybe that meant they approved of what he'd said. Maybe it didn't matter either way. *How can I know?* Istvan wondered. He didn't suppose he could, which didn't stop him from celebrating, too.

* * *

For once, the great square in front of the royal palace in Cottbus was packed with people. The Unkerlanters remained in holiday mood, too. *And why not?* Marshal Rathar thought. *We didn't just beat Algarve. We beat Gyongyos, too.* He looked back at the assembled might in the victory parade he was to lead. *We could lick the Kuusamans and the Lagoans, too. We could, if . . .*

If. The word ate at him. He hadn't gone into Gyorvar himself, but he'd had reports from men who had. The sorcery that had destroyed the capital of Gyongyos could fall on Cottbus, too. He knew that. He never forgot it. He had to hope King Swemmel also remembered it.

High and thin and spidery, a single note from a trumpet rang out: the signal for the parade to begin. *It should have been an officer's whistle, ordering the advance,* Rathar thought. But it was what it was. He thrust out his chest, thrust back his head, and marched forward as proudly and precisely as if he were on parade at the officer's collegium he'd never attended.

When he came into sight, the people who packed the square—all but the parade route through it—shouted his name again and again: "Rathar! Rathar! Rathar!"

Rathar had rather thought they would do that. He'd rather feared they would do that, in fact. He held up his hand. Silence fell. He pointed toward the reviewing stand, on which, surrounded by bodyguards, his sovereign stood. "King Swemmel!" he shouted. "Huzzah for King Swemmel!"

To his vast relief, most of the people started shouting Swemmel's name. He suspected they did so for the same reason he'd pointed to the king: simple fear. If a vast throng of folk started crying Rathar's name, Swemmel was too likely to think his marshal planned to try to steal his throne—and to make sure Rathar had no chance to do so. As for the folk who'd started yelling for Rathar, all of them had to know one of the men and women standing nearby was bound to be an inspector. The mines always needed fresh blood, despite the great glut of captives in them now. Inside a couple of years, most of those captives would be dead.

Behind Rathar came a block of footsoldiers. Behind them trudged weary, hungry-looking Gyongyosian captives. Most of those men would probably head for the Mamming Hills after their display here. Or maybe Swemmel had canals he wanted dug or rubble that needed carting away. The possibilities, in a kingdom ravaged by war, were endless.

After the Gongs marched a regiment of unicorn-riders, and then a regiment of behemoths. Rathar could hear the chain-mail clanking on the great beasts through the rhythmic thud of marching feet. Hearing that clank reminded him of reports the islanders had come up with behemoth armor better at stopping beams than anything his own kingdom had. One more project to keep the mages busy—as if they didn't have enough.

More behemoths hauled egg-tossers of all sizes through the square. Another shambling throng of Gyongyosian captives came after them, followed by more Unkerlanter footsoldiers. Those Gongs and soldiers might have to watch where they put their feet. Dragons painted rock-gray flapped past overhead. They were incontinent beasts, too; Rathar hoped none of them chose the wrong moment to do something unfortunate.

As he passed the reviewing stand—which, along with Swemmel and his guardsmen, held Unkerlanter courtiers and foreign dignitaries and attachés (the latter sure to be taking notes on the parade)—Marshal Rathar met the king's eye and saluted him. King Swemmel gave back his usual unwinking stare. But then, to the marshal's surprise, he deigned to return the salute.

Rathar almost missed a step. Did a formal, public salute from Swemmel mean the king truly trusted him? Or did it mean Swemmel wanted to lull his suspicions and put him out of the way? How could he tell, till the day came or didn't?

You could rebel, he thought. *Plenty would back you.* But, as always, he rejected the idea as soon as it crossed his mind. For one thing, he didn't want the throne. For another, he was sure Swemmel would win in a game of intrigue. He was doing what he wanted to do. He did it well. The crown? If Swemmel wanted it so badly, he was welcome to it.

Out of the square marched Rathar, out of the square and

down Cottbus' main avenue. The sidewalks there were packed, too; only a continuous line of constables and impressers held the crowd back. Men and women cheered much more enthusiastically than Unkerlanters usually did. If they were proud of what their kingdom had accomplished, they'd earned the right to be. And if they were relieved Unkerlant had survived, they'd also earned that right. How many of them had tried to flee west when Cottbus looked like falling to the Algarvians almost four years before? More than a few—Rathar was sure of that. How many would admit it now? Next to none, and the marshal was sure of that, too.

People who didn't have the pull to get into the central square shouted Swemmel's name more often than they shouted Rathar's. *These are the poor people, the ignorant people,* Rathar thought. *They don't really know who did what.*

That thought salved his vanity. Even so, he wondered how much truth it really held. Aye, Rathar had been the one who'd made the plans and given the orders that led to the defeat of the redheads and the Gyongyosians. But King Swemmel had been the one who refused even to imagine that Unkerlant could be beaten. Without such an indomitable man at the top, the kingdom might have fallen to pieces under the hammer blows the Algarvians struck during the first summer and autumn of the war.

Of course, if we hadn't been readying our own attack on Mezentio's men, if we'd paid more attention to defending our kingdom against them, they might not have been able to strike those hammer blows. Rathar shrugged. It was years too late to worry about such things now.

After the parade ended, a carriage waited to take Marshal Rathar back to the palace. Major Merovec waited in his office. Rathar set a sympathetic hand on Merovec's shoulder: no one cared about adjutants in victory parades. No one would ever know how important a job Merovec had had or how well he'd done it, either.

Perhaps not quite no one: Merovec said, "Thank you, sir—my promotion to colonel has finally come through."

"Good," Rathar said. "I put that in for you more than a year ago. One thing nobody can do, though, is hurry his Majesty."

"No, of course not," his adjutant replied. "What do they say, though? A rising tide lifts all boats? That's how things are right now."

"My boat has lifted me as far as I care to rise, thank you very much," the marshal said. He didn't know for certain that King Swemmel could sorcerously listen to his conversations, but had to assume the king could manage it. And there was only one higher rank to which a rising tide could lift him: the one Swemmel now held. He didn't want the king believing he aspired to the throne. Such notions, as he'd thought during the parade, were dangerous. He nodded to Merovec. "After putting up with me for so long, you deserve a promotion."

"Thank you, sir," Merovec said. "What rank do you suppose I'll have when the next war comes down the ley line at us?"

"The next war?" Rathar echoed.

His adjutant nodded. "Aye, sir. The one against the islanders, I mean. Whoever wins that will have all of Derlavai in his beltpouch."

"If it comes soon, we won't win it," Rathar said. "If it comes soon, they'll serve Cottbus as they served Gyorvar, and we can't hit back the same way. They can make us back away from whatever we try. We'd have to."

I hope we'd have to, the marshal thought. *If Swemmel gets a sudden attack of pride, he could throw this whole kingdom down the sewer.* He would have worried less with a calmer, more sensible ruler—not that Unkerlant had enjoyed a lot of calm, sensible rulers in her history.

A young lieutenant stuck his head into the office, spotted Marshal Rathar, and brightened. "There you are, lord Marshal," he said, as if Rathar had been playing hide-and-seek. "His Majesty wants to confer with you. At once."

At once should have gone without saying where Swemmel was concerned. Being king meant never having to wait. "I'm coming," Rathar said. That also went without saying. Merovec saluted as the marshal left the office. As always when summoned by Swemmel, Rathar wondered if he would ever come back here again.

He surrendered his ceremonial sword to Swemmel's

guards, let them frisk him, and then abased himself before his sovereign. "You may rise," the king said. "Did you see the Kuusaman and Lagoan vultures perched on the reviewing stand with us when you marched past?"

"Aye, your Majesty," Rathar replied. "I noticed the islanders' ministers and their attachés."

"What do you think they made of our might?" King Swemmel asked.

"Your Majesty, no matter how strong we are in soldiery, we dare not cross Lagoas and Kuusamo in any serious way till we can match them in magecraft, too," Rathar said. "They have to know that as well as we do."

Grimly, Swemmel nodded. "And so they laugh at us behind their hands. Well, we shall set our own mages to work, as indeed we have already done, and we shall see what spying can bring us, too."

"That will not be so easy," Marshal Rathar said. "How can one of our people pretend to come from Lagoas or Kuusamo?"

"One of our people would have a difficult time," the king agreed. "There are, however, some few Algarvians who speak Lagoan without a trace of accent. Some of them were Mezentio's spies. Paid well enough—and with their families held hostage to guard against betrayal—they should serve us well, too."

"Ah," Rathar said. "If we can bring that off, it will serve us well."

"Many Algarvians are whores who will do anything for money," Swemmel said. Rathar nodded. The king went on, "Our task is to find the ones who will be able to understand what they need to learn, and to slip them into the Lagoan Guild of Mages. It may not be easy or quick, but we think it can be done. As they say in cards, one peek is worth a thousand finesses."

Rathar laughed. He couldn't remember the last time he'd heard King Swemmel crack a joke. Then he realized the king wasn't joking. He nodded again all the same. Joking or not, Swemmel was right.

Nineteen

When the door to Lurcanio's cell opened at a time when he wasn't scheduled to be fed or exercised, he bit down on the inside of his lower lip. A break in routine meant trouble. He hadn't taken long to learn that. *How many captives in Algarvian gaols learned the same lesson?* he wondered. More than a few: of that he had no doubt. It didn't matter. Now it was happening to him. That mattered more than anything else in the world.

One of the Valmieran guards who came in pointed a stick at his face. "Get moving," he snapped.

Lurcanio got moving. He moved slowly and carefully, always keeping his hands in plain sight. The guards had made it very clear that they wanted him dead. He didn't care to give them any excuse to get what they wanted. "May I ask where we are going?" he inquired.

He got a nasty grin from that guard. Another one replied, "The judges have your verdict."

"Very well." Lurcanio did his best not to show the fear he felt. The judges could do whatever they pleased with him, and he had no chance of stopping them. He'd sung like a nightingale for his interrogators. Maybe that would count enough to keep him breathing. Of course, maybe it wouldn't, too.

Bright sunlight outside the gaol made him blink. His eyes watered. Not much light leaked into his cell. The guards hustled him into a carriage that carried more iron than a behemoth. A four-horse team had to draw it. Locks clicked and snapped on the doors after he got in.

In the passenger compartment, an iron grill separated him from the guard who rode with him. As the Valmieran locked it, Lurcanio asked, "What if I were a wizard? Could I conjure my way out of here?"

"Go ahead and try," the blond answered. "This here carriage is warded against anything a first-rank mage can do."

Lurcanio didn't believe him. Sorcerers were often more inventive than those who tried to stop them gave them credit for being. So were other people, come to that. Gaolers would have had an easier time were that not so. But Lurcanio himself was no wizard. He remained a captive. They hadn't even let him clean up before hauling him off to court. He didn't take that for a good sign.

He went into the courtroom through a hallway reserved for the accused—and even more lined with guards than usual today. When he entered, he found the place packed. Excitement filled the air. It was almost as palpable as sorcerous energy just before a major spell. The three judges, two in civilian costume, the third in uniform, strode in and took their places at the head of the courtroom. Everyone rose respectfully. Lurcanio bowed to them, as he would have done in an Algarvian lawcourt.

"Be seated," the bailiff intoned.

The chief judge, the soldier, sat in the center. He rapped loudly for order. "We have reached a verdict in the case of the Kingdom of Valmiera against Colonel Lurcanio of Algarve," he declared. "Is the accused present?"

"No, your Excellency. I am not here," Lurcanio declared. The scribe recording his words gave him a reproachful look. A few people giggled. Lurcanio thought he heard Krasta's voice. He looked around. Aye, there she was. *She wants to see me pay,* Lurcanio thought. She would likely get what she wanted, too.

Bang! The gavel stifled the giggles. "By speaking, the accused admits his presence," the senior judge said. "His display of levity is out of order, and will not be tolerated again."

"Will you do worse to me for making a bad joke than for any of the other things you claim I did while I served my kingdom?" Lurcanio asked.

"By no means, Colonel," the judge replied. "But we will bind and gag you. If that is what you want, you have but to say the word." He waited. Lurcanio said nothing. The judge nodded. "All right, then. Are you ready to hear the verdict of this court?"

Ready? Lurcanio thought. *Powers above, no!* But his dignity kept him from saying that out loud. He was sure they *would* bind and gag him. He was sure they would enjoy doing it, too. Refusing to give them the satisfaction, he nodded curtly. "I am ready, your Excellency, though I still insist this court has no legal jurisdiction over a soldier engaged in prosecuting a war."

"We have rejected that argument for others, and we reject it for you as well." The chief judge shuffled papers, then looked up at Lurcanio. "This court, Colonel, finds you guilty of facilitating the transportation of Kaunians through the Kingdom of Valmiera for the purpose of sacrifice. It also finds you guilty of facilitating the program known as Night and Fog, which seized Valmierans for the purpose of sacrifice. This court further finds that these programs constitute murder, not warfare. Accordingly, you are hereby sentenced to be blazed to death."

Lurcanio had been braced for it. It still came like a punch in the belly. So did the baying applause from the crowd in the courtroom. "I appeal this false verdict," he said, as steadily as he could.

"No." The chief judge shook his head. "This court was set up to deal with cases of this kind. There is no court to which to appeal our verdict."

"Very neat," Lurcanio said. The sarcasm got through; the judge flushed. Lurcanio went on, "No court to which to appeal, you say? May I not appeal to King Gainibu himself? I got to know him well during the occupation." *He turned out not to be quite so sottish and worthless as I thought he was, too. You never can tell.*

That request seemed to catch the panel by surprise. The judges put their heads together and argued in low voices. At last, the senior judge looked up. "Very well, Colonel. You will be furnished pen and ink for this purpose." He turned to the guards. "Take him back to his cell. Let him write what he will. Take the appeal to the king and let his will be done."

"Aye, your Excellency," the guards chorused. They

hauled Lurcanio from his seat. He blew Krasta a kiss as they led him away. Her scowl made him smile.

He wondered whether they would bother following the judge's orders, but they did. Lurcanio put his case as best he could. He wished he were writing Algarvian; being persuasive in a language not his own was hard. But then, how much difference would it make? Not much, he feared.

When he'd finished, he gave the appeal to the guards and asked for another leaf of paper. "What's this one for?" one of them asked suspiciously.

Lurcanio looked at him. "I am going to fold it into a ladder, stick it out the window, climb down it, and escape," he answered, deadpan. For a moment, the guards took him seriously; alarm flared on their faces. When they realized he hadn't meant it, they started to get angry. He wondered if he'd earned himself a beating.

But then, to his relief, one of them laughed. "Funny boy, aren't you?" the fellow said. "You aren't going anywhere, not till—" He drew the edge of his hand across his throat. "Enough jokes now. Tell me what you want it for."

"I want to write another letter," Lurcanio said. "Your censors will read it. You will probably read it yourself. By all the signs, I will not have many more chances to write letters."

"You've got that straight." The guard thought for a moment, then shrugged. "Well, why the blazes not? If we don't like what you write, the letter'll never get out of gaol."

"Exactly so." Lurcanio bowed. "I thank you."

He gnawed at the end of the pen when they gave him the new leaf of paper. He'd known exactly what he wanted to say to King Gainibu, even if he'd sometimes had trouble writing it in Valmieran. Here . . . *How do I even begin?* he wondered. But that solved itself. *By the time you read this, I expect I shall be dead,* he wrote. Coming out and saying that, even on paper, felt oddly liberating. He had an easier time going on from there than he'd thought he would.

The guards took away not only the letter but also the pen and the bottle of ink. "We don't want you turning this into a stick, now," one of them said, and laughed at his own joke.

Lurcanio dutifully chuckled, too. "If I could, I would," he said. "But a man would have to be more than a first-rank mage to bring that off, I fear. He would have to be what the Ice People call a god."

"Those stinking, hairy savages," the guard said, nothing but scorn in his voice. He took the letter out of the cell. The door slammed shut. The bar thudded into place to keep it shut.

Two afternoons later, the answer from the King of Valmiera to Lurcanio's appeal arrived. Lurcanio broke the seal and unfolded the leaf of paper. He recognized Gainibu's script, though the writing looked less shaky than it had when the king drank himself into a stupor almost every night.

Colonel Lurcanio: Greetings. I have read your appeal, King Gainibu wrote. *The essence of it seems to have two parts: first, that you were only obeying the orders your superiors gave you; and, second, that you might have done far worse than you did. The first falls to the ground at once. A man who murders again and again under orders remains a murderer. As for the second, it is probably true. No, I have no doubt that it is certainly true. I would not claim that I have forgotten our acquaintance. You might indeed have done more and worse. That you did not was surely due to the fact that you wanted to keep Valmiera as quiet as you could, but does remain so. It being so, I must ask myself whether it constitutes an adequately mitigating circumstance. With some regret, I tell you that, in my judgment, it does not. Aye, you might have done worse. What you did was quite bad enough. The sentence shall stand. Gainibu, King of Valmiera.*

Slowly, deliberately, Lurcanio folded the king's letter and set it down. Nothing left now but to die as well as he could. The guards had watched him read the letter. He nodded to them. "You will not have to worry about my complaints on the quality of accommodations and the dining much longer," he said.

"Did you really think his Majesty would let you off?" one of them asked.

Lurcanio shook his head. "No, but how was I worse off for trying?"

"Something to that," the guard said. "Tomorrow morning, then."

"Tomorrow morning," Lurcanio agreed. "Can you give me something worth eating tonight? As long as I am here, I aim to enjoy myself as best I can."

As the guards trooped out, one of them remarked, "Whoreson's got guts." Lurcanio felt a certain amount of pride. As soon as the door slammed shut, though, it evaporated. What difference did it make? When the sun came up tomorrow, he would stop caring—stop caring forever—what happened to him.

Time seemed to race. He'd hardly blinked before it got dark. His supper was no different from any other meal he'd had in gaol. He savored it just the same. He found himself yawning, but didn't sleep. With experience about to end forever, he didn't care to miss the little he had left. *They wouldn't have brought me a woman, even if I'd asked for one,* he thought. *Too bad.*

The sky, or the tiny scrap of it he could see through his window, began to grow light. The door opened. A squad of guards came in. Lurcanio got to his feet. "Can you walk?" the guard captain asked him.

"I can walk," he answered, and he did, though his knees wobbled from the fear he fought not to show. They led him to a courtyard and bound his wrists and ankles to a metal pole. He could smell terror seeping out from the old bricks behind him.

"Blindfold?" asked the guard captain. Lurcanio shook his head. A dozen men aimed sticks at him. The captain raised his hand, then let it fall. The Valmierans blazed. Even as Lurcanio braced himself, he thought, *How useless.* He cried out once. Then it was over.

"What's *this*?" Krasta asked irritably as the butler handed her an envelope on a silver tray.

"I don't know, milady," he answered, and did his best to vanish.

Muttering something unpleasant about the quality of help available these days, Krasta opened the envelope. It bore no return address, and she didn't recognize the hand that had written out her name and address. She was tempted to throw the envelope away unopened, but curiosity got the better of her.

The script of the letter inside was different from that of the address—different and familiar. *By the time you read this,* Krasta read, *I expect I shall be dead. I make no special plea for myself—what point to it? You know what you did, and you know what we did. You will try to deny it now, especially to yourself, but you went into our affair with your eyes open as wide as your legs.*

"Powers below eat you, Lurcanio," Krasta snarled. She almost tore the letter to pieces, but that first sentence kept her reading.

I have a favor to ask you—a deathbed favor, you might say, Lurcanio wrote. *It has nothing to do with me, so you need feel no pain in granting it.* Again, Krasta almost tore up the letter. Even beyond the grave, was the Algarvian trying to tell her what to do? Then she laughed unpleasantly. She could finish the whole wretched thing, find out exactly what he wanted, and then do just the opposite. She nodded to herself. The more she thought about it, the better that sounded.

"No one gives me orders," she said. "No one." She spoke louder than she had to, as if to persuade herself. For close to four years, Lurcanio had given her orders, and she'd—mostly—obeyed. She would be a long time forgetting that, however hard she tried.

You bore my son, Lurcanio wrote. Krasta's scowl darkened. She wished she could forget that, too. The little bastard's yowling made forgetting impossible, though. So did the shocking things being pregnant had done to her figure. For the moment, little Gainibu was mercifully asleep. Pretty soon, he would wake up and start being noisy again.

Even thinking about Lurcanio was easier than thinking about the baby. Because of the baby, because of what he'd turned out to be, she still had to wear this hot, uncomfortable wig whenever she appeared in public. Aye, Lurcanio and his bastard boy both had a lot to answer for.

What I ask you is, try to forget he is mine, the letter continued.

Krasta's lip curled. "Not bloody likely!" she said.

Try to treat him as you would have treated him were the charming Viscount Valnu indeed his sire, Lurcanio wrote. *You may think of me as you please. I made life inconvenient for you, I know, for I did not let you do just as you pleased—and what crime could be worse than that?* Krasta studied his words. She suspected a cut was hiding among them, but couldn't quite find it. Lurcanio had always enjoyed being obscure.

Moreover, he went on, *you were too friendly with me during the war to suit Valmiera as it is now. This, I know, has caused you some embarrassment. You must be sure the said embarrassment is all my fault, and so you will hate me for it.*

Krasta nodded savagely. "I certainly do!"

She could almost see Lurcanio shrugging. *Hate me if you will, then,* he wrote. *I can do nothing about it in any case. But I beg you, my former dear, do not hate the baby. Nothing that has happened here is the baby's fault.*

"Oh, you lying son of a whore," Krasta exclaimed. If little Gainibu hadn't been born with sandy hair, people now wouldn't think she herself had been a collaborator. Even Skarnu's peasant cow of a wife wouldn't have been able to keep scorning her, wouldn't have been able to crop her hair right after she gave birth. No, Lurcanio didn't understand much.

Or did he? *I know that, with his hair as it is, he will not have an easy time in your kingdom. During the war, some Kaunians tried to disguise themselves as Algarvians by dyeing their hair red. Going in the other direction might serve the child well here, at least for a time. Later, when passions have cooled, people may be better able to accept him for what he is.*

"Hmm." Krasta read that over again. It wasn't such a bad idea. Oh, certainly, people who knew her also knew she'd had an Algarvian bastard. But, with little Gainibu's hair dyed a safe blond, she would be able to take him out in public. She'd never before imagined being able to do that. Her free hand touched the curls of the wig. Before too long, she would be able to shed her disguise. Her son might have to keep his up his whole life long. "And that's your fault, Lurcanio, yours and nobody else's," Krasta said, as if Gainibu hadn't come forth from between her legs.

If the boy has your looks and my wit, he may go far in the world, given any sort of chance at all, Lurcanio wrote, arrogant to the end. *I hope you will give him that chance. My time is over. His is just beginning.* The squiggle he used for a signature sat under his closing words.

Now Krasta did tear the letter into tiny pieces. Once she'd done so, she put them down the commode, as she'd put the sheet in her brother's writing down the commode while the redheads still occupied Priekule. Then she would have got in trouble if Lurcanio had found Skarnu's words. These days, if anyone found Lurcanio's . . . She shook her head. It wouldn't happen. She wouldn't let it happen. She watched the water in the commode swirl away the soggy paper. Gone. Gone for good. She sighed with relief.

A moment later, almost on cue, little Gainibu started to cry. Krasta gritted her teeth. As far as she could see, a baby's cry was good for nothing but driving all the people within earshot out of their minds. Her first impulse, as always, was to turn around and get out of earshot as fast as she could. This once, though, she resisted that and went into the baby's bedroom instead.

Gainibu's wet nurse looked up in surprise. She was changing the baby's soiled linen and wiping his bottom. Krasta's nose wrinkled. Gainibu had done something truly disgusting. "Hello, milady," the wet nurse said. She deftly finished the job of cleaning and changing and picked up Krasta's son. The baby smiled and gurgled. The wet nurse smiled, too. "He's not a bad little fellow, even if . . ." She caught herself. "He's not a bad little fellow."

"Let me have him," Krasta said.

"Of course, milady." The wet nurse sounded astonished. Krasta had hardly ever said anything like that before. "Be careful to keep a hand under his head. It's still a little wobbly."

"I'll manage." Krasta took her son from the other woman. He smiled up at her, too. Before she knew what she was doing, she smiled back. *He tricked it out of me,* she thought, almost as if realizing a grown man had seduced her. When she smiled at him, Gainibu laughed and wiggled. "He likes me!" Krasta said in surprise. Because she had no use for the baby, she'd thought he wouldn't care for her.

"He likes everybody," the wet nurse said. "He's just a baby. He doesn't know anything about how mean people can be." She held out her hands. "Let me have him back, please. I was going to feed him after I got him cleaned up."

"Here," Krasta said. The wet nurse undid her tunic and gave the baby her right breast. Gainibu sucked eagerly. Krasta's breasts were dry again, though they still seemed softer and slacker than they had before she gave birth. Not till now, hearing the small, happy noises Gainibu made, had she wondered whether nursing him might have been a good thing. She shook her head. When he came out with hair sandy, not blond, she'd wanted him dead. Nurse him herself? No, no, no.

As casually as she could, Krasta asked, "Do you suppose he's still too young to dye his hair?"

"Dye his . . . ? Oh." The wet nurse blinked, then saw what Krasta was aiming at—what Lurcanio had been aiming at, though she wasn't about to admit it. The other woman said, "I don't know, milady. You might ask a healer about that. But when he gets a bit bigger, I'm sure it wouldn't hurt. And it would make things easier for him, wouldn't it?"

"It might," Krasta said. "I'm sure it would make things easier for me. I could show him in public without worrying about all the dreadful things that happen to . . . people with babies that have the wrong color hair." Her own convenience came first. That looking like everyone else might be better for little Gainibu was also nice, but distinctly secondary.

"Sooner or later, things will ease up," the wet nurse predicted. "People will get excited about something else, and then they won't care so much about who did what during the war. That's how it works."

"I hope so," Krasta said fervently. "As far as I'm concerned, people have made much too big a fuss about that already."

The wet nurse nodded sympathetically. Maybe she'd had an Algarvian boyfriend during the occupation. For all Krasta knew, she might have a little bastard at home herself. The wet nurse said, "Plenty of women were friendly with the redheads. That was just how things were back then. A baby? A baby was bad luck."

"He certainly was," Krasta said, giving her son a venomous stare. If he'd looked the way he was supposed to, or if he hadn't come along at all, she wouldn't have had nearly the troubles she'd had.

But the wet nurse said the same thing Lurcanio had: "It's not really his fault, milady. He can't help what he looks like."

"I suppose not," Krasta said reluctantly.

"And he is a nice little baby," the wet nurse went on. "Doing what I do, I see plenty of the little brats. He's sweeter than most. I think dyeing his hair is a good idea. You must be very clever, to have thought of that. If he looks like everybody else, he should be able to get on fine."

"Maybe," Krasta said. No, she wasn't about to admit that dyeing Gainibu's hair hadn't been her idea. If the wet nurse thought it was clever, she would take credit for it. Lurcanio? She snapped her fingers. *By the time you read this, I expect I shall be dead.* She didn't miss him. On the contrary; as long as he'd lived, she'd had to remember she hadn't always been able to do exactly as she pleased. Few thoughts could have been less pleasant to her.

"Let me have Gainibu again," she said. The wet nurse burped the baby before handing him to her. Krasta peered down into his little face. But for the color of his hair, he did look like her, as best she could tell.

He smiled again and then, without any fuss, spit up on her. The wet nurse hadn't burped him quite well enough.

For once, Krasta didn't get angry. She kept studying the baby. With blond hair, he might do after all.

If the boy has your looks and my wit, he may go far in the world. Krasta shook her head. She'd flushed those words down the commode. Since they were gone, they couldn't possibly be true . . . could they?

Leudast stood on the farther slopes of the Elsung Mountains, looking west into Gyongyos. No matter what his superiors said, he'd never expected to come so far so fast. He'd never expected the Gongs to lie down and surrender, either. He'd fought them before, and knew they didn't do things like that. But they had.

He also knew the Unkerlanters' onslaught hadn't been the only thing that made Gyongyos quit. Every new rumor said something different and horrible had happened to Gyorvar. Leudast didn't want to believe any of the rumors, because they all sounded preposterous. But if *something* truly dreadful hadn't happened to their capital, would the Gyongyosians have thrown in the sponge? He didn't think so.

His regiment had come far enough that, right at the edge of visibility, he could see the mountains sloping down toward the lowlands farther west still. He could also see the green in the bottom of a good many valleys. The Gongs, he'd heard, recruited a lot of their soldiers from such places. Unkerlant's broad, almost endless plains yielded many more men. He wasn't sure the average Unkerlanter made as ferocious a warrior as the average Gyongyosian, but that hadn't turned out to matter.

Captain Dagaric came up to stand beside him and look at the vast expanse of rock and snow and greenery. After staring a while in silence, Dagaric asked, "Do you know what you'll do next, Lieutenant?"

"No, sir," Leudast admitted. "I'm afraid I don't. I've been in the army a long time." It wasn't forever. It only felt that way.

"Aye, you've been in the army a long time," the regimental commander agreed. "If you were still a common soldier or a sergeant, I wouldn't worry about it so much. But you're an officer now, and you haven't been an officer all that long. You ought to think about it."

"I have been thinking about it, sir," Leudast replied. "If I weren't an officer, I'd be on my way home now. Well, trying to get home, anyhow. But . . . You don't mind my saying so, you're dead when they blaze you, regardless of whether you're a sergeant or a lieutenant."

"That's so," Dagaric said. Had he tried to deny it, Leudast would have ignored everything else he said. The captain went on, "A couple of things for you to think about, though. For one, nobody's going to be blazing at you for a while. After what we just went through, do you think anyone wants another war any time soon?"

Who can tell, with King Swemmel? But Leudast didn't trust Dagaric far enough to say that out loud. He did say, "You've got a point."

"You bet I do," Dagaric told him. "And my other point is, we need good officers, and you are one. Common soldiers and underofficers are conscripts. Officers are the glue that holds things together, especially in peacetime. Losing you after all you've done, all you've learned, would be a shame."

"I'm still thinking, sir." From his days as a common soldier and an underofficer, Leudast knew better than to come right out and tell a superior no.

"You should also remember, Marshal Rathar has his eye on you," Dagaric said. "Who knows how high you could rise with him behind you?"

Leudast gave a truly thoughtful nod. In the army as anywhere else, whom you knew counted for at least as much as what you knew. That he should know the Marshal of Unkerlant—and that Rathar should know him—still left him astonished. No denying that Dagaric had a point. Officers without patrons were liable to watch their careers wither. He wouldn't have to worry about that. But . . .

"Sir, I don't know that I want to be a soldier at all," Leudast said. "This isn't my proper trade."

"Well, what is your proper trade? Farmer?" Dagaric asked, and Leudast nodded again. The regimental commander snorted. "Do you really want to see nothing but your own village—whatever's left of it—the rest of your days? Do you really want to push a plow behind an ox's arse every year till you fall over dead?"

"It's what I know," Leudast answered. "It's about the only thing I do know."

Captain Dagaric shook his head. "You're wrong, Lieutenant. You know soldiering. You were in the army at the start, and you came out alive at the end. Have you got any idea how unusual that is? Millions of men know farming. Not very many have experience to match yours."

He was probably right. The only trouble was, Leudast didn't want most of the experience he had. He knew how lucky he was to have come through all the dreadful fighting he'd seen with only two wounds. But the wounds weren't all of it—in many ways, weren't the worst of it. Terror and hunger and cold and exhaustion and filth and the agony of friends . . . Did he want to stay in a trade that only promised more of the same?

Something else occurred to him, too, something that had been in the back of his mind ever since the Gyongyosians yielded. "Sir, there was this girl, back in a village in the Duchy of Grelz." Would Alize even remember who he was if he showed up there now, or would she be married to some local man? Plenty of wartime romances didn't mean a thing once the war was done. Some did, though. No way to find out which sort was which without going back there and seeing how things stood.

"A girl, eh?" Dagaric said. "You serious about her, or are you just looking for another excuse?"

"I'm serious, sir. I don't know if she is. I'd have to go back to Leiferde to find out."

"In peacetime, you know, a married officer isn't necessarily at a disadvantage," Dagaric remarked. "And who knows? She may be looking for a way to get off the farm and out of her village." He rubbed his chin. "I'll tell you what. You want to court her, do you?"

Leudast nodded. "Aye, sir, I do."

"You don't need to resign your commission to do that," Dagaric said. "I think the most efficient thing to do would be to give you, oh, a month's leave so you can sort out your personal affairs. At the end of that time, you'll have a better notion of what you want to do—and you'll have an officer's travel privileges to get to this Leifer-wherever-in-blazes-it-is. Does that suit you, Lieutenant?"

"Aye, sir! Thank you, sir!" Leudast said, saluting. The military ceremonial let him hide his astonishment. *Dagaric really must want me to stay in the army, or he wouldn't go so far out of his way to help me.* He still wasn't sure he wanted to remain a soldier, but knowing his superior wanted him to was no small compliment.

Leave papers in his beltpouch, he was two days in a wagon making his way back to the nearest ley line. Then he spent another nine days traversing Unkerlant from west to east, as he'd gone across the kingdom from east to west not so long before. The month of leave Dagaric had given him suddenly seemed less generous than it had when he'd got it: it left him about ten days in and around Leiferde.

He found he could tell exactly how far the Algarvians had come. All at once, the countryside took on the battered look with which he'd grown so familiar during the war. How long would it take to repair? So many men were gone. Every glimpse he got of life in the fields confirmed that. The old, the young, the female: they labored to bring in the harvest. He shivered anew when the ley-line caravan passed through Herborn, the capital of the Duchy of Grelz. There among those ruins King Swemmel had boiled false King Raniero of Grelz alive. *Thanks to me,* Leudast thought, and wondered if he would ever get the smell of Raniero's cooking flesh out of his nostrils.

Leiferde wasn't on a ley line, but didn't lie far from one. Leudast needed only half a day to get to the village. After so long cooped up on the wagon and the caravan, getting down and using his own legs felt good. The sun was sliding down the sky toward the western horizon when he strode up the dusty main street. Women peered at him from their vegetable plots and herb gardens. "A soldier," he heard them murmur. "What's a soldier doing here now?"

He knocked on the door at Alize's house. He'd hoped she would open it herself, but she didn't. Her mother did—a woman who looked much the way Alize would in twenty years or so. "Hullo, Bertrude," Leudast said, pleased he remembered her name.

The woman's jaw dropped. "Powers above!" she exclaimed. "You're *that* lieutenant. How are you, your Excellency?" She curtsied.

"I'm fine, thank you." Leudast had never said he was a nobleman. On the other hand, he'd never said he wasn't. He asked the question that needed asking: "Is Alize anywhere about?"

"She's out in the fields. She'll be back for supper," Bertrude answered. "That shouldn't be long, sir. Won't you come in and share what we have?"

"If it's not too much trouble, and if you have enough," Leudast said. "I know how things are these days."

But Bertrude shook her head. "It's no trouble at all, and we've got plenty," she said firmly. "Come have something to drink while you wait."

Leudast found the world a rosier place after pouring down most of a mug of spirits. He was fighting to stay awake when Alize and her father, Akerin, walked in. "Leudast!" Alize said, and threw herself into his arms. Her face against his shoulder, she added, "What are you doing here?"

"With the war over, I came back," he said simply. It had been a long time since he'd had his arms around a woman, even longer since he'd had them around one who wanted to be held.

Alize stared at him. "Men say they'll do that all the time. I didn't think anybody really would, though."

"Here I am," Leudast said. She seemed glad to see him. That made a good start.

Before he could go on from there, Bertrude broke in: "Supper's ready." Leudast sat down with Alize and her mother and father. The stew Bertrude served was full of oats and beets, not wheat and turnips, as it would have been in Leudast's village in the north. Mutton was mutton, though Bertrude flavored it with mint rather than garlic. Nothing at all was wrong with the ale she gave him to go with the supper.

After he'd eaten, Alize said, "I hoped you'd come back. I

didn't really think you would, but I hoped so. Now that you have come, what exactly do you have in mind? It can't be just . . . you know."

You can't have me for the sport of it, she meant. Leudast nodded. He'd already understood that. He said, "I came to wed you, if you'll put up with me."

"I think I can," Alize said with a smile. Leudast grinned with relief; he hadn't known how she would answer, though he wouldn't have returned to Leiferde if he hadn't had his hopes.

Her father asked, "You aim to settle down here and farm, then?"

The question went to the nub of things. "That depends," Leudast said. "I might, but then again, I might not. My other choice is staying in the army. The way the world looks, there'll always be jobs for soldiers."

"That's so," Akerin said, and Bertrude's head bobbed up and down. Alize's father asked another question: "How do you aim to make up your mind?"

"Well, if you really want to know, a lot of it depends on what your daughter wants." Leudast looked to Alize. "If you'd sooner stay in Leiferde, I know how to farm, or I did up north. It can't be too different here." He realized he'd just shown he was no noble. Shrugging, he went on, "Or if you'd rather be a soldier's wife . . ." Again, he shrugged the Unkerlanter peasant's businesslike shrug, so different from the fancy Algarvian variety. "I can do that, too."

"Go to a city?" Alize breathed. "Maybe even to Cottbus?" Her eyes glowed. "I've seen enough of a farming village to last me the rest of my days. However life turns out in a town, it has to be easier there than here."

Her father and mother didn't argue with her. In fact, they nodded solemnly. Leudast thought her likely right, too. He also nodded. "All right, then," he said. "I'll stay a soldier." Captain Dagaric would be pleased. Marshal Rathar might be pleased. Leudast wondered if he'd be pleased himself. *That depends on how long peace lasts,* he thought. Of course, if war came again, a peasant village near Unkerlant's eastern border wasn't safe, either. But if war came again, was any place at all safe? One way or another, he'd find out.

After supper, Ealstan tried to read the news sheet and play with Saxburh at the same time. That didn't work very well, because he couldn't give either one of them his full attention. The news sheet didn't care. His daughter did. "Dada," she said, and managed to put a distinct note of reproach in her voice.

"You're fighting a losing battle, son," Hestan said.

"What other kind is there, for a Forthwegian?" Ealstan answered. That earned him one of Hestan's slow smiles.

When he was talking to his own father, he wasn't paying attention to Saxburh, either. "Dada," she said again, and tugged at his hand. Laughing, he picked her up. She grabbed for his beard.

He managed to fend her off. "No, you can't do that," he told her. "That hurts."

Hestan said, "You got some pretty good handfuls of mine in your day."

"If I did, she's giving you your revenge." Ealstan tickled Saxburh, who squealed. "Aren't you?" She squealed again.

"If you're going to play with her, may I see the news sheet?" Vanai asked. Ealstan spun it across the room to her. As soon as Vanai started to read, Saxburh scrambled down off Ealstan's lap, toddled over to her, and started batting at the news sheet. "Cut that out," Vanai said. Saxburh didn't. Vanai rolled her eyes. "She doesn't want anybody reading—that's what it is."

"Maybe she thinks we'll get too excited when we see that King Penda vows he'll come back to Forthweg," Ealstan said.

"Not likely," Vanai exclaimed. "Who'd want him back, after he led the kingdom into a losing war?"

"That's the line the story takes," Ealstan said.

"I'm surprised the news sheet mentioned his name at all," Hestan said.

"It takes the same tone Vanai did," Ealstan repeated. "The feeling it wants to give is, *Oh, he can't possibly be serious, and who would care even if he were?* It's not a headline or anything—it shows up at the bottom of an inside page. That's one more way to show nobody thinks Penda's very important any more, I guess."

His father musingly plucked at his beard. "You know, that's clever," he said after he'd thought it through. "If they just ignored Penda, people would hear about this vow of his anyhow, and they'd think, *King Beornwulf is afraid. See how he's trying to hide things?* This way, they'll go, *Well, Beornwulf is king now, and Penda can make as much noise as he wants off in Lagoas.* Aye, clever."

"Mama!" Saxburh said indignantly, and swatted at the news sheet.

"You know you're not supposed to do that," Vanai said. "Are you getting fussy? Are you getting sleepy?"

"No!" Saxburh denied the mere possibility, and burst into tears when her mother picked her up.

"Most babies don't start saying no till they're a few months older than that," Hestan remarked. "Of course, my granddaughter is naturally very advanced for her age."

"I wish she were advanced enough to stop making messes in her clothes," Ealstan said. "Is she dry?"

Vanai felt the baby and nodded. "I think she'll go to sleep, too," she said, putting the critical word in classical Kaunian so Saxburh wouldn't follow it. But she'd done that once too often; her daughter had figured it out, and cried harder than ever. Vanai looked half pleased—one day, she did want Saxburh to learn the language she'd grown up speaking—and half annoyed. "There, there. It'll be all right." She rocked the little girl in her arms. Saxburh didn't think it was all right; she went on wailing. But the wails grew muffled as her thumb found its way into her mouth. After a little while, they stopped.

"Almost like the quiet after the fighting's over," Hestan said.

Ealstan shook his head. "No," he said positively. "That's different."

His father didn't argue. He just shrugged and said, "You'd know better than I, I'm sure. How's your leg these days?"

"It's getting better. It's still sore." Ealstan shrugged, too.

"When the rainy season comes, I'll make a first-rate weather prophet."

"I'm sorry about that. I'm more sorry than I can tell you," Hestan said. "But I'm glad you're still here to be able to predict bad weather before it comes."

"Oh, so am I," Ealstan said. "I'll tell you what gravels me, though." He laughed at himself. "I know it's a small thing, especially when you set it against all the evil that came during the war, but I wish I'd been able to finish my schooling. First the Algarvians watered everything down, and then I had to leave." He glanced over at Vanai, and at Saxburh, who'd started snoring around that thumb. "Of course, I learned a good many other things instead."

His wife was wearing her swarthy Forthwegian sorcerous disguise. She turned pink even so. "Everyone learns *those* lessons, sooner or later," she said. "I think it's very fine that you want to learn the others, too."

Her grandfather had been a scholar, of course. Considering how badly he and she had got along, it was a wonder she didn't hate the whole breed. But Kaunians had often looked down their noses at Forthwegians as being ignorant and proud of it. Vanai had never said any such thing to Ealstan, which didn't mean she didn't think it from time to time: not about him, necessarily, but about his people.

Hestan said, "If there hadn't been a war, I was thinking about sending you to the university at Eoforwic, or maybe even to the one at Trapani. I doubt either of them is still standing these days, and powers above only know how many professors came through alive."

"Trapani," Ealstan said in slow wonder. "If there hadn't been a war, I would have wanted to go there, too. That's very strange. The only thing I'd want to do now is drop an egg on the place. It's had plenty, but one more wouldn't hurt." He eyed his father. "Sending me to a university would probably ruin me as a bookkeeper, you know."

"Bookkeepers make more than professors ever dream of," added Vanai, sharply practical as usual.

Hestan shrugged. "I do know both those things. But a man who *can* dream should get his chance to do it. A careful man—which you've always been, Ealstan—doesn't need to be rich; he gets by well enough with a little less. Not having the chance to do what you really want can sour you for life."

Vanai carried Saxburh off and put her to bed. When she came back, she asked, "You're not talking about yourself, are you, sir? You don't seem soured on life, if you don't mind my saying so."

"Me? No." Hestan sounded a bit startled. "Not really, anyhow. But then, I've been lucky with my wife and—mostly—lucky with my children. That makes up for a good deal, believe me."

"*I* believe you," Ealstan said, and looked at Vanai in a way that made her turn redder than she had before.

His father smiled that slow smile. "That isn't what I meant, or not all of what I meant, though I expect you'll have a hard time believing me when I say so. But the truth is, I like moving numbers around. Maybe, if I'd had a chance, I'd be moving them around in different ways from those a bookkeeper uses. But if I tried to tell you I'm pining for a scholarly career I never had, that would be a lie."

Elfryth ducked her head into the dining room. "I just looked in on Saxburh. She's so sweet, lying there asleep."

"Sure she is," Ealstan said. "She's not making any noise."

His mother sniffed indignantly. His father chuckled and said, "Spoken like the proper sort of parent: a tired one."

"Stop that, Hestan," Elfryth said. "What were you saying there about telling lies?"

"I was telling them about running off and joining a traveling carnival when I was young," Hestan answered, deadpan. "Everything went fine till the elephant stepped on me. I used to be a much taller man, you know."

"Pity the beast didn't squash the silliness out of you, too," Elfryth observed.

Vanai looked from Ealstan's father to his mother and back again. "Is that where we'll be in twenty years?" she asked.

Ealstan didn't answer. He didn't know. Elfryth said, "Either something like this or you'll shout at each other all the time. This is better."

"I think so, too," Vanai said.

Hestan asked, "Are you still interested in going on to the university, Ealstan? We could probably afford it if you are."

"I don't know," he answered. "I never even graduated from the academy."

"You can always find ways around things like that." His father spoke with great assurance.

"Maybe," Ealstan said. "The other thing, though . . . Well, you said it yourself. I've got a family to worry about now—and I think I've been pretty lucky there, too." Having a wife and child would make his life as a student more complicated. Having a Kaunian wife and half-Kaunian child might make his life as a student much more complicated. That wasn't anything he could say to Vanai.

"It does make a difference, doesn't it?" Hestan said, and Ealstan nodded.

As Ealstan and Vanai lay down together that night, she said, "If you want to be a scholar, we could make it work, I think."

He shrugged. "Things aren't the way they were before the war. They're never going to be the same as they were before the war. I'm sorry." He took her hand. "I wish they could be, but it's not going to happen."

"I know," Vanai answered. "There are some things that, once you break them, you can't put them back together again."

That held nothing but truth. The ancient Kaunian population of Forthweg—more ancient here than the Forthwegians themselves—would never be the same again. Ealstan caught Vanai to him. "One thing, though," he said. "Because we met, I'm the luckiest fellow in the world."

She kissed him. "You're sweet. I wonder if we would have met anyhow. We might have. I came to Gromheort every now and then. And we—"

"We both knew about that oak grove where we found each other in mushroom season," Ealstan broke in. "We really might have."

"My grandfather wouldn't have approved. He *didn't* approve," Vanai said. "In peacetime, that might have mattered more."

"I hope not," Ealstan said.

"So do I," Vanai said. "But we don't know. We can't know. A lot of dreadful things have happened the past six years. I'm just glad we've got each other."

This time, Ealstan kissed her and hugged her to him. "I am, too."

Vanai let out a small laugh. "You're *very* glad, aren't you?" she said, and reached between them to show how she knew.

"And getting gladder every second, too," Ealstan told her. She laughed again. He started undoing her tunic. As often as not, that seemed to wake up the baby. Not tonight, though. He teased her nipple with his tongue. Her breath sighed out. In a bit, Ealstan poised himself above her. Not too long after that, he was as glad as he could possibly be that they had each other.

Count Sabrino, former and forcibly retired colonel of dragonfliers, had a roof over his head and, for the most part, enough to eat. In occupied, devastated Trapani, that made him a lucky man indeed. *As lucky as an aging cripple can be, anyhow,* he thought sourly. Day by day, his crutches seemed more a part of him.

Some men who'd lost a leg preferred a wheeled chair to crutches. Sabrino might have, too, in the Trapani he'd known before the war: a city of paved boulevards and smooth sidewalks. On the rubble-strewn, cratered streets of the Algarvian capital these days, such chairs got stuck too easily to seem practical to him.

He saw enough mutilated men, of all ages from barely bearded to older than he was, to have plenty of standards of comparison. Each one was an emblem of what Algarve had gone through. Taken together, they made a searing indictment of the darkness through which his kingdom had passed.

He stopped into a tavern not far from his home and ordered a glass of wine. The tapman's right arm stopped just below his shoulder: no possible hope of fitting him with a hook. But he handled the glass and the wine bottle with his remaining hand as well as anyone possibly could.

When Sabrino praised him, he let out a short, bitter burst of laughter. "It's not quite what you think, friend," he said. "I'm well off, if you want to call it that—you see, I've always been left-handed."

"If what you kept is more useful to you than what you lost, that is good fortune," Sabrino agreed. "Plenty of people have it worse."

"If a whole man said something like that to me, I'd punch the son of a whore in the nose—with my left hand, of course," the tapman said. "But you, buddy, you went through it, too. I'll take it from you. Where'd you get hurt?"

"Not far west of here, not long before the war ended," Sabrino answered. "I was on a dragon, and it got flamed out of the sky. Some of the flame got my leg, too, and so. . . ." He shrugged, then politely added, "You?"

"On the way to Cottbus, the first winter of the war in the west," the other cripple told him. "A flying chunk of eggshell tore the arm almost all the way off, and the healers finished the job. The same burst killed two of my pals."

Sabrino shoved a silver coin across the bar to him. "Have a glass of whatever you care for, on me."

"I usually don't, not when I'm working." But the tapman dropped the coin into the cash box. "Powers below eat it, once won't hurt. Thank you kindly, friend. You're a gentleman." He poured himself a shot of spirits, then took a shiny new copper coin from the box and gave it to Sabrino. "I wouldn't cheat you—here's your change."

Sabrino looked at the coin. It showed the profile of a plump man with a receding chin, not the strong, beaky image that had been stamped onto Algarve's currency for so many years. "So this is the new king, is it?" he said.

"If you believe the Unkerlanters, he is," the tapman answered. "Me, I don't know why they don't just put King Swemmel's face on the money and have done with it."

That would have been my face there, if I'd told Vatran aye, Sabrino thought as he put the copper in his beltpouch. It was a strange notion, and not one he'd had in the sanatorium bed when the Unkerlanter general came to call on him. He finished his wine, picked up his crutches (which he'd leaned against the side of the bar while he perched on

a stool and drank), left the tavern, and made his slow way
home.

When he got there, he found his wife more excited than
he'd seen her in years. "Powers above, Gismonda, what's
going on?" he asked, wondering what sort of calamity
could have upset her so.

But it turned out to be a different kind of excitement. "You
may be able to get your leg back," she said dramatically.

"What?" He shook his head. "Don't be silly. I'm an
abridged edition these days, and I'll stay that way as long as
I last."

"Maybe not," Gismonda said. "One of my friends—
Baroness Norizia, it was, whose husband got killed outside
Durrwangen—heard about this new healer called Pirello.
He's supposed to be able to restore lost limbs by sorcery.
Something to do with the law of similarity. Norizia didn't
know just what. What she knows about wizardry would fit
in a thimble, believe me, my darling. Pirello has something
or other, though."

"The law of similarity," Sabrino said musingly. He
looked down at himself. His surviving leg was indeed very
similar to the one he'd lost. A clever mage *might* be able to
use that resemblance. Or . . . "Odds are he's just a quack
preying on maimed men." Sabrino didn't want to let himself feel hope.

"Maybe." Gismonda was every bit as cold-blooded, perhaps more so. But she went on, "Shouldn't you talk to him
anyhow? What have you got to lose?"

"Money," Sabrino answered. He clicked his tongue between his teeth. *How much would I give to have my leg
back, really and truly?* The answer didn't take long to form.
Anything at all. "Might be worth seeing him, just to find
out."

Gismonda snapped her fingers. "I remember now what
Norizia called it. An elixir, that's what he uses. A miracle
elixir, she said."

"It would take a miracle," Sabrino said, "and miracles
aren't what magecraft is all about. Still . . ." He shrugged,
as well as he could with crutches bearing so much of his
weight. "I may as well take a look."

"I'll send one of the servants over to Norizia's and see if she knows where the fellow's offices are," Gismonda said.

From the word the servant brought back, the healer did business not far from the wreckage of the royal palace. Once the carriage had taken Sabrino to that part of town, finding his place of business proved easy. Broadsheets praising Pirello's miracle elixir were plastered to walls and fences.

Veterans missing arms and legs—and one man short his left ear—filled Pirello's waiting room. Sabrino gave his name to a pretty receptionist he wouldn't have minded knowing better, then eased himself down into a chair and got ready to wait till everyone ahead of him had seen the healer.

Before long, though, the receptionist gave him an inviting smile and said, "Count Sabrino? Master Pirello will see you now."

Sabrino struggled to his foot. Other mutilated men gave him sour looks, for which he didn't much blame them. His own suspicions flared. He hadn't given the receptionist his rank. How did Pirello know it? *He's likely a mage, after all,* Sabrino thought. And his own name and station hadn't been unknown in Trapani before the war. Still, he wasn't the only Sabrino around, either. *If he knows I'm a noble, maybe he thinks he can pry more money out of me than from ordinary men who've had bad luck. If I can get my leg back, though . . .*

"Here you are, your Excellency," the girl said. Her kilt was very short, showing off shapely legs. "Go right in."

"Thanks," Sabrino said. She beamed at him. He wondered if he ought to ask her name. *Later,* he thought. A hitching step at a time, he went into Pirello's sanctum.

It was lined with books, though not all of them had anything to do with healing or sorcery. The mage—*or is he just a mountebank?* Sabrino wondered—sprang from his chair and bowed himself almost double. "Your Excellency! What a privilege to meet you!" he cried. He was about thirty, with his mustaches and chin beard waxed to spikes. Plainly, he'd never missed a meal. "I hope I can help you."

"I hope you can, too," Sabrino said. "I've heard about

something to do with the law of similarity, and about some elixir of yours, and I decided to see what's going on here. What have I got to lose?"

"Exactly so, your Excellency. *Exactly* so!" Pirello beamed, as if Sabrino had been clever. "Do sit down, sir. I will tell you what I do. I will tell you in great detail, in fact." And he did. He went on and on and on, and grew more technical the longer he spoke.

Not all of what he said made sense to Sabrino, who wondered how much of it would have made sense to a first-rank mage. Before long, he held up a hand and said, "Enough, sir. Cut to the chase. You can help me, or else you can't. If you can, how long will it take and how much will it cost?"

"Between the spell and the elixir, which of course stimulates the regenerative faculty, you should see results—the beginning of results, I should say—within two months," Pirello replied. "As for the fee, I am the soul of reason. You pay me a third when I begin and the balance when completely satisfied." The price he named wasn't cheap, but wasn't exorbitant, either. "I would charge less, sir, but for the rare and costly ingredients in the miracle elixir, gathered from the land of the Ice People, from Zuwayza, from the most inaccessible and exotic islands of the Great Northern Sea. . . ."

"It sounds impressive." It sounded, in fact, a little too impressive for Sabrino to trust it fully. "How did you learn about this sorcery and your precious elixir, if I may ask?"

"Of course you may. I am the soul of truth as well as reason," Pirello said. "As the war neared an end, I was working on spells to help hold back the Unkerlanters. I realized that one of them—reversed, you might say—could prove a boon to mankind rather than a bane. Further research—and here we are."

"Here we are," Sabrino echoed. It had a certain amount of plausibility to it. As Sabrino knew to his own horror, Algarve had trotted out all sorts of desperate spells in the last days of the war. It could have been as Pirello claimed, no doubt of that. It could have been, but not necessarily. Sabrino found another question: "How long have you had this place open?"

"Not quite a month, sir," Pirello replied.

"All right." Grunting with effort, Spinello rose from the chair. "I may be back in a month or two, then. We'll see how things go."

"You have no confidence in me!" Pirello wailed. "I am insulted. I am outraged. I am furious. You have made me into a cheat, a criminal, a man without honor. In your mind, sir, this is what I am. Oh, the indignity of it!" He made as if to rend his garments.

Sabrino shook his head. "No, I'm just careful. I lived through the war. I want to see how things go before I jump in. Good day."

Behind him, Pirello expostulated volubly. The more the mage squawked, the less Sabrino trusted him. He made his slow way out of the office, past the receptionist—who'd stopped smiling at him—and out onto the street. His driver helped him up into the carriage. "Take me home," he said.

"Well?" Gismonda asked when he got back.

"He's a fraud," Sabrino answered. "I think he's a fraud, anyhow. If he's still in business six weeks from now, maybe I'm wrong."

Five weeks and three days after his visit to Master Pirello, news sheets—which had happily displayed his advertising—reported that his establishment was suddenly empty, as was the account he'd set up at a nearby bank. A warrant had been sworn out for his arrest, but the occupying authorities seemed more inclined to laugh at the Algarvians than to go after the trickster.

"Well, you were right," Gismonda said with a grimace.

"So I was. I've still only got one leg, but I've still got all my silver, too." Sabrino sighed. "But oh, how I wish I'd been wrong!"

Hajjaj eyed Tassi reproachfully. "You are extravagant, you know. You should come to me before you order jewels for yourself."

The Yaninan woman stamped her foot, which made her pale, dark-tipped breasts jiggle invitingly. "They were pretty. I wanted them. I got them," she replied in the throatily accented Algarvian she still spoke far better than Zuwayzi.

"You should have asked me first," Hajjaj repeated. "I am happy to give you a refuge here—"

Tassi twitched her hip. "I should hope so!"

"I did not let you stay here on account of *that*," the retired Zuwayzi foreign minister said. "I let you stay here on account of your trouble with Minister Iskakis. I am an old man: I make no bones about it. *That* does not matter to me nearly so much as it would have thirty years ago. And there is something you should know."

"And that is?" Tassi asked ominously.

"I divorced a wife not so very long ago—a young wife, a pretty wife, a wife most enjoyable in bed—because she spent more than she should have, because she ~~thought she~~ could take advantage of me," Hajjaj said. "I sent her back to her clanfather. I would send you away, too. You need to understand that, and to believe it."

"You wouldn't do such a thing to me." She sounded very sure of herself. As if by accident, she scratched her hipbone. Hajjaj didn't believe in accidents—certainly not in this one. The motion, he was sure, was aimed at guiding his gaze toward her patch of pubic hair. She'd noticed him noticing it; it stood out against her paleness much more than a darker-skinned Zuwayzi woman's did. Aye, she knew what her weapons were, and used them.

But those weapons wouldn't save her here. Hajjaj had to convince her of that. Wearily, he said, "You had better listen to me. I enjoy you. I am not infatuated with you. That I did not want Iskakis to punish you does not mean I am. You may not do whatever you like in my house. I do not have to keep you here, and I will not if I decide you abuse my hospitality. Have you got that?"

Tassi studied him. At last, she dipped her head—and then, a moment later, nodded. "You mean this, I think."

"You had best believe I mean it." Hajjaj nodded, too.

"How can you be so cold?" the Yaninan woman exclaimed.

"I ran my kingdom's affairs the whole of my adult life," Hajjaj said. "Did you think I would not be able to run my own?"

"But you ran your kingdom's affairs here." Tassi touched a painted fingernail to her forehead. "Your own affairs—

those belong here." Her finger came to rest near her left nipple.

"I find less difference between the two than you seem to," Hajjaj said. "If my wits tell me my heart is making me act like a fool, why should I go on doing it?"

"Because your heart drives you! Because you are passionate!"

She meant it. Hajjaj was sure of that. He shook his head even so. "I would rather be right."

"Right?" Tassi scornfully tossed her head. "Wouldn't you rather be happy?"

Hajjaj thought about that. "I *am* happy—or as happy as I can be with Unkerlant too strong in this land. If you mean, do I want to be head over heels in love . . . well, no. I have too many years and the wrong temperament for that." His chuckle was rueful. A good many of his own countrymen thought him cold-blooded, too.

Tassi snorted, but she also nodded again, this time without using a Yaninan gesture first. "I will remember," she said, and turned again. *Walked* wasn't quite the word; the twists her bare backside made did their best to refute everything Hajjaj had told her.

He chuckled. Enjoying someone in bed wasn't the same as falling in love with her—or with him, Hajjaj supposed. He'd needed more than a few years to reach that conclusion, but he was convinced of it now.

And besides, he thought, *any woman who wants to make me fall head over heels in love with her isn't going to have much chance to do it, because I'm already head over heels in love with someone else.*

How Kolthoum would laugh if he told her that! And why shouldn't she laugh? Her temperament was much the same as his own. That was one reason why he loved her, why the two of them fit like foot and sandal, why he wondered how he might go on living if anything happened to her. Arranged marriages didn't usually work out so. Then again, from what he'd seen, marriages springing from first fruits of passion didn't usually work out so, either. *Every once in a while, you get lucky.*

He rose to his feet and left the library. He wasn't much

surprised when Tewfik came up to him a few minutes later and said, "You put a flea in her ear, did you, young fellow?"

No one could have overheard his conversation with Tassi. But Tewfik might have been as much prophet as majordomo. Hajjaj was convinced the old man knew what went on well before it happened. "I hope I did," Hajjaj said now. "Maybe she'll listen. Maybe she'll go on thinking she can do just as she pleases, the way Lalla did."

"She's smarter than Lalla," Tewfik said.

"I think so, too," Hajjaj said. "I hope she is, for her sake. I don't want to give her back to Iskakis, but if she makes me not want to have her around, either. . . ."

"Pity Marquis Balastro didn't want to keep her," Tewfik said. "Pity Balastro got himself hauled down to Unkerlant, too. You could have sent her to him if he hadn't."

"For one thing, he didn't want her any more. That was part of the reason she came here, if you'll recall," Hajjaj said. The majordomo nodded. Hajjaj also thought it a pity the Algarvian minister to Zuwayza had been sent down to Unkerlant. Had that not happened, he wouldn't have been a retired diplomat himself. But . . . "A great pity Balastro got taken away. Swemmel's men blazed him, you know."

"I had heard that, aye, sir. Most unfortunate."

"I'm sure the marquis would be the first to agree with you," Hajjaj said.

Tewfik coughed. "If I may say so, sir, it is perhaps not the worst of things that the Unkerlanters' passion for vengeance should be aimed mostly at our late allies and not at us."

"Passion indeed," Hajjaj said—one more dangerous exercise of it. "And I fear you are right there, too, as you usually are."

The majordomo made a self-deprecating gesture. Inside, though, he would be preening. Hajjaj had known him all his own life, and was sure of it. But his praise of Tewfik hadn't been hypocritical. Had the Unkerlanters wanted to avenge themselves on Zuwayza as they were avenging themselves on Algarve, he might have been blazed alongside Balastro.

He wondered why Swemmel was so much more intent on punishing the redheads. Maybe there was some sense in Unkerlant that the Zuwayzin had had good reason for waging the war they did. After all, the Unkerlanters had invaded Zuwayza before the war with Algarve started. King Shazli owed them as much revenge as he could get, and if he lined up with the Algarvians to grab it, then he did, that was all.

Or maybe I'm imagining things, Hajjaj thought. *If I'm giving Swemmel a sense of justice, that's bound to be senility creeping up on me.*

"If I may make a suggestion, sir?" Tewfik said.

"By all means," Hajjaj said.

"You really should get the roofers out here, sir, before the fall rainy season begins," the majordomo said. "If the powers above be kind, they may perhaps find some leaks before the rain makes them obvious."

"And if they don't find any, they'll start some, to give them business later." Hajjaj hated roofers.

"Chance we take," said Tewfik, who did not admire them, either. "If we don't have them out, though, the rain is bound to show us where the holes are."

"You're right, of course," Hajjaj said. "Why don't you see to it, then?"

"I'll do that, sir," Tewfik said. "I expect they'll be out in the next few days." Ancient and bent, he shuffled away.

Hajjaj stared after him. What exactly was that last supposed to mean? Had the majordomo already summoned the roofers, and was he getting retroactive permission for it? That was what it sounded like. Hajjaj shrugged. He'd run Zuwayza's foreign affairs for a generation, aye. Tewfik had been running this household a lot longer than that.

What will happen when he finally falls over dead? Hajjaj wondered. His shoulders went up and down in another shrug. He wouldn't have been at all surprised to find Tewfik outlasting him. The majordomo seemed as resistant to change as the hills outside Bishah.

For a moment, that thought cheered Hajjaj. Then he frowned. What would happen to these hills if someone unleashed on them the appalling sorcery the Kuusamans and Lagoans had used against Gyorvar? Nothing good: Hajjaj was sure of that. The more he heard about that spell, the more it frightened him. He'd thought the first reports to come in to Bishah no more than frightened exaggerations, but they'd proved less than the dreadful reality. He'd never before known rumor to fall behind truth.

He'd heard Minister Horthy's aides had had to keep watch on the Gyongyosian minister day and night, to make sure he didn't slay himself. Hajjaj didn't know whether that was true; he did know Horthy hadn't been seen in public since Gyongyos surrendered to the islanders and to Unkerlant.

He sighed. So many things that had once seemed as changeless as these hills looked different, doubtful, danger-ous, in the aftermath of the Derlavaian War. For as long as he'd been alive, Algarve had been the pivotal kingdom in the east, the one around which events revolved, the one to-ward which her neighbors looked with awe and dread. That had remained so even after she lost the Six Years' War.

No more. Hajjaj was sure of that. It wasn't just that Mezentio's kingdom had been shattered, with one king in Algarve propped up by the islanders, the other by Swem-mel of Unkerlant. But Algarve had shattered herself morally as well. No one could look toward her now without disgust. That marked a great change in the world.

Would everyone turn to Unkerlant, then? Swemmel surely ruled the most powerful kingdom on the mainland of Derlavai. Would Yaninans and Forthwegians and Zuwayzin and even Algarvians start shouting, "Efficiency!" at the top of their lungs? The notion made Hajjaj queasy, but where else would folk look?

Kuusamo, maybe, he thought. Kuusamo and Lagoas were the only kingdoms that could hope to hold any sort of bal-ance against Unkerlant. *Kuusamo isn't even a kingdom, not really,* Hajjaj reminded himself. *How does it hold together under seven princes?* Somehow it managed, and more than managed. Its soldiers had done more than the Lagoans to beat Algarve in the east, and it had also beaten Gyongyos even without the final sorcery. Aye, Kuusamo was a place to watch.

Hard to have a vicious tyranny like Unkerlant's with seven lords in place of one, Hajjaj thought. And anything else, he was sure, made a better choice than Swemmel of Unkerlant.

Twenty

"Here, Vanai." Elfryth held out a platter. "Would you like another slice of mutton?"

"No, thank you," Vanai said. "I'm full."

Her mother-in-law frowned. "Are you sure? Powers above, you haven't even finished what you've got there. Now that we have enough food again, you really ought to eat."

"I'm full," Vanai repeated. She meant it, too. In fact, what she'd already eaten was sitting none too comfortably in her belly.

"*I'll* have some more mutton," Ealstan said. "And pass the porridge, too, please. Garlic and mushrooms and almonds . . ." He grinned and smacked his lips.

Hestan picked up the bowl and handed it to Vanai. "Pass this to your husband."

"All right," she said, and did. She'd had a helping of porridge herself, and liked it. But the odor of garlic wafting up from it now made her insides churn. "Here," she told Ealstan. Then, gulping, she left the table in a hurry.

When she came back, she'd got rid of what was bothering her—got rid of it most literally. She took a cautious sip of wine to kill the nasty taste in her mouth. She swallowed it even more cautiously, wondering if her stomach would rebel again. But the wine gave her no trouble.

"Mama!" Saxburh said from her high chair. Vanai gave

her a wan smile. The baby looked to be wearing more porridge than she'd eaten.

"Are you all right, dear?" Elfryth asked.

"I'm fine—now," Vanai said.

Something in her tone made her mother-in-law's eyes widen. "Oh," she said, and then, "If I'm wrong, you'll tell me, but . . . is Saxburh going to have a little brother or sister?"

So much for keeping it a secret a while longer, Vanai thought. Of course, bolting from the table in the middle of a good meal had a way of killing a secret dead. Vanai made herself nod. "Aye, I think she will."

And maybe it hadn't been such a secret after all. Hestan nodded and said, "You've been falling asleep pretty early lately. That's always a sign."

Ealstan said, "I thought so, too. I wasn't going to ask you for another little while, though. So we'll have a two-year-old and a baby in the house at the same time, will we?" He looked from his father to his mother. "How did you two manage?"

"It's simple enough," Hestan answered. "You go mad. Most of the time, though, you're too busy to notice you've done it." Elfryth nodded emphatically.

Saxburh plucked the spoon from her bowl of porridge and flung it on the floor. "Done!" she announced. Vanai grabbed the bowl before it followed.

Ealstan surveyed his daughter. "Before we turn her loose, I think we ought to take her to the public baths. They might have enough water to get her properly clean."

"She's not so bad as that," Vanai said. "A wet rag will do the job just fine." And so it did, though Saxburh liked getting washed no better than usual. Sometimes washing her face wasn't much different from wrestling.

"Another grandchild." Hestan smiled. "I like that."

"So do I," Elfryth said. "We can enjoy them, but Vanai and Ealstan have to do most of the work. What's not to like about an arrangement like that?"

"Ha," Ealstan said in a hollow voice. "Ha, ha, ha."

"What makes you think your mother was joking?" Hestan asked, sounding as serious as he did most of the time.

No matter how serious he sounded, Vanai knew better

than to take him seriously. "You—both of you—have given us lots of help with Saxburh. I know you'll help some with the new baby, too. Of course we'll do more—it's our child, after all."

"You married a sensible woman, son," Hestan said to Ealstan. "My only question is, if she's as sensible as she seems, why did she marry you?"

In a lot of families, a question like that would have been the opening blaze in a row. Here, Ealstan didn't even blink. "I fooled her. I told her I was rich and I came from a good family. She hadn't met you yet, of course, so she didn't know what a liar I was."

"Well! I like that!" Elfryth said. But her eyes twinkled, too.

"I'm sorry, Mother," Ealstan said. "I guess I'm only half a liar."

"Oh, stop, all of you," Vanai said. She'd seen how Ealstan and his family teased one another without angering or hurting anybody. She'd seen it, aye, but she didn't understand it or fully believe it. Had she and her own grandfather made cracks like that, the air around the two of them would have frozen for days. Brivibas appreciated a certain sort of dry wit, but he'd had no sense of humor to speak of. *And I always meant everything I told him, too,* Vanai thought. Looking back, some of the things she'd said didn't make her proud, but her grandfather had always had the knack for infuriating her.

Saxburh banged both little fists down on the high chair's tray, interrupting her mother's gloomy reflections. "Out!" she said.

"She's talking very well," Elfryth said as Vanai turned the baby loose. "She's going to be smart." She shook her head. "No, she's already smart."

"Must take after her mother," Hestan remarked.

"No doubt," Ealstan agreed. "Do you suppose I'm an idiot because I got it from you, or just because you raised me?"

"Both, I'd say," Hestan answered placidly. He turned to Vanai and shifted from Forthwegian to classical Kaunian: "When do you intend to teach the baby this language along with ours?"

"My father-in-law, I didn't do it before because of the

occupation," Vanai said in the same language. "If she'd spoken the wrong tongue while we were sorcerously disguised, that could have been . . . very bad."

"Of course," Hestan said. "But you can do it now—and you should, I think. With so many of your people gone on account of the cursed Algarvians, classical Kaunian is in danger of dying out as a birthspeech. After so many generations, *that* would be very bad, too."

"I've had the same thought," Vanai said. That a Forthwegian would feel as she did surprised her. *Ealstan would. Ealstan does,* she thought. But Ealstan was in love with her. His father wasn't. *But he gets a lot of his ideas from his father.* She shook her head, bemused at arguing with herself.

Hestan plucked at his thick gray beard. "I'm not my brother, and I thank the powers above that I'm not," he said. "We don't all hate Kaunians and Kaunianity, even if the war let too many who do run wild."

"I know that," Vanai said. "If I didn't know that, would I have married your son? Would we have a baby who's not one thing or the other, with another one on the way?"

"No, indeed," Hestan answered. "But sometimes these things do need saying."

"Fair enough." Vanai nodded. Saxburh scrambled up into her lap. The toddler looked curiously from her to Hestan and back again. They were talking, but they were using words she hadn't heard much before and couldn't understand. By her wide eyes, that was very interesting.

Ealstan said, "The next question is, how do I make enough money to feed a wife and two babies and maybe even myself?" He laughed. "After six years of questions like, *How do I stay alive?* and *How do I keep the cursed redheads from murdering my wife?*—after worrying about questions like those, thinking of money isn't so bad."

"I've never gone hungry, and neither did my children," Hestan said. "I don't think yours have much to worry about."

"If this were real peace, I wouldn't worry," Ealstan said. "But with everything all torn to pieces by the war, business just isn't what it used to be."

"Not now," his father agreed, "but it's bound to get better. It could hardly get worse, after all. And we're still willing to share, you know."

"Haven't we taken enough already?" Ealstan said.

"We're a family. This is what families are for." Elfryth nodded, most vehemently, toward Vanai. From personal experience, Vanai had only a vague notion of what families were for. She didn't want to shrug, so she just sat still.

Her husband still seemed unhappy. "You're not helping Conberge the same way you're helping us."

"So we're not, and do you know why?" Hestan asked. Ealstan shook his head. His father went on, "Because Grimbald's parents are helping the two of them—the three of them, soon—that's why."

"Oh," Ealstan said in a small voice.

Vanai said, "Thank you very much for everything you've done for us. I don't know what we would have done without you."

"This is what families are for," Elfryth repeated.

Hestan added, "And if you and Ealstan got by in the middle of Eoforwic in the middle of the war, I don't expect you would have had much trouble here in Gromheort in peacetime."

It's because he says things like that, Vanai realized, *that all his teasing doesn't pack a sting.* Ealstan couldn't doubt he really was loved, no matter how sardonic his father got. And the ley line ran in both directions. That was obvious, too.

Saxburh screwed up her face and grunted. No matter how clever she was, she was a long way from knowing how to wait when she needed to go. Vanai eagerly looked forward to the day when she learned. *But another baby's coming,* she thought in sudden dismay. *Even after Saxburh knows what to do, her little brother or sister won't.*

She carried her daughter away to clean up the mess. "Come on, you little stinker," she said. Saxburh thought that was funny. So did Vanai—but only after she'd washed her hands.

After Saxburh went to bed, Vanai soon followed. In this pregnancy as in the one before, she found herself sleepy all the time. "Another baby," Ealstan said in wondering tones. "I *had* thought you might be expecting again—your courses hadn't come."

"No, they hadn't," Vanai replied around a yawn. "They won't, not for a while now." She laughed a little. "I miss nine months of cramps, and then I get to make up for it all at once, and then some."

"If it's a boy, I'd like to name him Leofsig, for my brother," Ealstan said.

Vanai didn't see how she could quarrel with that, especially not when Leofsig, from all she'd heard, had got on with Kaunians as well as the rest of this remarkable Forthwegian family did—and when Sidroc, who'd gone into Plegmund's Brigade, had killed him. Nodding, she said, "I would like to give him—or her, if it's a girl—a Kaunian name, too."

"Of course," Ealstan said.

He hadn't quarreled. He hadn't even hesitated. He'd just said, *Of course.* Vanai gave him a hug. "I love you," she told him.

"I love you, too," he answered seriously. "That's what makes it all worthwhile. By the powers above, I do hope I'll be able to keep feeding everybody."

"I think you will," Vanai said. Ealstan still looked worried. She added, "Your father thinks you will, too. He's a very sharp man. If he thinks you can manage, he's likely right."

Ealstan kissed her. "You're the one who always knows the right thing to say."

She yawned again. "What I'm going to say now is, 'Good night.'" She rolled over onto her side and felt sleep coming down on her like a soft, dark blanket. She yawned one more time. Tomorrow, life would go on. It was an utterly ordinary thought—for anyone who hadn't been through what Vanai had. To her, the ordinary would never seem so again, not when she compared it to the years just past. Being able to have an ordinary life . . . Who, really, could want much more than that? *Not me,* she thought, and slept.

* * *

Pekka had run the largest, most complex sorcerous project the land of the Seven Princes had ever known. Over in the Naantali district, mages by the dozen had leaped to obey her. Thanks to the project, the Gyongyosians had surrendered and the Derlavaian War was over.

"Aye? And so?" Elimaki said when Pekka went over her accomplishments.

"And so? And so?" Pekka threw her hands in the air and scowled at her sister. "And so you'd think I'd be able to put together a simple wedding. That's *and so*. Wouldn't you?"

"Don't worry about it," Elimaki said soothingly. "You're doing fine. Everything will be wonderful. You're only getting upset because it's three days away."

"And because the caterer and the florist haven't got a clue—not even a hint—about what they're supposed to be doing," Pekka added. "They're both idiots. How do they stay in business when they're such idiots?"

"They've both been in business as long as we've been alive," her sister pointed out. "Come the day, everything will be perfect." Her mouth tightened. "A few years later, though, who knows?" Barristers and solicitors were still gnawing over the remains of her marriage, a marriage as much a wartime casualty as any wounded soldier.

Pekka wished Elimaki hadn't said that. "I'm nervous enough as things are," she said.

"If you don't want to go through with it—" Elimaki began.

"It's not that," Pekka broke in, shaking her head. "It's not that at all." She hoped she wasn't trying to convince herself as well as Elimaki. "But how can I help worrying about it? I worry about everything. I have to."

"I hope you're as happy ten years from now as you will be when you say your vows," Elimaki told her. "Uto thinks the world of Fernao, if that means anything to you."

"It means a lot," Pekka said. "The only question I have is whether it should make me happy or scare me."

Elimaki laughed. She knew Pekka's son as well as Pekka did herself. *She might know Uto better than I do*, Pekka thought. *The past few years, she's seen a lot more of him than I have.* "A little of both," she said. "You don't want him not to like Fernao. . . ."

"I certainly don't," Pekka said.

"But you wonder what he's liking if he likes him too much," her sister went on. "How much of a mischievous little boy can your fiancé be?"

"Some, I expect," Pekka answered. "Most men can, from everything I've seen." She thought of Ilmarinen, who still had a wide streak of mischievous little boy in him at more than twice her age. He and Uto had recognized each other as two of a kind. That was another frightening thought.

"If Uto's content with Fernao, that's good," Elimaki said. "A boy should have a man around, I think." She hesitated, then nodded to herself and went on, "And you don't have to tell him anything, either."

"No," Pekka said. "That crossed my mind, too." As far as she was concerned, it was far better that Uto never find out she and Fernao had been lovers before Leino died. Her son would have a much easier time accepting Fernao as a stepfather this way than as someone who might have displaced his real father even if Leino hadn't died.

"Simpler," Elimaki said.

"Aye." Pekka nodded. "And the world usually isn't simple, either."

"Don't I know it!" Elimaki exclaimed. "It's *never* simple once the solicitors get their claws into it, believe me it isn't. Powers below eat Olavin, why didn't he just walk in front of a ley-line caravan?"

Pekka thought she understood why Olavin had taken up with his secretary. He'd been away from his wife for a long time, so he'd found someone else. She'd done something not far removed from that herself. Since she saw no way to tell Elimaki anything of the sort without making her sister burst like an egg, she prudently kept her mouth shut.

Elimaki asked, "What sort of trouble is the caterer giving you?"

That made Pekka want to burst like an egg. "The moron! The idiot! The imbecile! He's telling me he can't get enough smoked salmon for the feast."

"Why not?"

"Why? I'll tell you why! Because his illiterate, crack-brained assistant who does his ordering didn't order enough, that's why," Pekka said. "He knew how much I'd asked for. He just forgot to get it. Incompetent bungler. Powers above, I wish we still took heads, the way our ancestors did in the old days. But his would be empty."

Elimaki went out to the kitchen. When she came back, she was carrying two mugs of brandy. "Here." She handed one of them to Pekka. "Drink this. You'll feel better."

"In the old days—"

"In the old days, this would have been fermented reindeer milk," her sister said firmly. Pekka found herself nodding. She took a sip, and nodded again. Sure enough, civilization *had* made progress in the past thousand years. Elimaki went on, "Everything will be fine at the wedding. You'll see. And I hope everything will be fine afterwards, but that's up to you—you and Fernao, I mean."

"We'll do the best we can," Pekka said. "That's all anybody can do."

By the time she'd finished the brandy, she did feel better. Her sister had poured her a hefty tot. She also felt sleepy, and let Elimaki put her to bed. She was sure she would be worried again in the morning, but she wasn't—only frantic, which wasn't quite the same thing. Frantic seemed to do the job. She approached the caterer with blood in her eye, and not only got a promise of all the smoked salmon she'd ordered, but got it at a reduced rate. "To make up for the problem our error caused you," the fellow said. *To get you out of the shop before you murder someone,* was what he probably meant.

The day of the wedding dawned fair and mild. Pekka let out a long sigh of relief. With summer past and autumn beginning, weather in Kajaani was always a gamble. Aye, a canopy behind Elimaki's house would have shielded the guests from the worst of it, but she didn't want everyone to have to come swaddled in furs, and she especially didn't want to bring the ceremony indoors. Old, old custom said weddings belonged outside, under the sun and the wind and the sky. If caught between old, old custom and an early snowstorm . . .

I don't know what I would have done, Pekka thought. *I'm glad I don't have to worry about it. We might almost be Gyongyosians talking about the stars.*

She was just getting into her leggings and elaborately embroidered tunic, a good hour before people were supposed to start arriving, when somebody knocked on the front door. "If that's Fernao, you can keep him," she called to Elimaki. "Otherwise, hit him over the head and drag him off to one side."

But it wasn't Fernao, and Elimaki didn't hit him over the head. "I need to speak to Pekka," Ilmarinen declared.

Pekka threw her hands in the air, thinking, *I might have known.* Fastening the last couple of bone toggles, she went out to the front room. "What is it?" she snapped. "It had better be interesting."

"Aren't I always?" he asked, with one of his raffish smiles.

She folded her arms across her chest. "What you always are, without fail, is a nuisance. I haven't got time for you to be a nuisance right now, Master Ilmarinen. Say your say and come back when you're supposed to, or you'll make me sorry I invited you."

"Here. Let me show you." He pulled a leaf of closely written calculations from his beltpouch and handed it to her. "It proves what I've been saying all along."

"I *really* haven't got time for this now." But Pekka took the paper—it was either that or throw him out bodily. She glanced through it . . . and stopped after a moment. It went from straight sorcerous calculation to purporting to prove by the same kind of calculations that she and Fernao would have a happy marriage. Not a dozen people in the world could have followed all of it—and she could imagine only one who could have written it. She wondered how much labor and thought had gone into it. In spite of herself, she couldn't stay annoyed. "Thank you very much," she told him. "I'll treasure it."

"Do better than that," Ilmarinen said. "Make it come true." He ducked out of the house. Pekka hoped he'd remember to come back at the right time.

Fernao did show up a few minutes later, along with the burgomaster of Kajaani, who would recite the marriage vows. The burgomaster, who was a plump little man, only a couple of inches taller than Pekka, looked odd standing beside her tall, lean Lagoan fiancé. "I hope you'll be very happy," the man kept saying.

"Oh, I expect we will," Pekka answered. "In fact, I have proof." She passed Fernao the paper Ilmarinen had given her.

He started looking through it, then did the same sort of double take she had. "Who gave you this?" he said, and held up a hand. "No, don't tell me. I'm a Zuwayzi if it's not Ilmarinen." Pekka nodded. Fernao got down to the bottom and shook his head. "There's nobody like him."

"Nobody even close." Pekka looked Fernao over. "How splendid you are!"

"Am I?" He didn't sound convinced, where any Kuusaman man would have. His tunic, his jacket, his leggings were even fancier than hers. All the embroidery looked done by hand, though it had surely had sorcerous augmentation. "So your Jelgavan exile did a good job?"

"It's—magnificent," Pekka said.

"Good." If anything, Fernao sounded amused. "It's not what I'd wear back at home, but if it makes people here happy, that's good enough for me."

"You are . . . most impressive," said the burgomaster, looking up and up at Fernao. "You will make an imposing addition to our fair city."

Someone else knocked on the door: an early arriving guest. There was always bound to be one. "Uto!" Pekka called. When her son appeared, she said, "Take the lady back out to the canopy."

"All right," Uto said, as docile as if he'd never got into trouble in his life. "Come with me, please, ma'am."

"Aren't you sweet?" said the woman, a distant cousin, which only proved how distant she was.

Before long, Pekka and Fernao walked up a lane through the seated guests and stood before the burgomaster. "As representative of the Seven Princes of Kuusamo, I am pleased to be acting in this capacity today," the fellow said. "It is far more pleasant than most of the duties I am called upon to fulfill. . . ."

He went on and on. He was a burgomaster; part of his job, pleasant or not, was making speeches. Uto stood beside Pekka and a pace behind her. He soon started to fidget.

A gleam came into his eyes. Pekka was keeping an eye on him, and spotted it. Ever so slightly, she shook her head. Her son looked disappointed, but, to her vast relief, nodded.

And then, at last, the burgomaster got to the part of his duties he couldn't avoid no matter how much he talked: "Do you, Pekka, take this man, Fernao, to be your husband forevermore?"

"Aye," Pekka said.

In Fernao's eyes, the burgomaster of Kajaani was a ridiculous little man: not because he was a Kuusaman—by now, Fernao took Kuusamans altogether for granted—but because he was absurdly self-important. But he didn't seem ridiculous at all as he asked, "Do you, Fernao, take this woman, Pekka, to be your wife forevermore?"

"Aye." Fernao did his best to make his voice something more than a husky whisper. His best proved none too good. But the burgomaster nodded, and so did Pekka. They were the people who really counted.

"By the authority vested in me by the people of Kajaani and by the Seven Princes of Kuusamo, I now declare you man and wife," the burgomaster said. *Forevermore.* That word seemed to roll down on Fernao like a boulder. He hadn't come to Kuusamo intending to find a wife—especially not a woman who was then married to somebody else. He hadn't even found Kuusaman women particularly attractive. But here he was. And what he'd just done did have certain compensations. Beaming, the burgomaster turned to him. "You may now kiss your bride."

When Fernao did, all the Kuusamans among the guests—everyone, in other words, except for a few cousins and an old uncle of his and Grandmaster Pinhiero—burst into cheers and shouted, "They are married!" Somebody had told him they would do that, but he'd forgotten. It made him jump. In Lagoas, as in most places, passing a ring marked the actual moment of marriage. The Kuusamans did things differently, as they often did.

"I love you," he told Pekka.

"I love you, too," she answered. "That's one of the better

reasons for doing this, wouldn't you say?" Her eyes sparkled.

"Well, now that you mention it . . ." Fernao said. Pekka snorted.

"If I may take my usual privilege . . ." The burgomaster kissed her, too. From some of the things Fernao had read, in the old days a Kuusaman chieftain's privilege had gone a good deal further than that. *One more reason to be glad we live in the modern age,* Fernao thought.

Where some Kuusaman customs were very different, the receiving line was just the same. He and Pekka stood side by side, shaking hands with people and accepting congratulations. "A pretty ceremony, my boy," said his uncle, a bony man named Sampaio. "I didn't understand a word of it, mind you, but very pretty."

"I'm glad you could come," Fernao answered. Speaking Lagoan felt distinctly odd; he didn't do it much these days. But his uncle, a successful builder, knew no Kuusaman and had long since forgotten whatever classical Kaunian he'd learned.

Sampaio stuck an elbow in his ribs and chuckled. "And that's one blaze of a suit you've got on, too," he said.

Fernao also thought he was on the gaudy side of splendid. But he shrugged and forced a grin. "It's what they wear here. What can I do about it?"

"Powers below eat me if I know." Sampaio gave Fernao a hug. "I hope you're happy with her, boy. She seems nice, even if we can't talk to each other."

"Well, I wouldn't marry her if I didn't like her," Fernao said, which made his uncle laugh. He suspected Pekka spoke a little more Lagoan than she let on. No point telling that to his uncle, though; he didn't think Sampaio would be coming down to Kajaani again any time soon.

Elimaki came up to him and gave him a fierce hug. "You take good care of my sister," she said. "You take good care of her, or you answer to me."

"I will. I intend to," Fernao said.

"You'd better." Elimaki made it sound like a threat. Remembering how her marriage had collapsed not so long before, Fernao supposed he understood why she sounded that way, which didn't make it any less unnerving.

Ilmarinen had a different take on things, as he usually did. Sidling up to Fernao, he said, "I hope it's still as much fun now that you've gone and made it official."

"Thank you so much for your good wishes," Fernao exclaimed.

"Always a pleasure, always a pleasure." Ilmarinen wagged a finger at him. "See what you get for saving me from myself? That's not the best recipe for getting a man to love you forever, you know."

"Don't be silly," Fernao said. "You didn't love me even before then."

Ilmarinen chuckled nastily. "Maybe we understand each other after all. Now I'm going to raid the feast. You have to stand here gabbing with the rest of these bores till half the good stuff's gone." And off he went, cackling like a broody hen.

Before Fernao could figure out what to say to that—not that it gave him much room for a comeback—he found himself clasping wrists with Grandmaster Pinhiero. The head of the Lagoan Guild of Mages said, "I didn't remember meeting her before. Now I've got at least some notion of why you were willing to move to the back of beyond. I wish you were still in Setubal, but I hope you'll be happy."

"Thank you, sir." Fernao hadn't been sure the grandmaster would be even that gracious.

But Pinhiero, he discovered, had other things on his mind besides this wedding. He asked, "Do you know a third-rank mage named Botelho, from down in Ruivaes?"

"I know the town—miserable little place," Fernao answered. "I've never heard of the man."

"Neither has anyone else," Pinhiero said grimly. "His documents are all perfect, he passed every obvious sorcerous test with ease—but he turned out to be an Algarvian on masquerade."

"Powers below eat him!" Fernao said. "Spying for King Mainardo?"

"Worse," Pinhiero replied. While Fernao was still wondering what could be worse, the grandmaster told him: "Spying for King Swemmel."

Fernao wished he hadn't cursed before. He really wanted to do it now. He contented himself with saying, "Swemmel really wants to know things, doesn't he?"

"Just a bit." Pinhiero's voice was dry. "The other interesting question is, how many other Guild members aren't what they're supposed to be?"

"You'd do well to find out," Fernao said. "Me, I'm just as well pleased to be down here, thank you very much."

"Aye, have a good time while the world's going down the commode around you," Pinhiero jeered.

Fernao gave him a bright, cheerful, meaningless smile. "If you think you can make me feel guilty on my wedding day, you'd better think again."

"Tomorrow won't be your wedding day, and you'll still be down here," the grandmaster said sourly. "You ought to come back to a place where things happen once in a while."

"If things didn't happen here, I never would have started working with the Kuusamans in the first place," Fernao pointed out. Grandmaster Pinhiero scowled at him. *I don't have to take his orders any more, or even listen to his complaints,* Fernao thought. He turned away from Pinhiero just in time to see Pekka drop to one knee before a Kuusaman younger than she was. *But her folk only do that for . . .* Fernao needed no more than half the thought before leaning on his cane to bow very low himself. "Your Highness," he murmured.

"As you were, both of you," Prince Juhainen said. Pekka rose; Fernao straightened. The prince went on, "Powers above grant that you spend many happy years together."

"Thank you very much, your Highness," Fernao and Pekka said together. They smiled at each other. Juhainen smiled, too, and moved on toward the reception inside Elimaki's house. In a low voice, Fernao said, "Well, sweetheart, if you have any kin who haven't been giving you enough respect, one of the Seven Princes at your wedding ought to do the job."

"I don't know," Pekka said. "People like that would complain because I didn't have two or three of the Seven down here."

Eventually, the last cousins, friends, and colleagues went inside, which meant Fernao and Pekka could, too. The caterer came up to Pekka with something like panic on his face. "The smoked salmon—" he began.

She cut him off. "If anything's gone wrong with *that* delivery—especially after all your promises—I won't just take it out of your fee. I'll blacken your name all over town. But don't bother me about it now, not on my wedding day." His face a mask of misery, the caterer fled.

"How much will it matter if you blacken his name?" Fernao asked.

His new bride looked surprised. "Quite a bit," she answered, and then must have realized why he'd asked the question, for she went on, "This isn't Setubal. There won't be thousands and thousands of people here who've never heard of him. When folks here find out about a fiasco, it'll hurt his business. And it should."

It's a small town, Fernao thought. That would take getting used to. As far as he could see, the caterer had set out a very respectable spread. Everything he ate was good, from prawns to slices of raw reindeer meat dipped in a fiery sauce. He didn't particularly miss the smoked salmon. But if it was supposed to be on the menu and wasn't there, the caterer deserved at least some of the trouble in which he'd landed.

A Valmieran wine washed down the delicacies. Fernao would have expected one from Jelgava, tangy with lemon and orange juice. Then he remembered that Pekka and Leino had gone on holiday to Jelgava. If Pekka didn't want to remind herself of days gone forever, he understood that.

Someone not far away let out a startled squawk. Someone else exclaimed, "How in blazes did a hedgehog get loose here?" People shooed the little animal out the door.

Voice even grimmer than when she'd dealt with the caterer, Pekka said, *"Where's Uto?"* Her son, once found, loudly protested his innocence—too loudly to convince Fernao. Pekka didn't look convinced, either, but a wedding reception was no place for a thorough interrogation. Uto escaped with a warning just this side of a threat.

And then the carriage that would take Fernao and Pekka to a hostel for their wedding night pulled up in front of Elimaki's house. Guests pelted them with little acorns and dried berries—symbols of fertility. "Careful," Pekka warned Fernao as they went down the walk to the carriage. "Don't slip."

With his bad leg, that was advice to take seriously. "I won't," he said. Pekka protectively took his arm to make sure he didn't.

At the hostel, another bottle of wine waited in a bed of snow. Pekka poured some for each of them. She raised hers in salute. "We're married. We're here. We're by ourselves. It's all right, or as all right as it can be."

"I love you," Fernao said. They both drank to that. He added, "What I'd bet you really feel like doing about now is collapsing."

"That's one of the things I feel like doing, aye," Pekka nodded. "But there's something else to attend to, too."

"Is there?" Fernao said, as if he had no idea what she was talking about.

Before long, they were attending to it. It was nothing they hadn't attended to a good many times before, but no less enjoyable on account of that—more enjoyable, if anything, because they knew each other better now, and each knew what the other enjoyed. And the first time after the ceremony made things official, as it were.

"I love you," Fernao said again, lazy in the afterglow.

"A good thing, too, after we just got married," Pekka replied.

"A good thing?" He stroked her. "You're right. It is."

A carpetbag by his feet, Ilmarinen stood on the platform at the ley-line caravan depot in Kajaani, waiting for the caravan that would take him back up to Yliharma. He was not very surprised when a tall Lagoan, his once-red hair now gray, walked up onto the same platform. "Hello, Pinhiero, you shifty old son of a whore," he said in fluent classical Kaunian. "Come on over here and keep me company."

"I don't know that I ought to," the Grandmaster of the Lagoan Guild of Mages replied in the same tongue. "You'd probably try to slit my beltpouch."

"That's what you deserve for wearing such a silly thing," Ilmarinen said.

Unperturbed, Pinhiero set his carpetbag down next to Ilmarinen's. "Besides, whom are you calling old? You were cheating people before I was even a gleam in my papa's eye."

"Don't worry—you've made up for it since," Ilmarinen said. "And you're the one who needs to steal from me more than I need to steal from you."

"A year ago, I would have," the grandmaster said. "Not now. Now I have what I need. You boys did play fair on that one, and I thank you for it."

"Don't thank me. Thank Pekka and the Seven Princes," Ilmarinen told him. "If I'd had my way, you'd still be out on the street corner begging for coppers. I wouldn't even have told you my name, let alone anything else."

He waited for Pinhiero to fly into a temper. Instead, the Lagoan mage said, "Well, maybe that's not so foolish as you usually are. Did you hear what I was telling Fernao at the wedding last night?"

"Can't say that I did," Ilmarinen answered. Pinhiero spoke of the Algarvian in Swemmel's pay whom the Lagoan Guild of Mages had unmasked. Ilmarinen scowled. "Oh, that's just what we need, isn't it? Might have known the Unkerlanters would try to steal what we've done. It's a lot faster and a lot cheaper than sitting down and doing the work themselves."

"I expected they would try to spy," Pinhiero said. "I didn't expect them to be so good at it. Who knows if this one whoreson is the only mage they planted on us? We'll have to do some more digging, but this bastard's credentials were *good,* and he speaks Lagoan as well as I do."

"That's not saying much," Ilmarinen remarked.

Pinhiero glared at him. "To the crows with you, my friend," he said, trotting out the curse as if he were a Kaunian from imperial days.

"Thank you so much." Ilmarinen gave the grandmaster a little half bow, which made Pinhiero no happier.

"If you're so confounded smart, what would you do about these fornicating Algarvians in Swemmel's pay?" the Lagoan demanded.

"Oh, I can think of a couple of things," Ilmarinen said lightly.

Pinhiero wagged a finger at him. "And those are? Talk is cheap, Ilmarinen, especially when you don't have to back it up."

Ilmarinen bristled. "Why should I tell you anything, you old fraud? All you do is insult me. As far as I can see, you *deserve* spies."

"Fine," Pinhiero said. "My first guess is, you haven't got any answers. My second guess is, you'd be happy to see Swemmel able to match the spells."

Those both struck home. Nettled, Ilmarinen snapped, "It'd be just like you Lagoan bunglers to let him have the secrets to them."

Before the grandmaster could answer, the ley-line caravan came into the depot from the north. Passengers got off. Along with the others waiting on the platform, Ilmarinen and Pinhiero got on. They went into an empty four-person compartment and glared so fiercely at the other people who stuck in their noses that they still had it to themselves when the caravan started back towards Yliharma. As soon as it began to move, they began to argue again.

"I'm tired of your hot air, Ilmarinen," Pinhiero said.

"If you weren't such a stupid clot, you'd be able to see these things for yourself," Ilmarinen retorted.

"See what things?" the Lagoan mage said. "All I see is a fraud who talks fancy and doesn't back it up. You say you have these magical answers"—he used the word with malice aforethought—"and then you don't say what they are. And the reason you don't say is that you haven't really got them."

"Five goldpieces say I do, and better than anything you've come up with," Ilmarinen said.

Grandmaster Pinhiero thrust out his hand. "You're on, by

the powers above." Ilmarinen clasped Pinhiero's hand and then took his wrist in an Algarvic-style grip. Pinhiero gave him a seated bow. "All right, your Magnificence. We've made the bet. Now talk."

"I will," Ilmarinen said. "The first thing you need to do is, you need to get Swemmel thinking the Algarvians he's hired to do his dirty work for him are going to pass whatever they find out to their own mages and not to him. If anything will give Swemmel nightmares, it's the idea of Algarve getting strong again. Am I right or am I wrong?"

He knew perfectly well he was right. King Swemmel saw plotters everywhere, and he had plenty of reason to dread Algarve. Even Pinhiero didn't deny it. All he said was, "You may be right."

"What I may be is on the way to winning my bet," Ilmarinen said, laughing. "Are you doing any of that now?"

"None of your business," the grandmaster said.

"Ha! That means you're not. I know you," Ilmarinen said, and Pinhiero didn't deny that, either. Ilmarinen went on, "The other thing you need to do is, you need to make some false results and put them where a spy who does a little work will come upon them. They can't be out in the open, or he won't trust them. But if he digs and digs and then finds them, he's bound to think they're real. And he'll send them back to Swemmel, and the Unkerlanter mages will try to use them, and either they won't work at all or they'll be a disaster, depending on how much effort you put into dreaming them up. Either way, the Unkerlanters will stop trusting what their snoops are feeding them. You're not doing that, either, are you?"

Grandmaster Pinhiero didn't answer right away. He shifted his weight so he could get at his beltpouch, then took out five gold coins and passed them to Ilmarinen. "Here," he said. "If I were wearing a hat, I'd take it off to you. You're twistier than an eel dancing with an octopus."

"Thank you very much," Ilmarinen said smugly.

"How in blazes do you come up with these things?" Pinhiero asked. "With a little luck, they'll tie the Unkerlanters in knots for months, maybe even years."

"You're supposed to think of them for yourself," Ilmarinen said. "Why are you grandmaster, if not to think of things like that? It can't be because you're such a brilliant wizard. We both know you're not. As far as magecraft goes, Fernao is worth ten of you."

"He's a clever fellow," Pinhiero admitted. "I thought he would sit in my seat one of these years, and then you Kuusamans went and kidnapped him. Grabbed him by the prong, by the powers above." He leaned forward and stared suspiciously at Ilmarinen. "Was that your idea, too?"

Ilmarinen shook his head. "Not a bit of it. I always thought he'd cause Pekka more trouble than he was worth. I hope I'm wrong, but I may be right yet."

"A likely story," Pinhiero said. "I don't know whether you're lying or not. You'll never admit it if you are."

"Who, me?" Ilmarinen did his best to look innocent. He hadn't had much practice at it, and didn't bring it off well. Pinhiero laughed raucously.

Ilmarinen muttered something under his breath. Here he'd told the unvarnished truth, and the Lagoan grandmaster hadn't believed him. As far as he was concerned, that was just like Lagoans. As did their Algarvian cousins, they often thought they knew everything there was to know. They couldn't get it through their heads that he and a lot of other Kuusamans trusted them no further than the Lagoans trusted folk from the land of the Seven Princes.

Of course, that cut both ways, as Pinhiero proved when he said, "Do you have any notion how much it galls us to follow your lead?"

"Some, maybe," Ilmarinen said. "We've been stronger than you for a while now. You just didn't notice, because most of what we did was out in the Bothnian Ocean and on islands in the Great Northern Sea where you don't have an interest. And besides, we're only Kuusamans—we don't make a big racket about what we do, the way Algarvic folk enjoy so much. We just go on about our business."

Grandmaster Pinhiero turned a dull red. He had to know Ilmarinen was right, however little he cared to admit it. He said, "The world is changing." By the way he said it, he wished the world weren't.

"Back in the days when the Kaunian Empire was tottering to a fall, a lot of nobles there would have said the same thing," Ilmarinen observed. "They would have said it in the same language we're using, as a matter of fact, so not everything changes."

"Easy for you to say such things, Ilmarinen—you're on the rising side," Pinhiero replied. "Me, I have to look at my kingdom shrinking."

"Not in size. Only in influence," Ilmarinen said. "Things would have looked a lot worse for you had Mezentio won the war. For that matter, the Algarvians didn't even manage a full sorcerous attack against Setubal. They did against Yliharma. I was there."

"You're always in the way of trouble," Pinhiero said.

The grandmaster subsided into gloomy silence as the ley-line caravan went through over the Vaattojarvi Hills. The weather was milder and the land fairer on the north side of the hills, but Pinhiero seemed no happier. At last, not too long before the caravan got into Yliharma, he burst out, "Is this what we fought so hard for? Is this why we spent so many men and so much treasure? To hand leadership in the world over to you?"

"Well, if you hadn't fought, you'd have handed it over to Algarve," Ilmarinen answered. "And you may not have handed it to us. You may have handed it to Unkerlant instead."

"You do so relieve my mind," the Lagoan grandmaster said, and Ilmarinen threw back his head and laughed. Pinhiero glared at him. "If the world does turn out to be Unkerlant's, you'll laugh out of the other side of your mouth, by the powers above."

"No doubt," Ilmarinen said. "No doubt at all. But I, at least, won't be wearing that foolish expression on my face, for it'll come as no surprise. And, I assure you, Kuusamo will work as hard against the rise of Unkerlant as we did against Algarve, and for most of the same reasons. Can you Lagoans say as much, when you can't even keep spies out of your guild of mages?"

"You cannot hold me responsible for the fact that Algarvians and Lagoans look much alike," Grandmaster Pinhiero ground out.

"No, but I can hold you responsible for forgetting that

that fact has consequences," Ilmarinen said. "This is why, during the war, we were so reluctant to train Lagoans in the new sorcery. We weren't sure they would all *be* Lagoans, if you take my meaning."

Pinhiero's glower grew darker than ever. Before he could say anything more, a conductor came through the caravan cars, calling, "Yliharma! Everybody out for Yliharma!" Ilmarinen laughed and clapped his hands. He'd managed to annoy the Lagoan grandmaster all the way up from Kajaani, *and* he'd got the last word. As the ley-line caravan slowed to a stop, he grabbed his carpetbag and hurried for the door.

The fields around Skarnu's castle were golden with ripening grain. Some of the leaves on the trees were going golden, too, with others fiery orange, still others red as blood. From the battlements, he could see a long way. A mild breeze stirred his hair. Turning to Merkela, he said, "It's beautiful."

His wife nodded. "Aye, it is." Her nails clicked as she drummed her fingers on the gray stone. "It's harvest time. I ought to be working, not standing around here like somebody who doesn't know a sickle from a scythe."

"When I walked onto your farm five years ago, *I* didn't know a sickle from a scythe," Skarnu reminded her.

"No, but you learned, and you worked," Merkela said. "I'm not working now, and I wish I were."

"You'd make a lot of farmers nervous if you did," Skarnu said.

"I know," Merkela said unhappily. "I've seen that. All the fairy tales talk about how wonderful it is for the peasant girl to marry the prince and turn into a noblewoman. And most of it is, but not all of it, because I can't do what I've been doing all my life, and I miss it."

Skarnu had never worked so hard in his life as when bringing in the harvest. He didn't miss it at all. Saying that would only annoy Merkela, so he kept quiet. She probably knew him well enough to understand it was in his thoughts. Valmiru came up on the battlements just then. Skarnu turned to the butler with something like relief. "Aye? What is it?"

"A woman with a petition to present to you, your Excellency," Valmiru replied.

"A petition? Really? A written one?" Skarnu asked, and Valmiru nodded. Skarnu scratched his head. "Isn't that interesting? Most of the time, people here just tell me what they've got in mind. They don't go to the trouble of writing it out." If nothing else had, that by itself would have told him he was in the country.

He went down the spiral staircase. The woman, plainly a peasant, waited nervously. She dropped him an awkward curtsy. "Good day, your Excellency," she said, and thrust a leaf of paper at him.

She would have retreated then, but he held up a hand to stop her. "Wait," he added. Wait she did, fright and weariness warring on her sun-roughened face. He read through the petition, which was written in a semiliterate scrawl and phrased as a peasant imagined a solicitor would put things: full of fancy curlicues that added nothing to the meaning and sometimes took away. "Let's see if I have this straight," he said when he was done. "You're the widow named Latsisa?"

She nodded. "That's me, your Excellency." She bit her lip, looking as if she regretted ever coming to him.

"And you have a bastard boy you want me to declare legitimate?" Skarnu went on.

"That's right," Latsisa said, looking down at her scuffed shoes and flushing.

"How old is this boy?" Skarnu asked. "You don't say here."

Latsisa stared down at her shoes once more. In a low voice, she answered, "He's almost three, your Excellency."

"*Is* he?" Skarnu said, and the peasant woman nodded miserably. Skarnu sighed. Sometimes being a marquis wasn't much fun. He asked the question he had to ask: "And does he have hair that's as much red as it is blond?" Latsisa nodded again, her face a mask of pain. As gently as he could, Skarnu said, "Then why do you think I would be willing to make him legitimate?"

"Because he's all I have," Latsisa blurted. She seemed to

take courage from that, for she continued, "It's not his fault what color his hair is, is it? *He* didn't do anything wrong. And I didn't do anything against the law, either. All right— I slept with an Algarvian. He was nicer to me than any Valmieran man ever was. I'm not even sorry, except that he had to go. But it *wasn't* against the law, not then. And it's not like I was the only one, either—*is* it, your Excellency?"

She knows about Krasta, Skarnu thought, and had to work to hold his face steady. But her other arguments weren't to be despised, either. He asked, "Didn't you care that you were sleeping with an enemy, an invader?"

Latsisa shook her head. "All I cared about was that we loved each other." Her chin came up in defiance. "We *did*, by the powers above. And if he ever came back here, I'd marry him in a minute. So that's why I want the boy made legitimate, your Excellency. He's what I've got."

"Even if he were made legitimate, he won't have an easy time growing up, not looking the way he does," Skarnu said.

"I know that," Latsisa answered. "But he'll have a harder time yet if he's a bastard. And you still haven't told me why it'd be against the law to make him all proper just on account of his father had red hair." Skarnu knew why he didn't want to do it. But the peasant woman was right; that was different from finding a reason in law why an Algarvian's bastard should be treated differently from any other. No sooner had that thought crossed his mind than Latsisa said, "Besides, the war's supposed to be over and done with now, isn't it?"

She was doing her best not to make things easy. Skarnu tried another tack: "What would your neighbors think?"

"One of my neighbors is Count Enkuru's bastard," Latsisa replied. "The count forced his mother, too, powers below eat him. He looks just like Enkuru, my neighbor does, but the count never gave his mother a copper for what he'd done. He was a noble, and his shit didn't stink—begging your pardon, your Excellency."

"That's all right," Skarnu said abstractedly. Aye, there were times when this job wasn't easy at all.

Latsisa went on, "So my neighbors don't get so up in arms about bastards as a lot of people would, maybe. Sometimes they happen, that's all, and a person who's a bastard doesn't usually act any different than anybody else."

Finding that ley line blocked, Skarnu went down another. He hardened his voice and said, "You do know that I was a Valmieran officer, don't you? And that my wife and I were both in the underground after the kingdom surrendered?"

"Aye, I know that. Everybody knows that—and what happened to your wife's first husband," Latsisa said. "But I thought I'd come and ask you anyways, on account of you'd got a name for judging 'fair." Her mouth twisted. "Maybe I heard that last wrong. Sure seems like I did."

Skarnu's cheeks and ears heated. "If you're going to ask me to set aside the whole war, you're asking a lot."

"War shouldn't have anything to do with it," Latsisa said. "I just want to make my little boy legitimate. Wouldn't have any trouble doing that if he was a blond like me, would I?"

I tried to get Merkela not to hate little Gainibu. I didn't have any luck, even though he's my nephew—maybe especially because he's my nephew, Skarnu thought. *Now here's a half-Algarvian bastard I've never even seen, and I'm ready to hate him, or at least to treat him differently from the way I would if he were all Valmieran.*

How many bastards had Valmieran women borne to Algarvian soldiers during the occupation? Thousands, surely—tens of thousands. Right now, he supposed, Algarvian women were lying down with occupying soldiers; they'd raise up another crop of bastards before long.

But that had nothing to do with the questions at hand. Would Latsisa have had any trouble legitimating a blond bastard boy? Skarnu knew she wouldn't; it would be a routine procedure, unless she had legitimate children who raised a fuss. Should her son's case be any different in law just because he had sandy hair? Try as he would, Skarnu could see no legal justification for denying the petition.

He ground his teeth; there was nothing he more wanted to see. But he couldn't find it. The peasant woman had argued him down. *And why not?* he gibed at himself. *Merkela does it all the time.* Thinking about Merkela made him wonder how he would explain himself to her. He didn't care to contemplate that right now. He took the petition, scrawled *I approve* on it, and signed his name. Then he thrust it at Latsisa. "Here."

Her jaw fell. Her eyes widened. "Thank you, your Excellency," she whispered. "I didn't think you would."

Skarnu hadn't thought he would, either. "I didn't do it for you," he said harshly. "I did it for honesty's sake. Take that, do whatever you need to do to register it with the clerks, and get out of my sight."

"Aye, your Excellency." The peasant woman didn't take offense. She dropped Skarnu another unpracticed curtsy. "What they say is true—you *are* a just man."

"I hope so," Skarnu said. "I do try." He gestured brusquely toward the door to the audience chamber. Latsisa, quite sensibly, left in a hurry. Skarnu sat where he was for a while, wondering if he'd done the right thing. At last, he decided he had, however little he liked it. That fortified him. He had the feeling he'd need fortifying.

Later that afternoon, Merkela asked, "What did the woman want?"

He tensed. "She had a bastard she wanted me to declare legitimate."

"A bastard?" Merkela was quick on the uptake. "An Algarvian's bastard?" Skarnu nodded. She said, "I hope you sent her away with a flea in her ear, the miserable, stinking whore."

"No," Skarnu said, and braced himself for trouble. "It's not the little boy's fault who his father was. If his father were Valmieran, there wouldn't be any question about making him legitimate. And so I did."

Merkela gave him a poisonous glare. "That's terrible," she said. "It's not just the boy. You might as well have told the woman it was all right for her to play the slut during the occupation."

"Even a whore can make a child legitimate," Skarnu said. "I know that for a fact. It hasn't got anything to do with whether she's good or not, only with whether the child is hers and whether anyone else in the family makes a stink. Here, there isn't anyone else in the family but her and the boy—she was a widow before she took up with the Algarvian."

"Did the redheads blaze her husband before she spread her legs for this one?" Merkela asked.

"I don't know the answer to that," Skarnu said. "I don't think so."

"Disgraceful," Merkela said.

"Is it? I don't think so," Skarnu said. "There are thousands of these bastards all over Valmiera. There's one in this castle—Bauska's little girl, remember? What are we going to do? Hate all of them for as long as they live? That's asking for trouble. The war is over. We can start to show a little pity."

"You can, maybe." No, Merkela had no yield in her.

With a sigh, Skarnu said, "I have to do things here as I think right. I would have caused more trouble by telling her no than I did by saying aye."

"I still think you made a mistake," Merkela told him. That was milder than most of the things she might have said. And she pushed it no further. Maybe, a tiny bit at a time, she *was* mellowing. If she was, she would never admit it. And Skarnu knew better than to say anything about it, which would only put her back up. Over these past five years, he'd learned to get along with his hot-tempered, stubborn wife. *And if that doesn't suit me for running a marquisate, powers below eat me if I know what would.* He gave Merkela a kiss, and wouldn't answer when she asked him why.

When Ealstan came out of the shop where he and his father had been casting accounts, he looked around in surprise. "School was right over there," he said, pointing down the street. "I didn't even notice when we got here this morning—my wits must be wandering."

Hestan looked over to the ruins of the academy—the Algarvians had used it for a strongpoint. "Not much left there, so I'm not surprised you didn't notice. And your wits were working fine. If they weren't, how did you catch that depreciation allowance I missed?"

"Oh. That." Ealstan shrugged. "I did plenty of those,

casting accounts for Pybba—he was a born thief, and he had me run them all the time, whether he deserved them or not." He shook his head in memory half fond, half furious. The pottery magnate turned underground leader had never done things by halves.

"You've spoken of him now and again," his father said. "He must have been something."

"Something, aye, but I still wonder what," Ealstan answered. "I would have liked him better if he'd had any use for blonds, but he was an old-line Forthwegian patriot—Forthwegians against the world, if you know what I mean."

"What finally happened to him?" Hestan asked.

"He surrendered when we couldn't hold out in Eoforwic any more," Ealstan answered. "The Unkerlanters just sat there on the other side of the Twegen and let Mezentio's men put us down. The redheads promised to treat the fighters who yielded as proper war captives, but I don't know what became of him after he went into the captives' camp. I wouldn't care to bet whether he's still alive."

"Depends on how good the Algarvians are at keeping promises." His father pointed toward some broadsheets printed in blue and white—Forthweg's colors—on a nearby wall. "Those weren't here this morning. I wonder what people are trying to convince us of now."

Ealstan only shrugged. "I've seen a million different broadsheets. I'm not going to get excited about another one." But, despite his words, he and his father both craned their necks toward the broadsheets as they came up to them.

KING BEORNWULF COMES TO GROMHEORT! the sheets declared. Below the caption was a portrait of Beornwulf, looking younger and handsomer and more kingly than Ealstan remembered him being back in Eoforwic. Of course, Ealstan had been dragged into the Unkerlanter army right after seeing Beornwulf, so his memories were liable to be biased.

"A parade," his father said, reading the smaller print below the King of Forthweg's picture. "A week from today." He glanced over to Ealstan. "We'll have to make sure we don't get stuck in traffic—unless you really want to go see him."

"No thanks—I *have* seen him," Ealstan said. "What with

what happened to me after I did, I'm not all that excited about doing it again." As if in sympathy, his wounded leg twinged. He took another look at the broadsheet. "No, we don't have to worry about it. The day will be a holiday, so nobody will go to work."

"Nobody who's looking for an excuse to stay home, anyway." Hestan took work very seriously indeed.

When Ealstan got home, he found that Vanai and his mother had already heard about the royal visit. "A crier was going through the streets shouting the news," Elfryth said. "Didn't you hear him?"

"Uh, no," Ealstan admitted. Maybe he took work too seriously himself. If the crier had gone by—and he probably had—he'd gone by unnoticed. Ealstan glanced over to his father. Hestan looked blank, too. *Who would have imagined columns of numbers could be so alluring?* Ealstan thought. He looked from his father to Vanai; at least he had good reason for finding her alluring. "How are you?" he asked.

"Not bad," she answered. "Breakfast stayed down. So did lunch. If dinner does, too, it will be a good day."

"Dada!" Saxburh said gleefully, and grabbed Ealstan by the leg, the only part of him she could reach.

He picked her up and gave her a big smacking kiss. She giggled. "Have you been a good girl today?" he asked.

"No." She sounded proud of herself. Then, as if to prove her point, she reached out for his beard with both hands.

He put her down in a hurry. "What else has she done? Or don't I want to know?" he asked Vanai.

"About what she usually does." His wife put a hand up to her mouth to hide a yawn. "The only trouble is, I'm so tired all the time, chasing after her wears me out more than it did."

Ealstan kissed her. "After you get through the first three months or so, you won't be so worn out any more. That's how it worked when you were carrying Saxburh, anyhow."

"I know," Vanai said. "But it's different now. Before I had Saxburh, I didn't have to chase a baby and keep an eye on her and nurse her. I'm still carrying Saxburh, even if she isn't inside me any more. I hope that won't make too big a difference this time around. It's bound to make some."

"You won't have to stay in hiding, though, and it won't matter if your masking spell wears off faster than it should because you're going to have a baby," Ealstan said. "You already found that out."

"Well, so I did," Vanai admitted. "No one bothered me at all. No one even yelled anything nasty at me. *That* surprised me. Maybe hating Kaunians has got to be bad manners for a while."

"I hope so," Ealstan said. "It always should have been. Kaunians are people, too." After the words were out of his mouth, he realized he was quoting his father.

Vanai sighed. "I don't think that has anything to do with why it might be out of fashion. If people thought like that, we never would have had much trouble. But the Algarvians hated Kaunians, and everybody hates the redheads right now, so whatever they did must have been wrong."

With a sigh of his own, Ealstan nodded. "You're probably right. I wish you weren't, but you probably are." Elfryth called them to supper then, which meant they dropped it. That also meant they had to capture Saxburh, who sometimes thought having to sit in a high chair was as cruel a punishment as going to the mines. This was one of those nights, which made supper, however tasty, something less than a delightful meal.

When Ealstan went off to cast accounts with Hestan the next morning, he noticed strangers on the streets of Gromheort—hard-faced, businesslike men who eyed how traffic went and who cast unhappy, suspicious glances toward every balcony and window above street level. After he spotted two or three of them, a lamp went on inside his head. "They must be King Beornwulf's bodyguards, coming to make sure nothing goes wrong when he has his parade."

"Mm, I daresay you're right," Hestan replied. "How—efficient of the new king." He and Ealstan both made faces. Beornwulf was Swemmel's puppet, and everyone knew it. The choice was between Swemmel's puppet and Swemmel undiluted by a puppet, and everyone knew that, too. Swemmel was rumored to think his own shadow plotted against him. If Beornwulf imitated him there, too, why should anyone be surprised?

More and more of Beornwulf's bodyguards came into Gromheort as the parade grew nearer. The afternoon before the King of Forthweg was supposed to go through the town, Ealstan stopped in surprise. "What is it, son?" Hestan asked.

"I know one of those fellows," Ealstan answered. "Why don't you go on ahead? I'd like to talk to him, but I don't want him to see what any of my kin look like."

His father plainly wanted to argue with him. After just as plainly wrestling with himself, Hestan didn't. "You make altogether too much sense," he said.

"I wonder where I got that from," Ealstan said. "Go on. I won't be long." Shaking his head and muttering to himself, Hestan went up the street.

After his father had turned a corner and got out of sight, Ealstan walked up to the bodyguard, stuck out his hand, and said, "Hello, Aldhelm. It's been a little while."

The guard studied him in some concern; he obviously hadn't expected to be recognized. Then his face cleared. "Ealstan, by the powers above!" He clasped Ealstan's hand. "I didn't know you were here. Last I saw you, we were both trying not to surrender to the cursed Algarvians back in Eoforwic."

"That's right." Ealstan nodded. "I managed to stay out of their hands, but I, ah, went into the Unkerlanter army a little while later." He didn't want to say anything too nasty about that, not if Aldhelm served Beornwulf and Beornwulf served Swemmel.

"Knew you weren't around." Aldhelm nodded himself. He looked Ealstan up and down. "Don't mean to pry, but did I notice a limp?"

"Aye," Ealstan said. "I got blazed in the leg in the street fighting here, and the Unkerlanters discharged me. I've been here ever since." He didn't say that Gromheort was his home town. True, he had an eastern accent, but this wasn't the only city in the eastern part of Forthweg. He went on, "It's not so bad these days. I get around on it pretty well."

"That's good. Glad to hear it." Aldhelm sounded more or less sincere. He continued, "You can guess what I'm up to these days."

"Unless I'm daft, you're one of Beornwulf's men," Ealstan said, and his former comrade in arms nodded again. Ealstan asked, "How does serving the king stack up against serving Pybba?"

"Ah, Pybba." A reminiscent smile spread over the guard's face. "He was a whoreson and a half, wasn't he?"

"He sure was. But he was *our* whoreson." Ealstan sighed. "I suppose the fornicating redheads blazed him once they got their hands on him, even if they promised they wouldn't. You never could trust those bastards."

"No, you couldn't," Aldhelm agreed, "but they didn't break their word there. You've been here in Gromheort all this time, have you?" He waited for Ealstan to nod, then continued, "After the war ended, Pybba came back to Eoforwic. He was skinny as a pencil and he'd lost most of this teeth, but he came back."

"Running his pottery again, is he? Good for him," Ealstan said.

But Aldhelm shook his head. "No, he's dead now. The Unkerlanters blazed him for treason, just a few weeks after he got home." He scowled: the expression of a man who feared he'd said too much. Sure enough, the next words out of his mouth were, "Listen, it's good to see you, but I've got business to take care of here. So long." He hurried away.

Pybba, dead? Pybba, surviving Mezentio's men to perish at the hands of Swemmel's? Slowly, Ealstan nodded. Pybba had risen against Algarve without leave and without help from Unkerlant. If that didn't make him a man who might rise against Unkerlant itself, what would? It was logical, if you looked at it the right—or was it the wrong?—way.

"Powers above," Ealstan said softly. But it wasn't the news of Pybba's death that made him exclaim, or not that alone. Six years earlier, he'd been here, right *here,* when the news racing through Gromheort that Alardo, the Duke of Bari, was dead had caught up with him: the death that had sparked the Derlavaian War. *A death before the war, a death after the war.* Ealstan kicked a stone. It spun away. *And too cursed many deaths in between.*

He hurried after Hestan. Back at home, Elfryth and Saxburh and Vanai would be waiting.

Look for

FIRST

HEROES

By HARRY TURTLEDOVE
and NOREEN DOYLE

Available in Trade paperback August 2005
from Tom Doherty Associates